THE BETROTHED

Alessandro Manzoni

THE BETROTHED
and
HISTORY OF THE
COLUMN OF INFAMY

Edited by
DAVID FORGACS AND MATTHEW REYNOLDS
University of Cambridge

J. M. Dent   London

First published in Great Britain in 1997 by J. M. Dent,
a division of the Orion Publishing Group,
Orion House, 5 Upper St Martin's Lane,
London WC2H 9EA

Introduction and other critical material
copyright © J. M. Dent 1997

History of the Column of Infamy © Oxford University Press 1964.
Reprinted from *The Column of Infamy* by Alessandro Manzoni translated
by Fr Kenelm Foster (1964) by permission of Oxford University Press

A CIP catalogue record for this book is available
from the British Library.

Printed and bound in Great Britain by
Butler & Tanner Ltd, Frome and London

CONTENTS

NOTE ON THE AUTHOR AND EDITORS

ALESSANDRO MANZONI was born in Milan on 7 March 1785. His mother Giulia separated from her husband, Count Pietro Manzoni, seven years later and soon moved to Paris with her lover, Carlo Imbonati: Manzoni was sent to boarding school. He began to make a name for himself as a lyric poet during the years 1801–5, which he spent mostly in Milan. In 1805 Imbonati died and Manzoni went to Paris to stay with his mother: they were to live together for the rest of her life. Manzoni joined the circle of intellectuals gathered around Sophie de Condorcet, forming a close friendship with the historian Claude Fauriel. In 1807 Pietro Manzoni died and the following year Manzoni married Henriette Blondel, a Calvinist. They would have ten children. Two years later Henriette was received into the Catholic Church, having taken instruction from the Jansenist Abbot Degola, who also had a strong influence on Manzoni. The family returned to Italy, to Brusuglio, near Milan, which was to be Manzoni's main home from now on. Between 1812 and 1815 he wrote his first major poems: the four *Inni sacri* and the political odes 'Aprile 1814' and 'Il proclama di Rimini'. In 1819 he published the first part of *Osservazioni sulla morale cattolica*, written on the advice of his confessor, and in 1820 the tragedy *Il Conte di Carmagnola*; the following year he composed 'Il Cinque Maggio', an ode on the death of Napoleon which made him known throughout Europe, and began work on *The Betrothed*. *Adelchi*, a second tragedy, was published in 1822, and the first edition of *The Betrothed* appeared, to wide acclaim, in 1827. Almost immediately Manzoni decided that the novel needed to be rewritten in the idiom of modern Florentine, and he spent the next thirteen years working on the revisions. In 1833 Henriette died, and four years later Manzoni married Teresa Borri Stampa. After the second edition of his novel in 1840 Manzoni did no more creative writing, but produced many works on the Italian language, as well as books of history and literary theory. In 1860 he became a senator of the new Italian Kingdom. He died in 1873, on 22

May. Verdi's *Requiem* was first performed exactly one year later in his memory.

DAVID FORGACS is a University Lecturer in Italian at Cambridge and a Fellow of Gonville and Caius College. His publications include *Rethinking Italian Fascism* (1986), *A Gramsci Reader* (1988) and *Italian Culture in the Industrial Era* (1990).

MATTHEW REYNOLDS is a Junior Research Fellow in English at Trinity College, Cambridge.

CHRONOLOGY OF MANZONI'S LIFE

Year	Age	Life
1782		Marriage of Giulia, daughter of Cesare Beccaria (the author of *Dei delitti e delle pene*), to Count Pietro Manzoni, 26 years her senior
1785		Alessandro Manzoni born in Milan (7 March). (His father was perhaps Giovanni Verri)
1792	7	Legal separation between his mother and her husband
1792–8	7–13	At school with the Somaschi friars, first in Merate, then, after the French invasion of 1796, in Lugano
1794	9	Death of Cesare Beccaria
1795	10	Giulia leaves Italy for Paris with Carlo Imbonati
1798–1801	13–16	At school with the Barnabite friars, first at the college of Castellazzo de' Barzi, then at the Collegio dei Nobili in Milan

CHRONOLOGY OF HIS TIMES

Year	Literary Context	Historical Events
1781	Kant, *Critique of Pure Reason*	
1782	Alfieri, *Saul*	
1783		End of war between Britain and the United States
1785	Cowper, *The Task*	
1788		Constitution of the United States of America
1789		French Revolution begins
1790	Burke, *Reflections on the Revolution in France*	
1791	Boswell's *Life of Samuel Johnson*; Marquis de Sade, *Justine, ou les malheurs de la vertu*	
1793	Vincenzo Monti, *La Bassvilliana*	Execution of Louis XVI; outbreak of war between Britain and France
1795–96	Goethe, *Wilhelm Meisters Lehrjahre*	
1796		French invasion of Milanese provinces
1798	Wordsworth and Coleridge, *Lyrical Ballads*	

Year	Age	Life
1801–5	16–20	At leisure, mostly in Milan. Gets to know Vincenzo Monti and Ugo Foscolo. Writes 'Il trionfo della libertà', 'Adda', the four 'Sermoni' and some shorter poems
1803–4	18	Winters in Venice, at the house of his cousin, Giovanni Manzoni
1805	20	Death of Carlo Imbonati (15 March). Goes to Paris to stay with his mother. Writes *Carme in morte di Carlo Imbonati* (published 1806). Meets Claude Fauriel, who was to be his friend for 20 years, as well as other intellectuals in the circle of Sophie de Condorcet
1807	22	March–May: Travels with mother to Milan and Turin. Death of Count Pietro Manzoni. September: returns with his mother to Milan in search of a wife
1808	23	Marries, by a Protestant rite, Henriette Blondel, a sixteen-year-old Swiss Calvinist (6 February); they have two months' honeymoon at the Beccaria villa on Lake Como, then go to Paris. In December, the birth of a daughter, Giulia (Giulietta)
1809	24	Giulietta is given a Catholic baptism. Henriette meets the Jansenist Abbot Degola. Publishes *Urania* (composed during the previous three years)
1810	25	Remarries Henriette by special dispensation, according to the Catholic rite (February). Has a religious revelation (April); he and Henriette begin instruction with Degola. Henriette is admitted into the Roman Catholic Church (May). Departure for the Villa Manzoni at Brusuglio, near Milan (June). This will be his main home for the rest of his life. Henriette's relatives are scandalized by her conversion. The Manzonis meet Monsignor Tosi who, on Degola's recommendation, becomes their confessor. Premature birth and death of a daughter, Vittoria Luigia Maria

Year	Literary Context	Historical Events
1799	Schiller, *Wallenstein*	France: Napoleon becomes First Consul
1801		Union of Britain and Ireland
1802	Foscolo, *Ultime lettere di Jacopo Ortis*	Napoleon head of 'Italian Republic'
1804		Napoleon proclaimed Emperor of France
1805		Battle of Trafalgar
1807	Hegel, *Phenomenology of Spirit*	
1808	Goethe, *Faust*, part I; Scott, *Marmion*	
1809–11	August Wilhelm von Schlegel, *Lectures on Dramatic Art and Literature*	
1810	Mme de Staël, *De L'Allemagne*	Wars of independence in South America

Year	Age	Life
1812	27	Henriette's father dies; Manzoni buys a house in Via Morone, Milan
1812–15	27–30	Four *Inni sacri*: 'La Risurrezione' (1812), 'Il nome di Maria' (1813), 'Il Natale' (1813), 'La Passione' (1814–15). Published together in 1815
1813	28	Birth of a son, Pier Luigi (Pietro)
1814	29	'Aprile 1814'. During the uprising in Milan, Manzoni sees a rioting crowd murder Prina, the finance minister. After the Austrian occupation troops are billeted in all three of his houses. He falls into debt
1815	30	Writes 'Il proclama di Rimini' and begins a fifth sacred hymn, 'La Pentecoste'. Refuses to contribute to *Biblioteca Italiana*, a magazine sponsored by the Austrian government. Birth of a daughter, Cristina
1816	31	Starts work on a historical drama, *Il Conte di Carmagnola*
1817	32	The Manzonis plan a trip to Paris: passports refused by the Austrian government. Another daughter, Sofia
1818	33	Sale of Il Caleotto, the house in Lecco
1819	34	Publication of the first part of *Osservazioni sulla morale cattolica*. The second part is left unfinished. Birth of a son, Enrico. In the autumn, Manzoni and his family succeed in visiting Paris, where they stay until July 1820
1820	35	Publication of *Il Conte di Carmagnola*. Seriously ill in May and June, but on his return to Italy his spirits improve in the company of his friends Berchet, Visconti and Grossi. He writes *Lettre à M. Chauvet*, an attack on the classical unities, not published until 1823, and begins work on a second tragedy, *Adelchi*
1821	36	Composes 'Marzo 1821' on the March uprisings in Italy, and 'Il Cinque Maggio', on the death of Napoleon, a poem which makes him celebrated throughout Europe. Another daughter, Clara. Henriette falls dangerously ill
1821–23	36–8	Works on *Fermo e Lucia*, the first version of *I promessi sposi*

Year	Literary Context	Historical Events
1812		The French army invades and then retreats from Russia
1813	Jane Austen, *Pride and Prejudice*	
1814	Scott, *Waverley*	Austria invades north Italy. Napoleon abdicates
1815	Napoleon's escape from Elba and final defeat at the Battle of Waterloo. Congress of Vienna	
1819	Schopenhauer, *The World as Will and Idea*	
1820	Revolution in Spain; uprisings in Italy. In Britain, death of George III and accession of George IV	
1821	Death of Keats	Death of Napoleon

Year	Age	Life
1822	37	Publishes *Adelchi*, together with *Discorso sopra alcuni punti della storia longobardica in Italia*; also poem 'La Pentecoste'. Another daughter, Vittoria. Death of Sophie de Condorcet
1823	38	Writes *Lettera sul Romanticismo* in response to an attack on Romanticism by Cesare d'Azeglio. (It is published without his consent in 1846, and with it in 1870.) Death of Clara
1824	39	A first volume of Manzoni's novel is printed as *Gli sposi promessi*, but not yet published
1824–25	39	The Manzonis are visited by Fauriel, his mistress Mary Clarke and her mother
1824–27	39–42	Turns the draft of his novel into *I promessi sposi*
1826	41	Death of Degola. Meets the philosopher Rosmini, who becomes his close friend and a strong influence on his thought. Birth of a son, Filippo
1827	42	Publication of *I promessi sposi*. The Manzonis visit Genoa and Livorno, where Henriette's doctor has ordered her to bathe, and then Florence, where Manzoni becomes convinced that his novel should be rewritten in the idiom spoken by cultivated Florentines
1828	43	*Il conte di Carmagnola* is performed in Florence, against Manzoni's will: it is not a success
1830	45	Birth of a daughter, Matilde
1831	46	Begins *Del romanzo storico*, a theoretical attack on works (such as *I promessi sposi*) in which history is mixed with fiction. Giulietta marries Massimo d'Azeglio

Year	Literary Context	Historical Events
1822	Death of Shelley	
1824	Death of Byron	
1826	Tommaso Grossi, *I Lombardi alla prima crociata*	
1827	Francesco Guerrazzi, *La battaglia di Benevento*; John Clare, *The Shepherd's Calendar*	
1829	Victor Hugo, *Les Orientales*	
1830	Stendhal, *Le Rouge et le Noir*	France: revolution deposes Charles X; Louis Philippe becomes king. Independence of Belgium. Uprisings throughout Europe. Britain: death of George IV and accession of William IV
1831	Leopardi, *Canti*	Uprisings in north and central Italy. Mazzini founds 'Young Italy'. Death of Carlo Felice, King of Piedmont. His successor is Carlo Alberto
1832	Silvio Pellico, *Le mie prigioni*; Goethe, *Faust*, part II	Britain: First Reform Act

Year	Age	Life
1833	48	Death of Henriette
1834	49	Death of Giulietta
1835	50	Begins *Sentir messa*
1837	52	Marries Teresa Borri Stampa
1838	53	Refuses an honour offered him by the Austrian government. Sofia gets married
1839	54	Marriage of Cristina. In the summer, Manzoni and Teresa visit Lesa, the home of Teresa's grown-up son, Stefano. (They will return there frequently during the next few years)
1840–42	55–57	Second, illustrated edition of *I promessi sposi*, together with *Storia della colonna infame*. It is published at Manzoni's own expense and is a financial failure
1841	56	Deaths of Cristina and of his mother Giulia
1842	57	Enrico marries an heiress
1844	59	Death of Fauriel
1845	60	Death of Sofia. Giuseppe Giusti visits for a month. Death of Monsignor Tosi
1845–55	60–70	Publication of *Opere varie*
1846	61	Pietro marries a ballerina without informing his father; Vittoria, too, gets married. Writes *Sulla lingua italiana*
1848	63	Manzoni's son Filippo, active in the revolution, is held prisoner by the Austrians. The Manzonis move to Lesa, where they stay until September 1850. A fire at Brusuglio destroys some of his property

Year	Literary Context	Historical Events
1833	Pushkin, *Eugene Onegin*	
1834		Slavery abolished in the British Empire
1837	Dickens, *Oliver Twist*	Britain: death of William IV and accession of Victoria
1839–42	The 'Opium War' between Britain and China	
1843	Vincenzo Gioberti, *Primato morale e politico degli Italiani*	
1844	Giuseppe Giusti, *Poesie*	
1846		Death of Pope Gregory XVI; election of Pius IX (Pio Nono). War between the U.S.A. and Mexico
1847	Charlotte Brontë, *Jane Eyre*; Emily Brontë, *Wuthering Heights*	
1848	Marx and Engels, *The Communist Manifesto*	Revolutions throughout Europe. Abdication of Louis Philippe. Resignation of Metternich. The 'Five Days' of Milan (18–23 March); war between Piedmont and Austria

Year	Age	Life
1850	65	Publishes *Del romanzo storico* and writes a dialogue, *Dell'invenzione* (published 1870)
1852	67	Filippo is arrested for debt. Visits Vittoria, her family and Matilde in Siena
1855	70	Death of Rosmini. Second, revised edition of the *Morale cattolica*
1856	71	Death of Matilde. Visits Tuscany and begins *Saggio di vocabolario italiano secondo l'uso di Firenze* (in collaboration with his friend Capponi)
1857	72	Enrico has financial difficulties (from which he will never emerge)
1858	73	Seriously ill (May–June)
1859	74	The Manzonis spend the weeks of the war in Torricella d'Arcellasco. Granted a pension by King Vittorio Emmanuele
1860	75	Cavour nominates Manzoni a senator of the new Italian Kingdom; Manzoni visits Turin in June to take his oath
1861	76	Death of Teresa. Attends Parliament for the proclamation of Vittorio Emmanuele II as King of Italy

Year	Literary Context	Historical Events
1849	Defeat of Piedmontese army at Novara. Abdication of Carlo Alberto; his successor is Vittorio Emanuele II. French troops besiege and conquer Mazzini's Roman Republic. Austria retakes Venice	
1850	Tennyson, *In Memoriam*; Hawthorne, *The Scarlet Letter*	China: Taiping Rebellion
1851	Ruskin, *The Stones of Venice*; Melville, *Moby Dick*	France: Louis Napoleon seizes power
1852		France: proclamation of the Second Empire. Cavour becomes head of the government of Piedmont
1854–56		Crimean War
1855	Browning, *Men and Women*; Whitman, *Leaves of Grass*	
1857	Flaubert, *Madame Bovary*; Baudelaire, *Les Fleurs du mal*	Indian Mutiny
1858		Secret alliance between France and Piedmont against Austria
1859	Darwin, *Origin of Species*	Piedmont and France declare war on Austria: peace is concluded after a series of quick victories for the allies; Piedmont makes large territorial gains
1860	George Eliot, *The Mill on the Floss*	Garibaldi lands in Sicily and conquers the whole of southern Italy, which is annexed to Piedmont
1861		The first parliament of united Italy (except for the Papal States and Venice) meets in Turin

Year	Age	Life
1864	79	Travels to Tuscany, and then to Turin, where he votes for Florence to replace Turin as the temporary capital of Italy
1868	83	A report for the government: *Dell'unità della lingua e dei mezzi per diffonderla*; and two letters: *Intorno al libro 'De vulgari eloquio' di Dante* and *Intorno al vocabolario*. Death of Filippo
1870	85	*Lettera al marchese di Casanova* (again on the language question; published posthumously, 1874). Begins work on *Saggio comparativo su la rivoluzione francese del 1789 e la rivoluzione italiana del 1859*, left unfinished at his death
1872	87	Accepts the honorary citizenship of Rome
1873	88	Death of Pietro. Manzoni dies in Milan on 22 May

Year	Literary Context	Historical Events
1861–65		American Civil War
1862	Christina Rossetti, *Goblin Market and Other Poems*; Hugo, *Les Misérables*	Bismarck becomes Chancellor of Prussia
1865	Birth of Yeats	
1866	Dostoevsky, *Crime and Punishment*; Ibsen, *Brand*	Austro-Prussian war; Venice is ceded to the Kingdom of Italy, of which Florence becomes the capital
1867	Ippolito Nievo, *Le confessioni d'un italiano*	
1869	Tolstoy, *War and Peace*	Opening of the Suez Canal
1870	Francesco De Sanctis, *Storia della letteratura italiana*	Franco-Prussian War; Rome becomes part of the Italian Kingdom.
1871	Birth of Proust	The Italian Parliament meets in Rome, the new capital. William I of Russia is proclaimed German Emperor at Versailles. The Paris Commune

INTRODUCTION

The plot of *The Betrothed* has many motifs of the traditional folktale: the threat to Lucia and to Don Abbondio which gets the story started; the separation of the two lovers; the tests and obstacles, including new threats, which they must confront before they can be married; the vow and the reuniting of the lovers at the end. It also shares some of the features of the Gothic romances of the early nineteenth century: the figure of the ogre-like nobleman in his hilltop castle (Chapter 20); the motif of the persecuted woman (Gertrude forced into the convent in Chapters 9 and 10; Lucia in the castle of the unnamed in Chapter 20). 'When one reads Manzoni,' D. H. Lawrence wrote, 'one wonders if he is not more "Gothic" or Germanic, than Italian.' Consistent with this romance dimension are the manufactured coincidences which occur at several points in the plot, such as Lucia just happening to be out when the *bravi* break in to abduct her, or everyone just happening to be in Milan at the end for the dénouement. The central motif of the sexual threat (the rape threat which hangs over Lucia for most of the novel) also belongs to the Romantic tale of terror.

Readers soon become aware, however, that there are other strands of narrative interwoven with this plot. The narration of historical events, for example, is intermittently present throughout but in Chapters 28 and 31–2, on the famine and the plague, it completely takes over the text in lengthy digressions from the main action. Some of Manzoni's readers objected to this. Goethe, for instance, complained on reading the first edition (1827) that in the last third of the text Manzoni had taken off his poet's robe to reveal the 'naked historian' underneath; he added that the German translation would need to cut these chapters drastically. (For this statement and those of most of the other critics cited here, see *Manzoni and his Critics*, p. 674 ff.) Whatever one thinks of this judgement, it is clear, in these and other parts of the narrative, that Manzoni is interested in writing history for its own sake and not just in writing a historical fiction. He is interested, too, in writing reflectively about history, comparing and commenting on the reliability of sources and weighing the evidence. He himself distinguished between what he called the 'positive truth' of historical writing and the 'verisimilitude' of 'poetry' or 'invention' (which included narrative fiction), but when he wrote *The Betrothed* he made it his business to deal in the former and not just the latter. In this respect, he is unique among the historical novelists of the nineteenth century – Scott, Stendhal, Tolstoy – for whom the narration of historical events was always enmeshed with the stories of the leading characters.

A striking example of Manzoni's interest in history for its own sake and in the problem of reliability is the *History of the Column of Infamy*. In 1823, when he was writing the first draft of the novel (published after his death and now known as *Fermo e Lucia*), Manzoni opened a digression within what was already a digression on the history of the plague, but it grew so big that he removed it and turned it into an appendix. The version included here is the one published with the novel in 1842. It deals with the case of a number of people arrested in Milan in 1630 on the suspicion of deliberately spreading plague by smearing a supposedly contagious unguent on walls and elsewhere. The suspected *untori* (smearers) were tortured, several were executed and the house of one of them, the barber Giangiacomo Mora, was ordered to be demolished. A column was erected in its place alongside which was a slab (now in the Musei Civici in the Castello Sforzesco, Milan) with a Latin inscription detailing the alleged crimes and the death sentence and warning passers-by to keep clear if they do not wish to be contaminated by the infamous ground. The transcripts of the trial had already been examined and the case against the suspects, as well as the use of torture, condemned by the Milanese Enlightenment reformer Pietro Verri (1728–97) in his *Osservazioni sulla tortura* (written in 1776–7 but not published until 1804). Manzoni reopened the case to argue that the investigating magistrates, in their determination to convict the suspects, had been guided by their passions and had wilfully ignored the many contemporary texts of legal procedure which restricted the use of torture. In addition, he wanted to demonstrate how seventeenth-century chroniclers and eighteenth-century historians almost unanimously reproduced the 'official' account of the case (the magistrates' view) which was itself founded on the oral rumours of frightened, uneducated people.

Historians had thus unthinkingly collaborated in forging new links in a chain of error that remained unbroken until Verri reopened the inquiry nearly 150 years later. Manzoni's re-reading of the case has been criticized, notably by Benedetto Croce and his pupil Fausto Nicolini in the 1930s, but it has more recently been defended, by Carlo Dionisotti and Leonardo Sciascia among others, as relevant to our own time in its indictment of the corruption to which all inquisitorial and accusatorial penal procedure is liable and of a 'bureaucracy of Evil' which reappeared in the Nazi extermination camps. The text also fits with the interest among social historians today in the use of inquisition documents to reconstruct a 'history from below', to piece together a picture of the language and mentality of the lower classes who were illiterate or semi-literate and who therefore left no traces of themselves in writing.

Indeed, *The Betrothed* as a whole is unusual for its time in the space it devotes to what Manzoni's English contemporary Macaulay called (in the essay 'History', 1828) the submerged 'under current' of society. There were precedents for the use of lower-class protagonists – for instance Scott's Jeanie Deans in *The Heart of Midlothian* – but Manzoni was more concerned than most historical novelists of the nineteenth century to show how ordinary people's lives were affected by such things as economic change, wars, famines and disease. He gives striking pictures, for instance, of the famine affecting the labouring poor both on the land (Chapters 4) and in the towns (Chapters 13 and 28) and of how the plague epidemic of 1629–31 hit the people of Milan (Chapters 31 and 32). He also draws attention, brilliantly, to the way that those excluded from access to literacy and formal learning are subject to the collusions and deceptions of the powerful, tricked by those who manipulate language and writing to their own ends. This is the fate of the suspects in the smearings trial. The lower classes may be aware and contemptuous of the deception (like Renzo confronted with Don Abbondio's Latin phrases in Chapter 2 or denouncing the use of 'paper, pen and inkwell' in Chapter 14) but this makes them no less weak in their dealings with the powerful.

Related to this is another strand of the narrative: that of political critique. *The Betrothed* – in this respect like other European historical novels of the nineteenth century – is at once a story set in the past and an indirect commentary on the present. The French Revolution and its sequel, the Napoleonic Wars, affected large areas of Europe and made nineteenth-century writers aware of the provisional nature of political systems and of frontiers between states, of people's potential for collective mobilization as crowds and of the strength of the new political ideologies: nationalism, liberalism and democracy. The historical novel, as George Lukács argued in his classic study of the genre written in the 1930s, grew out of these changes. It offered a way of interrogating the process of history itself, of looking into the past in order to try and make sense of the forces that had shaped the present and to understand the relations between large public events and the lives and actions of individuals.

Manzoni's novel was written and published during the restoration period (1815–48), when the old dynastic regimes had been returned to power in Europe after the defeat of Napoleon and before they were shaken again by revolution, and it makes an implicit criticism of foreign domination. In restoration Italy, the Habsburgs of Austria once again ruled Lombardy and Venetia in the north and some smaller states in the centre, the House of Savoy ruled Piedmont and Sardinia and the Spanish Bourbons the mainland south and Sicily. In this period, to write about a past time when Italians were oppressed by foreign rulers was to imply a similarity with Italy's present situation. Indeed, during the Risorgimento (the movement for independence from foreign rule which culminated in unification in 1859–61) one could write about any people oppressed at any time in history – as Verdi and his librettist Temistocle Solera did in the opera *Nabucco* (1842) about the Jews held captive in Babylon – and the audience would be able to draw a parallel with the Italians. Before the revolutions of 1848, such parallels were generally tolerated by the Austrian censors, who were more vigilant about blasphemy and the slandering of religious institutions than about these generally mild and wistful expressions of nationalist sentiment, which they seem to have accepted from the Italian cultural elites. Indeed, Verdi dedicated *Nabucco* to the daughter of the Austrian viceroy of Lombardy-Venetia. It is therefore difficult to evaluate this political aspect of Manzoni's novel and even his contemporaries were divided on it. Stendhal claimed the Austrian censors would never have allowed it to be printed had Manzoni not previously gained the protection of Metternich, the arch-reactionary chancellor of Catholic Austria, by virtue of his religious poems, the *Inni sacri* (*Sacred Hymns*) of 1812–22, whereas Luigi Settembrini said he and other Italian liberals regarded it as conservative for its time because it sent out a message of Christian resignation and passivity when they were struggling in Italy for political change.

In any case, one can argue that the most original and striking political aspect of the text lies not in its expression of nationalism but in what it says about the nature of power. Manzoni repeatedly draws attention to the workings of power and in particular to its abuses, to misrule and the misuses of authority, whether by a petty local tyrant like Don Rodrigo or a local priest like Don Abbondio, who fails to exercise responsibly the pastoral power with which he is invested, or by the lawyer Quibble-weaver who is in the pockets of the local elites (Chapters 3 and 5), or the Milanese magistrates who allow themselves to be led by what Manzoni sees as the folly of the multitudes into arresting, torturing and executing the presumed smearers during the plague. At the same time, Manzoni draws attention to the structures of power and inequality. He shows how some individuals, weak on their own, are given protection by their membership of powerful oligarchies – the clergy, the military, the nobility, merchants, lawyers, doctors – while others are excluded from and oppressed by the community of the powerful. He shows, too, how the relations between the powerful and the powerless line up with differences in status, wealth and learning: the last of these is measurable by whether or not one knows Latin or is able to read or write. In this way, Manzoni's text offers an intricate representation of society and social relations and of power in its cultural as well as its political dimensions.

Yet another strand of the text is provided by the narration of mental processes and psychic states, for which Manzoni's novel has been widely admired. His most detailed representations of the mind are those which deal with moments of heightened emotion: fear, inner conflict, tension, shame or embarrassment. Examples are the penitent visit of Fra Cristoforo, just after he has given up the secular life for the religious order, to the brother of the man he has killed (Chapter 4); the account of Lucia's fear during her incarceration by the unnamed (Chapter 20); and that of Don Abbondio's thoughts as he accompanies the unnamed to free Lucia (Chapter 23). The most celebrated example of all is the long digression on Gertrude's childhood and adolescence which occupies the second half of Chapter 9 and almost all of Chapter 10. The character of Gertrude was based on Sister Virginia Maria (convent name of Marianna de Leyva) whose story was recounted briefly in one of Manzoni's main historical source texts, Giuseppe Ripamonti's *Historiae patriae*, but the psychological details are Manzoni's own, mediated by a number of literary sources. If one looks closely at these passages, one can see that the narration of mental processes is done with a variety of techniques. These include interior monologue (Don Abbondio's journey), bold similes ('Such visions made Gertrude's mind stir and buzz as if a great basket of fresh flowers had been set down before a hive of bees'; 'all the other thoughts that had come crowding into Gertrude's re-awakened mind suddenly scattered, like a flock of sparrows at the sight of a hawk'), the close reporting of thoughts, gestures and facial appearance and the careful use of an early nineteenth-century map of the mind (Gertrude's consists of 'secret corners' and recesses, 'fantasies' and 'phantoms' which come to prominence, 'ideas' and 'images' which are displaced by others).

There is also a humorous strand. Some episodes – such as the botched attempt in Chapter 8 by Renzo and Lucia, assisted by Agnese, to pronounce themselves man and wife in front of Don Abbondio, with the parallel attempt by the *bravi* to abduct Lucia, or, at the end of Chapter 13, when Antonio Ferrer, the Grand Chancellor of Milan, helps the Commissioner for Supply out of a sticky situation in the bread riots – are masterpieces of comic narration. But there is also humour of a more restrained and complex kind, for instance in the characterization of Don Abbondio, whom Pirandello placed alongside Don Quixote as one of the great humorous creations of world literature. By 'humorous' Pirandello meant not simply comical but capable of generating a tension between contrary responses, a 'mixed feeling of laughing and crying'. The irony which pervades much of the narrative in Manzoni's novel and which is bound up with the peculiar self-sufficiency of its narrating voice – that is to say its ability to detach itself from the mere reporting of actions and thoughts and to comment, observe or generalize what is narrated – can also be considered a part of the novel's 'humour' in this sense.

The last strand, but by no means the least important, is that of Christian moralization. Many critics of the novel have drawn attention to the fact that it is not only on its final page that *The Betrothed* points a moral of Christian faith and resignation (which, according to their own convictions, they either approve or abhor) but that in many places the narrative is accompanied by judgements on the characters and their actions in terms of their selfish neglect of their obligations to others (Don Abbondio), their arrogant denial of God's authority (Don Rodrigo, the unnamed before his conversion), or, on the other hand, their piety (Lucia) and their charity (Fra Cristoforo). Through the contrasting characters of Fra Cristoforo and Don Abbondio, and through the examples of Gertrude and the unnamed, Manzoni criticizes all forms of outward obeisance to religious precepts which are not accompanied by inner faith, conviction and vocation. Antonio Gramsci, writing in the early 1930s, was among the critics who have complained that Manzoni is 'too Catholic', that he takes a paternalistic, condescending attitude towards the 'humble' people, seeing them as erring when left to themselves and in need of spiritual guidance by the Church. Alberto Moravia, in a provocative introduction to a modern edition of the novel, described it as a work of 'Catholic realism', analogous with the 'socialist realism' officially promoted in the Soviet Union under Stalin, and claimed it contained a 'ninety-five per cent' dose of religion. Even some Catholic critics have felt the book might be taken as pleading their cause too hard and have found the digression in praise of Cardinal Federigo Borromeo (Chapter 22) an awkward intrusion of pulpit oratory. The novel's coy treatment of sex, despite the centrality of Lucia's sexuality to the whole plot, has also been seen by certain readers (Jean-François Revel, for instance) as a sign of the text's excess of Catholic morality. It is true that certain discussions of the book, including that of Lukács, manage not to mention the religious element at all, but these are rare indeed.

What all these strands of the narrative add up to is a plural and disparate text, one in which the author is doing many things, performing different narrative functions, which involve him in diverse kinds of writing. Italo Calvino said it could be considered 'a polynovel in which various novels follow and cross over one another'. Sometimes these strands intertwine and work simultaneously; at other times the text switches from one to the other by means of digressions or parallel action, as in some film narratives. Much of the critical debate over Manzoni's novel since it was published has been directed towards establishing whether these different strands, the different types of writing, come together to produce a unified and coherent whole (for instance whether the history meshes with the fiction or pulls away from it – Manzoni himself felt this to be a problem) or whether one type (the social or psychological realism, the Gothic romance with its stereotypes and coincidences, the Catholic ideology) predominates over others. A whole tradition of criticism in Italy, from the mid-nineteenth to the mid-twentieth century, was influenced by the broadly Romantic aesthetics of Hegel (as mediated by the great nineteenth-century critic Francesco De Sanctis and subsequently by Benedetto Croce) according to which for a work of art or literature to be successful its raw 'content' (for instance abstract ideas and ideologies) must merge with and be wholly assimilated into its 'form'. De Sanctis himself felt that Manzoni had achieved this, but other critics, including Croce, dissented. In Manzoni, they held, there was an excess of raw Catholic 'oratory' or a residue of unassimilated raw history, or both. Croce, in addition, saw Manzoni as a poor historian, moralizing about the past and obsessed with quibbles over the interpretation of particular events rather than dealing impassively with the facts and having a grasp of the broad movement of history. Behind many of these critical arguments over Manzoni lies the running battle in modern Italian culture between Catholic and secular (or anti-clerical) ideologies, even though the arguments are not simply reducible to positions in this battle.

Not all these arguments and judgements are necessarily wrong – indeed some of them are persuasive – but I would claim that they have tended to produce closed readings of Manzoni's text, readings which have either broken it up into disconnected elements or, conversely, stitched it all together too neatly. Most of them are founded on the assumption that it is a good thing for a text to be coherent and unified, and that Manzoni's text ought to conform to this principle. Many of them assume that it is an aesthetic flaw if a novel contains too much 'real history', or if its narrator moralizes too much, or if the story strays too far from verisimilitude. But why should this be so? To treat a text in this way is not only to perform the questionable operation of seeking to improve or rewrite it rather than to understand and criticize it as it is, but also to remain imprisoned in those late eighteenth- and nineteenth-century categories and norms, such as 'coherence', 'wholeness', 'organic', 'historical truth' versus fictional 'verisimilitude'. It is also to posit the author as a simple, unified, coherent and stable subject.

But Manzoni was not a coherent subject. For much of his life, and most intensely during the twenty years in which he was intermittently involved in writing his novel, he was caught between competing intellectual and spiritual allegiances, conflicting desires and impulses. On the one hand he had grown up in the intellectual orbit of the Milanese Enlightenment and later moved in the liberal circles influenced by the moderate wing of the French Revolution (he maintained contacts in France throughout his life and much of his correspondence was written in French). His mother, Giulia Beccaria, was the daughter of Cesare Beccaria, the author of a treatise on penal reform, *Dei delitti e delle pene* (*Of Crimes and Punishments*, 1764), which had made an impact throughout Enlightenment Europe. Giulia's lover at the time Alessandro was born in 1785, and the latter's putative biological father, was Giovanni Verri, the younger brother of Pietro Verri. The guiding principle of the Milanese *illuministi* was that all human institutions and arrangements, from the economy and fiscal system to the state, the law and education, were capable of reform and improvement along rational lines by non-violent means. In moral terms, this view involved a utilitarian ethic, according to which human affairs could be regulated with mathematical precision so as to maximize goodness and pleasure and minimize evil and pain. Beccaria and Pietro Verri both argued for radical changes in the law and penal code, including the abolition of torture and of the death penalty, on the grounds of utility as well as humanity. On the other hand, Manzoni, from 1810 onwards, was a convert to Christianity (to be precise, a re-convert, since he had been baptized a Catholic before growing up as a freethinker) who embraced the Christian faith with great commitment, wrote an elaborate defence of Catholic morality (*Osservazioni sulla morale cattolica*, 1819–20) to refute the charges of the Swiss historian Sismondi that the Catholic Church had played a wholly negative role in medieval Italy and to repudiate utilitarian ethics, and, in later life, came to abjure the writing of works of 'poetry' and 'invention' (including novels, and thus by implication his own novel) as an idle occupation incompatible with moral, historical and religious truth.

It is certainly possible to see Manzoni as reconciling Enlightenment rationalism, liberalism and Christian faith in a coherent manner, just as it is possible to see him working out a coherent position on the historical novel. Kenelm Foster wrote with great elegance and conviction in 1967 of Manzoni as a Christian rationalist, his feet planted squarely on this earth, interested in human affairs and discerning God's traces within humanity. I would suggest, though, that this view smoothes over too neatly the contradictions that a 'Christian rationalism' or 'Christian humanism' can produce and did produce in Manzoni. It is actually very difficult to square the Enlightenment and liberal view of human actions as shaped and constrained by contingent institutions and beliefs, so that progressive reforms of those institutions will enable people to behave better towards one another, with a Christian view of human actions as the effect of individual conscience, of good or bad dispositions, of faith or lack of faith, all of which are taken to be relatively unchanging and indifferent to the social institutions of the moment. Similarly, it is very difficult for a historian to reconcile the notion, virtually a touchstone of all nineteenth-century historicisms, that societies evolve and that the present is therefore substantially different from the past, with the view that the capability of humans to act well or badly is much the same in all times and places. Yet it seems that Manzoni wanted to hold both these views simultaneously, to have it both ways. In the text of *The Betrothed* these contradictory positions are on display.

Twentieth-century literary criticism and theory has accustomed us to seeing literary texts as complex structures made up of plots and stories, characters, actions, devices, conventions and motifs, narrators who tell the story and 'focalizers' through whom the reader 'sees' events. It has also accustomed us to seeing authors no longer as the originators and guarantors of their texts' meanings but as writers who attempt to give shape to a language and to literary conventions and ideologies which are not of their own making and which tend to offer resistance to their efforts. Nineteenth-century novels are characteristically multi-purpose texts: they moralize, inform us about history, seek to amuse us, provide a view of human character, voice opinions about appropriate sexual and moral behaviour, make political judgements. Manzoni's novel bears out well the claim of Russian critic Mikhail Bakhtin that the discourse of the novel is inherently hybrid, made up of a mingling of many different voices and types of language. It is possible to argue (as the critic Vittorio Spinazzola has done) that the controlling presence of the narrator in *The Betrothed* is excessive. Yet it is also possible to argue (like Giovanni Macchia), that the author cannot fully control all the elements he brings into contact with one another, that he is obliged repeatedly to digress in an effort to bring his heterogeneous material into one place. Manzoni, that is to say, may have wanted to give his text artistic and ideological coherence, but there is much in it that resists such closure.

DAVID FORGACS

NOTE ON THE TEXT

The Betrothed (*I promessi sposi*) was Manzoni's only novel. It occupied him, on and off, for twenty years, from his mid-thirties to his mid-fifties. He wrote a first draft between 1821 and 1823. He never published this version (now known as *Fermo e Lucia*) in his lifetime but there have been several editions since his death; in the introduction to a recent one (Milan, SugarCo, 1992) veteran Manzoni scholar Giancarlo Vigorelli says 'Manzoni did not write two drafts of the same novel, as critics would still have us believe, but two quite different novels.' He reworked this version extensively to produce the first published edition of the novel (1825–7). Subsequently he made linguistic changes to the text, most of them guided by the principle that it should conform to the Italian spoken by educated people in contemporary Tuscany rather than to the traditional literary language or to that of his native Lombardy. These changes were incorporated into the second edition, which is the one translated here; it was published in instalments in 1840–2, with the appendix on the *History of the Column of Infamy* (*Storia della colonna infame*), which had not been included in the first edition. This is the first English-language edition since 1845 to reproduce the appendix together with the novel in accordance with Manzoni's definitive edition. The translation of the novel adopted is Archibald Colquhoun's, first published in Everyman's Library in 1951 and subsequently revised three times by Colquhoun himself. It has been substantially revised and annotated for this edition by Matthew Reynolds. The translation of the appendix is that of Kenelm Foster, originally published (as *The Column of Infamy*) by Oxford University Press in 1964 (the volume also contains a translation by Jane Grigson of Cesare Beccaria's treatise on penal reform *Of Crimes and Punishments*); it has been revised and annotated for this edition by David Forgacs. The Italian text used is that edited by Alberto Chiari and Fausto Ghisalberti in *Tutte le opere di Alessandro Manzoni*, Volume II/i (Mondadori, Milan, 1954).

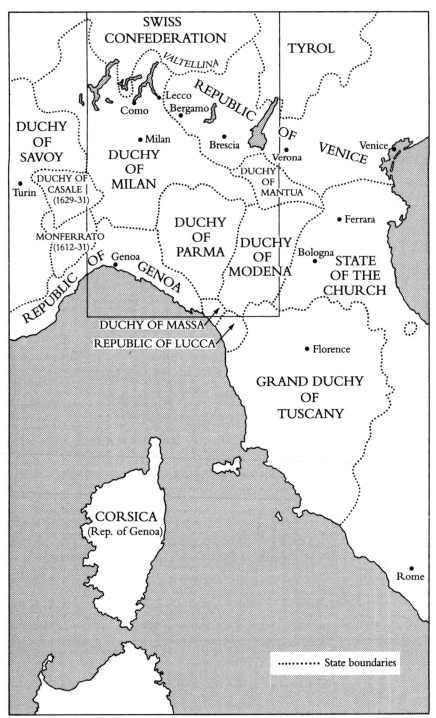

Northern and Central Italy c.1630

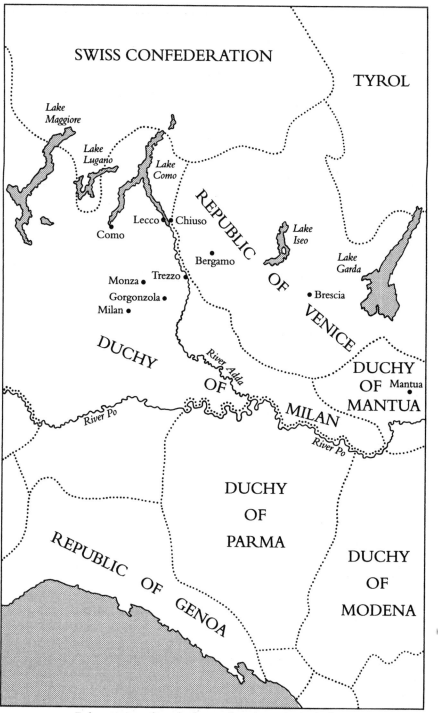

Enlargement of marked area showing principal places
mentioned in *The Betrothed*

THE BETROTHED

A MILANESE HISTORY OF THE
SEVENTEENTH CENTURY
DISCOVERED AND REWORKED
BY
ALESSANDRO MANZONI
EDITION REVISED BY
THE AUTHOR

AUTHOR'S INTRODUCTION

Historie may be verilie defined as a mightie war against Time, for snatching from his hands the years emprisoned, nay already slain by him, she calleth them back unto life, passeth them in review, and rangeth them once more in battle array. But the illustrious Champions who garner Palms and Laurels in this Arena bear off only the richest and most brilliant of the spoils, embalming in their ink the enterprises of Princes, Potentates, and mightie Personnages, and embroidering with the fine needle of their genius the threads of gold and silk which form an eternal tapestrie of glorious Deeds. To such arguments and perilous sublimities, ranging amid the Labyrinths of political Intrigue and the blare of warlike Trumpets, my feeble pen cannot, however, aspire; onlie, having learned of certain memorable events, though they be but concerned with persons of small import and low degree, I would fain preserve their memorie for Posteritie by setting down a clear, accurate and complete Account or Recital of them. Wherein will be seen, on a narrow Stage, grievous Tragedies of horror and Scenes of fearful wickedness, with interludes of Deeds of virtue and angelick goodness contrasted with these diabolick machinations. And verilie, considering that these climes of ours be under the sway of our Lord the most Catholick King, that neversetting Sun, and that over them also shineth with reflected Light that never-waning Moon, the Heroe of noble Lineage who ruleth pro-tempore in his place, and with him those fixèd stars the Magnificent Senators, and with them, spreading light in all directions like the wandering planets the other Worshipful Magistrates, thus forming a most glorious Firmament;* verilie then, there is no other cause to be found, on seeing this heaven changed into a hell of dark deeds, wickedness and crueltie practised more and more by rash men, but diabolick arts and agencies, as human evil could never by itself suffice to resist so many Heroes labouring ceaselessly for the publick weal with the eyes of Argus and the arms of Briarius.* For which reason, when setting forth *this Narrative of events that occurred in the times of my verdant youth, although the greater part of the personnages who play their parts therein have left the Stage of this World, and rendered themselves tributaries to the Fates, I shall, out of proper respect, withhold their names, that is their patronimicks, and do likewise with the names of places, onlie indicating the districts generaliter. Nor let anyone maintain that this be an imperfection in my Narrative or a deformity in this my rough progeny unless such a Critick be lacking in all Philosophie; for such as are versed in the latter will clearly see that nothing in the substance of the said Narrative is lacking. Foreasmuch as it be a thing self-evident and denied by none that names be nought but the purest of accidents....*

– But when I've had the heroic patience to transcribe this story from this scratched and faded manuscript, and brought it to light, as the saying goes, will I then find anyone with enough patience to read it? – *

This misgiving, born in the throes of deciphering a great blotch after the word *accidents*, made me suspend my copying and think more seriously about the best course to take. – It's true, of course – said I to myself, turning over the pages of the manuscript – it's true, of course, that this hail of conceits and metaphors doesn't go on as thickly as this throughout the whole work. The good man wanted, in his seventeenth century way, to show off his virtuosity at the start; but later on, in the course of the narrative, the style runs along much more naturally and smoothly, sometimes for long stretches at a time. Yes that's true; but, then, how commonplace and uncouth it is! What a lot of mistakes there are in it! Endless Lombard idioms, current phrases used wrongly, arbitrary grammar, sentences that don't hang together; then Spanish pomposities scattered about here and there; and, worst of all, at the most sublime or tragic points of the story, at anything arousing wonder or reflection – at all those passages, in short, that call for a bit of eloquence, to be sure, but an eloquence used with moderation, delicacy, and tact, he falls back unfailingly into the style of that opening preamble. And then, bringing together the most opposing qualities with remarkable ability, he manages to be at once crude and affected in the same page, the same sentence, the same word. Here it all is: that bombastic declamation, full of vulgar solecisms and with that clumsy pretension everywhere which is the characteristic of the writing of that century, in this country. It really isn't a work fit to present to readers of the present day; they're too sophisticated and too surfeited with this kind of extravaganza. It's lucky that the thought occurred to me at the outset of this grinding labour, and I wash my hands of it.

But just as I was closing up the tattered manuscript before putting it away, I felt a pang of regret that so beautiful a story should remain for ever unknown; for as a story (the reader may think differently) it seemed beautiful to me, yes, very beautiful. Why – I thought – couldn't the sequence of events be taken from the manuscript and the language recast? – Since no reasonable objection presented itself, I adopted this course forthwith. And there you have the origin of the present book, stated with a frankness equal to the importance of the book itself.

Some, however, of these events, and certain of the customs described by our author, seemed so novel, so odd – to put it mildly – that before placing any faith in them I decided to consult other witnesses; and I set to work rummaging among the records of that period, to make sure the world really went like that then. This research dispelled all my doubts: at every step I stumbled across similar things and even worse: and, what seemed still more conclusive, I even found a few characters of whose existence, never having met them outside our manuscript, I had been in doubt. I will cite some of these witnesses as the need arises, to vouch for things which the reader might, from their very strangeness, be most inclined to disbelieve.

But having rejected our author's style as intolerable, what kind of style have we substituted for it ourselves? That's the point.

Anyone setting himself to refashion another's work without being asked must be prepared to render a strict account of his own, even, in a way, contracts an obligation to do so; and this is a rule, both *de facto* and *de jure*, from which we in no way expect to be dispensed. We had intended, in fact, in order to conform to it with a good grace, giving detailed reasons here for the style of writing we have adopted: and with this object in view we have been trying during the whole of our labours to foresee every possible and probable criticism, with a view to refuting them all in advance. Nor would this have presented any difficulty, for (we must say in all truth) not a single criticism occurred to us without bringing a triumphant answer along with it, one of those answers which I wouldn't say solve problems, but change them. Often, also, we matched two criticisms up against each other, and made one knock the other out: or, after probing them deeply and comparing them carefully, we succeeded in discovering and showing that, opposed as they might be in appearance, they were of the same kind, and both arose from a careless disregard of the facts and principles on which a judgement should be based: so, lumping them together, to their great surprise, we sent them packing. Never would an author have produced such conclusive evidence of his being in the right. But, alas, when we were just going to put all these objections and all the replies to the objections together to get them into some sort of order, why, heavens, they came to a book in themselves. Seeing which, we gave up the idea, for two reasons with which the reader is sure to agree: the first, that a book written to justify another book – not to mention the style of another book – might seem rather ridiculous; the second, that one book at a time is enough, if indeed it is not too much. *

CHAPTER I

That branch of the lake of Como which extends southwards
between two unbroken chains of mountains, and is all bays and
gulfs as the mountains advance and recede, narrows down at one
point into the form of a river, between a promontory on one side
and a wide shore on the other; and the bridge which here links
the two banks seems to emphasize this transformation, and to
mark the point at which the lake ends and the Adda begins, only
to become a lake once more where the banks draw farther apart
again, letting the water broaden out and expand into new gulfs
and bays. The country bordering the lake, formed by the deposits
of three great torrents, is backed by two neighbouring mountains,
one called San Martino, and the other, in the Lombard dialect,
the *Resegone*, from its saw-like row of peaks; so that on first
seeing it so long as it is in profile – looking northwards, for
instance, from the ramparts of Milan – one can pick it out at
once, on the name alone, from the vast and lengthy range of
other mountains of obscurer name and more ordinary form. For
a considerable stretch the country rises slowly and continuously;
then it breaks up into little hills and valleys and into steep and
level tracts, following the structure of the two mountains and the
erosion of the water. The shore itself, intersected by the beds of
torrents, is almost entirely gravel and pebbles; the rest is fields
and vineyards, and scattered towns, villages and farms, with here
and there a wood extending right on up the mountain-side.
Lecco, which is the largest of these towns and gives its name to
the district, lies on the lakeside not far from the bridge, and is
even apt to find itself partly in the lake when this is high; it is a
big town nowadays, well on the way to becoming a city. At the
time of the events which we are about to describe, this township
which was already of some importance, was also fortified, and so
had the honour of housing a commandant and the advantage of
a permanent garrison of Spanish soldiers, who taught modesty to
the wives and daughters of the town, tickled up the shoulders of
an occasional husband and father, and, towards the end of
summer, never failed to scatter themselves among the vineyards,
to thin out the grapes and lighten the labours of the vintage for
the peasants. Paths and tracks used to run – and still do – from

one to another of these villages, from the mountain heights to the lakeside, and from one precipice to the other. Sometimes they run steep, sometimes level, and often drop suddenly and bury themselves between two walls, from which, when one looks up, only a patch of sky and some mountain peak can be discerned. Sometimes they come out on open terraces; thence the eye ranges over prospects of varying extent, always full of interest and always changing, as each point of vantage takes in different aspects of the vast landscape, and as one part or the other is foreshortened, or stands out, or disappears. One can see a piece here, another there, and then again a long stretch of that great varied mirror of the water; on this side the lake is shut in at one end, or rather lost among the ins and outs and groupings of the mountains, then spreads out again between more mountains, unfolding one by one, and reflected upside down in the water with the villages on the shores; on the other side is more river, then lake, then river again, losing itself in a shining coil among the mountains, which follow it, getting smaller and smaller until they too are almost lost in the horizon. The very spot from which so many different views can be seen itself appears in views from every side. The mountain on whose foothills you are walking unfolds its cliffs and pinnacles above and around you, each standing out on its own and changing at every step, turning what had just seemed a single ridge into a whole series of ridges, and showing on a height something that a moment before had seemed down on the shore; the quiet and cosy character of these foothills pleasantly tempers the wildness around, and is a foil for the grandeur of the rest of the landscape.

Down one of these paths, homeward bound from his stroll in the evening of the 7th of November of the year 1628, came Don Abbondio, the parish priest of one of the villages mentioned above; the manuscript does not give the name of the village or the surname of our character, here or later. He was calmly saying his office, every now and again, between one psalm and another, closing his breviary and leaving the index finger of his right hand in it as a bookmarker. Then he would clasp this hand in the other behind his back, look at the ground, and with one foot kick away towards the wall the pebbles which littered the path; then raise his head, let his eyes wander idly around and come to rest on part of a mountain which the rays of the setting sun, shining through the clefts of the mountain opposite were painting with large, irregular splashes of purple here and there on the outstanding bluffs. After which he opened his breviary again and recited another passage, and so came to a turn of the path where he was in the habit of raising his eyes from his book and glancing ahead of him: and he did the same that day. After the turning the path ran straight for about seventy yards or so, and then forked into two little tracks like an upsilon: the one to the right went up towards the mountains, and was the way to his parish; the other branched down to a torrent in the valley; on this side the wall was only waist-high to passers-by. The inner walls of the two paths, instead of joining up at the angle, ended in a shrine, on which were painted long, snaky shapes with pointed ends, supposed, in the mind of the artist and to the eyes of the local inhabitants, to represent flames; alternating with the flames were other shapes defying description, and these were meant to be souls in purgatory; souls and flames were painted in brick-colour on a greyish background, with the plaster flaked off here and there. As he turned the corner the priest glanced towards the shrine in his usual way, and saw something that was both unexpected and unwelcome. Opposite each other where the paths flowed, as it were, together, were two men: one of them was astride the low wall, with one leg dangling outwards and the other on the path; his companion was standing leaning against the wall, with his arms crossed on his chest. Their dress and manner, and what the priest from where he was could see of their faces, left no room for doubt as to their profession. On his head each wore a green net hanging over the left shoulder and ending in a large tassel; from this net a heavy lock of hair fell over their foreheads. They had long mustachios curled up at the ends; shining leather belts on which hung a brace of pistols; a small powder-horn dangled like a locket on their chests; the handle of a knife showed from a pocket of their loose wide breeches; they had rapiers with big, gleaming, furbished hilts of pierced brass, worked in monograms. It was obvious at first glance that they were men of the class known as bravi.

This class, now quite extinct, was then flourishing in Lombardy, and was already of considerable antiquity. Here, for the reader who may know little about it, are a few genuine examples, which may give an idea of its chief characteristics, of the efforts made to exterminate it, and of its obstinate and luxuriant vitality.*

On the 8th of April of the year 1583, the Most Illustrious and Most Excellent Don Carlo D'Aragon, Prince of Castelvetrano,

Duke of Terranuova, Marquis of Avola, Grand Admiral and Grand Constable of Sicily, Governor of Milan, and Captain-General of His Catholic Majesty in Italy,* '*fully aware of the intolerable state of misery in which this city of Milan has lived and is still living, by reason of the bravi and vagabonds*', published an edict against them. '*He declares and defines as being included in this ban as bravi and vagabonds ... all those, foreigners or otherwise, who have no settled occupation, or if they have any, do not exercise it ... but instead, engage themselves with or without payment, to some cavalier or nobleman, officer or merchant ... to render him aid and service, or, verily, as there is cause to presume, to plot against others. ...*' All these he orders to leave the country, within six days, on pain of the galleys, and gives all officers of justice the most extraordinarily wide and indefinite powers to carry out the order. But in the following year, on the 12th of April, the same nobleman, observing '*that this city is still full of the said bravi ... living as they did before, their ways wholly unchanged and their numbers undiminished*', issues another, even more energetically and vigorously phrased proclamation, in which, among other things, he orders:

'*That if any person at all, either of this city or a foreigner, shall be proved by the testimony of two witnesses, either to be, or to be commonly held to be, a bravo, and to have that reputation, even if he is not proved to have committed any crime ... may, solely on his reputation as a bravo, without other evidence be put by the said judges or by any one of them to the torture and the rack, in order to get further information ... and, although he may not confess to any crime, is even so to be sent to the galleys for three years, solely for being considered and having the reputation of a bravo, as aforesaid*'. All this (and more that is omitted) '*because His Excellency is determined to be obeyed by everyone*'.

Hearing such bold and confident words from so great a noble, and such orders going with them, one would be very much inclined to think that all the bravi disappeared for ever at their very sound. But the evidence of a nobleman no less authoritative and no less endowed with titles obliges us to believe quite the contrary. He was the Most Illustrious and Most Excellent Don Juan Fernandez de Velasco, Constable of Castile, Senior Chamberlain to His Majesty, Duke of the City of Frias, Count of Haro and Castelnovo, Lord of the House of Velasco, and of that of the

Seven Infantes of Lara, Governor of the State of Milan, etc. On the 5th of June of the year 1593, he also being fully aware '*how much harm and ruin is done by . . . the bravi and vagabonds, and of the great mischief this kind of person is to the public weal, in contempt of justice*', warns them once more that they must quit the country within six days, and repeats almost word for word the same measures and threats as used by his predecessor. Then on the 23rd of May of the year 1598, '*being informed with no little displeasure that . . . the number of these persons*' [bravi and vagabonds] '*is increasing day by day in this City and State, and that nothing is heard of them, day and night, but woundings, homicide, robbery, and crimes of every description, which they commit with the more ease because they are confident of the support of their masters and favourers . . .*', prescribes the same remedies again, increasing the dose as they do with obstinate diseases. '*Let everyone, therefore,*' he concludes, '*be fully on his guard against contravening the present decree in any way, or instead of His Excellency showing them his clemency, he will show them his severity and wrath . . . for he is resolved and determined that this shall be the last and peremptory warning.*'

But this opinion was not shared by the Most Illustrious and Most Excellent Lord, Don Pedro Enriques de Acevedo, Count of Fuentes, Captain and Governor of the State of Milan, and with good reason. '*Fully aware of the misery in which this City and State is living because of the great number of bravi who abound in it . . . and resolved utterly to uproot this pernicious seed*', he issues, on the 5th of December 1600, a new decree, full of severe penalties, '*with the firm intention that they will be carried out in their entirety, with all severity, and no hope of remission*'.

One is bound to think, however, that he did not throw himself into this with all the hearty goodwill he knew how to muster in plotting and stirring up trouble against his great enemy, Henry IV.* For history shows how he succeeded in arming the Duke of Savoy against that monarch, causing him thereby the loss of more than one city: and how he succeeded in bringing the Duke of Biron into a conspiracy, causing him thereby the loss of his head.* But, as for that pernicious seed, the bravi, it is quite certain that it was still sprouting on the 22nd of September of the year 1612. On that day the Most Illustrious and Most Excellent Lord, Don Juan de Mendozza, Marquis of Hynojosa, Nobleman, etc., Governor, etc., gave serious thought to their extirpation. To this end he sent off to the royal printers, Pandolfo and Marco

Tullio Malatesti, the usual decree, corrected and enlarged, for them to print, and so exterminate the bravi. But enough of these still survived on the 24th of December of the year 1618, to get the same and even heavier knocks from the Most Illustrious and Most Excellent Lord, Don Gomez Suarez de Figueroa, Duke of Feria, etc., Governor, etc. But as even these were not enough to kill them off, the Most Illustrious and Most Excellent Lord, the Lord Gonzalo Fernandez de Cordova, under whose governorship Don Abbondio's walk took place, had had to revise and republish the usual decree against the bravi, on the fifth day of October of 1627 – that is, one year, one month, and two days before that memorable event.

Nor was this the last publication; but we do not feel we need mention the later ones, as they lie outside the period of our story. We will only note one of the 13th of February of the year 1632, in which the Most Illustrious and Most Excellent Lord, 'and Duke of Feria', governor for the second time, tells us that 'the worst crimes are committed by the persons called bravi'. This is enough to prove that there were still bravi at the time of which we write.

That the pair described above were on the look-out for someone was all too obvious; but what was more unwelcome to Don Abbondio was the realization, from certain actions of theirs, that the person they were looking out for was himself. The moment he appeared they had exchanged glances and raised their heads with a movement which showed that both of them had suddenly exclaimed: 'Here's our man.' The one astride the wall had got up and swung his other leg on to the path: the other had detached himself from the wall: and both began to move towards him. He still held his breviary open in front of him, as though reading, and kept glancing ahead to watch their movements; and when he saw them coming straight towards him, a thousand thoughts came rushing suddenly into his head. He asked himself hurriedly if there were any path opening out to right or left between the bravi and himself; he saw at once that there was none. He made a rapid check to see whether he had offended anyone powerful or anyone vindictive; but even in this moment of alarm the consoling testimony of his conscience somewhat reassured him: yet the bravi were drawing near, and eyeing him fixedly. He put the index and middle finger of his left hand inside his collar as though he wanted to adjust it, and, running the two fingers round his neck, turned his head, twisting his mouth in the same direction, and looked as far as he could out of the corner of his eye to see if there was anyone coming; but no one was to be seen. He glanced over the low wall into the fields; no one: and again, more timidly, at the path ahead of him: no one but the bravi. What was he to do? There was no time to turn back; and to run for it was the same as asking to be pursued, or worse. As he could not avoid the danger, he hurried to meet it, for these seconds of uncertainty had already become so painful to him that all he longed for was to cut them short. He quickened his pace, recited a verse in a louder voice, set his face into as easy and cheerful an expression as he could muster, and made every effort to work up a smile. When he found himself face to face with the two worthies he said to himself, 'Here we go,' and stopped short in his tracks. 'Sir!' said one of them, staring him straight in the face.

'What can I do for you?' Don Abbondio answered at once, raising his eyes from his book, which remained propped up in both hands as if it were on a lectern.

'You're intending,' went on the other, with the threatening and angry manner of one catching out an inferior in the act of committing some offence – 'you're intending to marry Renzo Tramaglino and Lucia Mondella tomorrow?'

'That's,' answered Don Abbondio in a quavering voice – 'that's to say ... well, you gentlemen are men of the world, and know just how these things go. The poor priest doesn't come into it: people get things up on their own, and then ... then come to us as they'd go to the bank: and we ... we're just servants of the public.'

'Look here,' said the bravo at his ear, but in a solemn and commanding tone, 'this marriage isn't going to happen, not tomorrow nor any other day.'

'But, my dear sirs,' replied Don Abbondio in the gentle, soothing voice of one trying to persuade an impatient man – 'but, my dear sirs, do be so good as to put yourselves into my shoes. If it depended on me ... you know quite well I don't get anything out of it. . . .'

'Come on,' interrupted the bravo. 'If this had to be decided by chatter you'd have us all tied up in a minute. We don't know and don't want to know any more about it. A man forewarned is ... You get our meaning?'

'But you gentlemen are too fair, too reasonable . . .'

'But . . . but . . .' broke in the other bravo, who had not spoken before – 'but there'll be no marriage or . . .' here he gave a round oath – 'or whoever does it won't regret it, because he won't have time to and . . .' Another oath.

'Shut up . . .' went on the first speaker. 'His reverence is a man who knows the ways of the world; we're gentlemen, and don't want to do him any harm, as long as he's sensible. Your reverence, our master the most illustrious Lord Don Rodrigo sends you his kind regards.'

This name had the effect on Don Abbondio's mind of a flash of lightning at the height of a night-storm, illuminating everything for a confused second, and increasing the atmosphere of terror. As though instinctively, he made a low bow and said, 'If you could suggest . . .'

'What, suggest anything to a man who knows Latin!' interrupted the bravo again, with a laugh part savage and part uncouth. 'It's up to you. And above all don't you let out a word about this advice we've given you for your own good; or . . . ahem . . . it'd be the same as doing that marriage. Come on, what d'you want us to tell the most illustrious Don Rodrigo in your name?'

'My respectful . . .'

'Be clearer.'

'. . . Ready . . . always ready to obey . . .' And as he uttered these words, he himself was not at all clear if he was making a promise or paying a compliment. The bravi took them, or pretended to take them, at their more definite meaning.

'That's fine; and good night to you, sir,' said one of them, starting to set off with his companion. Don Abbondio, who a few seconds before would have given an eye from his head to get rid of them, now felt like prolonging the conversation and negotiations. 'Gentlemen . . .' he began, shutting his book with both hands; but without listening to him they took the path along which he had come, and were soon away, singing a low song which I would prefer not to set down. Poor Don Abbondio was left standing a moment with his mouth open, as if under a spell; then he took the path on the fork leading to his home, hardly managing to put one leg in front of the other, for they seemed to have gone numb. The reader will understand his state of mind better when we have said something about his temperament and the conditions of the period in which it was his fate to live.

Don Abbondio (as the reader will already have gathered) was

not born with the heart of a lion. But from his earliest youth he had observed that in those times no one was in a more awkward situation than an animal without tusks or claws, who yet was reluctant to be devoured. The laws afforded no protection of any kind to the quiet, inoffensive person, who had no means of making others fear him. Not that there was any lack of laws and penalties against personal violence. Laws, on the contrary, came pouring down: crimes were described and listed in the minutest detail and at greatest length; punishments were absurdly exorbitant, and, what is more, could be increased in almost every case at the will of any magistrate and of hundreds of other officials; legal procedure was arranged entirely so as to free the judge from anything that might hamper him in making a condemnation. The extracts we have given from the decrees against the bravi are a small but accurate example. In spite of this, or rather in many ways because of this, these decrees, which were reinforced and republished by governor after governor, only succeeded, with all their bombast, in making obvious the impotence of their authors. Their immediate effect, if any, was to add more vexations to those which the peaceful and weak already had to suffer at the hands of the turbulent, and to increase the latter's violence and cunning. Impunity was organized and had roots which the decrees did not touch, or could not move. The sanctuaries and privileges of certain classes, for example, were partly recognized by the law, partly tolerated in resentful silence, or opposed by vain protests, while they were upheld and defended by those classes with watchful energy and jealous punctilio. Now this impunity of theirs was threatened and attacked, but not destroyed, by the decrees, and at every threat and attack it naturally tended to make new efforts and find new ways to preserve itself. This was in fact what happened; as the decrees designed to suppress the violent appeared, these began to show their real strength and use any means that came to hand to go on doing what the decrees had just forbidden. The latter, on the other hand, had the effect of hampering at each turn and molesting the honest citizen with no power or protector of his own; for in trying to keep a tight hand on everyone, so as to punish or prevent any breach of the peace, they subjected the private citizen's every move to the arbitrary will of officials of every kind. But anyone who had taken the precaution, before committing a crime, to have a timely refuge ready in a monastery, or a palace where the police would not dare to set foot; anyone

who had taken no other precaution than wearing a livery which
bound the vanity and interests of some powerful family to defend
him, and so an entire section of society – such men were free to
do exactly as they liked, and could afford to laugh at all the
thunder of the decrees. Some who were assigned to carry these
out themselves belonged by birth to the privileged sections of
society, others were dependent on them for patronage; all were
on the side of the great by education, interests, habits, and
imitation, and would have been very careful not to offend them
simply on account of a piece of paper stuck up at the street-
corner. The men charged with the immediate execution of the
edicts could never have succeeded, even had they been as
resourceful as heroes, as obedient as monks, or as devoted as
martyrs, inferior as they were in numbers to those they were
supposed to suppress. They had, what is more, every likelihood
of being sacrificed and abandoned by those who, in the abstract
and, as it were, in theory, had given them their orders. But, apart
from that, these men were among the lowest and most squalid
creatures of their time; their job was held in contempt even by
those who should have feared it, and their very name was a term
of abuse. So it was not to be wondered at if, instead of risking,
indeed throwing away, their lives in a desperate enterprise, they
sold their inactivity and even their connivance to those with
power, reserving the use of their hated authority, and what
strength they did have, for the occasions when there was no
danger; for oppressing and grinding down, that is, peaceful,
defenceless citizens.

He who is out to cause trouble, or expects to be troubled
himself at any moment, is apt to look around for allies and
comrades. Hence at this period the tendency for individuals to
band themselves together in groups, form new ones, and get as
much power as they could for the group to which they belonged,
was enormously on the increase. The clergy were preoccupied
with defending and extending their immunity, the nobles their
privileges, and the military their exemptions. The merchants and
artisans were enrolled in unions and confraternities, the lawyers
formed a league, even the doctors had a corporation. Each of
these little oligarchies had its own special powers; in each of
them the individual enjoyed the advantages of being able to use
for himself, in proportion to his own authority and ability, the
united powers of the many. The most honest used these advantages only for defence; the cunning and criminal took advantage

of them to carry through abuses for which their personal resources were not sufficient, and to ensure their own impunity. But the powers of these various leagues were very unequal. The wealthy and turbulent noble – particularly in the country – surrounded by his troop of bravi and by peasants who were bound to him by family tradition and forced by interest or necessity to regard themselves almost as the subjects and soldiers of their master, wielded a power which no other kind of league could easily withstand.

Our Abbondio, who was not noble, nor rich – still less courageous – had realized, almost before he reached the age of reason, that in this society he was like an earthenware pot forced to travel among a lot of iron ones. So he had been very willing to obey his parents when they wanted him to become a priest. He had not, in point of fact, given much thought to the duties and noble aims of the office to which he was dedicating himself: to assure himself a way of living in some comfort, and to put himself in a class which was both strong and respected, had seemed to him two reasons which were more than sufficient for making such a choice. But no class can protect or look after the individual beyond a certain point; he must always set up his own private system of defence. Don Abbondio was continuously absorbed in thinking about his own peace and quiet, and had not bothered about advantages which were to be enjoyed only at the cost of a good deal of bother or a small amount of risk. His system consisted chiefly in avoiding all quarrels, and of giving way in those which he could not avoid: unarmed neutrality in all the struggles which broke out around him, from the controversies (very frequent at that time) between the clergy and the lay power, between military and civilians, between noble and noble, down to the scuffle between two peasants, started by a word and settled with fists or knives. If he found himself absolutely forced to take sides between two contending parties, he went with the stronger, but always in the rearguard, whence he tried to show the other that he was against him through no will of his own; but why, he seemed to be saying, aren't you the stronger; then I'd have come in on your side! By keeping well away from the arrogant, pretending not to notice their persecutions when they were only short-lived and capricious, and complying submissively when they were more serious and deliberate; by cajoling, with his bows and air of jovial respect, a smile out of even the surliest and most contemptuous when he met them on the road, the poor man had succeeded in passing his sixtieth year without running into any bad storms.

Not that he too did not have his share of bile; that continual exercise of patience, that agreeing so often with other people, all the bitter mouthfuls he had swallowed in silence, had gradually exasperated him to such a point that, had he not been able to let himself go now and again, his health would certainly have suffered. But as, after all, there were, when it came to the point, people in the world, and near him too, who he knew were absolutely incapable of doing him any harm, he was sometimes able to let out on them the ill-humour he had been repressing for so long, and indulge his own urge to have tantrums and do some unjust scolding. He was also a severe critic of those who did not behave as he did, but only when his criticism could be expressed without any danger, however remote. If a man was defeated, he had been rash, at the very least; if he got killed, he had always been a trouble-maker. If he stood up for himself against someone stronger and had his head split open as a result, he was always found to be in the wrong in some way by Don Abbondio; not a difficult thing to do, for right and wrong never divide up so neatly that any side can lay claim exclusively to one or the other. Above all, though, he denounced those of his brother-clergy who at their own risk took the side of the weak and oppressed against the tyrannical and strong. This he called rushing into trouble, or trying to straighten out a dog's leg; he would even say severely that this was getting mixed up with things profane and prejudicing the dignity of their holy office. Against all these he would inveigh, but only when he was alone with someone, or in a very small circle; and his vehemence on these occasions was in inverse proportion to the likelihood of his hearers resenting anything that concerned them personally. He had a favourite phrase with which he always ended his speeches on this subject: that unpleasant accidents do not happen to the honest man who keeps to himself and minds his own business.

Now, my five-and-twenty readers must just imagine the effect on the poor man's mind of the meeting we have described. Terror at those coarse faces and crude words; threats from a nobleman known never to threaten in vain; the sudden collapse of a system for living in peace which had cost him years of patience and study; a pass from which he could see no way out – all these thoughts were buzzing tumultuously through Don Abbondio's bowed head. If I could get rid of Renzo with a straight no, it'd be all right; but he'll want reasons; and what reasons, for heaven's sake, am I to give him? Oh ... oh ... oh ... he's headstrong too; as quiet as a lamb while left to himself, but if anyone puts his back up ... ugh ...! And then, and then, his head's quite turned by that girl Lucia, in love like ... What silly young fools they are, going and falling in love because they've got nothing better to do, and then wanting to get married, and not thinking about anything else. Little they care what trouble they let a poor honest man in for. Oh, poor me! Why should those two brutes go and plant themselves right in my path and take *me* on about it? Where do I come into it? Am I the one who wants to get married? Why didn't they go instead and talk to ... Oh, dear, what bad luck I've got! The right thing to say always comes into my head a minute after the chance's gone by. If only I'd thought of suggesting they should go and take their message ... But at this point he realized that to regret not having been an adviser in iniquity was itself rather too iniquitous, so he turned all the fury of his thoughts against the other person who had come and taken away his peace like this. He knew Don Rodrigo only by sight and reputation, and had never had anything to do with him, except to touch chin to chest and the ground with the brim of his hat the few times he had met him on the road. He had more than once found himself defending that man's reputation against people who were cursing one of his exploits under their breaths, with sighs and eyes raised to heaven. He must have said a hundred times that he was a respectable gentleman. But at that moment he called him in his heart by all the names that he had never heard others apply to him without hurriedly cutting them short with a 'Whoa, there'. Amidst this tumult of thoughts he reached the door of his home at the end of the village. He hurriedly put the key he had in his hand into the lock, opened the door, went in, shut it carefully behind him, and, longing to find himself in trustworthy company, called out at once: 'Perpetua! Perpetua!' making at the same time for the parlour, where she was sure to be laying the table for supper. Perpetua, as everyone will have realized, was Don Abbondio's servant: a faithful and devoted servant, who could obey orders and give them as the occasion required, put up for some time with her master's whims and grumbles, and make him put up with hers for some time too; these were becoming more and more frequent every day, since she had passed the canonical age of forty* and was still unmarried, because, according to her, she had refused every offer, and according to her women friends, she had never found even a dog willing to take her.

'Coming,' she replied, putting the little flask of Don Abbondio's favourite wine on the table in the usual place, and moving slowly in his direction. But before she had reached the parlour door in he came with a step so dragging and a look so clouded, a face so anguished, that it did not even need Perpetua's expert eyes to see at a glance that something really unusual had happened.

'Mercy on us! What's wrong, master?'

'Nothing, nothing,' replied Don Abbondio, letting himself drop, panting heavily, into his armchair.

'What, nothing? D'you expect me to believe that? You looking so upset and all! Something big's happened.'

'Oh, for heaven's sake! When I say nothing, either it *is* nothing, or it's something I can't talk about.'

'Something you can't even tell me? Who's going to look after your health? Who's to give you advice . . .'

'Oh, dear . . .! Do be quiet, and stop setting the table; give me a glass of wine.'

'And you trying to keep up that nothing's the matter,' said Perpetua, filling his glass, then holding it in her hand as if she intended giving it to him only in reward for the confidence which was so long in coming.

'Give it here . . . give it here,' said Don Abbondio, taking the glass with an unsteady hand, and emptying it quickly, as if it were medicine.

'So you want me to have to ask around to find out what's happened to my own master, do you?' said Perpetua, standing up in front of him with her arms akimbo and her elbows forward, and fixing him with a look as if she hoped to draw the secret out of his eyes.

'For heaven's sake! Don't go around gossiping and making a fuss. . . . It's a matter . . . it's a matter of life and death. . . .'

'Life and death!'

'Life and death.'

'You know perfectly well that whenever you've told me anything really frankly in confidence, I've never . . .'

'Oh really! Like that time . . .'

Perpetua realized she had struck a false note, so, quickly changing her tone: 'Master,' she said in a pathetic, melting voice, 'I've always been devoted to you, and if I want to know now, it's only out of consideration for you, so as to be able to help you and give you good advice, and cheer you up . . .'

The fact is that Don Abbondio was just as anxious to unburden himself of his woeful secret as Perpetua was to know it. And so, after repulsing more and more weakly a new series of pressing assaults from her, and after making her swear again and again that she would never breathe a word of it, finally, with many a pause, and many an alas, he told her the miserable tale. When he came to the fearful name of the man who was behind it, Perpetua had to take another and more solemn oath. And Don Abbondio, as he pronounced that name, flung himself back in his chair with a deep sigh, raised his hands in a gesture both of command and of entreaty, and said, 'For heaven's sake now!'

'Up to his usual tricks!' exclaimed Perpetua. 'Oh, the scoundrel! Oh, the bully! Oh, the godless man!'

'Be quiet, will you? Or d'you want to ruin me altogether?'

'Oh. We're alone here and no one can hear us. But what'll you do, my poor master?'

'There, you see,' said Don Abbondio in an angry voice. 'Just see what wonderful advice she gives me! She comes and asks me what I'm going to do, almost as if she was in this mess and it was up to me to get her out of it.'

'Well! I've got my own poor advice to give you, but then . . .'

'But then, but then. . . . Let's hear it.'

'My advice'd be: as everyone says our archbishop's a holy man, and a man with guts, too, who's not afraid of anyone, and just loves backing one of his parish priests and squashing one of these bullies, I'd say, write him a nice letter and tell him all about . . .'

'Be quiet, will you? Be quiet, will you? D'you think that's the kind of advice to give a poor man like me? When I might get a musket-shot in the back. . . . God save us! Could the archbishop put that right?'

'Oh! People don't scatter bullets like confetti; things would be in a bad way if these dogs bit every time they barked! And I've always seen them respect anyone who stands up to them and shows his teeth: but just because you never will stand up for yourself, we're reduced to this pass, when everyone feels they're free to . . .'

'Will you be quiet?'

'I'll be quiet in a minute, but it's a sure thing that when people realize a man's always ready at every encounter to haul down his bree . . .'

'Be quiet, will you? Is this the time to talk all this nonsense?'

'I've had my say; you just think it over tonight; but meanwhile don't go and make yourself ill and ruin your health; eat a mouthful . . .'

'Think it over!' grumbled Don Abbondio in reply. 'Of course I'll think it over; I've got enough to think over.' And he rose as he went on: 'I don't want to eat anything; nothing at all; I've got too much on my mind. I know I've got to think it over. Oh, that this should go and happen to *me*!'

'Try and get a drop of this down, at least,' said Perpetua, pouring it out. 'You know this always settles your stomach.'

'Oh! It'll take more than that . . . more than that . . . more than that!'

So saying he took the lamp, and still mumbling 'What a do! Fancy! A thing like that happening to an honest man like me. What about tomorrow? How will it go?' and other lamentations of the kind, he moved off on his way up to his room. On reaching the threshold he turned round towards Perpetua, put his finger to his lips, said in a slow and solemn tone, 'For heaven's sake,' and disappeared.

CHAPTER 2

We are told the Prince of Condé slept soundly on the night before the battle of Rocroi:* but in the first place he was very tired, and secondly he had already made all the necessary arrangements and settled what to do the next morning. All Don Abbondio knew as yet, on the other hand, was that next day was to be a day of battle; so most of the night was spent in agonized deliberation. To ignore the rascally warning and the threats, and carry out the marriage, was a course that he was not even willing to consider: to take Renzo into his confidence about what was necessary and try to find some means with him. . . . God forbid! 'Don't let out a word about this . . . or . . . ahem,' one of the bravi had said; and as he heard that 'ahem' echoing in his head, Don Abbondio, far from thinking of disobeying such an order, even began to regret having chattered to Perpetua. Escape? Where to? And what then? What a lot of difficulties and things to be borne in mind! At every line of action which he rejected, the poor man turned over in bed. The best, or rather the least bad, seemed to be to gain time by putting Renzo off. He remembered, just then, that it was only a few days before the closed season for marriages.* – If I can keep that boy at bay for these few days, I'd have two months' respite; and a lot of things can happen in two months. – He turned over the various excuses which he might use. They seemed a little flimsy, but he reassured himself with the thought that his authority would make up what they lacked in weight, and his long experience give him a great advantage over a callow youth. – We'll see – he said to himself. – He's thinking of his girl, but I'm thinking of my skin; I'm the more interested party, as well as being the shrewder. My dear son, if you're feeling all hotted up, well, there's nothing I can say – but I don't want to get mixed up in it. – When he had more or less settled his mind on this decision, he was finally able to get some sleep. But what sleep! What dreams! Bravi, Don Rodrigo, Renzo, paths, cliffs, escapes, pursuits, edicts, musket-shots!

The first moment of awakening after a misfortune or in a difficulty is always a very bitter one. The mind, as it begins to work again, falls back into the ideas normal to its previous calm existence. But the thought of the new state of affairs soon breaks rudely in, and is made all the more unpleasant by the sudden contrast. After tasting the bitterness of this moment in full, Don Abbondio quickly reviewed his plans of the night before, confirmed them once again, put them into better order, then got up and waited for Renzo fearfully, and at the same time with impatience.

Lorenzo – or Renzo, as everyone called him – did not keep him waiting long. As soon as the time came when he thought he could decently go, he set off for the priest's with the joyous impatience of a man of twenty who that day is going to marry the girl he loves. He had lost his parents when a boy and was a silk-spinner by trade, which was hereditary, as it were, in his family. This had been quite a lucrative trade in years gone by. It was now on the decline, though not so far that a good craftsman could not earn an honest living by it. Day by day work was dwindling; but the continual emigration of workers, attracted to the neighbouring states by promises, privileges and high wages, meant that there was still no lack for those who stayed at home. Apart from this, Renzo owned a small piece of land which he got someone to work or worked himself when the spinning wheel was at a standstill; so that he could call himself prosperous for his state in life, and though that year was even leaner than the ones before, and a real famine was already beginning to be felt, our young man, who had turned thrifty ever since he first set eyes on Lucia, was now well enough supplied not to have to struggle against hunger. He appeared before Don Abbondio in his best holiday clothes, with feathers of various colours in his hat, his dagger with its decorated handle in his breeches' pocket, and a certain gala air mingling with the slight swagger common at that period to even the quietest of men. Don Abbondio's uncertain and mysterious reception of him was in odd contrast to the young man's gay and resolute manner.

– He seems worried about something – guessed Renzo, then said:

'I've come, your reverence, to find out what's the most convenient time for us to be in church.'

'What day are you talking about?'

'What d'you mean, what day? Don't you remember it had been fixed for today?'

'Today?' replied Don Abbondio, as if this was the first he had heard of it. 'Today, today . . . You must be patient; I can't today.'

'You can't today? What's wrong?'

'I don't feel well, for one thing, d'you see.'

'I'm sorry about that; but what you've to do will take so little time, and be so little effort . . .'

'And then, and then, and then . . .'

'And then what?'

'And then there are complications.'

'Complications? What complications can there be?'

'You have to be in our position to realize the number of difficulties that come up in these matters, the number of things that have to be borne in mind. I'm too kind-hearted; all I think of is how to get over the obstacles and help everything along, and do what others want, and so I neglect my duty; and then I get reprimands, or worse.'

'But, in heaven's name, don't keep me in suspense like this. Tell me fair and square what's happened.'

'D'you realize how many formalities have to be gone through before a marriage can be properly carried out?'

'I jolly well ought to know something about them,' said Renzo, beginning to grow angry. 'You've been on enough about them to me these last few days. But hasn't it all been settled by now? Hasn't everything been done that had to be done?'

'Everything, everything, so you may think. For – be patient now – I'm the poor fool, who's been neglecting his duties so as not to put other people out. But now . . . that's enough, I know what I'm talking about. We poor parish priests are between the hammer and the anvil. You're impatient; I'm sorry for you, my poor lad; and my superiors. . . . but that's enough; there are things one can't talk about. And we are the ones who are stuck in the middle.'

'But do explain once and for all what this other formality is that's got to be done, as you say, and it'll be done straightaway.'

'D'you know what the nullifying impediments to marriage are?'

'How d'you expect me to know anything about impediments?'

Error, conditio, votum, cognatio, crimen.

Cultus disparitas, vis, ordo, ligamen, honestas.

'*Si sis affinis* . . .'* began Don Abbondio, telling off on the tips of his fingers.

'Are you making fun of me?' interrupted the young man. 'What d'you expect me to make of your *latinorum*?'

'Well, if you don't know these things, you'd better be patient and leave them to those who do.'

'Oh, come on now . . .'

'Come, come, my dear Renzo; don't go and get angry, as I'm ready to do . . . well – whatever depends on me. I – I'd like to see you happy; I'm fond of you. Yet . . . when I think how well off you were; what more did you want? And you go and get this bee in your bonnet about marriage. . . .'

'What kind of talk's this, sir?' burst out Renzo, part amazed and part enraged.

'I just mean be patient; that's all I mean. I'd like to see you happy.'

'And so . . .?'

'And so, my dear boy, it's not my fault; I didn't make the laws. And we've simply got to make lots and lots of inquiries before carrying out a marriage, so as to be sure there aren't any impediments.'

'But come on, now, tell me once for all what impediment has come up?'

'You must be patient! these things can't be worked out just like that. There won't be anything, I hope; but, all the same, we've just got to make these inquiries. The wording is clear as day: *antequam matrimonium denunciet* . . .'*

'I told you I won't have any Latin.'

'But I must explain to you . . .'

'But haven't you made all these inquiries already?'

'I haven't made all I should, I tell you.'

'Why didn't you make them in time? Why tell me it was all ready? Why wait . . .'

'There! You're reproaching me for being too kind. I've helped everything through for you as quickly as possible, but . . . but now I've had . . . Anyway, I know.'

'And what d'you expect me to do?'

'Be patient for a few days. My dear lad, a few days are not eternity; just be patient.'

'How long for?'

– We're getting into port – thought Don Abbondio to himself; and then, more graciously than ever, 'Come,' he said, 'in a fortnight. I'll try . . . I'll get . . .'

'A fortnight! That's a fine piece of news! I've done everything you wanted; the day's been fixed; the day arrives; and now you go and tell me to wait a fortnight! A fortnight,' he went on again, his voice getting louder and angrier, stretching out an arm and waving a fist in the air; and who knows what devilry he might have added to that word, had Don Abbondio not interrupted him by taking his other hand with timid, eager friendliness. 'Come, come, don't get angry, for heaven's sake. I'll try; I'll see if in a week . . .'

'And what am I to say to Lucia?'

'That it's been my mistake.'

'And to the gossip?'

'Tell them all I made a mistake, by being in too much of a hurry, by being too kind-hearted; put all the blame on me. Can I say more than that? Go on, for one week.'

'And then, there won't be any more impediments?'

'When I tell you . . .'

'All right, I'll be patient for a week; but remember this: once that's over, I won't be put off with chatter any more. Meanwhile, my respects.' And so saying, he went off, after making Don Abbondio a bow not as deep as usual, and giving him a look which was more expressive than it was reverent.

When he got outside and started walking, reluctantly for the first time in his life, towards the home of his betrothed, he began, in the midst of his anger, turning this interview over in his mind: and the more he thought of it the stranger it seemed. Don

Abbondio's cold and embarrassed reception: the hesitating and at the same time impatient way in which he had talked: those two grey eyes of his always shifting about while he was talking, as if they were afraid of meeting the words coming out of his mouth; his pretending to know almost nothing about the marriage, although it had all been so definitely arranged; and, above all, the way he had kept on hinting at something important without ever saying anything clearly – all this made Renzo suspect some mystery behind it all, different from what Don Abbondio would have had him believe. The young man was just on the point of turning back to pin him down and force him to talk more clearly, when, raising his eyes, he saw Perpetua walking ahead of him and going into a little garden a few yards from the house. He called out to her as she was opening the wicket, quickened his pace, caught her up and kept her at the entrance; then, hoping to find out something more definite, he paused to start a conversation with her.

'Good morning, Perpetua. I'd hoped we'd all have been enjoying ourselves together today.'

'Ah well! God's will be done, my poor Renzo.'

'Do me a favour, will you? That blessed man the priest has gone and given me some muddled reasons or other which I couldn't properly understand; do explain a bit better why he can't or won't marry us today.'

'Oh! d'you think I know my master's secrets?'

– Just as I thought, some mystery behind it – thought Renzo, and to bring it out to light he went on: 'Come on, Perpetua; we're friends. Tell me what you know; help a poor chap out.'

'It's a bad thing to be born poor, Renzo my dear.'

'That's true,' he went on, getting more and more confirmed in his suspicions, and trying to edge nearer to the subject. 'That's true,' he repeated; 'but d'you think it's for the priests to treat folk badly because they're poor?'

'Now look here, Renzo; I can't tell you anything, because ... I don't know anything. All I can do is assure you my master doesn't mean to do any harm to you or anyone else; and it's not his fault.'

'Whose fault is it, then?' asked Renzo, with apparent carelessness, but with ears cocked and heart in his mouth.

'When I tell you I don't know anything ... but I suppose I can stand up for my own master. It doesn't half hurt me to hear them say he's doing anyone harm on purpose. Poor old soul! If he's done anything wrong, it's through being too kind-hearted. There are some real scoundrels in this world, let me tell you, some bullies, some men without fear of God . . .'

– Bullies, scoundrels! – thought Renzo. – Those can't be his superiors. 'Come on,' he said then, hiding his growing agitation with difficulty – 'come on, tell me who it is.'

'Ah, you'd like to make me talk, and I can't talk because . . . I don't know anything; and when I don't know anything, it's the same as if I'd promised not to tell. You'd never drag a word out of me, not if you gave me the strappado! Good-bye; we're both of us wasting time.' And so saying she hurried into the orchard and shut the gate. Renzo gave a wave in reply, and then turned back very quietly, so that she should not realize in what direction he was going. But once out of the good woman's earshot he quickened his pace; in a minute he was at Don Abbondio's door; in he went, marched straight to the parlour where he had left him, found him still there, and rushed towards him with a reckless air and starting eyes.

'Hey! hey! what's up now?' said Don Abbondio.

'Who's the bully,' said Renzo, in the tone of a man determined to get a definite reply – 'who's the bully that doesn't want me to marry Lucia?'

'What? what? what?' stammered the poor man in his surprise, his face suddenly white and floppy as a wet dishcloth. And, still mumbling, he jumped up from his armchair to make a dash for the door. But Renzo must have been expecting this move, and was on the alert; he bounded there before him, turned the key, and put it in his pocket.

'Ah! ah! Are you going to talk now, your reverence? Everyone knows my own business except myself. It's about time I knew it myself, by Bacchus it is! What's the fellow's name?'

'Renzo! Renzo! Be careful what you're doing, for goodness sake; think of your soul!'

'I'm thinking I want to know right now, this very moment.' As he said this he put his hand, perhaps without realizing it, on the hilt of the dagger sticking out of his pocket.

'Mercy on us!' exclaimed Don Abbondio in a feeble voice.

'I want to know.'

'Who told you . . . ?'

'No, no, no more quibbling. Talk straight – now.'

'D'you want to see me dead?'

'I want to know what I've a right to know.'

'But if I talk I'm a dead man. Don't you expect me to value my own life?'

'Well, then. Talk.'

That 'well, then' was uttered with such energy, and Renzo's face had become so threatening, that Don Abbondio had to give up all hope of disobeying him any longer.

'Promise me, swear to me,' he said, 'not to tell anyone about it, never to say a . . .?'

'I promise I'll do something stupid if you don't tell me that man's name right away.'

At this new threat, with the face and look of a man who has the dentist's pincers in his mouth, Don Abbondio gasped out: 'Don . . .'

'Don?' repeated Renzo, as if he was helping the patient to get the rest out, and stooping down, with his ear close to the other's mouth, his arms tense and his fists clenched behind his back.

'Don Rodrigo!' blurted out the threatened man hurriedly, rushing the few syllables together and slurring over the consonants, partly from agitation, and partly because, using what was left of his wits to reach a compromise between his two fears, he seemed to be hoping to hide the word and make it disappear at the very moment he was forced to produce it.

'Ah, the swine!' shouted Renzo. 'And how did he do it? What did he tell you to . . .?'

'How, eh? How?' replied Don Abbondio almost indignantly, feeling that after making such a great sacrifice he had become a sort of creditor. 'How, eh? I wish it had happened to you, as it happened to me, who don't come into it in the least; then you certainly wouldn't have so many bees left in your bonnet.' Here he began to paint his unpleasant encounter in the most fearful colours; and as he talked he became more and more conscious of the rage welling up inside him, which until then had been wrapped up and hidden by his fear. At the same time, seeing Renzo standing motionless with his head down, between rage and confusion, he went on excitedly, 'A fine thing you've done! A nice way you've treated me! To play a trick of this sort on an honest man, on your parish priest! In his own house! On holy ground! A fine, brave thing you've done! To go and force out of me this misfortune of mine, this misfortune of yours! When I was keeping it from you out of prudence, for your own good! And now you know it, let's just see what you get up to. . . .! For heaven's sake! This is no joking matter. This isn't a question of

right or wrong; it's a question of might. And when I gave you a
bit of good advice this morning ... eh! In a rage at once. My
judgement was good enough for both of us; but there you are.
Open the door, anyway; give me my key.'

'Perhaps I was wrong,' answered Renzo, in a voice which had
softened towards Don Abbondio, although in it could be heard
the rage against his unmasked enemy. 'Perhaps I was wrong; but
just put your hand to your heart and think whether if you'd been
in my place . . .'

So saying, he took the key out of his pocket and went to open
the door. Don Abbondio followed him, came up beside him as
he turned the key in the lock, and, with a serious and anxious
look, raised the first three fingers of his right hand as if to give
him some help in return, saying, 'Swear, at least . . .'

'Perhaps I was wrong, and I'm sorry,' replied Renzo, opening
the door, and getting ready to leave.

'Swear . . .' replied Don Abbondio, clutching his arm with a
trembling hand.

'Perhaps I was wrong,' repeated Renzo, disengaging himself
from him; and off he rushed, so cutting short the discussion,
which, like a discussion on literature or philosophy or anything
else, might have lasted for centuries, as both sides did nothing
but repeat their own arguments.

'Perpetua! Perpetua!' cried Don Abbondio, after calling the
fugitive back in vain. Perpetua did not reply; Don Abbondio no
longer knew whether he was in this world or the next.

People of far greater importance than Don Abbondio have
more than once found themselves in situations so unpleasant,
and been so uncertain what to do next, that they have found the
best expedient was to take to their beds with a fever. Don
Abbondio did not have to search around for this expedient, as it
came up of its own accord. The fright of the day before, the
sleepless night of agony, the fright he had had that moment, the
dread of the future, all took their effect. He sat back breathless
and stunned in his armchair, and began to feel a shiver in his
bones. He looked at his nails, and sighed, calling out 'Perpetua!'
from time to time in a trembling, petulant voice. Finally she
arrived, with a big cabbage under her arm, and a look of
unconcern on her face as if nothing had happened. I will spare
the reader the lamentations and condolences, the accusations and
defences, the 'who else could have talked?' on one side, the 'I've
not said a word' on the other – all the muddles, in fact, of this

conversation. Suffice it to say that Don Abbondio ordered Perpetua to bar the front door, not to open it again for any reason at all, and to reply from the window, if anyone knocked, that the parish priest had gone to bed with a fever. Then he went slowly up the stairs, saying, 'I'm done for', at every third stair; and really did go to bed, where we will leave him.

Meanwhile Renzo was striding homewards at a furious pace, without having decided what to do, but with a mad longing to do something strange and awful. Those who provoke or oppress, all those who do any wrong to others, are guilty not only of the harm they do, but also of the twists they cause in the minds of those they have injured. Renzo was a peaceable young man and averse to bloodshed – an open youth who hated deceit of any kind; but at that moment his heart only beat to kill, and his mind turned only on thoughts of treachery. He would have liked to rush to Don Rodrigo's house, seize him by the throat, and ... But then he remembered it was like a fortress, garrisoned with bravi inside and guarded out; so that only friends and well-known servants could enter freely, without being looked over from head to foot; and an unknown little artisan could never get by without being examined: he more than anyone else ... he would be almost too well known. Then he imagined himself taking his musket, crouching behind a bush, and waiting to see if ever, ever, that man passed by alone. And, dwelling on this idea with ferocious pleasure, he imagined himself hearing a footstep – that footstep – and stealthily raising his head; he recognized the villain, levelled his musket, took aim, fired, saw him fall in his death-agony, flung him a curse, and rushed off towards the frontier and safety. And Lucia? – As soon as this word was thrown across these grim fantasies, the better thoughts with which Renzo's mind was familiar came crowding after it. He recalled the last memories of his parents; the thought of God, Our Lady, and the Saints came back to him; he remembered how often he had been solaced by knowing he had never committed a crime, and how often struck with horror at the story of a murder. And he woke from his bloodthirsty dream with terror, with remorse, and also with a kind of joy at having done no more than imagine it. But the thought of Lucia – what a train of others it brought with it! So many hopes, so many promises: the future they had so looked forward to, and been so certain of, and the day they had so longed for! And how was he to break this news to her? And then, what was he going to do next? How was he going to make her his, despite the power of that rascally grandee? And with all this there was, not a defined suspicion, but a tormenting shadow passing across his mind. This outrage of Don Rodrigo's could only have been caused by a brutal passion for Lucia. And Lucia? The idea that she had given him the smallest encouragement or the slightest hope was not a thought to do more than pass through Renzo's head. But had she known about it? Could that man have conceived his infamous passion without her realizing it? Would he have pushed things so far without making some approach to her? And Lucia had never said a word to him: to her betrothed!

Absorbed in these thoughts, he passed by his own home, which was in the middle of the village, went through it and on towards Lucia's, which was at the end, right on the outskirts. This cottage had a small yard in front, separating it from the road, and surrounded by a low wall. Renzo went into the yard, and heard a mixed, continuous buzz of voices coming from an upper room. He guessed this must be friends and neighbours come to attend Lucia; and he did not want to show himself to this gathering with that news all over his face and figure. A little girl who was in the yard ran to meet him, shouting: 'The bridegroom! the bridegroom!'

'Hush, Bettina, hush!' said Renzo. 'Come here; now go upstairs to Lucia, take her aside, and whisper in her ear . . . but so as no one hears or suspects anything, see? Tell her I must talk to her, that I'm waiting for her in the room downstairs, and tell her to come at once. . . .' The little girl went rushing up the stairs, happy and proud at having a secret commission to carry out.

At that moment Lucia was just coming, all dressed up, fresh from her mother's hands. Her friends were bustling round the bride and making her show herself off; and she was defending herself, with the rather aggressive modesty of peasant girls, shielding her face with her elbow, dropping it over her breast, and drawing her long black eyebrows down in a frown, yet with her lips parted in a smile. Her black young hair was divided over her forehead in a fine white parting, and wound round behind her head in multiple plaited coils, pierced by long silver hairpins which splayed out almost like the rays of a halo: a style which is still worn by the peasant women of Lombardy. Around her neck she had a necklace of garnets alternating with filigree gold beads; she wore a fine bodice of flowered brocade, with the cuffs open and laced with gaily-coloured ribbons, a short silk skirt with tiny tight pleats, scarlet stockings, and a pair of slippers also embroidered in silk. Apart from these special ornaments for her wedding day, Lucia had the daily one of her modest beauty, heightened and brought out at this moment by the various emotions crossing her face: joy tempered by a slight agitation, and the quiet melancholy which sometimes shows on the faces of brides, and, without marring their beauty, gives them an air of their own. Little Bettina thrust herself into the group, went up to Lucia, carefully made her see that she had something to tell her, and whispered her message in her ear.

'I'm going out a moment, and will be back,' said Lucia to the women; and hurried downstairs. When she saw Renzo's changed look and restless manner, 'What is it?' she said, not without a fearful presentiment.

'Lucia!' answered Renzo, 'it's all up in the air for today; and God knows when we'll be man and wife.'

'What!' said Lucia, in utter dismay.

Renzo briefly told her the story of the morning. She listened in anguish, and when she heard Don Rodrigo's name: 'Ah!' she exclaimed, blushing and trembling. 'So it's come to this!'

'Then you knew . . .' said Renzo.

'Only too well!' replied Lucia. 'But to come to this!'

'What did you know?'

'Don't make me talk about it now, don't make me cry. I'll run and call Mother, and send the women away; we must be alone.'

As she was leaving, Renzo muttered: 'And you never told me anything about it.'

'Ah, Renzo!' answered Lucia, turning to him a second without stopping. Renzo understood perfectly that his name, pronounced by Lucia at such a moment in that tone of voice, meant: Can you doubt that I only kept quiet about this from good and pure motives?

Meanwhile the good Agnese (as Lucia's mother was called), her suspicions and curiosity aroused by that whisper in the ear and by her daughter's disappearance, had come down to see what was happening. Her daughter left her with Renzo, went back to the group of women, and, composing her looks and voice as best she could, said: 'The priest is ill; and nothing'll be done today.' After saying this, she bade them all a hurried farewell, and came downstairs again.

The women filed out, and dispersed to tell others what had

happened. Two or three went right up to the priest's door, to make sure he was really ill.

'A high fever,' replied Perpetua from the window; and the sad news, as it was taken round to the others, cut short the conjectures which were already beginning to stir in their minds and to emerge as mysterious hints in their conversation.

CHAPTER 3

Lucia entered the room downstairs as Renzo was distractedly telling Agnese, who was distractedly listening. Both turned towards the one who knew more than they did, expecting an explanation from her that could not be anything but painful. Each of them showed through their grief, according to their different ways of loving Lucia, a different kind of pique at her having kept something from them, particularly something like this. Anxious as Agnese was to hear her daughter's story, she could not prevent herself from chiding her: 'Not to say a word about such a thing to your own mother!'

'I'll tell you all about it now,' replied Lucia, drying her eyes with her apron.

'Go on, talk! – talk, go on!' cried mother and bridegroom together.

'Holy Mother of God!' exclaimed Lucia. 'Who'd ever have thought things would come to this!' Then, her voice broken by sobs, she described how a few days before, as she was coming back from the spinner's, and had lagged behind her companions, she had been passed by Don Rodrigo, with another gentleman; how the former had tried to detain her with remarks which, as she said, were not at all nice; but, taking no notice, she had quickened her pace and caught up with her companions; as she did so she had heard the other gentleman laugh loudly and Don Rodrigo say, 'Let's have a bet on it.' They were there on the road again the day after; but Lucia was in the midst of her companions, with her eyes cast down. The other gentleman had given a guffaw, and Don Rodrigo said, 'We'll see, we'll see.' 'By the grace of God,' went on Lucia, 'that was the last day of the spinning. I at once told . . .'

'Who did you tell?' asked Agnese, meeting half-way, not

without a certain irritation, the name of the confidant preferred to her.

'Father Cristoforo, mother, in confession,' replied Lucia, in a tone of gentle apology. 'I told him all about it the last time we went to the convent church together; and, if you remember, that morning I kept on doing one thing after another, to hang back until other people from the village passed going in the same direction, so that I could go along with them; because I was so frightened of the road after that meeting. . . .'

Agnese's indignation subsided at the revered name of Father Cristoforo. 'You did the right thing,' she said. 'But why didn't you tell your mother all about it too?'

Lucia had had two good reasons: one was not to worry or alarm the good woman with something she could not prevent; the other was not to risk everybody gossiping about a story which she wanted carefully buried; all the more as Lucia hoped her marriage would stop this hateful persecution at its very beginning. Of these two reasons, though, she produced only the first.

'And you' – she turned then and said to Renzo in the tone we use to convey to a friend that he has been in the wrong – 'ought I to have told you about this? Anyway, you know it now, alas!'

'And what did the father say?' asked Agnese.

'He told me I should aim to hurry up the wedding as much as I could, and meanwhile keep indoors; and that I should pray well to the Lord; and that he hoped that man would lose interest in me if he didn't see me. And it's then I had to force myself,' she went on, turning to Renzo again, without raising her eyes to his face, and blushing all over – 'it's then I had to be brazen and beg you to try and hurry it on, and get it over and done with before the day that had been set. What you must have thought of me! But I was doing it for the best, and following advice, and felt sure . . . and the last thing I thought of this morning . . .' Here her words were interrupted by a violent fit of sobbing.

'Ah, the scoundrel! The damned swine!' Renzo began shouting, striding up and down the room, and clutching now and then at the hilt of his dagger.

'O God, what a mess!' exclaimed Agnese. The youth suddenly stopped in front of the sobbing Lucia, looked at her with sad and angry tenderness and said, 'This is the last thing that cut-throat's going to do!'

'Ah! no, Renzo, for heaven's sake!' cried Lucia. 'No, no, for heaven's sake! God's here for the poor too; and how d'you expect Him to help us if we do wrong?'

'No, no, for heaven's sake!' repeated Agnese.

'Renzo,' said Lucia, with an air of hope and calmer resolution, 'you've got your trade, and I can work; let's go so far away that that man'll never hear of us again.'

'Ah, Lucia! And what would we do then? We aren't husband and wife yet! D'you think our priest would give us the certificate to say that we are free to marry?* A man like that? If we were married already oh, then . . .'

Lucia began crying again; and all three fell silent, in a state of dejection which was in sad contrast to the festive gaiety of their clothes.

'Listen, children; listen to me,' said Agnese after a moment or two. 'I came into the world before you did; and I know a fair bit about it. We mustn't get into too much of a state about this; the devil's never as black as he's painted. The skein looks more tangled to poor folk like us than it really is, because we don't know how to get hold of the right thread. But sometimes a bit of advice or a little talk with someone who's studied . . . I know quite well what I mean. Now, do as I say, Renzo. Go to Lecco, ask for Doctor Quibble-weaver,* and tell him . . . But don't go and call him that, for heaven's sake; it's a nickname. You must say Doctor . . . what's his name now? Oh, dear! I don't know his real name; everyone calls him that. Anyway, ask for the doctor of law who's tall, gaunt, bald, with a red nose, and a raspberry birthmark on his cheek.'

'I know him by sight,' said Renzo.

'Good,' went on Agnese. 'Now, there's a man in a million for you! I've seen many a person in more of a mess than a chick in flax, and at their wits' end, and after an hour in private with Doctor Quibble-weaver (be very careful not to call him that, though!) I've seen them, I tell you, cracking jokes about it. Now, grab hold of those four capons – poor things! I was going to wring their necks for the feast on Sunday – and take them to him; as one mustn't ever go to these gentlemen empty-handed. Tell him everything that's happened; and you'll see he'll tell you straight off things that would never come into our heads if we thought about it a whole year.'

Renzo fell in with this advice very readily; Lucia approved of it, and Agnese, proud of having given it, took the unfortunate birds out of the coop one by one, put their eight legs together as if she was making a bunch of flowers, wound a piece of string round them, tied it, and handed them over to Renzo. After an exchange of encouraging remarks he went out through the orchard, so as not to be seen by any children, who would be sure to run after him, shouting, 'The bridegroom! the bridegroom!' So he cut across the fields (or, as they call them there, 'the places') and went along by the by-ways, fuming as he thought over his misfortune, and brooding over what he was going to say to Doctor Quibble-weaver. I leave the reader to imagine the kind of a journey which those poor birds must have had, tied together and held by the legs, with their heads hanging down, in the hands of a man troubled by so many emotions, who kept gesticulating at the thoughts rushing through his head. Sometimes he would stretch out his arm in rage, sometimes raise it in desperation, and sometimes brandish it threateningly in the air; giving them a series of fierce shocks all the time, and making those four dangling heads jump about; meanwhile they were trying to peck at each other, as too often happens among companions in misfortune.

On reaching the town he asked where the doctor lived; was shown, and went straight there. As he entered the house he began to feel coming over him the timidity that the poor and illiterate experience in the presence of a gentleman and a man of learning, and forgot all the speeches he had prepared; but a glance at the capons restored his courage. He went into the kitchen and asked the serving-woman if he could talk to the doctor. She eyed the birds, and laid hands on them as if she was used to such presents, although Renzo kept on drawing them away, as he wanted the doctor to see them and realize he had brought something with him. The latter arrived just as the woman was saying, 'Give'em here and go right in.' Renzo made a low bow; the lawyer greeted him benevolently with a 'Come along, my boy' and ushered him into his study. This was a large room, and had three of the walls hung with portraits of the twelve Caesars; the fourth was covered by a big bookcase full of dusty old volumes; in the middle of the room was a table piled with briefs, appeals, demands, and decrees, with three or four chairs ranged around it, and on one side a big armchair with a high square back and at the corners a pair of wooden ornaments shaped like horns; it was covered in cow-hide fastened with big studs, some of which had fallen off long ago, leaving the corners of the covering free to curl up here and there. The doctor was in his dressing-gown – that is, he was covered in a tattered old robe which he had worn many years ago to plead on the great occasions when he used to go to Milan on some important case. He shut the door, and encouraged the young man by saying, 'Now, my boy, tell me your story.'

'I want a word with you in confidence.'

'Here I am,' replied the doctor; 'talk away.' And he sat himself down in the big armchair. Renzo stood in front of the table with one hand in the crown of his hat, which he rotated with the other, and began once more, 'I'd like to know from a learned man like your honour . . .'

'Tell me the facts as they are,' interrupted the doctor.

'You must excuse me; poor folk like us aren't much good at talking. I'd like to know, then . . .'

'What a blessed lot you are! You're all alike. Instead of stating the facts, you all want to ask questions, because you've already got your own ideas in your heads. . . .'

'Excuse me, sir. I'd like to know if there's any law against threatening a priest so he doesn't carry out a marriage.'

– I get it – said the doctor to himself, although he had not really got anything at all. – I get it – and straightaway pulled a serious face, though mingling sympathy and solicitude with its seriousness. He pressed his lips tightly together and let out an inarticulate sound that suggested a feeling expressed more clearly in his first words. 'A serious matter, my boy; an actionable matter. You've done the right thing, coming to me. It's a clear case provided for in a hundred decrees, and . . . to be exact, in one of last year's from his lordship the present governor. I'll show it to you, and let you handle it straight away.'

So saying, he rose from his armchair, thrust his hands into the chaos of papers, and started shovelling them up from below as if he was mixing wheat in a bushel.

'Where's it got to, now? Come on out, come on out. One has to have so many things ready to hand! But it's sure to be here, as it's an important decree. Ah! Here we are, here we are.' He took it up, unrolled it, glanced at the date, and, looking more serious than ever, exclaimed, 'The 15th of October 1627! Yes, it's certainly last year's; a brand-new decree.* Those are the ones that frighten people most. Can you read, my boy?'

'A little, your worship.'

'Good! Now follow me with your eyes and you'll see.'

And he began to read, holding the decree spread up in the air, mumbling quickly over some parts and lingering with great emphasis on others, according to the needs of the case:

'*Whereas the decree published by order of the Lord Duke of Feria on the 14th of December 1620, and confirmed by the Most Illustrious and most Excellent Lord Gonzalo Fernandez de Cordova, etc., etc., announced the most extreme and severe penalties for the oppressions, exactions, and acts of tyranny which certain persons dare to commit against His Majesty's devoted Subjects, the frequency of these crimes and excesses, etc., etc., having in spite of this grown to such an extent that His Excellency has found it necessary, etc., etc. Hence, he has resolved, with the concurrence of the Senate and a Committee, etc., etc., to publish the present decree.*

'*And beginning with the acts of tyranny since experience shows that many both in the City and Countryside* are you listening? *of this State tyrannously cause disturbances of the peace and oppress the weaker in a variety of ways, as for instance by making forced deeds of sale, or rent ... etc., etc.,* where are you? Ah, here! listen: *by forcibly contracting or preventing marriages.* Eh?'

'It's my case,' said Renzo.

'Listen, listen; there's plenty more; and then we'll see the penalties. *By forcing them to give or not to give evidence; to make someone leave his place of residence, etc., etc., to pay a debt, or molest a debtor, to prevent a baker going to his mill;* none of this has anything to do with us. Ah! here we are: *forcibly to prevent a priest from carrying out the duties of his office, or to make him turn it to improper uses.* Eh?'

'They might have made the decree especially for me.'

'Eh? They might, mightn't they? listen, listen: *and other acts of violence of the kind, whether they are committed by feudal lords, nobles, burgesses, lower orders, or plebs.* No one can get out of that: they're all in it; it's a regular valley of Jehoshaphat.* Now listen to the penalties. *Although these and similar actions are already forbidden, nonetheless, as greater severity is needed, His Excellency by the present decree, without derogating, etc., etc., orders and commands that proceedings be taken by all the judiciary of the State, against all those who contravene under the above or other similar headings in any way, and that such financial and corporal punishment, deportation, the galleys, or even death ...* just a little bagatelle! *as His Excellency or the Senate may decide, according to the character of the case, persons or circumstances; and this irr-e-deem-ably, and with all severity,* etc., etc. Plenty of stuff here, eh? And here are the signatures: *Gonzalo Fernandez de Cordova*; and lower down: *Platonus*; and another one here: *Vidit Ferrer*; there's nothing missing.'*

While the lawyer was reading, Renzo was slowly following him with his eye, trying to get the meaning clear and to see for himself the magic words which seemed to help him. The doctor was astonished to see his new client more attentive than alarmed. – He must be past his apprenticeship, this fellow – he thought to himself. 'Ah! ah!' he said then. 'You've had your quiff cut off. That was prudent of you. But there was no need to, as you were coming to put yourself in my hands. The thing's serious; but you don't know what I'm capable of at a pinch.'

To understand this remark of the doctor's, one should know or remember that professional bravi and lawless characters of every kind used, at this period, to wear a long quiff, which they pulled over their faces like a visor when they were challenging anyone or thought a disguise necessary and the affair was one needing both force and circumspection. The proclamations had not been silent about this fashion. '*His Excellency* (Marquès de la Hynojosa) *commands that whosoever wears his hair so long that it covers his forehead as far as the eyebrows, and wears a lock of hair before or behind the ears, incurs the fine of three hundred crowns; and in case of inability to pay, of three years in the galleys for the first offence, and of such severer penalties, financial and corporal, than the above, for the second offence, as His Excellency may decide.*

'*However, he allows those who are bald or have other just reasons, such as marks or wounds, to wear, for their greater decorum and health, their hair just long enough to cover these defects and no more; he warns them solemnly not to exceed the limits of duty and pure necessity, or they will incur the same penalties as the others who contravene.*

'*He also orders all barbers, under pain of a fine of a hundred crowns and three strappados to be given in public, and other corporal punishment to be judged as above, to leave none of the said locks, tresses, or abnormally long hair, or hair over the forehead, temples or ears, on their customers; but they are all to be of equal length, as above, except in the case of those who are bald, or have other defects, as already stated.*' The quiff was therefore almost a part of the equipment, and a badge, of the bravi and vagabonds, so that from this they were commonly called quiffs (or *ciuffi*). This expression has survived, and is still used in dialect in a milder sense, and there is probably not one of our Milanese readers who does not remember having heard in his childhood his parents or teacher, or some family friend or servant, say of him: 'He's a *ciuffo*, he's a *ciuffetto*.'

'To tell the truth, on a poor chap's word,' replied Renzo, 'I've never worn one of those quiffs in my life.'

'We shan't get anywhere,' replied the doctor, shaking his head with a smile part sceptical and part impatient. 'If you don't trust me, we shan't get anywhere. You see, son, the man who tells lies to his lawyer is a kind of fool who'll end up telling the truth to the judge. A lawyer must be told things clearly; then it's up to us to muddle them up afterwards. If you want me to help you, you must tell me everything from A to Z, with your heart in your hand as though you were speaking to your confessor. You must tell me the name of the person who gave you the mission; he'll be a person of consequence, of course; in which case I'll visit him and pay him my respects. I shan't tell him, mind you, that you've told me you were acting under his orders, trust me. I'll tell him I've come to beg his protection for a poor young chap who's been slandered. And we'll make the necessary arrangements together to clear the matter up decently. You realize, of course, that in saving himself he'll be saving you too. If, on the other hand, it's entirely your own scrape, well, I won't let you down: I've got others out of worse messes. . . . As long, let it be understood, as you haven't offended anyone of consequence, I pledge myself to get you out of your fix; with a bit of outlay, of course. You must tell me who is the plaintiff, as they say; and, depending on our man's rank, state, and temper, we can see if it'd be best to hold him off by getting a protector, or by finding a way of fixing some criminal charge on him, and putting a flea in his ear. For, you see, if you know how to manipulate proclamations properly, no one's guilty, and no one's innocent. As for the priest, he'll keep quiet if he's a man of sense; if he proves stubborn, there're ways of dealing with that too. There's no hole one can't get out of; but it needs the right man to do it; and yours is a serious case, I tell you, a serious case. The edict's quite clear; and if it was a question of deciding between the law and you, I can tell you, between ourselves, you'd be for it. I'm talking to you as a friend; these scrapes have got to be paid for. If you want to get out of it with a whole skin, then it means money, frankness, trusting someone who likes you, being obedient, and doing everything I tell you.'

While the doctor was bringing all this out, Renzo was gazing at him with rapt attention, like a yokel in the village square gazing at a conjuror who, after cramming yards and yards of flax into his mouth, then pulls out an endless string of ribbons. But when he had fully grasped what the doctor was trying to say, and the misapprehension he was under, he cut the ribbons off short in his mouth by saying, 'Oh! your worship, how've you understood it? It's all just the other way round. I haven't threatened anyone; I don't do that kind of thing, I don't; you can ask everyone in my village, and they'll tell you I've never been up against the law. It's me who's been put upon; and I've come to you to find out how I'm to get redress, and very glad indeed I am to have seen that proclamation.'

'Devil take it!' exclaimed the doctor, his eyes widening. 'You've got me all tied up! It's always the way; you're all the same; can't you ever put things clearly?'

'Excuse me, but you never gave me time; now I'll tell you the story as it really is. Well, first of all I was supposed to be getting married today' – and here Renzo's voice trembled – 'I was supposed to be getting married today to a girl I'd been courting since last summer; and today, as I was saying, was the day we'd settled with the parish priest, and everything was ready. And then suddenly the priest began making excuses . . . well, anyway, to cut the story short, I got him to talk clearly, as I'd a right to, and he's confessed he'd been forbidden to carry out this marriage on pain of his life. That bully Don Rodrigo . . .'

'Hey! be off with you!' broke in the lawyer suddenly, frowning, wrinkling his red nose, and screwing up his mouth. 'Be off! Why d'you come and bother me with all this nonsense? Go and say that sort of thing among yourselves with people who can't control their tongues, and don't come and do it with a respectable man who knows what it's worth. Be off, be off; you don't know what you're talking about. I don't get myself mixed up with boys. I don't want to listen to talk of this kind – hot air.'

'On my oath . . .'

'Off with you, I say. What d'you think your oaths mean to me? It's not my business. I wash my hands of it.' And he began rubbing them together, as if he really was washing them. 'Learn to talk properly; and don't come intruding on a respectable man like this.'

'But listen, do listen,' Renzo went on repeating in vain. The doctor, still shouting, was pushing him towards the door; and when he got him there, opened it, called the serving-woman, and said to her, 'Give this man back what he brought at once; I don't want anything, I don't want anything at all.'

The woman had never carried out such an order since she had been in that house; but it was given so definitely that she did not hesitate to obey. She took the four wretched birds and gave them to Renzo, with a glance of contemptuous pity, which seemed to say: you must have done something pretty awful. Renzo tried to make polite objections; but the doctor was obdurate; and the young man, more bewildered and angrier than ever, was forced to take back the rejected victims, and return to the village to tell the two women the fine results of his expedition.

While he was away, the women had sadly taken off their wedding dresses and put on their workaday clothes, and then begun to discuss plans again, between Lucia's sobs and Agnese's sighs. When the latter kept on talking of the great results to be expected from the lawyer's advice, Lucia said that they ought to try to get all the help they could; that Fra Cristoforo was the man not only to give advice but to do something about it, when it was a question of helping those in distress; and that it would be a very good thing to let him know what had happened. 'It would, to be sure,' said Agnese; and together they set to thinking out some way of doing so, for they did not feel they had the courage to go off that day to the monastery, which was about two miles away; and certainly no one with sense would have advised them to do so. But as they were weighing up the various possibilities they heard a tap at the door, and at the same time a low but clear 'Deo gratias'.* Lucia, guessing who it might be, ran to open it; and at once, with a friendly little bow, in came a lay-brother collecting for the Capuchins, with his knapsack hanging from his left shoulder, its mouth twisted and held tight over his chest with both hands.

'Oh, Fra Galdino!' said the two women.

'The Lord be with you,' said the friar. 'I've come looking for walnuts.'

'Go and get some walnuts for the fathers,' said Agnese. Lucia got up and went towards the other room, but before going into it she stopped behind Fra Galdino's back, as he stood there in the same position, put her finger to her lips, and gave her mother a glance that tenderly, beseechingly, and also with a certain authority, asked her to keep the secret.

The mendicant gave Agnese a searching glance from a distance and said, 'What's this about the wedding? Shouldn't it have been today? I noticed a certain stir in the village as if there was something up. What's happened?'

'His reverence the priest's ill, and it had to be put off,' she replied hurriedly. Had Lucia not given that signal, the answer would probably have been different. 'And how's the collecting going?' she added, so as to change the subject.

'Not too well, my friend, not too well. This is the lot here.' And so saying he took off his knapsack and shook it in both hands. 'This is the lot; and I've had to knock at ten doors to put this fine pile together.'

'Ah, well! Crops are poor, Fra Galdino; and when one's short of bread, one can't afford to be open-handed about anything else.'

'And what's the best way to bring the good times back, my good woman? Giving alms. D'you know about that miracle of the walnuts that happened years ago at our monastery in Romagna?'

'No, I never have; tell me about it.'

'Oh! Well, then, in that monastery there was one of our friars who was a saint, called Fra Macario. One winter's day, as he was walking along a path by a field which belonged to one of our patrons – another good man – Fra Macario saw this benefactor standing under one of his big walnut-trees, and four labourers with raised spades just going to dig it up and lay bare the roots. "What are you doing to that poor old tree?" asked Fra Macario. "Father, it's not borne me any nuts for years and years, and now I'm going to make firewood of it." "Let it be," said the friar; "I tell you that this year it'll bear more nuts than it does leaves." Our benefactor, who knew what kind of man it was who had said this, at once ordered the workmen to throw the earth back on the roots again, and calling the friar as he was going on his way, said, "Fra Macario, half the yield will go to the monastery." The news of the prophecy got around; and everyone came rushing to look at the nut-tree. And in fact in the spring came blossoms galore, and in due course nuts galore. Our good benefactor did not have the satisfaction of gathering them; for before the harvest he had gone to receive the rewards of his charity. But the miracle was an even bigger one, as you'll hear. The good man had left behind him a son of a very different stamp. Now, at harvest time the collector went to draw the share due to the monastery; but this fellow pretended it was the first he had heard of it, and was rash enough to say that he'd never heard that Capuchins could make walnuts. And d'you know what happened then? One day (just listen to this) the rascal had invited a few friends of the same type as himself, and as they were carousing, he told the story of the nut-tree, and had a good laugh at the friars. The young fellows wanted to go and have a look at the great heap of nuts, and he led them up to the loft. But just listen; he opens the door, goes towards the corner where they'd piled the great heap, and just as he's saying, "Look," looks himself, and . . . what does he see? A great heap of dry walnut leaves. Wasn't that a lesson to him? And the monastery gained instead of losing by it; for after a prodigy like that the collection for walnuts brought in so many that a benefactor took pity on the poor collectors, and gave the monastery a donkey to help carry the nuts home. And so much oil was made, that all the poor came and took what they needed; for we're like the sea, which takes water in from everywhere, and distributes it back again to all the rivers.'

Just then Lucia reappeared with her apron so full of walnuts that she could only just hold them in by keeping the two corners high up and stretched out at arms'-length. As Fra Galdino was taking his knapsack off again, putting it down, and loosening the mouth to let the abundant offering in, her mother made Lucia a surprised and severe face for her extravagance. But Lucia gave her a glance which meant 'I'll justify myself.' Fra Galdino broke out into praises, good wishes, promises, and thanks, then hoisted the knapsack on to his shoulder again, and was just going off when Lucia called him back, and said, 'I'd like a favour of you; I'd like you to tell Fra Cristoforo that I need to talk to him urgently, and would he do us poor folk the kindness of coming to us straight away, for we can't go to the church ourselves.'

'Is that all you want? Fra Cristoforo shall know of your request within the hour.'

'I rely on you.'

'Don't you worry.' And so saying, off he went, rather more bowed and rather more happy than when he came.

Let no one think when he sees a poor girl sending for Fra Cristoforo with such confidence, and the collector accepting her message without surprise and without demur, that this Fra Cristoforo was just a friar like dozens of others, just someone to be treated anyhow. On the contrary, he was a man of great authority both among his own brethren and in the whole of the surrounding countryside; but such was the way of the Capuchins, to whom nothing seemed too low or too high.* Serving the lowly and being served by the great; going into palace and hovel with the same air of humility and confidence; being sometimes in one household at once an object of ridicule and a person without whom nothing could be decided; begging for alms from all and distributing them at the monastery to all who asked for them – a Capuchin was accustomed to everything. As he went along the street he might equally well run into a prince who would reverently kiss the end of his cord, or a group of urchins who, pretending to quarrel among themselves, would spatter his beard with mud. The word 'friar' was used at that period with the greatest respect and the most bitter contempt; and the Capuchins were the objects of these two opposing feelings and met with these two opposing treatments perhaps more than any other order; for owning nothing, and wearing a habit which was more than usually distinctive, making more open profession of humility, they exposed themselves more directly to the veneration and the scorn which these things can attract from men's different natures and different ways of thinking.

As soon as Fra Galdino had left, Agnese exclaimed, 'All those walnuts! In a year like this!'

'I'm sorry, mother,' answered Lucia; 'but if we'd given the same alms as the others the Lord knows how long Fra Galdino would have still had to tramp round before getting his knapsack full. The Lord knows when he would have got back to the monastery; and with all the gossip he'd have made and heard, the Lord knows if he'd have remembered . . .'

'Quite right; and besides it's all charity, and that always brings in a good reward,' said Agnese, who, for all her little defects, was a really good-hearted woman, and would have gone through fire, as the saying goes, for this only daughter of hers, in whom she had placed all her happiness.

Just then Renzo arrived; he came in with an expression of anger and humiliation on his face, and flung the capons down on a table; and this was the last of the poor birds' vicissitudes for that day.

'A fine bit of advice you gave me!' said he to Agnese. 'You sent me to a really good chap, a man who really helps the poor!' And he described his interview with the lawyer. The poor woman, dumbfounded at its turning out so badly, made an effort to show that her advice had been good even so, and that Renzo could not have gone about it in the right way. But Lucia interrupted this discussion by announcing that she hoped she had found someone who would be more of a help. Renzo welcomed this hope too, as is the way with people in trouble and misfortune. 'But if the father,' said he, 'doesn't find a solution, I'll find one myself in one way or other.'

The women advised peace, patience, and prudence. 'Tomorrow,' said Lucia, 'Father Cristoforo's sure to come; and you'll see he'll find some solution that us poor folk would never think of.'

'I hope so,' said Renzo. 'But in any case I'll get my rights, or have them got for me. There's justice in this world in the long run.'

Between the gloomy discussions and the comings and goings which we have described the day had passed away: and it was beginning to grow dark.

'Good night,' said Lucia sadly to Renzo, who could not bring himself to leave.

'Good night,' answered Renzo, more sadly still.

'Some saint will help us,' replied Lucia. 'Be prudent, and resign yourself.'

The mother added other advice of the same kind; and the bridegroom went off with a stormy heart, repeating those strange words to himself again and again. 'There's justice in this world in the long run.' How true it is that a man overwhelmed by grief no longer knows what he is saying!

CHAPTER 4

The sun had not yet fully risen on the horizon when Father Cristoforo left his monastery at Pescarenico to go up to the cottage where he was expected. Pescarenico is a small hamlet on the left bank of the Adda, or rather of the lake, a short way from the bridge; a little group of houses, mainly inhabited by fishermen, and decorated here and there with nets and trammels stretched out to dry. The monastery – the building is still standing – * was outside it, and facing the entrance to the village, with the road from Lecco to Bergamo running in between. The sky was all serene: as the sun gradually rose behind the mountain, its rays could be seen descending the tops of the opposite mountains and spreading rapidly down over the slopes and into the valley below. An autumn breeze was shaking the dead leaves from the branches of the mulberry-trees, and wafting them off to fall a few yards away. In the vineyards to right and left the vine-leaves were sparkling in varied shades of red on stems that were still stretched between their supports; and the fresh-turned furrows stood out in vivid brown amidst the fields of stubble, white and glistening with the dew. It was a cheerful scene; but every human figure that appeared in it saddened the eye and mind. Every now and again, ragged and emaciated beggars, who were either old hands at the profession or had been forced by recent necessity to beg for a living, came along. They passed Father Cristoforo silently, looking at him piteously, and although they had no hopes of anything from him, for a Capuchin never touched money, they made him a grateful reverence for the alms they had received or were on their way to solicit at the monastery. The workers scattered throughout the fields were an even more pathetic sight. Some were sowing their seed sparingly and grudgingly, as if they were risking something of great value. Others were plying their spades with difficulty, and listlessly turning over the clods. A skinny girl leading a thin, bony cow by a tethering-rope was looking ahead of it and stooping hurriedly down to snatch away as food for her family, some herb on which hunger had taught her that humans, too, could live. These sights increased at every step the melancholy of the friar, who was already walking along with the sad presentiment in his heart that he was on his way to hear bad news.

But why was he so concerned about Lucia? And why had he hurried off, at the first summons from her, as dutifully as at a call from the Father Provincial? And who was this Father Cristoforo?* – We must answer all these questions properly.

Father Cristoforo of * * * was a man nearer sixty than fifty years of age. His head was shaven, according to the Capuchin rules, except for a little fringe of hair encircling it: every now and again he would raise it in a movement which had something restless and haughty about it, then lower it at once in contrasting humility. The long white beard, hiding as it did his cheeks and chin, threw into relief the strong lines of the upper part of his face, which had gained in dignity, rather than lost in expression, from long habits of abstinence. A pair of sunken eyes was usually bent on the ground, but sometimes flared out into sudden animation, like a pair of mettlesome horses in the hands of a driver whom experience has taught they cannot master, though they give a caper now and then at the cost of a smart jerk of the bit.

Father Cristoforo had not always been like this, nor had Cristoforo always been his name; he had been baptized Lodovico. He was the son of a merchant of * * * (these asterisks are all due to the caution of my anonymous chronicler) who, finding himself in his latter years with an abundance of this world's goods, and an only son, had retired from business, and taken to the life of a gentleman.

In this new-found leisure of his there began to come over him a great shame of all the time he had spent doing something useful in this world. He became obsessed by this idea, and strove with every means to make people forget he had ever been a merchant; he longed to be able to forget it himself. But the draper's shop, the bales, the ledger, and the yard-stick kept on appearing to him in his memory, as the ghost of Banquo did to Macbeth, even amid the glamour of the banquet and the smiles of parasites. And these poor souls had to take indescribable care to avoid any word that might seem an allusion to their host's former condition. One day – to give one instance – towards the end of dinner, just when the gaiety was at its liveliest and freest, so that it was difficult to say who was enjoying themselves more, the host in loading the table, or the guests in emptying it, he was bantering in a friendly and patronizing way one of them who was the most honest trencherman in the world. This man, just to fall in with the joke, and without the least shadow of malice, rather with the candour of a child, replied, 'Ah! I'm turning a deaf ear, like a shopkeeper.' He was himself at once struck by the sound of the word he had just uttered, and looked uncertainly up at his host's face, which had clouded over; both would have liked to return to their former jollity, but it was impossible. The other guests were wondering, each on his own, how to smooth over the little awkwardness and create some diversion; but as they wondered they stopped talking, and in the silence the awkwardness became more obvious. Each avoided the other's eye; each felt everyone was busy thinking the thought they all wanted to conceal. Gaiety had fled for that day; and the tactless, or to be fairer, the luckless man never got another invitation. Thus Lodovico's father spent his last years in a continual state of worry and dread of being despised, without ever reflecting that selling is no more ridiculous than buying, and that for many years he had carried on the trade he was now ashamed of, in full view of the public, and without any regrets. He had his son brought up like a nobleman, as far as the conditions of the period and its laws and customs would permit; he gave him tutors in polite letters and knightly exercises, and died leaving him heir to a large fortune, and still a youth.

Lodovico had acquired lordly habits: and the flatterers among whom he was brought up had accustomed him to being treated with great deference. But when he tried to mingle with the aristocracy of the town he found a very different attitude from the one he had been used to: and he saw that if he was to be admitted to their set, as he wanted to be, he would have to learn a new lesson of patience and humility, always taking a back seat and putting up with snubs every moment. This way of life agreed with neither Lodovico's education nor his character. He drew away from these people with irritation. But he did so also with regret; for he considered that they ought really to have been his companions; all he wanted was for them to be more amenable. With this mixture of attraction and antipathy, not being able to mingle with them on friendly terms yet still wanting to be in some way in contact with them, he began to compete with them in splendour and extravagance, thus drawing on himself all at once enmity, envy, and ridicule. His temperament, which was both honest and impulsive, also led him in time into other more serious contests. He had a genuine and instinctive horror of violence and oppression, a horror he felt all the more strongly because of the rank of those who daily practised it – just the ones he had most grudge against. To appease or gratify all these passions at once, he readily took the side of the weak and oppressed, prided himself on countering some bully, and got himself drawn from one feud into another; so that, little by little, he came to set himself up as a protector of the oppressed and an avenger of wrongs. This was an arduous task, and there is no need to ask if poor Lodovico had his share of enemies, commitments, and worries. Besides this external struggle, he was continually torn by internal conflicts; for to carry some cause through successfully (not to mention the ones in which he failed) he had to use subterfuges and violence which his conscience could not approve. He had to keep a large number of bravi around him; and for efficiency, as well as for his own safety, to choose the boldest and most daredevil, which meant the most rascally, and to live among rogues, all for the love of justice. So that more than once, when discouraged by some failure or

anxious about an impending danger, wearied by continual precautions, disgusted with the company he kept, worried about the
future and about the way his fortune was daily dwindling away
in good works and bold enterprises, the idea of becoming a monk
had occurred to him more than once, such being a very common
way of getting out of difficulties at that time. But what might
have remained a mere notion for the rest of his life, became a
resolution as the result of an incident which was the most serious
of any that had yet happened to him.

One day he was walking along one of the streets in his city,
followed by two bravi and accompanied by a certain Cristoforo,
who had once been a clerk in the shop and had been made
steward of the household after it was shut. He was a man of
about fifty, and had been from his youth up devoted to Lodovico,
whom he had known from the cradle, and who gave him enough
with his salary and perquisites not only to live on but to raise
and maintain a large family. From some way off Lodovico saw a
certain noble appear, a notorious and arrogant bully to whom he
had never spoken in his life, but who hated him cordially, and
was as cordially hated in return; for it is one of the advantages of
this world that people can hate and be hated without knowing
each other. This person, followed by four bravi, was advancing
straight towards them with a haughty step, his head in the air,
and his mouth set in an expression of pride and disdain. Both
parties were walking next to the wall. But Lodovico (be it noted)
was grazing it with his right side, and this, according to one
custom, gave him the right (where on earth do these rights come
from?) to keep against this wall and not to make way for anyone
– an important point in those days. The other held, on the
contrary, that this was his due as a nobleman, and that it was for
Lodovico to turn out into the road – and this by virtue of another
custom. For there were two conflicting customs both in force in
this, as in so many other matters, without it ever having been
decided which of the two was the right one; this meant a struggle
every time an obstinate man came up against another of the same
temper. These two came towards each other, both keeping close
to the wall, like two moving figures in a bas-relief. When they
were face to face the noble eyed Lodovico up and down with his
head in the air and a haughty frown, and said in a corresponding
tone of voice, 'Make way.'

'It's for you to make way,' answered Lodovico; 'I have the
right.'

'With people of your rank the right's always mine.'

'Yes, if the arrogance of people of your rank were a law for people of mine.'

The bravi of both parties had stopped, each behind their own master, glowering at each other, with their hands on their swords, ready for a fight. People passing by drew back to see what was going on; and the presence of these spectators made the contestants more punctilious than ever.

'Get out into the open, you low tradesman: or I'll teach you once and for all how to treat a gentleman.'

'You lie in saying I'm low.'

'You lie in saying I'm a liar.' (This was the prescribed rejoinder.) 'And if you were a gentleman, as I am,' added the nobleman, 'I'd show you, with my cape and sword, who's the liar.'

'An excellent excuse to avoid backing up your insolent words by deeds.'

'Fling this knave into the gutter,' said the nobleman, turning to his men.

'We'll see about that!' said Lodovico, taking a quick step back and putting his hand to his sword.

'Insolent dog!' cried the other, drawing his own. 'I'll break this after it has been soiled by your low blood.'

At this they set on each other, and the attendants on both sides sprang to the defence of their masters. The contest was an unequal one both in numbers and also because, while Lodovico was more concerned with parrying the thrusts and disarming rather than killing his opponent, the latter was bent on killing him at all costs. Lodovico had already had a stab in his left arm from one of the bravi, and a scratch on one cheek, and his chief antagonist was pressing hard to finish him off, when Cristoforo, seeing his master in grave peril, fell on the nobleman with his dagger. The other turned all his fury against him and ran him through with his sword. On seeing this, Lodovico, beside himself, plunged his own sword into the vitals of the nobleman, who fell dying to the ground, almost at the same moment as did poor Cristoforo. The nobleman's bravi, seeing it was all over, took to their heels in disorder; Lodovico's men, who were also badly battered and slashed about, finding themselves in possession of the field, turned and ran off the other way, to avoid getting involved with the people already clustering round: and Lodovico found himself alone with the ghastly pair at his feet, in the midst of a crowd.

'What's happened? There's one – There's two – He's let some daylight into that one's vitals – Who's been killed? – That bully! – Oh, holy Mary, what a mess! – If you ask for it you get it. – You pay for everything in one go. – He's finished too. – What a blow! – It looks like being a serious business. – And that other poor devil! – Heavens! What a sight! – Save him, save him! – He's for it too. – Look what a state he's in! – Pouring with blood all over. – Beat it! beat it! Don't let 'em catch you.'

These last words were the ones most heard in the confused din of the crowd, and expressed the general opinion; and with the advice came help too. The affair had taken place near a Capuchin church, a sanctuary, as everyone knows, impenetrable at that period to the bailiffs and to the whole array of persons and things that went by the name of justice. The wounded man, almost senseless, was led or rather carried in there by the crowd; and the friars took him over from the hands of the people, who recommended him to them, saying, 'He's a decent chap who's killed an arrogant rascal; he did it in self-defence; he was forced into it.'

Lodovico had never shed blood before that moment; and although the taking of life was then so common that everyone was familiar with it by sight and hearsay, yet seeing a man killed by his hand and a man killed on his account had made a new and indescribable impression on him, and was a revelation of feelings unknown to him till then. The fall of his adversary, the sudden change of that face, in a moment, from threatening rage to the helplessness and the quiet solemn calm of death, was a sight which changed the soul of his slayer at one stroke. As he was dragged into the monastery he scarcely knew where he was or what he was doing, and on coming to, he found himself in bed in the infirmary, attended by the surgeon-friar (the Capuchins usually have one in every monastery), who was stanching and bandaging the two wounds he had received in the fight. One of the fathers whose special function was to assist the dying and who had often had to carry out this duty on the streets, had at once been called to the scene of the fray. He came back a few minutes later, went into the infirmary, and up to the bed where Lodovico lay, and said, 'Console yourself; at least he died a good death. He charged me to ask your forgiveness and to give you his.' These words brought poor Lodovico completely to his senses, and woke still more vividly and poignantly the confused feelings crowding through his mind: sorrow for his friend, remorse and consternation at the blow that had slipped from his hand, and, at the same time, agonized compassion for the man he had killed. 'And the other one?' he asked the friar anxiously.

'The other one had already died when I arrived.'

Meanwhile the approaches and precincts of the monastery were swarming with inquisitive crowds, until the bailiffs came, dispersed the mob, and posted themselves a little way from the gates but close enough to see that no one came out unobserved. There also arrived a brother of the dead man, two of his cousins, and an old uncle, with a great retinue of bravi; these began patrolling around, staring with airs and gestures of threatening contempt at the onlookers, who did not dare say it served him right, but had it written all over their faces.

As soon as Lodovico could collect his thoughts he called a confessor and asked him to go to Cristoforo's widow and implore her pardon in his name for having been the cause, however involuntarily, of her bereavement; and at the same time to assure her that he would assume responsibility for the family. Then, his mind reverting to his own affairs, he felt that idea of taking the cowl coming back to him more firmly and earnestly than ever. God Himself, it seemed to him, had set him on the path, and given him a sign of His will by bringing him to a monastery at such a juncture; and so the decision was made. He called for the Father Superior and made his desire known. The reply was that he should be careful of taking precipitous resolutions but that if he persisted he would not be refused. Then, calling in a notary, he made a deed of gift of everything he had left (still a considerable fortune) to Cristoforo's family: a sum to the widow, as if it were a marriage settlement, and the rest to the eight children whom Cristoforo had left behind him.

Lodovico's decision came very opportunely for his hosts, who found themselves in a grave dilemma on his account. To turn him out of the monastery, and thus hand him over to justice, or rather to the vengeance of his enemies, was a solution not even to be considered. It would have been equivalent to renouncing their own privileges, discrediting the monastery with the people, calling reproaches down on themselves from every Capuchin in the world for letting their common rights be infringed, and ranging against them all the ecclesiastical authorities, who regarded themselves as the guardians of these rights. On the other hand, the family of the dead man, who were very powerful both in themselves and by their connexions, had declared themselves determined to be avenged, and were proclaiming that anyone who tried to prevent it was their enemy. History does not say that they mourned the dead man very much, or even that a single tear was shed for him by any of his relations; it says only that they were all eager to get his slayer into their clutches, dead or alive. Now the latter had settled everything by donning the Capuchin habit. He was giving satisfaction of a kind, he was imposing a penance on himself, he was implicitly admitting his guilt, and he was withdrawing from the contest – in fact he was an enemy laying down his arms. The dead man's relations could also, if they liked, believe and boast that he had turned friar in desperation and from terror of their wrath. And anyway, to reduce a man to the point of stripping himself of all his possessions, shaving his head, walking barefoot, sleeping on straw and living on alms might seem punishment enough even to the vainest of injured parties.

The Father Superior called on the dead man's brother with a frank and humble air, and after innumerable protestations of respect for his illustrious family, and of his desire to oblige them in any way he could, spoke of Lodovico's repentance, and of his resolution, letting it be politely understood that the family should be satisfied with this, and hinting suavely and even more adroitly that, whether they liked it or not, so it was to be. The brother went into transports of rage, which the Capuchin allowed to expend itself, saying from time to time, 'Your grief is only too justified.' The nobleman let it be understood that, in any case, his family would be able to get redress; and the Capuchin, whatever he may have thought, did not deny it. Finally he requested, imposed rather, one condition: that his brother's slayer should leave the city at once. The Capuchin, who had already decided on this, said that it would be done, letting the other think, if he wished to, that this was an act of obedience; and so it was all arranged. The family were satisfied, for they came out of it with honour; the friars were satisfied, for they had saved a man as well as their privileges without making any enemies; the experts on chivalry were satisfied, for they saw an affair of honour ending in a proper way; the people were satisfied, for they saw a man they liked get out of a difficulty, and at the same time had a conversion to edify them; finally, satisfied more than anyone else, in the midst of his sorrow, was our Lodovico, who was about to begin a life of service and expiation, which might, if not repair, at least atone for the harm he had done, and deaden the intolerable pangs of remorse. The suspicion that his decision might be put down to fear distressed him for a moment, but he consoled himself at once with the thought that this unjust judgement would be for him another punishment and way of atoning. Thus he wrapped himself in sackcloth at the age of thirty; and as he had, according to the rules, to lay aside his own name and assume another, he chose one which would remind him at every moment of what he had to atone for; and called himself Fra Cristoforo.

As soon as the ceremony of taking the habit was over, the Superior told him he was to go and do his novitiate at * * *, sixty miles away, and that he was to leave next day. The novice gave a deep bow and asked for just one favour. 'Grant me permission, father,' he said, 'before I depart from this city where I have shed a man's blood and leave a family I have cruelly wronged, at least to make amends for what I have done; let me at least show my regret at not being able to repair the loss, by begging the brother of the man I have killed to forgive me, and taking, if God blesses my intention, the bitterness away from his heart.' It seemed to the Superior that such a step would not only be good in itself, but that it would help to conciliate the family to the monastery still more: and he went off at once to take Fra Cristoforo's request to the brother. The unexpected suggestion was received with amazement and with another upsurge of indignation, though not without a certain gratification too. After a moment's thought he said, 'Let him come tomorrow,' and gave a time. The Superior went back and took the novice the consent he wanted.

It had at once occurred to the nobleman that the more solemn and public this apology was, the more it would enhance his prestige with his whole family and with the people; it would also make (to use a fashionable modern phrase) a fine page in the family annals. He hurriedly notified all his relations to favour him (as they said then) with their company at noon next day, when they would have a general satisfaction. At midday the palace was teeming with gentry of every age and sex; they thronged about, with a swishing of big cloaks, a waving of tall plumes, and a dangling of rapiers, a poised movement of curled starched ruffs, a trailing and interlacing of brocaded robes. The ante-rooms, the courtyard, and the street were swarming with servants, pages, bravi, and spectators. When he saw all this show, Fra Cristoforo guessed the reason, and felt a slight trepidation; but the next instant he said to himself: – It's only right; I killed him publicly, with enemies all round him; that was a scandal in public, this is a reparation in public. – So, with his eyes cast down, and the other friar at his side, he went through the gate, crossed the courtyard, passing through a throng that gazed at him with impudent curiosity, climbed the stairs, and amidst another throng of nobles who drew back to make room for him to pass, finally, followed by a hundred eyes, came into the presence of the master of the house; the latter was standing in the middle of the saloon, surrounded by his nearest of kin, with his eyes on the ground and his chin in the air, clutching the hilt of his sword in his left hand and grasping the lapel of his cloak to his breast with his right.

There are times when a man's face and bearing have such a transparent air, such an open indication of the soul within, that a crowd of spectators could only judge it in one way. Fra Cristoforo's face and bearing told the bystanders quite clearly that he had not turned friar or come to humiliate himself from any human fears, and this began to conciliate everyone towards him. When he saw the person he had injured, he hurried towards him, went down on his knees before him, crossed his hands on his breast, and bowing his shaven head, said: 'I am your brother's murderer. God knows how gladly I would restore him to you at the cost of my own life; but as I can do nothing more but make these useless and tardy apologies, I implore you to accept them, for the love of God.' Every eye was fixed on the novice and on the person he was addressing; every ear was strained. As Fra Cristoforo stopped talking, a murmur of compassion and respect went round the hall. The nobleman, standing there with his air of forced condescension and suppressed rage, was disturbed by the words, and bent down towards the kneeling man. 'Rise,' he said in a softened voice. 'The injury ... the matter really ... but the habit you wear ... not only that but for yourself too ... get up, father. ... My brother ... I can't deny ... was a gentleman ... was a man ... who was apt to be rather impetuous ... rather hasty. But everything happens according to God's will. Let's say no more about it. ... But, father, you must not stay in that position.' And he took him by the arm and raised him up. Fra Cristoforo, standing now, but with his head bowed, replied, 'Can I hope then that you have granted me your pardon? And if I have yours, may I not hope for Another's? Oh, if only I could hear that word from your lips – pardon!'

'Pardon?' said the nobleman. 'You no longer need it. But, as you wish it, yes, yes, of course I pardon you with all my heart, and so do all of us. . . . '

'All of us! All of us!' shouted the bystanders together. The friar's face lit up with grateful joy, though under it there still showed the deep, humble remorse for a sin which no man's forgiveness could repair. The nobleman, won over by this look and carried away by the general emotion, flung his arms round his neck, and gave and received the kiss of peace.

'Bravo! Good!' burst out from all over the hall; everyone moved towards the friar and came pressing round him. Meanwhile servants arrived with copious refreshments. The nobleman approached our Cristoforo again, who was showing signs of wanting to withdraw, and said, 'Father, take something; do give me this proof of friendship,' and began serving him before anyone else; but the other drew back in friendly deprecation. 'Such things,' said he, 'are no longer for me; but never will I refuse a gift of yours. I am just about to set out on a journey; please let them bring me a loaf of bread, so that I can say I have partaken of your charity, and eaten your bread, and been given a token of your forgiveness.' The nobleman, deeply moved, ordered this to be done; and a footman in full dress soon appeared carrying a loaf of bread on a silver dish, and presented it to the friar, who took it, gave thanks, and put it into his knapsack. Then he asked leave to withdraw; and after another embrace from the master of the house and from all those near enough to get hold of him for a moment, he managed with difficulty to tear himself away; in the ante-rooms he had to struggle to free himself from the servants, and even from the bravi, who were kissing the hem of his robe and his cord and cowl. He reached the street borne along as if in triumph, and was accompanied by great throngs of people as far as one of the city gates, passing which he began his journey on foot towards the place of his novitiate.

The dead man's brother and kinsmen, who had been expecting that day to taste the deplorable pleasures of pride, found themselves filled instead with the serene delights of benevolence and forgiveness. The company stayed on some little while, discussing with quite unusual cordiality and amiability topics which none of them had been prepared for when they went there. Instead of satisfactions enforced, injuries avenged, and scores wiped off, their conversation ran on themes such as praises of the novice, on meekness and reconciliation. And one of them, who would probably have told for the fiftieth time the story of how his father, Count Muzio, had managed to get the better of that famous boaster Marquis Stanislao in their famous confrontation, held forth instead on the penances and marvellous long-suffering patience of a Fra Simone, who had died many years before. When the company had left, the master of the house, still in a state of deep emotion, began thinking over in wonder what he had heard and what he had said himself. 'The devil take that friar!' he muttered to himself – we must put down his exact words – 'The devil take that friar! If he'd stayed down on his knees a moment longer, I'd have been on the point of asking forgiveness from him, because he killed my brother.' Our story notes particularly that this nobleman was a little less hasty and a little more affable from that day onwards.

Father Cristoforo went on his way with a peace of mind he had never felt since that terrible day for which he was to dedicate his whole life to atone. He observed the silence imposed on novices without being aware of it, so absorbed was he in the thought of the labours, trials, and humiliations he would have to undergo to expiate his sin. He stopped at the house of a patron of the order at dinner-time, and ate the bread of forgiveness with almost voluptuous pleasure, but he retained a piece, and put it back into his knapsack, to keep as a perpetual reminder.

We do not intend to tell the story of his life as a friar; all we will record is that he carried out most carefully and cheerfully the ordinary duties assigned to him, of preaching and ministering to the dying; but he never lost an opportunity of carrying out two other duties he had imposed on himself: that of settling quarrels and that of protecting the weak. In this, without his realizing it, there entered something of his old self, and a spark of that warlike spirit which his humiliations and mortifications had not been able entirely to subdue. His language was usually humble and mild; but when truth and justice were at stake the old impetus would suddenly revive, and, strengthened and modified by a solemn emphasis due to the habit of preaching, give his language a character entirely its own. His whole bearing showed, as did his face, traces of a long struggle between a naturally fiery and violent temperament, and an opposing will that was usually victorious, always alert, and directed by higher motives and inspirations. One of his brother-friars and friends, who knew him well, once compared him to one of those words in the vocabulary which are rather too strong to use in the natural state, and which some (even educated people) use when carried away by passion, in a jumbled state, with a letter or so changed – words which remind one, even in this disguise, of their primitive energy.*

If any poor unknown girl in Lucia's plight had asked for Father Cristoforo's help, he would have hurried to her at once. As it was Lucia, he made all the readier haste because he knew and admired her innocence, was already worried about the danger she was in, and was full of indignation at the base persecution to which she was being subjected. In addition to this he was afraid that, having advised her to tell no one and keep quiet about it to avoid making things worse, his advice might have had some unfortunate effect; and to his natural kindliness were now added the torturing scruples which often afflict the good.

But while we have been telling Father Cristoforo's story he has arrived and appeared at the door; and the women have left the handle of the creaking spinning-wheel which they were turning, and started up, both crying with one voice: 'Oh, Father Cristoforo! Bless you!'

CHAPTER 5

Father Cristoforo stopped short on the threshold, and realized from his first glance at the women that his presentiments had not played him false. And so, in that tone of inquiry which anticipates bad news, his beard rising with a slight backward movement of his head, he said, 'Well, my children?' Lucia's reply was to burst into tears. Her mother began to apologize for their presumption ... but the friar came forward and sat down on a three-legged stool, and cut short the excuses by saying to Lucia, 'Calm yourself, my poor child. And you' – he turned to Agnese – 'tell me what's happened.' While the good woman was telling the sad tale as best she could, the friar changed colour again and again, raised his eyes to heaven, and sometimes stamped a foot on the ground. When the tale was told, he covered his face with his hands, and exclaimed, 'O blessed Lord! How long ...' But, without finishing the phrase, he turned to the women again and said, 'You poor things! God has indeed visited you. My poor Lucia!'

'You'll not abandon us, father?' said the latter between her sobs.

'Abandon you!' replied he. 'And if I abandoned you when you're in such a plight how would I ever dare to ask God for anything for myself again? You, whom He confided to me! Don't lose heart; He will help you; He is all-seeing; He can even make a worthless creature such as myself serve His purpose to confound a . . . Come now, let's think what can be done.'

So saying, he propped his left elbow on his knee, cupped his forehead in his palm, and grasped his beard and chin with his right hand, as if to bring all his spiritual powers firmly to bear. But the more carefully he examined it, the more he realized how serious and involved the matter was, and how few, uncertain, and dangerous were the resources. – Should I try to make Don Abbondio feel ashamed of himself and bring home to him how much he has failed in his duty? Shame and duty will not mean anything to him in his present state of fright. What about giving him a fright myself? What could I find that would frighten him more than a musket shot? Should I tell the cardinal archbishop about it all, and ask him to use his authority? That would take time; and what about meanwhile? What about afterwards? Even if this poor girl was married, would that curb this man? What lengths might he not go to? . . . And as for resisting him, how could we do that? Ah, if only, thought the poor friar, I could get our friars here and in Milan to do something! Ah! But this is no ordinary affair; they'd ignore me. That fellow pretends he's a friend of the monastery, and makes himself out to be a supporter of the Capuchins; have not his bravi come to us for asylum more than once? I'd be left in the lurch, and find myself being called a restless intriguer, and a troublemaker, too; and, what's more, I might also, by a misplaced effort, make things worse for the poor girl. – After weighing up the pros and cons of the various alternatives, he decided that the best course was to face Don Rodrigo himself, and try to put him off his infamous designs by imploring him and by frightening him with the terrors of the next life, and, if possible, of this one too. At the worst, he would at least this way get a clearer idea of how stubbornly he meant to carry on with his base engagement, find out more about his intentions, and be guided accordingly.

While the friar was thus brooding, Renzo, who could not keep away from the house, for reasons which anyone can guess, had appeared at the door; but on seeing the friar deep in thought, and the women signalling that he should not be disturbed, he stopped silent on the threshold. When the friar raised his head to tell the two women his plan, he noticed him, and greeted him with his usual familiar affection, given an added warmth by compassion.

'Have they told you, father?' Renzo asked him, in a broken voice.

'They have indeed, alas; and that's why I'm here.'

'What've you to say about that swine . . .?'

'It doesn't matter what I say. He's not here to listen; and what's the use of wasting words? I tell you, my dear Renzo, to put your trust in God, and He won't forsake you.'

'God bless you for those words!' exclaimed the youth. 'You're not one of those who always find the poor are in the wrong. But his reverence the parish priest and his worship the lawyer of lost causes . . .'

'Don't dwell on things that can only worry you pointlessly. I'm only a poor friar; but the little I can do for you – as I've just said to these women – I'll do willingly, and I won't desert you.'

'Oh, you're not like my friends out in the world! Just talkers! After all the offers they made to me when things were going well. Ah, ha! They were ready to give their very blood for me; they'd back me up against the very devil himself. If ever I had an enemy all I'd to do was give them a hint, and they'd soon have shut his mouth for him. And now you should see how they're drawing back. . . .' Raising his eyes to the friar's face at this point, he saw that it had clouded over, and realized that he should have kept quiet. But, in trying to set things right, he got more and more confused and involved: 'I meant . . . I didn't mean . . . that is, I meant to say . . .'

'What did you mean to say? Eh? So you've begun to spoil my work before it's even begun! It's a good thing for you you were undeceived in time. What! You were going round looking for friends. . . . And what friends! . . . They couldn't have helped you even if they had wanted to. And yet you were ready to lose one Friend who is both able and willing to do so. Do you not know that God is the Friend of the afflicted who put their trust in Him? Do you not know that the weak gain nothing by showing their claws? And even if . . .' At this point he grasped Renzo's arm firmly; and his look, without losing its authority, became touched by a solemn remorse. His eyes dropped, his voice became slow and almost sepulchral: 'and even if . . . what a terrible reward! Renzo! Will you put your trust in me? . . . What am I saying – in me? – a feeble mortal, a wretched friar? – Will you put your trust in God?'

'Ah, yes,' answered Renzo. 'He's really our Lord.'

'Good; promise me you won't attack or provoke anyone, and that you'll let yourself be guided by me.'

'I promise.'

Lucia heaved a great sigh, as if a weight had been lifted from her; and Agnese said, 'There's a good boy.'

'Listen, my children,' went on Fra Cristoforo. 'I'm going to talk to this man today. If God touches his heart and lends power to my words, well and good. If not, He will find some other solution. You meanwhile, keep quietly indoors, avoid all gossiping, and don't show yourselves. This evening, or tomorrow morning at the latest, you'll see me again.' So saying, he cut short their blessings and thanks, and went back to the monastery, where he arrived in time to recite sext in choir,* had lunch, and then set off at once for the lair of the wild beast which he wanted to try and tame.

Don Rodrigo's mansion stood alone, like a watch-tower, on top of one of the knolls scattered on that rugged side of the lake. To this indication our anonymous chronicler adds that the place (he would have done better to give its name clearly) was about three miles above the village where our couple lived, and four miles away from the monastery. At the foot of the knoll, on the south side looking over the lake, lay a little group of hovels occupied by Don Rodrigo's tenants, which was like the tiny capital of his petty kingdom. One had only to pass through it to get a clear idea of the habits and customs of the state. On glancing into a downstairs room through some door left open, one saw muskets, blunderbusses, spades, rakes, straw hats, hairnets, and powder-horns, piled higgledy-piggledy against the walls. The people one met there were scowling, powerful-looking fellows, with great quiffs of hair in nets thrown back over their heads; toothless old men who seemed ready to snarl and show their gums at the slightest provocation; women with masculine faces and brawny arms ready to back up their tongues if those were not enough; there seemed something surly and provocative in the looks and movements of the very children playing in the street.

Fra Cristoforo passed through the village, took a winding path up the hill, and came out on a small terrace in front of the mansion. The gate was shut, a sign that its master was at table and did not want to be disturbed. The few small windows looking on to the path were closed by shutters, dilapidated and eaten with age, but protected by thick iron grilles, although those on the ground floor were so high that a man could scarcely reach them by standing on another's shoulders. Deep silence reigned there; and the passer-by might have taken it for a deserted house, had not four creatures, two living and two dead, dispersed symmetrically outside it, given a sign of its being inhabited. Two great vultures, with spread wings and dangling heads, one stripped of its feathers and half eaten by time, the other still feathered and sound, were nailed up, one on each of the double gates; and two bravi lay sprawled on the benches to right and left of them, keeping guard and waiting to be called to enjoy the remains from their master's table. The friar stopped, as if he was prepared to wait. But one of the bravi got up and said to him, 'Father, father, go right in; we don't keep Capuchins waiting here; we're friends of the monastery; and I've been in there sometimes when the air outside wasn't too healthy; and things would have gone badly if you'd shut the door on me.' So saying, he gave two raps on the knocker, which sound was answered at once by the baying and howling of mastiffs and puppies within; and a few minutes later an old serving-man came grumbling to the door. But on seeing the friar he made him a low bow, quietened the dogs with coaxes and caresses, let the guest into a narrow courtyard, and shut the door again. Then he ushered him into a drawing-room, and looking at him with a mixture of surprise and respect, said, 'Aren't you ... Father Cristoforo of Pescarenico?'

'Yes, I am.'

'You, here?'

'As you see, my good man.'

'It'll be to do some good ... some good,' he went on, muttering to himself and setting off again. 'There's room for that every-where.' Passing through two or three other dark rooms, they reached the door of the dining-hall, from which came a confused din of knives and forks, of glasses and plates, but above all of raucous voices trying to shout each other down. The friar wanted to withdraw, and was trying, behind the door, to persuade the serving-man to leave him in some corner of the house until dinner was over, when the door opened. A certain Count Attilio who was sitting facing it (he was a cousin of the master of the house; and we have already mentioned him without giving his name), seeing a shaven head and cowl, and noticing the good friar's modest intentions, shouted out, 'Hey, hey! Don't run away, reverend father; come on in, come on in.' Don Rodrigo, without guessing exactly the purpose of this visit, had a vague presentiment, and would have preferred to dispense with it. But he could not very well hold back, once the thoughtless Attilio had shouted out so loudly; so he said, 'Come in, father, come in.' The friar came forward, bowing to the master of the house, and acknowledging the greetings of the guests with a wave of the hands.

People generally (I do not say everyone) like to picture the honest man facing the wicked with his head high, his gaze steady, his chest thrown out, and a ready tongue. In reality, however, many circumstances which rarely coincide are needed before he can take up this attitude. So the reader must not wonder if Fra Cristoforo, in spite of all the testimony of his conscience, his firm belief in the justice of the cause which he had come to champion, and a feeling of mingled repugnance and pity for Don Rodrigo, found himself standing timidly and almost in awe in the presence of the same Don Rodrigo, as he lounged there at the head of his table, in his own house and kingdom, surrounded by friends and flattery, by all the signs of power, with an expression on his face which was enough to discourage anyone from mentioning even a favour, much less any advice, much less a reproach, much less a rebuke. On his right sat Count Attilio, his cousin, and it scarcely need be added, his partner in rascality and debauch, who had come from Milan to spend a few days with him. On his left, at the other side of the table, with an air of deference, tempered, however, with a certain pomposity and presumption, sat his worship the mayor, the very man whose duty it was, in theory, to see that justice was done to Renzo Tremaglino and restrain Don Rodrigo within the bounds which we have mentioned above. Opposite the mayor, in an attitude of the purest and most exaggerated servility, sat our Doctor Quibble-weaver, with a black gown and a nose more rubicund than usual. Opposite the two cousins were a pair of obscure guests, who are mentioned in our story as doing nothing but eat, bow their heads, smile, and agree with whatever any of the other guests said, if another did not contradict it.

'Give the father a chair,' said Don Rodrigo. A servant brought a chair, on which Fra Cristoforo sat down, apologizing to the nobleman for having come at an inopportune moment. 'I should very much like to talk to you alone about something important, when it's convenient to you,' he added then in a low voice in Don Rodrigo's ear.

'Very well, we'll have our talk,' replied the latter. 'But meanwhile bring the father something to drink.'

The friar tried to excuse himself; but Don Rodrigo, raising his voice above the din, that had started up again, shouted, 'No, by Bacchus, you won't do me this wrong; never shall it be said that a Capuchin has left this house without tasting the wine from my cellar, or an insolent creditor without tasting the wood from my forests.' These words caused a general burst of laughter, and interrupted for a moment the heated discussion which the guests were having among themselves. A servant brought a salver with a flask of wine and a tall glass like a chalice to the friar; and he, not wishing to refuse so pressing an invitation from the person whom it was so important to conciliate, poured out some wine without hesitation, and started to sip it slowly.

'Tasso's authority doesn't bear out your thesis, worshipful Mr Mayor; in fact it goes against you,' Count Attilio began shouting again. 'For that learned and great man, who knew all the rules of chivalry backwards, made Argante's messenger ask the pious Buglione's leave before delivering the challenge to the Christian knights . . .'*

'But that,' answered the mayor, shouting as loudly – 'that's just an addition, a mere addition, just poetic licence, as a messenger is inviolable by law of nations, *jure gentium*; and, without looking too far afield, there's even a proverb which says that ambassadors can't be punished.* And proverbs, my Lord Count, are the wisdom of the human race. And as the messenger said nothing in his own account, but only handed over a written challenge . . .'

'But will you never understand that that messenger was an impudent ass, who didn't know the first thing . . .?'

'With your permission, gentlemen,' interrupted Don Rodrigo, who did not want the dispute to go too far, 'let us put it to Fra Cristoforo, and abide by his ruling.'

'Good! excellent!' said Count Attilio, who thought it most sophisticated to have a point of chivalry decided by a Capuchin; while the mayor, who felt more deeply about the point at issue, kept quiet with difficulty and an expression which seemed to say 'What childishness!'

'But as far as I can follow,' said the friar, 'those are not the sort of things I know about.'

'The usual modest excuses you friars make,' said Don Rodrigo. 'But you won't get out of it. Eh! Come along, father! We all know you were not born with that cowl on your head, and that you've known the world. Come, come; the point at issue is this . . .'

'The thing is . . .' Count Attilio began to shout.

'Let me tell him, cousin, as I'm neutral,' went on Don Rodrigo. 'This is the story. A Spanish knight sends a challenge to a Milanese knight; the messenger doesn't find the man at home, and delivers the letter to the knight's brother; the brother reads the challenge, and gives the messenger a thrashing in reply.* Now the question is . . .'

'Well done him!' shouted Count Attilio. 'It was a real inspiration.'

'Of the devil,' added the mayor. 'To beat a messenger! An ambassador! Whose person is sacred! Even you, father, can say if this was the action of a gentleman.'

'Yes, sir, the action of a gentleman,' shouted the Count. 'And allow me to say so, who ought to know what's becoming a gentleman. Now, if he'd used his fists, it'd be a different matter; but a stick doesn't soil anyone's hands. What I can't understand is why you're so concerned about a varlet's shoulders.'

'Who's mentioned shoulders, my lord Count? You're putting silly things into my mouth that have never come into my head. I was talking about his character, and not about his shoulders. Above all, I was talking about the law of nations. Just you tell me, please, if the *fetiales* of the ancient Romans sent out to carry their challenge to other peoples ever had to ask leave to deliver their message; and just you find me an author anywhere who mentions a *fetialis* being thrashed.'*

'What have the officials of ancient Rome got to do with us? An easy-going lot, and behind-hand, very much behind-hand, in such things. But according to the laws of modern chivalry, which is true chivalry, I say and still maintain that a messenger who dares to hand a gentleman a challenge without first asking his leave is an insolent rascal, who should not only be beaten, but who richly deserves it. . . .'

'Just try to answer this syllogism.'

'No, no, no.'

'Listen, listen, listen. To assault an unarmed man is an act of treachery. *Atqui*, the messenger, *de quo*, was unarmed; *ergo* . . .'*

'Slow, Mr Mayor, slow.'

'Why slow?

'Slow, I say. What's this you're telling me? It's an act of treachery to wound someone with a sword from behind, or to give him a musket-shot in the back; although there are certain precedents even for that. . . . But let's keep to the point. I grant you this could generally be called an act of treachery; but not giving a cad a few blows! Things would be at a pretty pass if he'd had to say, "Look, I'm going to beat you," as one would say to a gentleman, "Hands to your sword!" – And you, my worthy doctor of law, why don't you back me up with one of those fine speeches of yours, to help me persuade this gentleman, instead of just grinning at me to show you're on my side?'

'I . . .' stammered the lawyer in some confusion; 'I'm enjoying this learned argument; and I'm grateful for the chance that gave rise to such a nimble battle of wits. And then, it's outside my jurisdiction; his most illustrious lordship has already delegated a judge . . . the father here. . . .'

'True,' said Don Rodrigo. 'But how can you expect the judge to have his say when the litigants won't stop talking?'

'I'm dumb,' said Count Attilio. The mayor pursed his lips, and raised a hand in sign of resignation.

'Ah, thank heavens! Now the floor's yours, father,' said Don Rodrigo, with mock solemnity.

'I've already excused myself by saying I don't understand these things,' replied Fra Cristoforo, giving his glass back to a servant.

'Not a good enough excuse,' shouted the two cousins. 'We want your decision.'

'If that's the case,' the friar went on, 'then my humble opinion is that there should be neither challenges, nor messengers, nor thrashings.'

The company looked at each other in astonishment.

'Oh, that's rather tall!' said Count Attilio. 'I beg your pardon, father, but that's rather tall. It's obvious you don't know the world.'

'He?' said Don Rodrigo. 'Don't make me smile. Why, he knows it, my dear cousin, as well as you do. Isn't that true, father? Just tell us, father, just tell us, if you too haven't sown your wild oats?'

Instead of answering this playful little question, the friar had a word quietly with himself. – They're trying to get at you; but remember, friar, that you're not here on your own account, and that no personal considerations matter. –

'That may be,' said the cousin. 'But the father ... What's the father's name?'

'Father Cristoforo,' several replied.

'But, Father Cristoforo, my most respected sir, with maxims like those you'd turn the world upside down. No challenges! No thrashings! Then good-bye to the point of honour, and every cad will go unpunished. Luckily, the supposition's quite impossible.'

'Speak up, doctor,' exclaimed Don Rodrigo, who was trying to draw the argument farther away from the two original disputants. 'Speak up; it's your turn. You're a wonder at making a case out for everyone. Let's just see what sort of a case you make out for Father Cristoforo.'

'Really,' replied the doctor, brandishing his fork in the air, and turning to the friar – 'really I can't understand how it has not occurred to Father Cristoforo, who is the perfect combination of man of religion and man of the world, that his judgement – good, excellent, and of due weight in the pulpit though it may be – is worth nothing, if I may say so with all due respect, in a dispute about chivalry. But the father knows better than I do, that everything has got its right place; and I think that he has made a joke, to try and get out of the difficulty of making a judgement.'

What could one ever find to reply to arguments based on a wisdom so ancient, and yet always new? Nothing; and nor did our friar.

But Don Rodrigo, to put an end to this discussion, now started up another one. 'By the way,' he said, 'I hear there are rumours of a compromise going round Milan.'

As the reader knows, there was a struggle going on that year for the succession of the Duchy of Mantua, which, at the death of Vincenzo Gonzaga, who had left no legitimate issue, had passed into the possession of the next-of-kin, the Duke of Nevers. Louis XIII, or rather Cardinal Richelieu, was supporting this prince, who was a close friend, and a naturalized Frenchman. Philip IV, or rather the Count of Olivares, commonly known as the Count-Duke, was opposing him, for the same reason, and had declared war on him. As, however, this duchy was an imperial fief, both sides were putting pressure on the Emperor Ferdinand II, by petitions, intrigues, and threats, the one to confirm the investiture of the new duke, and the other to refuse it, or even get him expelled from the state.*

'I'm inclined to believe,' said Count Attilio, 'that things may be patched up. I've certain sources ...'

'Don't you believe it, my Lord Count, don't you believe it,' interrupted the mayor. 'I hear things even in this remote corner of the world; for his lordship the Spanish commandant, who is good enough to honour me with his friendship, and knows all about everything, as he's the son of one of the Count-Duke's dependants . . .'

'I tell you I come into contact with all sorts of important people in Milan every day; and I know on good authority that the Pope,* who's deeply interested in keeping the peace, has made certain proposals . . .'

'That may well be; it's only to be expected; His Holiness is just doing his duty; it's a pope's job to mediate between Christian princes; but the Count-Duke has his own policy, and . . .'

'And, and, and! D'you know, my dear sir, what the emperor's thinking of at the moment? D'you think Mantua's the only place in this world? There are a lot of things to bear in mind, my dear sir. D'you know, for instance, how far at the moment the emperor can trust that Prince of Wallenston, or Walliston, or whatever his name is,* and if . . .'

'The correct pronunciation in German,' the mayor interrupted again, 'is Vaglienstein, as I've often heard it pronounced by his lordship the Spanish commandant. But don't you worry, for . . .'

'Are you trying to teach me . . .?' the count was beginning, when Don Rodrigo gave him a glance imploring him to stop contradicting, for his sake. The count stopped, and the mayor, like a ship dislodged from a sandbank, continued his run of eloquence under full sail. 'Vaglienstein doesn't worry me much; for the Count-Duke's got eyes for everything and everywhere; and if Vaglienstein gets up to any tricks, he'll set him right, by fair means or foul. He's got his eye everywhere, I tell you, and a long arm; and if he's made up his mind – as he has, and rightly, like the great statesman he is – that the Lord Duke of Neevers is not going to take root in Mantua, then the Lord Duke of Neevers won't. And the Lord Cardinal of Riciliù* will make no more mark than a stone in water. It does rather make me laugh to think of that poor dear cardinal trying to cross swords with a Count-Duke, with an Olivares. In fact, I'd really like to be born again in another two hundred years' time, and hear what our descendants will have to say of such pretensions. Something more than envy's needed – what's needed is a brain, and there's only one brain in the world like the Count-Duke's. The Count-Duke, my dear sirs,' went on the mayor, still driving full sail before the wind, and a little surprised himself at not having run on to any reefs: 'The Count-Duke's an old fox, speaking with all due respect, who can throw anyone off the scent; and when it looks as if he's going right, you can be sure he's going left; so no one can boast of knowing his intentions, and the very people who put them into execution, the very people who write his despatches, are all in the dark. I speak with some knowledge of the facts, as our excellent commandant deigns to treat me with some confidence. The Count-Duke himself, on the other hand, knows exactly what's happening in every other court. Scarcely have these politicians (some of whom are wily enough, there's no denying) thought up a plan before the Count-Duke's already guessed it with that brain of his, and those secret sources and tentacles of his out everywhere. That poor fellow of a Cardinal of Riciliù tries here, sniffs there, toils, and sweats; and all to what purpose? When he's managed to bury his mine, he finds the counter-mine all laid ready by the Count-Duke . . .'

Heaven knows when the mayor would have touched land, had not Don Rodrigo, prompted also by the grimaces which his cousin was making, suddenly turned to a servant, as if on an inspiration, and told him to bring a particular bottle.

'Your worship the mayor and gentlemen,' said he then, 'let's drink a health to the Count-Duke; and you shall judge if the wine is not worthy of the person.' The mayor answered with a bow, as if acknowledging a personal favour; for everything done and said in the Count-Duke's honour he took as partly directed to himself.

'A thousand years of life to Don Gasparo Guzman, Count of Olivares, Duke of San Lucar, chief Private of our lord King Philip the Great!' exclaimed he, raising his glass.

('Private,' for those who do not know it, was the term used at that period for a prince's favourite.)

'A thousand years of life to 'im!' answered everyone.

'Serve the father,' said Don Rodrigo.

'Excuse me,' answered the friar. 'But I've already broken a rule, and I couldn't . . .'

'What!' said Don Rodrigo. 'It's a toast to the Count-Duke! D'you want to let us think you're on the side of the Navarese?'

(Such was the disparaging name given to the French at this time, from the princes of Navarre, who had begun reigning over them with Henry IV.)*

At an invitation put in these terms he thought it best to drink.

All the guests broke out into raptures and praises of the wine; all except the lawyer, whose raised head, fixed gaze, and pursed lips were more expressive than any words.

'Well, doctor, what d'you think of it?' asked Don Rodrigo.

The doctor drew from his glass a nose more rubicund and glistening than the wine itself, and replied, with great emphasis on every syllable, 'I state, pronounce, and decree that this is the Olivares of wines; *censui, et in eam ivi sententiam,* * that a similar liquor is not to be found in all the twenty-two kingdoms of our lord the king, whom God preserve. I declare and define that the dinners of our most illustrious lord Don Rodrigo eclipse the feasts of Heliogabalus;* and that famine is for ever banished from this palace, where splendour sits enthroned.'

'Well said! Well defined!' shouted the guests in chorus. But that word famine, which the doctor had uttered by chance, suddenly turned all their thoughts on to this melancholy subject; and they all began talking about the famine. Here everyone was in agreement – at the beginning, at least; but the noise was perhaps even louder than if they had disagreed. Everyone talked at once. 'There is no famine,' said one. 'It's the speculators . . .'

'And the bakers,' said another, 'who're cornering the grain. String 'em up!'

'That's right! String 'em up without mercy.'

'After fair trial,' shouted the mayor.

'Why trial?' shouted Count Attilio, even louder. 'Summary justice. Take three or four, five or six – the ones generally thought to be the richest and meanest – and string 'em up!'

'Make an example! Make an example! Nothing can be done without making an example.' 'Hang 'em! Hang 'em! And then grain'll come pouring out of every corner.'

If any of my readers has happened, on his way through a fairground, to have heard a troupe of fiddlers all tuning their instruments between numbers, each making as loud a noise as possible, so that they can distinguish their own instruments above the row made by the others, he can imagine the euphony of this conversation, if such it can be called. Meanwhile, that wine was flowing freely, and its praises getting mixed up, as was right and proper, with opinions on political economy; so that the words heard most often and more distinctly than any others were 'ambrosial!' and 'hang 'em!'

Don Rodrigo was giving an occasional glance, meanwhile, towards the only person who was silent there, and saw him sitting motionless, showing no signs of haste or impatience, making no move to remind him that he was waiting; but looking as if he had no intention of leaving until he had had his say. He would gladly have sent him off, and dispensed with the interview; but it was against his policy to dismiss a Capuchin without giving him a hearing. As the nuisance could not be avoided, he decided to face it at once and get it over; he rose from the table, the whole rubicund company rising with him, without interrupting the noise. Then he excused himself to his guests, and, rather stiffly approaching the friar, who had jumped up with the others, he said: 'I am at your service,' and led him into another room.

CHAPTER 6

'What can I do for you?' said Don Rodrigo, taking up a stand in the middle of the room. Such were his actual words, but the way he pronounced them clearly meant: take care who you're talking to, weigh your words, and hurry up about it.

There was no quicker or surer way of giving our Fra Cristoforo courage than to treat him arrogantly. He who had been hesitating, at a loss for words, passing the beads of the rosary on his girdle through his fingers as if hoping to find his preamble in one of them, now on Don Rodrigo's taking this line found more words than he needed come rushing to his lips. But realizing how important it was not to wreck his hopes, or – what was much more important – those of other people, he altered and toned down the phrases that had come into his mind, and said with studied humility, 'I have to suggest an act of justice to you, and appeal to your charity. Certain disreputable characters have been using your Excellency's name to frighten a poor priest and prevent him carrying out his duties, and so impose on two innocent people. A word from you can confound them, restore justice to its place, and relieve those who have been so cruelly wronged. This is in your power, and as it's in your power ... conscience, honour ...'

'You can talk to me about my conscience when I come to you for confession. As for my honour, I, and I alone, let me tell you, am its guardian; and I regard anyone who has the audacity to try to help me look after it as insolent and offensive.'

Fra Cristoforo, warned by these words that the lordling was trying to make the worst of what he said in order to turn the conversation to a quarrel and prevent him coming to the point, became all the more determined to be patient and to swallow every insult the other was pleased to make; so he quickly replied, in a subdued tone: 'If I have said anything to offend you, it was certainly unintentional. Do please correct me, rebuke me, if I do not speak with due respect; but deign to listen to me. For the love of heaven, of that God before whom we shall all have to appear . . .' – as he said this he took up the little wooden skull on his rosary in his fingers and held it before the eyes of his frowning listener – ' do not persist in refusing such a simple act of justice, and one that is so much due to these poor creatures. Remember that God always has His eye on them, and that their cries and groans are heard above. Innocence is a strong force in His . . .'

'No, father!' interrupted Don Rodrigo sharply. 'I have a great respect for the habit you wear; but the one thing that might make me forget it would be to see it on someone who has the audacity to come and spy on me in my own house.'

This word brought a flush to the friar's cheek; but, with the look of one swallowing a very bitter medicine, he went on: 'You cannot really think that is a proper thing to call me. You feel in your heart that my errand here is neither base nor contemptible. Listen to me, my Lord Rodrigo; and may heaven grant that you will not one day regret having failed to listen to me. Do not set your own glory. . . . What glory, Don Rodrigo! Glory before men maybe! But before God! You have much power down here; but . . .'

'Let me tell you,' said Don Rodrigo, interrupting him angrily, though not without a slight shiver of dread – 'let me tell you that when I've a fancy to hear a sermon, I can perfectly well go to church, like everyone else; but in my own house! Oh!' he went on, with an effort at a jeering smile, 'you're treating me as more important than I really am. A preacher in the house! Why, only princes have them.'

'And that same God who calls princes to reckoning for the words He addresses them in their palaces, that same God is now giving you a token of His mercy, by sending one of His ministers – a wretched and unworthy one, but still one of His ministers – to plead for an innocent girl . . .'

'Well, father,' said Don Rodrigo, making a move to go, 'I don't know what you're driving at: all I gather is there seems some girl you're very concerned about. Go and confide in whoever you please about it, but don't take the liberty of boring a gentleman with it any longer.'

As Don Rodrigo moved, the friar placed himself in front of him, though in an attitude of deep respect; and, raising his hands, as if to implore him and delay him at the same time, went on persistently: 'I am concerned about her, it's true, but not more than I am about you; both your souls concern me more than my own life does. Don Rodrigo! All I can do is pray to God for you: but that I'll do from the bottom of my heart. Do not refuse me; do not keep a poor innocent girl in anguish and terror. A word from you can settle everything.'

'Very well,' said Don Rodrigo. 'As you think I can do such a lot for this person; as you have her interests so much at heart ...'

'Well?' repeated Father Cristoforo anxiously, not feeling that Don Rodrigo's bearing and attitude did much to encourage the hope which these words seemed to convey.

'Well, advise her to come and put herself under my protection. She'll have everything she wants, and no one'll dare molest her, or I'm no gentleman.'

At this suggestion the friar's indignation, which he had held in check with difficulty till then, burst out. All his resolutions of prudence and patience went to the winds; his old self joined up with the new: in such cases, in fact, Fra Cristoforo really had the energy of two men. 'Your protection!' he exclaimed, recoiling a couple of paces, leaning proudly on his right foot, putting his right hand to his hip, pointing the other with outstretched forefinger towards Don Rodrigo, and fixing on him a pair of blazing eyes – 'your protection! It's a good thing you said that; it's a good thing you made such a suggestion. You've gone over the limit: and I'm not afraid of you any more.'

'How dare you talk to me like that, friar!'

'I'm talking as one talks to one abandoned by God, who cannot frighten any longer. Your protection! I well knew that innocent girl was under God's protection; but you – you've filled me with such a certainty of it now that I no longer need to take care what I say to you. Lucia, I say – see how I pronounce her name with head high and steady eyes.'

'What! In this house ...!'

'I pity this house. A curse hangs over it. You will see if the justice of God can be kept out by a few stones, or frightened off by a pair of sentries. You think God made a creature in His own image in order to give you the pleasure of tormenting her! You think God won't be able to defend her! You've spurned His warning. You are judged for it! Pharaoh's heart was as hard as yours, and God found a way to crush it.* Lucia is safe from you; I – a poor friar – I tell you that; and as for yourself, listen to what I foretell for you. A day will come . . .'

Up to now Don Rodrigo had been standing rooted there, speechless with rage and amazement; but when he heard this beginning of a prophecy being intoned, a vague, mysterious dread was added to his rage.

Quickly he seized that lifted, threatening hand, and, raising his voice to drown that of this prophet of ill omen, shouted: 'Get out of my sight, you impudent peasant, you lout in a cowl.'

Words so clear calmed down Father Cristoforo at once. Violence and insult had been so long and so closely associated in his mind with the idea of silence and suffering, that at this last compliment every trace of anger and excitement fell away from him, leaving him only with a wish to hear out quietly whatever Don Rodrigo might please to add. So, quietly withdrawing his hand from the nobleman's grasp, he bent his head and stood there motionless, as a battered tree, when the wind drops at the height of a storm, settles its leaves back naturally and waits for what hail the sky may send.

'You presumptuous upstart!' went on Don Rodrigo. 'You dare treat me as an equal! But you can thank the cassock on your rascally shoulders for saving you from the thrashing the likes of you get to teach them to keep a civil tongue in their heads. You can get out on your own legs this time; and we'll see about it.'

So saying he pointed, with imperious disdain, at a door opposite the one by which they had entered. Father Cristoforo bowed his head and went out, leaving Don Rodrigo pacing with furious strides up and down the field of battle.

When the friar had shut the door behind him, he noticed a man creeping quietly out of the room which he had just entered, keeping close to the wall, as if to avoid being seen from the room where the interview had taken place; and he recognized the old serving-man who had come to admit him at the gate. This man had been in that house for forty years or so – that is, before Don Rodrigo was born; he had entered it in the service of his father, who had been a man of quite a different sort. On his death the new master had dismissed the whole household and taken on a new set, but kept this man, both because of his age, and because, although his principles and habits were entirely different from his own, he had two qualities which made up for these defects: a lofty idea of the family dignity, and great experience in its ceremonial, whose most ancient traditions and minutest details he knew better than anyone else. In his master's presence the poor old man had never dared to hint, much less express, his disapproval of what he saw around him every day; the most that he ever did was to make some exclamation, or mutter a reproach between his teeth to his fellow-servants, who laughed at him for it, and sometimes even enjoyed egging him on in the subject, making him say more than he had meant to, and sing the praises once again of the old way of life of the house. His criticisms never reached his master's ears without an account of the laughter they had aroused; so that he, too, considered them only as harmless matters for jest. Then on days of entertaining or reception the old man became a serious and important personage.

Father Cristoforo looked at him as he passed, gave him a greeting, and was going on his way. But the old man came towards him with a mysterious air, put his finger to his lips, and then, with the same finger, beckoned him to follow him into a dark passage. Once there, he said in a whisper: 'Father, I heard everything, and I must talk to you.'

'Speak up quickly, then, my good man.'

'Not here; it'd be terrible if my master noticed. . . . But I know a lot, and I'll try and come to the monastery tomorrow.'

'Is there some plot on?'

'There's something in the wind, that's certain: I had noticed that already. But now I'll keep my ears open, and hope to find out all about it. Leave it to me. The things I see and hear . . .! Awful things! This house I'm in is . . .! But I want to save my soul.'

'May the Lord bless you!' and as the friar whispered these words he put his hand on the serving-man's white head, and he, older man though he was, stood bowing before him, like a son before his father. 'The Lord will reward you,' went on the friar. 'Do not fail to come tomorrow.'

'I'll come,' replied the serving-man. 'But you must leave at once, and – for the love of heaven – don't mention my name.' So saying, and looking around, he went out by the other end of the passage into a hall which gave on to the courtyard; then, seeing that the coast was clear, he beckoned the good friar, whose expression was a clearer answer to his last remark than any protestation. The serving-man showed him the way out, and the friar left without another word.

Now, this man had been listening at his master's door; had he done right? And had Fra Cristoforo done right to commend him for it? According to the most normal and generally accepted rules, it was a very bad thing to do; but could this not be regarded as an exception? And are there any exceptions to the most normal and generally accepted rules? Important questions, these; but the reader will have to decide them for himself, if he has a mind to. We do not intend to pass judgement; it is enough for us to record the facts.

Once outside and his back turned on that den of evil, Fra Cristoforo breathed more freely, and went hurrying down the slope, flushed in the face, and excited and upset, as may be imagined, both by what he had heard and by what he had said himself. But the old man's totally unexpected offer had been a great restorative; it seemed as if heaven had given him a visible sign of its protection. – Here's a thread, a thread put into my hands by Providence. And in that very house! Without my ever having dreamt of looking for it. – As he was thus ruminating, he raised his eyes towards the west, and seeing the sun low and already touching the tops of the mountains, he thought there was very little of the day left. Then, although his bones were aching and exhausted by the various fatigues of that day, yet he quickened his pace, so as to be able to take such news as he had to his protégés and be back at the monastery by nightfall; this being one of the strictest and most severely enforced rules of the Capuchin code.

Meanwhile at Lucia's cottage plans were being put forward and discussed, of which the reader should be informed. After the friar's departure the three of them had remained in silence for some time: Lucia sadly preparing the supper; Renzo on the point of leaving every moment, so as to avoid seeing her harrowed face, and yet unable to tear himself away; Agnese apparently all intent at the reel she was winding, though she was, in fact, turning a plan over in her mind, and when it seemed ready, she broke the silence by saying:

'Listen, my children! If you've got enough wit and courage, and if you trust your mother' (at that 'your' addressed to both of them Lucia gave a start), 'I can undertake to get you out of this hole, perhaps better and quicker than Fra Cristoforo, wonderful man though he is.' Lucia stood motionless and gave her a look more of surprise than of faith in such a magnificent promise. Renzo said at once: 'Wit? Courage? Go on, tell us – tell us what can be done.'

'It's true, isn't it,' Agnese went on, 'that we'd be a good step forward if you were already married? And that we could find a solution for everything else more easily?'

'There's no doubt of that, is there?' said Renzo. 'Once married, it's a wide world: and only a few steps from here, over the Bergamese border, a silk-worker's received with open arms. You know how often my cousin Bortolo's pressed me to go and live with him, and told me I'd make my fortune there, as he has; and the reason I never agreed to go was – why not say? – was because my heart was here. Once married, we could all go there together and set up house, and live in peace and quiet, out of this swine's clutches, and away from the temptation to do anything rash. Isn't that so, Lucia?'

'Yes,' said Lucia. 'But how . . .?'

'As I said,' went on her mother. 'Wit and courage and it's easy.'

'Easy!' exclaimed the pair together, for whom it had become so strangely and painfully difficult.

'Easy, if you know how to set about it,' replied Agnese. 'Just listen to me carefully, and I'll try to explain. I've heard it said by people who know, and I've seen a case myself, that for a legal marriage you must have a priest, but not necessarily his consent; it's enough if he's there.'

'What's all this?' asked Renzo.

'Just listen, and you'll hear. Two witnesses who're sharp and well-primed are needed. Then one goes to the priest; the important thing is to catch him unawares, so he's got no time to escape. The man says, 'Your reverence, this is my wife'; the woman says, 'Your reverence, this is my husband.' The priest must hear them, and the witnesses must hear them; and the marriage is all done, and as binding as if the Pope himself had done it. Once the words have been said, the priest can yell and shout and raise the devil; but it's all no use: you're man and wife.'

'Can it be really possible?' exclaimed Lucia.

'What!' said Agnese. 'You'll see I haven't learned nothing in the thirty years I spent in the world before you were born. It's just as I tell you; and in fact a woman I know who wanted to marry against her parents' wishes got what she wanted by doing this. The priest had his suspicions, and was on the look-out; but the young devils were smart enough to catch 'im at the right moment, said the words, and were husband and wife; though the poor girl regretted it afterwards within three days.'

Agnese was telling the truth, both about the possibilities and about the dangers of failure; for, as the only people who had recourse to this expedient were those who had found the ordinary way barred or refused, the parish priests took great care to avoid such forcible co-operation; and when one of them, even so, was surprised by one of these couples, with witnesses, he tried as hard to elude them as Proteus* did those who wanted to make him prophesy against his will.

'If only it were true, Lucia!' said Renzo, looking at her with an imploring air.

'What d'you mean, if only it were true?' said Agnese. 'You think I'm romancing too. I do my utmost for you both, and then I'm not believed. Very well, very well, get out of it as best you can; I wash my hands of it.'

'Ah, no! Don't forsake us!' said Renzo. 'I only said that because it seemed too good to be true. I'm in your hands; I look on you as if you were my real mother.'

These words dispelled Agnese's little gust of indignation, and made her forget a suggestion which had not, in truth, been made seriously.

'But then, why, mother,' said Lucia, in that demure way of hers – 'why didn't this occur to Father Cristoforo?'

'Occur?' replied Agnese. 'You can be sure it occurred to him! But he wouldn't have wanted to mention it.'

'Why not?' asked both the young people together.

'Why not? ... Well, if you really want to know, it's because the clergy don't think it's really quite right.'

'How can it not be quite right, and then all right once it's done?' asked Renzo.

'Don't ask me,' replied Agnese. 'They've made the laws as they wanted them, and poor folk like us can't understand them all. Like so many other things ... Look; it's like hitting someone; it's not right, but once it's done, not even the Pope can undo it.'

'But if it's not right,' said Lucia, 'one oughtn't to do it.'

'What!' said Agnese. 'D'you think I'd give you advice against God's will? If it was against your parents' wishes, and so's to marry some good-for-nothing ... But with me content, and to take this lad here, and with all the difficulties coming from a scoundrel; and his reverence ...'

'That's clear enough for anyone,' said Renzo.

'We needn't mention it to Fra Cristoforo beforehand,' went on Agnese. 'But once it's all over and done with, what d'you think he'll say? "Ah, my child! It was a naughty thing to do; but you've gone and done it." The clergy've got to talk that way. But, believe me, he'll be glad about it, too, in his heart of hearts.'

Lucia, without finding an answer to this reasoning, did not seem very convinced by it; but Renzo was all enthusiasm, and said: 'If it's like that, then it's as good as done.'

'Not too fast,' said Agnese. 'What about the witnesses? How're you going to find a pair who're willing, and who can keep quiet about it meanwhile? And how're we going to catch his reverence, who's locked himself up at home for the last two days? And keep him there? For I can tell you that although he's a slow man, he'll get as slippery as a cat when he sees you coming with that set-up, and will run off as fast as the devil does from holy water.'

'I've got it! I've got it!' said Renzo, banging his fist on the table and rattling the plates laid out for supper. Then he went on to explain his idea, which Agnese approved entirely.

'These are tricks,' said Lucia. 'They're not above-board. We've been straightforward up to now; let's go on, have faith, and God will come to our help. Fra Cristoforo said so. Let's get his opinion.'

'Be guided by those who know more about it than you do,' said Agnese, looking grave. 'What's the need of asking advice? God says He'll help those who help themselves. We'll tell the father all about it when it's done.'

'Lucia,' said Renzo, 'are you going to fail me now? Haven't we done everything that good Christians should? Oughtn't we to be man and wife already? Hadn't his reverence fixed the date and time himself? Whose fault is it if we've got to fall back on our own wits a bit? No, you won't fail me. I'll go off, and come back with the answer.' And with a parting look of entreaty at Lucia and of connivance at Agnese he hurried off.

Troubles sharpen the wits; and Renzo, who in the straight, even path of his life till then had never had much of an opportunity to make his brain any more flexible, had now, in this case, hit on a scheme which would have done credit to a lawyer. He went, according to plan, straight to the cottage of a certain Tonio, a short way away; he found him in the kitchen with one knee on the hob of the fire, holding the rim of a pot on the hot embers with one hand, and stirring with a wooden spoon a small mess of grey *polenta*, made with buckwheat.* Tonio's mother, brother, and wife were at table; and three or four small children were standing in front of their father, awaiting, with their eyes fixed on the pot, the moment when its contents were poured out. But there was none of that cheerfulness which the sight of an approaching meal usually gives to those who have earned it by hard work. The thickness of the *polenta* was in proportion to the year's harvest, not to the number and appetites of those sitting round the table. And each of them seemed to be thinking, as they gave side-glances of angry desire at the common dish, of the appetite that would survive it. As Renzo was exchanging greetings with the family, Tonio poured the *polenta* into a beechwood bowl standing ready to receive it, where it looked like a small moon in a big halo of mist. Even so, the women said politely to Renzo, 'Will you have some?' an invitation which the peasants of Lombardy (and of innumerable other places) never fail to give to anyone who finds them eating, even if the latter is a rich glutton just risen from table, and they themselves down to their last mouthful.

'No, thank you,' answered Renzo. 'But I only came to say a word to Tonio; and if you like, Tonio, we can go and feed at the inn, so as not to disturb the women, and talk there.' This suggestion was as welcome to Tonio as it was unexpected; and the women, and even the children (who reach the age of reason on this subject very early), were not unwilling to see the withdrawal of a competitor, and the most formidable competitor of all, too, for the *polenta*. The host did not wait to ask any more questions, and went off with Renzo.

They reached the village inn and sat down in complete freedom and perfect solitude, for poverty had banished all the regular customers from that place of delights. After eating what meagre fare there was and emptying a flask of wine, Renzo said to Tonio with an air of mystery: 'If you'd like to do me a small favour, I'd like to do you a big one.'

'Go on, speak out; anything you like,' replied Tonio, filling his glass. 'I'd go through fire for you today.'

'Don't you owe twenty-five *lire* to the parish priest, for the rent of his field that you were working last year?'

'Ah, Renzo, Renzo! You're ruining my treat. Why d'you bring that up now? You've spoilt my good mood.'

'The reason I mentioned the debt,' said Renzo, 'is that, if you like, I can give you the means of paying it.'

'D'you really mean that?'

'Really. Eh? Would you like that?'

'Like that? By Diana, would I like that! Apart from anything else, if only so as not to get those nods and shakes of the head his reverence gives me every time we meet. And then the everlasting: 'Tonio, don't forget! Tonio, when am I going to see you about that little business?' It's got so that when he fixes those eyes of his on me during the sermon I'm almost afraid he's going to say to me, right there in public, "What about that twenty-five *lire*?" Curse that twenty-five *lire*! And then he'd have to give me back my wife's gold necklace, which I could turn into *polenta*. But . . .'

'But, if you're willing to do me a little favour, the twenty-five *lire* are all ready for you.'

'Tell me what.'

'But . . .!' said Renzo, putting his finger to his mouth.

'There's no need for that. You know me.'

'His reverence has been producing one silly reason after the other to put off my wedding; but I want to get it over with. I'm told for sure that if the bride and bridegroom confront him, with two witnesses, and I say: "This is my wife," and Lucia says: "This is my husband," the marriage's all done. D'you get me?'

'You want me to come and be a witness?'

'Exactly.'

'And you'll pay off my twenty-five *lire* for me?'

'That's what I mean.'

'Anyone'd be a fool who didn't do it.'

'But we must find another witness.'

'I've found one. That half-witted brother of mine, Gervaso, will do whatever I tell him. You'll give him something to drink?'

'And to eat,' answered Renzo. 'We'll bring him here with us and give him a good time. But will he be able to do it?'

'I'll teach him; you know I've always had his share of the brains.'

'Tomorrow . . .'

'Good.'

'About dusk . . .'

'Fine.'

'But . . .!' said Renzo, putting his finger to his lips again.

'Bah . . .!' answered Tonio, giving his head a toss over his right shoulder, and raising his left hand with a look which said: You're wronging me.

'But if your wife asks questions, as she's bound to . . .'

'I owe my wife so many lies, I doubt if I'll ever be able to catch up with the arrears. I'll find some story or other to put her heart at rest.'

'Tomorrow morning,' said Renzo. 'We'll talk it all over and get everything properly fixed.'

With this they left the inn, Tonio going towards home, thinking up the tale to tell his womenfolk, and Renzo going to report on the arrangements he had made.

All this time Agnese had been making vain efforts to persuade her daughter. The latter was opposing every argument with one horn or the other of her dilemma: either it was wrong, in which case it should not be done; or it wasn't, in which case why not tell Fra Cristoforo?

Renzo arrived all triumphant, made his report, and finished it with an Mm? by which he meant, Am I a man or aren't I? Could anything better be found? Would it ever have occurred to you? And many other things of that kind.

Lucia was gently shaking her head; but the two enthusiasts took little notice of her, as one does with a child whom one does not expect to take in all the reasons for a thing, but whom one intends in due course to force by persuasion and authority to do what is required of it.

'Good,' said Agnese, 'good; but ... you haven't thought of everything.'

'What's been left out?'

'What about Perpetua? You haven't thought of Perpetua. Tonio and his brother she'll let in; but you! You two! Just think! She'll have orders to keep you at more of a distance than boys from a ripe pear-tree.'

'What shall we do about it?' said Renzo, rather perplexed.

'Here, I've thought of that. I'll come with you; and I've a secret way of drawing her out and getting her so excited she won't notice you others at all, and you'll be able to get in. I'll call her and touch her on such a chord that ... You'll see.'

'Bless you!' exclaimed Renzo. 'I've always said that you're our help in everything.'

'But all this is useless,' said Agnese, 'if we can't persuade Lucia; for she persists in saying it's a sin.'

Renzo used all his eloquence, too; but Lucia was not to be budged.

'I can't answer all your arguments,' said she. 'But I can see that to do this your way we'd have to get on by deceiving, lying, and tricking. Ah, Renzo ! We did not begin like that. I want to be your wife,' and she could not use this word or express that intention without blushing all over – 'I want to be your wife, but by straightforward, God-fearing means, and before the altar. Let us leave it to Him above. Don't you think He can find a way out and help us better than we can ourselves by all this deception? And why keep it dark from Fra Cristoforo?'

The discussion was still dragging on, and showed no signs of nearing its end, when the hurried clatter of sandals and the sound of a flapping cassock, like that made by puffs of wind in a sagging sail, announced Fra Cristoforo. They all fell silent; and Agnese just had time to murmur in Lucia's ear: 'Now, be very careful not to say anything to him.'

CHAPTER 7

Father Cristoforo arrived with the air of an able general who has lost an important battle through no fault of his own and goes hurrying off, distressed but not discouraged, worried but not overwhelmed, in haste but not in flight, to reinforce points that are hard pressed, rally his troops, and give out fresh orders.

'Peace be with you,' said he as he came in. 'There's nothing to be hoped from that man – we must put all the more trust in God; and already I've had a sign of His protection.'

None of the three had had very high hopes in Father Cristoforo's attempt; for to find a powerful person withdrawing from an act of oppression without being forced to, merely out of regard for unarmed entreaties, was a thing unheard-of rather than rare. Yet, even so, the melancholy certainty was a blow to them all. The women bowed their heads. But rage, with Renzo, overcame dejection. This announcement found him already embittered by so many painful surprises, so many abortive efforts and deluded hopes, capped moreover, at that moment, by Lucia's refusals.

'I'd like to know,' he cried, gnashing his teeth and raising his voice louder than he ever had before in Father Cristoforo's presence – 'I'd like to know what reasons that swine gave for maintaining ... for maintaining that my bride's not to be my bride.'

'Poor Renzo!' answered the friar in a grave and sympathetic

tone, and with a look that begged him affectionately to keep calm. 'If men of power wanting to commit acts of injustice always had to give their reasons, things wouldn't be as they are.'

'Then did that swine say that he doesn't want it just because he doesn't want it?'

'He did not even say that, my poor Renzo! It'd be another advantage if people would confess it openly when they're committing a crime.'

'But he must have said something. What did that hell-hound say?'

'I heard what he said, but I could not repeat it to you. The words of a strong and wicked man sting, but not for long. He can grow angry at your suspicions of him and yet make you feel at the same time that they are justified; he can insult you and make himself out to be the injured party, jeer at you and pretend he is in the right, bully and yet complain, flaunt his vices and yet be irreproachable. Do not ask me more about it than that. He never mentioned this innocent girl's name, or yours; he never made out he knew you, or that he wanted anything of you; but ... but, alas, I was forced to realize only too well that he is immovable. All the same, we must trust in God. You, poor souls, must not lose heart; and you, Renzo ... Oh! I can put myself in your place, believe me; I can feel what's going on in your heart. But be patient! Patience! It's a hollow word, a bitter word, for those who have no faith; but you ... won't you allow God one day, two days, as long as He needs, to make justice triumph? Time is His, and He has promised us so much of it! Leave it to Him, Renzo; and let me tell you ... let me tell all of you, that I've got a thread in my hand to help you. I can't say more about it at the moment. I won't be coming up here tomorrow; I'll have to be at the monastery all day, for your sakes. You, Renzo, try and come down there; and if for any unforeseen reason you can't come, send someone you trust, some young fellow with sense, by whom I can let you know what's happened. It's getting dark; I must hurry back to the monastery. Faith and courage, now; and God be with you.'

So saying, he hurried out and began running, almost leaping, down the twisting, stony path, so as not to arrive at the monastery late and risk a severe reprimand, or – what would have worried him still more – a penance that might prevent him being ready and free next day to do anything that his protégés' interests might require.

'Did you hear him say something about . . . about some thread he's got, to help us?' said Lucia. 'We ought to trust in him; he's a man who, when he promises ten . . .'

'If that's all,' interrupted Agnese, 'he might have spoken more clearly, or taken me aside and told me what this . . .'

'Just talk, all talk. I'll finish it off; I'll finish it off!' interrupted Renzo this time, pacing up and down the room, and with a look and tone that left no doubt what he meant by these words.

'Oh, Renzo!' exclaimed Lucia.

'What are you trying to say?' exclaimed Agnese.

'There's no need to say anything. I'll finish it off. Even if he's got a hundred or a thousand devils in him, he's still made of flesh and blood. . . .'

'No, no, for Heaven's sake!' Lucia was beginning, but sobs cut short her voice.

'You shouldn't say things like that, even as a joke,' said Agnese.

'As a joke?' shouted Renzo, stopping in front of Agnese's chair, and fixing her with a pair of starting eyes – 'As a joke! You'll just see if it's a joke.'

'Oh, Renzo!' said Lucia, between her sobs; 'I've never seen you in this state before.'

'Don't say such things, for Heaven's sake,' Agnese went on hastily, lowering her voice. 'Have you forgotten how many people the man's got at his command? And even if – which God forbid . . . There's always justice against the poor.'

'Justice, I'll do it for myself, I will! It's high time I did. It's not easy; I know that too. He guards himself well, the murdering swine; he knows he needs it; but it doesn't matter. Patience and resolution . . . and the right moment'll come. Yes, I'll do justice myself, I will; I'll rid the village of him, I will. How many people will bless me! . . . And then I'll hop off. . . .'

Lucia's horror at the obvious meaning of these words stopped her weeping and gave her strength to speak. Raising her tear-stained face from her hands, she said to Renzo in heartbroken but firm tones: 'So you don't care any more about having me for a wife. I'd promised myself to a God-fearing youth; but a man who had . . . Even if he was out of reach of all justice and vengeance, even if he was the king's son . . .'

'All right!' shouted Renzo, his face more convulsed than ever; 'I won't have you, then; but that man won't have you either. I'll be here without you, and he'll be in . . .'

'Ah, no, for pity's sake don't say such things; don't stare like that. No, I can't bear to see you like that,' exclaimed Lucia, weeping and imploring him with clasped hands, while Agnese was calling the youth by his name over and over again, and patting him on the shoulders and arms and hands to soothe him down. He stood there for some time motionless, deep in thought, gazing into Lucia's imploring face; then, all of a sudden, he gave her a stern look, drew back, stretched out an arm and finger towards her, and shouted, 'Her! Yes, it's her he wants. Death!'

'And what harm've I done you? Why d'you want to kill me too?' said Lucia, flinging herself on her knees before him.

'You!' answered he, his tone now full of a very different kind of anger, but anger none the less. 'You! How have you loved me? What proof have you given me? Haven't I begged you, and begged you, and begged you? And you? No, no!'

'Yes, yes,' replied Lucia precipitously. 'I'll come to the priest tomorrow, now, if you want me to; I'll come. Only be your old self again. I'll come.'

'D'you promise me?' said Renzo, his voice and look becoming all of a sudden more human.

'I promise you.'

'You've promised me, now.'

'Thanks be to thee, O Lord,' exclaimed Agnese, doubly content.

Had Renzo thought, in the midst of this fury of his, of taking advantage of Lucia's terror? Had he perhaps increased it and worked it up a little artificially? Our author protests that he knows nothing about this; and I think that not even Renzo himself was very clear. The facts are that he really was furious with Don Rodrigo and that he was longing for Lucia's consent; and when two strong passions are struggling together in a man's heart, no one, not even the man himself, can always clearly distinguish one voice from the other and say for certain which of them predominates.

'I've promised you,' replied Lucia, in a tone of timid and affectionate reproach. 'But you had promised, too, not to make any disturbance, to submit to Father . . .'

'Oh, come along! What did I lose my temper for? Are you going to go back on it now? And drive me to desperation?'

'No, no,' said Lucia, beginning to get frightened again. 'I've promised, and I won't go back on it; but you see how you've forced it out of me. Let's hope God may not . . .'

'Why're you wishing bad luck on us, Lucia? God knows we're doing no one any harm.'

'Promise me at least you won't do that again.'

'I give you my word, such as it is.'

'But keep to it this time,' said Agnese.

Here the author admits to something else that he does not know: whether Lucia's displeasure at being forced to give her consent was complete and absolute. We, like him, leave this in doubt.

Renzo would have liked to prolong the discussion and settle exactly what they were going to do next day, but it was already dark, and the women, not thinking it proper for him to stay longer at that hour, were bidding him good night.

But it was only as good a night for all three as can come after a day full of trouble and agitation, and before another destined to an affair of importance and uncertain result. Renzo came round very early and made plans for the evening's great operation with the women, or rather with Agnese, each suggesting and resolving difficulties, foreseeing obstacles, and each in turn beginning to describe the affair as if they were talking about something already over and done with. Lucia listened; and, without approving in words what she could not approve in her heart, promised to do her best.

'Are you going down to the monastery to talk to Father Cristoforo, as he told you to last night?' Agnese asked Renzo.

'Not on your life!' answered he; 'you know what eyes the father has: he'd read in my face, as if it was an open book, that there's something up; and if he began asking me questions I wouldn't know how to get out of it properly. And anyway, I must stay here to look after things. It'd be better for you to send someone.'

'I'll send Menico.'

'All right,' replied Renzo and went off, to look after things, as he had said.

Agnese went to a house nearby to look for Menico, a bright little lad of about twelve who was considered a sort of nephew through various cousins and in-laws. She asked his parents to let her borrow him, as it were, for the whole day, 'For a certain job,' she said. When she had got him, she took him to her kitchen, gave him his lunch, and told him to go to Pescarenico and see Fra Cristoforo, who would then send him back with a message when the time came: 'Fra Cristoforo, that fine-looking old man, you know, with the white beard, the one they call the saint. . . .'

'I know,' said Menico. 'The one who's always patting us children on the head, and gives us a holy picture now and then.'

'That's the one, Menico. And if he tells you to wait there near the monastery for a bit, don't wander off; be sure you don't go down to the lake with your friends, to watch the fishing or to play with the nets strung out on the walls to dry, or get up to that other favourite game of yours.'

Menico, it should be said, was an adept at stone-skimming; and it is well known that all of us, big and small, like doing the things which we are good at; and not only those, either.

'Pooh! Auntie; I'm not a kid.'

'Well, be sensible; and when you come back with the reply . . . look, here, these two bright new *parpagliole** are for you.'

'Give me them now; it's all the same thing.'

'No, no; you'd only go and gamble with them. Off you go now; be good, and you'll get even more.'

During the rest of that long morning certain odd things happened that aroused a good deal of suspicion in the women, worried as they already were. A beggar, whose appearance was not as exhausted nor as ragged as that of most of his kind, and which had something dark and sinister about it, came in to beg for alms, glancing furtively around as he did so. He was given a piece of bread, which he took and put away with ill-concealed indifference. Then he loitered, asking, with a mixture of impudence and hesitation, a lot of questions, to which Agnese was quick to answer the exact opposite of the truth. When he made a move as if to leave, he pretended to mistake the door, went through the one leading to the stairs, and glanced hurriedly round there as best he could. On their shouting after him, 'Hey, hey, where are you going, my friend? This way! this way!' he turned back and went out by the way which he was shown, excusing himself with an affected humility and meekness which accorded ill with his hard features. After this man other odd-looking figures kept appearing from time to time. It was not easy to tell what kind of men they were, but it was impossible to believe that they were the honest wayfarers who they pretended to be. One came in on the pretext of asking the way; others slowed down as they passed the door and glanced covertly into the room across the yard, as if they wanted to look without arousing suspicion. Finally towards midday the disturbing procession ended. Agnese would get up every now and then, cross the courtyard, go to the gate on the road, glance up and down, and come back saying, 'No one there'; she uttering the words with satisfaction and Lucia hearing them with satisfaction, without either of them knowing exactly why. But they both felt a vague disquiet on them which was sapping away, particularly with Lucia, most of the courage which they had been holding in reserve for the evening.

The reader however should be told something more definite about those mysterious prowlers; and in order to inform him of everything we shall have to retrace our steps a little, and return to Don Rodrigo, whom we had left the day before, after Father Cristoforo's departure, alone in a room in his mansion.

Don Rodrigo, as we have said, was pacing with long strides up and down this apartment, whose walls were hung with various generations of family portraits. When he reached a wall, and turned round, he would find himself facing one of his warrior ancestors, the terror of his enemies and his own men, with his grim aspect, cropped straight hair, twirling pointed mustachios standing out from his cheeks, and receding chin; the hero was standing encased in proof armour, with greaves, cuisses, breastplate, brassards, and gauntlets, his right hand on his hip and his left on the hilt of his sword. Don Rodrigo gazed at him; and on getting up to him and turning round, there he was facing another ancestor, a magistrate, the terror of litigants and lawyers, who sat in a great armchair upholstered in red velvet, wrapped in an ample black robe: everything about him was black, except for a white collar with two broad lapels and facings of sable (it was the distinctive senatorial dress, and worn only in the winter, which is why one never finds a portrait of a senator in summer clothes); he was spare, with frowning brows; in his hand he held a petition, and seemed to be saying: We'll just see about that. On this side was a matron, the terror of her servants: over there an abbot, the terror of his monks – all people, in fact, who had inspired terror, and still breathed it from their canvases. With such reminders around him, Don Rodrigo grew more angry and mortified and restless than ever that a friar should ever have dared to face him with the presumption of a Nathan.* He would form some plan for vengeance and then abandon it, and then wonder how he could satisfy at the same time his passion and what he was pleased to call his honour; and sometimes (just fancy!), when he heard the beginning of that prophecy ringing in his ears again, he felt goose-flesh, as they say, coming over him, and was almost on the brink of giving up the idea of getting either kind of satisfaction. Finally, to be doing something, he called a servant, and ordered him to make his excuses to the company and say that he was detained by urgent business. When the man came back to tell him that those gentlemen had left after sending him their compliments, 'What about Count Attilio?' asked Don Rodrigo, still pacing up and down.

'He's gone out with the other gentlemen, my lord.'

'All right. A guard of six men, then, at once; I'm going for a walk. My sword, cloak, and hat; at once.'

The servant withdrew, bowing in reply; and came back shortly afterwards with a rich sword, which his master buckled on; a cloak, which he flung over his shoulders; a hat with lofty plumes, which he put on his head and then clamped down fiercely with one hand – a sign of stormy weather. Off he started, and at the gate found his six ruffians fully armed, who made way and bowed, then fell in behind him. Surlier, haughtier, and more frowning than usual, he stalked out and off towards Lecco. At his approach the peasants and workers flattened themselves against the wall, doffing their caps and making him low bows, to which he did not reply. Even those whom the peasants would have called gentry bowed to him as inferiors; for there was no one in all those parts who could vie with him remotely in name, wealth, connexions, and the desire to use them all to be above others. To these he replied with proud condescension. It did not happen that day, but when he did happen to meet his lordship the Spanish commandant, the bows were equally low on both sides; it was like two potentates who have no dealings with one another but for the sake of appearances pay due honour to the other's rank. To get rid of his ill-humour, and offset the image of the friar which was haunting his imagination with other images of a very different order, Don Rodrigo that day entered a certain house which was usually much frequented, and where he was received with the assiduous cordiality and respect reserved for those who make themselves very much loved or very much feared: and returned to his mansion only after nightfall. As Count Attilio had also just that moment got back, supper was served, during which Don Rodrigo was deep in thought, and said little.

'Cousin, when are you settling this bet?' said Count Attilio in a malicious, jibing tone, as soon as the table was cleared and the servants had left.

'It's not St Martin's Day* yet.'

'You may as well settle it at once; for all the saints' days in the calendar will go by before . . .'

'That remains to be seen.'

'A politician's reply, cousin; but I understand it all, and am so sure of having won my wager, that I'm ready to lay you another one.'

'What's that?'

'That Father . . . Father . . . what's-'is-name? That friar, I mean, has converted you.'

'That's just another of your little mistakes.'

'Converted, cousin; converted, I tell you. As for me, I'm delighted. Think what a fine sight it will be to see you all penitent, with your eyes cast down! And what a triumph for that friar! How he must have stuck out his chest as he went home. Fish like you aren't caught every day, or with any old net. You can be sure he'll use you as an example, and talk about you whenever he goes preaching somewhere that's a little distant. I can almost hear him.' And here he began drawling through his nose, and waving his hands solemnly, as if he were preaching. 'In a part of this world which, out of proper respect, I will forbear to name, there lived, my dear listeners, and still lives, a certain dissolute nobleman, who was fonder of the society of women than he was of that of honest men. He was used to plucking every blade of grass for his sheaf, and had his eyes on . . .'

'That'll do, that'll do,' interrupted Don Rodrigo, with mingled amusement and annoyance. 'If you want to double the stakes I'm ready too.'

'Devil take it! You haven't gone and converted the friar?'

'Don't mention that man to me; and as for the wager, St Martin's Day will decide that.' The count's curiosity was aroused; he plied the other with questions, but Don Rodrigo managed to elude them all, by putting them off until the decisive day, not wanting to tell the opposing side about plans that were neither under way nor even fully formed.

The following morning Don Rodrigo awoke feeling his old self again. The apprehension which that phrase 'the day will come' had aroused in him had vanished completely with the dreams of night; only his rage remained, aggravated by shame for his passing weakness. The more recent memories of his triumphant promenade, of the bows and obeisances, and of his cousin's banter, had contributed not a little to his getting back his old spirit. As soon as he was up, he sent for Griso. – Big things on –

thought to himself the servant who took the order, for the man with this nickname was no other than the chief bravo, his master's most trusty agent, the one who was given the most dangerous and iniquitous tasks, the man who was bound to him entirely by gratitude and self-interest. He had come to beg Don Rodrigo's protection after killing a man in broad daylight in a public square; and Don Rodrigo had put him out of reach of the law by dressing him in his own livery. So, by pledging himself to carry out any crimes that he was ordered, he had insured himself immunity for the first he had committed. The acquisition had been of no small importance to Don Rodrigo; for Griso, apart from being far and away the ablest of his men, was also a proof of his master's successful defiance of the law; so that his power had grown thereby, in both reality and repute.

'Griso!' said Don Rodrigo; 'here's a chance to prove what you're worth. This Lucia girl must be in this house before tomorrow morning.'

'No one'll ever say that Griso shirked carrying out one of your illustrious lordship's orders.'

'Take as many men as you may need, and arrange and give whatever orders you think best; as long as it comes out all right. But above all take care no harm's done her.'

'A bit of a fright, my lord, so she doesn't make too much noise down there; it can't be done without that.'

'A fright, I realize, is unavoidable. But don't touch a hair of her head; and, above all, treat her with every respect. D'you understand?'

'My lord, we can't pluck a flower from its plant and bring it to your lordship without touching it. But it'll be no more than's absolutely necessary.'

'You will answer for it. And . . . how're you going to set about it?'

'I was just thinking, my lord. We're lucky the house is at the end of the village. We need some base; and right near there, now I come to think of it, there's that uninhabited cottage, isolated in the middle of the fields, the house . . . your lordship wouldn't know about such things . . . a house that got burnt out a few years ago, and has not been repaired for lack of money, and has been abandoned, and now no one but witches visit it; but it's not Saturday, and I don't care, anyway. These villagers are full of superstitions, and wouldn't go near it any night of the week for all the gold in the world; so we can go and stop there and be quite sure no one'll come and upset our plans.'

'Good! And what then?'

On this they both got down to it, Griso making suggestions and Don Rodrigo criticizing them, until they finally worked out how to carry the affair through without leaving any traces, even how to divert suspicion by a false trail, to impose silence on poor Agnese, and strike such terror into Renzo as to drive out his grief, or any idea of appealing to justice, and even any desire to complain; and all the minor villainies necessary to the success of the major villainy. We will refrain from giving details of these plans, for, as the reader will see, they are not necessary to an understanding of the story; and we are pleased also not to have to keep him listening any longer to these two arrant knaves discussing them. Suffice it to say that just as Griso was going off to put them into practice, Don Rodrigo called him back and said, 'Listen. If by any chance that insolent bumpkin gets into your clutches tonight, it wouldn't be a bad thing to give him a bit of a tickle across his shoulder in anticipation. Then the order he'll get tomorrow to keep quiet will be surer to take effect. But don't go out of your way to look for him in case you spoil things that're more important; you understand me?'

'Leave it to me,' answered Griso, making a bow with a gesture both obsequious and boastful; and off he went. The morning was spent reconnoitring the country. The false beggar who had insinuated himself in that way into the humble cottage was no other than Griso himself, come to see the plan of the house with his own eyes; the false wayfarers were his rascals, who only needed a superficial knowledge of the place, as they were to operate under his orders. After they had had their look, they were kept out of sight, so as not to arouse too much suspicion.

When they had all got back to the mansion, Griso made his report, settled on his definite plan of campaign, assigned parts to each of them, and gave his instructions. All this could not be done without the old serving-man, who was keeping his eyes and ears open, realizing that something big was in the air. By dint of listening and inquiring, by putting together a bit of information here and a bit there, puzzling out some obscure word, and interpreting some mysterious departure, he managed, finally, to get a clear idea of what was to take place that night. But by the time he had succeeded in doing this night was already near at hand and a small advance-guard of bravi had already gone off to hide themselves in the ruined cottage. Although the poor old man well realized what a dangerous game he was playing, and was also afraid of arriving too late he was determined not to fail in his engagement: so he went out under the pretence of going to take a little air and hurried off to the monastery as fast as he could, to give Father Cristoforo the promised warning. The other bravi moved off shortly afterwards, going one by one, so as not to look like a group; Griso came last, and all that remained behind was a litter which was to be brought to the hut later that night; as was done. When they had all assembled at the rendezvous, Griso sent three of them off to the village inn; one to station himself at the door, see what was happening in the street, and watch for the moment when all the inhabitants had gone indoors; the other two to stay gaming and drinking inside, as if they were there to pass the time, keeping a lookout meanwhile, if there was anything to look out for. He himself, with the main body of his forces, stayed in hiding to await events.

The poor old man was still shambling along; the three scouts were just reaching their posts; the sun was setting: when Renzo went into the women's house and said: 'Tonio and Gervaso are waiting for me outside; I'm going to the inn with them to have a bite of food; and we'll come and fetch you at the angelus. Come along, Lucia; courage! It all just hangs on one moment.' Lucia sighed, and repeated, 'Courage,' in a tone that belied the word.

When Renzo and his two companions reached the inn, they found the sentinel already at his post, taking up half the doorway as he leant his back against one of the door-posts, with his arms crossed on his chest. He kept looking to right and left, showing the glistening white or black of a pair of hawk-like eyes. A flat cap of crimson velvet, worn at an angle, covered half his quiff, which was parted over his swarthy forehead and came down under his ears on either side, ending in plaits held by a comb at the nape of the neck. In one hand he was dangling a thick cudgel; he wore no real weapons in sight, but even a child would have suspected, after one look at his face, that he had as many hidden away as he could carry. As Renzo, who was ahead of the others, was on the point of entering, this fellow stared at him fixedly, without making any effort to move. But the youth was determined to avoid any quarrel, as people usually are who have a tricky task on hand, and pretended not to notice him, not even saying: Make way; he managed to slide past sideways, flattening himself up against the other door-post, through the space left by this caryatid. His two companions had to make the same manoeuvre to get in. Once inside, they saw the others whose voices they had already heard; that is to say, the two ruffians who were sitting at a corner of the table, playing *mora*,* both were shouting at once (this time because of the game), now one now the other replenishing their glasses from a big flask standing between them. These also stared fixedly at the newcomers, particularly one of the pair, who had his hand in the air, three thick fingers splayed out, and his mouth still open from just shouting out a loud 'six', and who looked Renzo over from head to foot; he then gave a wink at his companion, and another at the man at the door, who answered by a nod of the head. Renzo, puzzled and suspicious, looked at his two guests as if hoping to find some explanation of all these signs in their faces; but all their faces showed was a hearty appetite. The landlord was looking at him as if awaiting his order; Renzo drew him off into another room and ordered supper.

'Who are these strangers?' he asked then in a low voice, as the landlord came back with a coarse table-cloth under his arm and a flask in his hand.

'I don't know them,' replied the landlord, spreading the cloth.

'What? Not one of them?'

'You must remember,' the man replied again, smoothing the cloth down on to the table with both hands, 'that the first rule in our business is never to ask about other people's affairs. So much so that even our womenfolk aren't inquisitive. Otherwise we'd soon be in trouble, with so many people coming and going; we're like a sea-port – in a decent year, I mean. But we mustn't lose heart, good times'll come back. It's enough for us if our customers are decent folk; who they are and who they aren't doesn't matter. And now I'll bring you a dish of meat-balls, the like of which you never tasted.'

'How can you tell . . .?' Renzo was rejoining, but the innkeeper was already on his way to the kitchen, and did not stop. There, as he was fetching the pan with the aforesaid meat-balls, the bravo who had looked our young man over came up to him very quietly and whispered: 'Who're those good people?'

'Honest folk from the village here,' replied the innkeeper, turning the meat-balls into a dish.

'Yes, but what are they called? Who are they?' the fellow insisted, in a rather rough tone.

'One's called Renzo,' replied the innkeeper, also in a whisper;

'a good steady young fellow. He's a silk-spinner, and knows his job well. The other's a peasant by the name of Tonio; a jolly chap, good company. A pity he's got so little to spend, or he'd spend it all here. The other's a half-wit who likes a good feed, though, when it's given him. By your leave.'

And with a little skip he passed between his questioner and the fireplace, and bore the dish off to where it was expected. 'How can you tell,' persisted Renzo, when he saw him reappear, 'that they're decent folk, when you don't know them?'

'By their actions, my friend; one tells a man by his actions. People who drink their wine without criticizing it, pay their bills without haggling, don't quarrel with the other customers, and if they've got to put a knife in someone, go and wait for him outside – away from the inn, so's the poor landlord keeps out of it – those are the decent folk. Though of course it's better if one knows people well – as we four know each other. But what the devil makes you want to ask so many questions, when you're a bridegroom, and ought to have your head filled with quite different things? And with those meat-balls in front of you, which would revive a corpse?' So saying, he went back to the kitchen.

Our author, remarking upon this man's different ways of answering questions, says that he was the sort of man who always made great profession of being on the side of decent folk in general, but who in practice paid much more attention to those with the reputation or appearance of knaves. What an unusual character! Eh?

It was not a very happy supper. The two guests would have liked to enjoy themselves at their ease; but their host, preoccupied for the reasons which the reader knows, and irritated and a little worried by the strange bearing of the unknown men, was longing to be off. They spoke in undertones because of them; and the conversation was jumpy, and disconnected.

'What a good thing,' Gervaso suddenly blurted out, 'that Renzo wants to get married, and needs . . .!' Renzo gave him an ugly look. 'Hold your tongue, you fool,' said Tonio, accompanying the epithet with a nudge of the elbow. The conversation lagged more and more until it died out altogether. Renzo was sparing in his eating and drinking, and was careful to pour out just enough wine for his two witnesses to make them lively without losing control of their wits. The table cleared, and the bill paid by the one who had taken least toll of the food, all three had to pass those faces again, which all turned to Renzo once more, as they had when he came in. He also turned round when he was a few yards away from the inn, and saw that the pair he had left sitting in the kitchen were now following him. Then he stopped with his companions, as if he had said to himself: Let's just see what these fellows want of me. But when the pair noticed that they had been observed they also stopped, whispered together, and turned back. Had Renzo been near enough to them to catch their words, he would have found them very strange. 'It'd be a fine feather in our caps, though, not to mention the tip we'd get,' one of the ruffians was saying, 'if we could tell them when we get back to the house that we'd given him a good hiding, all in a trice, and all on our own, without Signor Griso being here to lay it on.'

'And spoil the main job!' replied the other. 'There, he's noticed something; he's stopped to look at us. Oh, if only it was a little later! Let's turn back, so's not to arouse suspicion. People are coming along in all directions, see. Let 'em all go to roost.'

There was, in fact, that buzz and stir which is heard in a village at dusk, and which after a few minutes gives way to the solemn quiet of night. The women were coming from the fields, carrying their babies in their arms and leading by the hand the elder children, with whom they were repeating evening prayers; the men were coming in with their spades and hoes across their shoulders. When the doors opened, fires could be seen glimmering here and there, lit for the frugal suppers. There was a sound of 'good nights' being exchanged on the road, and a few words about the scarcity of the harvest and the hardships of the year. And above the voices could be heard the measured, booming strokes of the church bell tolling the close of day. When Renzo saw that the two intruders had turned back, he pursued his way in the gathering dusk, now and again whispering some reminder to one or other of the brothers. By the time they reached Lucia's cottage, it was quite dark.

As has been remarked by a barbarian not devoid of genius:

> Between the acting of a dreadful thing
> And the first motion, all the interim is
> Like a phantasma, or a hideous dream.*

Lucia had been in this agonizing dream for many hours; and Agnese, even Agnese, who had first thought of the idea, was preoccupied and could hardly find words to encourage her daughter. But at the moment of awakening – at the moment, that is, of starting to act – the spirits suddenly change completely. The terror and courage which formerly struggled there are followed by quite different terrors and courage; the enterprise looms before the mind in an entirely fresh light; what had seemed most alarming before often seems all at once to have become easy; while sometimes an obstacle that had previously been scarcely noticed suddenly becomes formidable; the imagination recoils in dismay; the limbs seem to refuse their obedience; and the heart fails to carry out promises which it had made with the greatest confidence. At Renzo's muffled knock, Lucia was assailed with such terror that she resolved at that moment to put up with anything, to be separated from him for ever, rather than carry out the decision which she had taken; but when he was before her, and had said: 'Here I am, let's go,' when they all seemed ready to set off without hesitation, as if to something settled and irrevocable; then Lucia had neither time nor strength to demur and, as if dragged along, tremblingly put one arm through her mother's, and another through that of her betrothed, and moved off with the venture some band.

Quietly, cautiously, they stole out of the cottage into the darkness and took the road leading away from the village. The shortest way lay across it and went straight to Don Abbondio's; but they chose this one so as not to be seen. By paths through orchards and fields they reached a point near the house; there they divided up. The two lovers stayed and hid behind a corner of the house, Agnese with them, but a little in front, so that she could catch Perpetua in time, and take charge of her; Tonio, with the halfwit Gervaso, who could do nothing by himself, yet without whom nothing could be done, went boldly up to the door and knocked.

'Who is it, at this hour of the night?' cried a voice from the window, which opened at the same moment; the voice was Perpetua's. 'There's no one ill, as far as I know. Has there been an accident?'

'It's me,' answered Tonio, 'with my brother, and we want to talk to his reverence.'

'D'you think this is a decent hour?' said Perpetua sharply. 'What manners! Come back tomorrow.'

'Listen; I may or I may not come back; I've got hold of some money, and I've come to settle that little debt you know about; I've got twenty-five new *berlinghe** here; but if I can't, never mind; I know how to get rid of these, and I'll come back when I've got some more together.'

'Wait, wait; I'll be back directly. But why come at this time?'

'I've only got hold of them myself a short time ago; and, as I told you, I thought that if I take 'em to bed with me, I shan't know how I'll feel in the morning. But if the time's not convenient, never mind. Anyway, here I am; and if I'm not wanted I'm off.'

'No, no, wait a moment; I'll come back with the answer.'

So saying, she shut the window again. At this point Agnese detached herself from the lovers, whispered to Lucia, 'Courage; it'll be all over in a moment – like pulling a tooth,' then joined the two brothers at the door, and began chatting to Tonio, so that Perpetua, on coming to open the door, should think she had happened along there by chance, and that Tonio had stopped her a moment.

CHAPTER 8

Carneades! Now who was he? – Don Abbondio was pondering to himself as he sat in his big armchair in an upstairs room, with a little book open in front of him, when Perpetua came in to give him the message. – Carneades!* I seem to've read or heard that name somewhere; he must be some scholar or man of letters of antiquity; it's one of those names; but who the devil was he? – So far was the poor man from foreseeing the storm about to burst over his head!

Don Abbondio, it should be known, enjoyed doing a little reading every day; and the priest of a nearby parish, who had a small library, used to lend him one book after the other – the first that came to hand. The one over which Don Abbondio was then poring (he was now convalescent from his fever and fears, in fact more recovered, as far as the fever was concerned, than he wanted people to think) was a panegyric in honour of San Carlo, which two years earlier, in Milan Cathedral, had been delivered with as much emphasis as it had been heard with admiration.* In it the saint was compared to Archimedes* for his love of study; and thus far Don Abbondio had not found himself in any difficulties, as Archimedes did so many strange things, and got himself so talked about, that no very vast erudition was required to know something about him. But after Archimedes the orator had compared him to Carneades; and here the reader had got stuck. It was at this moment that Perpetua came in to announce Tonio's visit.

'What, at this time of night?' said Don Abbondio also, naturally enough.

'What's one to expect? They've got no manners; but if you don't catch him on the wing . . .'

'Quite; if I don't catch him now, who knows when I will catch him! Let him in. . . . Hey ! hey! You're quite sure it's really him?'

'Of course,' replied Perpetua, and went down, opened the door and said: 'Where are you?'

Tonio came forward, and at the same moment Agnese appeared and greeted Perpetua by name.

'Good evening, Agnese,' said Perpetua. 'Where've you come from at this hour?'

'I've come from * * *,' and she named a nearby village. 'As a matter of fact,' she went on, 'I was kept there late all on your account.'

'Oh, why?' asked Perpetua; and, turning to the two brothers, 'Go in,' she said. 'I'm coming, too.'

'Because,' answered Agnese, 'one of those women who likes a gossip and doesn't know things kept on saying – would you believe it? – that the reason you never married Beppe Suolavecchia or Anselmo Lunghighna was because they wouldn't have you. I maintained that it was you who'd refused them, both of them. . . .'

'Of course. The liar! The big liar! Who is she?'

'Don't ask me that; I don't want to make mischief.'

'You shall tell me; you must tell me. Oh, the liar!'

'Anyway . . . but you can't think how sorry I was not to know the whole story, so as to put her in her place.'

'The things people make up!' exclaimed Perpetua again, then went on quickly: 'As for Beppe, everyone knows, and could see . . . Hey, Tonio! Leave the door to, and go on up; I'm just coming.'

A track opened out between two shacks opposite Don Abbondio's door, and turned past them into the fields. Agnese went towards this as if she wanted to get somewhere apart, so as to talk more freely; and Perpetua followed. When they had turned a corner and got to a spot from which it was impossible to see

what happened in front of Don Abbondio's house, Agnese gave
a loud cough. This was the signal. Renzo heard it, and gave Lucia
an encouraging squeeze of the arm; and then they both went
forward very quietly on tiptoe, creeping along close to the wall;
they reached the door, gave it a gentle push, and went into the
passage, where the two brothers were waiting for them. Renzo
quietly closed the door again; and all four went up the stairs,
without making as much noise even as a single person. On
reaching the landing, the two brothers went to the door of the
room, which was by the stairs, while bride and bridegroom
flattened themselves against the wall.

'*Deo gratias*,'* said Tonio, in a clear voice.

'Tonio, eh? Come on in,' answered the voice from inside.

Thus called, Tonio opened the door just wide enough to let
him and his brother through one at a time. The ray of light
suddenly coming through this opening and spreading over the
dark floor of the landing made Lucia start as if she had been
discovered. The two brothers went in, and Tonio drew the door
to behind him. The bride and groom stood motionless in the
darkness, with ears straining, holding their breath; the loudest
noise was the hammering of Lucia's poor heart.

Don Abbondio was sitting, as we have said, in an old armchair,
wrapped in an old dressing-gown, with an old night-cap on his
head which framed his face, in the dim light of a little lamp. The
two thick curls of hair escaping from his night-cap, the two thick
eyebrows, the two thick mustachios, and a thick beard, grizzled
and scattered all over his lined, brown face, looked very much
like bushes covered with snow, jutting from a rock in moonlight.

'Ah! ah!' was his greeting, as he took off his spectacles and put
them on to his book.

'Your reverence'll be saying we've come late,' said Tonio,
bowing, as also did Gervaso, rather more awkwardly.

'Of course it's late; late in every way. D'you realize I'm ill?'

'Oh, I'm sorry.'

'You must have heard; I'm ill, and don't know when I can
appear in public.... But why have you brought this ... this lad
along with you?'

'Just for company, your reverence.'

'All right; now, let's see....'

'They're twenty-five new *berlinghe*, the ones with St Ambrose
on horseback,' said Tonio, drawing a little parcel from his pocket.

'Let's have a look at them,' replied Don Abbondio; and, taking the packet, he put on his spectacles again, opened it, took out the coins, counted them, turned them over, turned them over again, and found no flaws in them.

'Now, father, you can give me back my Tecla's necklace.'

'Fair enough,' replied Don Abbondio; then he went to a cupboard, took a key from his pocket, and, looking around as if to keep spectators at a distance, partly opened the cupboard, filled the aperture with his person, put his head inside to see and an arm to take the necklace, found it, and, closing the cupboard door, handed it over to Tonio, saying: 'Is that all right?'

'Now,' said Tonio, 'perhaps you wouldn't mind putting something in black and white.'

'D'you want that, too!' said Don Abbondio. 'Everyone's so wise to these things nowadays. Eh! How suspicious the world's become! Don't you trust me?'

'What, not trust your reverence! You wrong me. But as my name's down in that book of yours on the debit side . . . so, as you've given yourself the trouble of writing it out once, well . . . from life to death . . .'

'All right, all right,' interrupted Don Abbondio, and with many a grumble drew a box on the table towards him, took out pen, ink, and paper, and began to write, repeating the words out loud as they came off his pen. Meanwhile Tonio and, at a sign from him, Gervaso had taken their stand right in front of the table, so as to prevent the writer from seeing the door, and begun scraping their feet on the floor out of apparent idleness, as a signal for the couple outside to come in, and at the same time as a cover for the sound of their footsteps. Don Abbondio, deep in his writing, was not attending to anything. At the sound of the scraping feet Renzo took Lucia's arm, gave it another encouraging squeeze, and moved forward, drawing with him the trembling girl, who could never have moved on her own. They came tiptoeing in very quietly, holding their breath, and hid behind the two brothers. Meanwhile Don Abbondio had finished what he was writing and was carefully re-reading it without raising his eyes from the paper; then he folded it in four, and said: 'Are you satisfied now?' took his spectacles off his nose with one hand, held the paper up to Tonio with the other, and looked up. Tonio, holding out a hand to take the paper, stepped back to one side; Gervaso, at a sign from him, stepped back on the other; and between them, as at a curtain opening at a play, appeared Renzo and Lucia. Don Abbondio saw them vaguely, then saw them clearly, was first alarmed, then amazed, then enraged, collected his wits, and made a decision – all this in the time it took Renzo to utter the words, 'Your reverence, in the presence of these witnesses, this is my wife.' His lips had hardly closed before Don Abbondio had dropped the paper, seized and lifted the lamp with his left hand, snatched the table-cover with his right, and pulled it hard towards him, flinging book, papers, ink-pot, and sand-box on to the floor; then, springing between the table and the armchair, he made for Lucia. The poor girl had scarcely been able, in that soft and now trembling voice of hers, to bring out, 'And this . . .' when Don Abbondio rudely flung the table-cover over her head and face to stop her saying the complete formula. Then, quickly dropping the lamp, which he held in his other hand, he used that, too, to wrap her up in the table-cloth, so that she was almost suffocated; meanwhile he was shouting at the top of his voice, 'Perpetua! Perpetua! Treachery! Help!' The wick dying on the floor threw a dim flickering light over Lucia, who, completely dazed, was not even making any effort to disentangle herself, and looked like a clay-model over which the sculptor has thrown a damp cloth. When the last glimmer of light had gone, Don Abbondio let the poor girl go, and began feeling his way towards the door of an inner room; he found it, went through, and locked himself in, still shouting, 'Perpetua! Treachery! Help! Out of this house! Out of this house!' In the first room all was confusion; Renzo, groping about with his hands, trying to stop the priest, as if he was playing at blindman's bluff, had found the door, and was knocking on it, shouting, 'Open up! Open up! Don't make such a row!' Lucia was calling Renzo in a feeble voice, and begging, 'Let's go; let's go! For the love of God.' Tonio was crawling about on all fours, scouring the floor with his hands, to try and find his receipt. Gervaso was screaming and jumping about like one possessed, looking for the door on to the stairs to get out to safety.

We cannot forbear pausing a moment to make a reflection in the midst of all this uproar. Renzo, who had raised all this noise in someone else's house, who had got in by a trick, and was now keeping the master of the house himself besieged in a room, has all the appearance of being the aggressor; and yet, if one thinks it out, he was the injured party. Don Abbondio, surprised, terrified, and put to flight while peacefully attending to his own affairs, might seem the victim; and yet, in reality, it was he who was doing the wrong. Such is often the way the world goes ... I mean, that's the way it went in the seventeenth century.

The besieged man, seeing the enemy showed no sign of withdrawing, opened a window looking over the church square, and began to shout, 'Help! help!' It was a clear, moonlit night; the shadow of the church, and beyond it the long, pointed shadow of the steeple, stood out dark and sharp on the glistening grass of the square; every object could be distinguished almost as clear as day. But as far as the eye could reach there was no sign of a living soul. But under the wall of the church – the one facing the priest's house – was a little room, a poky hole, where the sacristan slept. He was suddenly woken by the confused shouting, sat up, sprang hastily out of bed, opened the lattice of his little window, thrust out his head with half-glued eyes, and said, 'What's up?'

'Quick, Ambrogio! Help! People in the house!' Don Abbondio called across to him. 'Coming right away,' the man answered, pulled in his head, and shut his lattice. Though half asleep and more than half scared, he thought of an expedient on the spur of the moment to give even more help than he was asked, without getting himself involved in the fray, whatever it might be. Grabbing the breeches on the bed and tucking them under one arm, as if they were a dress hat, he went jumping down the wooden ladder, and rushed to the belfry, where he seized the rope of the bigger of the two bells and began ringing out an alarm.

Ton, ton, ton, ton. The peasants started up in bed; the youngsters in the hay-lofts pricked up their ears, listened, and jumped to their feet. 'What is it?' 'What is it?' 'The alarm bell! Fire? Thieves? Bandits?' Many of the women advised, begged their husbands not to stir, but to let the others do the running about; some of the men got up and went to the window; the more cowardly went back under the bed-clothes as if yielding to their wives' entreaties; the braver and the more inquisitive went down to get their pitchforks and muskets, and hurried off towards the noise. Others stayed to wait and see.

But before they were ready, even before they were well awake, the sound had reached the ears of the other persons who, not far away, were already up and dressed: the bravi in one place, Agnese and Perpetua in another. We will first give a brief account of what the former group had been doing from the moment when we left them, part at the ruined house and part at the inn. The latter three, when they saw all the doors closed and the road deserted, hurried out as if they had just noticed how late it was, saying that they had to get home at once. They made a turn round the village to make sure that everyone had gone indoors, met not a living soul, heard not the slightest noise. They also slipped furtively past our poor cottage, which was the quietest of all, as there was no longer anyone in it. Then they went straight on to the hut and made their report to Griso. The latter at once put a wide hat on his head and a palmer's cloak of waxed cloth covered with shells over his shoulders, took a pilgrim's staff, and said, 'Come along, now, be careful; quiet, and mind your orders,' then led off first, with the others behind. In a moment or two they were at the cottage, having taken a different path from the one our little group had used when they went off on their own expedition. Griso stopped his men a few yards away from it and went ahead alone to reconnoitre; then, seeing everything still and deserted outside, he beckoned two of his ruffians forward, and ordered them to climb carefully over the wall bounding the little yard, and, once inside, hide behind a thick fig-tree that had caught his eye that morning. This done, he gives a gentle knock intending to say that he was a pilgrim who had lost his way, and ask for shelter until daybreak. There is no reply; he knocks again a little louder; not a sound. Then he goes to fetch a third ruffian and gets him to climb into the yard like the other two, with orders to undo the bolt gently, so that they can get in and out easily. All this goes off with the utmost caution, and with gratifying success. He goes and calls the others, brings them in with him and sends them to hide with the rest; then stealthily closes the gate and posts two sentinels inside; thence he goes to the garden door. He knocks at this, too, and waits; – as well he may. Very quietly he undoes this bolt too; no one calls 'Who's there?' from inside; there is no one to be heard; things couldn't be going better. Forward, then: 'Sst,' he calls to those under the fig-tree, and with them enters the ground-floor room, where, the same morning, he had so treacherously begged that piece of bread. He pulls out steel, flint, tinder, and sulphur, lights his lantern, and goes into the inner room to see if there is anyone there: no one. He turns back, goes to the bottom of the stairs, looks, listens: all is solitude and silence. He leaves two other sentinels on the ground floor, and takes with him a bravo from Bergamo called Grignapoco who is to do all the threatening, coaxing, and giving of orders – all the talking, in fact, so that his dialect may make Agnese believe that the expedition has come from those parts. With this man beside him, and the others behind, Griso goes stealthily up the stairs cursing in his heart every creaking stair and every noisy step which his rascals make. Finally the top is reached. Here's where the hare is. Gently he tries the door leading into the first room; it gives, and opens a crack; he looks through it: all is dark; he puts his ear against it, to listen for anyone snoring, breathing, or moving inside; nothing. Forward, then. Holding the lantern before his face, so as to see without being seen, he flings the door wide, sees a bed, and rushes towards it. It is smooth and made up, with the coverlet turned neatly down over the pillow. With a shrug of the shoulders, he turns to his companions and signs to them that he is going to look in the next room, and that they are to come quietly in behind him. He enters it, goes through the same routine, and finds the same thing. 'What the devil's this mean?' he says then; 'has some swine of a traitor been spying on us?' Then they all begin looking about much less cautiously, poking into every corner, and turning the place upside down. While that part of the band are busy doing this, the two keeping guard at the street door hear a patter of little footsteps hurrying towards them; then, thinking that whoever it is will pass straight by, they keep quite still; but on the alert, just in case. In fact, the clatter stops right at the door. It was Menico running back with a message from Fra Cristoforo warning the two women to escape from home as soon as possible, for the love of heaven, and take refuge in the monastery, because ... the reader knows because of what. He takes the bolt-handle to knock with, and feels it dangling loose and undone in his hand. – What's this – he thinks, and pushes the door with trepidation; it opens. Menico sets a foot inside, in deep suspicion, and suddenly finds himself seized by both arms, with two low voices, to left and right of him, saying menacingly, 'Quiet! or you're a dead 'un.' Instead of which he lets out a yell. One of the ruffians claps a hand over his mouth; the other pulls out a great knife to frighten him. The poor boy trembles like a leaf, and does not try to cry out again. But all of a sudden there is heard a sound very different from his voice, as that first clap of the church bell booms out, followed by a whole storm of peals in succession. There's no one so suspicious as the guilty, says a Milanese proverb. Both those rogues seem to hear their Christian name, surname, and nickname being spelt out in those sounds. They let go of Menico's arms, hastily pull theirs back, look at each other with open hands and gaping mouths, and rush into the house to the main body of their companions. Off runs Menico down the road as fast as his legs can take him towards the belfry, where there is bound to be someone. The terrible peals have the same effect on the other rascals ransacking the house from top to bottom. They jostle against each other in panic-stricken disorder, each looking for the quickest way out. Tried men as they all are, and used to risking their necks, they cannot stand up to an indefinite danger, which they had not spied some way off before it came down on them. It needs all Griso's authority to keep them together, to save their retreat from becoming a flight. As a dog shepherding a herd of swine rushes about here and there after the strays, taking one by the ears and dragging it back into the herd, nosing in another, and barking at a third which is simultaneously getting out of line, so the pilgrim seizes and pulls in one man who is already on the threshold, shoves back with his staff one or two others making off in the same direction, and shouts at others who were rushing about without knowing where they were going; until he finally succeeded in collecting them all together in the middle of the yard. 'Quick! quick! Pistols in your hands, daggers at the ready, all together; and then we'll be off; that's the way to go. D'you think anyone'll dare touch us if we all keep together, you fools? But if we let ourselves be set on one by one, even the villagers'll have a go at us. Shame on you! Follow me, and keep together.' After which brief harangue he put himself at their head, and led the way out. The cottage was at the end of the village, as we have said; Griso took the road leading away from it, and the others all followed behind him in good order.

Leaving them on their way, let us go back a step to Agnese and Perpetua, whom we have left in that little lane. Agnese had been trying to get the other as far from Don Abbondio's house as possible; and it had all gone well up to a certain point. But suddenly the serving-woman had remembered the door which she had left open, and wanted to turn back. There was nothing to be done; Agnese had to turn back with her so as not to arouse her suspicions, and follow behind her; still trying to detain her, however, every time she saw that she was getting really warmed up on the subject of one of those abortive marriages of hers. She pretended to be paying close attention, and every now and again, to show that she was listening, and to keep the flow going, would say, 'Why, now I understand; that's all right; it's quite clear now:

and what happened next? And what about him? What about you?' But meanwhile she was carrying on another conversation with herself. – Will they be out by now? Or will they still be inside? What fools all three of us were not to have arranged some signal, so I could know when it's over. A really silly mistake! But it can't be helped; the only thing to do is to keep this woman away as long as I can. It's only time wasted, at the worst. – So, by little spurts and stops, they had got back quite close to the house, which, however, could not be seen because of the bend in the path. Perpetua had just reached an important part of her story and allowed herself to be stopped without making any fuss, and indeed without noticing the fact that she had, when, all of a sudden, echoing above through the still air and the deep silence of the night, she heard that first wild cry of Don Abbondio's, 'Help! help!'

'Mercy! What's happened?' cried Perpetua, and tried to run.

'What's up? What's up?' said Agnese, holding her by the skirt.

'Mercy! Didn't you hear?' replied the other, struggling to free herself.

'What's up? What's up?' repeated Agnese, clutching her by an arm.

'Devil take the woman!' exclaimed Perpetua, pushing her aside to free herself, and began to run. Just then, farther away, shriller, sharper, rang out Menico's scream.

'Mercy!' cried Agnese in her turn; and began running along behind the other. They had scarcely got their heels off the ground before out boomed the church bell; one stroke, then two, then three, then many more. These would have spurred them on if they had any need of it. Perpetua arrived a moment before the other. As she was about to push open the door, it was flung open from inside, and on the threshold appeared Tonio, Gervaso, Renzo, Lucia, who had just found the stairs and come leaping down them; and, hearing those terrible peals, were rushing to safety.

'What's up? What's up?' Perpetua breathlessly asked the brothers, whose only answer was to shove her aside and rush away. 'And you two? What? What're you doing here?' she then asked the other pair, when she had recognized them. But they also came out without answering her. Perpetua in her haste to get off where she was most needed asked no more questions, but quickly entered the passage, and ran, as best she could in the dark, for the stairs.

The bride and bridegroom, who were still no more than betrothed, now came face to face with Agnese, who was just panting up. 'Ah, there you are!' she gasped out. 'How did it go? What's the bell mean? I thought I heard . . .'

'Home, home,' said Renzo, 'before people come.' They were just setting off when Menico came dashing up, recognized them, stopped them, and still trembling all over, said in a hoarse voice: 'Where're you going? Back, back! This way, to the monastery.'

'Was it you . . .?' Agnese was beginning.

'Now what's happened?' asked Renzo. Lucia stood trembling in silence, completely overwhelmed.

'You've got devils in your house,' gasped out Menico. 'I've seen them myself – they tried to kill me – Fra Cristoforo said so – and that you were to come, too, Renzo, at once – and I saw them myself – what luck I found you all here! I'll tell you more about it when we're outside.'

Renzo, who was the most self-possessed of the party, thought that it would be best to make off immediately, one way or another, before people began arriving; and that the safest course was to do what Menico was advising, or rather ordering, with all the energy of one terrified out of his wits. Once they were on their way, and out of danger, the boy could be made to give a clearer explanation. 'You walk ahead,' he said to him, and 'Let's go with him,' he told the women. They turned and hastened towards the church and across the square, where, providentially, there was no living soul yet, down the lane between the church and Don Abbondio's house, through the first gap which they saw in the hedge, and away across the fields.

They were only about fifty yards from it, when a stream of people began running into the square, swelling in volume every moment. They looked into each other's faces; everyone had a question to ask, no one had an answer to give. The first arrivals ran to the church door – it was locked. Then they ran to the outside of the belfry; one of them put his mouth to a window, or rather a slit, and shouted in, 'What the devil is the matter?' On hearing a familiar voice, Ambrogio let go the rope and, assured by the buzz that there was a big crowd, answered, 'Just coming to open up.' He hastily slipped on the garment which he was carrying under his arm, went inside to the church door and opened it.

'What's all the row about? – What is it? – Where is it? – Who is it?'

'What d'you mean, who is it?' said Ambrogio, holding one of the doors with one hand and with the other grasping the top of the garment which he had hurriedly slipped on. 'What, don't you know? People in the priest's! Up, lads, to the rescue!' They all turned and swarmed below the house, looking up and listening – dead silence. Others ran round to the door; it was shut, and showed no traces of having been touched. They looked up; there was not a window open, not a sound to be heard.

'Who's inside there? – Hey, hey! – Y'r reverence! Y'r reverence!'

Don Abbondio, who had left the window and shut it as soon as he realized that the invaders had fled, and was at that moment busy rebuking Perpetua for leaving him alone in his ordeal, was forced to come to the window again on hearing himself called by the crowd; and when he saw the amount of help, began regretting having asked for it.

'What's happened? – What've they done to you? – Who are they? – Where are they?' fifty voices were simultaneously shouting at him.

'There's no one here any more – thank you – you can go back home now.'

'But who was it? – Where've they gone to? – What's happened?'

'People up to no good, people who go round by night – but they've fled – go back home – it's all over – another time, my children – thank you once again for your kindness.' And so saying he drew his head in again and shut the window. At which some of the crowd began to grumble, others to jeer, others to curse; and others were shrugging their shoulders and going off, when suddenly someone arrived so completely breathless that he could only just get his words out. This was a man who lived almost opposite our two women, who had gone to his window on hearing the noise, and seen the scattering bravi as Griso was trying to round them up. As soon as he had recovered his breath, he shouted: 'What're you doing here, lads? The devils aren't here, they're down the road, at Agnese Mondella's. Armed men; they're inside it; they seemed to be murdering a pilgrim; the devil only knows what it's all about!'

'What? – What? – What?' and tumultuous consultations began. 'We must go. – We must see. – How many are there? – How many are we? – Who are they? – The beadle! The beadle!'

'Here I am,' answered the parish beadle, from the middle of

the crowd; 'here I am. But you've got to help me, you've got to do what I say. Quick; where's the sacristan? To the belfry, to the belfry! Quick; one of you run to Lecco for help. Now come along, all of you.'

Some pressed forward, some slipped away through the crowd and made off; the confusion was tremendous, when another man arrived who had seen the band beating their hasty retreat, and shouted: 'Hurry, lads; thieves or bandits carrying off a pilgrim. They're out of the village already. After them! After them!' At this news they all moved off pell-mell down the road, without waiting for their leader's orders. Some of those in the vanguard dropped back as the army advanced, let others overtake them, and slipped into the main battle group; those in the rear pushed forward; finally the confused swarm reached the place indicated. The traces of the invasion were fresh and obvious: the door hanging open, the bolts undone; but the invaders had disappeared. They entered the yard and went up to the garden door; that too was open and unhinged. They called: 'Agnese! Lucia! The pilgrim! Where's the pilgrim? Stefano must've dreamt that pilgrim. – No, no; Carlandrea saw him, too. Hey, pilgrim! – Agnese! Lucia!' No answer. 'They've been kidnapped! They've been kidnapped!' At which some began shouting that they ought to follow the kidnappers, and that it was a scandal, a disgrace to the village if any rascal could come and kidnap women with impunity, like a kite snatching chickens from an unguarded yard. More tumultuous confabulations followed this; then someone in the crowd (no one ever really knew who it was) started a rumour that Agnese and Lucia had taken refuge in a house. The rumour rapidly grew, and was believed; no one said any more about chasing the fugitives; and the crowd dispersed, everyone going back to his own home. There was a general buzzing of voices, a tramping and knocking and opening of doors, an appearing and disappearing of lights, an asking of questions by the women at the windows and an answering back from the road. When this had become silent and deserted, the discussions continued indoors, until they ended in yawns, only to begin in the morning once again. There were no more incidents, however; except that that same morning, when the beadle was standing in his field, with his chin in his hand and an elbow leaning on a spade half-stuck into the ground, with one foot propped on its edge – standing, in fact, turning over in his mind the strange happenings of the previous night, and wondering whether his duty should have called him to do more than his caution suggested – he was approached by two burly-looking men with quiffs like those of the early French kings, * very like the pair who had accosted Don Abbondio five days before, if indeed they were not the same ones. These men warned the beadle even more brusquely to be very careful not to make a report to the mayor about what had happened, not to tell the truth if he was questioned about it, not to talk about it, and not to encourage the villagers to talk about it, if he valued his chances of dying in bed.

Our fugitives walked on in silence at a good pace for some time, each looking round in turn to see if anyone was following them. They were all overwrought by the stress of the flight, the excitement and suspense through which they had gone, the disappointment of their failure, and a confused apprehension of this new and unknown danger. But the continual tolling of those bells, which seemed, as distance weakened and muffled them, to take on something more and more gloomy and sinister, made them feel more overwrought than ever. Finally they ceased. Then the fugitives, who were just passing through a deserted field, not hearing a sound around them, finally slowed down. Agnese was the first to get back her breath and break the silence by asking Renzo how it had gone, and asking Menico what all the row at home had been. Renzo briefly told his sad story; and all three then turned to the boy, who passed on the friar's warning in more detail, and described what he himself had seen and the risk he had run, which was only too definite a confirmation of the warning. His listeners understood more than Menico could tell them; they shuddered at the discovery, and then suddenly stopped, looked at each other, and with one accord all three of them put out a hand to pat the boy's head and shoulders, as if to thank him tacitly for having been a guardian angel to them, and to show him how sorry they were for the anguish which he had endured and the danger which he had run for their sakes; and almost to apologize to him. 'Now go back home, as your family can't be allowed to worry about you any more,' said Agnese to him; and remembering the two *parpagliole* she had promised him, she took four from her pocket and gave them to him, saying: 'There; pray God we'll meet again soon,' and then Renzo gave him a new *berlinga*, and made him promise not to say a word about the message which the friar had given him. Lucia embraced him again and said good-bye in a sad voice. The boy, deeply moved, bade all of them a tender farewell and turned back. They went on their way again, deep in thought, the women ahead and Renzo behind, acting as guard. Lucia clung close to her mother's arm, gently but adroitly avoiding the help which the young man offered her in the difficult parts of that cross-country journey, feeling ashamed, even in this trouble, of having been alone with him so long and on such familiar terms when she had expected to become his wife a few moments afterwards. Now that the dream had been so cruelly dispelled she regretted having gone so far, and faced as she was with many reasons for trembling, trembled, too, with that modesty which does not spring from the painful knowledge of evil – that modesty which is ignorant of its own existence, like the fears of a child trembling in the dark without knowing why.

'And what about the house?' said Agnese suddenly. But, important as the question was, no one answered her, because no one could think of a satisfactory answer. They continued their way in silence, and shortly afterwards finally came out on the square in front of the monastery church.

Renzo went up to the door and gave it a strong push. It opened at once; and the moon streamed through the aperture upon the pale face and silvery beard of Fra Cristoforo, who had been standing there waiting for them. 'Thanks be to God!' said he when he saw there was no one missing, and beckoned them to enter. At his side was another Capuchin; this was the sacristan lay-brother, whom by entreaty and argument he had persuaded to wait up with him, to leave the door ajar, and stand watch to welcome the poor refugees; and all the friar's authority and prestige as a saint had been needed to get the lay-brother to do him so irksome, risky, and irregular a favour. Once they were inside, Fra Cristoforo softly closed the door again. Then the sacristan could contain himself no longer, and calling the friar to one side began muttering in his ear: 'But, father, father! At night – in church – with women – shut – the rules – but, father!' And he shook his head. – Just think! – Fra Cristoforo thought as the lay-brother was stammering out these words – if it was some rascal making his escape, Fra Fazio wouldn't make any difficulties at all; and yet a poor, innocent girl, who's escaping from a wolf's clutches ... '*Omnia munda mundis*,'* he said then, suddenly turning to Fra Fazio, and forgetting that the latter knew no Latin. But it was this very oversight that gave the words the right effect. If Fra Cristoforo had begun to argue and produce reasons, Fra Fazio would have been at no loss to find other reasons to oppose against his; and heaven knows how and when it would have ended. But at the sound of words so pregnant with mysterious meaning, and uttered with such an air of decision, he felt that they must contain the solution to all his doubts. He calmed down, and said: 'Ah, well! You know better than I do.'

'You can trust me,' answered Fra Cristoforo; then by the flickering light of the sanctuary lamp in front of the altar he went towards the fugitives as they waited there in suspense, and said to them: 'Give thanks to the Lord, my children, who has delivered you from so great a danger. Perhaps at this very moment...!' And here he began to explain what he had told the young messenger, little suspecting that they knew more than he did, and presuming that Menico had found them sitting quietly at home before the bravi had arrived. No one disabused him, not even Lucia, who did, however, feel a secret twinge of remorse at deceiving such a man; but it was a night of trickery and subterfuge.

'After this,' he went on, 'you must realize, my children, that this village isn't safe for you any longer. It's your village; you were born in it, you have done no one any harm; but such is God's will. It is a trial, my children; bear it with patience and faith and without rancour, and you can be quite sure that the day will come when you will find that you are glad of what is happening now. I have thought of a refuge for you for the present. Soon, I hope, you will be able to go safely back home; in any case, the Lord will do what is best for you; and I will certainly do my utmost not to fail in the trust He has put in me by choosing me as His instrument in the service of you His poor, afflicted creatures! You,' he went on, turning to the two women, 'can stay at * * *. You will be far enough away from any danger there, and at the same time not too far from your own home. Go to our monastery, ask for the Father Superior, and give him this letter; he'll be another Fra Cristoforo to you. And you, too, Renzo, my boy – you, too, must find a place where you're safe from the fury of others and from your own. Take this letter to Fra Bonaventura of Lodi, of our monastery at the Porta Orientale in Milan. He will be a father to you, he will advise you and find you work, until you can come back and live here in peace. Now go down to the shore of the lake, near the mouth of the Bione' (this is a stream near Pescarenico); 'there you'll find a boat. Call out: "Boat ahoy!" "Who for?" you'll be asked. Reply, "For Saint Francis." The boat will take you aboard and carry you over to the other shore, where you will find a cart that will take you straight to * * *.'

Anyone asking how Fra Cristoforo had managed to get such means of transport by sea and land put at his disposal so promptly would show how little he realizes the power which a Capuchin can wield when he has the reputation of a saint.

There was still the custody of the houses to be thought of. The friar took the keys, and arranged to hand them over to whomsoever Renzo and Agnese named. The latter heaved a great sigh as she took the key out of her pocket, reflecting that her home was open at that very moment, that it had been broken into, and who knew what there was still left to take care of.

'Before you leave,' said the friar, 'let us all pray to the Lord that He may be with you in this journey and for ever; and, above all, that He may give you strength and love, so that you yourselves may desire what He has desired for you.' So saying, he knelt down in the middle of the church, and all knelt with him. After praying for some minutes in silence, the friar uttered these words in a low but clear voice: 'We pray to Thee also for the poor wretch who has brought us to this pass. We should be unworthy of Thy mercy if we did not implore it for him from the bottom of our hearts; his need of it is so great! We, in our tribulations, have the solace of being on the road on which Thou hast set us; we can offer up our troubles to Thee, and they will turn to our good. But he! . . . he is Thine enemy. Oh, wretch that he is! He struggles against Thee! Take pity on him, O Lord; touch his heart, reconcile him to Thee, grant him all the blessings we could wish for ourselves.'

Then he arose, as if in haste, and said: 'Come, my children; there's no time to lose. May God guard you and His angel accompany you; go.' And, as they were setting off, filled with that emotion which has no words to express it and shows itself without them, the friar added in a deeply moved tone: 'My heart tells me we shall meet again soon.'

Certainly the heart has always something to tell about the future to those who listen to it. But what does the heart know? No more than a little of what has happened already.

Without waiting for a reply, Fra Cristoforo went towards the sacristy; the travellers left the church; and Fra Fazio shut the door, after saying good-bye in a voice that was also deeply moved. Very quietly they made their way to the spot on the lakeside to which they had been directed. They found the boat

ready, exchanged the password, and went aboard. The boatman
punted the boat away from the bank with one oar, then took up
the other and rowed out with both arms into the open lake
towards the opposite shore. There was not a breath of wind; the
lake lay flat and smooth, and would have seemed quite motionless
but for the gentle, tremulous swaying of the moon, reflected from
high up in the sky. The only sounds were the slow, sluggish
lapping of the waves on the pebbly shore, farther away the gurgle
of water swishing around the piles of the bridge, and then the
measured splash of those two oars as they cut the blue surface of
the lake, suddenly came out dripping, and then plunged in once
again. The wash of the boat, joining up behind the stern, left a
rippling furrow which drew farther and farther away from the
shore. The passengers sat silent, with their heads turned back,
gazing at the mountains, and at the moonlit countryside, dappled
here and there by great shadows. The villages and houses, even
the sheds, could be made out; Don Rodrigo's mansion, with its
squat tower, rising above the cottages huddled at the foot of the
headland, seemed like a wild beast standing there in the dark
amidst a group of sleepers, waiting and meditating some evil
deed. Lucia saw it and shuddered; she followed the slope down
with her eye, on down to her own village, gazed fixedly at the
end of it, and found her own cottage, found the thick top of the
fig-tree rising above the yard wall, found the window of her own
room; and as she sat in the bottom of the boat she leant her arm
against its side and her head against her arm, as if to sleep, and
secretly wept.

Farewell, mountains springing from the waters and rising to
the sky; rugged peaks, familiar to any man who has grown up in
your midst, and impressed upon his mind as clearly as the
features of his nearest and dearest; torrents whose varying tones
he can pick out as easily as the voices of his family; villages
scattered white over the slopes, like herds of grazing sheep;
farewell! How sadly steps he who was reared among you, as he
draws away! At that moment, in the mind even of him who
leaves you of his own accord, lured by the hope of finding fortune
elsewhere, the dreams of riches lose their charm; he finds himself
wondering how he could ever have resolved to leave you, and
would turn back even then, but for the hope of one day returning
rich. The more he advances into the plain, the more his eye
flinches away in weariness and disgust from its vast uniformity;
the air seems lifeless and heavy; gloomily and listlessly he enters

the bustling cities; the houses heaped on houses, the streets leading to more streets, seem to prevent him breathing there; and as he stands before the buildings which foreigners admire, he thinks with restless longing of a little acre in his own village, of a cottage which he has long marked for his own and will buy when he returns wealthy to his native mountains.

But what of one who has never even cast a passing wish beyond those mountains, who had set all the plans of her future among them, and is then driven far away from them by a perverse power! What of one who, suddenly torn from her dearest habits and thwarted in her dearest hopes, leaves those mountains to go and seek out strangers whom she has never wished to know, and can look forward to no definite time for her return! Farewell, home, where, sitting among her secret thoughts, she had learned to pick out from all others the sound of a footstep awaited with a mysterious trepidation. Farewell, house that was still not hers; house at which she had so often glanced hastily in passing, not without a blush; house in which the imagination had pictured a perpetual calm, married life. Farewell, church, wherein her soul had so often found serenity in singing the praises of the Lord; where a ritual had been promised and prepared; where the secret longing of her heart was to be solemnly blessed, and love ordained and called holy: farewell! He who gave you so much happiness is everywhere, and never disturbs the joy of His children, unless to prepare for them one greater and more certain.

Such – or more or less such – were Lucia's thoughts, and scarcely different were those of the other two pilgrims, as the boat drew nearer the right bank of the Adda.

CHAPTER 9

The knocking of the boat against the bank aroused Lucia, and, after secretly drying her tears, she raised her head as if she had just awoken from sleep. Renzo got out first and gave his hand to Agnese, who in turn gave hers to her daughter; and all three of them sadly thanked the boatman. 'What's there to thank me for?' the man replied. 'Aren't we down here to help each other?' and drew back his hand almost with horror, as if he was being asked to steal, when Renzo tried to slip into it some of the money that he had with him and had brought that evening with the intention of paying Don Abbondio generously for services rendered in his own despite. The cart was there ready for them; the driver greeted the trio for whom he had been waiting, made them get in, gave a shout and a shake of the whip at his beast, and off they went.

Our author does not describe this nocturnal journey, nor does he give the name of the town to which Fra Cristoforo had directed the two women; in fact, he expressly says that he does not intend to give it. The reason for this reticence transpires in the course of our story. Lucia's adventures during her stay there became entangled with the shady intrigue of a person belonging, it seems, to a family of great prestige at the period when our author wrote. To explain this person's strange conduct in this particular case, he has also had to give a brief account of her former life; and her family cuts a figure in it which anyone who reads on may see for himself. But research on our part has succeeded in discovering elsewhere what the poor man was trying, from caution, to conceal. A Milanese historian[†] who had occasion to mention this same person does not give, it is true, either her name or the name of the place; but he says of the latter that it was a noble and ancient town which lacked nothing of a city but the name; elsewhere he says that the river Lambro flows through it; and elsewhere, again, that it was the seat of an arch-priest. By putting all these facts together we have reached the conclusion that the place was certainly Monza. There may well among the vast treasures of historical deduction be subtler ones, but none, I think, more sure. We could also make a very well-founded guess as to the name of the family; but, although it has been extinct for some time past, we think it better to leave it unwritten, so as not to risk harming even the dead, and so as to leave some object of research for the learned.*

Our travellers arrived at Monza, then, shortly after sunrise. The driver went into an inn; and there, by right of familiarity with the place and acquaintance with the owner, he got them a room, and accompanied them to it. Renzo also tried, as he thanked him, to make this man take some money, but, like the boatman, he was thinking of another reward, remoter, but richer. He too drew back his hand and hurried out, as if escaping, to go and look after his beast.

[†] Josephi Ripamontii, *Historiae Patriae*, Decadis V. Lib. VI, Cap. III, pp. 358 et seq. (M.)

After an evening such as the one which we have described and a night such as everyone can imagine for himself, in the company of those thoughts, with the constant dread of some unpleasant encounter, under a more than autumnal breeze, continually jostled about in the uncomfortable vehicle which rudely awoke any of them who had just begun getting a moment's sleep, it seemed unbelievable to all three that they should be sitting on a firm bench and inside a room of any kind. They then made a frugal breakfast, as was dictated by the poverty of the times, the little money which they dared spend in view of the uncertain future, and their small appetite. The thought of the feast which they should have eaten two days before occurred to all three, and each gave a heavy sigh. Renzo would have liked to stay there for that day at least, to see the women lodged and attend to their first requirements; but the friar had advised the women to send him on his way at once. So they brought out these instructions, as well as a hundred other reasons – that people would begin talking, that the longer the separation was put off the more painful it would be, that he would be back soon to give his news and get theirs – so that he finally decided to leave. They made some tentative plans for meeting again as soon as possible. Lucia did not conceal her tears; Renzo kept his back with difficulty, wrung Agnese's hand hard, bade them 'Good-bye,' in a choking voice, and went off.

The women would now have been in great perplexity had it not been for the good carter, who had orders to guide them to the Capuchin monastery and give them any other help they needed. They set out with him, therefore, towards the monastery, which, as everyone knows, was a few paces outside Monza. On reaching the gate, their guide pulled the bell and asked for the Father Superior, who came at once; and took the letter there on the threshold.

'Oh! Fra Cristoforo!' said he, recognizing the handwriting. The tone of his voice and the expression of his face showed clearly that he was uttering the name of a great friend. It should be said, then, that our good Cristoforo had recommended the women most warmly in this letter, and given a most feeling description of their case, for the Superior made gestures of surprise and indignation from time to time, lifted his eyes from the paper and gazed at the women with a look of interest and pity. When he had finished reading, he stood there for some time deep in thought; then said: 'The only thing for it is the Signora; if the Signora will undertake this charge. . . .'

Drawing Agnese aside, on to the little square in front of the monastery, he asked her a few questions, to which she gave satisfactory replies; then he turned towards Lucia, and said to both of them: 'My good women, I will try; and I hope to be able to find you an asylum which will be more than safe and respectable, until it please God to provide in some other way. Will you come along with me?'

The women bowed respectful agreement, and the friar went on: 'Good; I'll take you to the Signora's convent straight away. But keep a few yards away from me, as people love talking scandal; and God only knows the gossip there'd be if the Father Superior was seen walking in the street with a pretty girl . . . with ladies, I mean.'

So saying, he went on ahead. Lucia blushed; the carter smiled and looked at Agnese, who could not help doing the same; and when the friar was some way ahead they all three moved off, and followed along ten yards or so behind him. Then the women asked the carter who the Signora was – a question they had not dared to ask the Father Superior.

'The Signora,' replied the other, 'is a nun; but she's not the same as other nuns. Not that she's the abbess, or the prioress – in fact, from what they say, she's one of the youngest there – but she's sprung from Adam's rib;* and her people were great folk in the olden days, and came from Spain, where the people who give the orders are; and that's why they call her the Signora, meaning she's a great lady; and the whole town calls her that, for they say they've never had a personage like her in that convent; and her folk count for a lot down in Milan now; and they're the kind who always have their own way in everything; and they count for even more here in Monza, for her father's the chief person in the town, although he's not here now; so she can order everyone about in the convent if she's a mind to; and even the people outside have a great respect for her; and when she takes something on, she always carries it through; so, if the good friar there manages to put you into her hands, and she accepts you, you'll be as safe as on the altar itself, I can tell you.'

When he was near the town gate, flanked at that time by an old half-ruined tower and the crumbling remains of a castle, which not more than ten of my readers are likely to remember having seen standing,* the Father Superior stopped, and turned round to see if the others were coming, then went through the gate and towards the convent. Reaching it, he stopped again at the gate and waited for the little party. He asked the carter to come back in a couple of hours for his reply: the man promised and took leave of the women, who loaded him with thanks and with messages for Fra Cristoforo. The Father Superior took the mother and daughter into the outer courtyard of the convent, put them into the stewardess's room, and went off alone to make his request. After some time he came back beaming, and told them to come along with him. It was high time, too, for mother and daughter were getting at their wits' end to ward off the pressing inquiries of the stewardess. As they were crossing an inner courtyard, he gave the women some advice as to how to behave with the Signora. 'She's well disposed towards you,' said he, 'and can help you as much as she wants to. Be humble and respectful, answer frankly any questions she likes to put to you, and when you're not being asked questions, just leave things to me.' They entered a room on the ground floor which gave on to the parlour. Before setting foot in it, the friar pointed towards the door and whispered to the women: 'She's in here,' as if to remind them of the advice which he had given them. Lucia, who had never before been inside a convent, looked round when she got into the parlour to see where the Signora was in order to curtsey to her, and was amazed to find no one there. Then she saw the friar and Agnese going towards a corner, looked in that direction, and saw a curiously shaped window, with two big, thick, iron gratings about a hand's breadth away from each other. Behind these was standing a nun. Her face, which might be that of a woman of twenty-five, gave a first impression of beauty; but of a beauty worn, faded, and, one might almost say, ravaged. A black veil, smoothed flat across her head, fell down somewhat away from her face on either side; under the veil a linen band of snowy white half-covered a forehead of a different, but not inferior whiteness: another pleated band surrounded her face and ended under her chin in a wimple that spread partly over her breast and covered the neck of a black habit. This forehead was continually puckering up, as if contracted in pain, when a pair of black eyebrows would draw together with a quick movement. A pair of eyes – jet black, too – would sometimes fasten on people's faces with an air of haughty curiosity, and sometimes suddenly drop, as if seeking to escape detection: at certain moments an attentive observer might have thought they were asking for affection,

sympathy and pity; at others he might think that he had caught
the sudden flash of a long-pent, inveterate hatred, a hint of
something threatening and savage. When they were at rest, and
not fixed on anything in particular, some might have read in
them a proud indifference, others suspected them to be gnawed
by a hidden thought, a familiar preoccupation of the mind, which
engrossed it more than any object around. Her cheeks were very
pale and delicately and beautifully shaped, but wasted and shrunk
by gradual emaciation. Her lips stood out against this pallor,
though barely suffused with a faint rosy tinge, and their movements were sudden and lively, like those of her eyes, full of
expression and mystery. The nobility of her well-formed figure
was spoiled by a certain carelessness of carriage, or disfigured by
certain abrupt, irregular movements, which were too resolute for
a woman, let alone a nun. Even her very dress showed a mixture
of thought and neglect which betokened a nun of a strange kind.
Her waist was drawn in tight with a certain worldly care, and a
curl of black hair escaped from her head-band on to one temple
– a sign of either forgetfulness or contempt of the rule that the
hair was always to be kept short from the moment when it was
cut during the solemn ceremony of investiture.

These things made no particular impression on the two women,
who were not used to distinguishing one nun from another; and
the Father Superior had often seen the Signora before and was
already used, as were so many others, to that hint of oddity
which appeared in her person as well as in her manner.

At that moment, as we have said, she was standing by the
grating, with one hand resting languidly on it, its white fingers
twined among the bars; and she was looking fixedly at Lucia
coming timidly towards her. 'Reverend mother, and most illustrious lady,' said the Father Superior, with his head bowed low
and his hand on his breast, 'this is the poor girl to whom you
have made me hope you will give your valuable protection; and
this is her mother.'

The two women he had presented made low bows, which the
Signora gestured at them to stop with a wave of the hand, and
said, turning to the friar: 'I am happy to be able to oblige our
good friends the Capuchin fathers. But,' she went on, 'tell me this
young woman's story in a little more detail, so that I can see
better what can be done for her.'

Lucia blushed scarlet and hung her head.

'You must know, reverend mother . . .' began Agnese, but the friar cut her short with a look and answered: 'This girl, most illustrious lady, has been recommended to me, as I told you, by one of our brethren. She has had to flee secretly from her village to escape certain grave dangers; and she needs a refuge where she can live for some time unknown, and where no one will venture to disturb her, even though . . .'

'What dangers?' interrupted the Signora. 'Please, Father Superior, don't make such a riddle of it all. You know we nuns like to hear a story in all its details.'

'They're dangers,' answered the Superior, 'which can only be vaguely hinted to the chaste ears of the reverend mother . . .'

'Oh, of course,' said the Signora hurriedly, blushing slightly. Was it modesty? Had anyone noticed the momentary expression of vexation that went with the blush, he might have doubted it, particularly if he had compared it to the blush which every now and again spread over the cheeks of Lucia.

'Suffice it to say,' went on the Superior, 'that a high-handed nobleman – not all the great ones of this world use the Lord's gifts to His glory and to their neighbours' advantage, like your illustrious ladyship – a high-handed nobleman had been persecuting this girl for some time with his unworthy advances, and then, seeing they were useless, went so far as to resort openly to force, so that the poor girl was reduced to fleeing from her own home.'

'Come nearer, girl,' the Signora said to Lucia, beckoning her with a finger. 'I know the Father Superior is the very soul of truth, but no one can know more about this affair than you yourself do. It is for you to tell us whether the attentions of this nobleman were odious to you.' Lucia obeyed the order to come nearer easily enough, but to answer this question was a different matter. She would have been embarrassed by a question on this subject even if it had been put by an equal; put to her by this lady, with a certain air, too, of malicious doubt, it took away all her courage to reply. 'Your ladyship . . . mother . . . reverend,' she faltered, and seemed at a loss for anything else to say. At this Agnese felt herself authorized, as being the person next-best informed, to come to her help. 'Your illustrious ladyship,' said she, 'I can bear witness that this daughter of mine detested that nobleman as the devil does holy water – he was the devil, I mean – you must excuse me if I don't talk well, but we're just plain folk; the fact is this poor girl was engaged to a God-fearing and steady young man of our own station, and if our parish priest had been a bit more what he ought to be . . . I know I'm talking about someone in holy orders, but Fra Cristoforo, the friend of the Father Superior here, is in holy orders, too, and there's a man as kind as could be, who could vouch, if he was here . . .'

'You're very ready to speak without being spoken to,' interrupted the Signora, with a haughty, angry look which made her seem almost ugly. 'Hold your tongue. I know well that parents always have an answer ready in their children's name!'

The mortified Agnese gave Lucia a look which meant: You see what I get for your being so flustered. The friar also signed to the girl, with a glance and a nod of the head, that this was the moment to come out of her shell, and not leave her poor mother in the lurch.

'Reverend lady,' said Lucia, 'what my mother has told you is the pure truth. The young man who was courting me' – and here she blushed scarlet – 'I took of my own free will. Excuse me for talking so shamelessly, but it's so as you don't think badly of my mother. And as for that gentleman (may God forgive him), I'd rather die than fall into his hands. And if your ladyship would be so kind as to keep us somewhere in safety now we're reduced to begging for shelter and bothering worthy folk – but God's will be done – you can be sure, your ladyship, that no one will pray for you more fervently than us poor women.'

'You I believe,' said the Signora, in a softened tone. 'But I'd like to hear your story when we are alone. Not that any more explanations or reasons are needed before meeting the Father Superior's wishes,' she quickly added, turning to him with studied courtesy. 'Indeed,' she went on, 'I've already thought it over, and this is what seems to be best for the present. The stewardess of the convent has just married off her youngest daughter a few days ago. These women can occupy the room which the girl has left free, and take over the few duties she used to do. Really' – and here she beckoned the Father Superior to come nearer the grating, and continued in an undertone – 'really, times are so bad that we had decided not to replace that girl, but I'll talk to the Mother Abbess about it, and a word from me . . . and to meet the Father Superior's wishes . . . in fact I can say it's certain.'

The friar began thanking her, but the Signora cut him short with: 'There is no need for compliments; I, too, in case of need, would call on the Capuchin fathers for help. After all,' she went on, with a smile with a hint of irony and bitterness about it – 'after all, aren't we all brothers and sisters?'

So saying, she called a lay-sister (two of whom were by a

particular distinction assigned to her personal service) and told her to inform the abbess and make the necessary arrangements with the stewardess and Agnese. She then dismissed the latter, gave the Father Superior leave to withdraw, and detained Lucia. The friar accompanied Agnese to the gate, giving her more instructions, and then went off to write his report to his friend Cristoforo. – A peculiar woman, the Signora! – thought he as he went along. – Really very odd! But one can get what one wants from her if one knows how to take her in the right way. My dear Cristoforo certainly won't be expecting me to have served him so quickly and thoroughly. The good brave man! He must always be taking on other people's troubles! But he does it all for the best. It's lucky this time he's found a friend to fix his affairs properly without any fuss or bother or ado, all in the wink of an eye. Good old Cristoforo will be pleased, and will realize we're worth something here, too. –

The Signora, who had been careful what she did or said in front of an elderly Capuchin, no longer bothered so much to restrain herself when left alone with an inexperienced peasant girl; and little by little her conversation became so strange that, rather than describe it, we think it better to give a brief account of the previous history of this unhappy woman – enough, that is, to account for the unusual and mysterious things which we have noted about her, and to make intelligible the motives for her behaviour later on.

She was the youngest daughter of Prince * * *, a great noble-man of Milan, who could reckon himself among the richest men in the city. But so high an opinion did he hold of his rank, that his wealth seemed only just sufficient, in fact scarcely adequate, to maintain its prestige; and his great preoccupation was to keep what there was all together in perpetuity, so far as lay in his power. History does not tell us exactly how many children he had; all it does is to give us to understand that he had destined all the younger children of either sex to the cloister, so as to leave the family fortune intact for the eldest son, whose function it was to perpetuate the family, to have children of his own, and so torture himself by tormenting them in the same way. The unhappy creature of our story was still hidden in her mother's womb when her state in life had already been irrevocably settled. All that remained to be decided was whether it was to be that of a monk or a nun, a decision for which her presence, but not her consent, was required. On her seeing the light of day, her father the prince, wishing to give her a name which would at once suggest to her the idea of the cloister and had also been borne by a saint of high rank, called her Gertrude.* Dolls dressed as nuns were the first toys to be put into her hands, then holy pictures representing nuns, such presents always being given with warm recommendations to treasure them as something precious, and with a 'Lovely, eh?' in a tone of affirmation and interrogation. When the prince, or the princess, or the heir – the only male child to be brought up at home – wanted to say how well the child was looking, they seemed only to be able to express what they felt by saying, 'What a mother abbess!' No one, however, ever told her directly that she had to become a nun. The idea was simply taken for granted and touched on incidentally every time her future prospects were discussed. If little Gertrude was ever found guilty of some slight act of arrogance or haughtiness, towards which her nature easily inclined her, 'You're only a little girl,' she was told. 'Such behaviour is unbecoming. But when you're a mother abbess, then you can rule with a rod of iron and order everyone about as you like.' Sometimes the prince would reprove her for certain over-free and familiar manners, to which she was equally prone, and say, 'Come! come! That's not the way for one of your rank to behave. If you want to be treated one day with the respect that's your due, you must begin to learn self-respect from now on. Remember that you must be the first person of the convent in everything; for one takes one's blood with one wherever one goes.'

Every remark of this kind impressed on the girl's mind the idea that she was to become a nun, but those coming from her father had more effect on her than all the others put together. The prince always bore himself like a severe master; but when it was a question of his children's future, his expression and his every word breathed a rigid resolution, a stern attachment to his authority, which impressed a sense of fatal necessity.

When she was six years old, Gertrude was put, both for her education and still more for the development of the vocation imposed on her, in the convent where we have seen her. The place was not chosen without design. The kind carter who had guided our two women had said that the Signora's father was the first man in Monza; and putting this evidence together with other hints inadvertently dropped by our anonymous chronicler here and there, we can also assert with some confidence that the town was a fief of his. However that may be, he certainly had very great authority there; and he thought that his daughter would be treated with more deference and distinction there than anywhere else, and that this might induce her to choose that convent as her perpetual abode. Nor was he proved wrong. The abbess and some of the other nuns – the busybodies who ruled the roost, as they say – were delighted at being offered the pledge of so useful and glorious a patronage. They accepted the suggestion with fulsome though not exaggerated expressions of thanks, and fully concurred with the intentions for his daughter's permanent establishment at which the prince had allowed himself to hint – intentions which agreed so entirely with their own interests. As soon as Gertrude entered the convent, she was called 'the Signorina' by antonomasia. She had a place apart at table and in the dormitory; her conduct was held up to the others as an example; sweets and caresses were lavished on her, and were seasoned with that mixture of respect and familiarity which is so flattering to a child who sees other children being treated by the same people with the usual air of superiority. Not that all the nuns were conspiring to draw the poor girl into the trap. There were many simple, guileless souls among them who would have recoiled in horror at the very thought of a daughter being sacrificed for financial considerations. But of these, busy as they were with their own occupations, some did not get any clear idea of the intrigue afoot, some did not realize how evil it was, some avoided looking into it too closely, and some kept quiet, so as not to stir up a useless scandal. One or two of them, remembering the similar arts by which they themselves had been led into taking a step which they had later regretted, pitied the poor, innocent girl, and showed their feelings by tender and melancholy caresses. But she was far from suspecting any mystery under this; and so things went forward. They might have gone forward to the end in this way had Gertrude been the only girl in the convent. But among her schoolfellows there were some who knew that they were destined for marriage. Little Gertrude, brought up with the idea of her own superiority, would talk grandly of her own future as abbess, as princess of the convent, determined at all costs to be an object of envy to the others; and it was with surprise and chagrin that she noticed that some of them had no such feeling at all. To the majestic, but cold and limited prospects called forth by the idea of being head of a convent, they would oppose the varied and glittering visions of weddings and banquets, of parties and balls, of summers in country-houses, of clothes and carriages.

Such visions made Gertrude's mind stir and buzz as if a great basket of fresh flowers had been set down before a hive of bees. Her parents and teachers had encouraged and inflated her natural vanity, to make the cloister attractive to her; but once this passion was excited by ideas so much more congenial to her character she threw herself into them more keenly and spontaneously. So as not to be outdone by her companions, and to gratify her new desires at the same time, she began to retort that, after all, no one could foist the veil on to her head without her own consent, and that she, too, could get married, live in a palace, and enjoy the world, and that better than any of them; that she could do so if she wanted to, that she might want to, that she did want to; and want to, in fact, by now she did. The idea of her own consent being necessary – an idea which had been as it were tucked away unobserved in a corner of her mind – now began to develop and to loom large in all its importance. She would call it every moment to her aid, so as to enjoy the visions of future delight in greater calm. Behind this idea, however, another never failed to appear: that it was a question of refusing this consent to the prince her father, who already took it, or pretended to take it, for granted; and at this idea his daughter was far from feeling the confidence which her words displayed. Then she would compare herself with her companions, whose confidence was of a very different kind, and began feeling the bitter envy which she had previously expected them to feel for her. And from envying them, she went on to hate them. Sometimes this hatred came out in irritability, rudeness or spiteful remarks; sometimes it would be allayed by the similarity of their hopes and desires, which would give rise to an apparent and transitory intimacy. Sometimes, longing for some real and present enjoyment meanwhile, she would console herself with the distinctions which she was shown, and flaunt this superiority of hers over the others; sometimes, when she could no longer endure the solitude of her own yearnings and fears, she would go and seek out the others and be all goodness to them, almost as if she was begging for their affection, encouragement and advice. Amidst these petty and deplorable struggles with herself and others, her childhood had passed away and she was entering that critical period, in which a mysterious power almost seems to enter the soul, arousing, colouring, developing all its inclinations and ideas, sometimes transforming them or turning them into unforeseen channels. Up till then what Gertrude had particularly dwelt on in those day-dreams of the future had been outward splendour and pomp: now vague soft and tender yearnings, diffused lightly at first like a sort of mist, began to spread and dominate her fancy. Deep in the most secret part of her mind she had made a kind of splendid retreat; there she would take refuge from the present, and entertain certain characters who were strangely made up from confused memories of childhood, the little she had seen of the outside world, and what she had gathered from the conversation of her schoolfellows. With these she would dally, talk, and answer herself in their name; there she would give orders and receive homage of every kind. Every now and again the thought of religion would come to disturb these brilliant but exhausting revels. But the religion which the poor girl had been taught, as she had understood it, turned pride into a virtue instead of banning it, and put it forward as a means of obtaining earthly happiness. Thus bereft of its essence it was no longer religion, but a phantom, like all the rest. During the intervals when this phantom took first place and predominated in Gertrude's mind, the unhappy girl would be overcome by confused terrors, and urged on by a confused idea of duty, to fancy that her aversion to the cloister and her resistance to the hints of her elders as to choice of her state in life were sins; and she would promise in her heart to shut herself into the cloister of her own free will in expiation.

There was a rule that no girl could be accepted as a nun without being examined by an ecclesiastic, called the nuns' vicar, or by someone delegated by him, to make certain that she was doing so of her own free choice; and this examination could not take place until a year after she had made her wishes known to the vicar by a written application. The nuns who had undertaken the odious task of getting Gertrude to commit herself for ever with the least possible realization of what she was doing, took advantage of one of the moments which we have described to get her to write and sign such an application. To induce her to do this more easily, they did not fail to point out and reiterate that it was only a mere formality, which – and this was quite true – could have no binding effect without her taking other steps later on, each of which would depend on her own free will. Even so the petition had probably not yet reached its destination before Gertrude already regretted having signed it. Then she regretted her regrets, and so the days and months passed in an endless see-saw of contrary emotions. For a long time she hid this step from her companions, now from fear of exposing a good decision to contradiction, and now from shame of disclosing a blunder. Finally the urge to unburden her mind and seek advice and encouragement prevailed. There was another rule by which a girl could not undergo the examination of her vocation without having spent at least a month outside the convent where she had been educated. A year had already passed since her request had been sent, and Gertrude was notified that she would shortly be fetched away from the convent to spend the month in her parents' house, and there take all the necessary steps to complete the deed she had already in fact begun. The prince and the rest of the family took this as much for granted as if it had already happened; but his daughter had quite other ideas in her head: instead of thinking of the next steps, she was wondering how she could retrace the first which she had taken. In these straits she decided to open her heart to one of her companions, who was the most outspoken and most apt to give daring advice. This girl advised Gertrude to inform her father of her new resolution by letter as she had not the courage to face him with a flat refusal. Free advice being very rare in this world, Gertrude was made to pay for this with a good deal of raillery about her poor spirit. The letter was concocted among four or five confidantes, written out secretly, and delivered by elaborate and roundabout channels. Gertrude waited in great suspense for a reply that never came. But a few days later the abbess summoned her to her cell, and, with an air of mystery, displeasure, and compassion, threw out dark hints of the prince being very angry, and of some great fault that she must have committed, but let her understand that she might hope to have it all forgotten if she behaved properly. The girl understood, and did not dare to inquire further.

The day so feared and so longed for came at last. Although Gertrude knew she was heading for a struggle, yet the sensation of getting away from the convent, of leaving those walls in which she had been shut up for eight years, of rolling through the open country in a carriage, and seeing the city and her home once more, filled her with tumultuous joy. As for the struggle, the poor girl had concerted measures with the help of her confidantes, and drawn up her plan of campaign, as the saying now goes. – Either they'll try and force me, – she thought – in which case I'll stand firm; I'll be humble and respectful but I won't consent: it's only a question of not giving another yes; and I won't give it – or they might try to touch me; in which case I'll be more touching than any of them; I'll sob and beg, I'll melt them to pity. All I want, after all, is to avoid being sacrificed. – But, as so often happens with anticipations of this kind, neither the one thing nor the other happened. The days passed without her father or anyone else mentioning the application or the retraction, and without any suggestions being made to her, either by coaxing or threats. Her parents were solemn, gloomy, and morose with her, without ever telling her why. All that was plain was that she was regarded as a culprit and as unworthy; a mysterious anathema seemed to hang over her and segregate her from her family, leaving her just sufficiently united to them to make her feel its weight. Only rarely, and then at pre-arranged times, was she allowed to see her parents and eldest brother. The three often seemed united in great mutual confidence, making Gertrude feel her isolation more painfully than ever. No one addressed a word to her; and if she ventured timidly some word not demanded by necessity, it was either ignored, or answered by a look that was careless, contemptuous, or severe. If, unable to endure this bitter and humiliating distinction any longer, she persisted and went on trying to ingratiate herself, if she seemed asking for a little love, she would at once get an indirect but clear hint about her vocation, and was covertly made to feel that there was only one way in which she could again win the affection of her family. Then Gertrude, not wanting it on such terms, was forced to draw back, to refuse the first signs of the kindness for which she had so longed, and of her own choice resume her place as an outcast. Moreover, she now found herself back there, with some appearance of being in the wrong.

These experiences in the world of reality were in painful contrast to the bright visions in which Gertrude had so much indulged, and was still indulging in the secrecy of her mind. She had hoped that in her splendid home with its flow of guests she would have enjoyed at least some real taste of the things which she had imagined; but she found herself utterly disappointed. Her confinement was as strict and complete as in the convent; there was not even a mention of going out; and a gallery opening from the house on to a neighbouring church even deprived her of the only possible occasion to leave it. The company which she kept was gloomier, more limited, and less varied than it had been at the convent. Every time a visitor was announced Gertrude was made to go up to the top floor and shut herself in with one or two old serving-women. There she also ate when there were guests. The servants conformed to the example and intentions of their masters in their way of speaking and behaving towards her; and Gertrude, who by inclination would have treated them with lordly familiarity, yet in her present situation would have been grateful for any show of affection as though she were their equal, and was even reduced to suing for it, suffered the additional humiliation of finding her advances treated with open indifference, glossed with a slight air of formal attention. She could not fail to notice, however, that a page, in striking contrast to the rest, treated her with respect, and showed a particular compassion towards her. The behaviour of this youth was the nearest approach that Gertrude had so far seen to the state of things she had so often pictured in her imagination – to the behaviour of those ideal beings of hers. Little by little something new showed in the girl's manner: both a serenity and a restlessness unusual to her, an air of having found something which she valued, which she wanted to contemplate every moment for herself and to keep away from others. She was watched more strictly than ever; and unexpectedly, all of a sudden one morning she was surprised by one of the serving-women as she was furtively folding up a piece of paper, on which she would have been wiser not to have written anything. After a brief scuffle the piece of paper remained in the hands of the serving-woman, and from hers passed into those of the prince.

Gertrude's terror at the sound of his footsteps can be neither imagined nor described; he was the father he was, he was angry, and she was guilty. But when she saw him standing before her with that frown on his brow and that piece of paper in his hand, she would gladly have been a hundred yards below ground – to say nothing of the cloister. His words were few, but terrible. Her immediate punishment was nothing more than to be locked into her room under the guard of the woman who had caught her. But this was only a beginning, a momentary expedient: some other grim and indefinite punishment, all the more terrifying for its vagueness, was promised, was hinted, for the future.

The page was immediately dismissed, as was to be expected, and threatened with some fearful vengeance if he ever dared to breathe a word of what had happened. As he gave this warning, the prince emphasized it by a couple of solemn boxes on the ears, so that the boy should have a memory associated with his adventure which would remove any temptation to boast of it. A pretext to account for the dismissal of a page was not difficult to find; as for the daughter, she was said to be indisposed.

She was now left filled with suspense and humiliation, remorse and dread of the future, and with no company but that of the woman whom she loathed as the witness of her guilt and the cause of her misfortune. In her turn, this woman hated Gertrude, through whom she was reduced, without knowing for how long, to the tedious life of a jailer and the perpetual custody of a dangerous secret.

The first confused tumult of these feelings gradually subsided; but each of them came back to Gertrude's mind one by one later, growing and staying to torture her more sharply at their leisure. What could be that punishment with which she had been so mysteriously threatened? Many and strange and various were those which came into Gertrude's vivid and inexperienced imagination. The one that seemed most likely was that she would be taken back to the convent at Monza, to reappear there no longer as the 'Signorina', but as a culprit, and be shut up there for God knew how long and on what awful terms. The dread of shame was the most agonizing part about this vision, agonizing as it all was. Again and again the phrases, the words, even the very punctuation points of that ill-starred letter went through her mind. She pictured them being scrutinized and weighed up by a reader so unexpected, so different from the one for whom they had been intended; she wondered if the letter had been seen by her mother's eyes or her brother's, and by how many others; and compared to that everything else seemed a mere trifle. The image of the youth who had been the origin of all the scandal did not fail, also, to come back often to haunt the poor recluse; and what a strange contrast this apparition must have been among all those other serious, cold, threatening ones so different from herself. Yet because she could not separate his image from theirs, nor return to those fleeting pleasures without her present sorrows, which were their consequence, coming back to her too, little by little she began to indulge in them more and more rarely, to thrust away their memory and wean herself off them. Nor did she, from now on, dwell long, or even willingly, on those gay and splendid fancies of before – they were too opposed to her actual circumstances and to every future probability. The only castle that was not a castle in the air in which Gertrude could conceive a quiet and honourable retreat was the convent, once she made up her mind to enter it for ever. Such a decision (she had no doubt) would set everything to rights, would cancel every score, and change her situation in an instant. Against this plan there rose up, it is true, the thoughts of her whole lifetime; but things had changed; and, in the abyss into which Gertrude had fallen, and in comparison to what she feared at certain moments, the role of a fêted, flattered, and obeyed nun seemed to her a very sweet thing. Two feelings of a very different nature also contributed at intervals to lessen her former aversion: at times remorse for her sin and a tender longing to be devout; at times embittered and exasperated pride at the treatment of her jailer, who (often, to tell the truth, provoked by her) vented her spite by frightening her with that threatened punishment, or by taunting her with the shame of her sin. Still more odious than her insults was the patronizing air which she would put on when she wanted to be agreeable. On all such occasions, the longing which Gertrude habitually felt to escape from her clutches and to find independence from her anger and pity became so acute and vivid, as to make anything that could help her satisfy it seem agreeable.

One morning, after four or five long days of prison, Gertrude, irritated and exasperated beyond measure by one of her jailer's little spites, had flung herself into the corner of the room, where she stayed some time devouring her rage, with her face hidden in her hands. An overwhelming desire to see other faces, to hear other words, to be treated differently then came over her. She thought of her father, of her family; her thoughts recoiled in terror. But then it occurred to her that it entirely depended on her to make friends of them, and she felt a sudden thrill of joy. This was followed by a confused and extraordinary repentance for her sin, and an equally strong impulse to atone for it. Not that her will had yet settled on this resolve, but never had she thought of it so warmly as she did now. She got up from her corner, went to a desk, took up that fatal pen again, and wrote her father a letter full of enthusiasm and submission, of hope and affliction, imploring his forgiveness, and showing herself vaguely ready to do anything to please him if he granted it.

CHAPTER 10

There are times when the mind, particularly the mind of the young, is disposed to yield to the slightest pressure of anything that has an appearance of virtue and self-sacrifice; it is like a newly opened flower, sinking languidly back on its fragile stem, and ready to yield its fragrance to the first breeze that plays around it. These moments, which should be regarded by others with delicate respect, are just the ones for which the cunning schemer watches, and catches on the wing, so as to ensnare the unguarded will.

On reading that letter, Prince * * * at once saw the loophole open to his old designs, still constantly before him. He summoned Gertrude to him; and as he waited, made ready to strike while the iron was hot. Gertrude appeared, and without raising her eyes to her father's face, flung herself down on her knees before him, with barely enough breath to gasp out, 'Forgive me!' He motioned her to rise; but, in a voice little calculated to reassure her, replied that forgiveness was not just a thing to be desired or implored; that this was only too easy and natural for one who found herself in the wrong and was afraid of being punished – in a word, it had to be deserved. All submissive and trembling, Gertrude asked what she ought to do. The prince (we have not the heart to call him at this moment by the name of father) did not give a direct reply, but instead launched out into a long speech about the sin which Gertrude had committed; and his words made the poor girl smart like the passing of a rough hand over a wound. He went on to say that even if ... if ever ... he had had any notion before of settling her in the world, she herself had now put an insuperable obstacle in the way; for no gentleman of honour – like himself – could ever bring himself to offer any respectable noble the hand of a young woman who had given such a proof of herself. His wretched listener was utterly overwhelmed. Then, gradually softening his voice and language, the prince went on to say that every sin, however, had its expiation and its atonement; that hers was one of those whose expiation was most clearly indicated, and that she ought to see in this unfortunate occurrence a warning that the life of the world was too full of dangers for her. . . .

'Ah, yes!' exclaimed Gertrude, shaken by fear, overwhelmed by shame, and swept away by a sudden gust of tenderness.

'Ah! You realize that, too,' went on the prince inexorably. 'Well, let us say no more about the past; it's all wiped out. You have chosen the only proper and honourable course open to you; but as you have chosen it with such good will and grace, it is for me to make it as pleasant as possible for you; it is for me to see that all the credit and advantage shall redound to you alone. I will take care of that.' So saying, he rang a bell on his desk, and said to the footman who answered it, 'I want the princess and the young prince at once.' Then he resumed to Gertrude, 'I want them to share my satisfaction at once, straight away. I want everyone to begin treating you at once with proper consideration. You have seen something of the sternness of a father; from now on you will see how loving he can be.'

Gertrude was left breathless at these words. One moment she wondered how a mere yes, escaping from her lips, could have come to mean so much, then she cast about to see whether there was any means of retracting it, or of restricting its meaning; but the prince's conviction seemed so complete, his delight so canny, his amiability so conditional, that Gertrude dared not utter a word that might in the slightest way disturb them.

A few minutes later the pair whom he had summoned arrived; and seeing Gertrude there, stared at her in uncertainty and surprise. But the prince, in a jolly, amiable way that gave them a lead, said 'Behold the lost sheep;* and let this be the last word to recall sad memories. Behold the consolation of the family. Gertrude no longer needs to be advised; what we wished for her own good she has chosen to do spontaneously. She has decided, she has given me to understand that she has decided' – at this point she raised a half-terrified, half-beseeching look towards her father, as if imploring him to stop, but he went on heartily – 'that she's decided to take the veil.'

'Good girl! Excellent!' exclaimed mother and son together, then one after the other embraced Gertrude, who received these demonstrations with tears, which were interpreted as tears of satisfaction. The prince then began to expatiate on what he was going to do to make his daughter's future happy and splendid. He spoke of the distinctions which she would enjoy in the convent and the town; how she would be treated as a princess there, as the representative of the family; how she would be raised to the highest dignities as soon as she reached a suitable age; and meanwhile would be a subject only in name. The princess and the heir renewed their praises and congratulations again and again. Gertrude felt as if she was in the grip of a dream.

'We must fix the day to go to Monza and make the formal application to the abbess,' said the prince. 'How pleased she'll be! I can assure you the whole convent will know how to appreciate the honour Gertrude is doing them. In fact . . . why don't we go today? Gertrude would be glad of a little air.'

'Yes, by all means,' said the princess.

'I'll go and give orders,' said the young prince.

'But . . .' ventured Gertrude timidly.

'Not too fast, not too fast,' went on the prince. 'Let her decide. Perhaps she doesn't feel quite up to it today, and would prefer to wait until tomorrow. Tell us: would you like us to go today or tomorrow?'

'Tomorrow,' answered Gertrude in a faint voice, feeling the little respite was at least something gained.

'Tomorrow,' said the prince solemnly. 'She's decided we're to go tomorrow. Meanwhile, I'll go and see the nuns' vicar and fix a day for the examination.' No sooner said than done. Out the prince went, and actually called in person (no small act of condescension on his part) on the aforesaid vicar; and they arranged for him to come two days later.

Gertrude did not have a moment's peace for the rest of that day. She would have liked to give her mind some repose, after so much excitement; to let her thoughts, as it were, clarify themselves; to take stock of what she had done and what she still had to do – to know her own mind, in fact, and to slow for a moment this machine which had scarcely started, and yet was already rushing along so speedily. But there was no chance. One occupation followed another, and overlapped, without an interruption. As soon as the prince had left, she was hurried off to the princess's dressing-room, to be combed and dressed by the princess's own personal maid, under her own personal direction. Before she had had the finishing touches, dinner was announced. Gertrude passed between the bowing servants, who congratulated her on her recovery, and found awaiting her a few of her closest relations, who had been hurriedly invited to do her honour and felicitate her on those two happy events: the recovery of her health, and the declaration of her vocation.

The 'little bride' (as girls who were about to become nuns were called, and it was by this name that Gertrude was greeted when she appeared) – the 'little bride' had a busy time answering all the compliments which were showered on her from every side. She was keenly conscious that every one of her replies was a kind of acceptance and confirmation. But how else could she reply? Shortly after they had risen from table, the hour for the drive came round. Gertrude entered a carriage with her mother and two uncles who had been at dinner. After making the usual turn, they came into the Strada Marina, which then crossed the space now occupied by the public gardens, and was where the gentry came in their carriages to disport themselves after the fatigues of the day. The uncles also talked to Gertrude, as was customary on such an occasion, and one of them, who seemed more than the others to know every person, every carriage, every livery, and had some remark to make every moment about my lord this or my lady that, suddenly turned to his niece, and said, 'Ah, you cunning little rogue, you! Turning your back on all these frivolities! What a shrewd one you are! Leaving us poor worldlings floundering about, and going off to lead a blessed life, and end by going to Paradise in a coach-and-six.'

They returned home after dark, and the footmen came hurrying down with torches to announce that there were numbers of visitors waiting for them. The news had gone around; and the friends and relations were coming to do their duty. They entered the drawing-room. The 'little bride' was the idol, the darling, the victim of everyone. They all wanted to monopolize her. Some promised her cakes and sweets, others promised visits; some talked of their relation Mother So-and-so, others of their friend Mother Such-and-such; some extolled the climate of Monza, others expatiated enthusiastically on the great figure she would cut there. Others, who had not been able to approach Gertrude through the besieging throng, stood waiting for a chance to get to her, feeling somewhat worried until they had done their duty. Little by little the company dispersed; everyone went, their worries over, and Gertrude remained alone with her parents and her brother.

'At last,' said the prince, 'I've had the satisfaction of seeing my daughter treated as becomes her rank. I must say, though, that she has borne herself very creditably. She has shown she'll have no difficulty in taking first place and in upholding the family dignity.'

They made a hurried supper, so as to get to bed quickly and be ready early the following morning.

Gertrude, saddened, out of humour, and at the same time a little heady from all those compliments, remembered at that moment all she had suffered from her jaileress; and seeing her father so ready to gratify her every wish except one, she decided to profit by her favour with him to appease at least one of the passions that were tormenting her. So she expressed a great aversion to being with this woman, and complained loudly of her ways.

'What!' said the prince. 'She has been lacking in respect! Tomorrow, tomorrow I'll give her a good talking-to. Just leave it to me, and I'll let her know who she is, and who you are. And anyway, a daughter I'm so pleased with should not have a person around her she dislikes.' So saying, he summoned another woman, and bade her attend Gertrude; who, in the meanwhile, chewing over and savouring the satisfaction which she had received, was surprised to find it so tasteless, compared to the longing which she had had for it. What was permeating her whole being in spite of herself was the realization of the great advances which she had made that day on the road to the cloister, and the thought that a withdrawal now would need much more strength and resolution than it would have a few days before, though even then she had not had enough.

The woman who accompanied her to her room was an old family servant, and had once been the nurse of the young prince, having taken him over when he was hardly out of swaddling-clothes, and brought him up till adolescence; and in him she had centred all her pleasure, hopes, and pride. She was as pleased at the decision made that day as if it were her own personal stroke of good fortune; and Gertrude was obliged, as a final entertainment, to listen to the old woman's congratulations, praises, and advice, and hear her tell of certain aunts and great-aunts of hers who had been very pleased to be nuns, because, being members of the family, they had always enjoyed the highest honours, as well as keeping a finger in many a pie outside, and achieved things from their convent parlours that the greatest ladies had not been able to do from their drawing-rooms. She talked about the visits which she would receive; and how one day the young prince would come with his bride, who was sure to be a great lady, too; and how then not only the convent but the whole town would be in a hubbub. The old woman talked all the time she was undressing Gertrude, and when Gertrude was in bed; she was still talking when Gertrude fell asleep. Youth and fatigue had proved stronger than her worries. Her sleep was feverish and troubled, full of agonizing dreams, but it was not broken until the strident voice of the old woman woke her, to prepare for the trip to Monza.

'Come along, come along, my lady bride; it's broad daylight, and it'll take at least an hour to dress you and do your hair. Madame the princess is dressing now; they've woken her four hours before her usual time. The young prince has already been down to the stables and back, and is all ready to leave at any moment. Quick as a hare, he is, the young rascal; but he's been like that since he was a child, as I can say, who've carried him in my arms. But one shouldn't keep him waiting, though, once he's ready to start; for although he has the best heart in the world, he's apt to get impatient then, and begin shouting. Poor child! He must be indulged; it's just his nature. And, then, he's got some reason this time, as he's putting himself out for you. Woe to anyone who crosses him at such moments! He hasn't any regard for anyone except his lordship the prince. But in the end, there's no one set over him except his lordship the prince, and one day he'll be his lordship the prince himself; as late as possible, though. Quick, miss, quick! Why're you looking at me like that? You ought to be out of your nest by this time.'

At the idea of the young prince being impatient all the other thoughts that had come crowding into Gertrude's re-awakened mind suddenly scattered, like a flock of sparrows at the sight of a hawk. She obeyed, dressed hurriedly, let her hair be combed, and appeared in the drawing-room, where her parents and brother were assembled. She was installed in an armchair, and served with a cup of chocolate, which was the equivalent at that time of being given the *toga virilis* among the ancient Romans.*

When they were informed that the carriage was ready, the prince drew his daughter aside, and said to her, 'Now, Gertrude, you did yourself credit yesterday; you must surpass yourself today. It's a question now of making a solemn entry into the convent and town where you're destined to be the chief figure. They're expecting you' – it goes without saying that the prince had sent off a message to the abbess the day before – 'they're expecting you, and all eyes will be on you. Be dignified, but easy. The abbess will ask you what you want; it is just a formality. You can reply that you've come to ask to be admitted to the veil in the convent where you have been so lovingly educated and where you have received so much courtesy; which is the pure truth. You must speak these few words naturally, so that nobody can say that they have been put into your mouth and that you cannot talk on your own. Those good nuns there know nothing of what's happened – it's a secret that must stay buried with the family – so don't look sorry or doubtful; it might make them suspect something. Show what blood you have in your veins; be affable and modest; but remember that in that place, away from the family, there will be no one above you.'

Without waiting for a reply, the prince started off down the stairs: Gertrude, the princess, and the young prince followed him, and they all got into the carriage. The troubles and trials of the world, and the blessed life of the cloister, particularly for young girls of the very noblest blood, were the subjects of conversation during the drive. As they were nearing their destination the prince renewed his instructions to his daughter, and repeated the formula of her reply a number of times. Gertrude felt her heart sink as they entered Monza; but her attention was momentarily distracted by some gentlemen who had stopped the carriage, and were reciting some complimentary speech or other. On starting off again, they went on to the convent almost at foot pace, among staring crowds who came hurrying on to the road from all sides. When the carriage stopped in front of that wall, in front of that gate, Gertrude felt her heart sink deeper than ever. They alighted between two rows of people, whom the footmen held back. All those eyes on her made the wretched girl take continual care how she bore herself; but more than all of them put together, she was held in subjection by the two eyes of her father, which she could not help continually turning to look at, terrified of them as she was: those eyes seemed to control her face and movements as if by invisible reins. They crossed the first court and entered another, and there they saw the gate of the inner cloister, wide open, and entirely filled with nuns. In the front row was the abbess, surrounded by the elders of the community; behind were the rank and file of the other nuns, some on tiptoe. At the very back were the lay-sisters, standing on benches. Here and there little eyes could be seen glittering, and little faces peeping half-way up among the habits. These were the most active and venturesome of the pupils, who had squeezed and squirmed themselves among the nuns, and succeeded in making openings through which they, too, could see what was going on.

The whole throng was buzzing with acclamations; many an arm could be seen waving in sign of welcome and of joy. They reached the gate; and Gertrude was face to face with the mother abbess. After the first greetings, the latter asked her, with a mixture of gaiety and solemnity, what it was she desired there, where no one could deny her anything.

'I am here...' began Gertrude; but just as she was on the point of uttering the words which would seal her destiny almost irrevocably, she hesitated a moment, and stood there with her eyes fixed on the throng in front of her. At that moment she caught sight of one of her old companions looking at her with a mixture of pity and scorn, and seeming to say, 'Ah! So the boaster's fallen to this!' This sight revived all her old feelings more vividly than ever, and also restored a little of her old courage. She was just casting about for any answer different from the one dictated to her, when, raising her eyes to her father's, as if to test their strength, she saw such deep disquiet there, such a threatening impatience, that her terror suddenly made her mind up for her, and as hurriedly as if she were escaping from some fearful object, she went on: 'I am here to request that I may take the religious habit in this convent, where I have been so lovingly educated.' The abbess replied at once that she was very sorry that, on such an occasion, the rules did not allow her to give an immediate answer, which must follow a general vote of the nuns and be authorized by her superiors, but that Gertrude, knowing what they all felt for her there, could foresee the reply with certainty; and that, meanwhile, there was no rule to prevent the abbess and nuns from showing the satisfaction which they felt at this request. Then broke out a confused chorus of congratulations and acclamations. At once great dishes full of cakes appeared, which were presented first to the 'little bride', and then to her family. While some of the nuns were surrounding her enthusiastically, others complimenting the mother, and others the young prince, the abbess asked the father to come to the parlour grille, where she was waiting for him, accompanied by two old nuns; when she saw him appear: 'My lord prince,' she said, 'to obey the regulations ... to carry out an indispensable formality, although in this case ... yet it is still my duty to tell you ... that every time a girl asks to take the veil ... the Mother Superior – in this case my unworthy self – is obliged to warn the parents ... that if, by any chance ... they had forced their daughter's will, they would incur excommunication. Your lordship will excuse me....'

'Of course, of course, reverend mother. I commend your punctiliousness; it's only right, too. . . . But you need have no doubt. . . .'

'Oh, of course, my lord prince. . . . I spoke from definite obligation. . . . Apart from that . . .'

'Yes, to be sure, to be sure.'

After this brief exchange of words the two interlocutors bowed to each other and separated, as if being there face to face was rather a strain for both of them, and each went back to rejoin their own party, one outside, and the other inside, the cloister threshold. Then, after some more chat, 'Come, come now,' said the prince. 'Gertrude will soon have plenty of opportunity of enjoying the society of these reverend mothers. We have put them to enough inconvenience for the moment.' So saying, he bowed; the family moved with him; more compliments were exchanged, and they set off.

Gertrude had little desire to talk on the way back. Appalled at the step which she had taken, ashamed of her cowardice, out of temper with herself and with the world, she was gloomily going over her remaining opportunities of saying no, feebly and confusedly promising herself that in this or that or the other of them she would be quicker and firmer. But with all these thoughts, her terror of her father's frown had not left her at all; so that, when a stealthy glance at him assured her that his face no longer showed any sign of anger, when she saw that, on the contrary, he looked very pleased with her, it seemed wonderful to her, and for a moment she was completely happy.

As soon as they reached home they had to wash and change. Then came dinner, then some visits, then the drive, a reception, then supper. Towards the end of this the prince brought up another subject: the choice of the sponsor. This was the name given to the lady who, at the request of the parents, became guardian and chaperon to a young novice in the period between her application and her entry into the convent. This period was spent in visiting churches, public buildings, salons, villas, and sanctuaries – all the most notable things, in fact, in the city and its environs; so that the girls, before making their irrevocable vow, could realize just what they were turning their backs on. 'We must think about a sponsor,' said the prince, 'as the nuns' vicar will be coming tomorrow for the formality of the examination, and immediately afterwards Gertrude will be put up for acceptance by the nuns as a candidate in the chapter.' In saying this he turned towards the princess, who, thinking she was being invited to make a suggestion, was beginning, 'Well, there's . . .' when the prince interrupted. 'No, no, madam; the sponsor must first of all be acceptable to the little bride; and although the choice, according to universal practice, is usually made by the parents, Gertrude has so much judgement, so much discernment, that she well deserves an exception being made in her favour.' And here, turning to Gertrude with the air of one announcing a singular favour, he went on: 'Any one of the ladies who were present at the reception this evening would be fully qualified to be a sponsor to a daughter of our house; there's none of them, I think, who would not consider it an honour to be selected. Choose for yourself.'

Gertrude realized perfectly well that to make this choice was to renew her consent; but the suggestion was made so conde- scendingly, that a refusal, however humble, would have seemed like contempt, or at least caprice or irresponsibility. So she took this step, too: she named the lady who had been most congenial to her that evening – the one, that is, who had most flattered and petted her, and treated her with all the familiar, engaging and affectionate ways which, in the first moments of an acquaintance- ship, counterfeit old friendship. 'An excellent choice,' said the prince, who had desired and expected this very one. Whether by chance or design, it had happened just as when a conjuror flicks through a pack of cards, tells you to think of one, and says that he will guess which it is: but he has flicked through them in such a way that you have seen only a single card. This lady had been so close to Gertrude all the evening, and had so completely engaged her, that it would have needed an effort of the imagin- ation to think of anyone else. All these attentions had not been without their motive: the lady had had her eye on the young prince for some time as a prospective son-in-law; so she regarded the concerns of this family as her own; and it was as natural for her to interest herself in dear Gertrude, as in her closest relations.

Gertrude woke next day thinking of the coming examination, and as she was brooding whether to seize this decisive occasion to turn back, and how best to do it, the prince summoned her. 'Now, my child,' said he. 'You've behaved very properly up to now; today it's a question of crowning the good work. Everything that has been done so far has been done with your full consent. If any doubts, or regrets, or childish misgivings have risen in your mind during this time, you should have expressed them before;

but at the stage things have got to now it's too late for any girlish nonsense. The worthy man who is coming this morning will ask you a great number of questions about your vocation, and if you're becoming a nun of your own free will, and the why and the wherefore, and I don't know what besides. If you hesitate in your replies, he'll keep on at you for any length of time. That would be irksome and distressing for you; but it might also have more serious results. After all the public demonstrations that have been made, the slightest hesitation on your part would throw doubt on my honour, and might make people think that I had taken some passing whim of yours for a firm resolution, that I had been precipitate, that I had . . . oh, anything! In such a case I should find myself forced to choose between two equally unpleasant alternatives: either to let the world form a low opinion of my conduct – a course which, in justice to myself, I simply cannot take – or else reveal the real motive for your decision and . . .' But at this point he saw Gertrude turn scarlet, her eyes fill, and her face contract like the petals of a flower in the sultry heat before a storm, so he dropped the subject, and went on serenely: 'Come, come, it all depends on you and on your good sense. I know you have a great deal of it, and that you're not a girl to spoil a good job at the last moment; but I have had to take every possibility into consideration. Let us say no more about it; and just agree that you will answer frankly, and in a way that will not arouse doubts in that worthy man's head. In this way you will also get it over all the quicker, too.' And here, after suggesting a few answers to the most likely questions, he started on the usual topic of the delights and joys awaiting Gertrude in the convent, and he kept on with this until a footman came and announced the vicar. The prince hurriedly renewed his most important warnings, and left his daughter with him, as the rules prescribed.

The worthy man had come somewhat predisposed to believe that Gertrude had a great vocation for the cloister; for so the prince had told him when he had gone to invite him. Of course the good priest, who knew that one of the most necessary virtues of his office was caution, made it a rule to be chary of these kind of statements and be on his guard against preconceptions. But it rarely happens that the positive and assured statement of a person of authority, whatever the subject, does not tinge the mind of his hearer.

After the first greetings were over: 'Young lady,' he said, 'I've come to play the devil's advocate; I've come to throw doubts on what, in your petition, you gave for certain; I've come to put the difficulties before your eyes, and find out if you have considered them properly. Would you mind my asking you a few questions?'

'Please do,' replied Gertrude.

The good priest then began to interrogate her in the prescribed form: 'Do you feel in your heart a free spontaneous resolve to become a nun? Have no threats or flattery been used? Has no authority been brought to bear on you to induce you to take this step? You can talk quite openly and sincerely to a man whose duty it is to find out your real wishes and to prevent pressure being put on you in any way.'

The real answer to such a question flashed into Gertrude's mind at once with terrible clarity. To make this answer she would have to give some explanation, say who she had been threatened by, and tell a story. . . . The wretched girl recoiled in horror from this idea, cast about hurriedly for another reply, found only one which could free her quickly and surely from this ordeal – the one farthest from the truth: 'I am becoming a nun,' she said, concealing her agitation – 'I am becoming a nun voluntarily, of my own free will.'

'How long have you had this idea?' the good priest went on to ask.

'I've always had it,' answered Gertrude, becoming, after that first step, bolder in telling lies against herself.

'But what is the chief reason for your wanting to become a nun?'

The good priest little knew what a terrible chord he was touching: and Gertrude made a violent effort not to let her face betray the effect which these words produced on her mind. 'My reason,' she said, 'is to serve God, and flee from the perils of the world.'

'It could not be due to some disappointment? Some – forgive me – caprice? Sometimes some transitory cause can make an impression that seems to be going to last for ever; and then, when the cause is removed and the mind's attitude changes, then . . .'

'No, no,' answered Gertrude precipitately; 'the reason is the one I told you.'

The vicar, more to carry out his duties fully than from any feeling that they were necessary, persisted in his inquiries; but Gertrude was determined to deceive him. Apart from the repugnance that she felt at the idea of revealing her weakness to this grave priest, who seemed so far from suspecting her of anything of the kind, it had also occured to the wretched girl that he could indeed prevent her from becoming a nun, but that there his authority and protection over her ended. Once he went she would be left alone with the prince. And, whatever she suffered in that house, the good priest would never hear of it, or, if he did hear, would be unable, with the best will in the world, to do anything but pity her: with that detached and measured pity generally accorded, as if by courtesy, to anyone who has given cause or pretext for the ills which they suffer. The examiner was tired of questioning before the wretched girl was tired of lying. Finding her replies invariably consistent, and having no reason to doubt their sincerity, he finally changed his tone, congratulated her, and virtually asked her pardon for having kept her so long carrying out these duties of his, added what he considered most suitable to confirm her in her good resolution, and took his leave.

As he was crossing the ante-rooms on his way out he ran into the prince, who seemed to be passing there by chance, and congratulated him, too, on the excellent disposition he had found in his daughter. The prince up to then had been in a most painful state of suspense. At this news he breathed again, and, forgetting his usual decorum, almost ran to Gertrude and loaded her with praises, caresses, and promises, with a cordial warmth and a tenderness that were largely sincere; of such a medley is the human heart.

We will not follow Gertrude through her constant round of spectacles and amusements. Nor will we describe in order and detail the feelings that passed through her mind during all this period. It would be a story of pain and wavering, too monotonous and too similar to what we have already told. The beauty of places, the constant change of scene, the pleasure which she felt driving about hither and thither in the open air, made more odious to her than ever the idea of the place where she would alight for the last time and for ever. Still more poignant were the impressions made on her by the receptions and balls. The sight of a bride in the more obvious and usual meaning of the word aroused in her an intolerable envy and gnawing anguish; and at times the looks of some man or other would make her feel that the very peak of happiness for her would be to hear herself called by that name. There were moments when the pomp of palaces, the splendour of their appointments, the buzz and joyous clamour of parties so intoxicated her, made her so long for a happy life,

that she would promise herself to recant, to suffer anything rather
than go back to the chill, dead shadow of the cloister. But all
such resolutions evaporated on a calmer consideration of the
difficulties, or simply on one glance at the prince's face. At times,
too, the thought of having to abandon these pleasures for ever
made even this little taste of them bitter and unpleasant, just as
the sick man burning with thirst looks furiously at, and almost
rejects with scorn, the spoonful of water which the doctor allows
him. Meanwhile the nuns' vicar had given the necessary certificate, and the authorization came for a chapter to be held for
Gertrude's acceptance. The chapter met, the two-thirds of secret
votes required by the regulations were given, as was to be
expected; and Gertrude was accepted. She herself, exhausted by
the long torment, then asked to enter the convent as soon as
possible. Obviously no one wanted to curb her impatience. She
had her wish, and was solemnly conducted to the monastery and
donned the habit. After twelve months of a novitiate full of
revulsions and repentances, she found herself at the moment of
profession – the moment, that is, when she would either have to
give a 'no' that would be stranger, more unexpected, more
scandalous than ever before, or repeat the 'yes' which she had
said so many times already. She repeated it, and was a nun for
ever.

One of the surprising and unique faculties of the Christian
religion is its ability to guide and console anyone who has
recourse to it in any juncture on no matter what terms. If there is
any remedy for the past, it prescribes and supplies it, gives the
light and strength to apply it, at whatever cost; if there is none, it
provides the means of carrying out in reality the proverb about
making a virtue of necessity. It teaches people to pursue steadily
what they have begun lightly; it inclines the mind to accept
willingly what has been imposed by force, and gives to a rash but
irrevocable choice all the sanctity, all the wisdom and, let us even
say boldly, all the joys of a vocation. It is a path so made that by
whatever labyrinth or precipice man may reach it, once he takes
the first step, he can thenceforward walk safely and cheerfully
along it and arrive happily at a happy end. By such means
Gertrude could have developed into a holy and contented nun,
whatever the manner in which she had become one. But instead
the wretched girl struggled against the yoke, so that she felt it
grow heavier and more galling. Continual regret for her lost
liberty, loathing of her present condition, wearisome hankering

after desires which would never be gratified – such were the chief
occupations of her mind. She brooded over her bitter past, going
back in her memory over all the various circumstances which had
brought her where she was; and pointlessly undid a thousand
times in her mind what she had done in fact. She accused herself
of cowardice, others of tyranny and perfidy: and she pined away.
She idolized and at the same time bewailed her beauty, lamented
her youth, destined to waste away in a slow martyrdom, and at
certain moments envied any woman, whatever her station, whatever her morals, who was free to enjoy these gifts out in the
world.

She hated the sight of those nuns who had had a hand in
ensnaring her there. She remembered the tricks and artifices
which they had used, and repaid them with rudeness, ill-temper,
and even open reproaches. Generally they had to endure this in
silence; for although the prince had been perfectly willing to
tyrannize over his daughter as much as was necessary to force
her into the cloister, he would not be so likely, once his purpose
was achieved, to allow others to prevail over anyone of his blood;
and any little rumour that they had done so might cause the loss
of a powerful patron, or even possibly change him from a patron
into an enemy. One might think that Gertrude would be drawn
towards the other nuns who had not taken part in those intrigues,
who liked her as a companion without having wanted her as one,
and who showed, by their pious, busy, and cheerful example,
how one could not only live but be happy there. But these, too,
were hateful to her, for different reasons; their air of piety and
content seemed a reproach to her restlessness and shrewishness,
and she never missed an opportunity of ridiculing them behind
their backs as bigots, or abusing them as hypocrites. She might
have been less against them had she known or guessed that the
few black balls found in the box which had decided her acceptance had been put there by them.

She seemed to find some satisfaction at times in giving orders,
in being flattered in the convent, in receiving visits from people
outside, in taking on some engagement, in extending her protection, in hearing herself addressed as 'the Signora'. But what
satisfactions were these! The heart that found itself so unap-
peased would have liked, every now and again, to add to them
and enjoy, too, the consolations of religion; but these only come
to those who renounce the others; as a shipwrecked man must
open his hand and let go the seaweed which he has seized by

instinct, if he is to grasp the plank that may bring him safely to the shore.

Shortly after her profession, Gertrude had been made mistress of the pupils. The situation of these young girls under a discipline like hers can be imagined. Her former confidantes had left; but she still retained all the impulses of that period; and in one way or another her pupils had to bear the brunt of them. Whenever the thought came into her mind that most of them were destined to live the kind of life from which she had been for ever excluded, she felt a grudge, almost a desire for vengeance, against those poor girls; and she would browbeat them, maltreat them, and make them pay in anticipation for all the pleasures which they would one day enjoy. Anyone hearing, in those moments, with what magisterial severity she punished any little fault, would have thought her a woman of fanatical and exaggerated piety. At other moments this same abhorrence of hers for the cloister, for rules, and for obedience would break out into fits of completely different humour. Then she would not only tolerate her pupils' noisy interruptions, but would incite them; she would enter into their games and make them more disorderly than ever; she would take part in their discussions and lead them far beyond any intentions with which they had started them. If one of the girls mentioned the Mother Abbess's love of gossip, their mistress would give a long imitation of it, and act it like a scene in a comedy; she would mimic the expression of one of the nuns, the walk of another; then she would laugh boisterously: but it was not a laughter that left her any happier than she was before. She had spent several years in this way, without having had the chance or the opportunity to do anything more, when, to her misfortune, an opportunity presented itself.

Among the other distinctions and privileges granted her as a compensation for not being abbess, was that of having her own separate apartments. That side of the convent adjoined a house in which lived a young man who was a professional rogue, one of the many who were able, at that period, with the help of their minions and of the alliance of other rogues, to defy justice and the forces of the law up to a point. Our manuscript simply calls him Egidio, without giving a surname. This fellow had noticed Gertrude from a little window that overlooked a courtyard in the wing of her apartments, as she sometimes idly passed or strolled there; and, attracted rather than alarmed by the dangers and

impiety of the undertaking, one day ventured to address her. The
wretched woman replied.

In that first period she had a feeling of keen, though certainly
not of open, satisfaction. The dreary void in her mind had
become filled with a constant, engrossing occupation – almost, I
might say, with a potent life. But this satisfaction was like the
restoring draught which the ingenious cruelty of the ancients
used to administer to the condemned, that they might have
strength to bear their tortures. At the same time a great change
came over the whole of her conduct; all at once she became more
equable and regular. Her grumbling and sneering stopped; and
she even began to show affability and affection, so that the nuns
rejoiced at the happy change, little suspecting the real motive, or
understanding that this new-born virtue of hers was no other
than hypocrisy added to her former faults. This outward show –
this exterior whitewash, as it were – did not last very long; at
least, not with any steadiness and consistency. Very soon the
usual spite and caprices returned once more, and with them her
sneers and imprecations against the prison of the cloister, sometimes expressed in language unusual in such a place and even
from those lips. But each of these outbreaks was followed by a
period of remorse and a great effort to efface their memory by
cajolery and fair words. The nuns put up with these vagaries as
best they could, and attributed them to the Signora's shrewish
and wayward disposition.

For some time no one seems to have suspected anything more.
But one day when the Signora was upbraiding a lay-sister about
some trifle or other, and abusing her beyond all measure and
reason, the lay-sister, after biting her lips and enduring it for a
time, finally lost patience and threw out a hint that she knew
something which she would tell at the right place and time. From
that moment the Signora had no more peace. Not long afterwards, however, the lay-sister was awaited in vain at her usual
duties. They went to look in her cell and did not find her. They
shouted for her – there was no reply. They looked here, there,
and everywhere, from attic to cellar – she was nowhere to be
found. And all kinds of conjectures might have been made had
not a breach been discovered in the garden-wall, which made
everyone think that she must have escaped that way. They
scoured Monza and the country around, particularly Meda,
where the lay-sister came from; they wrote off in various directions; but there was never the slightest news of her. Perhaps they

might have learnt more of her fate if, instead of searching afar, they had dug nearby. After much wondering – for no one had thought her capable of such a thing – and after much chatter, they came to the conclusion that she must have gone far, far away. And as one of the nuns happened to say, 'She must have fled to Holland,' it was at once said, and believed for some time both inside the convent and out, that she had fled to Holland. The Signora, however, does not seem to have been of this opinion: not that she showed in any way that she did not believe or that she contradicted the general opinion by putting forward any reasons of her own; certainly if she had any, never were reasons better concealed. Nor was there any subject which she so willingly avoided as this one, or any mystery she seemed less anxious to fathom. But the less she said, the more she thought about it. How many times a day did the vision of that woman suddenly come thrusting itself into her mind, and stay there, and refuse to move! How often would she have preferred to see the real living being there before her, rather than have her always in her thoughts, rather than find herself, day and night, in the company of that ghostly, terrible, impassible shade! How many times would she gladly have heard the woman's real voice, whatever it might threaten, rather than always hear the ghostly whispering of that same voice in the depths of her inner ear, repeating certain words with an insistence and a tireless perseverance that no living person ever had!

It was about a year after this event that Lucia was presented to the Signora, and had that interview with her at which we interrupted our story. The Signora asked more and more questions about Don Rodrigo's persecution, and went into certain details with a boldness which was quite new, as it was bound to be, to Lucia, who had never imagined that the curiosity of nuns could concern itself with such subjects. The comments, also, which the Signora interspersed with her questions, or which she implied, were no less strange. She seemed almost to laugh at Lucia's great horror of that nobleman, and asked if he was a monster, to frighten her so much; she seemed almost to consider that the girl's reluctance would have been silly and unreasonable, had it not been for her preference for Renzo. And about him, too, she asked questions that made the girl she was questioning gasp and blush. Then, realizing that she had let her tongue follow her vagrant fancies too far, she made an effort to correct herself and explain away her chatter; but she could not prevent Lucia remaining with an unpleasant, bewildered impression and a kind of vague dread. As soon as she was alone with her mother she told her all about it; but Agnese, with her greater experience, solved all her doubts, and cleared up the whole mystery in a few words. 'Don't be surprised,' she said. 'When you've known the world as long as I have, you'll realize these things aren't to be wondered at. All the gentry are a bit crazy. The best thing to do is to let them talk as they want, particularly if one needs them. Just look as if you're listening to them seriously, as if they were talking sense. You heard how she shouted at me, as if I'd said something silly? I didn't let it bother me. They're all like that. But, in spite of it all, thank heavens this Signora seems to have taken a liking for you, and really wants to protect us. And anyway, my child, the longer you live and the more you have to do with the gentry, you'll learn, you'll learn, you'll learn . . .'

The desire to oblige the Father Superior, the pleasure of playing the protectress, the thought of the credit to be got from championing so holy a cause, a certain liking for Lucia, and even a certain relief at doing good to an innocent creature, at helping and consoling the afflicted, had indeed disposed the Signora to take the cause of the two poor fugitives to her heart. At her request, and out of deference to her, they were lodged in the apartments of the stewardess next to the cloister, and treated as if they were in the service of the convent. Mother and daughter congratulated each other on having so quickly found such a safe and honourable refuge. They would also gladly have stayed there, ignored by everyone; but this was not easy in a convent, particularly as there was a man who was only too eager to have news of one of them, a man in whose mind fury at having been foiled and disappointed had now been added to his former lust and pique. And now, leaving the women in their asylum, we will go back to this man's house as he was awaiting the result of his iniquitous expedition.

CHAPTER II

Like a pack of hounds returning despondently to their master after chasing a hare in vain, with their snouts hanging down and their tails drooping, so, in that night of confusion, did the bravi, return to the mansion of Don Rodrigo. He was pacing in the dark up and down a disused room on the top floor which looked out over the terrace. Every now and again he would stop, strain his ears, look and peer through the chinks of the mouldering shutters, filled with impatience, and somewhat worried not only about the uncertainty of success, but also about the possible consequences; for this was the biggest and riskiest adventure on which the worthy man had ever embarked. He tried to reassure himself by thinking of all the precautions which he had taken to destroy the evidence, if not people's suspicions. – As to suspicions – thought he – I don't care a damn about them. I'd like to know who'd be bold enough to come up here to find out if there is or isn't a girl here. Let him come, let him, the impudent fool, and he'll get the right reception. The friar? – Let him come. The old woman? – The old woman can go to Bergamo. The law? – Bah, the law! The mayor's not a child or a fool. What about Milan? Who in Milan cares about these people? Who'd take any notice of them? Who knows they exist? They're as good as lost to the world; they haven't even got a landlord; – they're nobody's people. Come, there's no need to fear anything. What a shock Attilio will get tomorrow! He'll see – he'll just see whether I'm an idle boaster. And then . . . if by any chance there was any trouble – you never know, some enemy might try to seize this chance – Attilio'll be able to give me some advice, too; the honour of the whole family'd be at stake. – But the thought on which he dwelt the most – for he found it at the same time soothing to his doubts and nourishing to his principal passion – was the thought of the wiles, of the promises which he would use to win over Lucia. – She'll be so frightened at finding herself here alone, amongst those fellows and those faces, that . . . the most human face here's my own, by Bacchus . . . that she'll have to turn to me; and then she'll beg. And if she begs . . . –

As he was making up these fine accounts he heard a footstep, went to the window, opened it a little, and put his head out. There they were. – And the litter? The devil, where's the litter? – Three, five, eight; they're all there. There's Griso, too. The litter's not there; devil take it! Devil take it! Griso'll answer for this. –

On getting indoors Griso put his staff into a corner of a room downstairs, laid aside his cloak and pilgrim's hat, and, as was his responsibility, which no one envied him at that moment, went up to report to Don Rodrigo. The latter was waiting for him at the top of the stairs; and, seeing him coming up with the shambling gait of a disappointed rogue, 'Well,' he said or rather bawled at him – 'well, Sir boaster, Sir captain, Sir leave-it-to-me?'

'It's a bit hard,' said Griso, stopping with one foot on the top step – 'it's a bit hard to find oneself reprimanded, after working faithfully, and trying to do one's duty, and even risking one's skin.'

'How did it go? Let's hear, let's hear,' said Don Rodrigo, turning towards his room. Griso followed, and at once reported what he had arranged, done, seen, and failed to see; what he had heard, what he had feared, and how he had saved the situation – all described with the confusion and incoherence, the doubt and bewilderment, naturally reigning in his ideas.

'You're not to blame, and you did your best,' said Don Rodrigo: 'you did whatever could be done. But ... but ... can there be a spy under this roof? If there is, and I find out who he is – and find out we will if he exists – I'll settle him; I can tell you, Griso, I'll fix him black and blue.'

'The same suspicion had crossed my mind, my lord,' said Griso. 'If it's true, and we discover a swine of that sort, your lordship must put him in my hands. A man who's allowed himself the fun of making me spend a night like this! It'd be for me to pay him back. But I've got the idea, from various indications, that there's some other intrigue behind it, which I can't understand at the moment. Tomorrow, my lord, tomorrow we'll get it all clear.'

'Anyway, you weren't recognized?'

Griso replied that he hoped not; and the upshot of the interview was that Don Rodrigo ordered him to do three things next day that Griso was perfectly capable of thinking out for himself: to send two men off early in the morning to give the beadle that warning, which was done, as we have already noted; to send two others to the ruined house to keep guard there, chase off anyone who happened to come that way, and hide the litter from any prying eyes until it could be fetched the following night, as it was best for the moment not to make any other movements which might excite suspicion; next to go down himself, and send also a few of his most level-headed and plausible men to mingle with the villagers and try to find out something about the confused happenings of the night before. Having given these orders, Don Rodrigo went off to bed, and let Griso go, too, dismissing him with many praises, by which he obviously intended to make up for the hasty rebukes with which he had greeted him.

Go off to sleep, poor Griso, for you must need it. Poor Griso! Out and about all day and half the night, to say nothing of the risk of falling into the clutches of the peasants, or of having another price set on your head *'for the kidnapping of an honest woman'*, on top of all the others you've already got; and then to be greeted in that way! Ah, well! that's how men often repay their debts! You may have observed, though, from this incident, that justice, if it doesn't come at first, comes sooner or later in this world too. Go and sleep awhile! For one day you may be giving us another, more notable example of this.

The following morning Griso was already out and about again by the time Don Rodrigo arose. The latter at once went to find Count Attilio, who, on seeing him appear, made a face and gesture of derision at him, and shouted: 'St Martin's Day!'

'I don't know what to say,' answered Don Rodrigo, as he came up to him. 'I'll pay the wager; but that isn't what bothers me most. I hadn't told you anything about it because, I admit, I'd hoped to give you a surprise this morning. But ... anyway, I'll tell you all about it now.'

'That friar's had a hand in this,' said the cousin, after having heard the whole story, with more attention than might have been expected from such a feather-brain. 'That friar,' he went on, 'with that dead-cat look and those silly suggestions of his, is a hypocrite and intriguer, if you ask me. And you never confided in me, you never told me plainly what he came here to bother you about the other day.' Don Rodrigo described the interview. 'And you put up with all that?' exclaimed Count Attilio, 'You let him get away as he came in?'

'Did you expect me to bring all the Capuchins in Italy down on me?'

'I don't know,' said Count Attilio, 'if I'd have remembered at that moment that there were any other Capuchins in the world apart from that impudent rascal. But come, surely there's some way of getting one's own back within the bounds of prudence, even on a Capuchin? We'd have to double our civilities to the whole order, and then we could beat up one member of it with impunity. Anyway, he's escaped the punishment that suited him best. But I'll take him under my protection. I want to have the satisfaction of teaching him how to talk to people of our rank.'

'Don't go and make things worse.'

'Trust me just this once, and I'll serve you as a kinsman and a friend.'

'What are you thinking of doing?'

'I don't know yet; but I'll pay that friar off for sure. I'll think it over, and . . . our right honourable uncle of the Secret Council is the man who'll have to do the job for me. Dear old uncle! How I enjoy it every time I can get a big politician like that to do my little jobs for me! I'll be in Milan the day after tomorrow, and, in one way or the other, the friar will get his deserts.'

Luncheon was served meanwhile, which did not interrupt the discussion on an affair of such importance. Count Attilio talked about it all quite light-heartedly; and although he was playing the role that friendship for his cousin and the honour of their common name demanded – according to his ideas of friendship and honour – nevertheless he could not help laughing up his sleeve every now and again at such a complete fiasco. But Don Rodrigo, whose own affair it was and whose attempt at quietly bringing off a big coup had ended in such a resounding failure, was agitated by deeper emotions and distracted by more worrying thoughts. 'A fine lot those rascals will have to gossip about over the whole neighbourhood,' he was saying. 'But what does that matter? As for the law, I don't care a damn about that: there's no proof. Even if there were, I wouldn't care either. And, oh, by the way, I've had the beadle warned this morning to take care he doesn't put in a report on the affair. Not that anything would come of it; but gossip going too far irritates me. And it's a bit much, too, being made such a complete fool of.'

'You've done very well indeed,' answered Count Attilio. 'That mayor of yours – that stubborn, empty-headed bore of a mayor – is a good chap, though, a man who knows his duty; and they're just the people one should be most careful about not getting into embarrassing positions. Now, if a knave of a beadle goes and puts a report in to him, the mayor, however well disposed he may be, would simply have to . . .'

'But you,' interrupted Don Rodrigo, rather petulantly – 'you're messing up my affairs by your contradicting him in everything, and shouting him down; and jeering at him, too, sometimes. Why the devil shouldn't a mayor be a stubborn ass, if he's a good chap in every other way!'

'You know, cousin,' said Count Attilio, looking at him in amazement – 'you know, I'm beginning to think you've got the wind up. You're even beginning to take the mayor seriously . . .'

'Oh, come along! Didn't you yourself say we ought to take him into account?'

'Yes, I did say so; and when it's a serious matter I'll show you I'm no boy. D'you know what lengths I'd go to for you? I'm even ready to go and make a personal call on his worship the mayor. Won't he just be proud of the honour! And I'm ready to let him go on talking for an hour about the Count-Duke, and about his lordship the Spanish commandant, and to agree with him about everything, even with those silly blunders he makes. Then I'll throw in some little remark about our right honourable uncle of the Secret Council; and you know the effect these little remarks in the ear have on his worship the mayor. After all, when you come down to it, he needs our protection more than you do his patronage. I'll do things properly, and leave him better disposed than ever.'

After these and other similar remarks, Count Attilio went out hunting, and Don Rodrigo was left anxiously waiting for Griso's return. Finally, about dinner-time, the latter came to make his report.

The disorders of the previous night had made such a stir, and the disappearance of three people from a small village been such an event, that the inquiries both from solicitude and curiosity were bound to be numerous, eager, and insistent; and anyway there were too many people who knew something for them all to agree to keep everything quiet. Perpetua could not show her face at the gate without being pestered by someone or other to tell them who it was who had given her master such a fright; and Perpetua herself, on thinking over all the circumstances of the affair and finally realizing that she had been fooled by Agnese, was so furious at her perfidy that she badly needed a safety-valve. Not of course that she went round telling everyone how she had been fooled – about this she did not breathe a word – but she found it impossible to contain herself about the trick played on her poor master, particularly about how the trick had been planned and attempted by that honest young man, that good widow, and that little madonna-like Lucia. Don Abbondio might firmly order her and cordially beg her to keep quiet; she might repeat to him again and again that there was no need for him even to suggest anything so clear and obvious – the fact is that a great big secret like that in the poor woman's heart was like very new wine in an old, badly hooped cask, fermenting and gurgling and bubbling up, which, if it does not quite blow out the cork,

swishes round inside, and comes frothing or seeping out between
the staves, or dribbling out in sufficient quantities here and there
for people to taste it and tell more or less what wine it was.
Gervaso, to whom finding that for once he knew more than
others was an unbelievable discovery, to whom having a big
fright was no small glory, and who felt his having had a finger in
something criminal had made him into a normal man, was
bursting with the longing to boast of it. And although Tonio,
who was seriously worried about any inquiries, questionings, and
possible trials, ordered him, with a fist thrust in his face, not to
say a thing to anyone, there was no way of stifling every word
coming out of his mouth. Besides, Tonio himself, having been
away from home at such an unusual time that night, and come
back with such an unusual gait and air, in a state of excitement
that disposed him to frankness, had not been able to hide the
facts from his wife; and she, of course, was no mute. The one
who said least was Menico; for as soon as he told his parents the
story and the reason for his expedition, they were so horrified
that a son of theirs should have had any share in spoiling an
enterprise of Don Rodrigo's, that they would scarcely let the boy
finish his story. Then they ordered him most solemnly and
threateningly to take the very greatest care not to drop even the
least hint about it, and next morning, not feeling sufficiently sure
of him, they decided to keep him shut up indoors for that day
and a few days afterwards. But what of that? Why, they
themselves, when gossiping to their neighbours, and without at
all meaning to show that they knew more than others did, yet,
when they came to discussing the mysterious business and the
how and why and wherefore of the three poor fugitives' flight –
they themselves let fall, as if it were common knowledge, that
they had taken refuge at Pescarenico. So this fact, too, entered
into common discussion.

All these various scraps of information, when pieced together,
properly sewn up, and with the inevitable embroidery added,
made a simple and clear enough story to satisfy the most critical
mind. But it was that incursion of bravi – an incident too serious
and too notorious to be left out, and about which no one had
any definite information – that made the whole thing so confus-
ing. There was a muttered mention of Don Rodrigo's name:
everyone was agreed on that; but the rest was all darkness and
conjecture. The two bravi who had been seen on the road towards
evening, and the other who had been at the inn door, were

discussed a good deal; but what light could be drawn from that one meagre little fact? The innkeeper was questioned again and again as to who had been at the inn the night before; but he, if he was to be believed, did not even remember seeing any people that evening; and he did not fail to say that an inn was like a seaport where many people come and go. But what caused most puzzlement and disconcerted speculation was that pilgrim seen by Stefano and Carlandrea – that pilgrim whom those ruffians had tried to murder, and who had either gone off with them or been kidnapped by them. What had he come for? He was a spirit come from purgatory to help the women, said some; he was the condemned soul of some rascally impostor of a pilgrim, which came by night to join those who were doing what he had done during his lifetime; he was a real live pilgrim whom the others had wanted to kill for fear of his shouting and waking the village; he was (what strange notions come into people's heads!) one of those rascals themselves dressed up as a pilgrim. He was this, he was that, he was so many things, that Griso himself, with all his knowledge and experience, would not have been able to discover who he was if he had had to put this part of the story together from other people's talk. But, as the reader knows, the very thing that confused everyone else was the clearest to him. By using this as a key to interpret the information collected by himself directly, or by his subordinate scouts, he was able to put together quite a clear account for Don Rodrigo. He closeted himself with him at once, and told him about the stroke the unfortunate lovers had attempted, which naturally explained the empty cottage and the alarm-bell, without there being any need to suspect a traitor in the house, as the worthy pair had been thinking. He told him about their flight. And here again it was easy to find reasons: the lovers' fear at being caught red-handed, some warning of the raid after it was discovered and the whole village was topsy-turvy. Finally he told him of their having taken refuge at Pescarenico; farther than that his knowledge did not go. Don Rodrigo was pleased at the certainty that no one had betrayed him, and at finding his escapade had left no traces; but this was a brief and transient pleasure. 'Fled together!' cried he. 'Together! And that swine of a friar! That friar!' The word came out hoarsely; as he gnashed his teeth and gnawed his finger, his face looked as ugly as his passions. 'That friar shall pay for this! Griso! I want to know ... or my name is not Don Rodrigo ... I want to find out this very night ... I want to know where they are. I'll have no peace. . . . Go to Pescarenico, at once, to hear and learn and find. . . . Four *scudi* at once, and my protection for ever. I want to know tonight. That rascal . . . that friar . . .'

Off Griso set again; and by evening of the same day he was able to bring his worthy master the desired information; and this is how he did it.

One of the greatest joys in this life is friendship: and one of the joys of friendship is having someone in whom to confide a secret. Now, friends do not pair off in couples, like husbands and wives – everyone, generally speaking, has more than one, and this forms a chain whose end is impossible to find. When a friend, then, indulges in the joy of unburdening a secret on to another friend's bosom, he makes the latter, in his turn, feel the urge to taste the same joy himself. He implores him, it is true, not to tell a soul; but if such a condition were taken absolutely literally, it would at once cut off the flow of these joys at their very source. The general practice is for the secret to be confided only to an equally trustworthy friend, the same conditions being imposed on him. And so from trustworthy friend to trustworthy friend the secret goes moving on round that immense chain, until finally it reaches the ears of just the very person or persons whom the first talker had expressly intended it never should reach. Normally, though, it would be a long time on its way, if everyone had only two friends, one to make the confidence and the other to pass it on. But there are some favoured people who reckon their friends in hundreds; and when the secret gets to one of these, the chain takes so many twists and turns that it is no longer possible to keep track of it. Our author has not been able to find out exactly through how many mouths had passed the secret that Griso had been ordered to track. The fact is, that the good man who had taken the women to Monza was returning with his cart to Pescarenico towards five o'clock, when he ran into a trusted friend before getting home, and told him, in the greatest confidence, the good deed he had done, and its sequel; and the fact is, that two hours later Griso was able to hurry back to the house and tell Don Rodrigo that Lucia and her mother had taken refuge in a convent at Monza, and that Renzo had gone on to Milan.

Don Rodrigo felt a dastardly pleasure at this separation, and a revival of some of his dastardly hopes of achieving his aims. He spent most of the night brooding over the best means to do so; and got up early, with two plans in his mind, one settled and the other just sketched out. The first was to send Griso off to Monza at once to get more detailed information about Lucia and find out if any attempt could be made there. So, summoning his faithful henchman, he handed him the four *scudi*, commended him again for the ability with which he had earned them, and gave him the order that he had thought out.

'Your lordship . . .' said Griso, hesitating.

'What is it? Haven't I made myself clear?'

'If you could send someone else . . .'

'What?'

'Your most illustrious lordship, I'm ready to risk my skin for my master. That's my duty. But I know, too, that you don't want to risk the lives of your dependants too much.'

'Well?'

'Your most illustrious lordship knows how often I've had a price set on my head; and . . . Here I'm under your protection. We all pull together. His worship the mayor's a friend of the house. The bailiffs respect me; and I – it doesn't do me much honour, but it's just for a quiet life – I treat them as friends myself. In Milan your lordship's livery is known; but in Monza . . . it's I who am known there. And your lordship probably knows that, without boasting, anyone who hands me or my head over to the law would be bringing off a good thing. A hundred *scudi* down, and the privilege of freeing two criminals.'

'Devil take it!' said Don Rodrigo. 'Are you turning out just a cowardly cur with scarcely the guts to go for the legs of passers-by, that keeps looking round to see if his master's backing him up, and doesn't dare leave its own doorstep?'

'I think, my lord and master, that I've given proof . . .'

'And so?'

'And so,' went on Griso frankly, finding himself thus put on his mettle – 'and so your lordship may take it I've never spoken; brave as a lion, and fast as a hare I am, and ready to be off.'

'Mind you, I didn't say you were to go alone. Take a couple of your best men – Sfregiato and Tiradritto – and go off with a light heart, like the Griso I know. Devil take it! Three men like you, all going about their own business, who d'you think would dare stop you? The Monza bailiffs must be very bored with life to stake it for a hundred *scudi* at such a risky game. And besides . . . besides . . . I don't imagine I'm so completely unknown round there that being a servant of mine counts for nothing.'

Having put Griso somewhat to shame by this, he then went on to give him fuller and more detailed instructions. Griso took the two companions, and set off, looking bold and gay, but inwardly cursing Monza, prices on heads, women, and the whims of masters. He went stalking along as a wolf driven by hunger, with a pinched belly and ribs showing so clearly they could be counted, comes down from the snow-clad mountains, and edges suspiciously into the plain, stopping every now and again with one paw up, waving its mangy tail,

Raises its snout and sniffs the faithless breeze

for any scent of man or trap, pointing its sharp ears and rolling its bloodshot eyes, that shine with the lust for prey and the terror of pursuit. That fine line of poetry, by the way, if anyone cares to know whence it came, is from a small unpublished work on the Lombards and the Crusades,* which will not be unpublished much longer, and will make a great stir, too. I took this from it because it fitted in so well, and I have mentioned where it came from so that I might not be thought to be taking credit due to others. And I hope after this no one will think I am slyly trying to insinuate that the author of that little book and myself are like brothers, or that I can rummage among his manuscripts at will.

The other thing that worried Don Rodrigo was to find some way of preventing Renzo from ever being reunited with Lucia or setting foot in the village again. To this end he planned to spread rumours of threats and traps for Renzo, which, when they came to his ears through some friend, would drive away any desire to return to those parts. But the surest way, he thought, was to get him turned out of the state; and to succeed in this, he saw that law would be more use to him than violence. The attempt in the priest's house might be touched up a little, for instance, and made to look like an act of aggression or sedition, and then through the intermediary of the lawyer, the mayor persuaded to issue a warrant against Renzo. But he decided it would be wiser for him not to get involved in such a dirty business; and without puzzling his brain any farther, he decided to tell Dr Quibble-weaver just as much as was necessary for him to understand what was wanted. – There are so many proclamations! – thought he; – and the lawyer's no goose; he'll be able to find something that fits my case, some quibble to weave round that bumpkin, or I'll change his name for him. – But (how strangely things go in this world sometimes!) as Don Rodrigo was thinking that the lawyer was the best person to serve him, another person, the last anyone would have expected – Renzo himself – was working away with all his might to serve him, and that in a far quicker, surer way than any the lawyer could ever have found.

I have often watched a dear boy* (he's a bit too high-spirited, to tell the truth, but shows every sign of growing up into a decent citizen one day) busy driving his herd of guinea-pigs into their pen towards evening, after letting them run about free all day in a little orchard. He would try to get them all into the pen together, but it was labour wasted: one of them would stray off to the right, and as the little drover was running about to get it back into the herd, another, then two, then three others would go scurrying off all over the place to the left. Finally, after getting somewhat impatient, he would adapt himself to their ways, and push the ones nearest the door in first, then go and get the others, in ones or twos or threes, as best he could. We have to play the same sort of game with our characters; once we had Lucia under cover, we hurried off to Don Rodrigo; and now we must leave him to follow up Renzo, of whom we had lost sight.

After the painful separation we have described, Renzo was walking along from Monza towards Milan, in a state of mind that anyone can easily imagine. His home abandoned, his work gone, separated from Lucia – which was worse than anything – and now finding himself on the road without even knowing where to lay his head! And all because of that villain! When he allowed his thoughts to dwell on any of these things he felt himself overcome with rage and the longing for revenge; but then he would remember that prayer he had offered up with the good friar in the church at Pescarenico, and he would control himself. Just as his rage was welling up again he would see some shrine in a wall, doff his hat to it, and pause a moment to say another prayer: so that he must have killed Don Rodrigo in his heart and brought him to life again at least twenty times during that journey. The road then was buried down between two high banks, and was muddy, stony, and furrowed deep with wheel-ruts, which became like gutters after heavy rain, and flooded completely in some of the lower parts, so that one could have taken a boat on it. At these places a steep little track went zig-zagging up the bank, showing where other passers-by had made themselves a way across the fields. Renzo had gone up to the higher ground by one of these tracks, and found himself gazing at the great pile of the cathedral standing solitary in the plain, as if it were rising from a desert and not from the middle of a city; and he stopped short, forgetting all his troubles, to gaze even from afar at this eighth wonder of the world, which he had heard talked about so much ever since childhood. But, turning round after a few moments, he saw that rugged line of mountains on the horizon, saw his *Resegone* standing out high and clear among them, and felt the blood rush to his heart; he stayed there some time, looking sadly in that direction, then sadly turned and went on his way. Little by little he began to make out spires and towers, domes and roofs. Then, going down back into the road, he walked along it for some time, and when he found he was getting quite close to the city he stopped a passer-by, and bowing to him with all the grace he knew, said to him: 'Please, sir!'

'What do you want, my good youth?'

'Could you show me the shortest way to get to the Capuchin monastery where Fra Bonaventura is?'

The man to whom Renzo had addressed himself was a prosperous resident of the neighbourhood, who, having been to Milan on business that morning, was hurrying back without having done anything, longing to be home, and would gladly have dispensed with this delay. For all this, he showed no sign of impatience, and replied very politely: 'My dear boy, there's more than one monastery. You'll have to tell me more clearly which is the one you're looking for.' Renzo then took Fra Cristoforo's letter from his doublet, and showed it to the gentleman, who, reading 'Porta Orientale' on it, gave it back, saying: 'You're in luck, my good young fellow; the monastery you're looking for is not far from here. Take this lane on the left; it's a short cut, and in a few minutes you'll get to the corner of a long, low building; that is the lazaretto; follow the moat round it, and you will come out at the Porta Orientale. Go through it, and after three or four hundred yards you'll come to a small square with big elm-trees in it. The monastery is there; you can't miss it. God be with you, my good young fellow.' And, accompanying his last words with a pleasant wave of the hand, he went on. Renzo was left feeling amazed and edified at the civil way the townsmen treated the country-folk; he did not realize it was an exceptional day – a day when the cloak was bowing before the doublet.* He followed the road he had been shown, and found himself at the Porta Orientale. The reader, however, must not be led into picturing the scene which is nowadays conjured up by this name. When Renzo entered this gate, the road outside only ran straight for the length of the lazaretto, and then narrowed down, twisting along between two hedges. The gate consisted of two pillars, spanned

by a penthouse to protect the doors, and with a shack on one
side of it for the excise-men. The ramparts sloped down irregu-
larly to rough, uneven ground beneath, covered with rubbish and
broken potsherds dumped there at random. The street which
opened before anyone who entered by that gate was not unlike
the one now facing anyone entering by the Porta Tosa. A ditch
ran down the middle of it to within a short distance of the gate,
and divided it into two tortuous lanes, covered with dust or mud,
according to the season. Just where the alley called the Borghetto
ran – and still runs – the ditch emptied into a common sewer. At
this point there stood a column with a cross on it, called the
column of San Dionigi; to left and right ran gardens bordered by
hedges, and a few hovels at intervals, inhabited mainly by washerwomen. Renzo went into and through the gate, none of the
excise-men taking any notice of him, which he thought rather
strange, because the few people from his part of the world who
could boast of having been to Milan had told great stories of the
searchings and questionings that anyone arriving from the
country was subjected to. The street was deserted, so that, if he
had not heard a distant buzz which suggested that some big
movement was afoot, he might have thought he was entering an
uninhabited city. As he went on, not knowing what to think, he
noticed the ground streaked with some soft white substance like
snow – only it could not be snow, which neither falls in streaks,
nor, usually, at that time of the year. He stooped down to look
at some of it, touched it and found it was flour. – There must be
a great glut in Milan – said he to himself – if they scatter the gifts
of God about in this way. They'd given us to believe there was a
famine everywhere. Just see what they do to keep the poor
country-people quiet. – But on reaching the foot of the column a
few yards farther on, he saw an even stranger sight. There,
scattered over the steps of the pedestal, were certain objects
which were certainly not stones, and which, if they had been on
a baker's counter, he would not have hesitated a moment in
calling loaves of bread. But Renzo dared not believe his eyes so
readily; for, the deuce take it, that was not the place to find
bread. – Let's just look into this – he said to himself; and going
up to the column, bent down and took one up; it really was
bread: a round loaf of the very white kind that Renzo usually ate
only on feast-days. 'It really is bread!' he said out loud – such
was his amazement. 'Is this how they scatter it about here? And
in this year too? And don't even bother to gather it up when it

falls? Is this the land of milk and honey?' After a ten-mile walk
in the fresh morning air that bread had aroused his appetite as
well as his amazement. Shall I take it? he deliberated. Pooh!
they've gone and left it here at the mercy of the dogs; a human
being may as well enjoy it, too. After all, if the owner appears I'll
pay him for it. – So thinking, he put the loaf he was holding into
one pocket, took a second one and put it into the other pocket,
then picked up a third and began eating it as he set off again,
more mystified than ever, and longing to clear up what it was all
about. Just as he was starting he saw people coming from inside
the city, and looked intently at the ones who appeared first.
These were a man, a woman, and a small boy a few steps behind
them; all three were carrying burdens that looked beyond their
strength, and all three had a very odd appearance. Their clothes
– or the remains of them – were white with flour; so were their
faces, which also looked wild and inflamed; and they were
walking along not only bowed under their loads, but painfully,
as if their bones were aching. The man was staggering under a
great sack of flour, which had rents in it here and there, through
which the flour was dribbling at every jolt or lurch. But the
woman looked even more misshapen; she had an enormous belly,
which she seemed barely able to support on two arms curved
round it like the handles on a jar; under this great belly was a
pair of legs, bare to above the knee, coming tottering forward.
On looking more closely, Renzo saw that that huge mass was her
skirt, which the woman was holding up by the hems, with as
much flour inside as it could contain – and a bit more besides;
for at almost every step the wind was blowing some of it off. The
boy was holding a basket full of bread on to his head with both
hands; but, as his legs were rather shorter than those of his
parents, and he was gradually lagging behind, every now and
again he would run a little to catch them up, when the basket
would lose its balance and a loaf fall out.

'Go and throw some more away, you good-for-nothing,' said
his mother, grinding her teeth at the boy.

'I'm not throwing them away; they're falling out by themselves.
What can I do?' answered the boy.

'Eh! It's a good thing for you my hands are full,' rejoined the
woman, shaking her fist as if she were going to give the poor boy
a good clout, and spilling enough flour with this movement to
make up the two loaves the boy had just dropped. 'Oh, come
along,' said the man. 'We'll come back and pick 'em up, or

someone else will. We've been starving so long, now there's a bit of plenty, let's enjoy it in peace.'

Meanwhile more people were coming from the direction of the gate: one of these accosted the woman and asked: 'Where does one go to get bread?'

'Farther on,' she replied, adding in a mutter when they were ten yards away: 'these rascally peasants'll come and make a clean sweep of all the bakeries and shops, and there won't be anything left for us.'

'Something for everyone, you old terror,' said her husband – 'plenty, plenty.'

From these and other things he saw and heard Renzo began to realize he had come into a city in a state of rebellion, and that this was a day of conquest, meaning that everyone was taking according to his wishes and strength and giving a blow or two in payment. Much as we want our poor country boy to cut a good figure, historical accuracy obliges us to admit that his first feeling was one of pleasure. He had found so little to commend in the ordinary course of things that he was inclined to approve of whatever changed them in any way at all. And besides, not being in any way superior to the ideas of his age, he also shared the common opinion or prejudice that the scarcity of bread was due to the speculators and bakers; and he was inclined to approve of any method which tore from their grasp the food which, according to this view, they were so cruelly denying to the whole starving populace. Even so, he decided to steer clear of the tumult and congratulated himself on being on his way to a Capuchin who would find him shelter and be like a father to him. So thinking, and watching meanwhile more conquerors coming along, loaded with booty, he covered the short distance still separating him from the monastery.

On the site of the present fine building, with its lofty portico, there was at that period, and until only a few years ago, a small square, with the church and monastery of the Capuchins at the end behind four great elm-trees.* We congratulate, rather enviously, those of our readers who have not seen things in that state, for it means that they must be very young, and have not yet had time to commit many follies. Putting the half-loaf he had left back into his doublet, and taking out his letter ready in his hand, Renzo went straight up to the door and pulled the bell. A small wicket with a grating opened, and the face of the porter appeared at it, asking who it was.

'Someone from the country, bringing an urgent letter for Fra Bonaventura from Fra Cristoforo.'

'Give me it here,' said the porter, putting a hand up to the grating.

'No, no,' said Renzo. 'I must put it in his own hands.'

'He's not in the monastery.'

'Let me come in, and I'll wait for him.'

'You follow my advice,' replied the friar: 'go and wait in the church, where you can do your soul a bit of good meanwhile. No one's allowed into the monastery for the moment.' And, so saying, he shut the wicket. Renzo was left standing there with his letter in his hand. He walked a few steps towards the church, intending to follow the porter's advice, then thought he would first go and have another look at the riot. Crossing the little square, he went to the street corner, and paused there with his arms crossed on his chest, looking to the left towards the interior of the city, where the crowds were swarming thicker and noisier. A whirlpool always attracts the spectator. – Let's go and have a look – he said to himself; and, pulling out his piece of bread, he moved off in that direction, munching as he went. As he is on his way we will give as brief an account as possible of the causes and beginnings of this turmoil.

CHAPTER 12

That was the second year of bad harvests.* During the first the surplus from preceding years had more or less made up the deficiency; and the population had reached the harvest of 1628 – the year we are at in our story – without having either starved or stuffed, but certainly quite without any reserves. Now, this eagerly awaited harvest turned out even poorer than the one before, partly owing to the worse weather (not only in the area round Milan, but also over a good part of the surrounding country), and partly due to the fault of man. The ravages and wastage of war (that glorious war we have mentioned above) were such that many more farms than usual in the part of the country nearest the fighting were abandoned and left untilled by the peasants, who, instead of labouring to produce bread for themselves and others, were forced to go and beg it from charity.

I have said many more than usual, because the intolerable
exactions, levied with a greed paralleled only by their senseless-
ness, the habitual conduct, even in peace-time, of the troops
billeted in the villages – compared by the melancholy chronicles
of the time to that of an invading enemy – and other reasons
which this is not the place to mention, had been gradually
working for some time to produce this wretched effect throughout the whole of the Milanese provinces; the particular circumstances of which we are now speaking were like the sudden
aggravation of a chronic disease. And the harvest, poor as it was,
had not even been fully gathered, before the provisioning of the
army, and the waste that always goes with it, had made such big
inroads into it that a scarcity began to make itself felt very
quickly, and with the scarcity its distressing, but healthy as well
as inevitable result, a rise in prices.

Now, when this reaches a certain point, the general belief
always arises (or at least has always arisen up to now; and if it
still does after all that has been written on the subject, just think
of those times!) that this is not caused by the scarcity of supply.
People forget having feared and foretold it; all at once they begin
assuming that there is plenty of grain, and that the evil is really
due to not enough being sold in the shops – assumptions without
any foundation in heaven or earth, but which at the same time
arouse anger and excite hope. The real or imaginary hoarders of
grain, the landowners who did not sell out their whole stock in
one day, the bakers who bought it up – all those, in fact, who
had, or were rumoured to have, a little or a lot of it, were blamed
for the scarcity and the rise in prices, and were the objects of
universal complaint and loathing by rich and poor. People told
each other with certainty where warehouses and granaries, piled,
crammed, brimming over with grain, were to be found; a fantastic
figure was given for the number of sacks; people talked confidently of the immense quantity of grain secretly being sent to
other parts, where others were probably complaining with equal
assurance and indignation of the grain there being sent to Milan.
The magistrates were implored to enact those measures which
have always seemed to the people – or have at least always
seemed up to now – to be so fair, so simple, so well able,
according to them, to draw out corn that was hidden away, or
walled-up, or buried, and restore plenty once again. The magistrates did do something; for instance, they fixed a ceiling price
for some commodities, threatened with penalties anyone refusing

to sell, and issued other edicts of the kind. As, unfortunately, no edicts in the world, however bold they may be, have the power to reduce the need for food or to produce crops out of season, and as these edicts in particular were certainly not able to extract corn from whatever superfluity might have existed, so the evil went on and grew worse. The people attributed this to the scantiness and feebleness of the remedies, and clamoured loudly for ampler and more radical edicts. And, unfortunately for them, they found the very man after their own heart.

In the absence of the governor, Don Gonzalo Fernandez de Cordova, who was directing the siege of Casale in Montferrat, his functions in Milan were taken over by the Grand Chancellor, Antonio Ferrer, also a Spaniard. The latter saw – and who would not have seen? – that a fair price for bread was a most desirable thing in itself; and thought – which is where he made his mistake – that an order from him would be enough to produce it. He fixed the *meta* (as the tariff for foodstuffs is called here) of bread at the price which would have been just if wheat were being sold at thirty-three *lire* the bushel, when in fact it was being sold as high as eighty. He acted like a woman past her first youth who thinks she will grow younger by altering her birth certificate.

Orders less stupid and iniquitous than these have often remained dead letters through their inherent contradictions; but the people were watching over the execution of these, for, having seen their wishes finally converted into law, they were determined not to be tricked. They rushed off to the bakeries at once, to demand bread at the fixed price; and they demanded it with the threatening, determined air that comes from a union of passion, strength, and legal backing. That the bakers complained goes without saying. To be mixing, kneading, thrusting loaves in and out of the oven without a moment's respite (for the people, vaguely realizing that things had been forced, besieged the bakeries continuously, to make the most of that milk and honey while it lasted); to be toiling and drudging away far more than usual, only to find themselves out of pocket – anyone can see that this was not much fun for them. But with the magistrates threatening penalties on one side, and the people determined to be served on the other, urging them on and complaining with those loud voices of theirs if any baker demurred, and threatening to take justice into their own hands (the worst justice there is in this world), there was nothing for it but to go on kneading, thrusting loaves in and out, and selling them. But it was not enough for them just to be bullied or intimidated into going on performing these tasks: they had to be able to do them: and things had only to go on like this a little longer for them to become quite impossible. They pointed out to the magistrates how iniquitous and intolerable was the burden imposed on them, and protested that they were ready to throw their shovels into the ovens and quit. Meanwhile, they went ahead as best they could, always hoping that some time or other the Grand Chancellor would listen to reason. But Antonio Ferrer, who was what would nowadays be called a man of character, replied that the bakers had made big profits in the past, and would soon be making big profits again with the return of plenty; that even so, he would consider giving them some subsidy: and that meanwhile they must carry on. Did he really convince himself by the arguments he put forward to others? Or did he, realizing from its results how impossible his edict was to maintain, want to throw the odium of revoking it onto others? But who can now enter into the mind of Antonio Ferrer? The fact remains that he held firm by his decisions. Finally the *Decurions* (a municipal magistrature composed of nobles, which lasted right up until 1796) wrote and told the governor about the state things were in, and asked him to find some solution that would get them going again.

Don Gonzalo, up to the ears in military affairs, did what the reader is sure to have guessed: he appointed a commission with full powers to fix a feasible price for bread; something that would allow both sides to rub along. The deputies held a meeting (or as it was called here in the would-be Spanish official jargon of the day, a *junta*), and after many bows and compliments, hems and haws, preambles, tentative suggestions, and hesitations, they were finally forced into a decision by the necessity felt by all; and knowing well that they were playing a very high card, but convinced there was nothing else for it, decided to raise the price of bread. The bakers heaved a sigh of relief, but the populace was infuriated.

The evening before the day of Renzo's arrival in Milan the streets and squares were swarming with men in the grip of a common rage, and dominated by a common idea; friends and strangers all fell into groups, without any pre-arrangement, almost without realizing it, like drops of water scattered over the same slope. Every conversation strengthened the convictions and fanned the passions of the listeners, as it did those of the speakers. Among all these excited people there were also a few with cooler heads, who were observing this troubling of the waters with pleasure, and doing their best to trouble them still more, by means of arguments and stories which the cunning know how to invent and overwrought minds are so apt to believe; and they determined not to let the waters settle without doing a little fishing in them. Thousands of men went to bed that night with a vague feeling that something ought to be done, that something would be done. Before daybreak the streets were again scattered with knots of people; children, women, men, old folk, workers, beggars, all met together at random. Here there was a confused murmur of many voices; there one man was making a speech, while others applauded; here a man was asking his nearest neighbour the same question the latter had just had put to him: another there was repeating some exclamation he had just heard echoing in his ears; complaints, threats, astonishment were everywhere; and the total vocabulary of all this talk was just a few words.

All that was needed now to convert words into actions was an occasion, a little push, any sort of start; and this was not long in coming. About daybreak the apprentices began coming out of the bakeries, carrying baskets full of bread, to take to their usual customers. The first appearance of one of these unfortunates near a group of people was like a lighted squib falling into a powder-magazine. 'There, just see if there's any bread!' cried a hundred voices at once. 'Yes, bread for the tyrants, who're wallowing in plenty, and would like us to die of starvation!' said one; and went up to the boy, put his hand on the rim of the basket, gave it a jerk, and said, 'Let's have a look.' The boy went red, then white, trembled, wanted to say, 'Let me go,' but the words died on his lips; he loosened his arm, and hastily tried to extricate himself from the straps, while the people around cried, 'Down with that basket!' Many hands grabbed it, and bore it to the ground; the cloth covering it was flung aside; a warm fragrance was diffused all round. 'We're Christians, too, and have a right to eat bread as well as others,' said the first man, taking out a round loaf, and waving it in the air to show it to the crowd, then plunging his teeth into it; in a minute all hands were at the basket, the loaves were being flung into the air, and in less time than it takes to tell it, the basket was empty. Those who had not managed to get any, exasperated at seeing that others had, and spurred on by the ease of it, moved off in squads, looking for other baskets; and no sooner met one than they emptied it. There

was no need even to assault the bearers; those of them who had
the bad luck to be going their rounds saw the turn things were
taking, set their burdens down of their own free will, and took to
their heels. In spite of all this, the vast proportion of the people
remained hungry. Even the victors were dissatisfied with so
meagre a spoil: and mingling with both were those others who
were set on disorders on a much bigger scale. 'To the bakery! To
the bakery!' the cry went up.

In the street known as the Corsia de'Servi there was, and still
is,* a bakery that has kept the same name – a name which in
Tuscan means the bakery of the crutches, and in Milanese is
made up of such ill-assorted, cacophonous, and barbarous syllables that the alphabet lacks symbols to indicate their sound.†
This is where the crowds were making for. The shopkeepers were
just questioning the apprentice who had come back empty-
handed; and he, all dishevelled and dismayed, was stammering
out an account of his mishap, when a sound of tramping feet and
a roar of voices came to their ears. The noise came nearer; then
the vanguard of the mob hove into sight.

Shut up shop, shut up shop; quick, quick; one of them rushed
off to get help from the sheriff; the others hastily shut the shop
and bolted the doors.

Outside, the crowd was beginning to thicken, shouting, 'Bread!
bread! Open up! Open up!'

A few minutes later the sheriff arrived with an escort of
pikemen. 'Make way, lads, make way; get home, get home. Make
way for the sheriff!' shouted he and his men. The crowd, which
was not yet too thick, made just enough room for them to be
able to reach the shop and place themselves all together, though
in no good order, in front of the door.

'Why, my lads,' the sheriff began addressing the crowd from
there, 'what are you doing here? Go home, go home! Where's
your fear of God? What will our lord the king say? We don't
want to hurt you, but just go off home, like good fellows, now.
What the devil are you doing here, crowding up like this? No
good, either to your souls or bodies. Go home, go home!'

But how could those who saw the speaker's face and heard his
voice have obeyed him, even if they had wanted to, jostled and
squeezed as they were by those behind, who were being squeezed
by others in turn, piling up, in wave after wave, right up to the

† El prestin di scansc. (M.)

very edge of the crowd, which was growing all the time? The sheriff began to feel suffocated. 'Get 'em back so I can have a breath of air,' he told his pikemen. 'But don't hurt anyone. Let's try to get into the shop. Knock; keep 'em back.'

'Back, back!' shouted the pikemen, flinging themselves all together on those in front, and pushing them back with the butts of their pikes. They screamed and pulled back as best they could – by stubbing their shoulders into the chests, their elbows into the stomachs, and their heels on to the toes of those behind them. There was such a press and squash that the people who found themselves in the middle would have given a great deal to be elsewhere. Meanwhile a small space had been cleared in front of the shop. The sheriff knocked; knocked again; and shouted for them to open. Those inside saw him from the windows, hurried downstairs and opened up. The sheriff went in and called the pikemen, who edged in one by one, the last of them holding the crowd back with their pikes. When they had all got in, they bolted and barricaded the door again, and the sheriff ran upstairs and went to a window. Uh, what a swarm!

'Lads,' he bawled; many looked up. 'Go home, my lads! A general pardon to those who go home at once.'

'Bread! Bread! Open up! Open up!' were the words most clearly distinguished in the fearful roar the crowd raised in reply.

'Be sensible, now. Be very careful. You've still got time. Go on, off with you, back home. You'll get your bread; but this isn't the way. Hey, hey! What are you doing down there? What! At that door! Hey, hey! I'm looking! I'm looking! Careful now, it's a serious crime. I'm just coming down. Hey, hey! Drop those iron bars – hands off! Shame on you, Milanese like you, who're known for your goodness the world over. Listen, listen! You've always been good la . . . Hah, you scum!'

This abrupt change of style was caused by a stone from the hands of one of those good lads, which struck the sheriff on the forehead, on the left bump of his metaphysical cavity. 'Scum! Scum!' he went on shouting, hastily closing the window and drawing in. But even if he had shouted with all the power in his lungs, his words, had they been good or bad, would all have been drowned and lost in the storm of yells from down below. What he said he had seen was a great activity with stones and bars (the first that had come to hand on the way) to try and batter down the door and wrench the grilles from the windows. The work was already well under way.

Meanwhile, the owners and apprentices of the shop were at the upstairs windows, armed with stones (probably torn up from the paving of the yard), shouting and grimacing at those below to stop, showing their stones, and signing that they intended to use them. Then, seeing they were wasting their time, they began to throw them in real earnest. Not a single one missed its mark; for the mob was now so dense that a grain of millet, as the saying is, could not have reached the ground.

'Hah, yer swine! Hah, yer villains! Is this the bread you give the poor? Oh! Ow! Ouch! Now, now!' were the screams from down below. A number were badly hurt; and two boys were killed. Fury gave the crowd new strength; the door was soon burst open, the grilles twisted back, and the torrent streamed in through every breach. Those inside, seeing how black things looked, fled into the attics; the sheriff, the pikemen, and some of the shop-people crouched up there under the tiles, while others escaped through a skylight and took to the roofs, like cats.

The sight of the spoil made the victors forget their plans for a bloody vengeance. They flung themselves on the bins and snatched at the bread. Others, however, rushed to the counter, broke open the lock, seized the tills, took out handfuls of money, stuffed it in their pockets, and went out loaded with coins, to come back later to steal bread, if there was any left. The crowd spread through the warehouses. They laid hands on the sacks, dragged them about, turned them over; some thrust a sack between their legs, undid the top, and threw away some of the flour to reduce it to a portable load, while others shouted 'Wait, wait,' and stooped down to catch the manna in their aprons, handkerchiefs, or hats. Another ran to the kneading-trough, and took out pieces of dough, which lengthened and oozed out in all directions. Another had snatched up a sieve, and was brandishing it about. Men, women, children, pushed and jostled and shouted, while a white dust rose everywhere, settled everywhere, veiling the whole scene in mist. Outside, a throng made up of two opposing queues – those coming out with their spoils, and those trying to enter and get some – were entangling and jostling with each other.

While this bakery was being turned upside down, none of the other bakeries in the city was quiet and out of danger. But crowds had not made for any of the others in sufficiently large numbers to be able to attack them; in some the owners had collected help and were in a state of defence; others, finding themselves too few, came to some sort of terms, and distributed bread to those beginning to collect in front of their shops, on condition they went away. And they went away, not so much because they were satisfied, as because the pikemen and the bailiffs, while keeping at a safe distance from the terrible affair at the Bakery of the Crutches, showed themselves in sufficient strength elsewhere to over-awe the unlucky groups who were not enough to form a mob. So the confusion at that first ill-fated bakery was constantly increasing; for all those whose hands were itching to do some mischief hurried off there, where their friends were strongest and the danger negligible.

Such was the state of affairs when Renzo, having munched most of his loaf by this time, was wandering down the street from the eastern gate, and approaching, without knowing it, the very centre of the tumult. He was walking along, sometimes hurried, sometimes held back by the crowd, and watching and keeping his ears open as he went, to try and gather, from the confused buzz of talk around, some more definite news of what was happening. These are more or less the sort of remarks he succeeded in catching during that walk.

'Now it's all come out,' one man was shouting. 'The filthy trick these rogues have been playing on us, about there being no bread, or flour, or corn. Now it's all quite plain and obvious: they can't try and deceive us any more. Hurrah for plenty!'

'I tell you, this is no good at all,' said another; 'it's just a drop in the ocean; things will get worse, in fact, if proper justice isn't done once and for all. Bread will get cheap, but they'll put poison in it, to kill the poor off like flies. They're already saying there are too many of us. They've said so at the Junta, and I can vouch for it, as I've heard it with these very ears from a woman I know who's a friend of a relation of someone who works in one of those gentlemen's kitchens.'

Another man's language was unrepeatable, as he foamed at the mouth, and with one hand held a ragged handkerchief to his disordered, bloodstained hair. And one or two bystanders were echoing him, as if to console him.

'Make way, make way, gentlemen, please; make way for the poor father of a family, who's carrying home something to eat for his five children,' a man was saying as he came staggering along under the load of a huge sack of flour; and everyone tried to draw back and let him pass.

'Me?' another was saying, almost in a whisper, to his companion. 'I'm beating it. I've a bit of experience, and know how these things go. These oafs who are making such a noise now will be hiding at home in terror tomorrow. I've already noticed certain faces, certain gentlemen going spying around and seeing who's here and who isn't here. Then when it's all over the reckoning will come along, and those who have been up to anything will be for it.'

'The man who's protecting the bakers,' shouted a sonorous voice that attracted Renzo's attention, 'is the Commissioner of Supply.'

'They're all rascals,' said one bystander.

'Yes, but he's the chief one,' answered the first.

The Commissioner of Supply was elected every year by the governor from among six nobles proposed by the Council of *Decurions*, and was the president of this council, as well as of the Commission of Supply. The latter was also composed of twelve members, also noble, and its chief duty – among others – was to control the provision of food. Anyone occupying such a post in times of famine and ignorance is bound to be considered the author of these evils – unless he did what Ferrer had done; which was not within their powers to do, even if it had been in their thoughts.

'Scoundrels!' another was exclaiming. 'Is there anything worse they could do? They've even got to the point of saying the Grand Chancellor's an old man in his second childhood, to destroy his prestige and get all the power themselves. We ought to make 'em a great sty and shove 'em all inside, to live on vetch and rye-grass, which is what they want us to do!'

'Bread, did you say?' another man was saying as he hurried away. 'Why, there are heavy stones – stones this big – coming down like hail. The ribs that got broken! I'm longing to get home.'

Amidst talk like this, by which it would be difficult to say whether he was more enlightened or confused, and amidst jostling and pushing, Renzo finally arrived in front of the bakery. The people had already thinned out a lot, so that he could observe the ugly remains of the recent havoc: the wall scarred and pitted by stones and bricks, the windows off their hinges, the door torn away.

– This surely isn't a good thing – said Renzo to himself – if they go and smash up all the bakeries like this, where do they reckon to make the bread? In the wells? –

Every now and again someone came out of the shop carrying a piece of a bin, or trough, or sieve, a rolling-pin, a stool, a pannier, a ledger – anything, in fact, that happened to be in that ill-fated bakery; and, shouting 'Make way, make way,' would pass out through the crowd. All these, he noticed, were going off in the same direction, and, it was plain, to some pre-arranged spot. – What's this now? – Renzo wondered; and he followed in the wake of a man who had made a bundle of broken boards and splinters, hoisted it on his back, and was making his way, like the others, along the street flanking the northern side of the cathedral (the one which took its name from the flight of steps that used to be there, and was removed a short time ago). His curiosity to see what was happening did not prevent our country lad from pausing when he found himself facing the vast pile, and gazing up at it open-mouthed. Then he quickened his pace to catch up with the man he had taken as guide; he turned the corner, and glanced up also at the façade of the cathedral, which was still in the rough at that time, and far from finished; and kept on close behind the man, who was going towards the middle of the square. The farther they advanced, the thicker the crowds got, but they made way for the laden man. He cleft through the waves of people, and Renzo, still following closely in his wake, reached the very centre of the crowd with him. Here was an empty space, and in the middle of it a heap of embers, remains of the implements mentioned above. Hands were clapping and feet were stamping all around, and a thousand throats shouting cries of triumph and imprecation.

The man with the bundle threw it on the heap; another man stirred up the fire with the charred butt of a pole. The smoke thickened and grew denser. The flames mounted, and with them the cries grew louder. 'Long live plenty! Death to the starvers! Death to the famine! Death to the supply people! Death to the Commission! Long live bread!'

In truth, destroying sieves and kneaders, pillaging bakeries and routing bakers, are scarcely the promptest ways of ensuring 'bread for ever'; but this is one of the metaphysical subtleties which a multitude does not grasp. Sometimes, however, a man can grasp this without being a great metaphysician, when he is still fresh to the problem; and it is only by discussing it, and hearing it discussed, that he becomes incapable of understanding it. This thought had, in fact, occurred to Renzo from the very first, as we have seen, and was recurring to him every minute. He kept it to himself, however, for among all the faces around there was not one which seemed to say: Brother, correct me if I'm wrong, and I'll be glad of it.

The flames had died down once more; no one could be seen coming with any more fuel, and people were just beginning to get bored, when the rumour went round that a bakery was being besieged at the Cordusio – a square or cross-roads not far from there. Often in such circumstances the rumour of something is enough to bring it about. As it spread, so did the urge among the crowd to rush off there. 'I'm going; you, are you going? Coming; let's go,' was heard on all sides; the crowd broke up and became a procession. Renzo hung back, hardly moving, except when he was dragged along by the current, and wondering to himself meanwhile whether he ought to get out of the tumult and return to the monastery to look for Fra Bonaventura, or go and see this other one, too. His curiosity won again. He decided, however, not to get into the thick of the crowd and risk having his bones broken or worse, but to keep some distance away and look on. And finding he already had a little elbow room, he took his second loaf out of his pocket, bit off a mouthful, and tacked himself on to the rear of the tumultuous army.

This was already moving from the square into the short, narrow street of the old fish-market, and thence, by that crooked arch, into the Piazza de' Mercanti. And there were very few, as they passed in front of the niche that stands midway along the portico of the building then known as the Doctors' College, who did not glance up at the great statue inside it, and at that solemn, morose, frowning face of Philip II, which even in marble imposed a kind of awe, and, with its outstretched arm, seemed to be on the point of saying: 'I'm just coming after you, you rabble.'

By a strange chance that statue no longer exists. About a hundred and seventy years after the events we are describing, one day its head was changed, the sceptre was taken from its hand, and a dagger put in its place; and the statue was re-named Marcus Brutus. It stood in this state for a couple of years or so; but one morning certain people who had no sympathy for Marcus Brutus, and who must in fact have had a secret grudge against him, threw a rope around the statue, pulled it down, and committed all sorts of outrages on it; then they dragged it, mutilated and reduced to a shapeless torso, through the streets, with their eyes and tongues straining out, and when they were completely exhausted, rolled it down no one knows where. If anyone had told Andrea Biffi this, when he was carving it!*

From the Piazza de' Mercanti the mob passed through, by that other arch, into the Via de' Fustignai, and thence spread out into the Cordusio. As everyone turned the corner they at once looked towards the bakery about which they had been told. But instead of the crowds of friends they had expected to find at work there, all they saw were a few people hovering apparently in hesitation some distance from the shop, which was shut, and had armed men at the windows, getting ready to defend themselves. At this sight some were amazed, some cursed and some laughed; some turned round to tell others who were just arriving; others stopped; others tried to turn back; others said, 'Forward, forward.' There was a swaying to and fro, a kind of lull, a hesitation, a confused buzz of discussion and consultation. At this moment an ill-fated voice called out from the middle of the crowd: 'The Commissioner of Supply's house is nearby! Let's go and do justice, and sack it!' It seemed like the general reminder of an old plan rather than the adoption of a new suggestion. 'To the Commissioner's! To the Commissioner's!' was the only cry to be heard. The crowd surged all together towards the street in which stood the house named at such an unlucky moment.

CHAPTER I3

The unfortunate Commissioner was at that moment taking a bitter, troubled rest, after a meal which he had eaten without any appetite and without any fresh bread; and was waiting, in great suspense, to see how the storm would end up – although he was far from suspecting that it was just about to burst so appallingly over his own head. Some kindly person ran on in front of the crowd to warn him of what was hanging over him. The servants, already attracted to the door by the noise, were looking in consternation up the street in the direction from which it was approaching. As they were listening to the warning, they saw the advance guard appear; up rushed some to warn their master; and while he was wondering whether to flee and how, another came to tell him it was too late. The servants scarcely had time enough to shut the gates. They bolted them, barred them, and ran to shut

the windows, as when one sees the sky getting black and expects
the hail any minute. The shouting swelled, coming down from
above like thunder, and reverberating through the empty courtyard; every hole in the house echoed with it; and in the midst of
the vast confused uproar a shower of stones was heard falling
thick and fast upon the door.

'The Commissioner! The tyrant! The starver! We want him,
dead or alive!'

The wretched man was running about from room to room,
pale and breathless, wringing his hands, appealing to God and to
his servants to stand by him and find him some way of escape.
But how, and where? He climbed up into the lofts, peered
anxiously down into the street through a slit, and saw it crammed
full of furious people; he heard the voices clamouring for his
death, and, more beside himself than ever, drew back and went
to search for the safest and remotest hiding-place he could find.
Crouching down in it, he listened and listened to hear if the
ghastly sounds were getting weaker or the tumult was abating a
little; but instead he heard the bellowing getting louder and
fiercer and the bangs on the door redoubling, so that his heart
turned another somersault, and he hurriedly plugged up his ears.
Then, completely losing control of himself, he clenched his teeth
and twisted up his face, braced his arms and fists, as if he hoped
they would hold the doors firm, then . . . But what else he did we
cannot tell, as he was alone; and history can only guess. Luckily,
it is quite used to doing so.

Renzo found himself this time in the very thick of the tumult,
and carried there not by the tide, but by his own purpose. At the
first suggestion of bloodshed he had felt his own blood curdle
within him. Whether the sacking was a good or a bad thing in
this case he could not say: but the idea of murder aroused pure,
instant horror in him. And although he was quite certain – such
is the fatal way the inflamed opinions of a crowd can influence
an excited mind – that the Commissioner was the main cause of
the famine and the enemy of the poor, yet, having overheard
some remarks as the crowd first moved off that showed there
were some people who intended to make every effort to save
him, he had at once decided to take a hand in this good work
himself; and with this intention he had pushed forward, almost
as far as that door, just as it was being assailed in a variety of
ways. Some were pounding at the nails of the lock with flints, to
wrench it out; others were setting to work more methodically

with crow-bars and chisels and hammers; others, again, were scraping and scratching away at the wall with stones, broken knives, nails, sticks, and even finger-nails, if they had nothing else, trying to loosen the bricks and make a breach. Those who could not help were shouting encouragement to the others; but at the same time, by pressing and shoving, they further hampered an undertaking already hampered by the disorderly rivalry of the workers. For what only too often happens in a good cause – that its most ardent supporters become a hindrance – can sometimes, by the grace of God, also happen with a bad.

The first magistrates to get the news of what was happening at once sent off an appeal for help to the commandant of the castle, then known as the castle of Porta Giovia, and he despatched a few soldiers. But between warning, orders, mustering, getting under way, and the way itself, by the time they arrived the house was already besieged by a vast mob. They halted a long way off, at the very edge of the crowd. The officer commanding them did not know what steps to take. There was only a hotch-potch – if I may use the expression – of people of various ages and sexes, looking on. On their being told to disperse and make way, their only answer was a deep, prolonged mutter; no one moved. To fire into this rabble seemed to the officer not only a cruel, but a very dangerous thing to do, which would only harm the less offensive minority and infuriate the more violent majority; and anyway, he had no such orders. It would have been better to break through the outer ring of the crowd, scatter them to right and left, and advance to give battle to the real belligerents; but the difficulty was to succeed in this. Who could tell if the soldiers would keep together in good order? Who could tell that they would not themselves be scattered about in the crowd instead of breaking it up, and, after provoking it, find themselves at its mercy? The irresolution of the commander and the inactivity of the soldiers looked, rightly or wrongly, like fear. The people nearest them contented themselves with staring at them with an air of 'devil we care.' Those a little farther away did not hesitate to make provocative faces and shout taunts at them. Farther away still, few knew or cared whether they were there or not. The demolition squad went on breaking down the wall, with no thought beyond getting it done quickly. The bystanders went on encouraging them with shouts.

Conspicuous among these was an old rogue who was a spectacle in himself; his fiery eyes starting from their cavernous

sockets, his face contracted in a grin of diabolic glee, he was
brandishing above his shameful white hairs a hammer, a rope,
and four great nails, with which he said he meant to crucify the
Commissioner on his own door-post, once he was killed.

'Hey! Shame on you!' burst out Renzo, horrified at these words
and at the looks of approval he saw on many faces around, as
well as encouraged at seeing others showing the same horror that
he felt himself, silent though they were. 'Shame! Do we want to
do the executioner's job? Commit murder? How d'you expect
God to give us bread if we go and do atrocities like that? He'll
send thunderbolts down on us, not bread!'

'Ah, you dog! Ah, you traitor to your country!' shouted one of
those who had caught these blessed words in the din, turning on
Renzo with the face of a demoniac. 'Wait, wait! He's one of the
Commissioner's men, disguised as a peasant; he's a spy. At him,
at him!' A hundred voices echoed all round: 'What is it, where is
he? One of the Commissioner's men! A spy! The Commissioner
escaping disguised as a peasant! Where is he? Where is he? At
him! At him!'

Renzo went dumb, made himself as small as he could, and
longed to vanish altogether. Some of his neighbours put him
between them, trying to drown those hostile and murderous cries
by shouting other and different cries. But what stood him in
better stead than anything was a shout of 'Make way, make
way!' which was raised nearby: 'Make way! Help's coming!
Make way there, hey!'

What was it? It was a long ladder some were bringing to prop
up against the house so as to get in through a window. But by
good luck this means of simplifying entry was not itself simple to
put into practice. The bearers at each end and along the sides of
the ladder, pushed, confused, shoved apart by the press, were
loosed from their moorings. One weighed down as if under a
struggling yoke, with his head between two of the rungs and with
the struts on his shoulders, was bellowing hard. Another was
pushed away from his load, and the abandoned ladder went
knocking against shoulders, arms, ribs; what their owners had to
say can be imagined. Others then raised the dead weight up with
their hands, thrust themselves beneath it, and bore it up on their
shoulders, shouting, 'Courage! Come on!' The fatal machine
went forward in jumps and twists, arriving just in time to distract
and confuse Renzo's enemies. He took advantage of this confusion within the confusion, and first almost creeping along, then

using his elbows for all he was worth, he got away from the neighbourhood which was so unhealthy for him, intending also to get out of the tumult as soon as possible, and really go this time to find or to wait for Fra Bonaventura.

But suddenly an extraordinary movement began at one edge and spread through the whole crowd, and a cry went echoing from mouth to mouth, 'Ferrer! Ferrer!' Amazement, delight, fury, approval, disgust, broke out wherever this name reached: some shouting it, some trying to drown it, some blessing it, and others cursing it.

'Ferrer here? – It's not true, it's not true! – Yes, yes; long live Ferrer! He's the man who got bread cheap. – No, no! – He's here, he's here in a coach. What's it matter? What's he got to do with us? We don't want anyone! – Ferrer! Long live Ferrer! The friend of the poor! He's coming to take the Commissioner off to prison. – No, we'll take the law into our own hands! Back, back! – Yes, yes; Ferrer! Let Ferrer come on! To prison with the Commissioner!'

And everyone rose up on tiptoe and turned to look in the direction where this unexpected arrival had been announced. As they all rose up, they saw exactly the same as if they had kept their heels on the ground; but so it was, they all rose.

In fact the Grand Chancellor, Antonio Ferrer, had arrived in a coach at the very edge of the crowd, on the opposite side to the soldiers. Probably his conscience had been gnawing at him for having, by his folly and obstinacy, been the cause or at least the occasion of the riot, and he was now coming in the hopes of allaying it, or at least of averting its most terrible and irreparable effects; he was coming to spend well an ill-gotten popularity.

In all popular tumults there are always a certain number of men who, either from excited passions, or fanatical conviction, or evil intentions, or just from a cursed taste for disorder, do all they can to push things as far as possible: they propose and support the wildest suggestions, and fan the flames whenever they begin to languish: nothing is ever enough for them; they want the riot to burst all bounds and go on forever. But, to balance these, there are always a certain number of others who are working with equal ardour and persistence to produce the opposite results; some moved by friendship or partiality for the people threatened, others with no other motive than a pious and instinctive horror of bloodshed and atrocity. May Heaven bless them! In each of these rival parties unanimity of desire creates, even without any prior arrangements, an immediate uniformity of action. The mass or, one might almost say, the material for the tumult consists of a haphazard mixture of people who tend in indefinite variations towards one or the other of these extremes; moved partly by hot-headedness, partly by knavery, partly by a desire to see justice done as they understand it, partly by the urge to see something exciting happen; ready for savagery or pity, for hatred or adoration, as the opportunity for wallowing in any of these feelings comes up; longing to hear and to believe astounding news every moment, needing someone to shout at, to applaud, or to deride. 'Long live' and 'Death to' are the words they bring out most readily. And anyone who has succeeded in persuading them that such and such a person does not deserve to be drawn and quartered, need use no more words to convince them that he is worthy of carrying in triumph. They are actors or spectators, instruments or obstacles, according as the wind is blowing; ready to keep quiet when they hear no more cries to repeat, to stop when there is no longer anyone to incite them, and to disperse when they hear many voices agreeing and no one contradicting that it is time to go; and on getting back home they ask each other what it was all about. Now, as it is this mass that has the most power, and can give it to anyone it likes, both the active parties use every art to try and win it over to their side and to gain control of it; they are almost like two hostile spirits trying to get into that gross body and make it move. They compete in spreading the rumours most likely to stir its passions, in directing the movements that further their own intentions; and whichever of them is most capable of kindling or lulling its indignation, or of awakening its hopes or terrors, whichever of them can find the catchword that is repeated loudest and most often, is the one which expresses, affirms, and at the same time creates the preference of the majority for one side or the other.

All these remarks are merely made to introduce the fact that, in the struggle between the two parties contending for the preference of the crowds outside the Commissioner's house, the appearance of Antonio Ferrer gave an almost immediate advantage to the humane party, which was obviously the weaker, and would have lost both the power and the incentive to fight had help been delayed much longer. He was popular with the mob, because of the tariff he had thought out which was so favourable to the consumers, and because of the heroic stand he had made against all the arguments opposed to it. Those already biased in

his favour were drawn to the old man more than ever by the bold
confidence with which he had come, without any escort, without
any retinue, to face an excited and turbulent mob. Then, hearing
that he was coming to take the Commissioner off to prison had
an admirable effect; with the result that the fury against the
latter, which would have been made fiercer by any brusqueness
or refusal to make concessions, now, with this promise of
satisfaction, with this bone in its mouth, calmed down a little,
and gave way to other contrary feelings welling up in many
minds.

The partisans of peace took heart again, and began helping
Ferrer in a hundred different ways – those near him by rallying
the general applause, and trying at the same time to get the crowd
to draw back and make room for the coach; others by clapping,
by repeating and passing on his words, or the words they thought
best suited him, by shouting down those still obstinately angry,
and turning against them the new passions of the fickle crowd.
'Who doesn't want to say, "Long live Ferrer"? Don't you want
bread to be cheap, eh? They're rogues, the people who don't
want decent justice; and some of those making most row are
doing it to let the Commissioner escape. To prison with the
Commissioner! Long live Ferrer! Make way for Ferrer!' And as
the number of those shouting thus increased, the boldness of the
opposing party abated, so that the others passed from talk to
action and laid hands on those still continuing the work of
demolition, pushed them aside and snatched the tools from their
hands. These fumed, threatened, and tried to retaliate; but the
cause of bloodshed had lost the day. The cries now predominating were: 'Prison!' 'Justice!' 'Ferrer!' They were routed after a
short struggle; the others took over the doorway, both to protect
it from any new assaults and to prepare an entry for Ferrer. Some
of them called in to those in the house (there was no lack of
holes), to tell them help was arriving and to get the Commissioner
ready: 'To go off at once . . . to prison; ahem, d'you understand?'

'Is that the Ferrer who helps to make out the proclamations?'
Renzo inquired of a new neighbour, remembering the *Vidit
Ferrer* the lawyer had shouted in his ear as he showed it to him
at the bottom of that edict.

'That's right; the Grand Chancellor,' was the reply.

'He's a good man, isn't he?'

'Of course he's a good man! He's the one who made bread

cheap; the others didn't want to; and now he's come to take the
Commissioner off to prison, for not doing things right.'

It goes without saying that Renzo was all for Ferrer at once.
He wanted to go straight off to meet him. It was no easy matter;
but he managed to make his way, with some of those rustic
pushes and shoves of his, and reach the front rank, right beside
the coach.

This had already advanced some way into the crowd. At that
moment it was halted, held up by one of the frequent obstacles
inevitable in a progress of that kind. The aged Ferrer was
showing, first at one window and then at the other, a countenance
that was all humility, smiles, and affection, a countenance that
he had always kept in reserve for when he found himself in the
presence of Philip IV; but now he was forced to use it on this
occasion, too. He was also talking away, but the clamour and
buzz of so many voices, the very applause being shouted at him,
allowed very little of what he said to be heard, and then by only
very few people. So he was helping himself out by gestures, now
putting his hands to his lips to kiss them, then splaying them out
and distributing the kisses to right and left in acknowledgement
of this public kindness; now reaching his hands out of the
window and waving them slowly to and fro, to ask for a little
room; then lowering them in a graceful gesture, to ask for a little
silence. When he had succeeded in obtaining some, those nearest
to him could hear and repeat what he was saying: 'Bread; plenty;
I've come to do justice. A little room, if you'd be so kind.' Then,
overwhelmed and, as it were, stifled by the din of so many voices,
the sight of so many faces crowded together, of so many eyes
fixed on him, he drew in a moment, puffed out his cheeks, heaved
a great sigh, and muttered to himself, '*Por mi vida, que de
gente!*'*

'Long live Ferrer! Don't be afraid. You're a good man! Bread,
bread!'

'Yes, bread, bread,' answered Ferrer. 'Plenty; I promise it' –
and he put his hand to his heart.

'A little room,' he added quickly. 'I'm coming to take him off
to prison, to give him the punishment he deserves!' and added
under his breath, '*Si es culpable.*'* Then he leaned forward
towards the coachman and said hurriedly, '*Adelante, Pedro, si
puedes.*'*

The coachman was also beaming at the crowds with affable
condescension, as if he were some great personage himself; and

was waving his whip very slowly to left and right, with ineffable politeness, to ask his inconvenient neighbours to tighten up and draw back a bit. 'Please, gentlemen,' he was saying, too – 'a little room, just a very little – just enough to let us pass.'

Meanwhile the most active of the well-wishers were exerting themselves to make the room so courteously requested. Some went ahead of the horses and made people draw back by fair words, by putting their hands to their hearts, and by sundry gentle pushes: 'Over there, come, a little room, gentlemen'; some were doing the same each side of the coach so that it could pass without crushing any feet or bruising any noses; which, besides doing injury to others, would also have exposed to great danger the reputation of Antonio Ferrer.

Renzo, after standing for some time admiring the dignified old man, ruffled a little by his ordeal, worn by fatigue, but animated by solicitude and almost transfigured by the hope of saving a fellow-creature from mortal anguish – Renzo, I say, put aside all idea of leaving, and decided to help Ferrer, and not to leave him until his purpose was accomplished. This was no sooner said than done; and he set to work helping the others to make room for him; and was certainly not the least active of them. A space was made. 'Now come on,' several people said to the coachman, drawing back or going on to make more room farther ahead. '*Adelante, presto, con juicio,*'* his master said; and the coach began to move. Ferrer, amidst the salutations he was lavishing over the public at large, also made others of special acknowledgement, with a meaning smile, to those he saw working to help him; and several of these smiles fell to the share of Renzo, who did, in fact, really deserve them, and served the Grand Chancellor that day better than the best of his secretaries could have done. The young rustic was captivated by this graciousness, and almost began to feel that he had made a personal friend of Antonio Ferrer.

The coach, once started, continued to move, more or less slowly, and not without sundry other little halts. The total distance was not much more than a musket-shot; but it would have seemed a long journey with regard to the time it took, even to one not in the holy haste of Ferrer. The crowds were surging round the coach in front and behind, to right and to left, like white-flecked billows around a ship plunging on in the midst of a storm. But the din was even louder, more raucous, more deafening, than a storm. Ferrer was looking out now on one side, now

on the other, beckoning, gesticulating, trying to catch what was
being said, so that he could make the right reply. He was also
trying as best he could to keep up some sort of conversation with
that group of friends outside; but it was a difficult thing to do –
the most difficult thing, perhaps, that he had ever had to do in all
his years of Grand Chancellorship. Every now and again, however, some word, even some phrase, repeated by a knot of people
as he passed, made itself heard, like a stronger rocket above a
great explosion of fireworks. And he was trying to give a
satisfactory answer to these cries, making great play with the
phrases he knew would be most acceptable, or that some
immediate necessity seemed to demand, and talking continuously
the whole of the way. 'Yes, gentlemen, bread; plenty! I'll take
him off to prison myself; he'll be punished . . . *si es culpable*. Yes,
yes, I'll order it; cheap bread. *Asi es* . . .* so it shall be, I mean;
our lord the king does not want such very faithful subjects to go
hungry. *Ox! Ox! Guardaos;** don't get hurt, gentlemen. *Pedro,
adelante con juicio*. Plenty, plenty! A little room, please. Yes,
bread, bread! To prison, yes, to prison! What's that?' he then
asked a man who had thrust his head and shoulders through the
window to shout at him some advice, or request, or praise. But
even before he had heard the 'What's that?' the man had been
pulled back by someone else who saw that he was just on the
point of being crushed by one of the wheels. Amidst these sallies
and replies, amidst the incessant acclamations, amidst a shout or
two rising here and there from the opposition, but instantly
suppressed, Ferrer finally reached the house, chiefly thanks to the
work of those good helpers of his.

Others with the same good intentions were already on the spot,
as we have said, and had meanwhile been working away at
making and maintaining a clear space. They begged, exhorted,
threatened, pushed, shoved, even kicked out here and there, with
that increased zest and renewed energy that come from seeing a
desired end getting nearer. Finally they had succeeded in dividing
the throng in two, and then in pushing back both throngs far
enough to make a small empty space between the door and the
coach, which had now stopped opposite. Renzo, who had been
acting as pathmaker and escort in turns, had arrived with the
coach, and was now able to join one of the two front rows of
well-wishers, who were acting at the same time as a flank to the
coach and as a breakwater against the two surging waves of
people. And as he was helping to keep back one of these with his

strong shoulders, he also found himself in a good position to see
what was going on. Ferrer drew a great sigh of relief when he
saw that empty space, and the door still shut. 'Shut' in this case
simply means not open; for the hinges were almost torn off the
posts; the battered and splintered doors were forced and burst
open in the middle, showing through the gaping hole a piece of
twisted chain, slack and almost torn from its sockets, holding
them, if so it can be called, together. Some worthy man had put
his mouth to this gap, and was shouting for them to open;
another hurriedly flung back the door of the coach. The old man
put out his head, rose, and grasping this worthy man's arm with
his right hand, came out on to the step of the coach.

The crowd on both sides were standing on tiptoe to see; a
thousand faces, a thousand beards were upturned: the general
curiosity and attention produced a moment of general silence.
Ferrer, as he paused for that moment on the step, glanced around,
saluted the crowd with a bow, as if from a pulpit, and, putting
his left hand on his heart, called, 'Bread and justice!' Then, frank,
upright, clad in his official robes, he stepped to the ground, amid
acclamations ringing to the stars.

Meanwhile those inside had opened the door, or rather opened
what was left of the door, by drawing out the chain with its half-
detached staples and widening the breach just enough to admit
this most-welcome guest. 'Quick; quick,' said he. 'Open it
properly so I can get in; and you, like good people, do keep the
crowds back; don't let them come on top of me . . . for heaven's
sake! Keep a little space open, as soon . . . Hey! Hey! Gentlemen,
a moment!' he said again to those inside. 'Slow with that door;
let me pass. Eh! My ribs! Remember my ribs! Now shut it; no!
Hey! Eh! My robe! My robe!' This would in fact have been
caught between the doors, had not Ferrer, with great presence of
mind, gathered in the train, which disappeared like the tail of a
snake darting back into its hole when pursued.

Once closed, the doors were barred again as best they could
be. Outside, Ferrer's self-constituted bodyguard were working
away with shoulders, arms, and voices to keep the space open,
praying to the Lord in their hearts that he would be quick.

'Quick! Quick!' Ferrer was also saying under the portico inside,
to the servants standing breathless around him, calling out:
'Blessings on you! Ah, your Excellency! Oh, your Excellency! Uh!
Your Excellency!'

'Quick, quick!' repeated Ferrer. 'Where's that blessed man?'

The Commissioner was coming downstairs, half dragged, half carried by other servants. He was as white as a new-washed sheet. On seeing his saviour he heaved a great sigh. His pulse began beating again, a little life began coming back to his legs and a little colour to his cheeks; and he hurried unsteadily towards Ferrer, saying, 'I am in God's and your Excellency's hands. But how can we get out of here? It's surrounded everywhere by people who want to kill me.'

'*Venga usted con migo,** and take courage. My coach is outside here. Quick, quick!' And taking him by the hand, he led him towards the door, reassuring him the while, but saying to himself as he went, '*Aqui esta el busilis; Dios nos valga!*'*

The door opened. Ferrer went out first. The other followed behind him, crouching, clinging, glued to the robe that was his salvation, like a child to its mother's skirts. Those who had been keeping the space clear now formed a kind of net, or cloud, by raising their hands and hats to screen the perilous sight of the Commissioner from the crowd. He got into the coach first, and hid himself in a corner. Ferrer got in after him; the carriage door was shut. The mob confusedly saw this, guessed what had happened, and let out a yell of applause and curses.

The stage of the journey still to be done might be thought to be the most difficult and dangerous. But public opinion had obviously shown it was in favour of the Commissioner's being taken off to prison, and during the halt many of those who had helped Ferrer to arrive had been working very hard to prepare and keep open a passage through the middle of the crowd, so that, this second time, the coach was able to get ahead a little more quickly and continuously. As it progressed, the two crowds dammed up on each side of it closed in and mingled in its wake.

As soon as Ferrer sat down, he lent over to warn the Commissioner to keep himself well back in the corner, and not to show himself, for the love of God; but the warning was superfluous. He himself, on the other hand, had to show himself so as to occupy and draw on to himself all the attention of the crowd. And again during the whole of this trip, as of the first, he kept making to his changeable audience the most continuous speech in time, and the most disconnected in sense, there has ever been: but now and again he would interrupt himself with some little word in Spanish, which he would hurriedly turn to whisper in the ear of his huddled companion. 'Yes, gentlemen. Bread and justice! To the castle! To prison! Under my own guard! Thank

you, thank you, thank you so much. No, no; he won't escape.
*Por ablandarlos.** It's only too true; we'll look into it, we'll see. I
love you all, too. A severe punishment. *Esto lo digo por su bien.**
A fair price, an honest price, and punishment for all starvers!
Pray draw aside a little. Yes, yes, I'm an honourable man, a
friend of the people. He'll be punished. It's true, he's a rascal, a
scoundrel. *Perdone, usted.** He'll have a bad time, a bad time of
it ... *si es culpable.* Yes, yes, we'll see all the bakers do their
duty. Long live the king and the good Milanese, his most faithful
subjects. He's for it, he's for it. *Animo; estamos ya quasi fuera.'**

They had, in fact, got through most of the crowd, and were
nearly clear of it altogether. There Ferrer, as he was beginning to
give his lungs a little rest, found his tardy relief, the Spanish
soldiers, who had not, however, been completely useless in the
end, as they had helped, with the support and direction of one or
two citizens, to send a few people off quietly, and kept the
passage clear for the final exit. As the coach arrived, they drew
up in line and presented arms to the Grand Chancellor, who
waved a hand to left and right here, too; and said to the officer
who approached to salute him, '*Beso a usted los manos*':* words
which the officer understood for what they really meant – namely,
You've given me a fine lot of help! In reply, he saluted again and
shrugged his shoulders. It would have been an appropriate
moment to say, *Cedant arma togae*;* but Ferrer was not in the
mood for quotations at that moment; and anyway, the words
would have been wasted, for the officer did not understand Latin.

Pedro, as he passed between those two rows of soldiers,
between those muskets so respectfully raised, began to feel his
old courage return to his breast. He recovered completely from
his consternation, remembered who he was, and who his passengers were; and began shouting, 'Hey, there, hey!' without more
pretence at ceremony, to the crowds who were now scattered
enough to tolerate such treatment; then, whipping up his horses,
he put them to the gallop, and off they went towards the castle.

'*Levantese, levantese; estamos ya fuera,'** Ferrer said to the
Commissioner, who, reassured by the cessation of the shouting,
by the rapid movement of the carriage, and by these words,
turned, straightened out, and got up. Then, pulling himself
together a little, he began to thank his liberator again and again
and again. The latter, after condoling with him on his danger,
and congratulating him on his escape, exclaimed 'Ah!', running
his hand over his bald pate. '*Que dirà de esto su excelencia,**

who's already at his wits' end about that cursed Casale which just won't surrender? *Que dirà el Conde-Duque*, who gets annoyed if a leaf makes more noise than usual? *Que dirà el Rey, nuestro señor*, who's bound to come to hear of an upset like this? And will that be the end of it? *Dios lo sabe.*'*

'Ah! As for myself, I want to have nothing more to do with it,' said the Commissioner. 'I wash my hands of it; I resign my office into your Excellency's hands, and am going to live in some cave on a mountain-top and become a hermit, far away from all this bestial rabble.'

'*Usted* will do whatever is best *por el servicio de su magestad*,'* the Grand Chancellor replied gravely.

'His Majesty doesn't want me to die,' replied the Commissioner. 'A cave, a cave for me! Far from all this rabble.'

Our author does not tell us what happened about this resolution of his, and after accompanying the poor man as far as the castle, makes no more mention of his concerns.

CHAPTER 14

The crowd left behind began dispersing and ebbing away to left and right down one street or another. Some went home to attend to their own affairs; some went off to get a breath of air after so many hours of being squeezed up, some to look for friends to talk over the great events of the day. The same dispersion was going on at the other end of the street, where the crowd had thinned out enough to allow the squad of Spanish soldiers to advance and station itself outside the Commissioner's house without meeting any resistance. The dregs, as it were, of the rioters were still congregated near this – a group of rascals who, discontented at so tame and abortive a conclusion to so great a show, were complaining, cursing, or consulting each other to see if some other attempt could still be made, and, by way of experiment, pounding and pushing at that wretched door, which had been barred up again as best it could be. On the squad's arrival all these people moved off in the opposite direction, some straight away, some hesitating reluctantly, leaving the field clear to the soldiers, who took it over and stationed themselves there to guard the house and street. But knots of people were scattered all round the neighbouring streets; wherever two or three people had stopped, three, or four, or twenty others would gather round them. Here one man would break away; there a whole group would move off together. It was like the clouds still remaining scattered and scudding about a clear sky after a storm, making anyone looking up say that the weather has not yet settled. And you can imagine what a babel of talk there was. Some were giving exaggerated accounts of particular incidents they had seen; some were describing what they had done themselves; some were congratulating each other that it had all ended so well, and praising Ferrer, and foretelling dire trouble for the Commissioner. Some said scoffingly, 'Don't you worry, they won't kill him – wolf doesn't eat wolf'; some were muttering angrily that things had not gone as they should have, that they had been tricked, and that it had been madness to go and make such a fuss only to let themselves be hoodwinked in this way.

Meanwhile the sun had gone down, things were all becoming a uniform colour, and many people, tired by the day and bored with gossiping in the dark, were turning towards home. Our young man, after helping the passage of the coach as long as it needed help, and after passing with it also through the two ranks of soldiers as if in triumph, had been delighted to see it rolling along freely and out of danger. He went with the crowd a little way, and then left it at the first corner to get a breath of air himself. After a few steps in the open he began to feel, amidst all the excitement of so many confused new emotions and impressions, a great need of food and rest; and began looking about him for the sign of some inn, for it was now too late to go to the Capuchin monastery. As he was walking along like this, with his head in the air, he came up against a knot of people, and, stopping, found they were discussing plans and ideas for the next day. He stood listening a moment, and then could not resist having his say; for it seemed to him that anyone who had done as much as he had could make a suggestion without presumption. Convinced by everything he had seen that day that all that was needed to put a project into effect was to get it taken up by those going round the streets, 'My good sirs, may I give my humble opinion?' he shouted, by way of preface. 'My humble opinion is this: there's not only cheating going on with bread. And as we've seen plainly enough today that we can get our rights by making ourselves heard, we ought to go on like this, until we've set all the other wrongs to rights, and made the world a decenter place to live in. . . . Aren't I right in saying, sirs, that there are a handful of tyrants who turn the ten commandments upside down, and go out of their way to find quiet, unsuspecting folk to do them all the harm they can, and then are always in the right? – Why, after doing something worse than usual they even walk about with their heads higher. Even Milan must have its share of them.'

'Only too many,' said a voice.

'That's what I said,' went on Renzo. 'We hear stories round our way, too. Besides, it stands to reason. Suppose, for example, one of the people I'm talking about spends some of his time in the country and some in Milan. If he plays the devil there, he won't be an angel here, it seems to me. And just tell me, sirs, if you've ever seen a single one of these people with his nose between bars? And the worst of it is – I can tell you this for sure – that there are decrees – printed ones – to punish them; and not just vague decrees, really good ones, so's you couldn't want anything better; all the rackets set down clearly, just as they happen; and each of them with a good stiff penalty. And they say "whosoever he may be, lower orders or plebs", and a lot more besides. Now you just go to the lawyers – those scribes and pharisees – and ask them to get your rights according to the decrees: they'll pay you about as much attention as the Pope does a vagabond. It's enough to turn any decent man's head. It's plain enough that the king, and the government, would like the rascals punished; but nothing can be done, because they're all in league. So the thing is to break it; to go tomorrow morning to Ferrer, who's a good man, a gentleman who doesn't give himself airs. We could see today how glad he was to be amongst the poor, and how he tried to listen to the things that were said to him and give a fair answer. We ought to go to Ferrer and tell him how things are. I can tell him some fine things for my part: how with my very own eyes I've seen a proclamation with lots of coats-of-arms on top, with the names of three important people all printed clear underneath, and one of the names was Ferrer's. I saw it with my very own eyes. Now, this decree said just what I needed, and a lawyer I went to to try to help me get my rights, according to the intentions of those three gentlemen (and Ferrer among them) – this lawyer, who had shown me the decree himself: that's the best part about it, ha! ha! – he thought I was mad. I'm sure that when that good old man hears about this – he can't know everything that goes on, particularly outside in the country – he won't want things like that going on any longer, and will find some good remedy. And then they themselves, if they make the decrees, must like to see them obeyed; for it's an insult, a slur on their names, too, to treat them as if they're worth nothing. And if those bullies won't climb down, and get up to any tricks, we can help him, as we did today. I'm not saying he should go round in his coach collecting all the rogues, bullies, and tyrants; why, Noah's Ark would be needed for that. All he need do is issue orders to those whose job it is – and all round, not only in Milan – so's the decrees are carried out; and have a big trial of all those who have committed these rackets; and prison where it says prison, and the galleys where it says galleys; and tell all the mayors to do things properly; if not, sack 'em, and put better ones in. And then we would also be there to lend a hand, as I say. And order the lawyers to pay some attention to the poor and raise their voices to defend the right. Don't you agree, sirs?'

Renzo had been speaking with such sincerity that from the moment he began most of the group had stopped their other discussions and turned towards him; and at a certain point they had all become his listeners. A confused clamour of applause, of 'Bravo'; 'Of course'; 'He's right'; 'Only too true', was the audience's reply. But critics were not lacking. 'Oh, yes?' said one of them; 'agree with a bumpkin? Why! they're all lawyers!' and off he went. 'Now,' muttered another, 'every ragamuffin will want to have his say; and we'll have so many irons in the fire we'll never even get our bread cheap, which is why we started this.' But Renzo heard only the compliments. People shook him by one hand and the other. 'Good-bye until tomorrow. Where? ... in the cathedral square? All right, all right; and we'll do something.'

'Which of you good gentlemen could show me an inn where I can get a bite to eat and a simple bed?' said Renzo.

'I'm at your service, my good young fellow,' said a man who had been listening attentively to the speech, and had not yet said anything. 'I know the very inn to suit you; and I'll recommend you to the landlord, who's friend of mine, and a good man.'

'Near here?' asked Renzo.

'Not far away,' the man replied.

The meeting broke up; and after shaking many an unknown hand Renzo went off with the unknown man, thanking him for his kindness.

'What's there to thank me for?' said the man. 'One hand washes the other, and both of them wash the face. Aren't we

bound to help our neighbours?' And as he walked along he began
asking Renzo, by way of making conversation, one question after
the other. 'Not that I want to be inquisitive, but you seem to be
very tired. Whereabouts have you come from?'

'I've come,' replied Renzo, 'all the way, all the way from
Lecco.'

'All the way from Lecco? You're from Lecco, are you?'

'From Lecco. . . . Near there, that is.'

'My poor young chap! From what I could understand, by what
you said, you seem to've been very badly treated.'

'Eh! My dear sir! I had to be a bit careful what I said, so as not
to talk about my affairs in public; but – enough, they'll come out
one day; and then . . . But here's an inn-sign – faith, I don't feel
like going any farther.'

'No, no! Come along to where I said; it's only a short way on,'
said the guide. 'You won't find it so good here.'

'Ah, well,' the young man answered, 'I'm not a young gentleman, who's used to being coddled. A bit of something to stoke
me up and a straw mattress are enough for me. What I'm keen
on is finding them both soon. Here's luck,' and he turned into a
dirty-looking door, above which hung the sign of the full moon.

'All right, I'll take you in here, as that's what you want,' said
the unknown man, following him in.

'Don't put yourself out any more,' answered Renzo. 'But,' he
added, 'I'd be pleased if you'd come and drink a glass of wine
with me.'

'I'll accept your kind offer,' replied the man; and, as one more
used to the place, went ahead of Renzo through a small yard, to
the kitchen door. He raised the latch, opened it, and went in with
his companion. A couple of lamps, hanging by two hooks from
the ceiling rafters, cast a dim light over the room. A good number
of men were sitting, busily engaged, on two benches each side of
a long, narrow table, which occupied nearly the whole length of
the room. Here and there cloths and plates were scattered over
it, and here and there cards being turned over and back, dice
being thrown and gathered; but flasks and glasses were everywhere; coins of *berlinghe*, *reali*, and *parpagliole* were also being
bandied about, and, if they had been able to talk, would probably
have said, 'We were in a baker's till this morning, or in the pocket
of some spectator at the riot, who was so intent on watching the
progress of public affairs that he forgot to look after his own
private interests.' The noise was terrific. A waiter was dashing

about to and fro, serving tables and game-boards at the same time. The landlord was sitting on a small stool under the chimney-hood, apparently engrossed in certain shapes he was drawing in and rubbing out in the ashes with the tongs, but in reality alive to everything going on around him. He rose at the sound of the latch, and went to meet the new arrivals. On seeing Renzo's guide, he said to himself – Curse you, always coming and getting underfoot when I least want you! – Then he gave Renzo a hasty glance, and said, still to himself – Don't know you; but coming with such a huntsman you must be either hound or hare; I'll know which, when you've said a couple of words – But no trace of these reflections appeared on the landlord's face, which was motionless as a portrait; it was a full, shiny face, with a thick, reddish beard, and a pair of clear, steady eyes.

'What would you gentlemen like?' he said out loud.

'A flask of decent wine to begin with,' said Renzo. 'And then a bite to eat.' So saying, he flung himself down on a bench towards the end of the table, and let out a resounding 'Ah!', as if to say: a seat feels good after being up and doing for so long. But suddenly the memory of the bench and table at which he had sat the last time with Lucia and Agnese came into his mind; and he heaved a sigh. Then he gave his head a shake, as if to drive the thought away, and saw the landlord coming along with the wine. His companion had sat down opposite Renzo, who filled his glass at once, saying 'Just to wet the lips.' Then he filled the other glass, and emptied it in one draught.

'What can you give me to eat?' he said to the landlord then.

'I've got some stew. Would you like that?' said the innkeeper.

'Yes, fine. Some stew.'

'You'll be served at once,' said the landlord to Renzo; and to the waiter, 'Serve this stranger.' And he turned back towards the chimney. 'But . . .' he went on then, turning back to Renzo, 'I haven't got any bread today.'

'As for bread,' said Renzo, in a loud voice, laughing, 'Providence has thought of that.' And drawing out the third and last of the loaves he had picked up under the cross of San Dionigi, he waved it in the air, and cried, 'Look at it, the bread of Providence!'

At the exclamation, many people turned round, and seeing that trophy in the air, one of them cried, 'Hurrah for cheap bread!'

'Cheap?' said Renzo. '*Gratis et amore*.'*

'Better still, better still.'

'But,' added Renzo at once, 'I wouldn't like you gentlemen to think badly of me. It's not that I fiddled it, as they say. I found it on the ground; and if I could find the owner, am ready to pay him for it.'

'Bravo! bravo!' shouted the company – to none of whom had it even occurred that these words were true – grinning more broadly than ever.

'They think I'm joking, but it's quite true,' said Renzo to his guide; and turning the loaf over in his hand, he added, 'Just look at the state they've got it into. It's like a pancake. But what a squeeze there was! Anyone with bones a bit tender must've got hurt,' and he quickly devoured three or four mouthfuls of the bread, and sent a second glass of wine down after it, adding, 'This bread won't go down by itself. I've never felt so dry. How we shouted!'

'Prepare a good bed for this honest fellow,' said the guide, 'as he's intending to sleep here.'

'D'you want to sleep here?' the landlord asked Renzo, going up to the table.

'Sure,' answered Renzo. 'Any bed will do, as long as the sheets are fresh from the wash; for though I'm a poor chap, I'm used to a bit of cleanliness.'

'Oh, as for that,' said the landlord; he went to the desk in a corner of the kitchen, and came back with an inkwell and a sheet of paper in one hand, and a pen in the other.

'What does this mean?' exclaimed Renzo, swallowing a mouthful of stew that the waiter had set in front of him; then he added with a smile of surprise, 'Is this the sheet fresh from the wash?'

The landlord put the inkstand and paper down on the table without replying, then leant his left arm and right elbow on it, and with the pen in the air, and his face raised towards Renzo, said, 'Would you please tell me your Christian name, surname, and residence?'

'What?' said Renzo. 'What has all this to do with the bed?'

'I'm just doing my duty,' said the landlord, giving the guide a look. 'We have to give an account of everyone who comes to lodge here: "*His Christian name and surname, nationality and business, whether armed . . . how long he is staying in the city.*" . . . Those are the words of the decree.'*

Renzo drained another glass before replying. It was his third, and I am afraid we shall be unable to count them any more from now on. Then he said, 'Ah! ah! You've got a decree! I pride myself on being a bit of a lawyer: so I know at once how much notice to take of decrees.'

'I'm telling the truth,' said the innkeeper, still looking at Renzo's silent companion; then he went back to the desk, took a great sheet of paper out of it – a genuine copy of the decree – and came and spread it under Renzo's eyes.

'Ah, look!' exclaimed he, raising his newly-filled glass with one hand and emptying it again, and pointing at the decree with the other. 'There's that fine page of a missal. Very glad indeed to see it. I know those arms; I know that heretic's face, with the rope round his neck.' (The governor's coat-of-arms was then put at the top of the proclamations; and conspicuous in those of Don Gonzalo Fernandez de Cordova was a Moorish king chained by the throat.) 'That face means "Let those who can, give the orders, and those who want, obey them." When that face has managed to send Signor Don . . . never mind, I know who, off to jail; when it's managed, as another sheet of missal like this says, to let an honest chap marry an honest girl who wants to marry him, then I'll give this face my name. I'll even give it a kiss, what's more. I might have good reasons not to give it – my name, I mean. Why! And if a certain blackguard with a pack of other blackguards under him – for if he was alone' – here he finished the phrase with a gesture – 'if a certain blackguard wanted to know where I was, to play me a dirty trick, would this face here move a finger to help me? I wonder. I've got to give my business, have I? That's a new one on me. I've come to Milan to go to confession, let's say; but I want to go and confess to a Capuchin friar, let's say, and not to an innkeeper.'

The landlord was silent, and kept his eyes on the guide, who made no sign of any kind. Renzo, we are sorry to say, gulped down another glass and went on, 'I can give you a reason, my dear host, that'll satisfy you. If the decrees that speak up in favour of honest citizens don't count at all, then the ones that don't ought to count even less. So take this litter away, and bring another flask instead: for this one's a dead 'un.' So saying, he gave it a gentle tap with the knuckles, and added, 'Listen, listen, landlord, how it tinkles.'

This time also Renzo had gradually attracted the attention of the people round; and this time also he was applauded by his audience.

'What am I to do?' said the landlord, looking at the unknown man, who was not unknown to him.

'Come along, come along,' shouted a number of the boisterous company. 'The young fellow's right; they're all nuisances, traps, and frauds. New laws today, new laws.'

Amidst these cries the unknown man gave the innkeeper a reproving glance for making his questioning too obvious, and said, 'Let him have his own way; don't make a scene about it.'

'I've done my duty,' said the innkeeper out loud, then to himself – Now I've my back to the wall – and took the pen, ink, paper, decree, and empty flask, the last to hand over to the waiter.

'Bring another of the same,' said Renzo. 'I find it's good company, and we'll put it to bed like the other one, without asking its surname, Christian name and nationality and business, and if it's staying a bit in this city.'

'More of the same,' the landlord said to the waiter, handing him the flask, and went back to his seat under the hood of the fireplace. – What a hare! – thought he, beginning to stir the ashes again – and what hands you've got into! You silly fool! Drown, if you want to drown; but the landlord of the Full Moon's not going to get involved in your follies. –

Renzo thanked the guide and all the others who had taken his side. 'You're good friends!' said he. 'Now I really see that decent folks give each other a helping hand and support each other.' Then, stretching his right hand out over the table, and taking up the stance of an orator once more, he exclaimed, 'Why is it that the people who rule this world want to drag pen, ink, and paper in everywhere! Always brandishing a pen! A great mania those gentry have for using the pen!'

'Ah, my good friend from the country! D'you want to know the reason?' laughingly said one of the players, who was winning.

'Let's hear it,' answered Renzo.

'The reason is this,' said the fellow. 'That as those gentry are the ones who eat all the geese, they've got such a lot of quills, such a lot that they just have to find something to do with them.'

Everyone burst out laughing, all except his companion who was losing.

'Ooh!' said Renzo, 'he's a poet, that one. So you've got poets here, too. They're cropping up everywhere nowadays. I'm a bit in that line myself, and can let out some peculiar . . . but that's when things are going well with me.'

To understand this nonsense of poor Renzo's, the reader

should know that among the common people in Milan, and even more in the country, the word 'poet' does not mean what it means among all respectable folk – a sacred genius, an inhabitant of Pindus,* a votary of the Muses: it means a peculiar person who's a bit crazy, and talks and behaves with more wit and oddity than sense. What an impertinent habit this is of the common people's of manhandling words and making them say things so very far from their legitimate meaning! For what, I ask you, has writing poetry got to do with being a bit crazy?

'But I'll tell you the real reason,' added Renzo. 'It's because they're the ones who hold the pen; and so what they say can fly off and vanish into thin air; but they're very careful about what a poor man says, and soon skewer it and nail it down on paper with that pen of theirs, to use it later, at the right time and place. Then they've got another little habit; when they want to get into a mess some poor chap who's never been educated, but who's got a little ... I know what I mean ...' And here, to make himself understood, he began tapping, almost battering, his forehead with the tip of his forefinger. 'And they realize he's beginning to see through their tricks, then bang! they throw some word in Latin into the conversation to make him lose the thread and muddle him up. Enough; the practices that ought to stop! Today, luckily, everything was in plain language and without pen, ink, or paper; and tomorrow, if people know how to set about it, things will be done even better – without touching a hair of anyone's head, though, all done legally.'

Meanwhile some of the company had gone back to their gaming, others to their eating, most of them to their shouting; some were leaving; new ones were arriving; the landlord was attending to both – none of them things that have anything to do with our story. The unknown guide was also longing to get away; he had no particular business in that place, as far as could be seen, but did not want to leave before having another little private chat with Renzo. He turned to him, and began talking about bread again; and after producing a few of the phrases that had been going round from mouth to mouth for some time, came out with a suggestion of his own. 'Eh! If I was in authority,' he said 'I'd find a way of putting things to rights.'

'What would you do?' asked Renzo, looking at him with a pair of eyes that were shining brighter than they ought, and twisting up his mouth a little in an effort to pay attention.

'What would I do?' said the man. 'What I want to see is enough bread for everyone, rich and poor alike.'

'Ah! That would be fine,' said Renzo.

'This is what I'd do. Fix a decent price, so that everyone could get along on it. And then, ration the bread according to the number of mouths; for there're some greedy gluttons who want to get everything for themselves, and try and grab as much as they can; and then there's not enough bread for the poor. So the thing to do is to ration the bread. And how can that be done? Well, by issuing a card to every family, in proportion to the number of mouths, for them to go and get the bread at the baker's. Me, for instance, they would give a card made out in this way: Ambrogio Fusella, by trade a cutler, with a wife and four children, all old enough to eat bread (note that well). He is to be given so much bread, and pay so much for it. But it should be done fairly, always according to the number of mouths. To you, for instance, they would issue a card for . . . your name?'

'Lorenzo Tramaglino,' said the young man, who, carried away by the idea, did not notice it was entirely based on pen, ink, and paper; and that the first thing to do to put it into execution would have to be to collect people's names.

'Fine,' said the unknown man. 'But have you got a wife and children?'

'I ought to by rights . . . not children . . . too soon for that . . . but a wife . . . if things went as they ought to. . . .'

'Ah, you're single! Then patience, a smaller ration for you.'

'That's fair. But if soon, as I hope . . . and with God's help . . . Anyway, what if I had a wife, too?'

'Then your ticket would be changed, and the ration increased. Always in proportion to the number of mouths, as I said,' replied the unknown man, getting up.

'That'd be fine,' shouted Renzo; and went on, shouting and banging his fists on the table: 'And why don't they make a law like that?'

'How can I tell? Meanwhile I'll bid you good night, and be off; for my wife and children must have been waiting for me some time.'

'Another little drop, another little drop,' bawled Renzo, hurriedly filling the man's glass, then getting up and catching him by the end of his doublet, and pulling hard to make him sit down again. 'Another little drop; don't go and insult me like this.'

But his friend freed himself with a jerk, and, leaving Renzo pouring out a jumbled mixture of entreaties and reproaches, said 'Good night' again, and left. Renzo went on begging him until he was out in the street and then dropped back on the bench again. He stared fixedly at that glass he had filled, and, on seeing the waiter passing the table, beckoned him to stop, as if he had something to tell him; then, pointing to the glass, 'There!' he said, enunciating slowly and solemnly, articulating each word very carefully – 'there, I'd prepared this for that good chap. You see, brimful, right for a friend; but he didn't want it. People get strange ideas sometimes. It's not my fault; I showed him my good heart. Now, as it's already there, it mustn't be wasted.' So saying, he took it and drained it at one gulp.

'I understand,' said the waiter, moving away.

'Ah! You've understood, too,' went on Renzo. 'Then it's true; when arguments are sound . . .!'

Here all our love of truth is necessary to make us proceed faithfully with a narrative which does so little credit to a character of such importance that he might almost be called the hero of our story. But for the same reason of impartiality, we must also state that this was the first time such a thing had happened to Renzo; and it was his very inexperience in such excesses that made this first one of his turn out so fatally. He had tossed down those first few glasses one after the other, contrary to his usual habits, partly because he felt very parched, and partly because of a certain exaltation of mind that prevented him from doing anything in moderation; and they had gone straight to his head; they would have done nothing more than slake the thirst of a practised drinker. Here our anonymous chronicler makes an observation which we repeat for what it is worth. Temperate and honest habits, he says, have this advantage among others, that the more they are settled and rooted in a man, the more sensitive he is to any slight departure from them; so that he remembers it for some time afterwards; and even a folly becomes a useful lesson to him.

However that may be, when those first fumes rose to Renzo's brain, wine and words went on flowing, one down and the other up, without restraint or moderation; and at the point we left him he was already pretty far gone. He felt a great urge to talk; there was no lack of listeners, or at least of men present whom he could take as such; and for some time his words, too, had been coming out without waiting to be asked, and getting themselves strung together into some sort of order. But gradually the

business of finishing his sentences began to become most infer-
nally difficult for him; a thought which had come clear and vivid
to his mind would suddenly fade and disappear; and words
would keep him waiting and then turn out not to be the proper
ones. In these straits, by one of the false instincts that so often
lure men to their ruin, he had recourse to that blessed flask. But
anyone with a grain of sense can say what help the flask would
be in such a situation.

We will record only a few of the vast number of words he
brought out during that disastrous evening; many more that we
omit would be too unseemly, for not only did they not make
sense, but they did not even make a pretence of any – a necessary
condition for a printed book.

'Ah! landlord, landlord!' he began again, following him with
his eyes round the table or to his place under the hood of the
fireplace, sometimes fixing them on some place where he was
not, and talking continuously amid the uproar. 'What a landlord
you are! I can't swallow that . . . that trick about the Christian
name, surname, and business. To a chap like me . . .! You didn't
behave decently. What's the satisfaction, what's the fun, what's
the pleasure . . . of getting a poor lad down on paper? Am I right,
sirs? Landlords ought to be on the side of the honest folks. . . .
Listen, listen, landlord; I just want to make a comparison . . . for
the reasons. . . . You're all laughing, eh? I'm a bit tipsy, I know,
but I can reason right. Just tell me: who is it keeps your place
going? The poor folks, don't they? Aren't I right? Just you tell
me if those gentry of the decrees ever come here to drink a glass
of wine?'

'All water-drinkers,' said one of Renzo's neighbours.

'They want to keep their heads clear,' added another, 'so as to
tell their lies properly!'

'Ah!' shouted Renzo. 'That was the poet who spoke then. So
you people get my arguments, too. Answer, then, landlord, has
Ferrer, who's the best of the lot, ever come here to drink a health
and spend a single farthing? And that swine of an assassin Don
. . . I must be quiet, though; I'm a bit beyond myself. Ferrer and
Father Chrr . . . I know who; they're two honest gents; but there
are very few honest gents. The old are worse than the young; and
the young even worse than the old. But I'm glad there's been no
blood spilt. Shame! That kind of barbarity should be left to the
hangman. Bread; oh yes; bread! I got some pretty hard shoves;
but . . . I gave some, too. Make way! Plenty! Hurrah! And yet

even Ferrer . . . a few words in Latin; *siés baraòs trapolorum.**
. . . A cursed habit! Hurrah! Justice! Bread! Ah, those are the
right words. . . . Those good gents should have been on hand . . .
when that ton, ton, ton broke out, and then ton, ton, ton. . . .
We wouldn't have fled then. Hold that priest there . . . I know
who I'm thinking of!'

At these words he lowered his head and remained for a time as
if absorbed in some thought. Then he heaved a great sigh, and
raised a face with two damp, glistening eyes in it, and such a
languishing, grotesque look of tenderness that it was well the
object of his thoughts could not see him at that moment. But the
wretches who had made fun of Renzo's passionate involved
eloquence before, now made more fun than ever of his woebegone air; those nearest him told the others to look, and they all
turned towards him, so that he became the butt of the whole
company. Not that any of them were in their full senses, whatever
those may have been; but none of them, to tell the truth, was as
far gone as poor Renzo; and besides, he was a peasant. One after
the other they began to tease him with coarse and silly questions,
with mocking buffoonery. Renzo at one moment showed signs of
getting angry, at another of taking them as a joke, and at another
began talking of something quite different, without taking any
notice of all those voices, and answering and asking questions
himself, but all by fits and starts, and all quite wide of the mark.
Fortunately, among all his ravings he had kept a sort of instinctive
care to avoid mentioning the names of people: so that even the
one which must have been most prominent in his memory was
not pronounced; and very sorry we should have been if that name
for which we too feel a certain respect and affection had been
bandied about those coarse mouths and become a laughing-stock
of those foul tongues.

CHAPTER 15

The landlord, seeing that the game was going on rather long, had
gone up to Renzo and, politely asking the others to leave him
alone, begun shaking him by the arm, to try to make him
understand and persuade him to go off to bed. But Renzo kept
on going back to Christian names, surnames, decrees, and honest

folks. However the words bed and sleep repeated in his ear finally
got into his head; they made him feel a little more clearly the
need for what they meant, and produced a moment of lucid
interval. The gleam of returning sense made him realize dimly
how much of it had left him; rather as the last taper remaining
alight in a candelabra shows up the others that have gone out.
He pulled himself together, spread out his hands and braced them
against the table, tried once or twice to get up, sighed, swayed,
and at the third attempt, supported by the landlord, succeeded in
getting to his feet. Steadying him, the latter steered him between
the table and the bench; then, taking a lamp in one hand, partly
led him, partly pulled him with the other, as best he could,
towards the door giving on to the stairs. There, at the volley of
farewells that the others were shouting after him, Renzo wheeled
round: and but for his supporter's dexterity in holding him up by
one arm, this move would have meant his going head over heels;
anyway, he turned, and with his free arm began tracing and
waving greetings in the air, like one of Solomon's knots.

'Let's go to bed, to bed,' said the landlord, dragging at him.
He squeezed him through the door; and with even more effort,
pulled him to the top of the stairs and then into the room he had
assigned to him. Renzo was pleased at the sight of the waiting
bed; he gave the landlord an affectionate look from two eyes that
were shining and blinking like a couple of glow-worms. He tried
to balance on his legs, and stretched a hand out towards the
landlord's face to pinch his cheek in sign of friendship and
gratitude, but could not manage it. 'Good landlord!' he did
manage, however, to say. 'Now I see you're an honest gent. A
kind thing to do this – to give a lad a bed. But that trick of yours
about Christian name and surname, that wasn't like an honest
gent. Luckily I'm quite sharp myself . . .'

The landlord had not expected him to be so coherent still, and
knowing from long experience how often men in that condition
are apt to change their minds, he decided to profit by this lucid
interval to make another attempt. 'Now, sonny,' said he, putting
on his kindliest look and manner; 'I didn't do it to annoy you, or
to pry into your affairs. What d'you expect? It's the law, and
we've got to obey it, too; otherwise we'd be the first to get
punished. It's better to satisfy them, and . . . after all, what's it all
about? Nothing very much! Just a couple of words. Not for
them, but as a favour to me. Come along; let's have it now, here

between ourselves, just you and me. Tell me your name and . . . then go to bed with a quiet mind.'

'Hah, you scoundrel!' exclaimed Renzo; 'you swindler! To come back at me now with all that stuff about surname, Christian name, and business!'

'Quiet, you clown; go to bed,' said the landlord.

But Renzo went on louder than ever, 'I get it; you're in the league, too. Just you wait, just you wait, and I'll fix you,' and, turning his head towards the stairs, he began to bellow louder than ever, 'Hey, friends! The landlord's in the . . .'

'I was only joking,' cried the latter in Renzo's ear, pushing him towards the bed – 'only joking; didn't you realize I was only joking?'

'Ah, joking! Now you're talking sense. If you were only joking – it really is a joke,' and he fell face-downwards on the bed.

'Come on now, get undressed; quick,' said the landlord, and added help to advice – for he had to.

When Renzo had got off his doublet – which was pretty difficult – the landlord snatched it up and went through the pockets to see if there was any money in them. He found some; and thinking that next day his guest would have quite different accounts to settle, and that this money would probably fall into hands from which no landlord was likely to retrieve it, he decided to try to see if he could at least get this affair through.

'You're a good lad, an honest gent, sonny, aren't you?' he said.

'A good lad, an honest gent,' repeated Renzo, his finger still fumbling with the buttons of the garments he had not been able to take off.

'Good,' replied the landlord. 'Then just settle my little account now, as I have to go out tomorrow on some business . . .'

'That's fair enough,' said Renzo. 'I'm sharp, but I'm honest. . . . But what about the money? How can we find the money now?'

'Here it is,' said the landlord; and by bringing to bear all his experience, all his patience, all his skill, he succeeded in settling his bill with Renzo and getting himself paid.

'Give me a hand, so that I can finish undressing, landlord,' said Renzo. 'I can tell myself I'm very sleepy now.'

The landlord gave him the required help. He also drew the covers over him, and bade him a rough good night, as he was already snoring. Then, drawn by the kind of attraction that sometimes makes us regard an object of our dislike as attentively as an object of our love, and which is only the desire to know what it is that affects our sensibilities so strongly, he paused a moment to gaze at this irksome guest, raising the lamp over his face, and shading it with a hand so that the light fell on him, almost in the attitude in which artists depict Psyche gazing stealthily at the features of her unknown spouse.* 'You big fool!' he said inwardly to the poor sleeper. 'You just went and asked for it. And then, just tell me how you like it tomorrow. You louts, you, trying to go round the world without even knowing the direction the sun rises: and getting both yourselves and your neighbours into trouble.'

So saying, or rather thinking, he drew back the lamp, moved away, left the room and locked the door. From the landing he called to his wife and told her to leave the children in the care of a servant-girl and go down into the kitchen, to take his place. 'I've got to go out, thanks to a stranger who's happened in here – unluckily for me – the devil knows how,' he added; and told her briefly about the tiresome incident. Then he said once more, 'Keep an eye on everything; and above all be very careful, on a cursed day like this. We've got a bunch of ruffians down there who, between drinking and being loose-tongued by nature, are capable of saying anything. All that's needed is for some reckless . . .'

'Oh! I'm not a child, and I know what's to be done, too. Up to now you can hardly say, it seems to me . . .'

'Good, good; and see they pay; and as for all the speeches they're making, about the Commissioner of Supply and the governor and Ferrer and the *Decurions* and the gentry and Spain and France and all that nonsense; just pretend you haven't heard them. For to contradict might be to ask for trouble at once, and to agree might be to ask for it in the future. And you know yourself how sometimes it's the people who say the worst things who . . . Anyway, when you hear certain remarks, just turn your head away and say "I'm coming," as if someone was calling you from another part. I'll try and get back as soon as I can.'

So saying, he went down to the kitchen with her, gave a glance around to see if there was anything new, took his hat and cloak down from a peg and a cudgel from a corner, recapitulated the instructions he had given by another glance at his wife, and went out. But even while he was going through all these motions, he had taken up again, inwardly, the thread of the apostrophe he had begun at poor Renzo's bedside; and went on with it as he was walking along the street.

– You stubborn bumpkin! – (for however much Renzo had tried to hide his origins, they were betrayed by his words, pronunciation, looks, and movements). – On a day like this, when by a bit of tact and good sense I was just managing to get through clear, you must come along at the end of it and break all the eggs in the basket. Are there so few inns in Milan, that you must go and hit on just mine? If you'd come alone, at least, I'd have winked an eye for this evening, and given you a bit of advice in the morning. But no, sir: you must needs bring someone with you: and bring a police agent, what's more! –

At every step the innkeeper met passers-by either singly or in pairs or groups, going round whispering together. At this point in his mute soliloquy he saw a patrol of soldiers coming towards him, and as he drew aside to let them pass, looked at them out of the corner of his eye, and went on to himself, – There are the ones who are going to punish fools. And you, you poor idiot, just because you've seen a few people gadding round making a row, you've gone and got it into your head that the world must change its ways. And on this fine foundation you've gone and ruined yourself, and almost ruined me, which isn't fair. I did my best to save you; and you, you oaf, nearly turned the inn upside down in exchange. Now it's up to you to get out of your mess; I'll look after myself. As if I wanted to know your name from any curiosity of mine! What do I care if you're called Taddeo or Bartolomeo? As if I enjoy using a pen all that much! But you're not the only ones who wants things your own way. I know perfectly well that some of the decrees aren't any use; a fine bit of news for a bumpkin to come and tell us! But what you don't know is that decrees against innkeepers do mean something. And you think you can go round talking, not even knowing that if you want to do that and make light of the decrees, the first thing is to be very careful what you say about them. And d'you know what would happen to a poor innkeeper who was of your way of thinking, and didn't ask the name of those who happened to favour him with their company? 'Under pain, for any of the aforesaid innkeepers, tavern-keepers or others, as above, of the sum of three hundred scudi.' Yes, that's how they get three hundred scudi out of us, and all to spend them so well: 'to be handed over two-thirds to the Royal Chamber, and the other third to the denouncer or informer.' What a fine rogue! 'And in the case of inability to pay, five years in the galleys, or such *greater penalties, pecuniary or corporal, as His Excellency may decide.'* Much obliged to him for his kindness. –

As he was saying this, the innkeeper reached the threshold of the Palace of Justice.

Here, as in all the other offices, the whole place was astir; they were all busy issuing the instructions for the following day that were most likely to calm ardour, avoid pretexts for more rioting, and keep power in the hands of those who usually exercised it. The troops at the Commissioner's house were reinforced; the approaches were barricaded with beams and blocked by carts. All bakers were ordered to make bread without a pause. Messengers were dispatched to villages nearby with orders to send grain into the city. Nobles were deputed to take up their station at every bakery from early in the morning, to superintend the distribution, and to restrain the turbulent by the authority of their presence, and by fair words. But so as to give, as the vintners say, a knock on the hoops and another on the cask, and reinforce the advice with a little awe, they were trying to find ways of laying hands on some seditious element. This was chiefly the task of the High Sheriff, whose feelings towards the riot and the rioters can be guessed, with the soaked piece of lint he was wearing over one of the organs of his metaphysical cavity. His minions had been going around since the beginning of the rioting; and the so-called Ambrogio Fusella was, as the innkeeper had said, a police agent in disguise sent out to catch some easily recognizable person red-handed, note him, and track him, so as to seize him during the quiet of that night or next day. As soon as he had heard a few words of Renzo's speech, this man had immediately marked him down as just the guileless type that was wanted. Then, finding he was fresh from the country, he had tried to bring off the master-stroke of guiding him straight to the jail as the safest lodging-house in town; but this had failed, as we have seen. He had been able, however, to bring back definite information about his surname, Christian name, and home, besides a large amount of other information based on guesswork; so that when the innkeeper arrived to say what he knew about Renzo, they already knew more about him than he did. He went into the usual room, and made his statement; that a stranger had come to lodge with him who kept on refusing to give his name.

'You've done your duty by coming and telling the authorities,' said a criminal notary, laying down his pen. 'But we already knew about him.'

– Not much of a secret! – thought the innkeeper – no genius needed for that! –

'And we also know,' went on the notary, 'what his precious name is.'

– The devil! His name, too. How did they get that? – thought the innkeeper this time.

'But you,' went on the other, with a severe expression – 'you're not telling us everything frankly.'

'What more's there for me to say?'

'Ah! ah! We know quite well that this man brought a quantity of stolen bread into your inn – stolen violently, too, by looting and sedition!'

'If someone comes along with a loaf in his pocket I can't possibly tell where he went and got it. For I swear on my life, I saw only one loaf.'

'Ah, always defences and excuses; to hear you people, one'd think you were all law-abiding citizens. How can you prove that loaf was come by honestly?'

'What have I got to prove? I don't come into it; I'm just the innkeeper.'

'You can't deny, though, that this customer of yours had the temerity to say insulting things against the decrees and to make coarse and disrespectful remarks about His Excellency's coat-of-arms.'

'Please, your worship, how could he be my customer if this was the first time I'd seen him? It was the devil, speaking with all due respect, who sent him to my house. If I'd known him, your worship can see I would not have had to ask for his name.'

'But there've been inflammatory things said in your inn and in your presence; presumptuous speeches, seditious proposals, complaints, grumbling, outcries.'

'How can your worship expect me to take any notice of all the foolish things said by so many people shouting all at once? A poor man like me has to look after his own affairs. And then your worship well knows that anyone who's free with his tongue is usually ready with his fists, particularly when there's a group of them, and . . .'

'Yes, yes, let 'em do and say what they like; tomorrow, tomorrow we'll see if their fancies have passed. What do you think?'

'I don't think anything.'

'That the mob will get mastery of Milan?'

'Oh, of course not.'

'You'll see, you'll see.'

'I know what's what; the king will always be king; but those who've gained will get away with it, and naturally a poor father of a family doesn't want to get mixed up. You gentlemen have the power; it's up to you.'

'Have you many people in the house still?'

'A pretty good number.'

'And what's that customer of yours doing? Still wrangling and inciting people to plan riots for tomorrow?'

'That stranger, your worship means? He's gone to bed.'

'So you have a lot of people. . . . Right; be careful you don't let him escape.'

– What, have I got to act the bailiff – thought the landlord, but said neither yes nor no.

'Go back home, then, and be careful,' went on the notary.

'I always am careful. Your worship can say if I've ever had anything to do with the law.'

'And don't you go thinking the law has lost its power.'

'I? For Heaven's sake! I don't think anything; I just look after my inn.'

'The usual cry; have you nothing else to say?'

'What else should I have to say? There's only one truth.'

'All right. We have your declaration for the moment. If anything comes up, you must tell us in detail anything you are asked.'

'What should I have to tell you? I don't know anything; I've only just got head enough to look after my own affairs.'

'Be careful you don't let him go.'

'I hope his excellency the High Sheriff will be told I came along straight away to do my duty. I kiss your worship's hands.'

At daybreak Renzo had been snoring away a good seven hours, and was still, poor fellow, sound asleep, when he was roused by a couple of rough shakes at his arms and a voice shouting, 'Lorenzo Tramaglino,' from the foot of the bed. He woke up, pulled his arms back, reluctantly opened his eyes, and saw a man in black standing at the foot of his bed, and two armed men one each side of his pillow. And, between surprise, drowsiness, and hangover from that wine you know about, he lay there a moment dazed. Then, thinking he was dreaming, and not liking that particular dream, he stretched, as if to wake himself completely.

'Ah! So you've heard at last, Lorenzo Tramaglino?' said the man with the black coat, who was the same notary of the night before. 'Come on, then, get up, and come with us.'

'Lorenzo Tramaglino?' said Lorenzo Tramaglino. 'What does that mean? What d'you want with me? Who told you my name?'

'Less talk, and hurry up,' said one of the bailiffs beside him, grasping his arm again.

'Hey! What's this rough stuff?' shouted Renzo. 'Landlord! landlord!'

'Shall we take him off in his shirt-tails?' said the same bailiff, turning to the notary.

'Did you understand?' said the latter to Renzo; 'they will do it that way, if you don't get up right away, and come along with us!'

'But why?' asked Renzo.

'You'll hear the why and wherefore from the High Sheriff.'

'I? I'm an honest citizen, I haven't done anything; and I'm amazed . . .'

'All the better for you, all the better for you; then a few words will clear you, and you'll be able to go about your business.'

'Let me go about it now,' said Renzo. 'I have nothing to do with the law.'

'Come off it, let's get it over,' said one of the bailiffs.

'Shall we really carry him away?' said the other.

'Lorenzo Tramaglino!' said the notary.

'How d'you know my name, sir?'

'Do your duty,' said the notary to the bailiffs, who forthwith laid hold of Renzo to pull him out of bed.

'Hey! Hands off a decent citizen or . . . I can dress myself.'

'Well, dress yourself at once, then,' said the notary.

'I'm dressing,' answered Renzo; and began to gather up here and there the clothes that were littered over the bed like wreckage on a sea-shore. And he continued, as he began putting them on, 'But I don't want to go before the High Sheriff. I have nothing to do with him. As you have insulted me unjustly like this, I want to be taken before Ferrer. Him I do know, and that he's a good chap, too; and he's under an obligation to me.'

'Yes, yes, sonny; you'll be taken before Ferrer,' answered the notary. In other circumstances he would have had a really hearty laugh at such a request; but this was not the moment to laugh.

On his way there he had already seen certain movements in the streets which might have been the remains of an insurrection not completely died down or the beginning of a new one, it was difficult to judge which: people coming out of doorways, conferring with each other, walking along in groups and forming knots. And at that moment he was listening intently without seeming to, or at least trying not to seem to, and it seemed to him that the noise was getting louder. So he wanted to speed things up; but he also wanted to get Renzo away willingly and friendlily; for if it came to an open fight with him, he was not at all sure that once they were in the streets they would still be three to one. So he winked at the bailiffs to tell them to be patient and not aggravate the young man, while, on his part, he was trying to persuade him with fair words. Meanwhile the youth, as he was very slowly dressing, was going over in his mind, as best he could, the events of the day before, and more or less guessed that the decrees and the business of the Christian name and surname must be at the bottom of it all. But how the devil had this man got hold of his name? And what the devil had happened during the night for the authorities to have gathered enough assurance to come and lay hands on one of the good lads who had had such a say in things the day before? – and who were not all asleep, for Renzo also was now becoming aware of a growing noise in the street. On glancing at the notary, he began to descry the hesitation the man was vainly trying to conceal. Then, to find out if he had guessed right, and to discover the lie of the land as well as to gain time and to have a go, he said, 'I see just what is at the back of all this; it's all because of my Christian name and surname. I was a bit tight last night, it's true; these landlords have some treacherous wines sometimes; and sometimes, as I say, it's the wine inside a man that does the talking. But if that is all it's about, I'm ready to give you every satisfaction. And, then, you know my name already. Who the devil could have told you it?'

'Fine, sonny, fine!' replied the notary, making himself very pleasant. 'I see you've got sense; and take it from me who's in the business, you're wiser than most. It's the best way to come off well and quickly. With such a good disposition, you'll be through it all and free after a few words. But you see, sonny, my hands are tied. I can't release you here, as I would like to. Come along, then; be quick, and don't be afraid; for when they see who you are – and then I'll put in a word. . . . Just leave it to me. . . . Anyway; hurry up, sonny.'

'Ah! You can't; I see,' said Renzo, going on with his dressing, and waving away the bailiffs, who were making as if to lay hands on him to get him to hurry.

'Shall we pass by the cathedral square?' he then asked the notary.

'Wherever you like; the shorter the way, the sooner you'll be free,' said the latter, cursing inwardly at having to let pass this mysterious question of Renzo's, which could have become the theme of a hundred interrogations. – How unlucky I am! – he thought – Just think: here's someone fallen into my hands who obviously wants to do nothing but talk; and if I only had a little time, I'd get him to confess *extra formam** to speak academically, by way of a friendly chat, everything I wanted with no strappado at all; he's the sort to take off to prison already thoroughly interrogated without his even realizing it; and a man like that goes and falls into my hands at such a difficult moment. Eh! there's no help for it – he went on thinking, listening intently and turning his head round – there's no way out; it looks like being a worse day than yesterday. – What made him think this was an extraordinary noise coming up from the street, and he could not resist opening the lattice and peeping out. He saw a group of citizens, who, on being told to disperse by a patrol, first answered back insultingly, and finally dispersed grumbling; and what struck the notary as a fatal sign was that the soldiers were all civility. He shut the window, and stood there a moment wondering whether to carry the affair through to the end, or leave Renzo under guard of the two bailiffs and run off to the High Sheriff to give him an account of what was happening. – But – he thought at once – he'll tell me I'm a good-for-nothing, a coward, and that I should have carried out my orders. There's no help for it. We're in the dance, and dance we must. A plague on all this hurry! Curse this job! –

Renzo was now up; the two satellites were standing one on each side of him. The notary signed to them not to use too much force, and said to him, 'Now, like a good boy; come along; hurry up.'

Renzo, too, had been listening, looking and thinking. He was entirely dressed by now, except for his doublet, which he was holding in one hand, while rummaging through his pockets with the other. 'Hey!' said he, giving the notary a very significant look. 'There was some money and a letter here, my dear sir!'

'Everything'll be given to you promptly,' said the notary, 'after you've been through these little formalities. Let's go. Let's go.'

'No, no, no,' said Renzo, shaking his head; 'that won't do; I want my property, my dear sir. I'll account for my actions, but I want my own property.'

'I want to show I trust you. Here you are, and let's be quick,' said the notary, taking the sequestrated papers from his bosom and handing them over to Renzo with a sigh. The latter put them back in their place, muttering between his teeth, 'Hands off! You've had such a lot to do with thieves, you've learnt the job a bit yourselves.' The bailiffs could contain themselves no longer; but the notary curbed them with a glance, saying to himself meanwhile – If you ever get your foot inside that threshold you'll pay for that, you'll pay for that with interest. –

As Renzo was putting on his doublet and taking his hat, the notary signed to one of the bailiffs to lead the way downstairs, sent the prisoner down after him, then the other friend, then went himself. In the kitchen, as Renzo was saying, 'And where's this blessed landlord gone and hidden himself?', the notary made another sign to the bailiffs. They seized the young man by each arm and quickly fastened his wrists with certain instruments, called by that euphemism handcuffs. These consisted (we are sorry to have to descend to particulars unworthy of the gravity of our story, but clarity demands it) of a thong a little longer than the width of a normal wrist, with two small pieces of wood at the end, like pegs. The thong went round the patient's wrist; the pegs were passed between the middle and the third finger of the captor's hand and were held closed up in his fist, so that he could tighten the thong at will by giving it a twist. By this means he was able not only to keep his prisoner secure, but also to torture him if he was recalcitrant; for this purpose the thong was scattered over with knots.

Renzo struggled to free himself and shouted, 'What treachery's this? To do this to an honest man . . .!' But the notary, who had fair words for every unpleasant event, said, 'Patience; they're only doing their duty. What would you have? These are all just formalities: even we can't always treat people as we'd like to. If we didn't do what we're told we'd be in worse trouble than you. Be patient.'

As he was speaking, the two whose job it was gave the pegs a twist. Renzo quietened down like an unruly horse feeling the jerk of a bit, and exclaimed: 'Patience!'

'Good lad!' said the notary. 'That's the best way to get out of it well. What would you have? It's a nuisance; I can see that, too. But just behave yourself, and you'll be out of it in a moment. And as I see you're well-disposed, and I feel inclined to do you a good turn, let me give you another little bit of advice for your own good. Believe me, as I've had a lot of experience in all this: walk absolutely straight ahead, without looking here and there, and without attracting attention; in that way no one will notice you, no one will realize what's going on; and you'll keep your good name. An hour from now you'll be free; they've got so much to do they'll also be in a hurry to get you over and done with; and then I'll put in a word, too. . . . You'll be able to go on your way, and no one will ever know you've been in the hands of the law. And you there,' he went on, turning to the bailiffs, with a severe look, 'be careful not to hurt him, for he's under my protection. You have got to do your duty; but remember he's a good fellow, a well-behaved young chap who will be free very shortly; and that his good name is important to him. Walk along so that no one notices anything; as if you were three respectable citizens out for a walk.' And with a commanding tone and a threatening frown, he concluded, 'D'you understand me?' Then, turning to Renzo, with his brow smooth, and his face suddenly beaming, as if to say: oh, we're real friends! he whispered again, 'Now, be sensible, do what I suggest; go along quietly and collectedly. Trust one who wishes you well. Let's go.' And the party set off.

But of all these fine words Renzo did not believe a single one: neither that the notary liked him better than the bailiffs, nor that he was so anxious about his good name, nor that he had any intention of helping him. He realized perfectly well that the good man was afraid some opportunity to escape might come up in the street, and was putting up all these fine reasons to prevent him watching out and taking advantage of it. So that all these exhortations did was to confirm the intention he already had, of doing exactly the reverse.

Let no one conclude from this that the notary was a clumsy novice in guilery; for he would be much deceived. Our historian, who seems to have been one of his friends, tells us that he was a past-master at the game; but at that moment he was in a state of agitation. In cooler moments he would have jeered, I can tell you, at anyone trying to induce another to do something suspicious by suggesting and recommending it warmly to his intended victim

under the miserable pretence of giving disinterested friendly
advice. But there is a general tendency when men are excited or
in serious straits, and see how another could get them out of their
difficulties, to ask the other for it insistently and repeatedly and
under every sort of pretext; and tricksters, when they are excited
or in straits, also follow this general rule. Hence it is that they,
too, cut so poor a figure in those circumstances. Those masterly
contrivances, those clever tricks by which they are used to gaining
their point, have become almost second nature to them, so that
by applying them at the right moment with the necessary
calmness and tranquillity of mind, they strike their blow so surely
and secretly that they arouse universal applause when the successful issue is finally known. But when the poor things are in a
fix they apply them hastily, rashly, and without suavity or tact.
So that they would excite pity and laughter in anyone seeing
them labouring and struggling in this way; and the victim they
are trying to deceive, however less shrewd he is than they, can
see through their game quite easily and turn their ruses to his
own use, and against them. And that is why one can never
sufficiently impress on professional tricksters the importance
either of always keeping a cool head, or else of always keeping
the upper hand, which is the surest method.

Scarcely, therefore, had they set foot in the street than Renzo
began glancing around, turning to right and left, and keeping his
ears open. But there was no great press of people; and although
something of a seditious air was easily discernible on the faces of
a number of passers-by, they were all keeping straight on their
way; and of sedition proper, there was none.

'Be sensible, now, be sensible!' the notary was whispering
behind his back. 'Think of your good name, your good name,
sonny.' But Renzo was intently watching three men with flushed
faces coming along, and when he heard them talking about a
bakery, hidden grain, and justice, he began to grimace at them,
and to cough in the way that indicates anything but a cold. The
men looked at the party more carefully, and stopped; others
passing by also stopped; still others who had gone by turned
round when they heard muttering, came back, and lined up
behind them.

'Take care now. Be sensible, sonny. It'll be worse for you,
remember. Don't go and ruin your own case, your good name,
your reputation,' the notary was still whispering. Renzo went on
worse than before. The bailiffs exchanged a look, and, thinking

they were doing the right thing (everyone is liable to make mistakes), gave the handcuffs a twist.

'Ouch! ouch! ouch!' cried their victim. At the cry, people came flocking round; more came hurrying up from all over the street. The procession found itself surrounded. 'He's a bad character,' murmured the notary to those crowding in around him. 'He's a thief caught red-handed. Please get back, and make way for the law.' But Renzo saw the right moment had arrived, saw, too, that the bailiffs had turned white, or at least pale, and thought, – It's all up with me, unless I help myself now – and raised his voice at once: 'Friends! They're taking me off to prison, because yesterday I cried: bread and justice. I haven't done anything wrong. I'm an honest citizen. Help me, friends; don't abandon me.'

A favourable murmur, clearer cries of protection rose in reply. The bailiffs first ordered, then asked, then begged those nearest to get out of the way and make room; instead of which, the crowd pushed and pressed in all the more. Seeing things looking black, they let go the handcuffs, and thought of nothing any more but losing themselves among the crowd and getting away unobserved. The notary was fervently longing to do the same, but had trouble because of his black coat. The poor man, pale and terror-stricken, trying to make himself as small as possible, twisted about in an attempt to slither out of the crowd. But every time he raised his eyes he saw twenty other eyes on him. He did his best to look like a stranger who had been passing there by chance and got wedged in the crowd, like a straw in ice; and when he found himself face to face with a man gazing fixedly at him and frowning worse than the rest, he shaped his mouth into a smile and, with a simple air, asked him: 'What's up?'

'Ugh, carrion-crow!' answered the man. 'Carrion-crow! Carrion-crow!' echoed all round. The shouts were followed by shoves; so that in a short time, partly thanks to his own legs, partly to the elbows of others, he managed to achieve what he most longed for at that moment – to be out of that crush.

CHAPTER 16

'Beat it, young fellow, beat it. There's a monastery, here's a church. This way, that way . . .!' was shouted at Renzo from all sides. As for escaping, you can just imagine if he needed any advice about that. From the first moment that the hope of getting out of those clutches had crossed his mind he had been making plans, and had decided, if he succeeded in getting away, to go on and not stop until he was not only out of the city but out of the duchy as well. – For – he had been thinking – they've got my name on their books, however they came by it; and with the surname and Christian name, they can come and get me when they want to. – And as for sanctuary, he would only have taken to that if he had the bailiffs right on his heels. – For, as long as I can be a bird of the woods – he had also thought – I'll not become a bird in a cage. – So he had decided to take refuge in the village near Bergamo where his cousin Bortolo lived – who, if you remember, had more than once invited him to go there. But the difficulty was finding the way. Left to himself in an unknown part of an almost unknown city, Renzo did not even know by which gate to leave to go to Bergamo, and had he known, would not have been able to get to it. He was just on the point of asking one of his rescuers the way; but as he had formed certain suspicions, in the short time he had had to think over his adventures, about that obliging cutler with the four children, he did not want to advertise his plans to so many people, among whom there might be another of the same kidney; so he at once decided to get away from there quickly, and ask the way later in some part where no one knew who he was or why he was asking. 'Thank you, friends, God bless you,' he said to his rescuers, and going through the space that was immediately opened for him, took to his heels, and away – into an alley – down a side-street – along he galloped for some time, without knowing where. When he thought he had got far enough away, he slackened his pace, so as not to arouse suspicion; and began to look around to choose someone to whom to put his question, some face that inspired confidence. But there were difficulties here, too. The question was a suspicious one in itself; time pressed; the bailiffs, once out of that little difficulty, were sure to get on the trail of their fugitive again. The news of his flight might have reached as far as there; and in these straits Renzo had to make about ten judgements of physiognomy before he found what looked like a suitable face. That fat man over there, standing at the door of his shop, with his legs apart, his hands behind his back, his paunch sticking out, and his chin in the air with a great dew-lap hanging from it, and who, for lack of anything else to do, was alternately raising his quivering bulk on his toes and letting it fall back on his heels – he had the face of an inquisitive gossip who would be more likely to ask questions than answer them. That other man coming towards him with fixed eyes and a hanging lip, so far from being able to point out another's way promptly and accurately, seemed scarcely to know his own. That boy over there did, in point of fact, look bright enough, but also showed signs of being still more mischievous, and would probably take great delight in sending a poor countryman in the opposite direction from the one he wanted. How true it is that to a person in difficulties, almost everything seems a fresh difficulty! Finally, seeing a man come hurrying along, it occurred to him that this one might give him a quick answer without doing too much talking, as he probably had some urgent business of his own on hand; and on hearing him talking to himself he thought he must be an honest man. He went up to him and said, 'Excuse me sir, which way does one go for Bergamo?'

'For Bergamo? By the Porta Orientale.'

'Thanks very much; and to get to the Porta Orientale?'

'Take this street to the right; you'll find yourself in the cathedral square. Then . . .'

'That's enough, sir; I know the rest. May God reward you.' And off he set at once in the direction indicated. The other looked after him an instant, and putting that way of walking and that inquiry together in his mind, said to himself – Either he's been up to things, or others are trying to get up to things with him. –

Renzo reached the cathedral square, and crossed it, passing by a heap of ashes and burned embers in which he recognized the remains of the bonfire he had watched the day before. He skirted the cathedral steps, seeing the 'Bakery of the Crutches' once again, half dismantled, and guarded by soldiers; then went straight up the road he had come along with the crowd, and so reached the Capuchin monastery. He glanced at the square and church door, and said to himself with a sigh, – That friar, though, gave me some good advice when he told me to go and wait in the church and do myself a bit of good. –

Here, on pausing a moment to make a careful survey of the gate through which he had to pass, and seeing from that distance a great many people guarding it, he felt, in his over-excited state of mind (pity him, he had good reason for it), a certain reluctance to face the passage. He had a place of sanctuary so handy, where, with that letter, he would be sure of a welcome; and he was strongly tempted to enter it. But quickly plucking up courage, he thought, – A bird in the woods – as long as I can. Who knows me here? Those bailiffs can't have cut themselves up into pieces so as to go and watch all the gates. – He turned round, to see if by any chance they were coming along that way; but saw neither them nor anyone else who seemed to be taking any notice of him. He went forward, keeping in check those blessed legs of his, which were always wanting to run when the wise thing was only to walk, and very slowly, whistling in an undertone, he reached the gate.

There was a group of excise-men right in the entrance, with a reinforcement of Spanish soldiers also. But their attention was all concentrated outwards to prevent the entry of that element which always gathers at the news of an uprising, like vultures to a field of battle. So that Renzo, walking with an air of indifference, downcast eyes, and a gait between that of a man setting out on a journey and one just going for a stroll, passed through without anyone saying a word. But inside his heart was beating furiously. Seeing a lane running off to the right, he went into it to avoid the main road; and walked on for some time without even turning round.

On and on he walked, passing farms, passing villages, pushing on without asking their names: he was sure of getting farther away from Milan, and hoped he was going towards Bergamo; and that was enough for the moment. Every now and again he would turn round; every now and again, too, he would look at and rub one or other of his wrists, which were still rather numb, and bore all round them a scarlet weal left by the thong. His thoughts, as anyone can imagine, were a jumble of regrets and anxieties, of rage and tenderness. He made painful efforts to piece together the things said and done the night before, to discover the hidden part of his unfortunate adventure, and find out, above all, how they had been able to discover his name. His suspicions naturally fell on the cutler, to whom he clearly remembered blabbing it out. And as he thought over the way the man had got it out of him, and of his whole manner, and all those suggestions which had always led to his wanting to know something, his suspicions became almost certainty. Then he had a confused memory of having gone babbling on after the cutler's departure; who with, he had not the faintest idea; what about, his memory, however much he examined it, could not tell him; all it could tell him was that it was not at home at the time. The poor fellow was quite lost among these speculations. He was like a man who has signed a number of blank cheques and entrusted them to someone he thought was completely honest; and when he finds out the other is a cheat, tries to discover how his affairs stand. But what is there to discover? It's all a chaos. Another nagging worry was to make some satisfactory plan for the future; the ones which were not up in the air were all cheerless.

But very soon his most nagging worry of all became to find the way. After walking along for some time, almost, one might say, at random, he saw that he could not succeed entirely on his own. He felt a certain reluctance to uttering the word Bergamo, as if there were something suspicious, something shameful about it; but there was nothing else to be done. So he decided to apply, as he had done in Milan, to the first passer-by whose face appealed to him – which is what he did.

'You're off your road,' replied this man, and after a moment's thought, described to him, partly in words and partly in gestures, the detour he would have to make to get back on the main road. Renzo thanked him, and actually made off in that direction as if following the route the man had told him, though intending to get near that blessed main road, keep it in sight, and skirt it as much as possible, but without setting foot on it. This plan was easier to conceive than it was to carry out. Eventually, by tacking from left to right in what is called a zig-zag, and partly by following other directions which he plucked up courage to ask for here and there, correcting them according to his own lights, and adapting them to his own ends; partly by letting himself be guided by the road along which he happened to be walking, our fugitive had covered about twelve miles without being more than six from Milan; and as for Bergamo, he was lucky not to have got farther away from it. He began to realize that he would never succeed in getting there this way either, and tried to think of some other method. The one he hit on was to discover, by some roundabout means, the name of a village near the frontier which he could reach by main roads, and have the way shown him by asking for this, without scattering about that inquiry for Bergamo which seemed to him to reek so much of flight, expulsion, and crime.

As he was wondering how to set about getting this information without arousing suspicion, he saw a leafy branch* hanging over the door of an isolated house outside a little hamlet. He had for some time also been feeling a growing need to restore his energies, and thought this would be the place to kill two birds with one stone; so he went in. There was no one there but an old woman with a distaff by her side and a spindle in her hand. He asked for something to eat; was offered a piece of stracchino cheese and some good wine; accepted the cheese and declined the wine with thanks (a loathing for it had come over him since the tricks it had played on him the night before), and sat himself down, asking the woman to be quick. She had the food on the table in a moment, and then at once began showering her guest with questions about himself and about the great doings in Milan, rumours of which had reached even there. Renzo not only succeeded in parrying her questions with great presence of mind, but even managed to profit by his very difficulties and make the old woman's curiosity serve his purpose, when she asked him where he was going.

'I have to go to lots of places,' he answered, 'and if I have a moment I would like to go to that biggish village on the Bergamo road, near the frontier, but in the state of Milan. . . . What's its name?' There's sure to be one – he thought to himself.

'Gorgonzola, you mean,' replied the old woman.

'Gorgonzola,' Renzo repeated after her, partly to fix the word in his memory. 'Is it very far from here?' he went on then.

'I don't know for sure; maybe ten, maybe twelve miles. If one of my sons was here he could tell you.'

'And d'you think it can be reached through these nice side lanes, without taking the main road? It's so dusty, so very dusty there! Such a time since it rained.'

'I should think so. You can ask at the first village you come to going straight ahead,' and she gave him the name.

'Fine,' said Renzo, and got up, taking a piece of bread left over from his meagre breakfast – a very different piece of bread from the one he had found the day before at the foot of the cross of San Dionigi. He paid his bill, left, and went straight ahead. And, not to draw things out longer than necessary, by going on from village to village with the name of Gorgonzola on his lips, he reached it about an hour before nightfall.

As he walked along he had planned to make another little halt there to have a rather more substantial meal. His body would have liked a little rest, but Renzo rather than humour it in this would have preferred to let himself fall exhausted by the wayside. His plan was to find out at the inn how far it was to the Adda, adroitly to discover if there was any side road that led to it, and to set off again in that direction after having refreshed himself. Born and raised at the second source, as it were, of that river, he had often heard it said that at a certain point and for a certain stretch in its course it formed the frontier between the states of Milan and Venice; where this point and stretch might be he had no clear idea, but things being as they were, his most urgent need was to get over it, wherever it was. If he did not succeed in doing this that day, he was determined to keep on walking as long as time and strength would allow; and then wait for dawn, in some field, some desert, wherever God pleased, so long as it was not an inn.

After a few steps in Gorgonzola, he saw an inn-sign, and entered. When the landlord came up, he asked for something to eat and half a litre of wine; time and the extra miles had made his extreme fanatical loathing for it pass away. 'Do please be quick,' he added, 'as I have to be on my way again at once.' This he said not only because it was true, but also for fear the landlord should think he wanted to sleep there, and begin to ask him for his Christian name, surname, and where he came from, and what his business was. . . . Keep off all that!

The innkeeper promised Renzo he would be served at once, and the latter sat down at the end of the table, near the door – the place of the shy.

In the room there were a few idlers from the village who had been discussing and commenting on the great news from Milan of the day before, and were longing to hear something of what had happened that day, too, particularly as those first reports had done more to whet than to satisfy their curiosity – an uprising neither subdued nor successful, suspended rather than ended by the fall of night, a thing interrupted, the end of an act rather than of a play. One of these men detached himself from the group, went up to the new arrival, and asked if he had come from Milan.

'Me?' asked Renzo, taken by surprise, to gain time to answer.

'You, if you don't mind the question'.

Renzo shook his head, pursed his lips, made some inarticulate sound, and said, 'Milan, from what I've heard . . . isn't the sort of place to go to at the moment, unless you've absolutely got to.'

'So the rioting is going on today as well, then?' asked the inquisitive man more insistently.

'You'd have to be there to know,' said Renzo.

'But you, haven't you come from Milan?'

'I've come from Liscate,' answered the young man promptly, having thought up his reply in the meanwhile. He had, in fact, come from there, strictly speaking, for he had passed through there; he had learned its name at one point on his journey from a passer-by who had pointed out this village as the first to pass to reach Gorgonzola.

'Oh!' said his friend, as if meaning – Better if you had come from Milan, but patience. – 'And at Liscate,' he added, 'had they no news from Milan?'

'Very likely someone there had,' answered the man from the mountains, 'but I didn't hear any.'

He said these words in the particular tone which means 'that's enough of that.'

The inquisitive man went back to his place; and a moment later the landlord came to lay the table.

'How far is it from here to the Adda?' Renzo said to him, mumbling the words and looking half asleep, as we have seen him do on another occasion.

'To the Adda, to cross over?' said the landlord.

'That is, yes . . . to the Adda.'

'D'you want to cross by the Cassano bridge, or the Canonica ferry?'

'Anywhere. . . . I'm just asking out of curiosity.'

'Eh! I meant because those are the places where honest folk cross – those who can give an account of themselves.'

'Good. How far's that?'

'You can take it that to one place and the other it would be about six miles, a little more, a little less.'

'Six miles! I didn't think it was as much as that; and I suppose,' he went on then, with an air of indifference carried to the point of affectation – 'and I suppose, if one had to take a short-cut, there'd be other places to cross, too?'

'Sure there are,' replied the landlord, fixing him with a pair of eyes full of malicious curiosity. This was enough to stifle back the other questions the young man had ready. He pulled his plate to him, looked at the half-litre of wine the landlord had put down with the plate on the table, and said, 'Is the wine pure?'

'As gold,' said the landlord. 'Ask anyone in the village and round about who knows anything about wine; and then you can taste it for yourself.' So saying, he turned back towards the other group.

– Curse these innkeepers! – exclaimed Renzo to himself – the more of them I know, the worse I find them. – None the less, he settled down to eating with a hearty appetite, keeping his ears open at the same time without seeming to, to gather any information and find out what was thought there of the great event in which he had played no small part, and, above all, if there was any decent fellow among the talkers from whom a poor lad could ask his way without being cross-questioned and forced to discuss his private affairs.

'Ah, well!' one man was saying, 'it really does look as if the Milanese meant business this time. Anyway, we'll hear something tomorrow, at the latest.'

'I'm regretting not having gone to Milan this morning,' said another man.

'If you go tomorrow I'll come along with you,' said a third, and another, then another.

'What I'd like to know,' went on the first man, 'is whether those gentry in Milan will give a moment's thought to the poor country folk, or if they'll make decent laws just for themselves alone. You know what they are, eh? Stuck-up people from the city – everything for themselves, and others might as well not exist.'

'We have mouths of our own to eat with, and to have our say, too,' said another, in a voice as modest as the proposition was daring, 'and once the ball is set rolling ...' – but he thought it best not to finish the sentence.

'It's not only in Milan there's grain hidden,' another was beginning, with a dark, malevolent look; when a horse was heard approaching. They all rushed to the door, and, recognizing the new arrival, went out to meet him. He was a merchant from Milan whose business took him to Bergamo several times a year, and who was in the habit of spending the night at that inn on the way: and as he nearly always found the same company there, he knew them all. They crowded around him, one holding his bridle, another his stirrup.

'Welcome, welcome!'

'Well met.'

'Have you had a good journey?'

'Excellent. And how are you all?'

'Fine, fine. What news do you bring from Milan?'

'Ah! Always wanting news,' said the merchant, dismounting, and leaving his horse in the hands of an ostler. 'Besides, besides,' he went on, entering with the company, 'you probably know more about it than I do by now.'

'We know nothing, really we don't,' said several of them, putting their hands to their hearts.

'Is it possible?' said the merchant. 'Then you'll hear some rather wonderful ... and some rather dreadful things. Hey, landlord, is my usual bed free? Good. A glass of wine, and my usual bite to eat, at once, as I want to get to bed early, to make an early start tomorrow morning and reach Bergamo in time for lunch. So you people,' he went on, sitting down at the opposite end to where Renzo sat silent and attentive – 'so you people don't know about all the goings-on yesterday?'

'Yesterday, yes.'

'There you are,' went on the merchant. 'Of course you've got news. What I say is that, always being on the watch here, to give every passer-by the once-over. . . .'

'But today, how did things go today?'

'Ah, today. You don't know anything about today?'

'Nothing at all; no one's been by.'

'Then just let me wet my lips, and I'll tell you what happened today. You'll hear.' He filled his glass, took it up in one hand, raised the end of his moustache with the first two fingers of the other, stroked his beard, drank, and resumed: 'Today, my dear friends, came very near being as rough a day as yesterday, or worse. And I can scarcely believe I'm here talking to you all; as I'd put aside every idea of travelling, to stay and look after my poor shop.'

'What the devil happened?' said one of his hearers.

'The devil's the right word! Listen.' And carving, then eating the dish put in front of him, he went on with his story. The company was standing on either side of the table, listening with open mouths. Renzo in his place was, without seeming to, probably listening more eagerly than any of the others, as he very slowly chewed his last few mouthfuls.

'Well, this morning the blackguards who'd made that frightful uproar yesterday met at pre-arranged places (there was already an understanding; everything was planned). They met, and started the old business of going round the streets, shouting to attract other people. You know what happens when a room's swept out – saving your presence? The farther you go, the higher the dirt piles up. When they thought they'd got enough of a crowd together, they set off for the house of his lordship the Commissioner of Supply; as if their outrages yesterday were not enough. To a gentleman like that! Oh, the blackguards! And the things they said against him! All made up, of course. A real proper, punctual-paying gentleman like him; as I can say, for I'm quite at home there, and supply the cloth for the servants' liveries. Off they started for that house. Then you should have seen what a rabble, what faces! Just think, they passed right in front of my shop – faces that ... the Jews of the Via Crucis* aren't in it at all. And the things that came out of those mouths of theirs! Enough to make you stop your ears up, if it hadn't been unwise to attract their attention. So there they were, going along, bent on sacking the house. But...' And here he raised his left hand, spread it out, and put the point of his thumb to the tip of his nose.

'But?' echoed almost every one of his listeners.

'But,' went on the merchant, 'they found the street barred with logs and carts, and a fine row of soldiers behind the barricade, with their muskets at the ready, to give them the reception they deserved. When they saw all this fine show ... What would you all have done yourselves?'

'Turned back.'

'Of course; and that's what they did. But just you see if they hadn't the devil in them. They had got to the Cordusio, when they saw that bakery they had been wanting to sack ever since yesterday. And what d'you think was going on in that shop? They were busy distributing bread to their customers; there were gentry there, too, the very flower of the gentry, supervising to see everything went well. And those swine (they had the devil in them, I tell you, and then there were agitators urging them on) – those swine went rushing in like furies; there was a catch-as-catch-can; in the twinkling of an eye, everything was upside down – gentry, bakers, customers, loaves, counter, benches, troughs, bins, sacks, sieves, bran, flour, dough. . . .'

'What about the soldiers?'

'The soldiers had the Commissioner's house to look after; you can't sing and whistle at the same time. It was all in the twinkling of an eye, I tell you; snatch – grab; everything good for anything at all was taken. And then they got again that fine idea they had yesterday – of taking the remains to the square and making a bonfire of them. And they'd already begun, the scoundrels, to bring stuff out – when a bigger scoundrel than any of the others – just guess the fine suggestion he came out with?'

'What was that?'

'To pile everything up in the shop and set fire to pile and house together. No sooner said than done. . . .'

'Did they set fire to it?'

'Wait. An honest man of the neighbourhood had an inspiration from Heaven. He rushed upstairs for a crucifix, found one, fixed it to the arch of one of the windows, then took two blessed candles from the head of one of the beds, lit them, and put them on the window-sill, either side of the crucifix. The crowd looked up. There's still some fear of God in Milan, I must own, for they all came to their senses – or most of them did, anyway; some of them, of course, were devils who'd have set fire to Paradise itself, for loot. But when they saw the crowd wasn't with them, they had to stop and keep quiet. Then just guess what suddenly arrived unexpectedly! The whole cathedral chapter in procession, in full canonicals, with the cross on high. And Monsignor Mazenta, the arch-priest, begins preaching on one side, and Monsignor Settala, the penitentiary, on the other, and others, too. "But, good people, what are you trying to do? But, is this the example to set your children? Come, get back home; why, don't you know bread is cheap again – cheaper than before? Go and look, and you'll see the notice on the street corners."'

'Was it true?'

'Deuce take it! Would the canons of the cathedral come along in *cappa magna** to tell lies?'

'And what did the people do?'

'Bit by bit, they went off, hurried to the street corners; and there was the tariff for anyone who could read. Just fancy what it was; an eight-ounce loaf for a *soldo!*'

'What a bargain!'

'All right as long as it lasts. D'you know how much flour has been wasted between yesterday and this morning? Enough to keep the duchy going for two months!'

'And have no decent laws been made for the parts outside Milan, too?'

'What's been done in Milan is all at the city's expense. I don't know what will happen about you. It'll be as God wills. Anyway, the rioting's over. But I haven't told you everything; now comes the good part.'

'What else?'

'This last night, or this morning, a lot of people were arrested; and it was learned at once that the ringleaders will be hanged. As soon as this news began to get round, everyone took the shortest cut home, so as not to risk being one of them. When I left it, Milan was like a monastery of friars.'

'Will they really hang them?'

'Of course! And soon, too,' answered the merchant.

'And what'll the people do?' the man who had put the other question asked.

'The people? They'll go and watch,' said the merchant. 'They were so longing to see someone dying in the open air that they tried, the rascals! to get their fun out of his lordship the Commissioner of Supply. Instead of him, they'll have four wretches, attended with every formality, accompanied by Capuchins and by the confraternities for a good death; they're people who deserve it. It's an act of providence, you see; it was necessary. The people were already beginning to get into the habit of entering shops and helping themselves without putting their hands in their pockets; if they'd been allowed to go on, wine would have been next after bread, and so from one thing to another. . . . D'you think they'd ever stop such a useful habit of their own free will? And I can assure you that it wasn't a very happy prospect for an honest man who kept his shop open.'

'Of course not,' said one of his listeners. 'Of course not,' echoed all the others in chorus.

'And,' went on the merchant, wiping his beard with his napkin, 'it had all been planned some time ago. There was a conspiracy behind it, did you know that?'

'A conspiracy?'

'A conspiracy. All an intrigue set going by the Navarese, by that French cardinal – you know the one I mean; the one with a sort of Turkish-sounding name.* He thinks things up every day to harm the crown of Spain. But he wants, above all, to bring off a stroke in Milan; for he knows perfectly well – the wily old dog – that this is the king's stronghold.'

'I see.'

'D'you want a proof? The people who made the most disturbance were foreigners. There were faces going around that had never been seen in Milan. Oh, that reminds me. I forgot to tell you a story I was told as absolutely true. One of them was arrested in some inn.' . . . Renzo, who had not lost a syllable of this discourse, when this chord was touched felt himself go cold all over, and gave a start before he had time to think of pulling himself together. But no one noticed; and the speaker went on without interrupting the thread of his narrative: 'They're not quite sure yet exactly where this man came from, or who had sent him, or what kind of man he was; but he was certainly one of the ringleaders. He'd been raising the devil the day before in the middle of the rioting; and then, not content with that, he had begun to make speeches, and put forward the gallant idea that the whole of the gentry should be murdered. The blackguard! Who'd keep the poor going if the gentry were all murdered? The police had marked him down, and got their clutches on him. They found a bundle of letters on him, and were just taking him off to prison. But what d'you think happened then? His confederates, who were patrolling round the inn, came up in large numbers, and freed him, the scoundrel.'

'And what happened to him?'

'No one knows; he's either escaped, or is hiding in Milan. People like that haven't a house or home, and find food and lodging everywhere: but only as long as the devil can and wants to help them: they get caught when they least expect it; for when the pear's ripe, it must fall. At the moment it's known for sure that the letters remained in the hands of the law and that the whole conspiracy is described in them; they say a lot of people will be involved. So much the worse for them; for they've turned half Milan upside down, and would have done even worse. People say the bakers are rascals. I know that, too; but let them be hanged after proper trial. There's grain hidden. Who doesn't know that? But it's for the authorities to keep a good look-out and go and unearth it, and send the hoarders to the gallows with the bakers. And if the authorities don't do anything, it's up to the city folk to protest about it. And if they don't listen the first time, protest again. For one gets what one wants if one protests enough. But don't let this vile habit catch on of people going into shops and warehouses and helping themselves.'

The little food Renzo had eaten had all turned to poison. He longed to get out and far away from that inn, from that village; more than ten times he must have said to himself, 'Let's be off; let's be off'; but his old fear of arousing suspicion, now increased beyond measure, had begun tyrannizing over every other thought and kept him nailed to his seat. In his perplexity he thought this gossipy fellow was bound to have done with talking about him sometime; and decided in his own mind to move as soon as he heard the conversation change to another subject.

'And that's why,' said one of the group, 'knowing how these things go, and that honest folk aren't safe in riots, I wouldn't let myself be carried away by curiosity, and stayed at home.'

'And I, did I move?' said another.

'Or I?' added a third. 'Why, if by any chance I'd been in Milan, I'd have left my business unfinished and come back home at once. I've got a wife and children; and then, to tell the truth, I don't like uproars.'

At this point the landlord, who had also been listening, went towards the other end of the table to see what that stranger was doing. Renzo seized the opportunity, beckoned the landlord over to him, asked him for his bill, and paid it without looking it over, although he was in pretty low water. Then, without saying another word, he went straight to the door, crossed the threshold, and taking Providence for his guide, set off in the opposite direction to the one by which he had come.

CHAPTER 17

One longing is often enough to destroy a man's peace of mind; think, then, of two each conflicting with the other. Our poor Renzo, as the reader knows, had had two such longings in him for many hours: the longing to rush ahead, and the longing to hide away; and the merchant's ominous remarks had increased both of them immeasurably at one stroke. So his adventure had made a stir, had it? So they wanted to catch him at any cost? Who knows how many bailiffs must be out hunting for him! or what orders must have gone round to ransack inns and villages and roads for him! Then he thought that, after all, there were only two bailiffs who knew him, and that he did not wear his name written on his forehead. But various stories he had heard came back to him of fugitives found and caught by strange coincidences, recognized by their gait, or their suspicious air, or some other unforeseen signs; all this plunged him into gloom.

Although the clock was striking twenty-four* as he left Gorgonzola and the approaching darkness was lessening those dangers
all the time, yet it was with reluctance that he took to the main
road: and he determined to turn into the first lane that seemed to
lead towards the part he was so anxious to reach. At first he met
an occasional passer-by; but, full as he was of those ugly
apprehensions, he had not the heart to accost any of them to ask
the way. – Six miles, that man said – he thought – if it becomes
eight or ten by going out of my way, the legs that did the others
will do those too. I'm certainly not going towards Milan; so I
must be going towards the Adda. If I go walking on and on,
sooner or later I'll get there. The Adda has a good loud voice,
and I shan't need to ask the way any longer, when I'm near it. If
there is any boat to cross by, I'll cross at once; if not, I'll stop in
a field or in a tree, like the sparrows, till morning. Better up a
tree than in a prison-cell. –

Quite soon he saw a small lane opening off to the left, and
turned into it. If he had come across anyone at that hour he
would not have had so many scruples about asking to be shown
the way; but not a living soul was to be seen or heard. So he went
on wherever the road led him, thinking.

– Me raise the devil! Me want to murder all the gentry! Me
with a bundle of letters! My confederates keeping guard over me!
I'd pay a good bit to meet that merchant on the other side of the
Adda (ah, when shall I be across that blessed Adda?) and stop
him, and ask him at my ease just where he picked up all that
precious information. Let me tell you now, my dear sir, that this
and this is what really happened, and that the only devilry I ever
got up to was helping Ferrer as if he'd been my own brother. Let
me tell you that the rascals who, according to you, were my
friends, wanted to play me a dirty trick, just because at one
moment I spoke up like a good Christian. Let me tell you that
while you were looking after your shop I was getting my ribs
crushed to save your Commissioner of Supply, whom I'd never
even seen before. Just you see if I ever put myself out again to
help the gentry . . . tho' it's true we must do it for the good of
our souls; they're fellow-creatures, too. And what about that
great bundle of letters in which the whole plot was described,
that's now in the hands of the law, as you know for certain?
Shall we have a bet on my making it appear here, without any
help from the devil? You'd be curious to see that bundle,
wouldn't you? Here it is, then. . . . What? Only one letter? . . .

Yes, sir, only one letter; and that, if you'd like to know, was written by a friar who could teach you more Christian doctrine than you ever knew; a friar a single hair of whose beard – with no offence to you – is worth the whole of yours put together. And it's written, this letter is, as you see, to another friar, another man. . . . You can see now what blackguards I've got for friends. And just you learn to be a bit more careful what you say another time, particularly about a fellow-creature. –

But after a time these and other thoughts of the kind ceased altogether. The present circumstances of our poor pilgrim absorbed all his faculties. The dread of being pursued and discovered, which had darkened his journey during daylight, no longer worried him, but so many things made this journey much more trying now than before! The darkness, the solitude, the growing weariness, now beginning to tell on him; a slight but keen and steady breeze, which was anything but pleasant to one still wearing the clothes he had put on to go and marry round the corner and then come triumphantly back to his own home. And what made everything worse was this walking along at random, and as it were by touch, looking for a place of rest and safety.

When he found himself passing through a hamlet he would creep along very softly, keeping a look-out for some door that might still be open; but he never saw any sign of people stirring, other than an occasional light shining through a window. Every now and again, when he was far from any houses, he would stop and listen for that blessed sound of the Adda: but in vain. Nor was any other sound to be heard, except a baying of dogs from some isolated farm, floating mournfully and at the same time menacingly through the air. When he went nearer, the baying changed into quick, furious barking; and as he passed by the gate, he could feel and almost see the beast with its muzzle in the crack of the door, redoubling its howls, and quickly driving away any temptation to knock and ask for shelter. And, perhaps, even without the dogs, he would never have brought himself to it. – Who's there? – he thought – What d'you want at this hour? How did you get here? Who are you? Aren't there any inns for you to put up at? That's what they'll say to me, at the best, if I knock; even if there wasn't some timid sleeper there who'd at once begin shouting: 'Help! Thieves!' One would have to have some clear answer ready at once; and what answer have I got? No one who hears a voice in the night thinks of anything but thieves, rogues, and treachery. They never think any honest man could be on the

road at night except for a gentleman in his carriage. – So he kept
this as a last resort in case of extreme necessity, and went
plodding on, in the hope of at least finding the Adda, if not
crossing it, that night; and of not having to look for it in broad
daylight.

Trudge, trudge, trudge. The cultivated land now merged into
moorland strewn with fern and broom. This seemed to him, if
not an absolute indication, at least some sort of argument for a
river being near, and he started off by a path that ran through it.
After a few steps he stopped to listen: but still in vain. The
irksomeness of the journey was intensified by the wildness of the
spot, by there not being in sight a mulberry, or a vine, or any
other sign of human cultivation, which had been a kind of
company for him. On he went, in spite of this, and to quieten
various fancies, various apparitions which were beginning to
beset his mind – the vestiges of tales told him as a child – he
began as he walked along to recite the prayers for the dead.

Gradually he found himself getting into higher undergrowth of
thorn, scrub-oak, and gorse. On he walked, quickening his pace
more from impatience than desire, and began to see an odd tree
or two scattered among the bushes; and still farther along the
same path, he realized that he was entering a wood. He felt a
certain aversion to plunging into it, but overcame it and pushed
on unwillingly; but the deeper he plunged in, the more his
aversion grew, the more everything unnerved him. The trees he
could just discern seemed like strange, deformed monsters; he
was alarmed by the shadow of the gently swaying tree-tops,
quivering on the path, lit up here and there by the moon; the very
rustling of the dry leaves stirred or trampled by his feet had
something hateful to his ear. His legs had a kind of urge, an
impulse to run, and at the same time seemed barely able to
support him. He felt the night breeze beating more fiercely and
bitterly against his brow and cheeks; he felt it piercing between
his clothes and his bare flesh, and penetrating more sharply into
the very marrow of his bruised, exhausted bones, quenching the
last spark of his energy. At one moment the repugnance, the
vague horror with which his mind had been battling for some
time seemed suddenly about to overwhelm him. He nearly
succumbed altogether; but terrified by his own terror more than
by anything else, he summoned his former spirits to his aid and
bade them hold firm. Thus momentarily reinvigorated, he
stopped short to take thought, and decided to get out of there at

once by the path he had come, return straight to the last village he had passed, get back among human beings again, and seek some shelter, even at an inn. As he stood still there, the rustling of his feet in the leaves hushed, and all quiet around him, he began to hear a sound – a murmur – a murmur of running water. He strained his ears – now he was sure of it. 'The Adda!' he exclaimed. It was like finding a friend, a brother, a saviour. His weariness almost disappeared; he felt his pulse beat again, the blood course freely and warmly through his veins once more, his confidence return, and most of his uncertainty and dejection disappear. Without hesitation now he plunged deeper and deeper into the wood towards the friendly sound.

In a few moments he reached the edge of the flat ground and the brink of a high bank; and peering down through the bushes that covered the whole slope, he saw the gleam of running water. Then raising his eyes, he saw a vast plain stretching out from the opposite bank, scattered with villages, and beyond them hills on one of which was a big whitish splodge which, he thought, must be a town – Bergamo for sure. He went a little way down the slope, and, pushing aside and parting the brushwood with his hands and arms, looked down to see if there was any boat stirring on the river, and listened for the splashing of oars. But he saw and heard nothing. Had it been anything smaller than the Adda, Renzo would have gone straight down and tried to ford it; but he well knew that the Adda was not a river to be treated so lightly.

So he then began to consider, very calmly, what the best thing was to do. To climb up into a tree and stay there waiting for the dawn for perhaps another six hours, in that breeze and that frosty air, was more than enough to numb him in good earnest. To walk up and down for the whole of that time, apart from being very little use against the rigours of the night, was asking too much of those poor legs of his, which had already done more than their duty. He remembered having seen in a field near the heath one of those straw-thatched cabins made of logs and wattle plastered with clay, which the peasants around Milan use to deposit their harvest in the summer, and shelter at night to watch over it. At other seasons of the year they are deserted. He quickly marked this out for his lodging, and retracing his steps along the path, passed the wood, the bushes, and the heath once more, and went towards the cabin. A worm-eaten door half off its hinges, without key or chain, stood half open. Renzo opened it and went in. He saw a wicker hurdle swung in the air like a hammock and propped up on cleft branches, but did not bother to get up into it. On the ground he saw some straw; and thought that a little nap would taste very sweet even there.

But before stretching himself out on this bed which Providence had provided for him, he knelt down to thank God for this blessing and for all the help which he had had from Him during that terrible day. Then he said his usual prayers, asking God's pardon, moreover, for not having said them the night before – for having – to use his own words – gone to bed like a dog or worse. – And that was why . . .! – he added to himself then, leaning his hands on the straw and stretching out from kneeling to lying – and that was why I had that fine awakening this morning. – Then he gathered up all the straw left around him and arranged it over himself, making the best blanket he could to temper the cold which even in there made itself quite keenly felt, and curled himself up underneath it, intending to have a really good sleep, which he felt he had earned over and over again.

But scarcely had he closed his eyes than back and forth across either his memory or his imagination (I could not give the exact place) began such an incessant, such a crowded coming and going of people, that it was good-bye to sleep. The merchant, the notary, the bailiffs, the cutler, the landlord, Ferrer, the Commissioner, the party at the inn, the mob in the street, then Don Abbondio, then Don Rodrigo – all people to whom Renzo had something to say.

Only three of the images that came to his mind had no bitter associations, were clear of all suspicion, pleasant in every way; two particularly, certainly quite different from each other, but closely linked in the young man's heart – one a black tress, and the other a white beard. But even the satisfaction he got from letting his thoughts dwell on these was anything but pure and tranquil. Thinking of the good friar made him feel more ashamed than ever of his own follies, of his shameful drunkenness, of the fine use he had made of all that fatherly advice. And contemplating the image of Lucia – we will not venture to describe his feelings: the reader knows the circumstances, and can picture them for himself. And poor Agnese, how could he forget her? Agnese, who had chosen him, who already regarded him as one with her only daughter, who had spoken and behaved to him with a mother's heart, before even being called so by him. But it was another, no less poignant, pang of grief to think that because of those very same loving intentions, and because of the affection she had for him, the poor woman now found herself homeless, almost vagrant, uncertain of the future, and reaping troubles and trials from the very things that she had hoped would be the joy and comfort of her declining years. Poor Renzo, what a night! One that should have been his fifth night of marriage! What a room! What a marriage bed! And after what a day! And what a day the next one was to be, and all the series of other days after that! – God's will be done! – he would answer the thoughts that bothered him most. – God's will be done! He knows what He is doing; it's for our own good. May it all go to expiate my sins! Lucia is so good. God will not let her suffer for long, for long, for long! –

Amid all these thoughts, and despairing now of ever getting to sleep, with the cold making itself felt more and more, so that he could not prevent himself from shivering and his teeth from chattering every now and again, he yearned for the coming of day, and followed impatiently the slow movement of the hours. I say followed, as every half-hour he heard the strokes of a clock reverberating through the vast stillness; I suppose it must have been the one at Trezzo. And the first time that unexpected clang fell on his ears, without his having the least idea where it came from, it made an impression of mystery and solemnity on him like a warning from a person unseen in a voice unknown.

When at last that bell had tolled eleven times,* which was the hour Renzo had decided to get up, he rose half numb, knelt down, and said his morning prayers with more fervour than usual. Then he stood up and stretched wide and long, shook his waist and shoulders as if to put its members in touch with each other again, for they all seemed to have gone off on their own, blew into one hand after the other, rubbed them together, and opened the door of the cabin. First he gave a glance around to see if there was anyone about; then, seeing no one, he looked for his path of the night before; he recognized it at once and set off along it.

The sky held promise of a fine day. Away in a corner the moon, rayless and pale, stood out even so against the vast background of greyish-blue, which way down towards the east was merging gently into a rosy yellow. Farther down still, right on the horizon, stretched a few clouds in long, uneven layers between blue and brown, the lowest of them tipped beneath with a streak almost of flame, which was gradually becoming sharper and more vivid. To the south other clouds, piled up in light and fleecy masses, were glowing with a thousand nameless colours: that Lombard sky so really lovely on a lovely day, so radiant, so peaceful. Had Renzo been there for pleasure he would certainly have looked up and admired that dawn, which was so different from the one he was used to seeing in his own mountains. But his attention was on the path, and he was walking with long strides, to warm himself up and to arrive quickly. He passed the fields, the heath, the bushes, he crossed the wood, looking around here and there as he did so and smiling rather shamefacedly at the horrors he had felt there a few hours before. He reached the edge of the bank and looked down; and there, through the branches, he saw a fishing-boat coming very slowly upstream, close to the near bank. He hurried down among the brambles, the shortest way he could, and reached the water's edge; very quietly he called out to the fisherman; and intending to give the impression of someone asking an unimportant favour, but unconsciously with almost an air of entreaty, he beckoned the man to draw in. The fisherman surveyed the bank, looked carefully upstream, and turned to look down it, then headed the prow of the boat towards Renzo, and came to the bank. Renzo, who was standing on the very verge, almost with one foot in the water, seized the prow, jumped in and said, 'Could you do me the favour of rowing me across – for a consideration?' The fisherman had guessed, and already turned in that direction. Renzo seeing another oar at the bottom of the boat bent down and grasped it.

'Careful, careful,' said the owner, but on seeing how deftly the young man was handling the instrument and preparing to use it, 'Ah, ah,' he said, 'you're in the trade.'

'A bit,' answered Renzo, and set to work, rowing with more strength and skill than an amateur. Without ever relaxing, every now and again he would give a suspicious glance at the bank from which they were drawing away, and then another impatient one at the bank for which they were bound, fuming at not being able to go the shortest way – for the current was too strong at that point to be able to go straight across, and the boat had to go diagonally, partly cutting across and partly following the flow of the water. As with all complicated affairs where the difficulties present themselves at first as a mass, and then come out one by one as we go on, Renzo, now that the Adda was as good as crossed, was only worried at not knowing for certain if this was the frontier, or if, now that he had got over this obstacle, there was still another one to overcome. So he called to the fisherman, and, nodding towards the whitish splodge he had seen the night before and which showed up now much more clearly, said, 'Is that Bergamo, that place over there?'

'The city of Bergamo,' answered the fisherman.

'And that bank, is that Bergamese territory?'

'Land of Saint Mark.'

'Long live Saint Mark!' exclaimed Renzo. The fisherman said nothing.

They reached that bank at last. Renzo leapt on to it, thanking God to himself, and the boatman with his lips; then he thrust a hand in his pocket, pulled out a *berlinga*, which in the circumstances was no small loss to him, and offered it to the good man, who gave another glance at the bank on the Milanese side, and yet another up and down the river, stretched out his hand, took the tip, set it down, then pursed his lips, and put his finger to them, accompanying the gesture with a significant look, said, 'Good journey to you,' and turned back.

Lest the reader be unduly surprised at this man's prompt and discreet courtesy, we should inform him that he had often been asked to do a similar service for smugglers and bandits, and usually did it, not so much for the small and uncertain earnings he might make from it, as to avoid making any enemies among such people. He did it, I say, every time he was sure he was not seen by customs-men, bailiffs or spies. So, without liking one any more than the other, he tried to satisfy everyone with the impartiality usually shown by those who have to deal with one set of people, while being liable to give an account of themselves to another.

Renzo paused a moment on the bank to gaze at the opposite shore, that land that had been burning under his feet a short time before. – Ah! Out of it at last! – was his first thought. – Glad to be rid of you, cursed country – was his second, his farewell to his native land. But his third went to those he was leaving in it. Then he crossed his arms over his chest, heaved a sigh, looked down at the water flowing at his feet and thought, – It has flowed under The Bridge (as the one at Lecco was usually called in his own part of the world by way of pre-eminence). Ah, what a wicked world it is! Ah well! God's will be done! –

He turned his back on these sad things, and set out, taking the whitish mark on the mountain slope as a reference point, until he found someone to show him the right road. And it was worth seeing the open way in which he now accosted passers-by, and how he named the village where his cousin lived, without all those subterfuges. He learned from the first person to whom he applied that he still had nine miles to go.

That journey was not a happy one. Apart from the troubles Renzo was carrying along with him, his eye was saddened every moment by gloomy sights, which made him realize that he would find the same scarcity in the country he was entering as he had left at home. The whole way along, and particularly in the fields and villages, he met beggars at every step – not professional beggars, for they showed their distress more by their faces than by their clothes – peasants, mountain-dwellers, artisans, complete families, from whom came a confused mutter of entreaties, lamentations, and sobs. Besides moving him to pity and sadness, this sight also made him worry about his own prospects.

– Who knows – he began brooding – if I'll get along all right? If there's work now, as there was in the years before? Anyway, Bortolo used to be fond of me, and he's a good fellow, he's made money, he's invited me so many times; he won't let me down. And then Providence has helped me up to now and will help me in the future too. –

Meanwhile his appetite, which he had been feeling for some time now, was growing from mile to mile. And although Renzo, when he began paying it attention, felt he could hold out without great discomfort for the two or three miles that were left, it occurred to him on the other hand that it would not be quite the thing to present himself to his cousin like a beggar, and to let his first greeting be: 'Give me something to eat.' He took all his worldly wealth out of his pocket, rolled it in the palm of one hand, and counted it. It was not an addition that required a great amount of arithmetic; but there was quite enough for a modest meal. So he went into an inn to restock his stomach; and when he had paid, in point of fact he still had a *soldo* or two over.

As he was going out he saw two women, half sitting, half lying, by the door, so close that they almost blocked it; one was elderly and the other younger, holding a baby that was crying and crying as it sucked in vain, first at one breast and then at the other. All three were the colour of death. Standing near them was a man whose face and frame showed traces of former vigour, now wasted and well-nigh consumed away by long want. All three of them stretched a hand out towards the man they saw coming out with an elastic step and refreshed air. But none of them spoke: could any entreaty say more?

'Here's to Providence!' said Renzo, and quickly thrusting his hand into his pocket, he emptied it of its few coppers, put them in the palm nearest him, and went on his way again.

The meal and the good deed (for we are made up of body and soul) had gladdened and cheered all his thoughts. Certainly his stripping himself of his last *soldo* in this way had given him more confidence in the future than finding ten times that sum would have done. For if Providence, to sustain for that day those poor wretches fainting by the roadside, had kept in reserve the very last coppers of a stranger who was himself a fugitive, far from his own home, and uncertain how he was going to live, who could believe it would forsake the person it had used for this, in whom it had inspired such a lively, effective, positive trust? Such were more or less the young man's thoughts, although they were even less clear than the one I have tried to express. For the rest of the way, as he thought over his problems, everything seemed to look more cheerful. The famine must come to an end some time. There was a harvest every year. Meanwhile he had his cousin Bortolo, and his own ability; and, on top of that, he had some money at home which he would send for at once. With it, if the worst came to the worst, he could get along from day to day until the return of plenty. – And then, once plenty has come back at last – Renzo went on daydreaming – work will begin humming again; the owners will compete for Milanese workmen, who are the ones who really know their job. The Milanese workers will raise their crests: for anyone who wants skilled men will have to pay for them. A man will earn enough to feed more than one person, and to put a bit aside, too, and I'll get someone to write to the women to come over. . . . But then, why wait so long? Isn't it true that with the little we have in reserve we'd have kept going back home this winter too? We'll do the same here. There are parish priests everywhere. So these two dear women will come, and we'll set up house. How pleasant to go strolling, all of us together, along this very road! And go right up to the Adda in a cart, and picnic on the bank, right on the bank, and show the women the place I embarked, the brambles I came down through, the place where I stood looking for a boat. –

He reached his cousin's village. As he went into it, or rather before he even set foot in it, he noticed a very tall building, with several rows of very long windows. He recognized this as a spinning-mill, went in, and in a voice loud enough to be heard above the noise of machinery and falling water, asked if there was a certain Bortolo Castagneri there.

'Signor Bortolo! There he is.'

– Signor? That's a good sign – thought Renzo; then saw his cousin and ran towards him. The latter turned round and recognized the youth as he was saying: 'Here I am.' He gave an 'Oh!' of surprise, and they both raised their arms and threw themselves on each other's necks. After these first greetings, Bortolo drew our young man into another room, away from the noise of machinery and from inquisitive eyes, and said to him, 'I'm glad to see you; but what a strange chap you are! I'd invited you to come time and time again, and you never wanted to; and now you've arrived at rather a ticklish moment.'

'The fact is, I must tell you, I didn't come away of my own free will,' said Renzo – and then, very briefly, though not without great emotion, he told him his sad story.

'That's another kettle of fish,' said Bortolo. 'Oh, you poor Renzo! But you've relied on me, and I'll not let you down. Actually, there's no demand for workmen at the moment. It's all anyone can do to keep their own on, so as not to lose them and put the business out. But my master here is fond of me, and he's got the resources. And, to tell you the truth, boasting apart, he owes it largely to me. He supplies the capital, and I supply the little ability I have. I'm the foreman. Did I tell you that? And, between ourselves, the right-hand man, too. Poor Lucia Mondella! I remember her as if it were only yesterday. A good girl she was! Always the best-behaved in church. And when one passed by that cottage of hers . . . I seem to see it now, that cottage, just outside the village, with a big fig-tree hanging over the wall . . .'

'No, no; don't let's talk about it.'

'I was only going to say that whenever one passed that cottage one always heard the spinning-wheel turning and turning. And that Don Rodrigo! He was getting like that even in my day. But now he's playing the devil outright, as far as I can see, for as long as the Lord leaves him a loose rein. Anyway, as I was saying, we're suffering a good deal from the famine here too. . . . That reminds me, how's your appetite?'

'I ate a short time ago, on the way.'

'And how are we off for money?'

Renzo stretched out his hand, brought it up to his mouth, and blew over it lightly.

'That doesn't matter,' said Bortolo; 'I've got some. And don't give it a thought; for things will change for the better very soon, God willing, and you'll be able to repay me, and still have enough over for yourself.'

'I've got a little at home; and I'll get it sent.'

'Good; and meanwhile draw on me. God has been good to me, so that I can do good to others; and if I don't do it to friends and relations, who shall I do it to?'

'I said trust in Providence!' exclaimed Renzo, squeezing his cousin's hand affectionately.

'So,' went on the latter, 'they've gone and made all that row in Milan. They seem a bit crazy to me, those chaps. Yes, the rumour had already got here; but I'd like you to tell me about it in more detail. Oh, we've got plenty to talk about. Now, here, as you see, it's all much quieter, and things are done with a bit more sense. The city has bought two thousand loads of grain from a merchant in Venice – grain that comes from Turkey; but when it's a question of going hungry, one isn't so finicky. Now just listen to what happens next – what happens is that the governors of Verona and Brescia shut their gates, and say, "No grain is going to pass this way." And what do the Bergamese do then?* Send a lawyer – Lorenzo Torre – to Venice: one of the best. He went rushing off, presented himself before the Doge, and began, 'Now, what are those governors up to?' What a speech he made! A speech fit to be printed, they say. What it means to have someone who knows how to talk! Straight away the order was given to the governors to let the grain through, and not only that, but to provide an escort; and it's on its way now. And the countryside hasn't been forgotten either. Giovanbatista Biava – the Bergamese representative in Venice (that's another good man) – has made the Senate realize that people are starving in the country as well, and the Senate has granted four thousand bushels of millet. That helps to make bread, too. And then, you know, if there isn't any bread, we can find something else. The Lord has treated me well, as I told you. Now I'll take you to my master. I've often talked about you to him, and he'll give you a good reception. He's a good Bergamese of the old sort – large-hearted. He's not really expecting you now; but when he hears your story . . . Besides, he knows how to value a good worker, for famine passes, but business goes on. But first of all I must warn you of one thing. D'you know what they call us Milanese in this country?'

'What do they call us?'

'They call us blockheads.'

'Not a very nice name.'

'There it is. Anyone born in the Milanese provinces who wants to live in Bergamese territory has just got to put up with it. For these people round here calling a Milanese a blockhead is the same as calling a nobleman "most illustrious".'

'They only say it to people who let 'em, I fancy.'

'My lad, if you aren't prepared to swallow being called a blockhead the whole time, don't reckon on being able to live here. You'd have to have your knife in your hand always. And, even supposing you had killed two, three, or four people, someone would finally come along and kill you; and it wouldn't be a very nice prospect, coming up before the Judgement Seat with three or four murders on your soul.'

'And a Milanese who has a bit of . . .' – here he tapped his forehead with his finger, as he had done at the Inn of the Full Moon – 'I mean, someone who knows his job well?'

'All the same thing; here he's a blockhead, too. Do you know what my master says when he talks about me to his friends? "That blockhead has been an absolute godsend to my business; if I hadn't got that blockhead, I'd be in a fine mess." It's just the custom here!'

'It's a silly custom. And considering what we know how to do (after all, it's us who brought this industry out here and keep it going), isn't there any chance of their changing it?'

'Not so far. They might in time; with the children growing up now. But there's not a chance with full-grown men; they've got the habit, and they won't ever give it up. What is it, after all? It's nothing to the tricks our dear fellow-countrymen played on you, and particularly to the ones they wanted to play on you.'

'Yes, that's true enough. If there's nothing else wrong . . .'

'Now you're convinced on that point, everything will go all right. Come along to my master, and cheer up.'

Everything did, in fact, go all right, and so exactly as Bortolo had promised that a detailed account seems unnecessary. And it really was a dispensation of Providence: for as to the money and belongings Renzo had left at home, we shall see now how much they were to be relied upon.

CHAPTER 18

That same day, the 13th of November, a courier for his worship the mayor reached Lecco, and handed him a dispatch from the High Sheriff, which contained instructions to make all possible and needful inquiries to ascertain whether one Lorenzo Tramaglino, a young silk-weaver, who had escaped from the power of the *praedicti egregii domini capitanei*,* had returned *palam vel clam*,* to his own village, *ignotum*,* exactly which, *verum in territorio Leuci*;* and *quod si compertum fuerit sic esse*,* the said mayor was to make every effort *quanta maxima diligentia fieri poterit** to seize his person; and having secured him properly, *videlizet*,* with strong manacles – as thonged handcuffs for the said person had proved insufficient to hold him – to have him taken off to jail, and there kept under strong guard, until he was handed over to those who would be sent to fetch him; and whether he was found or not, *accedatis ad domum praedicti Laurentii Tramaliini; et facta debita diligentia, quidquid ad rem repertum fuerit auferatis; et informationes de illius prava qualitate, vita, et complicibus sumatis*;* and everything said and done, found and not found, taken and left, *diligenter referatis.** The mayor, after doing everything humanly possible to make sure that the person in question had not returned home, summoned the beadle of the village, and was conducted by him to the aforesaid house, with a great retinue of notaries and bailiffs. The house was shut up; whoever had the keys was either not there, or not to be found. The door was broken in, and the premises searched with all due diligence, which meant that they were treated like a city taken by assault. The news of this expedition went round the whole neighbourhood at once. It reached the ears of Fra Cristoforo, who, no less astounded than distressed, made inquiries everywhere to try to throw some light on the reasons for such an unexpected event; but all that he gathered was vague speculations. So he wrote off at once to Fra Bonaventura, hoping to get some more definite information from him. Meanwhile, Renzo's friends and relations were summoned to make statements giving everything that they knew about his 'evil character'. To bear the name of Tramaglino became a misfortune, a disgrace, and a crime. The whole village was upside down. Gradually it became known that Renzo had escaped from the bailiffs right in the middle of Milan, and then vanished. Rumour said that he had committed some offence; but what the offence was people either could not say, or else had a hundred different versions. The more heinous the offence, the less it was believed in the village, where Renzo was known as a good youth. Most people presumed, and whispered among themselves, that it was all a plot organized by that tyrant Don Rodrigo to ruin his humble rival. For sometimes, it is true, even rogues may be wronged by people forming judgements without the necessary knowledge of the facts.

But we, with, so to speak, all the facts before us, can affirm that even though Don Rodrigo had had no hand in Renzo's misfortunes, he was as pleased about them as if they had been his own work, and was triumphant with his intimates, particularly with Count Attilio. The latter, according to his original plans, should have been in Milan by now, but at the first news of the rioting, and of the rabble roaming the streets in anything but a mood to submit to a beating, he had thought it better to stay in the country until things quietened down; particularly because, having given offence to very many people, he had reason to fear that some of those who had kept quiet only from helplessness might feel encouraged by the circumstances and consider it a good moment to take revenge for all of them. This suspense did not last long. The arrival from Milan of the warrant to search Renzo's house was already an indication that things had resumed their normal course; and since positive confirmation of this came almost at the same time, Count Attilio left at once, after encouraging his cousin to persist in his undertaking and carry it to a conclusion, and promising, for his part, to set about getting rid of the friar without delay: to which end, the lucky accident to his lowly rival should play admirably into his hands. Scarcely had Attilio left than Griso arrived safe and sound from Monza, and told his master what he had been able to find out: that Lucia had taken refuge in such-and-such a convent, under the protection of such-and-such a noble lady; and that she was always hidden in there as if she was a nun herself, never setting foot outside the door, and assisting at the church services through a grating in a window; which was a disappointment to many people who, having heard rumours of her adventures and great things of her face, would have liked to have had a look at it.

This account put the devil into Don Rodrigo, or rather, gave an extra stimulus to the devil already there. So many circumstances favourable to his design fanned his passion more than ever – that is, the mixture of pique, pride, and infamous caprice of which his passion was composed. Renzo was away, banished, outlawed, so that anything done against him became lawful, and even his bride could be considered in a way as rebel's property. The only man in the world who was able and willing to take her side, and make a noise loud enough to be heard afar off and by people of importance – the angry friar – would probably also soon be out of harm's way. And here was a new obstacle which not only outbalanced all these advantages, but made them, one might say, worthless. A convent in Monza, even without a princess in it, was too tough a nut for the teeth of Don Rodrigo to crack; and however much he buzzed around this refuge of hers in the imagination, he could think of no means or way of breaching it, either by force or fraud. He very nearly threw up the whole enterprise; he was on the point of going off to Milan, making a detour to avoid even passing through Monza, and in Milan flinging himself into the midst of friends and amusements to try to drive away with thoughts of unalloyed gaiety this thought which had now become a torment. But – but – those friends – careful with those friends, now. . . . He might find that their company only brought him new vexations rather than distractions: for Attilio was sure to have trumpeted it all about by now, and alerted them all. He would be asked for news of the fair peasant girl on all sides; and would have to have an answer ready. He had intended . . . he had tried . . . but what had he succeeded in doing? He had taken on a pledge (rather a shady one, it is true; but there it was – one can't always control one's whims; the point is to satisfy them), and how had he gone through with it? By giving in. To a peasant and a friar? Ugh! And when a piece of unexpected good luck had got rid of one of them without any help from the good-for-nothing and a clever friend got rid of the other, the good-for-nothing had not even known how to profit by this, but had beaten a cowardly retreat. It was more than enough to prevent him from ever holding up his head among his peers again; either that or to make him have his sword in his hand the whole time. And then how could he ever return to this house and village; how could he ever remain there, where leaving aside the poignant and incessant reminders of his passion, he would be branded by failure? Where the public hatred for him would grow and his reputation for power decline both at the same time? Where he would read in every ragamuffin's face, even amidst their bows, an acid: 'You've been beaten, have you? Glad of that.' The road of iniquity, observes our manuscript here, is a broad one, but that does not mean that it is comfortable. It has its stumbling-blocks and rough passages: and its course can be irksome and wearing, for all that it leads downhill.

Don Rodrigo was in this state of not wanting to pull out, to stop, or to go backwards, yet unable to go forward on his own, when a means of doing so occurred to him. This was to ask for the help of a certain person, whose tentacles often stretched farther than others could see: a man – or a devil – for whom the difficulties of an enterprise were often an incentive to his under-taking it. But this course also had its risks and inconveniences, the graver for their not being calculable beforehand; for no one could foresee how things would end, once he had embarked on them with this man, who was certainly a powerful ally, but was no less an arbitrary and dangerous guide.

These reflections kept Don Rodrigo hesitating for some days between a yes and a no, both of which were equally unpleasant. In the meantime, a letter came from his cousin telling him that the plot was well under way. Shortly after the lightning came the thunder, which means that one fine morning he heard that Fra Cristoforo had left the monastery of Pescarenicò. This happy result so promptly attained, and Attilio's letter encouraging and at the same time threatening him with its chaff, inclined Don Rodrigo more and more towards the risky course. What gave him the final push was the unexpected news that Agnese had come back home – one obstacle the less around Lucia. Let us give some account of these two events, beginning with the latter.

The two unfortunate women were hardly settled into their place of retreat than the news of the great riots in Milan spread throughout Monza, and consequently throughout the convent, too; and in the wake of the big news came an infinite series of details which multiplied and varied every moment. The steward-ess, who from her quarters could keep one ear in the street and another in the convent, picked up bits of information from here, there, and everywhere, and passed them on to her lodgers. 'They've put two, six, eight, four, seven of them in jail. They're going to hang them, some in front of the "Bakery of the Crutches", and some of them at the top of the street where the Commissioner of Supply lives. . . . Hey! hey! Just listen to this one! One of them escaped, who's from Lecco, or those parts. I don't know his name; but someone will come along who'll be able to tell me – to see if you know him.'

This announcement, together with the fact of Renzo having arrived in Milan just on the fatal day, made the women, particularly Lucia, rather uneasy; but just imagine their state of mind when the stewardess came along to tell them: 'That man who beat it to save his neck comes from your very own village – he's a silk-spinner called Tramaglino; d'you know him?'

Lucia, who was sitting hemming something or other, let the work drop, turned pale, and looked so changed that the stewardess would certainly have noticed it had she been nearer. But she was standing at the door with Agnese, who – shaken herself, though not so much as her daughter – was able to put up more of a front. To give some sort of answer, she said that everyone knew everyone else in a small village, and she knew him; but she could not conceive how he ever got involved in anything like that; for he was a steady young man. Then she asked if it was certain he had escaped, and where to.

'Escaped – everyone says that; where to, is not known. They may catch him yet, or he may be in safety. But if he falls into their clutches again, this steady young man of yours . . .'

Here the stewardess was luckily called away, and went off, leaving the mother and daughter in the state of mind that you can imagine. The poor woman and the afflicted girl had to remain in this suspense for some days, going over the possible whys and wherefores and consequences of that unfortunate event, and commenting to themselves, or in whispers to each other when they could, on these terrible words.

Finally one Thursday a man came to the convent asking for Agnese. He was a fishmonger from Pescarenico on his regular trip to Milan to dispose of his wares, who had been asked by good Fra Cristoforo to go and call at the convent on his way through Monza, give the women his greetings, and tell them all he knew about Renzo's sad affair, recommending them to have patience and trust in God; to say that he, poor friar though he was, would certainly not forget them, and would look out for some way to help them; and meanwhile, that he would never fail to give them his news every week by this means or some other. The only fresh and definite news which the messenger had to give of Renzo was about the visitation of his house and the search for him; but this had been quite fruitless, and it was known for certain that he was safe on Bergamese soil. This assurance, it is unnecessary to say, was a great balm for Lucia. From that moment she wept more easily and less bitterly; she found more comfort in those secret outpourings to her mother, and mingled thanks with all her prayers.

Gertrude often summoned her to her private parlour, and sometimes kept her talking there for long periods, taking pleasure in the poor girl's innocence and sweetness, and in hearing herself thanked and blessed at every moment. She also told her, in confidence, a part (the clean part) of her own story, of what she had suffered, only to enter this life of suffering; and Lucia's first suspicion and wonder began turning to pity. She found in this story more than sufficient to explain her benefactress's rather strange behaviour; particularly with the help of that theory of Agnese's about the minds of the gentry. But however much she felt the urge to reciprocate the confidences which Gertrude made her, it never even crossed her mind to tell her about this new anxiety and misfortune, or to tell her who the escaped spinner was, for fear of spreading around a tale so full of pain and scandal. She also tried to avoid replying to Gertrude's inquisitive questions about her story before her engagement. But here the reason was not prudence. It was because to the poor innocent girl this story seemed a thornier and more difficult one to describe than anything which she had heard or thought she was likely to hear from the Signora. Those dealt with tyranny, treachery, and suffering – ugly, painful things, yet things which could be expressed; but hers was pervaded by a feeling, a word, which she felt she could not possibly pronounce when speaking of herself, and for which she would never have been able to find a substitute that would not seem shameless – the word love!

Sometimes Gertrude would almost resent this defensiveness of hers, but then so much affection and respect, so much gratitude and trust shone through it! Sometimes, perhaps, she disliked that shy, delicate modesty even more for another reason; but it was forgotten in the sweetness of the thought that recurred to her every time she looked at Lucia: 'I'm helping this girl'; and it was true; for besides the refuge she provided, those talks and familiar endearments were of no small comfort to Lucia. She found another in continuous work, and was always asking to be given things to do; even in the parlour she always had some work to keep her hands busy. But how painful thoughts have a way of seeping through everywhere! As she sewed and sewed – almost a new occupation for her – every now and again the thought of her spinning-wheel would come back to her – and how many other things would come in its wake!

The next Thursday the fishmonger or another messenger came with Fra Cristoforo's greetings and a confirmation of Renzo's successful flight. Other positive news about his troubles there were none; for, as we have told the reader, the Capuchin had been hoping to get some from his colleague in Milan, to whom he had recommended Renzo; but this friar had answered that he had seen neither the letter nor the bearer; that someone from the country had come to the monastery to look for him; but that, not finding him in, he had gone off and not appeared again.

The third Thursday no one appeared. And this for the poor women was not only the loss of a comfort for which they had been longing and hoping, but, as every trifle is apt to do with those in affliction or difficulties, became a source of disquiet and of a hundred torturing suspicions. Even before this Agnese had been thinking of making a visit home. Not seeing the promised messenger decided her. For Lucia it was a serious matter to be taken from her mother's apron-string; but her longing for some news, and the security which she felt in her guarded and holy asylum, overcame her reluctance. They decided between them that Agnese would go next day and wait in the street for the fishmonger, who should pass that way on his journey back from Milan, and would ask him to be so kind as to give her a seat in his cart to take her back to her native mountains. She met him according to plan, and asked if Fra Cristoforo had sent no message for her? The fishmonger had been out fishing all day before he left, and had not heard anything from the friar. She did not need to beg for the favour which she wanted, and bidding the Signora and her daughter farewell, not without tears, and promising to send news of herself at once and to return soon, off she went.

Nothing particular happened on the journey. They rested for part of the night at an inn, as was usual, and setting off again before daybreak, reached Pescarenico early in the morning. Agnese got out in the little square in front of the monastery, letting her conductor go off with many a 'God reward you.' Then, as she was on the spot, she decided to see her good benefactor the friar before going home. She rang the bell; the friar who came to open it was Fra Galdino – the one of the walnuts.

'Oh! My good woman, what wind brings you here?'

'I've come to see Fra Cristoforo.'

'Fra Cristoforo? He's not here.'

'Oh! Will it be long before he's back?'

'Long . . .' said the friar, shrugging his shoulders and burying his shorn head in his cowl.

'Where's he gone to?'

'To Rimini.'

'To . . .?'

'To Rimini.'

'Where's that?'

'Eh, eh, eh!' replied the friar, slicing the air up and down with an extended hand to signify great distance.

'Oh, woe is me! But why's he gone off so suddenly?'

'Because the Father Provincial wanted him to.'

'And why send him away? When he was doing so much good here. Oh, Lord above!'

'If superiors had to give reasons for their orders, where would obedience be, my good woman?'

'Yes; but this will be the ruin of me.'

'D'you know what probably happened? What probably happened is that they needed a good preacher at Rimini (we've got them everywhere, to be sure; but sometimes a particular man's needed). The Father Provincial there will have written to the Father Provincial here, to ask if he's got such and such a kind of person, and the Father Provincial will have said: Fra Cristoforo's the man for this. That's what must have happened, you know.'

'Oh, poor us! When did he leave?'

'The day before yesterday.'

'There! If only I'd acted on my intuition to come a few days sooner! And it's not known when he may come back? More or less?'

'Ah, my good woman, only the Father Provincial knows that – if even he does. When once one of our preaching friars takes wing, no one can tell what branch he'll go and settle on. They'll want him here, there, and everywhere, and we have monasteries in all four quarters of the globe. Suppose now Fra Cristoforo has a great success in Rimini with his Lenten sermons – for he doesn't always preach extempore, as he did here for the fisher-folk and peasants – he's got sermons all written out, for town pulpits – wonderful they are. The news of this great preacher will go round those parts, and they may want him . . . oh, anywhere. And then he'll have to go; for we live by the charity of the whole world, and it is right we should serve the whole world.'

'Oh, Lord above! Lord above!' exclaimed Agnese once again,

on the verge of tears. 'What am I to do without him? He was like a father to us! It will be the ruin of us!'

'Listen, my good woman. Fra Cristoforo was a really fine man; but we've got others, you know: men of parts, with hearts full of charity, who can deal equally well with the gentry and the poor. Would you like Fra Atanasio? Would you like Fra Girolamo? Would you like Fra Zaccaria? He's a man of real worth, you know, is Fra Zaccaria. And don't go taking any notice, as certain ignorant folk do, of his being so gaunt, and having such a weak voice, and such a thin, straggly little beard. I don't say he's good at preaching, for everyone has his particular gifts; but he's a marvel at giving advice, you know.'

'Oh, please!' exclaimed Agnese, with that mixture of gratitude and impatience which one feels at offers that show someone's good intentions more than they suit our own convenience. 'What do I care whether another man is a marvel or not, when it was the poor man who's gone who knew all about our affairs, and had made all sorts of arrangements to help us?'

'Well, then, you must be patient.'

'That,' replied Agnese, 'I know. Sorry for troubling you.'

'No trouble at all, my good woman. I'm sorry for your sake. And if you decide to come and see one of our fathers, the monastery's always here, and won't run away. Ah, well, I'll see you soon, when I go collecting oil.'

'Good-bye,' said Agnese; and began walking towards her own village, feeling as forlorn, confused, and upset as a poor blind man who has lost his staff.

Being somewhat better informed than Fra Galdino, we are able to explain what really happened. As soon as Attilio arrived in Milan, he went, as he had promised Don Rodrigo, to call on their mutual uncle, of the Secret Council. (This was an advisory committee composed of thirteen important legal and military figures, whom the governor consulted, and which, if he died or was transferred, temporarily assumed the reins of government.) Their right honourable uncle the count was a lawyer, one of the senior members of the Council, and enjoyed a certain prestige in it; but at exploiting this prestige, and impressing others with it, he was unrivalled. Ambiguous language, significant silences, sudden pauses in the middle of a sentence, winks that meant 'My lips are sealed,' raising hopes without committing himself, conveying a threat amidst elaborate politeness – all were techniques used to this end, all went to increase his own importance; so that, eventually, if he said 'I can't do anything about this' (sometimes because it happened to be the absolute truth), he said it in such a way that it was not believed, and that, too, served to increase the conception, and hence the reality, of his power – like those boxes still occasionally to be seen in some chemists' shops, which have certain words in Arabic on the outside, and nothing inside, but serve to maintain the prestige of the shop. That of the right honourable uncle, which had been growing by imperceptible stages for a very long time, had recently made a giant's stride, as they say, due to the unusual occasion of a journey to Madrid on a mission to the Court. To form an idea of his reception there one would have had to hear its description from his own lips. We shall only mention that the Count-Duke had treated him particularly graciously, and admitted him into his confidence to the extent of once asking him, in the presence, it might be said, of half the court, how he liked Madrid, and of another time telling him, as they were alone together in the embrasure of a window, that the cathedral of Milan was the biggest church in the king's dominions.

After paying his own respects to his uncle, and giving him those of his cousin, Attilio put on a serious air, which he knew how to assume at the proper time, and said, 'I think I am doing my duty, and not betraying Rodrigo's confidence, if I warn my right honourable uncle of a matter which, unless you intervene, may become serious, and have consequences . . .'

'One of his usual scrapes, I suppose.'

'In all justice to my cousin, I must say that the fault's not on his side. But he's got his blood up about it, and, as I say, there's only our right honourable uncle who can . . .'

'Let's hear about it, let's hear about it.'

'There's a Capuchin friar in those parts who has a grudge against Rodrigo; and things have got to such a point that . . .'

'How often have I told you that the friars must be left to stew in their own juice? They've given enough trouble as it is to those who have to . . . whose duty it is . . .' Here he sighed. 'But you people who can steer clear of them . . .'

'My lord and uncle, it is my duty to tell you here and now that Rodrigo would have steered clear of this if he possibly could. It's the friar who's got a grudge against him, and has taken to provoking him in every way he can. . . .'

'What the devil has this friar got to do with my nephew?'

'First of all, he's known to be a restless character, who makes a practice of taking sides against the gentry. This man protects, directs, and I don't know what else besides, a little peasant girl down there; and he's got such an affection, such an affection for this girl . . . I don't say an interested affection, but still it's a very jealous, a very suspicious affection.'

'I understand,' said the right honourable uncle; and across the background of clumsy stupidity painted on his face by nature, hidden and overlaid later by thick layers of diplomacy, there shone a sudden flash of malice, making a very pretty sight indeed.

'Now, for some time,' went on Attilio, 'this friar has got it into his head that Rodrigo has some sort of designs on this . . .'

'Got it into his head! Got it into his head! I know my lord Don Rodrigo, too; and it would need another advocate than you to defend him on this subject!'

'My lord and uncle, I can well believe that Rodrigo made some joking remark to this girl when he met her on the road. He's young, and anyway, he's not a Capuchin. But these are just trifles, not worth detaining my right honourable uncle with; the serious thing is that the friar has been talking about Rodrigo as if he were an ordinary common fellow, and is trying to incite the whole village against him. . . .'

'And what about the other friars?'

'They don't take any part, as they know him to be a hot-head, and have every respect for Rodrigo; but, on the other hand, this friar has great influence with the peasants, for he also sets up as a saint. . . .'

'I imagine he does not know that Rodrigo is my nephew.'

'Doesn't he just! It's that, in fact, that's spurring him on more than ever.'

'What? What?'

'Because, as he goes around boasting, he gets all the more fun from taking it out of Rodrigo just for the very reason that he has a family protector of as much authority as your lordship. He says he snaps his fingers at grandees and politicians, and that St Francis' cord can tie swords up, too, and that . . .'

'Oh, the impudent friar! What's the fellow's name?'

'Fra Cristoforo of * * *,' said Attilio; and the right honourable uncle took a little note-book out of a drawer of his table, and wrote that poor name down, sighing again and again. Meanwhile Attilio was going on, 'He's always been like that. His former life is known. He was a plebeian who found himself with a little money, and wanted to compete with the gentry of his own town, and from rage at not being able to get where he wanted with all of them, killed one of them, then turned friar to save his neck.'

'Fine! Excellent! We'll see to him, we'll see to him,' said the right honourable uncle, still sighing.

'Now,' went on Attilio, 'he's angrier than ever, as he's failed to carry out a plan he was very keen on; and from this my right honourable uncle will understand the kind of man he is. He wanted to get this girl of his married off; whether it was to save her from the dangers of the world, if you understand what I mean, or for some other reason, he was determined to get her married; and he had found the . . . the man. This was another creature of his whose name my lord uncle may, in fact, certainly will, have heard; for I am sure the Secret Council must have had to occupy itself with this worthy person.'

'Who's that?'

'A silk-spinner, Lorenzo Tramaglino, the one who . . .'

'Lorenzo Tramaglino!' exclaimed the right honourable uncle. 'Fine! Excellent indeed, friar! To be sure, in fact he had a letter for . . . What a pity that . . . But it doesn't matter. All right; and why doesn't our Don Rodrigo tell me anything about all this? Why has he let things go so far and not had recourse to one who is both able and willing to guide and support him?'

'I'll be frank with you about that, too,' went on Attilio. 'For one thing, knowing how many worries and cares our right honourable uncle has in his head' – the latter sighed and put his hand to it, as if to show what a great strain it was to hold them all in – 'he had scruples about adding another one to them. And then, to tell you the whole truth, from what I can gather, he's so exasperated, so beside himself, so sick of the friar's insults, that he feels more like taking some summary justice of his own, rather than getting it in the regular way, through the prudence and power of our noble uncle. I've tried to smooth him down; but seeing things were getting worse and worse, I thought perhaps it was my duty to warn our right honourable uncle about it all, who, after all, is the prop and pillar of the family . . .'

'You would have done better to have spoken a little sooner.'

'That's true; but I was hoping that it would blow over by itself, or that the friar would finally come to his senses again, or that he would leave the monastery, as is apt to happen with these friars, who are here one moment and there the next. And then it would all have been done with. But . . .'

'Now it's for me to set things to rights.'

'That is what I thought, too; our right honourable uncle, with his shrewdness, with his authority, will know how to prevent a scandal and save Rodrigo's honour at the same time which is, after all, also his own. This friar, I said to myself, is always harping on about the cord of St Francis; but one can use it quite well, that cord of St Francis, without having it round one's belly. My noble uncle has many means of which I know nothing; I know the Father Provincial has a great respect for him, as it's right he should; and if our noble uncle thought that the best course in this case would be to get the friar a change of air, with just a few words he could . . .'

'Leave the thinking to those whose business it is, sir!' said his right honourable uncle rather brusquely.

'Ah, that's true,' exclaimed Attilio, with a shake of his head and a look of self-pity. 'As if I was one to give our noble uncle advice! But it was the deep regard I have for the family honour that made me speak. And I'm also afraid I've done something else wrong,' he added with a thoughtful air. 'I'm afraid of having wronged Rodrigo in the eyes of our noble uncle. I would feel no peace if I thought I'd been the cause of your thinking Rodrigo lacks any of that faith and submissiveness to you that is due from him. Believe me, my lord uncle, in this case it was simply . . .'

'Come, come! Not much chance of you two not backing each other up! You'll always go on being friends until one of you gets a little sense. Feckless, feckless, always getting into some scrape or other; and then it's for me to get you out; why . . . you almost make me say something silly . . . why, you give me more to worry about, the pair of you, than' – and his sigh here can be imagined – 'than all these blessed affairs of state.'

Attilio made a few more excuses, promises, and compliments, then he took his leave, and came away accompanied by a 'Be sensible, now,' which was his right honourable uncle's usual formula of dismissal for his nephews.

CHAPTER 19

Anyone who saw a weed – a fine yellow dock, for instance – growing in an untilled field, and really wanted to know if it came from a seed ripened in the field itself, or from a seed borne there by the wind, or dropped by a bird, would never come to any conclusion, however long he pondered over the matter. So we, too, cannot tell if the right honourable uncle's decision to make use of the Father Provincial to cut the tangled knot in the most satisfactory way, sprang naturally from his own brain, or from Attilio's insinuation. Attilio had certainly not thrown it out just by chance, and although he must have expected that his uncle's touchy vanity would react to so open a hint, he wanted to dangle the idea of this solution in front of him, and to put him on the road which he wanted him to follow. This solution, on the other hand, was so adapted to the right honourable uncle's disposition, and so plainly indicated by circumstances, that one might wager that he would have found it for himself without any suggestion from anybody. The important thing was that someone of his name, a nephew of his, and in a struggle which seemed only too open, should not be worsted: this was absolutely essential to the prestige which he had so much at heart. Whatever satisfaction his nephew could get on his own would be a worse cure than the disease itself, and sow troubles far and wide; this must be prevented at all costs and without loss of time. He could order him to leave that country-house of his at once; but he would not obey, and if he did it would mean abandoning the field of battle, and a retreat on the part of the family before a monastery. Orders, legal powers, threats of that kind were useless against an adversary like this. The regular and secular clergy were completely immune from all lay jurisdiction not only in their persons but in the places where they lived, as even someone who had read no other story than the present one – (poor fellow) would know. All that could be done against such an adversary was to try to get him removed, and the means of doing this was the Father Provincial, on whom Fra Cristoforo's going or staying depended.

Now, there was a long-standing acquaintance between the Father Provincial and the right honourable uncle. They seldom saw each other, but when they did it was with great demonstrations of friendship and extravagant offers of service. There are times when it is easier to deal with someone with a large number of people under him than with a subordinate who can only see his own point of view, heed his own feelings, and care for his own ends; while the former at once sees hundreds of connexions, consequences, and interests, hundreds of things to be avoided or safeguarded, and can therefore be approached in a hundred different ways.

When he had pondered it all over, the right honourable uncle one day invited the Father Provincial to dinner, and to meet him asked a galaxy of guests chosen with exquisite subtlety. There were some of his most heavily titled kinsmen, whose surnames alone were titles enough; and who by their very bearing, natural assurance, and lordly haughtiness, managed, without even trying, to impress and renew every minute an idea of superiority and power, as they talked about the highest matters in the most familiar terms. Then there were a few clients bound to the family by hereditary dependence, and to its head by life-long service, who began at the soup to say 'yes' with lips, eyes, and ears, with their whole head, with their whole bodies and souls, so that by the time the fruit came round they were reduced to forgetting how anyone ever managed to say 'no'.

At table the noble host soon brought the conversation round to the subject of Madrid. Many roads lead to Rome; but with him they all led to Madrid. He talked about the court, the Count-Duke, the ministers, the governor's family; about the bull-fights, which he was able to describe admirably, having seen them from a privileged place; about the Escurial* of which he was able to give a minute account, as one of the Count-Duke's dependants had taken him round every nook and corner. The whole company sat listening to him alone for some time as if they were in a lecture-hall, then divided up into private conversations; and he went on describing more of these splendours, as if in confidence, to the Father Provincial, who was sitting beside him and let him go talking on and on and on. But at a certain point the priest gave the conversation a turn, drew it away from Madrid, and so from court to court, from dignitary to dignitary, got it on to Cardinal Barberini, who was a Capuchin and a brother of the reigning pope, Urban VIII, no less. The count then had to sit and listen and let him talk a little, and remember that, after all, there were other grandees in this world as well as the ones whose names he could use. Shortly afterwards, on rising from table, he asked the Father Provincial to accompany him into another room.

Two powers, two grey heads, two ripe experiences were now face to face. The magnificent nobleman asked the very reverend priest to take a seat, sat down himself, and began: 'In view of the friendship there is between us, I thought I might venture to speak to your reverence about a matter of common interest to us both – a matter to be settled between ourselves, without resorting to other means which might ... And so with a frank heart I will tell you as best I can what it is about, and I am sure we will find ourselves in agreement after a few words. Tell me: is there in your monastery at Pescarenico a certain Father Cristoforo of * * *?'

The Provincial nodded assent.

'Now tell me frankly, your reverence, as friend to friend ... this person ... this father ... I do not know him personally, although I do know several Capuchin fathers, sterling men, zealous, prudent, humble; I've been a friend of the order since I was a boy.... But as in all rather large families ... there is always some individual, some wild ... And I know from certain reports this Father Cristoforo to be a man ... with rather a quarrelsome nature ... not endowed with all that prudence, all that tact.... I would wager he has given your reverence cause for worry more than once.'

– I understand; it'll be some pledge he's made – the Father Provincial was thinking meanwhile. – My fault; I knew that blessed Cristoforo was a type to be kept moving from pulpit to pulpit, and not left in one place for six months, particularly in a country monastery. –

'Oh!' he said then, 'I am really sorry to hear your magnificence has such a poor opinion of Father Cristoforo; for, as far as I know, he is ... exemplary in the monastery, and highly thought of outside.'

'I understand perfectly; your reverence has to ... But, but as a sincere friend I would like to warn you of something which you would find it useful to know; and even if you know about it already I can, without failing in respect, put forward certain consequences that are ... possible; I won't say more than that. We know this Father Cristoforo is protecting a man from those parts, a man ... your reverence will have heard him spoken of; the one who escaped so scandalously from the hands of the law, after having done things on that terrible St Martin's day, things – things that ... Lorenzo Tramaglino!'

– Oh dear! – thought the Provincial; and said, 'That circumstance is new to me. But your magnificence well knows that part of our duties is to find those who go astray, and to bring them back ...'

'Yes, of course. But protecting those who have gone astray in certain ways ... These are thorny matters, delicate matters....' And here, instead of blowing out his cheeks and sighing, he compressed his lips, and drew in as much air as he usually let out in one sigh, then went on: 'I thought it best to give your reverence some inkling of these circumstances, because if His Excellency should ever ... some move might be made at Rome ... I don't know ... and Rome might send up ...'

'I am much obliged to your magnificence for the warning: but I am sure that if inquiries are made about this, it would be found that the only dealings Father Cristoforo had with the man you mention was to try to bring him to his senses. I know my Father Cristoforo.'

'You know better than I do, of course, what he was like as a layman, and about the little escapades of his youth.'

'The glory of this habit, my lord count, is that whatever cause for talk a man has given as a layman, he becomes a different person once he assumes it. And since Father Cristoforo donned this habit ...'

'I would gladly believe that, I say it from my heart; I would gladly believe that. But sometimes, as the proverb says ... "it's not the cowl that makes the monk".'

The proverb did not fit exactly; but the count had hurriedly substituted it for another that was on the tip of his tongue: 'no wolf changes by dressing as a sheep'.

'I have evidence,' he went on. 'I have proof ...'

'If you know definitely,' said the Provincial, 'that this priest has committed some fault (all of us may err), I should consider it a real favour to be told of it. I am his superior – though an unworthy one – but I am that precisely in order to correct and remedy things.'

'I will tell you. In addition to the unpleasant circumstance of this priest's open protection of the person mentioned, there is another distasteful fact, and one which might ... But we can settle it all together between ourselves. The fact is that this same Father Cristoforo has taken against my nephew, Don Rodrigo * * *.'

'Oh! I'm very sorry about that – very sorry, very sorry indeed.'

'My nephew is young and impetuous; he has a strong sense of who he is, he's not used to being provoked ...'

'I will make it my duty to get thorough information about such a thing. As I have already said to your magnificence – and I am speaking to a nobleman no less just than he is experienced in the world – we are all made of flesh and blood, we are all liable to make mistakes ... as much on one side as on the other; and if Father Cristoforo has erred ...'

'You see, your reverence, these are matters, as I said before, that ought to be settled between ourselves and buried there, matters which with too much probing ... only get worse. You know what happens then. These bickerings, these wranglings which are often started by some quite trifling thing, go on and on and on.... Try to get to the root of it, and either you never get down there, or a lot of other complications start. Smooth 'em down, nip 'em in the bud, most reverend father, nip 'em in the bud, smooth 'em down. My nephew is young. The priest, from what I hear of him, still retains all the spirit, all the ... er ... inclinations of youth; and it is up to us, who are getting on in years ... alas, eh – most reverend father?'

For anyone watching at this point it was just as when a backdrop is raised prematurely by mistake in the middle of a serious opera, and some singer is surprised having a cosy chat with a friend as if there was never an audience in the world. The look and voice of the right honourable uncle as he said that 'alas' were completely natural. There was no diplomacy in that. It was really true that his years bothered him. Not that he regretted the pastimes, the fire, the grace of youth; that was all frivolous, ridiculous nonsense! The reason for his sorrow was much more solid and important: it was that he was hoping for a higher appointment when it fell vacant, and was afraid of not reaching it in time. Once that was obtained, one can be certain he would no longer bother about his age and die content without wanting anything more, as everyone who wants something very much protests that he will do when he has eventually obtained it.

But let him go on talking. 'It's up to us,' he went on, 'to have sense for the young and to put their misdeeds to rights. Luckily we are still in time. This affair has not made any stir yet; it's still a case of a good *principiis obsta*:* and getting the spark away from the straw. Sometimes a person who has not done well in one place, or has caused some trouble there, gets on surprisingly well in another. Your reverence doubtless can find just the proper niche for this priest. There is that other business, too, which might have incurred the suspicions of those who ... might like him moved. And by placing him in some post a good way away, we'll be killing two birds with one stone, or, to put it better, everything'll be settled and no harm done.'

The Father Provincial had been expecting this conclusion ever since the beginning of the conversation. – Ah, well! – he was thinking to himself – I see your drift. It's the old story. When a poor friar falls foul of your class, or just one of your class, and worries them, his superior has to get him moved at once, without even finding out if he is right or wrong. –

And when the count had finished, and let out a long sigh, which was equivalent to a full stop: 'I understand perfectly,' said the Provincial, 'what your lordship means; but before taking a step . . .'

'It's a step and it's not a step, very reverend father. It's a natural thing, an ordinary thing; and if you don't take this solution, and take it at once, I can foresee a whole heap of trouble, an Iliad of misfortunes. Some rash folly . . . I don't believe my nephew would ever . . . I am here to see to that. . . . But at the point this thing has reached, if we don't cut it short now, without wasting time, with one clean stroke, things can't possibly stay where this is and remain a secret . . . and then it won't be only my nephew. . . . It would be stirring up a hornet's nest, most reverend father. We are a powerful family, you see; we have connexions . . .'

'Illustrious ones.'

'You understand me; all people with good blood in them, which in this world . . . counts for something. Family honour will come into it. It will become a communal affair; and then . . . even for anyone peace-loving . . . It would be a real blow to me to have to . . . to find myself . . . I who have always been so well disposed to the Capuchin fathers. . . . To go on doing good, as your friars have up to now, to the great edification of the public, you need peace, you need to be free from strife, and on good terms with those who . . . And then you have relations in the world . . . and these family feuds, as soon as they begin, spread and branch out, and draw half the world . . . into them. I find myself in this blessed office, which obliges me to maintain a certain dignity. . . . His Excellency . . . my lords and colleagues . . . they would all make common cause . . . particularly with that other circumstance. . . . You know how these things go.'

'In truth,' said the Father Provincial, 'Fra Cristoforo is a preacher; and I had already thought . . . In fact I have just been asked . . . But at this moment, and in circumstances like these, it might look like a punishment; and a punishment before it is quite clear . . .'

'Not a punishment, no. Just a wise precaution, a solution of mutual convenience, to avoid any unfortunate accidents that might . . . you know what I mean.'

'The matter remains on those terms between your lordship and myself; I understand. But if the facts are as they were reported to your magnificence, it is impossible, it seems to me, that something should not have got about the village. There are instigators and mischief-makers, or at least malicious busybodies, everywhere, who take an insane delight in seeing the gentry and the clergy at loggerheads. And they pry about, put two and two together, discuss it. . . . Everyone has his own dignity to maintain; and I, as superior – an unworthy one – have an express duty . . . the honour of the habit . . . it is not my private concern . . . it is a trust which . . . Your noble nephew, if he is as angry as your magnificence says, might take it as a satisfaction made to himself, and . . . I don't say boast or triumph about it, but . . .'

'D'you think so, most reverend father? My nephew is a gentleman who is considered in the world . . . according to his rank and due; but he is a mere boy before me; and he will do just exactly what I tell him. But I will go farther; my nephew shall know nothing about it. Why need we give any explanation? These are things we have settled between ourselves, like good friends; and between us they should remain. Don't worry about that. I ought to be used to keeping secrets,' and he sighed. 'As for the gossips,' he went on. 'What can they say? It is such a normal thing for a friar to go and preach at another town! Besides, we who can tell . . . we who can foresee . . . we whose duty it is . . . we ought not to pay attention to gossip.'

'Still, it would be well to forestall them on this occasion by your noble nephew making show, giving some obvious proof of friendship and esteem . . . not for us, but for the habit.'

'Of course, of course, that's only right. . . . But there is no need of it. I know the Capuchins are always received by my nephew in a proper way. He does it by inclination: it's quite a family trait; and, besides, he knows he is doing something that pleases me. But anyway, in this case . . . something out of the ordinary . . . it's only right. Leave it to me, most reverend father, and I shall order my nephew . . . that is, I shall have to hint at it rather discreetly, so that he does not realize what has passed between us. For I would not like us to put a salve where there is no wound. And as for what we have decided, the sooner it's done the better. And if you happen to find some niche rather far away . . . to avoid the very least chance . . .'

'It just happens I have been asked for a preacher for Rimini, and I might, even without any other reasons, have had my eye on ...'

'Most opportune, most opportune. And when?'

'As it must be done, it may as well be done soon.'

'Soon, soon, very reverend father; better today than tomorrow. And,' he went on, rising from his chair, 'if I or my family can do anything for our good Capuchin fathers ...'

'We know the kindness of your family by experience,' said the Father Provincial, rising in his turn, and following his conqueror towards the door.

'We have put out a spark,' said the latter, pausing – 'a spark, most reverend father, that might have started a big conflagration. A few words between friends can settle great affairs.'

On reaching the door, he flung it open, and absolutely insisted on the Father Provincial going ahead of him. They entered the other room and joined the rest of the company.

A great deal of study, a great deal of dexterity, a great deal of eloquence, did that nobleman put into the managing of such an affair; but he also produced corresponding results. In fact, by the conversation we have described, he succeeded in sending Fra Cristoforo on foot from Pescarenico to Rimini, which is a good long walk.

One evening a Capuchin from Milan arrived at Pescarenico with a package for the Father Guardian. It contained the order for Fra Cristoforo to proceed to Rimini, where he was to preach the Lenten sermons. The letter to the Guardian bore instructions that he was to intimate to the said friar that he was to give up all thought of whatever activities he might be engaged on in the village he was leaving and to maintain no correspondence about them. The friar bearing the message was to be his travelling companion for the journey. The Guardian said nothing that evening. Next morning he summoned Fra Cristoforo, showed him the order, and bade him go and get his wallet, staff, cloak, and girdle and with the friar, whom he presented, set off on his journey at once.

The reader can imagine the blow this was for our friar. The thought of Renzo, Lucia, Agnese, came to his mind at once, and he exclaimed, as it were, within himself – Oh, God! What will those poor wretches do when I am not here? – But then he raised his eyes to heaven, and accused himself of lack of confidence and of presumption at having thought himself necessary for anything.

He crossed his hands on his chest in token of obedience, and bowed his head before the Father Guardian, who then drew him aside and gave him the rest of the message in words of advice and a tone of command. Fra Cristoforo went to his cell, took his wallet, put into it his breviary, his Lenten sermons and the bread of forgiveness, bound up his gown with his leather girdle, took leave of those of the other friars who happened to be in the monastery, then finally went to receive the Father Guardian's blessing, and with his companion set out on his appointed road.

We have said that Don Rodrigo, more than ever bent on carrying through his precious enterprise, had decided to seek the help of a terrible ally. We cannot give the name, surname, or title of the latter, or even make a guess at them;* which is all the stranger as we find this personage mentioned in many books (printed books, too) of that period. The similarity of the facts does not leave much room for doubt that this is the same person, but everywhere great care has been taken to avoid giving his name, almost as if it would scorch the pen and hand of the writer. Francesco Rivola, when he has to mention this person in his life of Cardinal Federigo Borromeo, calls him 'a nobleman as powerful by riches, as he was illustrious by birth,' and leaves it at that.* Giuseppe Ripamonti, who in the fifth book of the fifth decade of his *Storia Patria* mentions him more extensively, refers to him as 'one', 'the latter', 'the former', 'this man', 'that personage'. 'I will relate,' he says in his elegant Latin, which we translate as best we can, 'the case of one who was among the first grandees of the city, and had established his residence in the country near the frontier; and there he flouted the judgements of law cases, the judges, every tribunal, even of sovereignty, making his very crimes his security. He led a life of complete independence, harbouring outlaws, and an outlaw himself at one time, then returning as if nothing had happened. . . .'* We shall take other extracts from this writer, when they happen to confirm and clarify the story of our anonymous author; with which we will now push ahead.

To do whatever the laws forbade or any power at all opposed; to be arbiter and dictator of the affairs of others, from no other motive than a pleasure in power; to be feared by all, and to dominate those who usually dominated others – such had been this man's chief passions at every period of his life. Ever since his youth he had felt a mixture of contempt and impatient envy at seeing or hearing all the bullying, rivalry, and tyranny around him. As a young man, living in the city, he never missed – he even went out of his way to seek – opportunities of quarrelling with the most celebrated exponents of these arts, and thwarting them so as to measure his strength against theirs and either curb them or make them seek his friendship. Superior to most of them in wealth and retinue, and to all, perhaps, in daring and determination, he forced many of them to withdraw from all rivalry, gave many others a lesson, and made friends of many more – not, however, as equal friends, but as the only kind he liked: subordinate friends, who acknowledged themselves his inferiors and always gave him the right of way. In fact, however, he became himself the agent, the tool of them all. They never failed to ask for the help of so powerful an ally for all their affairs: and withdrawal would have meant for him forfeiting his reputation or failing in his chosen role. So that finally he went to such lengths, both on his own account and others', that neither his name nor his family nor his friends nor even his daring could sustain him against the public decrees of exile: and he had to bow before so much powerful animosity and leave the state. I believe this is the event referred to in a remarkable passage in Ripamonti. 'Once when this person had to leave the country, this was the secrecy, respect, and timidity with which he did so; he crossed the city on horseback, followed by a pack of hounds, with horns blowing; and as he passed in front of the palace, he left with the sentries an insolent message for the governor.'

During his absence he did not interrupt his dealings or his correspondence with those of his friends who had still remained linked to him – to translate Ripamonti literally – 'in secret alliance of atrocious plans and ghastly deeds'. He also seems to have contracted certain new and terrible relations with people of the highest rank, of whom the aforesaid historian speaks with mysterious brevity. 'Even certain foreign princes,' he said, 'used his services more than once to carry out some important assassination, and often sent him from afar reinforcements of people to serve under his command.'

Finally (how much later is not known), either because the sentence against him was raised by some powerful intercession, or because his audacity gave him immunity, he decided to return home; which he did – not, however, to Milan, but to a castle on the borders of the Bergamese territory, which, at that time, as everyone knows, belonged to Venice. 'That castle' – I quote from Ripamonti again – 'was a kind of workshop of bloodthirsty orders. The very servants had a price on their heads, and had spent their lives severing those of others. There was not a cook or a scullion exempt from murder. The hands of boys were stained with blood.' Besides this amiable domestic circle, he had, as our historian states, another of similar characters scattered over various parts of the two states on whose borders he lived, stationed there, and always ready to carry out his orders.

All the petty tyrants for a good part of the surrounding country had been forced, on one occasion or another, to choose between the friendship and the enmity of this super-tyrant. But the first to attempt resistance had fared so badly that none of them felt like putting themselves to the test again. Nor could any of them remain independent of him by keeping to themselves and looking after their own affairs. Some messenger of his would arrive to tell them to abandon a certain undertaking, stop molesting a certain debtor, and the like. They had to answer yes or no. When one party had gone to do him fealty as a vassal and asked him to arbitrate in some affair, the other party had the hard alternative of either bowing to his decision, or declaring himself his enemy; which was equivalent, as they used to say once, to being in the third stage of consumption. Many who were in the wrong applied to him to be put effectively in the right; many who were in the right applied to him to ensure themselves the protection of so powerful a patron and to keep out their adversary; both became more completely his dependants than ever. Sometimes it happened that a weak victim of oppression would turn to him; then he would take the part of the weak and force the oppressor to desist, repair the harm which he had done, and ask for pardon. And if the other held out, he would start such a war against him that he would either be forced to quit the scene of his depredations or else be made to pay a speedier and more terrible penalty. And in such cases the name so dreaded and so abhorred was blessed just for a moment; for from no other power, public or private, could such an act of – I will not say of justice – but of relief and compensation, have been looked for at that period. More frequently, indeed usually, his power had been, and was then still being used to minister to iniquitous passions, atrocious revenges, and arrogant caprices. But its different uses always had one same effect: that of impressing on everyone's minds how much he was willing and capable of doing in defiance of right and wrong – those two things which are such an obstacle to men's wishes, and so often force them to turn back. The fame of the ordinary petty tyrants was mainly restricted to the small area in which they were richest and strongest: each district had its own; and they all resembled each other so much that there was no reason for people to concern themselves with any others apart from their local one. The fame of our tyrant, however, had long been diffused throughout the whole of the Milanese provinces. Everywhere his life was a subject for popular tales, and his name bore with it the idea of something compelling, strange, and fabulous. The suspicion that he had his agents and hired assassins everywhere also contributed to keeping his memory alive everywhere. These were only suspicions – for who would openly avow such a dependence? – but every petty tyrant might be his colleague, every little malefactor one of his men. And this very uncertainty made the conception of it vaster, and the fear of it deeper. Whenever a set of unknown and unusually savage-looking bravi put in an appearance anywhere, whenever some appalling crime was committed whose author could not be pointed out or guessed at once, people muttered the name of the man whom, thanks to that blessed circumspection of our authorities, we shall be obliged to call the unnamed.

From his castle to the mansion of Don Rodrigo was no more than seven miles; and the latter had no sooner become master and tyrant, than he was forced to realize that, at so short a distance from such a personage, he would not be able to carry on business without coming either to grips or to peaceful terms with him. So he had offered his friendship, and been accepted; in the same way, be it understood, as did all the others. He had done him more than one service (the manuscript does not say more); and each time he had been rewarded by promises of help on any occasion. But he took great care to hide such a friendship, or at least not to disclose how close and of what nature it was. Don Rodrigo certainly wished to play the tyrant, but not the wild and savage tyrant: the profession was with him a means, not an end. He wanted to live freely in the city, and enjoy the comforts, pleasures, and honours of society. This meant that he had to take certain precautions, consider his relations, cultivate the friendship of important people, and keep one hand on the scales of justice so as to be able to tip them in his favour when necessary, or push them aside, or bang them over the head of someone who could be settled more easily that way than by private violence. Now, his intimacy, or rather his collusion, with a man of that sort, an open enemy of public authority, would certainly not have been much of a recommendation for such favours, particularly with his right honourable uncle. But such traces of this friendship as it was impossible to conceal might pass as an indispensable relationship with a man whose enmity was too dangerous, and so make an excuse out of necessity. For those who assume responsibility for others and are unwilling or unable to do anything about it, eventually have to consent up to a point to those others shifting for themselves – or, if they do not consent in so many words, they wink an eye at it.

One morning Don Rodrigo rode out on horseback, dressed for hunting, with a small escort of bravi on foot, Griso at his stirrup and four others in line behind, and set off towards the castle of the unnamed.

CHAPTER 20

The castle of the unnamed was perched above a dark and narrow valley, on top of a bluff jutting out from a rugged chain of mountains, and joined to them or separated from them – it is difficult to say which – by a mass of crags and precipices, and a labyrinth of caverns and chasms, which also extended on both sides of it. The side overlooking the valley is the only practicable one; it is a steepish but even and unbroken slope, with uplands of meadow and, farther down, tilled fields dotted here and there with cottages. The base is a bed of flints, over which, according to the season, runs a rivulet or a roaring torrent. It then served as the border between the two states. The ridges opposite, which form, as it were, the other wall of the valley, also have a little cultivation on their slopes; the rest is rock-splinters and boulders, and precipices without track or vegetation, except for an occasional bush in a cleft or along some ridge.

From the castle heights, like the eagle from its blood-stained nest, the savage nobleman dominated every spot around him where the foot of man could tread, and never saw anyone higher or above him. A single sweep of his eye could embrace the whole of that enclosure, the slopes, the base, and the tracks inside it. The track which climbed in twists and turns up to this terrible abode unrolled itself to the onlooker from above like the folds of a ribbon; from his windows and loopholes the nobleman could count at his leisure the steps of anyone coming up, and level a gun at him a hundred times over. And with the garrison of bravi that he kept up there, he could have stretched many even of a large company out on the path or hurled them to the bottom, before a single one succeeded in reaching the top. But no one dared set foot there, or in the valley either, even to pass through, unless he was on good terms with the master of the castle. And any bailiff who dared show himself there would have been treated like an enemy spy caught inside a camp. Grim tales were told of the last ones who had attempted the enterprise; but these were old tales by now; and none of the young men remembered ever having seen one of that ilk in the valley, dead or alive.

Such is the description that our anonymous chronicler gives of the place – of the name, not a word. What is more, so as not to give us any clue with which to find it, he says nothing about Don Rodrigo's journey, and carries him straight into the middle of the valley, to the foot of the bluff, just at the beginning of the steep winding path. Here there was a tavern, which might well have been called a guard-house. A blazing sun was painted on both sides of an old sign hanging over the door; but the only name given to it by public opinion, which sometimes repeats the names it is taught, and sometimes alters them to please itself, was the Inn of Malanotte.*

At the sound of an approaching cavalcade, a young lout appeared on the threshold armed to the teeth like a Saracen. He looked them over, then went in to tell a trio of ruffians who were gaming with a filthy crumpled pack of cards. The one who seemed to be the leader got up, went to the door, and, recognizing one of his master's friends, gave him a respectful greeting. Don Rodrigo returned this greeting very civilly, and asked if his master was up at the castle; when the sort of corporal replied that he thought so, he dismounted and threw his reins to Tiradritto, one of his escort. He then unslung his musket, and handed it to Montanarolo, as if relieving himself of a useless weight so as to climb more easily, but in reality because he was well aware that no one was allowed up that slope with firearms. Then he took a few *berlinghe* out of his pocket, and gave them to Tanabuso, saying, 'You others stay and wait for me here; and enjoy yourselves meanwhile with these good fellows here.' Last of all he took out some gold *scudi* and handed them to the corporal, half for himself and half to divide among his men. Then, with Griso, who had also put his musket aside, he began the ascent on

foot. Meanwhile the three bravi mentioned above, and Squinter-
notto who made up the fourth (Ah! you see what fine names,*
and how carefully we have preserved them!), stayed behind with
the three henchmen of the unnamed and the young gallows-bird,
gaming, drinking, and bandying exploits with each other.

Another of the unnamed's bravi who was on his way up
overtook Don Rodrigo shortly afterwards, recognized him at a
glance, and went on in his company, thus sparing him the
annoyance of having to give his name and render an account of
himself to others he might meet who did not recognize him. On
reaching the castle and being admitted (leaving Griso, however,
at the door), he was taken through a labyrinth of dark passages,
and a series of rooms hung with muskets, sabres and halberds,
with a bravo or two on guard in each of them, and after waiting
awhile, he was ushered into the presence of the unnamed.

The latter came towards him, returning his greeting, and at the
same time looking at his face and hands, as he did from force of
habit, almost an involuntary one by now, even with his oldest
and most tried friends. He was tall, swarthy, and bald; his few
remaining hairs were white, and his face was wrinkled, which
made him look, at first sight, rather older than his sixty years.
But his bearing and movements, the animation of his strongly
pronounced features, the sinister but vital flash of his eye,
indicated a vigour of body and mind which would have been
remarkable in a young man.

Don Rodrigo said that he had come for advice and help; that,
finding himself with a difficult undertaking from which his
honour did not allow him to withdraw, he had remembered the
promises of one who was known never to promise too much or
in vain: and he then laid bare the whole abominable intrigue. The
unnamed, who already knew something of the story, but only
vaguely, listened attentively, both because he had a natural
interest in such tales, and because in this one was implicated a
name that he knew and hated – that of Fra Cristoforo, the open
enemy of tyrants in word, and, where possible, in deed. Don
Rodrigo, knowing his man, began to exaggerate the difficulties
of the undertaking: the distance of the place, a convent, the
Signora.... At this the unnamed suddenly interrupted, as if
commanded by some demon hidden in his heart, and said he
would take on the affair. He made a note of poor Lucia's name,
and dismissed Don Rodrigo, saying, 'You'll shortly hear from me
what you are to do.'

The reader may remember the profligate Egidio who lived next door to the convent which sheltered poor Lucia; he should now be told that this was one of the unnamed's closest and most intimate partners in crime; which is why the latter had given his word so promptly and decidedly. Yet as soon as he was alone he began to – I will not say repent – but regret having given it. For some time he had been feeling, not exactly a remorse, but a certain disquiet at his crimes. These, accumulating in his memory if not in his conscience, rose up before him again in all their number and ugliness every time he committed a new one; it was like the gradual increase of a weight that was already uncomfortable. A certain repugnance, which he had felt at his first crimes, but had then overcome until it had almost completely disappeared, now began making itself felt once more. But in those early days the prospect of a long, indefinite future, the consciousness of vigorous vitality, had filled him with carefree confidence; whereas now, on the contrary, it was the thought of the future which made the past more irksome. – To grow old! To die! And then? – And, strange! The idea of death, which, in moments of danger, facing an enemy, usually redoubled his spirits and filled him with a frenzied courage – this same idea, when it came to him in the silence of the night, in the safety of his own castle, now threw him into instant consternation. It was not a death threatened by an enemy mortal like himself; it could not be repulsed by a superior or readier arm. It was coming alone, springing from within him. It might still be far away, but each moment was bringing it a step nearer: and even as his mind was struggling painfully to rid itself of the thought, it was approaching. In the early days, the frequent examples, the almost continual sight, of violence, revenge, and murder had inspired him with a fierce competitiveness, and had also served him as a kind of authority against the voice of conscience. Now the confused but terrible idea of an individual responsibility, of a reason independent of example, would rise before his mind. Now the very fact of his having left the ordinary run of malefactors behind and outstripped them all sometimes gave him a feeling of tremendous solitude. The God of Whom he had heard speak, but Whom he had long ceased either to acknowledge or deny, occupied as he was only in living as if He did not exist, now, in certain moments of depression without reason, of terror without danger, seemed to be crying within him: But I do exist! In the first flush of his passions the laws which he had heard proclaimed – if nothing else – in His name had seemed merely odious. Now, when they came back to his mind unexpectedly, in spite of himself he began to see them as something inexorable. But, rather than reveal this new uneasiness to anyone, he covered it over deeply, and masked it with an appearance of greater ferocity than ever; hoping, too, by this means to disguise it from himself, or to stifle it. Regretting (since he could not destroy or forget them) the days when he used to commit crimes without remorse, and when his only worry was their success, he made great efforts to bring them back, to grasp and recover once again that former ready, daring, proud, and imperturbable will of his, so as to convince himself that he was still the same man.

So on this occasion he had pledged his word to Don Rodrigo at once, in order to shut the door on any possible hesitation. But scarcely had the other left, than he began to feel oozing away the resolution which he had summoned up to make the promise; he began to feel thoughts seeping into his mind tempting him to default, which would have meant losing face before a friend, before a minor accomplice. To cut short this painful contrast, he summoned Nibbio, who was one of the ablest and most daring agents of his enormities, and his usual go-between with Egidio; and with a resolute air ordered him to mount a horse at once and go straight off to Monza to tell Egidio of the pledge which he had undertaken, and ask for his help in carrying it out.

The rascally messenger returned with Egidio's reply quicker than his master expected. This was that the enterprise was a safe and easy one, that the unnamed was to send a coach at once with two or three well-disguised bravi; and that he would take care of the rest and arrange the whole matter. At this news the unnamed, whatever he felt like inside, hurriedly gave orders to Nibbio himself to do everything as Egidio had said, and with two others, whom he named, to set off on the expedition.

If to carry out the horrible service requested him Egidio had had only his ordinary resources to reckon on he would certainly not have given so prompt and definite a promise. But in that very sanctuary where it seemed that everything should be an obstacle, the atrocious youth had a resource known only to himself; and what would have been the greatest difficulty for others was for him a tool. We have mentioned that the wretched Signora had once lent ear to his addresses. The reader may have realized this was not the last time, and was only a first step on the road of abomination and of bloodshed. That same voice which had acquired weight, and I might almost say authority, from the crime, now imposed on her the sacrifice of the innocent girl in her charge.

The suggestion appalled Gertrude. To lose Lucia by some unforeseen chance and through no fault of hers would have seemed a misfortune and a bitter punishment to her; and now she was being ordered to deprive herself of the girl by a base act of treachery, and so change a means of expiation into a fresh subject for remorse. The wretched woman tried every way she could to evade the horrible command – every way, except the only sure one, which was always there open in front of her. Crime is an exacting, inflexible master, against which no one can be strong unless he rebels completely. This Gertrude could not bring herself to do; and she obeyed.

It was the day that had been agreed on. The appointed hour was drawing near. Gertrude was alone in her private parlour with Lucia, lavishing more endearments on her than usual, which Lucia was receiving and reciprocating with growing tenderness – like the lamb fearlessly trembling under the shepherd's hand as he gently strokes and coaxes it, and turns to lick his hand, unaware that outside the pen waits the butcher to whom the shepherd has just sold it a moment before.

'I need an important service done; and only you can do it for me. I've so many people at my command, but not a single one I can trust. I must talk about something very important, that I'll tell you about, with that Father Guardian of the Capuchins who brought you here, my poor Lucia: but no one must know that I've sent you to get him, either. I've no one but you who can take this message secretly for me.'

Lucia was terrified at such a request; and modestly, but without hiding her astonishment, began putting forward all the reasons against her going which the Signora would understand and should have foreseen: without her mother, all alone, along a lonely road, in an unknown town. . . . But Gertrude, trained in a diabolic school, showed herself in her turn so surprised and displeased at finding such reluctance in the person whom she regarded as most dependable, and pretended to find her excuses so flimsy: why! in full daylight! a mere step! a road over which Lucia had been a few days before, and which even if she had never seen it she could not mistake, when given the directions . . .! She went on so much that the poor girl was both touched and ashamed, and let fall, 'All right; what am I to do?'

'Go to the Capuchin monastery' – and she described the road again – 'call for the Father Guardian, and tell him in private to come to me at once, at once; but not to tell a soul that it was I who sent for him.'

'But what am I to say to the stewardess, who has never once seen me go out, and will ask me where I'm going?'

'Try and get past without being seen. And if you don't manage to, tell her you're going to some church or other, where you've promised to offer some prayers.'

This was a fresh difficulty for the poor girl – to tell a lie. But the Signora seemed so afflicted by her refusals, and made it seem so mean of her to put a vain scruple before gratitude, that Lucia, overwhelmed rather than convinced, and above all more affected than ever, answered, 'All right; I'll go. May God help me!' And moved to go.

When Gertrude, who was following her from her grille with fixed, troubled eyes, saw her set foot on the threshold, she opened her mouth, as if overcome by an irresistible impulse, and exclaimed, 'Listen, Lucia!'

The girl turned round and went back to the grille. But already another thought – a thought that was used to predominating – had prevailed again in Gertrude's unhappy mind. Pretending that she was not satisfied with the instructions she had given, she once more described to Lucia the road which she must take, and dismissed her, saying, 'Now do everything as I've told you, and come back soon.' Lucia set off.

She passed through the cloister gates unobserved and went on to the street, her eyes lowered, keeping close to the wall. She found the town gate from the instructions which she had been given and from her own memory, passed through it, then, keeping herself to herself and trembling a little, took the main road, and in a few minutes reached and recognized the one leading to the monastery. This road was then, and still is, sunk like the bed of a stream between two high banks fringed with big bushes which form a kind of roof over it. On entering it and finding it completely deserted Lucia felt her fears increase and quickened her step; but she breathed more freely a little farther on at seeing a travelling coach standing still in it, with two travellers by the open door, looking up and down as if they were not sure of the way. As she drew near she heard one of the two say, 'There's a good lass who'll show us the way.' In fact, when she reached the carriage the same man turned round with a more courteous air than his looks seemed to warrant, and said, 'Young lady, could you show us the road to Monza?'

'You're going away from it that way,' replied the poor girl; 'Monza is over here . . .' and she was just turning to point with her finger when the other man (this was Nibbio) suddenly seized her by the waist and lifted her off the ground. Lucia turned her head round in terror and let out a shriek. The ruffian thrust her into the carriage. Another who was sitting inside seized her and pushed her, in spite of her cries and struggles, onto the seat opposite him. Another put a handkerchief round her mouth and stifled her cries. Meanwhile Nibbio had jumped hurriedly into the carriage, too; the door shut; and the carriage set off at full gallop. The other man who had asked that treacherous question stayed behind in the road, glancing up and down to see if anyone was answering Lucia's shriek. Not a soul was in sight. He jumped on to one of the banks, drew himself up by the branch of a bush, and disappeared. This was one of Egidio's men. He had been watching out from his master's door for the moment when Lucia left the convent, had taken a good look at her so as to be able to recognize her, and then run off by a short cut to wait for her at the appointed spot.

Who can describe her terror and anguish, or express what passed through her mind? She opened wide eyes terror-stricken with anxiety to know more about her fearful plight, and then shut them quickly with horror and apprehension on seeing those brutal faces. She writhed about, but was held fast on all sides. She gathered all her strength together and made a desperate effort to throw herself towards the door; but a sinewy pair of arms pinned her to the bottom of the carriage, while four powerful hands held her as if in a vice. Every time she opened her mouth to scream the handkerchief stifled it in her throat. Meanwhile three devilish mouths were repeating in the most human tones they could assume, 'Quiet, quiet; don't be afraid, we don't want to do you any harm.' After a few moments of this agonizing struggle, she seemed to quieten down. Her arms slackened; her head fell back; the lids only just managed to keep open over her staring eyes; and those horrible faces surrounding her seemed to mingle and wave about in front of her in a monstrous tangle. The colour fled from her cheek. A cold sweat covered her. She succumbed, and fainted.

'Come, come, courage,' said Nibbio.

'Courage, courage,' echoed the other two ruffians. But the loss of all her senses prevented Lucia at that moment from hearing the comforting sounds from those horrible voices.

'The devil! She seems dead,' said one of them. 'Supposing she really is dead?'

'Oh! Dead!' said the other. 'It's just one of those fainting fits women get. I've known that whenever I've wanted to send anyone, man or woman, off into the other world, it's needed a good deal more than this.'

'Come along!' said Nibbio. 'Get on with your jobs, and don't mind anything else. Pull the blunderbusses out of the case, and have them ready. There are always some rascals hiding in this wood we're just coming into. Don't hold them in your hands like that, devil take it! Put them behind you there, laid out. Can't you see the girl's a softie and faints at nothing at all? If she sees firearms, she's capable of really dying on us. And when she comes to, take care not to frighten her. Don't touch her unless I give you a sign; I'm enough to hold her. And keep quiet; leave the talking to me.'

Meanwhile the coach, still at full gallop, had plunged into the wood.

After a time poor Lucia began coming to, as if from a deep and troubled sleep, and opened her eyes. She had to make an effort to distinguish the terrifying objects around her and to collect her thoughts. At last once more she realized her terrible situation. Her first use for the little strength which had come back to her was to make another lunge towards the door, to fling herself out. But she was held back, and all that she was able to do was get a momentary glimpse of the wild solitude through which they were passing. She let out another shriek; but Nibbio, raising his hefty hand with the handkerchief in it, said as gently as he could, 'Come, keep quiet, and it'll be better for you. We don't want to do you any harm, but if you don't keep quiet we shall have to make you.'

'Let me go! Who are you? Where are you taking me to? Why've you captured me? Let me go, let me go!'

'Don't be afraid, I tell you. You're not a child, and ought to realize we don't want to do you any harm. Don't you see we could have killed you a hundred times over, if we'd had bad intentions? So keep calm.'

'No, no, let me go on my way; I don't know you.'

'We know you.'

'Oh, Most Blessed Virgin! How d'you know me? Let me go, for pity's sake. Who are you? Why've you captured me?'

'Because we were ordered to.'

'Who by? Who by? Who could have ordered you to?'

'Hush!' said Nibbio with a stern look. 'You must not ask us questions like that.'

Lucia made another sudden attempt to fling herself at the door; but finding it useless, fell back on entreaties once more. And bowing her head, with tears coursing down her cheeks, her voice broken by sobs, her hands clasped before her lips, 'Oh!' she said – 'oh, let me go, for the love of God and the Most Holy Virgin! What harm have I done you? I'm a poor girl who's never done anything to you. What you've done to me I forgive from the bottom of my heart; and I'll pray to God for you. If you've a daughter, too, or a wife or a mother, think what they would be suffering if they were in this state. Remember we must all die, and one day you will want God to be merciful to you. Let me go, leave me here. The Lord will help me to find my way.'

'We can't.'

'You can't? O Lord! Why can't you? Where do you want to take me? Why . . .?'

'We can't. It's useless. Don't be afraid, we don't want to hurt you. Just keep quiet and no one will touch you.'

More and more distressed and distraught, more terrified than ever at finding her words making no impression, Lucia turned to Him who holds the hearts of men in His hands, and can, when He wishes, soften the hardest. She shrank back as far as she could into the corner of the coach and, crossing her arms over her breast, gave herself up for some time to silent prayer. Then she drew out her rosary and began to tell it, with more faith and fervour than she had ever done in her life before. Every now and again, hoping that she had been granted the mercy which she had implored, she turned and begged the men once more: but always in vain. Then she would again swoon away, and again revive to live through more anguish. But we have not the heart to describe this at any length. An overpowering pity makes us hasten this journey, which lasted more than four hours, to its end; and there are other painful hours to get through after it. Let us transport ourselves to the castle where the unhappy girl was being awaited.

She was awaited by the unnamed with an uneasiness and uncertainty of mind quite unusual to him. How strange! This man, who had despatched so many lives in cold blood, who in all those deeds of his had never considered the suffering which he was causing save at times to relish the savage joys of revenge, now, in laying hands on this poor unknown peasant girl, felt a horror, almost a kind of terror. From a window high up in his grim fortress he had been gazing for some time down one of the defiles into the valley. There came the coach at last, drawing slowly ahead; for that first gallop had subdued the fire and exhausted the strength of the horses. And although, from the point where he stood watching, it seemed no larger than a child's toy carriage, he recognized it at once, and felt his heart beat faster.

– Will she be in it? – he thought at once; and went on to himself, – How this girl is bothering me! Let's get rid of her. –

And he was on the point of calling one of his ruffians, sending him straight down to meet the coach, and ordering Nibbio to turn round and take the girl to Don Rodrigo's. But an imperious 'No' resounding in his head banished the idea. Tormented, however, by the need to give some order, finding it intolerable to stand idly waiting for that coach as it came nearer step by step, like a betrayal – or could it be? – like a retribution, he called for an old serving-woman of his.

This old woman had been born in this same castle, was the daughter of one of its former custodians, and had spent all her life within it. What she had seen and heard there since her cradle had impressed on her mind a tremendous and terrible conception of the power of her masters; and the chief maxim which she had learnt from precept and example was that they must be obeyed in all things, for they could do very great harm and very great good. The idea of duty, which lies like a seed in the hearts of all men, had developed in hers and become linked and associated in her mind with feelings of respect, of dread, and of servile devotion. When the unnamed became her master and began turning his power to such fearful uses, she had felt horror at first, together with a deeper sense of submission. In time she grew accustomed to what she saw and heard around her all day long; and the potent, unbridled will of such a great lord became a kind of fatal justice for her. When she grew up, she had married one of the servants of the house, who shortly afterwards, in the course of a dangerous expedition, left his bones down by a roadside and her a widow up in the castle. The vengeance which her master had promptly taken had given her a savage consolation, and increased her pride at being under so powerful a protector. From thenceforward she had only very rarely set foot outside the castle; and gradually there had faded from her mind almost all ideas of how human beings lived save within its precincts. She had no particular duties assigned to her, but one or another of that crew of ruffians was always keeping her busy off and on, which made her grumble continuously. Sometimes she had rags to patch, sometimes a hasty meal to prepare for one returning from an expedition, and sometimes wounds to dress. Then the orders, complaints, and thanks of those men were seasoned with crude jests and coarse oaths; 'old woman' was what she was usually called – the qualifying adjectives, which were always attached, varying according to the speakers' mood and circumstances. Sometimes, when her sloth was disturbed and her anger provoked – her two ruling passions – she would return these compliments in terms in which Satan would have recognized more of his own spirit than in those of the men provoking her.

'D'you see that coach down there?'

'I see it,' replied the old woman, thrusting out her sharp chin and straining her sunken eyes, as if she was trying to force them from their sockets.

'Have a litter prepared at once, get into it, and have yourself taken down to Malanotte. Quick, now, so that you arrive there before the coach. It's only coming on at a funeral's pace. In that coach there is . . . there should be . . . a girl. If there is, tell Nibbio in my name to put her into the litter and come on up here himself at once. You will stay in the litter with the . . . girl; and on getting up here, you will take her to your own room. If she asks you where you're taking her, and whose the castle is, take care not to . . .'

'Oh!' said the old woman.

'But,' went on the unnamed, 'cheer her up.'

'What am I to say to her?'

'What are you to say to her? Cheer her up, I tell you. Have you reached your age without knowing how to cheer a fellow creature at need? Haven't you ever felt faint of heart? Haven't you ever felt afraid? Don't you know the words that soothe most at such moments? Just say a few of those words; find some, dammit. Go.'

When she had gone, he stood at the window some time with his eyes fixed on the coach, already getting much larger; then he raised them towards the sun, which was just at that very moment hiding behind the mountain; then up at the clouds scattered above it, which from brown had changed almost in a moment to flame. He drew back, closed the window, and began pacing up and down the room with the step of a traveller in a hurry.

CHAPTER 21

The old woman had hurried away to obey orders and to issue them with the authority of that name which, whoever pronounced it in that place, set everyone hurrying; for it never entered their heads that anyone would dare to use it without authorization. She reached Malanotte, in fact, a short time before the coach arrived; and when she saw it coming she got out of the litter, beckoned the coachman to stop, and, going up to the door, whispered their master's orders to Nibbio, who put his head out.

Lucia gave a start as the carriage stopped, and awoke from a kind of lethargy. She felt her blood running cold again, and looked about with eyes staring and mouth open wide. Nibbio had drawn back; and the old woman, with her chin on the door, was looking at Lucia and saying, 'Come along, my good girl; come along, you poor thing; come along with me, as I've orders to treat you well and to cheer you.'

At the sound of a woman's voice the poor girl felt a momentary comfort and courage, but relapsed at once into a deeper terror than before. 'Who are you?' she said in a trembling voice, fixing her astonished gaze on the old woman's face.

'Come along, come along, you poor thing,' the latter kept on repeating. Nibbio and the other two, guessing their master's intentions from the old woman's unusually kindly words and soft tone, tried as nicely as they could to persuade their captive to obey. But she went on gazing out; and although the wild and unknown place and the assurance of her guards did not give her much hope of there being any help near, she opened her mouth, in spite of this, to scream, but held it back on seeing Nibbio give a meaningful glance at the handkerchief; she trembled, writhed, was taken out and put into the litter. The old woman got in after her. Nibbio told the other two ruffians to follow behind it, and himself began hurrying up the slope to hasten to his master's summons.

'Who are you?' Lucia anxiously asked the unknown and deformed face beside her. 'Why am I with you? Where am I? Where are you taking me?'

'To someone who wants to help you,' answered the old woman. 'To a great . . . They're lucky folk, the ones he wants to help! Lucky for you! Lucky for you! Don't be afraid; be jolly, now, for he's told me to try and cheer you. You'll tell him, eh? That I've cheered you?'

'Who is he? Why? What does he want with me? I've nothing to do with him. Tell me where I am; let me go; tell these people to let me go – to take me to some church. Oh! You who are a woman, in the name of the Virgin Mary . . .!'

That sweet and holy name, once repeated with veneration in her early years, and then never invoked or perhaps even heard for so long, made on the mind of the wretch who heard it at that moment a strange, confused, halting impression, dim as the memory of light in an old man blind from childhood.

Meanwhile the unnamed was standing at the castle gate looking down and watching the litter advancing step by step, as he had watched the coach before, with, at a distance that increased every instant, Nibbio running ahead of it. When the latter reached the top, the nobleman beckoned him to follow, and went into one of the castle rooms with him.

'Well?' he said, stopping short.

'All without a hitch,' answered Nibbio, with a bow. 'The warning on time, the girl on time, no onlookers, only one scream, no one appeared, the coachman ready, the horses good, the road clear, but . . .'

'But what?'

'But . . . to tell the truth, I had much rather the orders had been to put a shot in her back, without hearing her talk, without looking her in the face.'

'What? What? What d'you mean?'

'I mean that the whole time, the whole time . . . She made me pity her so much.'

'Pity! What d'you know about pity? What is pity?'

'I'd never really understood so well before. It's rather like fear, pity is; once you let it get hold of you, you're quite unmanned.'

'Let's hear how this girl managed to move you to pity.'

'Oh, illustrious master! For so long . . . Weeping, begging, making such piteous eyes, going pale as death, and then more sobbing, and begging, and saying things . . .'

– I don't want that girl in the house – the unnamed was thinking meanwhile – I was a fool to let myself in for this. But I've given my word, I've given my word. When she's far away . . . – And, raising his head with a commanding air towards Nibbio, 'Now,' he said – 'Now just you put aside your pity, get on a horse, take a companion – two if you like – and gallop off to the house of that Don Rodrigo, you know. Tell him to send . . . but to be quick about it, otherwise . . .'

But inside him another 'No', even more imperious than the first, prevented him finishing. 'No,' he exclaimed in a firm tone, almost as if he was expressing to himself the order of that secret voice – 'No; go and rest; and tomorrow morning . . . you'll do what I tell you.'

– That girl must have some demon of her own – he began thinking when he was alone, standing with his arms crossed on his chest and his gaze fixed on a spot on the floor where the rays of the moon, coming through a high window, were casting a pale square of light, chequered by the massive iron grilles and fretted delicately by the small window-panes. – Some demon, or . . . some angel protecting her. . . . Nibbio feeling pity . . .? Tomorrow, tomorrow morning early, out of here that girl goes to her fate, and that's the last I'll hear of her, and – he went on to himself, rather in the spirit in which one gives an unruly boy an order which one knows he will not obey – and that's the last I'll think of her. But that fellow Don Rodrigo mustn't come and pester me with thanks; as . . . I don't want to hear any more mention of that girl. I helped him because . . . because I had promised, and I had promised because . . . that's my destiny. But I'll see the fellow pays me well for this. Now let's see . . . –

And he tried to think up some particular enormity to ask him to do, as a compensation and almost as a punishment; but the words 'Nibbio feeling pity!' went through his mind again. – What could that girl have done? – he went on, drawn along by that thought – I want to see her. . . . Eh! No . . . Yes. I want to see her. –

And he went from one room to another until he reached a narrow flight of stairs, groped his way up, went to the old woman's room, and kicked at the door by way of a knock.

'Who is it?'

'Open.'

At the sound of that voice the old woman bounded up. The bolt was at once heard grating through the sockets, and the door was thrown open. From the threshold the unnamed cast a glance around the room, and, by the light of a lamp burning on a small table, saw Lucia huddled down on the floor in the farthest corner of the room.

'Who told you to fling her down there like a bundle of rags, you wretch?' he said to the old woman, with an angry frown.

'She went where she wanted to,' replied the latter humbly. 'I did all I could to cheer her up, as she can tell you herself; but it wasn't any use.'

'Get up,' said the unnamed to Lucia, approaching her. But she, whose panic-stricken soul had been thrown into fresh panic by the knocking, the opening door, and the appearance of this man, crouched deeper in her corner than ever, with her face buried in her hands, motionless except that she was trembling all over.

'Get up. I won't do you any harm . . . and I can do you some good,' repeated the nobleman. 'Get up,' his voice thundered out, irritated then at having twice given an order in vain.

As though galvanized by terror, the unhappy girl at once raised herself on her knees and, joining her hands together as she would before a sacred image, raised her eyes to the unnamed's face, and lowering them quickly, 'Here I am,' she said. 'Now kill me.'

'I told you I wanted to do you no harm,' replied the unnamed in a softer tone, gazing fixedly at that face, distorted by anguish and terror.

'Courage, courage,' said the old woman. 'If he tells you himself that he won't do you any harm . . .'

'Then why,' went on Lucia in a tone in which a tremble born of fear mingled with a courage born of desperate indignation – 'why have you made me suffer the tortures of hell? What have I done . . .?'

'Have they ill-treated you, then? Speak up.'

'Ill-treated me! They've seized me by treachery, by force! Why? Why did they seize me? Why am I here? Where am I? I'm just a poor, harmless girl. What have I done? In the name of God . . .?'

'God, God,' interrupted the unnamed – 'always God. Those who can't defend themselves, who haven't the power to, are always bringing up this God of theirs, as if they'd spoken to Him. What do you expect from this word of yours? To make me . . .' and he left the sentence unfinished.

'Oh, my lord! Expect! What can a poor girl like me expect,

unless it's for you to have mercy on me? God forgives so much for one deed of mercy. Let me go; for pity's sake let me go! Don't let the suffering you have caused a poor, harmless creature be on your conscience when you die one day. Oh! you who can give the order, do tell them to let me go. They've brought me here by force. Send me with this woman to * * * where my mother is. Oh, Most Holy Virgin! My mother! My mother, for pity's sake, my mother! Perhaps she's not far away from here. . . . I have seen my own mountains. Why d'you make me suffer? Have me taken to a church. I'll pray for you for as long as I live. What does one word cost you? Ah, there! I see you are moved to pity. Say one word, just one word. God forgives so much for one deed of mercy!'

– Oh, if only she was the daughter of one of those swine who outlawed me! – the unnamed was thinking – of one of those curs who would like to see me dead! How I'd gloat over this wailing of hers; but instead . . . –

'Do not reject a good inspiration,' Lucia went on fervently, encouraged by a certain air of hesitation in the tyrant's face and bearing. 'If you don't grant me this mercy, the Lord will grant it. He will let me die, and it will all be over for me: but you! Perhaps some day you, too – But no, no; I'll always pray that the Lord may preserve you from all harm. One word – what will that cost you? If you knew the agony I . . .'

'Come, take heart,' interrupted the unnamed, with a gentleness that made the old woman start with amazement. 'Have I done you any harm? Have I threatened you?'

'Oh no! I see you have a kind heart, and feel some pity for this poor creature that I am. If you wanted you could frighten me more than any of the others, you could kill me . . . and instead of that you have . . . lightened my heart a little. May God reward you for it. Complete your work of mercy; set me free, set me free!'

'Tomorrow morning . . .'

'Oh, set me free now, right away . . .'

'Tomorrow morning we shall meet again, I tell you. Come, be of good heart meanwhile. Have a rest. You must need something to eat. They'll bring you some right away.'

'No, no; I'll die if anyone comes in here. I'll die. Take me to a church. . . . God will reward you for every step I take.'

'A woman will come to bring you food,' said the unnamed, and as he said this was astonished himself at such an expedient occurring to him, or at his feeling any need of finding one to reassure a little peasant girl.

'And you,' he went on then quickly, turning to the old woman, 'encourage her to eat; put her to sleep in your bed; and if she wants your company, well and good; otherwise you can sleep on the floor for one night. Cheer her, I tell you; cheer her up. And see she has no complaints to make of you!'

So saying, he moved rapidly towards the door. Lucia got up and ran to detain him and renew her appeals; but he was gone.

'Oh, woe is me! Shut the door, shut it, quick,' and when she heard the door slam and the bolts drawn, she went back and crouched in her corner again. 'Oh, woe is me!' she sobbed again. 'Who can I appeal to now? Where am I? Tell me, tell me, please, who that gentleman is . . . the one who was talking to me?'

'Who is he? Who is he? You'd like me to tell you that, eh? You wait and see if I tell you. Just because he's protecting you, you're beginning to give yourself airs. You must get what you want, and drag me into it, also. Ask him yourself. If I did this for you, too, I wouldn't get the kind words you've heard. – I'm old, old' – she went on, muttering between her teeth. – 'A curse on the young, who look pretty whether they're laughing or weeping, and are always in the right.' – But when she heard Lucia sobbing, her master's words came back to her threateningly, and stooping over the poor huddled girl, she went on in a gentler tone, 'Come, I haven't said anything nasty to you. Cheer up. Don't ask me to tell you things I can't. Anyway, pluck up your courage. Oh, if you knew how many people would be pleased to hear him talk as he talked to you! Cheer up: soon they'll be bringing you something to eat; and I who know can tell you, from the way he spoke, it will be something good. And then you must go to bed and . . . you'll leave a corner for me, I hope,' she added in a tone that was peevish in spite of herself.

'I don't want to eat, I don't want to sleep. Leave me alone. Don't come near me. Don't go away!'

'No, no, there,' said the old woman, drawing away and sitting on a broken-down chair, whence she shot at the poor girl an occasional glance of mingled fear and resentment. Then she would give a look of vexation at her bed, thinking of the possibility of being excluded from it the whole night, and grumble at the cold. But she cheered herself with the thought of the supper, and the hope that there would be some to spare for her. Lucia was not conscious of either cold or hunger, and as if stunned, felt even her griefs and terrors only in a confused way, like feverish dreams.

On hearing a knock she started; and raising a terrified face, cried, 'Who is it? Who is it? Don't let anyone in!'

'No, no; it's good news,' said the old woman. 'It's Martha bringing the food.'

'Shut the door, shut the door!' cried Lucia.

'Ugh! Right away, right away,' replied the old woman, taking a basket from Martha, then sending her off, shutting the door after her, and putting the basket on a table in the middle of the room. Then she invited Lucia again and again to come and partake of the good things, and broke into exclamations about how tasty the food was, using the words most likely, in her opinion, to arouse the poor girl's appetite. 'Lovely morsels such as the likes of us remember a long time when we get a chance of tasting them! The wine the master drinks with his friends . . . when any of them come . . .! And they want to have a good time! Ahem!' but, finding all her lures were in vain, 'It's you who don't want to,' she said. 'Don't you go and tell him tomorrow that I didn't encourage you. I'll eat; and there'll be more than enough left over for you for when you come to your senses and decide to do as you're told.' So saying, she began eating greedily. When she had had her fill she rose, went towards the corner and, stooping down over Lucia, repeated her invitation to eat, and then to go to bed.

'No, no, I don't want anything,' replied the girl in a feeble, almost drowsy, voice. Then she went on more firmly, 'Is the door bolted? Is it bolted properly?' Then she glanced around the room, arose, and went towards it with faltering step and hands in front of her.

The old woman ran there before her, took hold of the bolt, shook it, and said, 'D'you hear? D'you see? It's properly bolted, isn't it? Now are you content?'

'Oh, content! Contented here!' said Lucia, going back to her corner again. 'But the Lord knows I am here!'

'Come to bed. What are you doing there, crouching down like a dog? Why refuse a bit of comfort when you can get it?'

'No, no: leave me alone.'

'Well, it's your choice. Look, I'm leaving you the best place. I'm on the very edge: I'll make myself uncomfortable for your sake. If you want to come to bed, you know what to do.

Remember I asked you again and again.' So saying, she got under the covers fully dressed; and all was silence.

Lucia remained motionless, huddled in her corner, with her knees drawn up, her hands resting on her knees, and her face buried in her hands. As far from sleeping as from waking, across her mind was flitting a rapid succession, a turbid series of thoughts, fancies, and fears. Sometimes her mind would clear, the horrors which she had seen and suffered during the day would come back to her more clearly, and she would dwell agonizingly on the grim and formidable realities of her situation. Sometimes her mind was carried off to even darker regions, where it wrestled with the phantasms born of uncertainty and terror. For some time she remained in the throes of this anguish; finally, more weary and worn than ever, she stretched out her tortured limbs and lay or rather fell down, remaining there some time in a state almost akin to real sleep. But all of a sudden she was aroused as if by some internal call, and felt she must arouse herself completely, retain all her scattered senses, and find out where she was, and how and why she had got there. A sound made her prick up her ears; it was the slow, hoarse snoring of the old woman. She opened her eyes wide, and saw a faint light alternately shining out and disappearing; it was the expiring wick of the lamp, whose tremulous gleams were rising, then quickly falling, like waves ebbing and flowing on a shore, and whose light withdrew from the surrounding objects before they could take clear shape or colour from it, leaving only a succession of muddled glimpses. But recent impressions very soon came back to her, and helped her to make out what her senses found confused. The unhappy girl awoke completely and recognized her prison. All the memories of the horrible day behind her, all the terrors of the future, assailed her together. Even this calm around her now after so much agitation, this semblance of rest, this abandon into which she had let herself fall, inspired her with new terror; and such dread overcame her that she longed for death. But at that moment she remembered that she could at least pray, and with this thought a sudden hope began to dawn in her heart. She took up her rosary again, and began to tell the beads; and as the prayers fell from her trembling lips, she felt a vague confidence growing in her heart. Suddenly another thought crossed her mind: that her prayers would be more acceptable and more likely to be granted if she were to make some offering from the midst of her desolation. She thought of what was dearest to

her on earth, or rather of what had been dearest to her on earth,
for at that moment her mind was capable of feeling no other
emotion than fear and of conceiving no other desire than
freedom: then she remembered what it was, and decided to make
a sacrifice of it at once. She got up on to her knees, and clasping
her hands on her breast, with the rosary dangling from them,
raised her face and eyes to heaven, and said, 'Oh, Most Holy
Virgin! Thou to whom I have so often commended myself, and
who hast so often solaced me; thou who hast borne so many
sorrows, and art now so glorious, and hast performed so many
miracles for the poor and afflicted; help me! Rescue me from this
danger, take me back safely to my mother, oh, Mother of the
Lord! and I make a vow to you to remain a virgin; I renounce my
poor Renzo for ever, in order to be henceforth yours and yours
alone.'

After uttering these words she bowed her head and put her
rosary round her neck as a kind of token of consecration and a
safeguard at the same time, as part of the armour of the new
militia in which she had enlisted. She sat down on the floor again,
and felt a certain calm, a deeper confidence coming over her. The
tomorrow morning repeated by that powerful unknown came
back to her, and she seemed to hear in those words a promise of
deliverance. Her senses, exhausted by so much struggle, were
gradually lulled by these soothing thoughts; and finally, towards
daybreak, with the name of her protectress on her lips, Lucia
sank into a profound unbroken sleep.

But there was another in the same castle who would have liked
to do the same, and could not. After leaving, or almost escaping
from Lucia, and giving orders for her supper, the master of the
house had made his customary visits to the different posts of the
castle, with that image vivid in his mind and those words
resounding in his ears all the time. Then he had flung into his
room and hastily locked himself in, as if he was barricading
himself against a troop of enemies; and after undressing in the
same haste, had thrown himself on his bed. But that image, more
present in his mind now than ever, seemed to be saying to him,
'No sleep for you!' – What silly womanish curiosity – thought he
– was it that made me see her? That fool Nibbio was right; it
unmans one...! I?... I – I unmanned? What has happened?
What the devil has got into me? What's new? Didn't I know
before that women whine? Even men whine sometimes, when

they can't rebel! Devil take it! Haven't I ever heard a woman bleat before? –

And here, without his making much effort to delve into his memory, it produced of its own accord many occasions in which neither entreaties nor laments had been able to deter him from carrying out his purpose. But the memory of these exploits, far from restoring to him the firmness he was now lacking to carry this present one through, far from extinguishing this disturbing sense of pity, stirred up instead a kind of terror, a sort of frenzy of repentance. So that it seemed a relief to go back again to that image of Lucia, against which he had been trying to brace his courage. – She's still alive – he thought. – She's here; I'm still in time. I can still say to her: Go, and be happy again; I can still see that face change, I can still say: forgive me. . . . Forgive me? I ask for forgiveness? And of a woman? I . . .? And yet! If a word – just a word like that – could make me feel well and lift this devilry from my heart, I would say it. Eh! I feel I would say it. See what I'm reduced to. I'm unmanned. Unmanned! . . . Oh, come – he said then, turning angrily over in a bed now become so hard, under blankets now become so heavy – Oh, come! These foolish ideas have passed through my head before. This one will pass, too. –

And to make it pass, he began casting about in his mind for something important to him, something that used to occupy him strongly, so that he could become engrossed in it. But he could find none. Everything seemed changed to him: the things that had always stimulated his desires before no longer had anything desirable about them. His passions, like a horse suddenly become restive at a shadow, refused to carry him forward. When he thought of various enterprises embarked on and not yet concluded, instead of feeling spurred to finish them off, or irritated at any obstacles (for even anger would have been soothing for him at that moment), he felt saddened, almost appalled, at the steps already taken. Time stretched before him void of all purpose, of all occupation, of all desire, full only of intolerable memories, every hour of it like the one which was now passing so slowly, so draggingly over his head. He lined up all his ruffians before him in his imagination, and could think of no order to give them that mattered to him at all – in fact the very thought of seeing them again and being among them was another burden, an idea that revolted and unnerved him. And when he tried to find an occupation for next day, some practicable task, all he

could think of was that next day he could set that poor girl at
liberty.

– I'll set her free; yes. As soon as it's dawn I'll hurry along to
her, and I'll say: Off with you, off with you! I'll give her an
escort. . . . And what about my promise? And my pledge? And
Don Rodrigo? . . . Who's Don Rodrigo, anyway . . .? –

Like someone caught by an unexpected and embarrassing
question from a superior, the unnamed hastily tried to think of
an answer to this query put by himself – or rather by that new
self which had grown so alarmingly all of a sudden, and was
rising up to judge his former self. Then he began searching
around for the reasons which could have led him to assume the
task, almost before being asked, of causing so much suffering to
a wretched unknown girl, without any incentive of hate or fear,
just to do a favour to Don Rodrigo. But, far from being able to
find reasons which now seemed to him valid enough to excuse
his action, he could scarcely explain to himself what had induced
him to make that promise at all. His assent, rather than deliberate, had been the instantaneous reaction of a mind conditioned
by his former habits and feelings, a consequence of a thousand
former actions. And the tormented self-examiner, so as to
account for this one fact, found himself involved in the examination of his whole life. Back, back he went, from year to year,
from feud to feud, from murder to murder, from crime to crime;
each of them came back to his new conscience isolated from the
feelings that had made him want to commit them, so that they
reappeared in all the monstrousness which those feelings had
prevented him noticing. They were all his: they were him; the
horror of this thought, reviving at each fresh memory, clung to
them all, and grew at last to desperation. He sat up, frenzied,
flung out a frenzied arm to the wall by the bed, snatched a pistol,
pulled it down, and . . . just at the moment of finishing off a life
that had become insufferable, his thoughts, assailed as it were by
a posthumous terror and dread, jumped forward into the time
which would still be flowing on after his death. With a shudder
he pictured his mutilated corpse lying motionless at the mercy of
the most abject of his survivors; the surprise and confusion in the
castle next day; everything upside down; and himself, powerless,
speechless thrown down anywhere. He imagined the talk there,
around, far away; and the joy of his enemies. The darkness and
silence around him also made death seem all the gloomier and
more ghastly. He would not have hesitated, it seemed to him, if

it had been day-time, out in the open, facing people; he could fling himself into a river and disappear. And, absorbed in these tormenting reflections, he was raising and lowering the hammer of his pistol with a convulsive movement of the thumb, when another thought came flashing into his mind. – If that other life they used to talk about when I was a boy, and are always talking about still as if it were a sure thing – if that life doesn't exist at all, and it's all an invention of the priests, then what am I doing? Why die? What's it matter what I've done? What difference does it make? It's madness, this.... And if there is that other life....? –

At such a doubt, at such a risk, a blacker, deeper despair than ever came down on him, a despair from which there was no escape – not even in death. He let his weapon drop, and began clawing his hair, his teeth chattering, trembling all over. All of a sudden the words which he had heard repeated again and again a few hours before came back into his mind: – God forgives so much, for one deed of mercy! – And they no longer came back to him in those accents of humble supplication in which they had been uttered, but in a tone full of authority, which induced at the same time a far-away hope. That was a moment of relief. He took his hands from his temples, and with a rather more composed air, fixed his mind's eye on her who had uttered these words; and he saw her, not as his prisoner, not as a suppliant, but in the attitude of one dispensing grace and consolation. He longed for daybreak so that he could rush to set her free, and hear other refreshing, life-giving words from her lips; he imagined himself escorting her back to her mother himself. – And then? What shall I do tomorrow for the rest of the day? What shall I do the day after tomorrow? What shall I do the day after that? And at night? The night, which will come back in twelve hours! Oh, the night! No, no, not the night! – And he fell back to thinking of the empty void of the future, searching in vain for some employment to fill up his time, some way of getting through the days and nights. One moment he thought of abandoning the castle and going away to some far country where no one would know him, even by name; but he realized that his own self would always be with him. Now a dark hope would revive in him of being able to return to his old spirit and inclinations, and that his present state was a passing delirium. Then again he would dread the day, which would show him to his household so miserably changed; then he would long for it, as if it would throw light also into his thoughts. And lo! just as day was breaking, a few minutes after Lucia had fallen asleep, as he sat there motionless, there was borne to his ears a wave of sound, faint, confused, but with something indefinably gay about it. He listened, and made out the distant ringing of festive bells; and a few seconds later he heard the mountain echo languidly repeating the music and blending into it. Shortly afterwards he heard more bells chiming nearer by, these also ringing in celebration; and then more. – What is all this gaiety? What have they got to be so happy about? – He sprang from his bed of thorns, threw on some clothes, ran to open a window, and looked out. The mountains were half veiled in mist; the sky was not so much cloudy as all one ashen-coloured cloud; but in the slowly gathering light people could be distinguished passing along the road at the bottom of the valley; others were coming out of their houses and moving off, all in the same direction towards the defile to the right of the castle, all dressed in holiday clothes, and with unusual alacrity.

– What the devil's up with those people? What reason can there be for this gaiety in this cursed country? Where is all that rabble going? – And he called out to a trusted bravo who always slept in the next room, to ask him for the cause of this stir. The fellow, who knew as little about it as he did, said he would go and find out. The nobleman stood there leaning on the window-sill, all intent on the moving spectacle below. There were men, women, and children, some in groups, some in couples, some alone; one man would catch up with another ahead and go on in his company; another joined the first person he ran into as he left his house; and they went on together, like friends bound on a common journey. Their actions plainly showed a haste and joy common to them all: and that uncoordinated but blended pealing of the various bells, some near, some farther away, seemed, as it were, to be the voice of those gestures and the interpreter of the words which could not carry up there. He looked and looked; and something more than curiosity grew up in his heart to know what it was that could give the same transport of happiness to so many different people.

CHAPTER 22

Shortly afterwards the bravo came back and told him that Cardinal Federigo Borromeo, Archbishop of Milan, had arrived at * * * the day before, and would be there all that day; that the news of his arrival had spread round the surrounding villages that evening and made everyone eager to go and see such a person, and that the bells were ringing more from joy than to inform people of the occasion. Left to himself again, the nobleman went on gazing down into the valley, more thoughtful than ever. – All for one man! All these people eager and happy, just to see one man! And yet each one of them must have his own devil to torment him. But none of them – none of them can have one like mine. None of them will have spent the sort of night I have. What has that man got, to make so many people happy? A few coins to distribute here and there . . . but they can't all be going for alms. Maybe for some sign in the air, some word. . . . Oh, if only he had the words that could soothe me! If only . . .! Why shouldn't I go, too? Why not? . . . I will go, I will go. And I want to talk to him; I want to talk to him alone. What shall I say to him? Oh, well, whatever, whatever . . . I'll hear what he has to say to me first, this man! –

Having come to this confused resolution, he hastily finished dressing, donned a jacket of rather military cut, took the pistol still lying on the bed, hung it on one side of his belt and on the other side another which he took from a nail on the wall, and thrust his dagger into the same belt; next he took down from the wall a carbine whose fame almost rivalled his own, slung it across his shoulders, took up his hat and left the room. First he went straight to where he had left Lucia. Putting his carbine down outside in a corner near the door, he knocked, at the same time calling out. The old woman jumped down from her bed and ran to open the door. Her master entered, glanced round the room, and saw Lucia huddled still and quiet in her corner.

'Is she asleep?' he asked the old woman in a whisper. 'Asleep there? Were those my orders, you old hag?'

'I did my very best,' she replied. 'But she wouldn't eat anything, and she wouldn't come . . .'

'Let her sleep in peace. Take care not to disturb her; and when she wakes up . . . Martha will wait in the next room, and you will send her to get anything the girl asks for. When she wakes

up ... tell her that I ... that the master of the house has gone
out for a little while, and will be back soon, and that ... he'll do
whatever she wants.'

The old woman was astounded. – Can the girl be some
princess? – she was left wondering to herself.

The nobleman went out, took up his carbine again, then sent
Martha to wait in the next room, and the first bravo he met to
mount guard and see that no one except her set foot inside the
room: after which he left the castle and set off down the slope at
a run.

Our manuscript does not say how far it was from the castle to
the village where the cardinal was staying; but judging from the
events which we are about to describe, it could not have been
more than a good walk away. This could not be inferred simply
from the fact that people were flocking there from that valley and
from even farther, for we find in the memoirs of the period that
they would come in crowds for twenty miles and more to see
Federigo.

The bravi whom the unnamed met on the way down stopped
respectfully as their master passed, waiting to see if he had any
orders for them, or if he wanted to take any of them with him on
an expedition, and were at a loss to know what to make of his
manner, and of the scowls which he gave in reply to their bows.

When he got to the highroad, what astonished the passers-by
was to see him without an escort. But they made way for him all
the same, leaving him a wide enough space for an escort to pass
too, and raising their hats respectfully at the same time. On
reaching the village he found a large crowd assembled; but his
name passed quickly from mouth to mouth, and the crowd
opened before him. He stopped someone and asked him where
the cardinal was to be found. 'At the parish priest's,' the man
replied with a bow, and told him where it was. The nobleman
went there and entered a little courtyard in which there were
many priests, who all looked at him with surprised and suspicious
attention. Opposite he saw an open door giving on to a small
parlour, also filled with priests. He took off his carbine, propped
it up in a corner of the courtyard, and entered the little parlour.
There was more staring and whispering there, too, a name being
repeated, then silence. He turned to one of the priests, asked him
where the cardinal was, and said he wanted to speak to him.

'I'm a stranger here,' replied his interlocutor, then glanced
round and called the cardinal's chaplain and cross-bearer, who

was just whispering to a colleague in the corner of the room, 'That man? That notorious man? What's he doing here? Let's give him a wide berth!' But at this call for him resounding in the general silence, he had to come forward. He bowed to the unnamed and stood waiting to hear what he wanted, raising his eyes with uneasy curiosity to the other's face, then lowering them quickly, hesitated a moment, then said, or rather stammered, 'I don't know if his Illustrious Grace ... just at this moment ... is free ... if he can ... but anyway I will go and see.' And very reluctantly he went off to take the message to the cardinal in the adjoining room.

At this point in our story we cannot refrain from pausing awhile – like a traveller wearied and exhausted by long plodding through wild and arid country, who halts and lingers for a time on the grass under the shade of a noble tree, by a stream of running water. We have now fallen in with a person whose name and memory soothe the mind with a sense of quiet reverence and pleasant sympathy, whenever they come back to it – and now more than ever, after so many scenes of pain, and after the contemplation of such manifold and wearisome evil! About this character some few words must be said: anyone who does not care to hear them, but is anxious nevertheless to get on with the story, should skip straight on to the following chapter.

Federigo Borromeo, born in 1564, was one of those men, rare at any period, who have used outstanding talents, all the resources of great wealth, all the advantages of a privileged position and an unflagging diligence, in the quest and practice of the good. His life is like a brook, gushing limpid from the rock without ever going stagnant or turbid, until, after a long passage through many a field, it flows limpid into the river. Since childhood, amidst all the luxury and pomp surrounding him, he had heeded those words of humility and self-denial, those maxims about the vanity of pleasure, about the injustice of pride, about true dignity and true riches, which are handed down from one generation to the next (whether heeded or not by men's hearts) as the most elementary teaching of religion. He listened, I say, to these lessons and maxims, he took them seriously, tested them, and found them true; he saw that, in that case, other opposing lessons and maxims which had also been handed down from generation to generation with the same certainty, and sometimes by the same lips, could not be true: and he resolved to take the ones that were true as guides for his thoughts and actions.

Convinced that life was not destined to be a burden for the many and a holiday for the few, but a responsibility for all, of which each one will have to render an account, he began from childhood to consider how he could make his life useful and holy.

In 1580 he signified his resolution to dedicate himself to the ministry of the Church, and took the habit from the hands of his cousin Carlo,* already proclaimed for some time by universal renown as a saint. Shortly afterwards he entered the college founded by the latter at Pavia, which still bears the name of their family. There he not only applied himself assiduously to the tasks laid down, but assumed two others of his own free will: teaching Christian doctrine to the roughest and most forsaken of the population, and visiting, serving, comforting, and helping the sick. He used the authority which was invested in him by everything about that place to attract his companions into helping him in this work; and he exercised a kind of primacy of example in all that was honest and useful, a leadership which he would probably have gained by his own personal gifts had he come from the lowest station in life. He not only did not seek, but did his best to shun the advantages of other kinds which his station could have procured him. The table he kept was poor rather than frugal, his clothes were poor rather than plain; and the whole tenour of his life and conduct was in conformity with this. Nor did he ever consider changing it, in spite of the complaints and lamentations of some of his relations that he was lowering the family dignity by acting in this way. He also had another struggle to wage with his instructors, who were always trying to foist on or around him, by surprise, some nobler appendage, something to make him stand out from the others and figure as the prince of the place. Either they thought by this to ingratiate themselves in the long run, or they were moved by that servile attachment which takes pride and enjoyment in the splendours of others; or they may have been the kind of prudent folk who shrink from virtue as from vice, and are for ever preaching that perfection lies in the middle – and fix the middle just at the exact point where they have arrived themselves and are comfortably settled. Federigo, far from letting himself be won over by these attempts, reproved those who made them; and this between his boyhood and adolescence.

It is not to be wondered at during the lifetime of Cardinal Carlo, his senior by twenty-six years, whose grave and solemn presence seemed the living expression of holiness and a continual reminder of his works, and whose authority was increased (if that was possible) by the open spontaneous homage of those surrounding him whoever and however many they might be, that Federigo should try to model his childhood and youth on the thought and behaviour of such a superior. But it is certainly remarkable that after his death no one would have noticed that Federigo, then twenty, was now bereft of a critic or a guide. The growing renown of his talents, learning and piety, his relationship and connexion with a number of powerful cardinals, his family standing, his name itself, which Carlo had almost identified with sanctity and pre-eminence – everything, in fact, that should and could lead men to high ecclesiastical dignity, combined to predict it for him. But he was convinced in his heart of what no professing Christian can deny with his lips, that the only real superiority one man can have over others is in his willingness to devote himself to their service, and he both dreaded elevation and tried to avoid it; not certainly because he shrank from serving others – few lives were as much spent in this as his – but because he did not consider himself worthy or capable of such high and perilous service. So when, in 1595, he was offered the archbishopric of Milan by Clement VIII,* he seemed greatly perturbed, and refused without hesitation. Later he yielded to the express command of the pope.

Demonstrations of this kind – and who does not know it? – are neither difficult nor rare; and it requires as little effort of ingenuity each time for hypocrites to make them as it does for wits to deride them. But do they cease, because of that, to be the natural expression of a wise and virtuous impulse? Life itself is the touchstone of words; and words that express such an impulse, even if they have been on the lips of all the impostors and scoffers in the world, will always be beautiful when they are preceded and followed by a disinterested life of sacrifice.

As archbishop, Federigo showed a remarkable and constant care to reserve for himself only such of his wealth, time, and care – only such of himself, in short – as was absolutely necessary. He would say, as everyone says, that the revenues of the Church were the patrimony of the poor; but his way of understanding this may be seen from what follows. He had an estimate made of how much he needed for his personal and household expenses; and on being told it was six hundred *scudi* (*scudo* was the name at that period of the gold piece which was afterwards called a *zecchino*, retaining the same weight and value), he gave orders that this sum should be paid every year from his privy purse into that of his household account, not considering it right that he, with his immense riches, should live on his patrimony. So sparing and niggardly was he with himself that he was careful not to discard any clothes before they were completely worn out; uniting with this taste for simplicity, however, as contemporary writers noted, one for exquisite cleanliness – two habits which were indeed remarkable in that dirty and showy age. In the same way he assigned the remains from his frugal table to a hospital for the poor, so that they should not be wasted, one of the inmates coming into the dining-room every day to collect whatever was left over. These are preoccupations which would, perhaps, suggest a mean, petty, narrow kind of virtue, a mind wrapped up in details and incapable of higher ideas, were it not for the existence of the Ambrosian library,* which Federigo had projected with so much boldness and liberality and so munificently built up from its foundations. In order to stock this library with books and manuscripts (apart from giving his own collection, which he had built up at great trouble and expense), he sent off eight of the most cultivated and expert scholars he could find to buy up others throughout Italy, France, Spain, Germany, Flanders, Greece, the Lebanon, and Jerusalem. In this way he succeeded in getting together about thirty thousand printed volumes and fourteen thousand manuscripts. To the library he attached a college of learned men (there were nine of them at first, maintained at his expense during his lifetime, after which, the ordinary revenues not being enough for this outlay, they were reduced to two); their duties were to cultivate various studies, theology, history, letters, ecclesiastical history, and oriental languages, each of them being obliged to publish some work on the studies assigned to them. To this he also added what he called a 'trilingual college', for the study of Greek, Latin, and Italian, and a school where the pupils were taught these various languages and subjects so as to teach them in their turn one day. To this he added a printing-press for oriental languages – that is, Hebrew, Chaldaic, Arabic, Persian, and Armenian – a gallery of paintings, another of sculpture, and a school for the three principal visual arts. For the latter he was able to find teachers already trained; for the rest, we have seen to what pains he went for the collecting of books and manuscripts. It must certainly have been even more difficult to find the type-fonts of the various languages, which were much less cultivated in Europe then than they are now, and more difficult still than the fonts, the men who could teach them. Suffice it to say that eight of the nine professors were taken from among the young seminarists; from which we may infer his opinion of the scholarship and the reputations made at that period – an opinion that seems to agree with that of posterity, which has let both of them fall into oblivion. The rules which he laid down for the use and organization of the library show the intention of making it perpetually useful, an intention not only fine in itself, but in many particulars far more enlightened and considerate than the ideas and customs usual at that period. He enjoined the librarian to keep in touch with the most learned men in Europe, so as to have news from them of the latest scientific developments, to find out the best works issued on any subject, and to buy them. He also directed him to point out to readers books which they did not know, and which might be useful to them. He laid down that everyone, whether citizen or stranger, should have the time and opportunity to consult the books as much as they wanted. Such a regulation may now seem obvious and inherent in the foundation of a library. But it was not so then. In a history of the Ambrosian written (with all the elaboration and elegance common to the age) by one Pierpaolo Bosca,* who was librarian after Federigo's death, it is expressly noted as something very unusual that in this library, formed by a private citizen almost entirely at his own expense, the books could be seen by the public and given to anyone who asked for them, as were also a chair, and pen, ink, and paper, to take any notes that he might need. In some of the celebrated libraries of Italy of the period, on the other hand, the books were not even visible, but were shut away in cupboards, whence they were taken only by courtesy of the librarian when he felt like showing them for a moment; and the idea that any of those frequenting the library should be given facilities for study never even crossed their minds. So that to enrich libraries of this kind meant to withdraw books from normal circulation – one of those methods of cultivation, of which there were and still are many, and that only make the soil more sterile.

Do not ask what were the effects on the general level of culture of this foundation of Borromeo's. It would be easy to prove in a few phrases, as things are proved, that they were either miraculous or nothing at all; to try and explain more or less what they really were would be wearisome, unconstructive, and irrelevant. But just consider what a generous, wise, benevolent, persevering lover of human betterment must have been the man who planned all this, and planned it in such a way, too, and carried it through amid all the ignorance and inertia and general antipathy for every form of scholarship: in the midst, that is, of remarks like '*What does it matter? Aren't there more important things to think about? What an absurd idea! This is really the limit*', and others of the kind, which were, it is quite certain, far more numerous than the *scudi* spent by him on the undertaking, which amounted to one hundred and fifty thousand, most of them his own.

A man like that could be called supremely beneficent and generous, without our having to add that he spent many other *scudi* on the immediate relief of the needy; and there may still be those who consider that expenditure of the kind I have just described, or even expenditure of any kind, is the best and most useful form of charity. But Federigo considered alms-giving proper as a very first duty; and here, as in everything else, his actions were in accordance with his principles. His life was spent in the continual lavishing of money on the poor. We shall soon, in connexion with this same famine to which our story has already alluded, have occasion to mention several actions of his which show the wisdom and delicacy which he could put into his liberality. We will cite only one of the many outstanding examples of this virtue of his that is noted by his biographers. On hearing once that a certain nobleman was using trickery and pressure to make one of his daughters become a nun when she preferred to get married, he sent for the father; and on getting him to admit that the real motive for his insistence was that he had not got the four thousand *scudi* which he considered necessary to marry off his daughter decently, Federigo gave her a dowry of four thousand *scudi*. This may seem to some people to be rather excessive, rather ill-advised generosity, and over-complaisant towards the foolish caprices of a vain man; and that the four thousand *scudi* could have been better employed in a hundred other ways. To this we have nothing to reply unless it be to wish that we could more often see such excesses of virtue, so free from the prevailing opinions (every age has its own), so independent of the general tendency, as the one which, in this case, moved a man to give four thousand *scudi* so that a young girl should not become a nun.

This man's inexhaustible charity showed not only in his giving but in his whole bearing. Easy of access to all, he felt it a special duty to have a pleasant smile and an affectionate courtesy towards those who are called the lower classes, particularly as they find so little of it in the world. And here he also had to struggle against the gentlemen of the 'ne quid nimis' school,* who would have liked to have kept him within limits in everything – that is, of course, within their own limits. Once, during a visit of Federigo's to a wild and mountainous part of the country, as he was giving some poor children instruction and fondly caressing them between question and answer, one of these people warned him to be more careful in caressing such filthy, repulsive children; almost as if he supposed, the good man, that Federigo had not enough common sense to make this discovery or enough acumen to think of this recondite piece of advice for himself. Such is the misfortune of men in high stations in certain periods and conditions – for while they seldom find anyone to tell them of their failings, they have no lack of people courageous enough to reprove them for their good deeds. 'They are my souls,' replied the good bishop, not without some irritation: 'they may never see my face again, and you don't want me to embrace them?'

But he was very rarely irritated, and was admired for the sweetness of his manner, and for his imperturbable calm; this might be attributed to an unusually happy temperament, but was in fact the result of constant discipline over a disposition naturally lively and impulsive. If there were times when he showed himself severe, even harsh, it was towards those of his subordinate clergy whom he found guilty of avarice or negligence or any other conduct opposed to the spirit of their noble ministry. For anything that affected his own interest or temporal glory he never showed any sign of joy, regret, eagerness, or anxiety; this was, indeed, wonderful if his soul was not stirred by any of these feelings but even more wonderful if it was. Not only did he carry away from the many Conclaves* at which he had assisted the reputation of never having aspired to that office which is so tempting to ambition and so disastrous to piety, but once when a colleague of great influence came to offer him his vote and that of his faction (an ugly word, but the one which they then used), Federigo rejected the suggestion in such a way that the other abandoned the idea and turned elsewhere. This same modesty, this dislike of predominating over others, was equally apparent in the commonest occurrences of life. Assiduous and indefatigable in organizing and commanding when he considered it his duty, he always avoided intruding in other people's affairs, and even did all that he could to avoid doing so when he was asked to; a discretion and restraint unusual, as everyone knows, in men zealous for good like Federigo.

If we allowed ourselves to continue the pleasant task of collecting the remarkable traits in his character, the result would certainly be a strange mixture of merits in apparent contrast to each other, and certainly difficult to find combined. We must not, however, omit to notice another singularity of that admirable life: that, full as it was of every kind of activity, of organizing, functions, teaching, audiences, diocesan visits, of journeys and of controversies, not only did study play a part in it, but it played as much part as would have sufficed for any professional literary man. And in fact, among all the other varied titles for praise, Federigo also enjoyed among his contemporaries that of a man of learning.

We must not conceal, however, that he held firmly in principle and maintained perseveringly in practice certain opinions which would strike everyone at the present day as being not merely ill-founded but odd* – even those most eager to find them sound. There is always, for anyone who wants to defend him on this score, the current accepted excuse, that they were errors of his period rather than his own – an excuse which might have some, even great value, in certain cases, and when deriving from a detailed examination of the facts – but when applied, as it generally is, baldly and at random, means just nothing at all. And that is why, not wishing to solve complicated problems with simple formulas, or lengthen out this episode unduly, we will desist from setting them down; letting it suffice that we have mentioned cursorily that we do not claim everything as being equally admirable in a man so admirable on the whole. For we do not want it to seem as if we meant to write a funeral oration.

We shall certainly not be doing our readers an injustice in supposing that some of them may ask if such a man has not left some monument of all this genius and learning. He has indeed! About a hundred of his extant works, big and small, in Latin and Italian, printed and in manuscript, are preserved in the library which he himself founded; treatises on morals, sermons, dissertations, on history, sacred and profane antiquities, on literature, the arts and various other subjects.

– And how comes it – this reader will ask – that so many works are forgotten, or at least so little known, so little sought after? How comes it that with such talent, such learning, such knowledge of men and affairs, such meditation, such passion for the good and the beautiful, such candour of soul, and with so many other qualities which make up a great writer, this man has not left among those hundred works a single one which is considered outstanding even by those who do not agree with it, and known by its title even by those who have not read it? How comes it that, collectively, they have not been enough to gain, at least by their number, a literary fame with posterity? –

The inquiry is undoubtedly a reasonable one, and the whole question very interesting; because the reasons for this phenomenon are to be found by the observation of many general laws; and when found, they would lead to the explanation of many other similar phenomena. But these reasons would be both numerous and lengthy; and then what if they were found not to be agreeable? What if they made the reader turn up his nose? So it will be better for us to take up the thread of our story once more, and, instead of chattering away about this man any longer, to go and watch him in action, under the guidance of our author.

CHAPTER 23

Cardinal Federigo was studying – as he usually did in any leisure interval – until it was time to go to church and celebrate divine service, when the chaplain came in, looking very disturbed.

'A strange visitor, a very strange visitor indeed, your most Illustrious Grace.'

'Who is it?' asked the cardinal.

'No less a person than the Lord . . .' answered the chaplain, and, accenting the syllables with great significance, he uttered the name which we are unable to write for our readers. Then he added 'He's here outside in person; and is actually asking for an audience, your Illustrious Grace!'

'Him!' exclaimed the cardinal, his face lighting up, and shutting his book as he rose from his chair. 'Let him come in! Let him come in at once!'

'But . . .' replied the chaplain, without stirring, 'your most Illustrious Grace must realize who this man is; he's that outlaw, that notorious . . .'

'And is it not a happy chance for a bishop that a man like that should feel a wish to come and see him?'

'But . . .' insisted the chaplain, 'there are certain things we can't ever mention, because your lordship says they're nonsense. Even so, I feel it my duty, when a case comes up . . . Zeal makes enemies, your Grace; and we know for certain that blackguards have dared to boast that one day or other . . .'

'And what have they done?' interrupted the cardinal.

'I repeat that this man is a dealer in crime, a desperado in contact with the most violent desperadoes, and he may be sent . . .'

'Oh, what kind of discipline is this!' interrupted Federigo, still smiling, 'when troops exhort their general to be timid?' Then, becoming serious and thoughtful, he went on, 'San Carlo would never have found himself in the position of discussing whether or not to receive such a man; he would have gone to him himself. Let him in at once; he has already waited too long.'

The chaplain withdrew, saying to himself, – There's no help for it; these saints are all pigheaded. –

On opening the door, and entering the room where he had left the nobleman and the other priests, he saw the latter drawn on one side, whispering together and giving covert glances at their visitor, who was left alone in a corner. He went towards him, looking him over as best he could out of the corner of his eye, and wondering what arsenal of weapons might be lurking under that jacket of his, and whether really, before admitting him, he ought to suggest that he should at least . . . But he could not get up enough courage. On coming up to him, he said, 'His Grace awaits your lordship. Would you be so good as to come with me?' And as he preceded him through the little crowd, which made way at once, he kept giving glances to right and left which meant, What can I do? Don't you all know yourselves that he always goes just his own way?

Hardly had the unnamed entered the room than Federigo went forward to meet him, with a frank and eager look, and arms outstretched as if to a welcome guest. Then he quickly signed to the chaplain to withdraw; the latter obeyed.

The two of them stood there in silence for a while, each hesitating for different reasons. The unnamed, who had been carried there by an inexplicable urge rather than led there by any definite purpose, now remained there as if under compulsion, torn between two contending emotions, one a longing and a confused hope of finding some relief from his inner torments, and the other shame and annoyance at coming there like some submissive and miserable penitent, to confess his guilt and implore another man's pardon. No words would come, and he scarcely tried to find any. But on raising his eyes to the other's face, he found himself penetrated more and more by a peremptory yet sweet feeling of veneration, which increased his confidence, soothed down his vexation, and subdued, almost, as it were, silenced his pride without making any frontal attack on it.

Federigo, in fact, had one of those presences which proclaim their superiority, yet make themselves beloved. His bearing was naturally dignified, with an unconscious majesty, and was in no way bowed or slackened by age. His eye was grave and lively, his forehead open and thoughtful. In spite of his pallor and grey hairs, in spite of the traces of abstinence, meditation, and labour, there was still a kind of virginal bloom about him. His features showed that he had once been handsome in the strict sense of the word. Now the habits of solemn and benevolent thought, the inward peace of a long life, the love of his fellow-creatures, the continuous joy of ineffable hope, had substituted for this a kind of beauty of old age, thrown into stronger relief by the sumptuous simplicity of the purple.

He, too, kept his penetrating gaze fixed for some time on the countenance of the unnamed, and, long used as he was to deducing thoughts from appearances, seemed to find under that dark and troubled mien something that corresponded more and more with the hopes which he had conceived at the first announcement of this visit. 'Oh,' he said, with animation, 'what a welcome visit this is! And how grateful I should be to you for making such a good decision; although for me it comes as a bit of a reproach!'

'A reproach!' exclaimed the nobleman in great surprise, but softened by those words and that manner, and pleased that the cardinal had broken the ice and got the conversation under way.

'Certainly it's a reproach to me,' went on the latter; 'for letting myself be forestalled by you; when for such a long time, for so many times, I should have come to see you myself.'

'*You* come to *me*! Do you know who I am? Did they tell you my name?'

'Do you think that I should have felt this joy, which must certainly show on my face, at the announcement and the sight of a stranger? It is you who have made me feel it; you, I say, whom I should have sought out; you whom at least I have so long loved and lamented and so often prayed for; you whom of my children, much as I love them all, I should most have longed to welcome and embrace, had I ever felt there was any hope of it. But God alone can perform miracles and make up for the weakness and slowness of His poor servants.'

The unnamed was amazed at this impassioned speech, at these words which replied so definitely to what he had not yet said or quite made up his mind to say, and stood there in silence, moved but dumbfounded. 'What!' went on Federigo, still more affectionately; 'you have good news to give me, and keep me in suspense for so long?'

'*I* have good news, I? I whose heart is a hell; how can I have good news for you? Tell me, if you know it, what is this good news you are expecting from a man like me?'

'That God has touched your heart, and wants to make you His,' replied the cardinal calmly.

'God! God! God! If only I could see Him! if only I could feel Him! Where is this God?'

'You ask me that? You? And who is nearer to Him than you? Don't you feel Him in your heart, weighing you down, worrying you, never letting you be, and drawing you on at the same time, tempting you with a hope of tranquillity and consolation, a consolation which will be full, immense, as soon as you recognize Him, acknowledge Him, implore Him?'

'Oh yes, truly! I have something here weighing me down, eating me away! But God! If there is this God, if He is what they say, what use do you expect Him to have for me?'

These words were spoken in accents of despair; but Federigo replied in solemn tones, as of quiet inspiration: 'What use can God have for you? What use has He for you? To be a sign of His power and His goodness. He wants to derive a glory from you that no one else could give Him. If the world has been crying out against you for so long, if thousands upon thousands of voices have been raised to execrate your misdeeds . . .' (the unnamed started, seized for a moment with amazement at hearing language to which he was so unused, and even more at finding that he felt no indignation but almost relief at it). 'What glory,' went on Federigo, 'will that bring to God? Those are cries of terror, of self-interest; of justice, too, maybe, but of such an easy, obvious justice! Some of them, perhaps, spring from envy of your appalling power, and of that certainty of mind that has been so deplorable until today. But when you yourself rise up and condemn your past life, and become your own accuser, ah, then!

then shall God be glorified indeed! And you ask what use God can have for you? Who am I, a poor mortal, to tell you the use such a Lord can have for you? what use He can make of your impetuous will and your dauntless perseverance, when He has animated and inflamed them with love and hope and repentance? Who are you, a poor mortal, to think yourself capable of devising and doing greater evils than the good God can make you will and perform? What use can God have for you? Can He not pardon you? Save you? Carry out the work of redemption in you? Are these things not magnificent and worthy of Him? Ah, just think! If I, a creature so weak and miserable, who am yet so full of myself, if I, such as I am, so long now for your salvation that (let Him be my witness) I would gladly give these few remaining days of mine for it – think – how great, how deep, must be the love of Him who inspires me with a love so imperfect and yet so lively. How He must love you, how He must want you, when He orders and inspires in me a love for you that devours my being!'

As these words came from his lips, his face, his expression, his every movement, was instinct with his feelings. His listener's face, from being anguished and convulsed, had become at first astonished and intent, then composed itself into a look of deeper, less agonizing emotion. His eyes, which had never wept since childhood, swelled with tears; and when the words ceased he covered his face with his hands, and gave himself up to unrestrained weeping, which was his final and clearest reply.

'Great and good God!' exclaimed Federigo, raising his eyes and hands to heaven, 'what have I, Thy useless servant, Thy idle shepherd, done that Thou shouldst call me to this banquet of grace, that Thou shouldst think me worthy to assist at such a joyful miracle?' So saying, he stretched his hand out to take that of the unnamed.

'No!' cried the latter. 'No! Keep away, away from me. Do not soil that innocent, generous hand. You do not realize all that has been done by this one you want to clasp.'

'Let me,' said Federigo, taking it with affectionate violence – 'let me clasp this hand that will repair so many wrongs, that will dispense so many benefits, that will succour so many afflicted, and will be stretched out unarmed, in peace and humility, to so many enemies.'

'It is too much,' sobbed the unnamed. 'Leave me, your Grace; leave me, good Federigo. Crowds of people are awaiting you; so

many innocent souls, so many who have come from afar to see
and hear you just once; and you stay back talking . . . to me!'

'Let me leave the ninety-nine sheep,' replied the cardinal. 'They
are safe on the mountain-side; I want now to be with the one
that was lost.* Those others are much happier now, maybe, than
looking at this unworthy bishop of theirs. Perhaps God, who has
wrought a miracle of mercy on you, may be diffusing over them
a joy of which as yet they do not know the cause. These people
are perhaps united to us without being aware of it; the Holy
Spirit may be filling their hearts with an undefined glow of
charity, a prayer in your favour, a thanksgiving of which you are
the as yet unknown object.' So saying, he threw his arms around
the unnamed's neck. The latter, after making an effort to extricate
himself and putting up a momentary resistance, yielded, as if
overborne by this impetus of love, and embraced the cardinal in
his turn, burying his trembling, altered features on his shoulder.
His burning tears fell on the unstained purple of Federigo, whose
guiltless hands affectionately clasped those arms, and pressed
against the jacket used to bearing the weapons of violence and
treachery.

When the unnamed finally disengaged himself from this
embrace, he covered his eyes again with one hand, and, raising
his face at the same time, exclaimed, 'God is great indeed. God is
indeed good. Now I know myself. Now I understand what I am.
My crimes stand before me. I shudder with horror at myself. And
yet . . . and yet I feel a relief, a joy that I have never felt in all this
horrible life of mine.'

'This is a foretaste,' said Federigo, 'that God gives you to draw
you into His service, to encourage you to enter resolutely upon
the new life in which you will have so much to undo, so much to
repair, so much to regret.'

'Wretch that I am!' exclaimed the nobleman. 'How many –
how very many – things there are that I can do nothing but
regret! But at least I have undertakings, scarcely begun, which I
can break off in the middle, if nothing else. There's one I can
break off and undo and repair at once.'

Federigo became all attention; and the unnamed then described
briefly, but in terms of even stronger execration than those which
we have used, the outrage done to Lucia, the poor girl's anguish
and terror, and how she had begged him, and the frenzy into
which these entreaties had thrown him, and how she was still up
at the castle. . . .

'Hah, let us lose no time!' exclaimed Federigo, breathless with pity and compassion. 'How blessed you are! This is an earnest of God's pardon. He has enabled you to become an instrument of salvation where you intended to be one of ruin. May God bless you. God has blessed you already. Do you know where she comes from, this poor, unhappy girl of yours?'

The nobleman named Lucia's village.

'It is not far from here,' said the cardinal. 'May God be praised; and probably . . .' So saying, he hurried to a table and rang a little bell. The chaplain came anxiously in, and his first glance was at the unnamed. At the sight of that changed face and those eyes red with weeping, he looked at the cardinal; and noticing under that unalterable composure a look on his face of a kind of grave contentment and almost impatient concern, he was just about to go into open-mouthed ecstasy, had not the cardinal quickly roused him from his contemplation by asking him if the parish priest of * * * was among the priests assembled in the other room.

'He is, your most Illustrious Grace.'

'Bring him in at once,' said Federigo, 'and the priest of this parish here with him.'

The chaplain withdrew, and entered the room where all those priests were gathered. All eyes turned towards him. And he, with his mouth still open and that look of rapture still all over his face, said, raising his hands and waving them in the air, 'Friends! friends! *Haec mutatio dexterae Excelsi!*'* and stood there a moment without uttering another word. Then, reassuming the tone and manner of his office, he added, 'His most illustrious and most reverend lordship wants to see the priest of the local parish here, and the priest of the parish of * * *.'

The first one summoned came forward at once; and at the same time from the middle of the crowd there came a long-drawn 'Me?' in a tone of amazement.

'Aren't you the parish priest of * * *?' the chaplain went on.

'Yes, to be sure; but . . .'

'His most illustrious and most reverend lordship wants to see you.'

'Me?' said the same voice again, the monosyllable clearly expressing, What have I to do with it? But this time, with the voice emerged the man himself, Don Abbondio in person, with a dragging step, and an expression of mingled wonder and disgust. The chaplain beckoned him with a hand as if to say: Here, come along; why all the fuss? And, going ahead of the two priests, he went to the door, opened it, and ushered them in.

The cardinal let go the hand of the unnamed, with whom he had been meanwhile arranging what was to be done, drew a little aside, and beckoned to the local priest. He told him the story briefly, and asked him if he could find a trustworthy woman at once to go off in a litter to the castle and fetch Lucia – a sensible woman with a warm heart, who would know how to behave on such a novel expedition, and would have the right manner and find the words most likely to hearten and soothe the poor girl, who might find herself after so much suffering and distress, thrown into confusion once more by liberation itself. The priest thought a moment, said that he knew the very woman for it, and withdrew. The cardinal then beckoned the chaplain again, and ordered him to get a litter and postilions ready at once, and two mules saddled. When the chaplain had also left, he turned to Don Abbondio.

The latter was already close to him, in order to keep as far away as he could from that other nobleman, and was giving covert glances meanwhile first at one and then at the other, trying to puzzle out what all this bustle was about. Now he came still closer, made a bow, and said, 'They have given me to understand that your most Illustrious Grace wanted me; but they must have been mistaken, I think.'

'They were not mistaken,' replied Federigo. 'I have good news to give you, and a most pleasant and agreeable task for you. One of your parishioners, whom you will have lamented as lost, Lucia Mondella, has been found, and nearby, at the house of this dear friend of mine here. And you will go with him now, together with a woman whom the priest here has gone to find – you'll go, I say, fetch this poor member of your flock, and accompany her back here.'

Don Abbondio did all he could to conceal the vexation, nay, the alarm and dismay which this suggestion, or order rather, gave him; and not having time to smooth off or wipe away a grimace that had already formed on his face, he hid it by bowing his head down deeply in sign of obedience. And he only raised it to make another deep bow to the unnamed, with a piteous look in his eye which seemed to say: I'm in your hands; have pity on me; *parcere subjectis.*

The cardinal then asked him what relations Lucia had.

'The only close relation she has, who lives or lived with her, is her mother,' replied Don Abbondio.

'And she's at her own village?'

'Yes, your Grace.'

'As,' went on Federigo, 'this poor girl cannot be restored to her own home right away, it would be a great consolation to her to see her mother without delay; so if the local priest here has not come back before I go into church, please ask him to find a cart or a horse, and send a responsible person to fetch the mother and bring her here.'

'How about if I went?' said Don Abbondio.

'No, no, not you; I have already asked you to do something else,' replied the cardinal.

'I meant,' rejoined Don Abbondio, 'to break the news to the poor mother. She's a very sensitive woman; and someone's needed who knows her, and can treat her in the right way, or he'll do more harm than good.'

'That is why I asked you to tell the priest here to choose a tactful person; you are much more necessary elsewhere,' answered the cardinal. What he meant was: that poor girl has far more need to see a face which she knows, a person whom she trusts, after so many hours of agony and ghastly uncertainty about the future in that castle; but this was not a reason that could be so bluntly put before the third party present. The cardinal, however, found it strange that Don Abbondio had not guessed or thought of this for himself, and his suggestion and insistence seemed so much out of place that he thought there must be something behind it. He looked him in the face, and easily read there the fear of travelling with that alarming person-age, and of entering that fearful house, even if only for a few minutes. Wishing therefore to dispel these cowardly apprehen-sions, and being loath to take the priest aside and whisper to him secretly in the presence of his new friend, he decided that the best thing to do was what he would have done without this motive, and talk to the unnamed himself; and Don Abbondio would then realize from his replies that he was no longer a man to be frightened of. So he went up to the unnamed, and with that air of spontaneous familiarity which goes with strong new affections as well as with intimacies of long standing, 'Don't think,' he said, 'that I'm going to be satisfied with this one visit for today. You will come back, won't you, with this good priest here?'

'Come back?' answered the unnamed. 'Even if you refuse to

see me, I should stay stubbornly outside your door like a beggar. I need to talk to you; I need to listen to you, to see you! I need you!'

Federigo took his hand, pressed it and said, 'Then please stay and dine with us. I shall expect you. Meanwhile, I am going to pray, and to offer up thanks with the people; and you are going to reap the first-fruits of mercy.'

At these demonstrations Don Abbondio stood there like a timid boy who sees a huge shaggy dog, with red eyes and a great reputation for biting and snarling, being patted confidently on the head by its master, and hears him say that his dog is really a nice, very quiet beast; he looks at the master and does not contradict or assent; he looks at the dog, and dares neither to approach him, for fear that the nice quiet beast might show his teeth if only in jest, nor to withdraw for fear of attracting attention; and he says in his heart – Oh, if only I were safe at home! –

As the cardinal, still holding the unnamed by the hand and drawing him along with him, started for the door, he gave another glance at the poor man, who was hanging back, looking woebegone and discontented, and making a long face in spite of himself. And thinking that this vexation of his might come from a feeling that he was being overlooked and put in a corner, particularly by contrast with the warm reception given to a malefactor, he turned in passing, paused a moment with an amiable smile, and said, 'Father, you are always with me in the house of our good Lord; but this . . . this man *perierat et inventus est.*'*

'Oh, I'm so pleased to hear it!' said Don Abbondio, making a deep bow to both of them in common.

The archbishop went on ahead, and pushed at the door, which was at once flung open from outside by two footmen, one on each side of it; and the remarkable couple appeared before the eager eyes of the clergy assembled in the room. They gazed on those two faces, each of them with a different but equally profound emotion depicted on it: tender gratitude and a humble joy on the venerable features of Federigo; confusion tempered with relief, a new modesty, a keen remorse on those of the unnamed, which still showed, however, the vigour of his wild and fiery nature. Several of the spectators, so it turned out afterwards, had been reminded of that saying of Isaiah, '*The wolf also shall dwell with the lamb; and the lion shall eat straw like the ox.'* Behind them came Don Abbondio, of whom no one took any notice.

When they were in the middle of the room, the cardinal's chamberlain came in from the other side and approached to tell him that he had carried out the orders given him by the chaplain, that the litter and the two mules were ready, and that they were only awaiting the arrival of the woman whom the priest was to fetch. The cardinal told him to tell the priest to talk to Don Abbondio as soon as he arrived; everything was under the direction of the latter and of the unnamed, whose hand he shook again in farewell, repeating, 'I shall expect you.' He turned to greet Don Abbondio, then set off in the direction of the church. The clergy followed after in something between a procession and a mob, and the two travelling companions were left behind alone in the room.

The unnamed was standing there all absorbed, deep in thought, impatiently waiting for the moment to go and set his Lucia free from her anxieties and her prison – his Lucia now in so different a sense from the day before; and his face expressed an intense agitation, which might easily seem something worse to the suspicious eye of Don Abbondio, who was looking at him out of the corner of his eye, and would have liked to start a friendly conversation with him; but – What am I to say to him? – he was thinking. – Ought I to say, I'm so glad, again? But what am I so glad about? That, after being a fiend up to now, you've finally decided to become a decent person like everyone else? Some compliment! Oh, oh, oh! However I twist them, my congratulations can't mean anything else but that. And then, has he really become a decent person? All of a sudden like that! So many demonstrations are made in this world, and for so many reasons. How can I know, anyway? And meanwhile, it's fallen on me to go with him! Into that castle! Oh, what a thing to happen! Who could have guessed it this morning! Ah, if only I can get out of this safely Perpetua shan't hear the end of it for forcing me to come along here, when there was no need to, all the way from my parish; telling me all the parish priests from round about and even farther away were hurrying here – and that I mustn't lag behind – and this, and that, and the other; and then she goes and gets me involved in an affair like this! Oh, woe is me! And yet I'll have to say something to him. – And, after thinking it over and over, he had found something he could have said – that he had never expected to have the good fortune to travel in such honourable company – and was just opening his mouth to say it, when the chamberlain came in with the village priest. He announced that the woman was waiting in the litter, and then turned to Don Abbondio to get the cardinal's other instructions from him. Don Abbondio conveyed them as best he could in his confused state of mind, and then went up to the chamberlain and said, 'Do at least give me a quiet beast; for, to tell the truth, I'm not much of a horseman.'

'Of course,' answered the chamberlain with a half-grin. 'It's the secretary's mule, and he's a literary man.'

'That will do . . .' replied Don Abbondio, still thinking inside himself – Pray Heaven it's gentle. –

The nobleman had strode quickly off on first hearing the news; when he got to the door he remembered Don Abbondio, who had stayed behind. He paused to wait for him, and when he came bustling up looking apologetic, bowed to him and made him pass through the door first, with a courteous and humble air: which calmed the poor afflicted man's nerves a little. But scarcely had he set foot in the courtyard than he saw another novelty which spoiled his little satisfaction: he saw the unnamed stride to a corner, grasp his carbine by the barrel in one hand and by the strap in the other, and then, with a brisk movement, as though he were at drill, sling it over his shoulder.

Oh dear! Oh dear! Oh dear! – thought Don Abbondio – what's the fellow going to do with that contraption? A find kind of hair shirt and penance for a new convert! And suppose some little whim takes him? Oh, what an errand! What an errand! –

Had the nobleman the least suspicion of the kind of thoughts passing through his companion's mind, we cannot say what he might have done to reassure him; but he was a thousand miles away from any such suspicion; and Don Abbondio was carefully avoiding making any movement that would clearly mean: I don't trust your lordship. On reaching the street door, they found the two animals ready waiting. The unnamed leapt on to one which had been led up to him by a groom.

'He's not got any bad habits?' Don Abbondio asked the chamberlain, lowering to the ground again a foot which he had already raised towards the stirrup.

'You can mount with an easy mind; he's a lamb.' Don Abbondio, clinging to the saddle, was hoisted up inch by inch by the chamberlain, until finally he was astride.

The litter, which was some paces ahead borne by two mules,

moved off at a word from the postilion; and the convoy got under way.

They had to pass in front of the church, crammed full of people, and through a little square, full also of more people from the village and outside, who had not been able to get into the church. The great news had already got round; and at the appearance of the party, and of the man who, only a few hours before, had been an object of hatred and terror, and was now one of delighted amazement, a murmur of something like applause went up among the crowd; and as they made way, they jostled each other to get a close view of him. The litter passed, the unnamed passed; and before the open door of the church he raised his hat and bowed that dreaded forehead down to the mane of his mule, amid a hundred voices murmuring 'God bless you!' Don Abbondio also raised his hat and bowed down, recommending himself to Heaven; but when he heard his brother-priests solemnly chanting in chorus, he felt such envy, such melancholy tenderness, such grief, that he only just managed to restrain his tears.

When they were beyond human habitation and in the open country, going along the twists and turns of a road that was sometimes entirely deserted, a blacker cloud than ever settled over his thoughts. The only object on which he could rest his eyes with any confidence was the postilion, who, being in the cardinal's service, was presumably an honest man, and did not look like a coward. Every now and again passers-by would appear, also in groups, hurrying to see the cardinal. These were a relief for Don Abbondio; but only a transitory relief, for he himself was going towards that fatal valley, where there was no one to be met but the subjects of his friend there – and what subjects! More than ever he longed to enter into conversation with this friend, both to sound him out a little more, and to keep him in a good humour; but this desire left him on seeing him so deep in thought. So he had to fall back on talking to himself; and here is just a part of what the poor man said to himself during that journey; for to put it all down would be enough to fill a book.

– How true the saying is that saints as well as sinners must have quicksilver running through them, and, not content with always being on the move, would like to set the whole human race rushing about too if they could. And then the biggest busybodies of the lot must needs go and light on me, who never bothers anyone, and lug me into their affairs by the hair, me who asks for nothing else than to be left alone. That mad rascal of a Don Rodrigo! What's to prevent him from being the happiest man on earth, if only he had just a bit of sense? He's rich, he's young, he's respected, he's courted; he's bored with being too well-off; so he has to go and make trouble for himself and others; he could do the same job as Michelaccio;* but no, sir; he must needs go and take to molesting women; which is about the maddest, silliest, wildest job in this world; he could ride to Paradise in a coach and six, and prefers to go to hell on his own limping feet. And this other fellow! – and here he gave a look as if he suspected that that other fellow could read his thoughts – this other fellow, after turning the place upside down with his villainies, is now turning it upside down with his conversion . . . if it's a real conversion. Meanwhile, it's I who have to test it out! . . . But there's nothing for it; when people are born with that fever in their bodies, they must always be causing some upset or other. Is it really so difficult to be a decent citizen all one's life, as I've been? But no, sir. They must needs be slashing and killing and playing the devil . . . oh, poor me! . . . And then causing another upset, even with their repentance. One can repent in one's own home, if one wants to, quietly, without making so much fuss about it, and without being such a nuisance to one's neighbours. And then his Illustrious Grace is all open arms straightaway, and it's dear friend, sweet friend; drinking in everything he said as if he'd seen him do miracles; and then rushing into decisions right off, throwing himself into them with both hands and feet, with a 'quick here', and a 'quick there'; in my book that's called being hasty. And then, without the slightest security, he goes and delivers a poor priest right into his hands! That's what's called playing heads or tails with a man's life. A bishop, as holy as him, ought to value his curates like the apple of his eye. A bit of level-headedness, a bit of prudence, a bit of consideration, can go with saintliness, too, it seems to me. . . . And supposing it's all just a sham? Who can fathom all men's motives? Particularly men like this? To think I've got to go with him into his own house! Can there be any devilry behind it? Oh, poor me! It's best not to think about it. How did Lucia get mixed up in this? Was there some understanding with Don Rodrigo? What people! But at least that would be something you could make sense of. But how did she get into this man's clutches? Who can tell? It's all a secret with his Grace. And they don't tell me a thing, when they're making me trot about like this! I don't want to pry into other people's affairs, but when one's risking one's life one has a right to know something. If it really was only to go and fetch that poor girl, then patience! Though he might as well have brought her down with him in the first place. And besides, if he's really so converted, if he's become such a holy father, what need is there of me? Oh, what a mess! Ah, well, let's hope to heaven that it is true. It will have been most inconvenient, but there it is. I'd be pleased for that poor Lucia's sake also; she must have had a narrow escape, too. Heaven only knows what she's been through; I'm sorry for her; but she was born to be my undoing. . . . If only I could see what this man thinks right in his heart. How can one fathom him? There he is, looking like Saint Anthony in the desert one moment, and Holofernes in person the next.* Oh, poor me! Poor me! Anyway; heaven's under an obligation to help me out, as I didn't come into this from any whim of my own. –

The thoughts could, in fact, be seen chasing each other across the unnamed's face, like the clouds over the face of the sun during a storm, alternating one moment to the next from dazzling light to black gloom. His mind, still intoxicated by Federigo's sweet words, and as if renewed and rejuvenated with new life, would rise to those ideas of mercy, pardon, and love; then it would fall back again under the weight of the terrible past. He searched anxiously about to find any crimes that were still reparable, which could be stopped half-way, and to find the quickest and surest way of doing so; how to disentangle so many knots, and what to do with so many accomplices. It made him dizzy to think about it. Even on this present expedition, which was the easiest and nearest to completion, he was going along with mingled impatience and anguish, as he thought of what that poor girl was suffering meanwhile – God only knew how much – and that it was he, although he was now hurrying to free her, who was responsible for her suffering. At every fork in the road the postilion would turn round to find out which way to take: the unnamed would point with a hand and sign to him to hurry at the same time.

They entered the valley. And what a state poor Don Abbondio was in then! That notorious valley, about which he had heard so many horrible tales; and now to be inside it! Those notorious men, the flower of the bravi of Italy, those men who were without fear and without pity. To see them in flesh and blood! To meet

one or two of them at every turn of the road! They bowed down
to their master humbly enough. But oh, those weather-beaten
faces! Those bristling mustachios! Those glances that seemed to
Don Abbondio to be saying: Shall we give this priest a little treat?
Such a point of extreme consternation did he reach that he even
began saying to himself, – I wish I *had* married them! I couldn't
have fared worse! – Meanwhile they were going along a stony
path skirting the torrent, with the view of harsh, dark, barren
rocks on one side and a population which made any desert seem
desirable on the other. Dante was in no worse case in the midst
of Malebolge.*

They passed in front of Malanotte; bravi, at the door; bows to
their master, glances at his companion and at the litter. Those
men did not know what to think; already the unnamed's departure all alone that morning had been extraordinary enough; his
return was no less so. Was this some prize he was bringing with
him? And how had he managed all on his own? And why a
strange litter? And whose livery could that be? They looked and
looked, but none moved, for such was the order they read in
their master's glance.

They climb the slope, they reach the top. The bravi, on the
terrace and at the gates draw back on either side to let them
through. The unnamed signs to them not to make any other
move, spurs, and passes ahead of the litter; beckons the postilion
and Don Abbondio to follow him; passes through an outer
courtyard, and thence into another; goes towards a small doorway, waving back a bravo who is hurrying to hold the stirrup,
and says to him, 'You stay here, and see no one comes.' He
dismounts, hurriedly ties the mule to an iron grille, goes to the
litter and up to the woman, who has drawn back the curtain, and
whispers to her, 'Try to comfort her at once; make her understand
she's free and in friendly hands. God will reward you for it,' and
signs to the postilion to open the door. Then he turns to Don
Abbondio, and with an air of greater serenity than the latter had
ever seen or ever thought to see on his face, transfigured with the
joy of seeing the good work finally nearing completion, says to
him, still in a whisper, 'Your reverence, I must apologize for the
inconvenience you are being put to on my account. You are
doing it for One who repays well, and for this poor creature of
His here.' So saying, he takes the bridle in one hand, and the
stirrup in the other, to help Don Abbondio dismount.

That look, those words, that action, had put new life into Don

Abbondio. He let out a sigh, which had been turning round inside him for the last hour without ever finding a way out, bowed towards the unnamed, and answered in a faint voice, 'Not at all! Please, please, please...!' and scrambled down from his mount as best he could. This the unnamed also tied up, and telling the postilion to wait for them there, took a key from his pocket and opened the door. He entered, ushered in the priest and the woman, then went ahead of them to a stairway, which all three mounted in silence.

CHAPTER 24

Lucia had woken a short time before; and of that time, part had been painfully spent in struggling to wake completely and separate the turbid visions of her dreams from the memories and images of a reality which was only too like the horrible visions of sickness. The old woman had approached her at once, and said in that forced humble tone of hers, 'Ah, you've slept? You could have slept in the bed; I told you so again and again last night too.' And, not getting any reply, she had gone on, always in that same tone of peevish entreaty, 'Now do eat something, won't you? Be sensible. Ugh, how awful you look! You need to eat up. And suppose when he comes back, he blames it on me?'

'No, no; I want to go away, I want to go to my mother. Your master promised me I should; tomorrow morning, he said. Where is he now?'

'He's gone out; but he told me he'd be back soon, and he'd do whatever you wanted.'

'Did he say that? Did he say that? Then, I want to go to my mother, at once, at once.'

And just at that moment there was the sound of footsteps in the adjoining room; then a tap at the door. The old woman ran to it, and asked, 'Who's there?'

'Open,' the well-known voice answered in subdued tones. The old woman drew the bolt; the unnamed opened the door slightly with a gentle push and told the old woman to come out and let in Don Abbondio and the good matron. Then he pulled the door to again, and waited outside it, sending the old woman off to a remote part of the castle, as he had already done with the other servant who had been keeping guard outside.

All this stir, that momentary suspense, the first appearance of newcomers, had made Lucia's heart bound with agitation, for to her, intolerable as her present situation was, every change was a cause for suspicion and fresh alarm. She looked, saw a priest and a woman, and took heart a little. She looked more closely; was it he or wasn't it? Then she recognized Don Abbondio, and stayed there with staring eyes, as if she were under a spell. The woman went up to her, and, bending over her with a look of compassion, took hold of her hands as if to caress her and raise her up at the same time, saying, 'Oh, my poor child! Now come, come along with us.'

'Who are you?' Lucia asked her; but, without waiting for her reply, she turned back to Don Abbondio, who had stopped a few paces from her, with an expression that was also full of compassion; she gazed at him fixedly again, then exclaimed, 'You! It's really you? Our parish priest? Where are we? . . . Oh, woe is me, I'm out of my senses!'

'No, no,' answered Don Abbondio. 'It really is me. Cheer up! We've come to take you away, d'you see? It really is your priest, come on purpose, astride a mule too. . . .'

As if suddenly getting all her strength back, Lucia started quickly to her feet, gazed fixedly at those two faces again, and said, 'Then it's Our Lady who must have sent you.'

'I think it must be,' said the good woman.

'But can we go away, can we really go away?' went on Lucia, lowering her voice and giving a timid and suspicious look around. 'What about all these people . . .?' she went on, her lips still contracted and quivering with terror and horror. 'And that lord . . .? That man . . .? Oh, yes, he did promise me . . .'

'He's here in person, too, come with us on purpose,' said Don Abbondio. 'He's waiting outside. Let's get going: we mustn't keep a man of his rank waiting.'

Just then the person of whom they were speaking pushed open the door and showed himself. A short time before, Lucia had been longing for him to appear – in fact, since she had had no other hope in the world, she had been longing for nothing except him; but now, after seeing friendly faces and hearing friendly voices, she could not restrain a sudden shudder; she started, gasped, hugged the good woman close, and buried her face in her bosom. The unnamed, when he saw that face on which he had been unable to gaze steadfastly the evening before, and which prolonged suffering and abstinence had made paler, more dejected, more wasted than ever, had stopped short almost on the threshold. Now, seeing her attitude of terror, he cast down his eyes, and stood there another moment silent and motionless; then, answering the question which the poor girl had not put into words, 'It's true,' he exclaimed. 'Forgive me!'

'He has come to free you. He's not the same person. He's become good. Don't you hear him asking you to forgive him?' said the good woman in Lucia's ear.

'What more could he say? Come, up with that head. Don't be a baby. And we can get off at once,' said Don Abbondio to her. Lucia raised her head, looked at the unnamed, and seeing that forehead bowed, those eyes lowered and abashed, she was moved by mixed feelings of relief, gratitude, and pity, and said, 'Oh, my lord! May God reward you for your mercy!'

'And you, a hundredfold, for the good these words of yours do me.'

So saying, he turned towards the door, and went out first. Lucia, now completely reassured, followed leaning on the woman's arm; Don Abbondio brought up the rear. They went down the stairs, and reached the door giving onto the courtyard. The unnamed threw it open, went to the litter, opened the door, and with a gentleness bordering on timidity (two things new for him) held Lucia's arm and helped her into it, and the good matron after her. He then untied Don Abbondio's mule, and helped him to mount.

'Oh, what condescension!' said the latter; and mounted much more nimbly than he had the first time. The party moved off when the unnamed was also in the saddle. His brow was high once more, his eye had resumed its wonted look of command. The bravi they met read the signs of deep thought and unusual preoccupation on his face; but more than that they did not, and could not, understand. At the castle nothing was yet known of his great change of heart; and certainly none of them could ever have reached such a conclusion by guesswork.

The good woman had at once drawn the curtains of the litter. Then, taking Lucia's hands affectionately, she set to work to comfort her with words of pity, tenderness, and congratulation. And, seeing how the confusion and obscurity of all these happenings, as well as the exhaustion from so much suffering, was preventing the poor girl from tasting the joy of her liberation to the full, she told her what she thought was most likely to disentangle, as it were, and settle her poor scattered thoughts. She named the village where they were bound.

'Really?' said Lucia, who knew it was not far from her own; 'oh, thank you, Most Holy Virgin! My mother! My mother!'

'We'll send and fetch her at once,' said the good woman, who did not know that this had already been done.

'Yes, yes; may God reward you. . . . And you, who are you? How did you come . . .?'

'Our priest sent me,' said the good woman; 'for God, blessed be His name, touched the heart of this lord, and he came to our village to talk to his Grace the Cardinal Archbishop (who's with us on a visit, the holy man), and he has repented of his dreadful sins, and wants to change his way of life; and he told the cardinal that he had abducted a poor girl – that's you – with the connivance of some other godless person, but the priest didn't tell me who it was.'

Lucia raised her eyes to heaven.

'You may know yourself,' the good woman went on. 'Anyway, the cardinal thought that, as it was a girl, it would be a good thing to have a woman go along for company, and told the priest to find one. And the priest, in his goodness, came to me . . .'

'Oh! May the Lord reward you for your kindness.'

'Don't mention it, my poor child. And our priest told me to try and cheer you and raise your spirits at once, and explain to you how the Lord has saved you by a miracle. . . .'

'Ah, yes! A real miracle: by Our Lady's intercession.'

'And so, he says make your mind easy, and forgive the man who wronged you, and be thankful God has been merciful to him; yes, and pray for him too – so that, as well as reaping merit from it, you will also feel a lightening of the heart.'

Lucia answered with a look that said 'yes' as clearly as any word could have done, and with a sweetness which no words could have expressed.

'There's a good girl!' went on the woman. 'And as your own priest happened to be in our village (there are any number of them there from the whole neighbourhood, enough to perform in concert four general offices), the cardinal thought of sending him with the party too; but he hasn't been much help. I'd already heard he was not worth much; but I could see how, in this instance, he's as panicked as a chick in flax.'

'And this ...' asked Lucia, 'this man who's had a change of heart ... who is he?'

'What! Don't you know?' said the good woman, and told her his name.

'Oh, mercy on us!' exclaimed Lucia. How often had she heard that name repeated with horror in many a story in which he had played the role which the ogre plays in other tales! And now, at the thought of having been in his dreaded power, and of being at that moment under his merciful protection; at the thought of her appalling danger, and of her unexpected deliverance; at the thought of whose face it was she had seen pass from haughtiness to compassion, and then to humility, she fell into a kind of ecstasy, only saying every now and again, 'Oh, mercy on us!'

'It really is a great mercy!' said the good woman. 'It's bound to be a great relief for lots of people. To think of all the lives he's turned upside down; and now, from what our priest told me ... and then, why, one's only got to look at his face to see he's become a saint! And then we'll soon tell by his works!'

It would not be true to say that this worthy woman did not feel a great deal of curiosity to know more details about the adventure in which she found herself playing a part, but it must be said to her credit that, restrained as she was by her respectful sympathy for Lucia, and having some feeling for the responsibility and dignity of the charge entrusted to her, it never even occurred to her to ask an indiscreet or idle question. Every word she spoke throughout that journey was of comfort and concern for the poor girl.

'Heaven alone knows how long it is since you've eaten!'

'I don't remember any more ... not for a long time.'

'You poor thing! You must need something to pull you together.'

'Yes,' replied Lucia in a faint voice.

'At home, thanks be to God, we'll find something straight away. Bear up, for it's not far now.'

Lucia then sank languidly back into the depths of the litter, as if overcome by drowsiness, and the good woman left her undisturbed.

As for Don Abbondio, this return was certainly not as agonizing for him as the outward journey a short while before; yet even this was not a pleasure trip. When that overwhelming fear had stopped, he had felt complete relief at first; but very soon a hundred other worries began springing up in his heart – as after a great tree is uprooted, the ground beneath remains bare for some time, but then gets all overgrown with weeds. He now became more sensitive to everything else; and found no dearth of material for self-torture in his thoughts, about both the present and the future. He was feeling the discomfort of this mode of travel which he was little used to, much more now than on the outward journey, particularly at the beginning during the descent from the castle to the bottom of the valley. The postilion, urged on by signs from the unnamed, was driving his animals at a smart pace; the two mules were following close behind at the same pace; so that in some of the steeper bits poor Don Abbondio would be pitched forward, as if pushed by a lever from behind, and have to steady himself by clutching at his pommel. He did not dare to ask them to go slower; and then he was longing to get away from that neighbourhood as soon as possible. Moreover, whenever the track ran over a bank or ridge, the mule, according to the habit of its kind, seemed to take a spiteful pleasure in always keeping to the outside and planting its hooves on the very brink; and Don Abbondio would see almost perpendicularly beneath him a drop, although to him it appeared a precipice. – You too – he muttered to the animal in his heart, – have got this cursed craze for going out of your way to look for danger when the path's so broad! – and he would pull the bridle in the opposite direction, but in vain; so that in the end, grumbling with rage and fear, he let himself be led along, as usual, by the will of others. The bravi no longer alarmed him so much, now that he was more certain what their master was thinking. – But – he reflected next – who knows how they will take it if the news of this great conversion gets round these parts too, while we're still here. Anything might happen! Supposing they get some idea I've come here to play the missionary! Poor me! Why, they'd martyr me! – The frown of the unnamed worried him no longer. – Nothing less than that's needed to keep these brutes round here in order – thought he – I can see that. But why should I be the one to get among all these people! –

At last they reached the foot of the descent, and finally came out of the valley too. The forehead of the unnamed was clearing. Don Abbondio also took on a more natural expression, freed his head a little from where it was wedged between his shoulders, stretched his arms and legs, and straightened his back so that he began to look quite different, and breathe more freely again; then, with a mind more at ease, he set himself to review other more remote dangers. – What will that brute Don Rodrigo say to this? First to have his nose put out of joint like this, then be jeered at, he won't like it a bit. He will really play the devil now. Now we'll see if he takes against me too, for being mixed up in this little trip. If he didn't hesitate before to send those two rascals of his to treat me like that right on the road, what won't he do now! He can't take it out of his Illustrious Grace – who's a much bigger nob than him – he'll have to gnaw at his bit there. But he'll still be full of spleen, and he'll want to vent it on somebody. What always happens in such cases? It's the underdog who always gets the kicks; it's the rags that get sent flying. Lucia, his Illustrious Grace will naturally see is put somewhere in safety; that other poor chap's out of reach and has already had his share; so I'm the one who'll be the scapegoat. It would really be cruel, if after all this worry and inconvenience, which I haven't got a bit of credit for, I had to bear the brunt! What will his Grace do to protect me now, after having got me into the middle of it? Can he make sure that cursed man doesn't do me a worse turn than before? And then, he's got so much to think about. He has a finger in so many pies. How can he take care of everything? People like that sometimes leave things in a worse mess than they were before. When they go in for doing good, they do it all in one lump; when they've had their satisfaction from it, they've had enough, and don't feel like worrying about all the consequences: whereas those with a taste for doing harm are much more diligent about it, and follow things right through to the end, and never give themselves a rest, as they have got that canker eating away at them. What about going and telling him I came here at his Grace's express command, and not of my own free will? That would look as if I was taking sides with evil. Oh, Heavens above! Me on the side of evil! Just for the fun of it! Ah, well! The best thing to do would be to tell Perpetua the whole story just as it is, and leave it to her to spread it round. As long as his Grace doesn't get the idea of advertising it about, creating some useless scene, and dragging me into it too. Anyway, as soon as we arrive I'll go and pay my respects hurriedly, if he's come out of church; if not, I'll leave my excuses, and go straight off back home. Lucia is in good hands; there's no need for me any more; and after all this hardship I've the right to a bit of rest too. And then . . . I only hope his Grace doesn't get curious to know the whole of the story, and call me to account for that business of the marriage. That would be the last straw. And suppose he comes to visit my parish too. . . . Ah, well, what must be, will be; I won't worry about it before it happens. I've got enough troubles as it is. For the present I'll go and shut myself up at home. As long as his Grace is in these parts, Don Rodrigo won't dare get up to any tricks. And then . . . and then? Ah! I can see my last years are going to be bad ones! –

The convoy arrived before the church services were over. It passed through the midst of the same crowd, which was no less moved than the first time; and then it split up. The two on mules turned aside into a small square, at the end of which stood the priest's house; the litter went on towards that of the good matron.

Don Abbondio did as he had planned. As soon as he had dismounted, he paid the unnamed the most effusive compliments and asked him to make his excuses to his Grace, as he had to go straight back to his parish on urgent business. He then went to find what he called his horse, that is the stick which he had left in a corner of the parlour, and set out on his way. The unnamed stayed waiting for the cardinal to return from church.

The good matron had sat Lucia down in the cosiest corner of her kitchen, and busied herself preparing her some refreshment, turning away with rustic cordiality the thanks and excuses which her guest kept on repeating to her.

Quickly rekindling the fire under a pot, in which a fat capon was floating, she soon brought the broth to the boil; then, filling up a bowl in which she had already put some pieces of bread, she was finally able to set it before Lucia. And as she saw the poor girl reviving with every spoonful, she congratulated herself aloud on all this happening on a day when, as she said, 'there was something on the hearth beside the cat. . . . Everyone's made an effort to have some little special thing today,' added she, 'except for the very poor, who can only just manage to get vetch bread and millet *polenta*; but they're all hoping to get something today from such a generous gentleman. We, for our part, aren't in their case, thanks be to heaven. What with my husband's trade and a little plot of land we have, we manage to get along. So you can eat up without worrying: the capon will soon be ready, and you'll be able to revive yourself better.' So saying, she turned her attention back to preparing the meal and laying the table.

Lucia, meanwhile, now that her strength had returned to her somewhat, and her mind was calmer, was beginning to tidy herself up from an instinctive habit of cleanliness and modesty; she tied and plaited her loose, dishevelled tresses, and adjusted the handkerchief on her bosom and around her neck. In doing so her fingers touched the rosary which she had put there the night before; her eyes went to it at once; instantly her mind was in tumult: the memory of her vow, suppressed and stifled by all the emotions of the moment, suddenly rose and stood clear and distinct before her. Then all the powers of her mind just barely reviving were suddenly overwhelmed again, and had she not been so well prepared by a life of innocence, resignation, and trust, the consternation which she felt at that moment would have been despair. After a boiling-up of thoughts without words, the first to take shape in her mind were: – Oh, woe is me! What have I done! –

But scarcely had she thought this, than she recoiled as if in terror. All the circumstances of her vow came back to her – the intolerable anguish, the despair of any help, the fervour of her prayer, the depths of feeling with which the promise had been made. And to regret her promise after having obtained the favour seemed to her sacrilegious ingratitude, an act of perfidy towards God and Our Lady. It seemed to her that such infidelity would draw new and more terrible misfortunes down on her, amidst which she could no longer hope even in prayer; and she hastened to disavow her momentary regret. She took the rosary reverently from her neck, and holding it in her trembling hand, confirmed and renewed her vow at the same time, imploring with heart-broken earnestness to be granted the strength to carry it out and spared the thoughts and occasions which might be likely, if not to change her mind, at least to harass it beyond endurance. Renzo's absence, with no likelihood of return – that absence which had hitherto been so bitter to her – now began to seem like a dispensation of Providence which had made the two events coincide with one aim in view; and she tried hard to find in the one a reason for being content with the other. Following this came the thought that this same Providence might complete its work by finding some way of reconciling Renzo too, and of making him forget . . . But this solution had scarcely entered her head than it threw into confusion the mind that had gone looking for it. Poor Lucia, feeling she was on the very verge of regretting the vow again, fell to praying, to confirming it and struggling once more, from which she arose, if we may be allowed the expression, like a tired and wounded victor from above an enemy defeated – I do not say killed.

All of a sudden there was a scampering of feet and a sound of happy voices. It was the little family coming back from church. Two little girls and a small boy came bounding in, stopped a moment to give an inquisitive glance at Lucia, then ran to their mother and clustered around her. One of them asked who their unknown guest was and why and how she was there; another tried to describe the wonders they had seen. The good woman answered each and every one of them with a 'Hush! Hush!' Then, with a more sedate step, but with cordial solicitude written all over his face, in came the master of the house. He was, if we have not already said so, the tailor for the village and neighbourhood – a man who knew how to read, who had in fact read the *Lives of the Saints*, the *Guerrin meschino* and the *Reali di Francia,** and passed in the neighbourhood for a man of parts and learning – praise, however, which he modestly disclaimed, saying only that he had mistaken his vocation, and that if *he* had gone in for study instead of so many others . . .! For all this, he was the best-natured fellow in the world. Happening to be present when his wife had been asked by the priest to undertake the errand of mercy, he had not only consented to her going, but would have encouraged her had there been any need. And now that the service, the pomp, the crowds, and above all the cardinal's sermon had, as the saying is, aroused all his best feelings, he was coming home with eager anticipation and longing to know how it had all gone off, and to find the poor innocent victim safe.

'Just look over there,' the good woman said to him as he came in, pointing towards Lucia, who blushed, rose, and began stammering out apologies. But, going up to her, he interrupted with enthusiastic greetings, exclaiming, 'Welcome, welcome! You're Heaven's blessing on this house! How glad I am to see you here! I was pretty sure you'd get out safely, for I've never known the Lord begin a miracle without finishing it well. But I'm really glad to see you here. You poor girl! Still, it's a great thing to be the object of a miracle.'

It should not be thought that he was alone in calling that event by such a name, just because he had read the *Lives of the Saints*. In all the village and neighbourhood around no other term was used for as long as the memory of it lasted. And to tell the truth, with all the embroidery that was added, no other name would have been suitable.

Then, sidling quietly up to his wife, who was just lifting the pot off its chain, he whispered to her, 'Did everything go off well?'

'Perfectly: I'll tell you all about it later.'

'Yes, yes; time enough.'

Quickly putting the dish down on the table, the mistress of the house went and fetched Lucia, led her to it, and sat her down; then she cut a wing off the capon and put it before her, after which she and her husband sat down too, both of them encouraging their shy and dispirited guest to eat. At the first mouthful the tailor began to hold forth with great emphasis, amidst interruptions from the children eating around the table, who had seen too many wonders themselves to play the part of mere listeners for very long. He described the solemn ceremonies, then digressed to talk about the miraculous conversion. But the thing which had made most impression on him, and to which he returned most often, was the cardinal's sermon.

'To see him there in front of the altar,' said he, 'a noble of that rank, like a parish priest . . .'

'And with that gold thing on his head . . .' one of the little girls said.

'Be quiet! To think, I say, that a noble of that rank and such a learned man – from what they say, he's read every book there is – and that's something no one else has managed to do, even in Milan – to think he could adapt himself to saying those things in a way everyone could understand . . .'

'I understood too,' said another little chatterbox.

'Be quiet! What d'you think you could understand?'

'I understood he was explaining the gospel instead of our priest.'

'Be quiet! I don't mean people with a bit of education, who'd be bound to understand anyway, but even the dullest-witted, the stupidest, could follow the sense of what he was saying. If you go now and ask them to repeat his words, you'll find, of course, they won't remember a single one – but they've got the whole feel of them inside. And then, without his ever mentioning that nobleman by name, how well one understood he was alluding to him! And besides, to understand that, one only had to see when he had tears in his eyes. And then everyone began to cry too . . .'

'Yes, they really did,' burst out the little boy. 'But why were they all crying like that – like babies?'

'Be quiet! And there are some pretty hard hearts in this village. And then he really made us see that even though there is a famine, we ought to thank the Lord and be content – do what we can, work hard, help each other, and be content. Because suffering and being poor's not the real misfortune: the real misfortune's doing harm. And those are not just fine words either; for it's a known fact that he lives like a poor man himself, and takes the bread from his own mouth to give to the hungry; when he could lead a life of luxury better than anyone. Ah! that's when hearing a sermon gives a man satisfaction – not like so many others, with their: "do as I say, and not as I do." And then he made us really see that even those of us who aren't gentry, if they've got more than they need, are bound to share with those in want.'

Here he interrupted his monologue of his own accord, as if struck by an idea. He paused a moment, then filled up a plate from the food on the table, added a loaf of bread, wrapped the whole lot in a napkin, and taking it by the four corners, said to the elder of his little girls, 'Here, take this.' In her other hand he put a flask of wine, and added, 'Go down to the widow Maria's; leave her these things, and tell her to enjoy them with her children. But do it nicely, now. Don't make it look as if you're giving alms. And don't mention it to anyone you meet; and take care not to break anything.'

Lucia felt her eyes fill with tears and a wave of tenderness refresh her heart, just as the conversation before had soothed her more than any speech of sympathy could have done. Fascinated by those descriptions, by those visions of pomp, by the emotions of pity and of wonder, swept by the same enthusiasm as the speaker himself, her mind was drawn away from the painful thoughts about herself; so that when they returned, she found herself better able to cope with them. Even the thought of her great sacrifice, while it had not lost its bitterness, now seemed to be mingled with a kind of austere and solemn joy.

Shortly afterwards the village priest came in, and said he had been sent by the cardinal to inquire after Lucia and to tell her that his Grace wished to see her that day, and also to thank the tailor and his wife in his name. So grateful and confused were Lucia and her hosts that they could find no words in which to reply to such attentions from so great a personage.

'And your mother has not arrived yet?' said the priest to Lucia.

'My mother!' exclaimed she.

And when the priest told her that she had been sent for on the archbishop's orders, she put her apron up to her eyes and burst into a flood of tears, which lasted for some time after the priest had gone. When the tumult of emotions aroused by this announcement had begun to give way to calmer thoughts, the poor girl remembered that this approaching happiness of seeing her mother again – a happiness so unexpected a few hours before – had been one which she had expressly implored during those terrible hours, and almost made a condition of her vow. *Bring me safely back to my mother*, she had said – the words now stood out clearly in her memory again. She confirmed herself then more than ever in her intention of keeping the promise, and felt another and more bitter twinge of conscience for that *Woe is me*! which had escaped her at that first moment.

Agnese in fact was only a short way off while they were talking about her. The poor woman's feelings at that unexpected summons can easily be imagined, and at hearing the news, necessarily meagre and confused, of some appalling danger (over now, so much could at least be said), of some terrible adventure of which the messenger could give no details or explanation, and of which she had no clue to any explanation herself. After clawing her hair, and crying, 'O Lord! O Blessed Lady!' again and again, after asking the messenger a lot of questions which he could not answer, she jumped hurriedly into the cart, exclaiming and asking useless questions the whole way. Then at a certain point they had met Don Abbondio trudging slowly along, putting his stick ahead of him at every step. After an 'Oh!' on both sides, he had halted, she had called a halt and got out, and they had both drawn aside into a chestnut grove flanking the road. Don Abbondio informed her of what he had been able to hear and of what he had been forced to see. It was not clear to her; but at least Agnese was assured that Lucia was quite safe; and breathed a sigh of relief.

After this Don Abbondio tried to broach another topic, and to give her long instructions on how to behave to the archbishop, if he – as he probably would – wanted to talk to her and her daughter; and how, above all, it would not do for her to say a word about the marriage. . . . But Agnese, seeing that the good man was only speaking in his own interests, had left him standing there without promising, and indeed without deciding anything; for she had other things on her mind. And she had resumed her journey.

Finally the cart arrived and drew up at the tailor's. Lucia jumped up hastily. Agnese got out, rushed inside, and they were in each other's arms. The tailor's wife, who was the only person present, cheered, soothed, and congratulated them both, and then, discreet as ever, left them to themselves, saying that she was going to prepare them a bed, that it was no inconvenience to her at all, and that anyway both she and her husband would rather sleep on the ground than let them go seeking shelter elsewhere.

After the first transports of sobbing and kissing were over, Agnese asked to hear about Lucia's adventures, and the girl began to recount them with difficulty. But, as the reader is aware, it was a story which no one knew in its entirety; and there were parts that were obscure and quite inexplicable to Lucia herself. This was particularly the case with the fatal coincidence of that terrible coach being there on the road just when Lucia happened, by an extraordinary chance, to be passing along it; about this both mother and daughter made endless conjectures, without ever hitting the mark or even getting near it.

As for the chief author of the plot, neither of them could avoid thinking that this must be Don Rodrigo.

'Ah, the black villain! The firebrand of hell!' exclaimed Agnese. 'But his time will come too. The Lord God will pay him out as he deserved, and then he will also feel . . .'

'No, no, mother; no!' interrupted Lucia. 'You must not hope he suffers, you must not hope it for anyone. If you knew what suffering is like! If you had felt it! No, no; let's rather pray to God and Our Lady for him: that God may touch his heart, as He has that other poor noble's, who was worse than him; and who's now a saint.'

The revulsion Lucia felt at going back over memories so recent and so cruel made her break off her story more than once. More than once, too, she said that she had not got the heart to go on, and only managed to continue with difficulty and after many tears. But at one point in her tale – when she came to the vow – she was held back by a different feeling. This was the fear that her mother would tax her with having been hasty and rash; or that she might bring out one of her broad rules of conscience as she had about the wedding, and try and force her to agree with it; or that she would tell someone about it in confidence, poor woman, if only to get ideas and advice, and so let it become public knowledge, the very thought of which made Lucia blush all over. Also she felt a certain shyness of her mother, an inexplicable aversion to mentioning the subject at all. All these things together made her hide that important fact, and resolve to take Fra Cristoforo into her confidence first of all. So it can be guessed what a blow it was to her when she asked after him and discovered that he was no longer there, that he had been sent off to some far-away town, to a town with some peculiar name.

'And Renzo?' said Agnese.

'He's safe, isn't he?' said Lucia anxiously.

'That much is certain, as everyone says so. It's held for sure that he's taken refuge in Bergamese territory; but no one seems to know the exact place; and he hasn't sent a word so far; hasn't found a way to yet, probably.'

'Ah, if he's safe, thanks be to God,' said Lucia; and was trying to change the subject, when it was changed for her by an unexpected event – the appearance of the cardinal archbishop.

The latter, on returning from church, where we had left him, had heard from the unnamed that Lucia had arrived safe and sound. He had then taken him into dinner with him, and sat him at his right-hand side, in the midst of a circle of priests who could not take their eyes off that countenance so softened without being weakened, so humbled without being humiliated, or stop comparing it with the idea which they had so long had of this personage.

At the end of dinner the two of them had again retired in private together. After a conversation lasting much longer than the first, the unnamed had set off for his castle on the same mule of that morning; and the cardinal had called the village priest, and told him that he wanted to be taken to the house where Lucia was sheltering.

'Oh, your Grace,' had replied the priest. 'Please don't disturb yourself. I'll send off at once to tell the girl and her mother, if she has arrived, to come here, and her hosts too, if your Grace wishes, and anyone else your most Illustrious Grace may want to see.'

'I want to go and visit them myself,' Federigo had replied.

'Your most Illustrious Grace must not put yourself out; I'll send for her at once. It'll only take a moment,' had insisted the offcious priest (a good man on the whole), not understanding that the cardinal wanted by this visit to pay homage to misfortune, to innocence, and to his own ministry at the same time. But when the superior again expressed the same desire, the subordinate bowed and led the way.

When the two personages were seen appearing in the street, everyone in it turned towards them; and in a few moments more came hurrying from every side, those who could walking beside them, while the rest came flocking along behind. The parish priest kept on calling out, 'Come, get back, back there; come, come!' and Federigo kept on saying, 'Let them be,' and went ahead, now raising a hand to bless the crowd, then lowering it to fondle the children running around his feet. In this way they arrived at the tailor's, and went in, while the crowd piled up outside. But also in the crowd was the tailor himself, who had been tagging along behind with the rest, with eyes fixed and mouth agape, without knowing where he was going. When he saw the unexpected destination, he forced his way through, with what bustle can be imagined, shouting out again and again, 'Make way for someone who's got to pass,' and went in.

Agnese and Lucia heard a growing buzz in the street; they were still wondering what it could be when they saw the door burst open, and the prelate and the parish priest appear on the threshold.

'Is that her?' asked the former of the latter, and, at his affirmative nod, went towards Lucia, who had stayed there by her mother's side, both of them rooted and mute with surprise and shyness. But the tone of voice and the look and bearing, and, above all, the words of Federigo had re-animated them at once. 'My poor child!' he began. 'God has allowed you to be sorely tried; but He has also shown you that He had never ceased to have His eyes on you, that He had not forgotten you. He has brought you back to safety again; and He has made use of you for a great work, to do a great mercy to one person, and to relieve many others at the same time.'

Here the mistress of the house appeared in the room. She had been looking out of the window, and when she saw who was entering her house, had hurried downstairs, after tidying herself up as best she could; and almost at the same time the tailor came in at another door. Seeing that the conversation had already started, they withdrew into a corner together, and waited there with deep respect. The cardinal, after a courteous greeting to them, went on talking to the women, mingling an inquiry or two with his words of comfort to see if he could learn from the replies some way of helping one who had suffered so greatly.

'If only all priests were like your lordship, taking sides with the poor a bit, instead of getting them into messes so as to save their own skins!' said Agnese, emboldened by Federigo's kindly and familiar manner, and annoyed at the thought that Don Abbondio, after always sacrificing others to his own interests, should expect on top of it to be able to prevent them venting their feelings a little when there was this rare chance of complaining to someone above him.

'Do say whatever is in your mind,' said the cardinal. 'Talk freely.'

'I mean that, if our priest had done his duty, things wouldn't have gone this way.'

But when the cardinal insisted on her explaining more fully, she began to find herself somewhat in difficulties at having to tell a story in which she herself had played a part that she did not care to have known, particularly by such a personage. She managed, however, to save the situation by making a small cut: she described how the marriage had all been arranged and how Don Abbondio had refused, not omitting that excuse about *his superiors* that he had used (ah, Agnese!); then she skipped straight on to Don Rodrigo's attempt, and how being warned beforehand, they had managed to escape. 'But there,' she finally added, 'it was escaping only to get into another mess again. Though, if his reverence had only told us the whole thing frankly and married up my poor children then and there, we'd have gone away at once, all together, secretly, to some distant part where even the air wouldn't have been any the wiser. So time was lost; and everything went the way it did.'

'Your priest shall render me an account of this,' said the cardinal.

'No, my lord, no, my lord,' said Agnese quickly. 'I didn't tell you for that. Please don't scold him, for what's done is done. And besides, it won't do any good; he's made that way. If the chance came up again, he'd do exactly the same thing.'

But Lucia, not satisfied with this version of the story, added, 'We too have done wrong; it's plain it was not God's will that it should happen.'

'What wrong could you have done, my poor child?' said Federigo.

Lucia, in spite of the winks which her mother was secretly trying to give her, then told the story of the attempt made in Don Abbondio's house, and ended by saying, 'We have done wrong; and God has punished us.'

'Accept from His hands the sufferings you have endured, and be of good heart,' said Federigo. 'For who else has reason to rejoice and hope if not those who have suffered and are ready to accuse themselves?'

Then he asked her where her betrothed was, and on hearing from Agnese (Lucia was silent, with downcast head and eyes) that he had fled the country, he looked surprised and disappointed, and asked the reason.

Agnese told him as best she could the little she knew of Renzo's story.

'I've heard speak of this young man,' said the cardinal. 'But however can it be that someone implicated in things of that kind could have won the hand of a girl like this?'

'He was a good boy,' said Lucia, her face blushing scarlet, but her voice firm.

'He was a quiet boy – almost too quiet,' added Agnese. 'And you can ask anyone at all about that, even the parish priest. Who knows what they trumped up against him by tricks and confusion down there! It doesn't take much to make the poor out to be knaves.'

'That's only too true, alas,' said the cardinal. 'I'll certainly find out about him,' and he made them give him the youth's name and surname, and noted it down in his memorandum book. Then he added that he planned to visit their village in a few days' time, when Lucia could go there without fear, and that meanwhile he would think about providing her with a safe retreat until everything was properly arranged.

He then turned towards the master and mistress of the house, who came forward at once. He renewed the thanks he had sent through the priest, and asked if they would mind sheltering for a few days the guests whom God had sent them.

'Oh, yes, your lordship,' replied the woman, but with a tone of voice and a look that expressed much more than this curt response choked by shyness. But her husband, thrown into a state of frenzy by the presence of such a questioner and by the desire to do himself honour on such an occasion, was anxiously trying to think up some fine reply. He screwed up his forehead, rolled his eyes, pursed his lips, stretched the bow of his intellect with all his might, and ransacked his brain: all he found there was a medley of unfinished phrases and half-formed ideas. But time was pressing; the cardinal was already showing that he had interpreted his silence. The poor man opened his mouth and said, 'Of course!' Nothing else would come out. This not only humiliated him severely at the time, but the memory of it always obtruded ever afterwards to spoil his satisfaction in the great honour which he had received. And how often, when going over it again and putting himself back into that situation in his mind's eye, there would come into it, almost as if out of spite, words which would all have been better than that insipid: *Of course*! But, as an old proverb says: many are the ditches filled with afterthoughts.

The cardinal left, saying, 'May the Lord's blessing be upon this house.'

That evening he asked the village priest how he could best recompense the tailor, who could not be rich, for his costly hospitality – particularly in those times. The priest replied that, in truth, neither the good tailor's earnings from his trade nor the rents from some little fields he had would have been enough this year for him to be liberal with others; but that, having managed to lay something aside from former years, he now found himself better off than most others in the neighbourhood, and could spend a little extra without hardship, as he was certainly doing very willingly this time; and that, besides, it would be impossible to get him to accept any recompense.

'He probably,' said the cardinal, 'has accounts with people who can't pay.'

'Just think, your most Illustrious Grace: these poor people pay with their surplus crops. Last year there was no surplus at all; and this year everyone has less than they need.'

'Very well,' said Federigo. 'I'll make myself responsible for all those debts. Will you please get a list of them from him, and settle them.'

'It will come to a considerable sum.'

'So much the better. And then you must have only too many in even greater need, who have no debts because they can't get credit.'

'Ah, yes, alas! One does what one can; but how can one ever meet all their needs, in times like these?'

'Get him to clothe them at my expense, and pay him well for it. Really this year anything not spent on bread seems like robbery; but this is a special case.'

We do not want to close the story of this day without giving a brief account of how it ended for the unnamed.

This time the news of his conversion had gone into the valley before him. It had spread around at once, everywhere causing consternation, anxiety, muttering, and dismay. The first bravi or servants whom he saw (they were all the same thing) he signed to follow him; and the same with the others. They all flocked along behind him, with a new apprehension, but with their usual deference, until, with an ever-growing retinue, he arrived at the castle. He signed to the men at the gates to follow behind with the others, entered the outer court, and, going towards the middle of it without dismounting, there gave a thunderous halloo. This was his usual signal for all those within hearing to come hurrying to him. In a moment the men scattered throughout the castle came to answer the call, and joined the others already assembled: all were looking at their master.

'Go and wait for me in the great hall,' he said to them; and from the height of his saddle watched them moving off. Then he dismounted, led his animal to the stables himself, and went to the place where they were waiting for him. At his appearance the loud buzz of whispering died away at once; all drew to one side, leaving a large part of the hall empty for him; there were about thirty of them.

The unnamed raised his hand, as if to hold that sudden silence – raised his head, which towered over the whole company, and said, 'Listen, all of you, and none of you speak unless you're asked a question. My children! The road we have been treading up to now leads to the depths of Hell. I am not trying to reproach you, as I have been the foremost of you all, the worst of you all; but hear what I have to say to you. God in His mercy has called on me to change my life. I shall change it; I have already changed it. May He do the same with all of you. You must know, then, and must take it as certain, that I am determined to die sooner than do anything more against His holy laws. I release each and all of you from the iniquitous commissions you have had from me. You understand me? What is more, I order you not to carry out anything that you were ordered to do before. And you can take it as equally definite that none of you from now on will be able to do evil under my protection or in my service. Those of you who want to stay under these conditions will be like sons to me; and I should be happy at the end of a day when I have eaten nothing so as to give my last loaf to the last man of you. Those who do not wish to remain will be given whatever salary is due to them, and a present on top of it. They may go. But let them never set foot in here again, unless it be to change their way of life; in which case they will always be received with open arms. Think it over during the night. Tomorrow I shall call you, one by one, for a reply; and then I shall give new orders. For the moment each of you go back to your posts. And may God, who has been so merciful with me, send you the right thoughts.'

Here he ended, and all were silent. However varied and

tumultuous the thoughts seething in their rough brains, no
outward sign of them appeared. They were accustomed to taking
their master's voice as the declaration of a will from which there
was no appeal; and that voice, in announcing that his will had
changed, gave no sign at all of its having weakened. It never even
entered their heads to try to take advantage of him and answer
back to him like any other man, now that he had been converted.
They saw him as a saint, but as one of those saints who are
painted with head erect and sword in hand. Besides the awe in
which they held him, they also (particularly those born in his
service, as many of them had been) felt the affection of vassals.
Then they also had a warm admiration for him; and felt in his
presence some of that, I might almost say, bashfulness, which
even the roughest and most turbulent spirits feel before a
superiority which they have once recognized. Also, what they
had just heard from his lips might be odious to their ears, but
was neither false nor in the least foreign to their understanding.
If they had mocked at such things a thousand times in the past, it
was not because they disbelieved them, but in order to forestall
by their mockery the fear that would have seized them had they
come to thinking them over seriously. And now, seeing the effect
of this fear on a spirit like their master's, there was not one who
was not infected by it to some degree, at least for a time. In
addition to this, those of them who had been outside the valley
that morning and had been the first to hear the great news had
also seen and reported the joy and elation of the population, and
the love and veneration that had taken the place of the former
hatred and terror for the unnamed. So that the man they had
always regarded, as it were, as a superior being, even though they
themselves were the main source of his power, they now saw as
the wonder, the idol of the crowd. They saw him still above the
rest of men, very differently from before, but no lower – still out
of the common herd, still a leader.

So they stood there, bewildered and uncertain of each other
and of themselves. Some complained; some began to make plans
about where to go and look for work and shelter; some examined
themselves to see if they could adapt themselves to becoming
respectable citizens; some, too, had been touched by his words
and felt a certain inclination to do so; some, without coming to
any decision, thought of promising everything readily, and staying meanwhile to eat the bread offered them so generously, which
was then so scarce, in order to gain time. No one breathed a

syllable. And when the unnamed, at the end of his speech, raised that imperious hand of his again to tell them that they were dismissed, they slunk off silently together, like a flock of sheep. He went out in their wake, and, stationing himself in the middle of the court, stood watching them scattering in the twilight, each of them going towards his post. Then he went upstairs and fetched a lantern, and again made the rounds of the courtyards, passages, and halls, visited all the entrances, and seeing that all was quiet, finally went off to sleep. Yes, to sleep; for he felt sleepy.

Never before had he, who had so often gone in search of them, been so burdened with tangled and at the same time urgent affairs as he was then; and yet he felt sleepy. The regrets that had kept him awake the night before were not only not silenced, but were louder, sterner, more inexorable than before; and yet he felt sleepy. The discipline, the kind of government which he had established in the castle for so many years and with such care, with such a singular combination of audacity and perseverance, he had now himself, perhaps, overthrown, with a few words. The unbounded devotion of his dependants, their readiness to do anything for him, their ruffianly loyalty, on which he had been used to depending for so long – all these he had now himself shaken; his resources he had now changed into a mountain of perplexities, he had brought confusion and uncertainty within his gates; and yet he felt sleepy.

So he went to his room, approached the bed which had been so strewn with thorns the night before, and knelt down beside it, with the intention of praying. He did, in fact, find in a deep and hidden corner of his mind the prayers he had been taught to say as a child. He began to recite them; and those words, so long furled up inside him, now came out after each other as if they were unwinding. It gave him an indefinable mixture of sensations: a certain sweetness at this return to the habits of innocence; a heightened sorrow at the thought of the abyss which he had put between that time and this; a longing to attain to a new conscience by works of expiation, to a state nearer that innocence to which he could never return; gratitude, and a confidence in the mercy that could bring him to this condition, and had already given him so many signs of wanting to do so. Then, rising from his knees, he went to bed, and fell asleep at once.

So ended that day, so celebrated even when our anonymous author was writing. And now, were it not for him, nothing of it,

or at least of its details, would be known; for all that Ripamonti
and Rivola, both quoted above, say, is that a certain notorious
tyrant, after an interview with Federigo, changed his whole
course of life, marvellously and for ever after. And how many
have ever read the books of those two? Still fewer than those
who will read ours. And who knows if, in the valley itself,
suppose anyone had the desire to search for it and the ability to
find it, there still survives some vague and confused tradition of
this event? So many things have happened since that time!

CHAPTER 25

On the following day nothing was talked about in Lucia's village
and the whole countryside round Lecco but her, the unnamed,
the archbishop, and one other person, who, much as he delighted
in having his name on the lips of others, would willingly have
done without it on this occasion – we mean his lordship Don
Rodrigo.

Not that his doings had not been talked about before, but it
had been disjointed, surreptitious talk; two people had to know
each other very well before opening up on such a topic. And even
then they did not put into it all the feelings of which they were
capable; for, generally, when men can vent their indignation only
at grave risk, they not only show less of it and keep their feelings
completely to themselves, but even feel it less in reality. But who
now could refrain from inquiring or abstain from discussing an
event so notorious, in which the hand of Heaven had been seen,
and in which two such personages had cut such a good figure?
One who united so warm a love of justice with so much authority;
the other, whose repentance made it seem that tyranny itself had
been so humbled that it had come, as it were, to hand in its arms
and ask to withdraw. In comparison with these, Don Rodrigo
seemed rather insignificant. Now at last everyone understood
what it meant to molest innocence in order to dishonour it, to
persecute it with such shameless persistence, with such atrocious
violence and abominable treachery. Now, as a result, all that
gentleman's numerous other exploits were reviewed, and everyone said what they felt about them, emboldened by finding
themselves in agreement with everyone else. There was a general

muttering and whispering; at a safe distance, however, because of all the bravi whom the man had around him.

A good share of this public odium fell also on his friends and flatterers. The mayor was well-cursed for always being deaf, blind, and dumb to the tyrant's misdeeds – but this also at a distance, for if he had no bravi, he had bailiffs. With Doctor Quibbleweaver who had nothing but scheming and talking to support him, and with the other little hangers-on of his rank, no such care was needed; they were pointed at and given such black looks that they thought it best not to show themselves in the streets for some time.

Don Rodrigo, thunderstruck at the unforeseen news, so different from the message that he had been expecting from day to day, from moment to moment, had shut himself up in his mansion for two days, alone with his bravi, grinding his teeth; on the third he left for Milan. Had it been only this muttering among the people, he might, as things had gone so far, have stayed to face it out, and also to try and make an example of some of the most daring; but what drove him away was the definite news that the cardinal was coming to those parts. His right honourable uncle, who only knew what Attilio had told him of the story, would certainly expect Don Rodrigo to cut a great figure on such an occasion and to receive the most distinguished public attentions from the cardinal; anyone can see how this would have gone now. He would have expected it, and have required a minute description; for it was an important opportunity of showing how highly the family was esteemed by one of the foremost authorities. To avoid this unpleasant difficulty Don Rodrigo had risen one morning before daybreak, got into his carriage, with Griso and the other bravi outside, in front, and behind it, and, leaving orders that the rest of the servants were to follow, departed like a fugitive, like (if we may exalt our characters by so illustrious a comparison) – like Catiline from Rome,* fuming and swearing to return very soon, in different circumstances, to take his revenge.

Meanwhile the cardinal was visiting, at the rate of one a day, the parishes in the territory of Lecco. On the day when he was due to arrive at Lucia's village most of the inhabitants had gone out along the road to welcome him. At the entrance to the village, right beside Agnese and Lucia's cottage, there was a triumphal arch, made of beams for the uprights and poles for the traverses, the whole covered with straw and moss, and decorated with green boughs of butcher's broom and holly vivid with red berries. The façade of the church was draped with brocades; from every window-sill hung extended quilts and sheets, and swaddling bands arranged like streamers – all the little necessities, in fact, that could be made to look like decorations. Towards three in the afternoon, which was the hour when the cardinal was expected, those who had stayed at home – old folk and women and children for the most part – also set out to meet him, partly in procession, and partly in a horde, with Don Abbondio at their head, ill at ease in the midst of all the festivity, both because of the noise that was stunning him and the continuous scurrying of people to and fro, which made his head go round, as he kept saying; and also because of his secret anxiety that the women might have talked, and that he would have to render an account of the marriage.

Then into sight hove the cardinal – or rather the crowd in the midst of which he was being carried in his litter, with his suite around him; for the only sign of him to be seen was a piece of the cross, above everyone's heads, being carried by the chaplain astride a mule. The crowd advancing with Don Abbondio broke up and rushed to join the other one; and he, after saying three or four times, 'Slow; into line; what are you doing?' turned back in vexation; and muttering, 'It's an absolute Babel, an absolute Babel,' again and again, went into the church, which was quite deserted, and stayed there to wait.

The cardinal advanced, distributing blessings with one hand, and receiving them in turn from the lips of the crowd, whom his attendants had great difficulty in keeping back. As it was Lucia's village, these people would have liked to make some extraordinary demonstration in honour of the archbishop, but this was no easy matter, for wherever he went all usually did their utmost. Even at the very beginning of his episcopate, at his first solemn entry into the cathedral, the press and surge of the crowds round him had been so great that his life was feared for; and some noblemen nearest him had drawn their swords to frighten off the crowd and push it back. So unruly and violent were the manners of the period that even a demonstration of goodwill for a bishop in church, and its control, had to come close to bloodshed. And even that defence might not have proved sufficient had not the master of ceremonies and his assistants, two young priests as strong in body as in mind, called Clerici and Picozzi,* hoisted him on their shoulders and carried him bodily along from the doors to the high altar. From that time onwards his first entry into church on all his episcopal visits may without joking be counted among the hardships of his office, and sometimes among the perils to which he was exposed.

This church too he entered as best he could. He went up to the altar, and remained there for some time in prayer; then, according to his usual habit, he gave the people a short talk about how he loved them and wanted their salvation, and how they were to prepare themselves for the functions of next day. Afterwards, when he had withdrawn to the priest's house, he asked, in the course of conversation, among other things, about Renzo. Don Abbondio said that he was rather a quick, stubborn, hot-tempered young fellow. But on more detailed and precise questions being put him, he had to answer that he was a good youth, and that he too could not understand how he had ever got up to all the devilry they said he had in Milan.

'As for the girl,' went on the cardinal. 'Do you also think she can come and live safely now at her own home?'

'For the moment,' answered Don Abbondio, 'she can come and stay as she likes. For the moment, I say, but,' he added with a sigh, 'your most Illustrious Grace would have to be always here, or at least near at hand.'

'The Lord is always near at hand,' said the cardinal. 'But anyway, I shall think of somewhere safe to put her.' And he at once gave orders for the litter to be sent early next morning, with an escort, to fetch the two women.

Don Abbondio came out feeling very pleased that the cardinal had talked to him about the young pair without calling him to account for his refusal to marry them. – So he doesn't know anything – said he to himself – Agnese held her tongue: what a miracle! It's true, they have to see each other again; but I'll give her some more instructions, that I will, – not realizing, poor man, that Federigo had not broached this subject because he intended to talk about it at length when he had more time. And before giving him what he deserved, he wanted to hear his reasons.

But the good prelate's preoccupations about putting Lucia in safety had become superfluous; since he had left her, there had been certain developments which we must now relate.

The two women, during the few days they had to spend in the tailor's hospitable house, had each resumed, as far as they could, their former way of life. Lucia had at once asked for some work; and she sewed and sewed away, as she had done in the convent, withdrawn in a little room, far from prying eyes. Agnese went out a little, and worked a little in her daughter's company. Their conversation was as melancholy as it was affectionate. They were both prepared for separation, for the lamb could not go back and live so near the lair of the wolf; and when and what would be the end of this separation? The future was dark and involved, particularly for one of them. Agnese would go on making happy conjectures about it: how Renzo would soon be finally sending news of himself, if he had not come to any harm; and how if he had found work and somewhere to settle, and if (and who could doubt it?) he held to his promises, why shouldn't they go and live with him? Over and over again she would talk about such hopes to her daughter, for whom it is hard to say if it was more painful to listen or difficult to reply. Her great secret she had kept always to herself; and disturbed as she was at deceiving so good a mother, not for the first time, she was held back, as if invincibly, by shyness and the various fears which we have mentioned above, and went on from day to day without saying a word about it. Her plans were very different from those of her mother – or it would be truer to say that she had no plans at all; she had abandoned herself to Providence. So she would always try to let this subject drop, or to avert it. Or she would say, in general terms, that she had no hope or desire left for anything more in this world, beyond being reunited with her mother as soon as possible. Most often her tears would come just in time to drown her words.

'D'you know why you feel that?' Agnese would say. 'It's because you've suffered so much, and can't believe things can ever take a turn for the better. But leave it to the Lord, and if . . . Wait till there's a ray – just a ray – of hope, and then you can tell me if there's nothing you're thinking of.' Lucia would kiss her mother and weep.

Besides this, a close friendship had quickly sprung up between them and their hosts; and where should such a thing spring up if not between benefactors and benefited, when both one and the other are good people? Agnese in particular had many long chats with the mistress of the house. Then the tailor would entertain them with stories and moral disquisitions. At dinner, particularly, he always had some wonderful tale to tell about Bovo d'Antona or the Desert Fathers.*

Not far away from this village was the country seat of a couple of great consequence: Don Ferrante and Donna Prassede; their surname, as usual, is left in our anonymous chronicler's pen. Donna Prassede was an old lady with a strong propensity for doing good – certainly the worthiest profession that man can ply, but one which, like all others, is open to abuse. To do good, one must know what it is; and, like everything else, we can only know this by means of our own passions, our own judgements, our own ideas – which often do not amount to very much. Donna Prassede's attitude towards ideas was the same as they say one should have towards friends; she had few but was strongly attached to the few she had. Among these few there were unfortunately many mistaken ones; and these were not the ones which she cherished least. Hence it happened that she would either take as good what was not so in reality, or use means which were apt to have the very opposite effect to her intentions, or think some of these means legitimate when they were not so at all, all from a vague presumption that those who go beyond their duty can also go beyond their rights. She often tended either not to see the realities of a situation, or to see realities that were not there at all; and made many other similar mistakes which can and do happen to all, not excepting the best of us; though with Donna Prassede they were apt to happen far too often, and not infrequently all at the same time.

When she heard of Lucia's great adventure, and all that was said of her on that occasion, she was taken with curiosity to see her; and sent a coach with an old retainer to fetch both mother and daughter. The latter shrugged her shoulders, and asked the tailor, who had brought the message, to find some way of excusing herself. So long as it was only a question of turning away ordinary people wanting to meet the girl of the miracle, the tailor had helped her out very willingly. But to refuse in this case seemed to him almost a subversive act. He protested and exclaimed and gave so many reasons: how that was not the way to behave and that it was an important family, and that one doesn't say no to the gentry, that it could make their fortune and that Donna Prassede, apart from anything else, was a saint – he was so insistent, in fact, that Lucia had to yield, particularly as Agnese was supporting every reason with 'Of course, of course.'

When they entered her presence the old lady gave them a most gracious reception, and congratulated them again and again, then questioned them and advised them; all with a superiority that was almost innate, though it was offset by so many expressions of humility, tempered by so much solicitude for them, and flavoured with so much piety, that Agnese almost immediately, and Lucia soon after, began to feel relieved of the oppressive respect which was induced in them at first by the presence of the gentry; they even began to find a certain attraction in it. Anyway, to cut a long story short, Donna Prassede, hearing that the cardinal had undertaken to find Lucia a refuge, urged on by a desire to second and also to forestall that good intention herself, offered to take the girl into her household, where, without being bound to any particular service, she could help the other women at their tasks when she wanted to. She added that she would inform his Grace of this herself.

Apart from the obvious and immediate good in this deed, Donna Prassede also saw and proposed to herself another which perhaps to her outweighed the first: that of reforming a young mind, and of bringing back to the right path one who was in sore need of it. For, from the moment when she had first heard Lucia mentioned, she had been convinced at once that a young woman who could promise herself in marriage to a ne'er-do-well, to a seditious element – a gallowsbird, in fact – must have some defect or secret failing in her. Tell me who your friends are, and I'll tell you who you are. The sight of Lucia had confirmed this conviction. Not that at bottom, as they say, she did not seem a good young woman, but there were many reservations. That hanging head, with its chin always on the base of her neck, that way of not replying, or of replying in short little phrases, as if forced to, might denote modesty, but they could also denote a great deal of stubbornness; it did not take much to see that that head had its own ideas. And that continuous blushing, and those stifled sighs.... Then a pair of great eyes which Donna Prassede did not like at all. She felt as sure as if she had heard it on good authority that all Lucia's misfortunes were a punishment from Heaven for her attachment to that good-for-nothing, and a warning to her to break away from him completely; and this being the case, she proposed to co-operate herself towards so good an end. For, as she often told herself and others, her whole object in life was to help to carry out the will of Heaven; but she often made the great mistake of taking for the will of Heaven her own brain. She was very careful, however, not to give the least hint of the second intention we have mentioned. One of her maxims was that to succeed in doing people good, the first rule, in most cases, was to keep one's plans to oneself.

Mother and daughter looked at each other's faces. As they

were under the painful necessity of separating, the offer seemed
an acceptable one to both of them, if only because the house was
so near their village; so that, if the worst came to the worst, they
would be near each other and meet when the family came down
to the country again the next summer. Seeing assent in each
other's eyes, they both turned to Donna Prassede with the thanks
that mean acceptance. The latter repeated her kindnesses and
promises; and said she would send a letter down at once for them
to take to the cardinal.

On the women's departure, she had the letter composed by
Don Ferrante, whom she would use as a secretary on important
occasions, as he was a man of letters – of which more later. Don
Ferrante put all his knowledge into a communication of such
importance, and when he handed the draft over to his consort to
copy, warmly recommended her to take great care with the
handwriting; this being one of the many things which he had
studied and one of the few in the house over which he had any
control. Donna Prassede copied it out very carefully, and sent the
letter down to the tailor's. This was a day or two before the
cardinal sent his litter to bring Lucia and Agnese back to their
own village.

On their arrival, they got out at the priest's house, where the
cardinal was. Orders had been given for them to be introduced
to his presence at once. The chaplain, who was the first to see
them, carried these out, only detaining them long enough to give
them a hurried lesson on the etiquette to be used with his Grace
and the titles to be given him – which he usually did every time
that he could do so without the cardinal knowing. It was a
continuous torment to the poor man to see the disorder in this
respect reigning around the cardinal. 'All,' as he would say to
others of the suite, 'because the blessed man is too good to
people, because he's so very familiar.' And he would relate how
with his own ears he had several times heard people answer him
with a 'Yes, sir,' 'No, sir.'

The cardinal was at that moment discussing the affairs of the
parish with Don Abbondio; so that the latter did not have an
opportunity to give the women his instructions also, as he had
hoped to do. He was only able, as he passed near them on his
way out and their way in, to give them a wink to show that he
was pleased with them, and that like good folk they should go
on holding their tongues.

After the first greetings on one side, and the first bows on the other, Agnese took the letter from her bosom and gave it to the cardinal, saying, 'It's from Donna Prassede, who says she knows your illustrious lordship well, your Grace; as is only natural all you grandees should know each other. When you've read it, you'll see.'

'Good,' said Federigo, after reading it and extracting the honey from Don Ferrante's flowers. He knew that family well enough to be sure Lucia had been invited there with the best intentions, and that she would be safe there from the intrigues and violence of her persecutor. We have no positive knowledge of what his opinion was of Donna Prassede's brain. Probably she was not the person he would have chosen for this particular purpose; but, as we have said or hinted elsewhere, it was not his habit to undo things which did not concern him, in order to do them up better.

'Accept peacefully this new separation, and the uncertainty you are in,' he added then. 'Trust that it will all be over soon, and that the Lord will guide things towards that end to which He seems to have directed them; but you can be sure that whatever He wishes will be best for you.' He then gave to Lucia in particular a few more kind words of advice, some more of comfort to them both, blessed them, and dismissed them. As soon as they were outside they found themselves beset by a waiting swarm of friends – almost the whole population of the village, one might say – who bore them off home as if in triumph. The women all competed with each other in congratulations, sympathy, and inquiries; and there were cries of regret from everyone when they heard that Lucia was leaving next day. The men vied with each other in offers of service; every one of them wanted to stand guard over the cottage that night. At which our anonymous author has thought fit to make a proverb: D'you want lots of people to help you? Then try not to need it.

All this welcome confused and bewildered Lucia; Agnese was not so easily put out. But on the whole it did Lucia good too, taking her mind somewhat off the thoughts and memories which assailed her even in the midst of the excitement, at passing that door, entering those little rooms, at the sight of every object.

When the bell rang to announce that the service was about to begin, everyone moved off towards the church, and this was another triumphal march for our two women.

After the service, Don Abbondio, who had hurried off to see that Perpetua had arranged everything properly for the meal, was summoned by the cardinal. He presented himself at once before his lofty guest, who waited until he was near, and then began 'Father,' saying the word in such a way that the other realized that it was the beginning of a long and serious talk – 'Father, why did not you marry that poor girl Lucia to her betrothed?'

– They've let the cat out of the bag this morning – thought Don Abbondio, and stammered out in reply, 'Your Illustrious Grace will doubtless have heard of the various entanglements that arose from this affair. It's all been such a confusion that I can't get it all clear even today; as your illustrious lordship may also conclude from the fact of the girl being here, after all these adventures, as if by a miracle; and the young man, after other adventures, no one knows where he is.'

'I am asking,' went on the cardinal, 'if it is true that before all these things happened you had refused to celebrate the marriage on the appointed day when you had been asked to; and why?'

'Really . . . if your Illustrious Grace only knew . . . what threats . . . what terrible orders I had not to talk . . .' and he stopped there without finishing the sentence, respectfully implying by his manner that it would be indiscreet to inquire further.

'What!' said the cardinal, his voice and manner graver than usual. 'It is your bishop who, from his duty and for your justification, wants to know why you did not do what in the regular course of things it was your obligation to do.'

'Your Grace,' said Don Abbondio, making himself as small as possible, 'I didn't mean . . . But it seemed to me with it all being so confused and so long ago, and with nothing to be done about it, that there would be no point in raking it all up. . . . Still, still I'm sure . . . your Illustrious Grace wouldn't want to betray a poor parish priest. For you see, your Grace, your illustrious lordship can't be everywhere; and I stay here exposed to . . . But of course if you order me to, I'll tell you everything.'

'Tell me; my only wish is to find you blameless.'

Then Don Abbondio began to tell his doleful story; but he suppressed the chief name and substituted 'a great nobleman' for it, thus making what little concession to prudence he could in this tight corner.

'And had you no other reason?' asked the cardinal, when Don Abbondio had finished.

'Perhaps I didn't make myself quite plain,' replied the latter. 'They forbade me to carry out that marriage under pain of death.'

'And does that seem a sufficient reason for you not to carry out a definite duty?'

'I've always tried my best to do it – my duty, I mean – even at great inconvenience, but when one's life is at stake!'

'And when you presented yourself to the Church,' said Federigo in an even more solemn tone, 'to take this ministry upon yourself, did it give you a guarantee of life? Were you told that the duties of the ministry were free from every obstacle and immune from every danger? Were you told that your duty ended wherever danger began? Or were you not told exactly the opposite? Were you not warned that you were being sent out like a lamb among wolves? Did you not realize there were men of violence who might object to what you were ordered to do? Did He whose doctrine and example we follow, in imitation of Whom we call ourselves and let men call us shepherds – did He, when He came down to earth to carry out His mission, lay it down as a condition that His life should be safe? And did He need the Holy Unction, the laying-on of hands, the sacrament of priesthood to save and preserve that life for a few more days on earth at the expense of charity and duty? Let the world teach that as a virtue, and advocate it as a doctrine! What am I saying? Oh, shame! For even the world rejects it; the world also makes its own laws which prescribe evil as well as good; it has its own gospel – the gospel of pride and hatred – and it will not have it said that the love of life is a good reason for transgressing its precepts. It will not have it; and it is obeyed. And we! We, the children and the heralds of the promised land? What would become of the Chruch if such language as yours was that of all your brethren? Where would she now be if she had appeared in the world with such doctrines?'

Don Abbondio's head hung down. Before such arguments as these his spirit felt like a chick swept off in the talons of a hawk, to an unknown region, into an air which it had never breathed. But seeing that he had to make some sort of reply, he said with rather forced submissiveness, 'Your most Illustrious Grace, I may be in the wrong. When life isn't supposed to count, I don't know what to say. But I don't see what's to be gained by it, even if one did go and try and be brave, when one has to deal with people with might on their side, who don't want to listen to reason. And that lord is a person with whom one can't either win or come to terms.'

'And don't you realize that suffering for the cause of justice is our way of conquering? If you do not know this, what is it you preach? What is it you teach? What are the *good tidings* you have to announce to the poor? Does anyone expect you to conquer might by might? You will certainly never be asked one day if you managed to check the strong; for you were not given either the mission or the means for that. But you will assuredly be asked if you have used the means you had at your disposal to do what was prescribed, even when the strong had the temerity to try to forbid you.'

– These saints are peculiar too – Don Abbondio was thinking meanwhile. – Really, what it boils down to is that he's more concerned about the loves of two young people than about the life of a poor priest. – And for his part, he would have been only too glad for the conversation to end there; but at every pause he saw the cardinal waiting and looking as if he expected a reply, a confession, or an apology: something anyway.

'I can only repeat, your Grace,' he therefore replied, 'that I'm in the wrong. . . . But courage isn't a thing one can give oneself.'

'And why, then, I might ask you, have you bound yourself to a ministry which pledges you to a continual struggle with the passions of the world? But why, I would rather ask, have you forgotten that whenever you need courage to carry out your obligations in this ministry, however you started in it, there is One who will give it infallibly if you but ask for it? Do you think that all those millions of martyrs were courageous by nature? That they naturally held life of so little account? So many young people who were beginning to enjoy it, so many old ones who were used to regretting its drawing near its close? So many virgins, and so many wives, and so many mothers? They all had the courage, because courage was necessary; and they had trust. Knowing your own weakness and your own duties, did you ever think of preparing yourself for the difficult situations that might overtake you, that have overtaken you? Ah! If you have loved (as you must have loved) your flock for so many years of pastoral labours, if you have put all your heart and your cares and your delight in them, then courage ought not to fail you in the moment of need. Love is bold. Surely, then, if you loved those who have been entrusted to your spiritual care, those whom you call your children, surely, when you saw two of them threatened together with yourself, ah, surely then love must have made you tremble for their sakes, as the weakness of the flesh had made you tremble for your own? You must have felt humiliated at those first fears, because they were the result of your cowardice. You must have begged for the strength to overcome them, to expel them as a temptation. At least you must have felt that holy and noble fear for others, for your own children, that fear which must have given you no peace, that must have prompted you, urged you to think, to do everything possible to avert the danger that was threatening them. . . . What did this fear, this love, inspire in you? What did you do for them? What did you think of doing?'

And he fell silent as if awaiting a reply.

CHAPTER 26

At such a question Don Abbondio, who had been struggling meanwhile to find something to reply to the other less precise ones, stood rooted there without uttering a word. And, to tell the truth, even we, sitting with our manuscript in front of us and a pen in our hands, and nothing to contend with except phrases, or anything to fear but the criticisms of our readers – even we, I say, feel a certain reluctance to proceed. We find something rather strange in this proposal with so little effort of a series of such admirable precepts of heroism and charity, of keen solicitude for others, and of unlimited sacrifice of self. But reflecting that these things were said by one who actually practised them, we will forge bravely ahead.

'You don't answer?' resumed the cardinal. 'Ah, if you had done, on your part, what charity and duty required of you, then, whatever the turn things took, you would not be without an answer now. Just see for yourself, then, what you have done. You have obeyed the behests of evil, unmindful of what was prescribed for you by duty. You have obeyed them without hesitation. Evil had shown itself to you to intimate its desires; but it wished to remain hidden from those who could have taken precautions and been on guard against it. It wanted to avoid any noise, it wanted secrecy to mature at leisure its designs of treachery and violence. It ordered you to transgress and to be silent. You have transgressed and you have not spoken. I ask now if you have not done more; you must tell me if it is true that you have given false pretexts for your refusal, so as not to reveal your motive for it.' And here he paused, again awaiting a reply.

– These sneaks have gone and reported that to him too – thought Don Abbondio; but he gave no sign of having anything to say: so the cardinal went on, 'If it is really true that you have told these poor people what was false in order to keep them in the ignorance and obscurity in which iniquity wanted them . . . then I must believe it; then it only remains for me to blush with you, and for you, I hope, to weep with me. See where you have been led (kind heavens, and you have even brought it up now as an excuse!) by your regard for this life that must end. It has led you. . . . Refute these words freely if you think them unjust, and take them in salutary humility if they are not . . . it has led you to deceive the weak, to lie to your own children.'

– So that's the way things go – Don Abbondio was saying to himself meanwhile: – with that devil incarnate – and he was thinking of the unnamed – he flings his arms round his neck; and with me, only for telling a half-lie just to save my skin, he makes all this fuss. But they're our superiors, they're always in the right. It's just my unlucky star that everyone sets on me, even the saints. – Aloud he said, 'I've done wrong; I realize I've done wrong; but what *was* I to do in a predicament like that?'

'You can still ask that? And have I not told you? Was there any need to tell you? To love, my son; to love and to pray. Then you would have felt that the forces of evil can threaten and can strike, but they cannot command. You would have joined together, according to the laws of God, what man wished to put asunder. You would have done those poor unhappy creatures the service they had a right to ask of you. For the consequences God Himself would have been surety, for you would have been treading in His path; by taking another, you have made yourself your own surety; and see what the consequences are! But had all human resources failed you? Was there no way out, had you been willing to look around you, and think about it, and seek for it? You know now that those poor creatures would have found their own solution had they been married: they were ready to flee from the face of their oppressor, and had already decided on their place of refuge. But even apart from that, did it never occur to you that after all you had a superior? A superior who could never have this authority to reprimand you for failing in your office unless he also had the obligation to help you carry it out? Why did you not think of informing your bishop of the obstacles put up by an infamous violence against the exercise of your ministry?'

– Perpetua's advice! – thought Don Abbondio irritably; what he had most vividly before him during this speech was the picture of the bravi and the thought that Don Rodrigo was still alive and healthy, and would be bound to come back one day or the other in glory and triumph and rage. And although the dignified presence, the appearance and language of the prelate, confused and rather frightened him, it was a fear that did not overwhelm him completely, or drive out all idea of resistance; for at the back of his mind was the thought that the cardinal, when all was said and done, had neither musket nor sword nor bravi.

'How was it you did not think,' went on the latter, 'that if there was no other asylum open to these innocent refugees, I was there to receive them and put them in a place of safety, had you sent them to me, sent those outcasts to your bishop as his own, as a precious part, I do not say of his duties, but of his riches. And as for you, I should have taken your anxiety on myself; I would not have been able to sleep until I was sure that not a hair of your head would be touched. Did I not have the means, or the place, to safeguard your life? Do you not think that that man, with all his daring, would have found that daring ebbing away entirely when he knew his plots were known outside of here, were known to me, that I was watching him and was determined to use all the means in my power in your defence? Did you not know that just as men often promise more than they can maintain, so they frequently threaten more than they are prepared to perform? Did you not know that the forces of evil depend not only on their own strength, but also on the credulity and fears of others?'

– Just Perpetua's arguments – thought Don Abbondio here again, without ever reflecting that his servant and Federigo Borromeo finding themselves in agreement on what he could and should have done told very much against him.

'But you,' pursued the cardinal in conclusion. 'Did you see nothing, did you want to see nothing but your own temporal danger? What wonder, then, that it should seem so great as to outweigh for you every other consideration!'

'It was because I saw those awful faces,' blurted out Don Abbondio, 'and heard what they said. Your Illustrious Grace talks well; but you should have been in a poor priest's shoes, and on the spot yourself.'

Hardly were these words uttered than he bit his tongue. He realized that he had let his irritation carry him too far, and said to himself – Now for the hail. – But on timidly raising his eyes, he was utterly amazed to see the aspect of this man, whom he would never succeed in fathoming or understanding, pass from that solemn air of authority and reproof to one of sorrowful and pensive gravity.

'Yes, alas!' said Federigo. 'Such is our miserable and terrible lot. We must exact rigorously from others what only God knows if we are ready to give ourselves; we must judge, correct, reprove; and only God knows what we ourselves would do in like case, what we have done in like cases! But woe to me if I was to take my own weakness as a measure of others' duty, or as a standard for my own teaching! And yet it is certainly my duty to set an example to others, as well as preaching to them, and not be like the scribes and pharisees who load others with the burdens which they cannot carry themselves and would not touch with a finger.* Therefore, my son, my brother, since the errors of those in high places are often better known to others than to themselves, tell me frankly if you know that I have failed in any duty of mine through cowardice, through any other consideration; confront me with it, so that at least a confession can make amends where an example had been wanting. Reprove me freely for my weaknesses; and then my words will acquire more value in my mouth, for you will have a livelier feeling that they do not come from me, but from One who can give both you and me the necessary strength to do what they prescribe.'

– Oh, what a holy man! But what a worrier! – Don Abbondio was thinking. – Even with himself; for ever prying and fussing, criticizing and cross-questioning; even with himself. – Then he said aloud, 'Oh, your Grace! Are you making fun of me? Who does not know your illustrious lordship's firm courage and intrepid zeal?' And to himself he added – Only too well. –

'I was not asking for praises, which make me tremble,' said Federigo; 'for the Lord knows my failings, and those I know myself are enough to confound me. But I wanted – I still want – us to be confounded together before Him, that we may take confidence together. I want you, for your sake, to realize how opposed your conduct has been, and your language still is, to the laws which you preach, and by which you will be judged.'

'Everything falls on me!' said Don Abbondio. 'But the people who came and told you this, they didn't tell you how they got into my house by treachery, so as to take me by surprise, and carry out a marriage against the rules.'

'They did tell me, my son; but this grieves me, this alarms me
– that you should still want to excuse yourself by accusing others,
and use for your accusals what ought to be part of your own
confession. Who put them, I will not say under the necessity, but
under the temptation, of doing what they did? Would they have
ever tried that devious way, had the lawful one not been closed
to them? Would they have ever thought of tricking their pastor,
if they had been taken into his arms, been helped and advised by
him? Of surprising him, had he not concealed himself? And then
you lay the blame on them? And then you are indignant because,
after so many misfortunes – nay, in the very midst of misfortune
still – they gave vent to some words of complaint to their – to
your pastor? That the appeals of the oppressed and the complaints of the afflicted are odious to the world is to be expected,
for the world is like that; but not to us! And what advantage
would it have been to you had they remained silent? Would it
have been any gain for you for their cause to go up entire before
the judgement of God? Is it not another reason for your loving
these people – and you have so many reasons already – that they
have given you this opportunity of hearing the sincere voice of
your bishop, that they have given you a means of realizing better,
and partly discharging, the great debt you owe them? Ah, even
had they provoked you, harmed you, persecuted you, I would tell
you (and should it be necessary to tell you?) to love them for that
very reason. Love them because they have suffered, because they
are still suffering, because they are yours, because they are weak,
because you are in need of forgiveness, and to obtain it, think
how potent their prayers could be!'

Don Abbondio was silent; but it was no longer the sullen,
impatient silence of before: it was the silence of one who has
more things to think about than he has to say. The words which
he had heard were the unexpected conclusions, the new applica-
tions of a doctrine which he had long believed in his heart and
never disputed. The misfortunes of others, which he had always
been distracted from considering by preoccupation with his own,
now came to him with a new impact. And if he did not feel all
the remorse which the sermon was intended to produce in him
(for that same fear was always there to act as counsel for the
defence), he did at least feel some: he felt a certain dissatisfaction
with himself, a sense of compassion for others, a mixed and
confused tenderness. He was – if the comparison be allowed to
pass – like the damp, crushed wick of a candle, which, when put

near the flame of a torch, first smokes and spits and splutters and refuses to light, but finally catches, and begins to burn more or less well. He would have accused himself openly, he would have wept, had it not been for the thought of Don Rodrigo; but even so, he showed himself sufficiently moved for the cardinal to notice that his words had not been without effect.

'Now,' went on the latter, 'one is a fugitive from his home, the other on the point of abandoning hers, both of them with only too strong reasons for keeping away, and no likelihood of ever reuniting here again, content to hope that God will reunite them elsewhere. Now, alas, they do not need you; now, alas, you have no opportunity to help them, nor can any be discovered in the short distance we can see into the future. But who knows if God in His mercy is not preparing some? Ah, do not let the chance slip! Seek it out, be on the watch for it, pray Him to make it come.'

'I won't fail to, my lord; I won't fail to, really I won't,' replied Don Abbondio in a tone which came at that moment from his very heart.

'Ah, yes, my son, yes!' exclaimed Federigo; and with a dignity full of affection, concluded, 'Heaven knows how much I would have preferred to have quite a different conversation with you. Both of us have now lived long; Heaven knows how hard it has been for me to have to inflict reproaches on your white hairs, and how much more gladly I would have preferred us to console each other in our common cares and troubles with talk of a blessed hope which is now so near us. May God grant that what I have had to say to you may help both you and me. Do not make me have to answer, on the judgement day, for allowing you to retain an office in which you have so unhappily been wanting. Let us redeem the time; midnight is near; the Bridegroom cannot be far off; let us keep our lamps alight.* Let us offer our hearts, wretched and empty as they are, to God, that He may be pleased to fill them with that charity which amends the past, which ensures the future, which fears and trusts, weeps and rejoices in its knowledge; which becomes in every instance the virtue of which we stand in need.'

So saying, he moved from the room; and Don Abbondio followed along behind.

Here our anonymous chronicler tells us that this was not the only interview between these two personages, nor was Lucia the only subject of their discussions, but that he had confined himself to this so as not to stray too far from the main subject of the story. And he says that for the same reason he does not mention other notable things said by Federigo in the course of his visit, nor his liberality, nor the quarrels he composed, nor the ancient feuds between individuals, families, complete districts, which he settled or (much more frequently, we fear) temporarily lulled, nor the various tyrants and bravi whom he tamed, either for life or at least for a time – all of which things occurred in varying degrees in every place in his diocese where that excellent man spent some time.

Our chronicler then goes on to say that Donna Prassede came next morning, as had been arranged, to fetch Lucia and pay her respects to the cardinal, who praised the girl and recommended her warmly to her care. You can imagine Lucia's tears at her parting from her mother; and she left her cottage and bade farewell to the village a second time with that sense of doubly bitter sorrow that one feels on leaving the only place that one has ever loved, and that can be so no longer. But this was not her last farewell to her mother; for Donna Pressede said that she was staying on at her country house, which was not far away, for a few days longer, and Agnese promised her daughter to go and see her there, to give and to receive an even sadder farewell.

The cardinal also was just starting off to continue his tour, when the priest of that parish in which lay the castle of the unnamed arrived and asked to speak to him. On being admitted, he presented a packet and a letter from that nobleman, asking Federigo to persuade Lucia's mother to accept the hundred gold *scudi* in the packet, to serve as a dowry for the girl or for whatever use they thought best; he asked the cardinal at the same time to tell them that if ever at any time they thought there was anything he could do for them, the poor girl knew, only too well, where he lived; and that for him this would be one of the greatest pieces of good fortune. The cardinal sent for Agnese at once, and gave her the message, to which she listened with no less amazement than satisfaction; then he handed her the packet, which she took without much persuasion. 'May God reward that lord,' said she. 'And please, your Illustrious Grace, thank him very kindly. And don't tell anyone about it, for this is a village where ... Excuse me, please; I'm sure someone of your rank wouldn't go and gossip about a thing like that; but ... you know what I mean.'

She then went very quietly home, locked herself in her room, and undid the package; and, though prepared, she was spellbound at seeing all in a heap, and all her own, so many of those coins which she had perhaps only seen before one by one, and then very rarely. She counted them, and had some difficulty in stacking them up and keeping them there, for they kept on falling down and sliding between her inexpert fingers; finally she managed to make them up into a roll again, wrapped them up in a cloth, tied them round with string, and tucked them securely into a corner of her mattress. The rest of that day she spent in a reverie, making plans for the future, and longing for the next day. On going to bed, she lay awake for some time, her thoughts with the hundred *scudi* underneath her; on falling asleep, she saw them in her dreams. At break of day she got up and set off at once towards the country house where Lucia was.

The latter, on her side, although her great aversion to talking about her vow had not abated, had decided even so to force herself to tell her mother all about it during this interview, which would be the last they would have for a long time.

No sooner were they alone, than Agnese, with a look of animation, and at the same time in a low voice, as if there were someone present whom she did not want to hear, began, 'I've got something wonderful to tell you,' and told her about their unexpected good fortune.

'God bless him, that lord,' said Lucia. 'So you'll have enough to be comfortable yourself, and to help others.'

'What?' said Agnese. 'Can't you see what a lot of things we can do with all this money? Listen; all I have is you – you two, I might say, for I've always regarded Renzo as my own son ever since he began courting you. I only hope nothing awful's happened to him, seeing as he's not let us know anything; but it can't all have gone badly, eh? Let's hope not, let's hope not. As for me, as for me, I'd have liked to have left my bones in my own village; but now that you can't be here, thanks to that villain – and anyway, the very thought of his being near makes me begin to hate my own village – I can be happy wherever you two are. I've been ready from the first to go with you two to the end of the world, if need be; and I've always been of that mind; but how could it be done without money? D'you understand now? That little money the poor boy had laid aside with so much pinching and scraping, the law officers came and swept it all away; but the Lord has sent us some good luck to make up for it. So when he's found a way of letting us know he's still alive, and where he is, and what his intentions are, I'll come to Milan and fetch you –

yes, I'll come and fetch you myself. I would have thought twice about doing it before; but misfortune makes one more self-reliant; I've been as far as Monza, and know what travelling is. I'll take some sensible companion with me, some relation, like Alessio from Maggianico, for instance; for there's no really sensible man in our own village; I'll come with him; we'll pay all the expenses, and . . . d'you understand?'

But seeing that Lucia, instead of brightening, was looking more dejected and showing only a tenderness without gaiety, she broke off her speech in the middle, and said, 'But what's the matter? Don't you agree?'

'Poor mother!' exclaimed Lucia, throwing an arm round her neck and burying her face in her bosom.

'What's the matter?' asked her mother anxiously once more.

'I should have told you before,' replied Lucia, raising her face and drying her tears. 'But I never had the heart to; have pity on me.'

'Tell me what; come.'

'I can't be that poor boy's wife any longer!'

'What? what?'

Then Lucia, with head low and heaving breast, weeping silently, like one describing something which is irrevocable however unpleasant it may be, told her about the vow; and clasping her hands together at the same time, and begging her mother's forgiveness once again for not having spoken till then, she implored her not to tell a living soul about it, and to help her carry out what she had promised.

Agnese was dumbfounded and filled with consternation. She would have been indignant at its having been kept from her; but a realization of the gravity of the case stifled her personal annoyance. She would have said: What have you done? but this, it seemed to her, would be quarrelling with Heaven itself; particularly as Lucia began describing the horrors of that night in more vivid colours than ever, her black desolation, her unforeseen liberation, between which her promise had so explicitly, so solemnly, been made. And meanwhile various examples also occurred to Agnese of strange and terrible punishments brought down by the violation of some vow, which she had heard tell of, and had herself told her daughter. After a moment or two as if in a trance, she said, 'And what will you do now?'

'Now,' replied Lucia, 'it is for the Lord to provide – for the

Lord and for Our Lady. I've put myself into their hands; they haven't abandoned me so far, and they'll not forsake me now that ... The only favour I ask of the Lord, after the salvation of my soul, is that He will let me come back to you again; and He will grant me that – yes, He will grant me that. That day ... in that coach ... Oh, Most Holy Virgin! ... Those men! ... Whoever could have thought they were leading me to someone who'd take me to meet you the next day?'

'But not to tell your mother all about it at once!' said Agnese, with a slight irritation tempered by tenderness and pity.

'Pity me; I had not the heart.... And what use would it have been to distress you before?'

'And Renzo?' said Agnese, shaking her head.

'Ah!' exclaimed Lucia, starting, 'I must never think of that poor boy again. It seemed before as if he wasn't destined to ... See how the Lord seems to have wanted to keep us apart. And who knows...? But no, no. He will have preserved him from danger, and will make him even happier without me.'

'But meanwhile,' went on her mother, 'if only you hadn't gone and bound yourself for good and all, and if Renzo hasn't come to any harm, I'd have arranged everything with that money.'

'But would that money ever have come,' replied Lucia, 'if I hadn't spent that terrible night? It's the Lord who's willed that it should all fall out like this; His will be done,' and her voice was drowned in tears.

At this unexpected argument Agnese became silent and thoughtful. After a moment or two, Lucia repressed her sobs, and went on, 'Now that it's done, we must resign ourselves to it with a good heart; and you, poor mother, you can help me, firstly by praying to the Lord for your poor daughter, and then ... that poor boy will have to be told. Can you take that on? Do, please; for you know how to do it. When you find out where he is, get someone to write a letter to him, find someone who ... your cousin Alessio's just the one, he's a prudent, kindly man, and he's always been friendly, and won't talk about it. Get him to write what's happened, where I was taken to, how I suffered, and how it was God's will; and how he's to resign himself, for I can't ever marry anyone. And see it's broken to him kindly; explain that I've promised, that I've made a real vow. When he knows what I've promised to Our Lady ... he's always been God-fearing. And the first time you have news of him, do get someone to write to me, and let me know he's safe and well, and then . . . don't let me know anything more.'

Agnese, very tenderly, assured her daughter that everything would be done as she wished.

'There's something else I'd like to say,' went on Lucia. 'If that poor boy hadn't had the misfortune to think of me, nothing that's happened to him would have come about at all. He's a wanderer on the earth. They've cut him off from his livelihood. They've taken away his belongings – those savings he had made, you know why, poor boy . . . and we've so much money! Oh, mother! As the Lord has sent us so much, and it's really true you look on that poor boy as your own . . . Yes, as your own son! Oh, then, divide it between you; for God will surely not fail us. Try and find some bearer you can trust, and send it to him, for Heaven knows how much he must need it!'

'Very well, bless your heart!' replied Agnese. 'Of course I'll send it to him. Poor boy! Why d'you think I was so glad of the money? Ah, well . . . I came along here feeling so happy. Anyway, I'll send it him. Poor Renzo! But he too . . . I know whom I'm talking about; of course money's welcome to those that need it; but this won't be the kind to make him any fatter.'

Lucia thanked her mother for her prompt and generous acquiescence, with such gratitude and affection that an observer would have realized that her heart was still clinging to Renzo, perhaps more than she herself would have believed.

'And what'll a poor old woman like me do without you?' said Agnese, weeping in her turn.

'And I without you, poor mother? And in a strange house, too? And down there in Milan . . . But the Lord will be with us both, and will bring us together again afterwards. We'll see each other again in eight or nine months; and by that time, perhaps sooner, He will have arranged things so that we come together again. Let us leave it to Him. I shall always ask the Madonna for that favour. If I had anything else to offer her, I would do so; but she is so merciful that she will grant me this for nothing.'

With these and other similar oft-repeated words of lament and comfort, complaint and resignation, with many an exhortation and promise to secrecy, with many a tear, and after long and oft-renewed embraces, the women separated, each promising in turn to see each other the following autumn at the latest; just as if the fulfilment of this depended on them, and yet just as people always do in similar circumstances.

After this a long time went by before Agnese was able to get any news of Renzo. No letter or message from him reached her; and none of those whom she could consult in the village and neighbourhood knew any more than she did.

She was not the only one making these inquiries in vain. Cardinal Federigo had not just told the poor woman as a matter of form that he wanted to find out about the young man, but had in fact written off at once to do so. On his return to Milan from his tour he had received a reply to say that nothing could be discovered about the whereabouts of the person named; that he had certainly stayed some time in the house of a relative of his at such-and-such a village, where he had given no one any occasion to talk about him; but that one morning he had suddenly disappeared, and even his relative did not know what had become of him, and could only repeat some vague and contradictory rumours current round there, that he had enlisted for the Levant, that he had crossed over into Germany, or perished fording a river; but that they would not fail to be on the watch, in case something more positive ever came to light, and pass it on at once to his most illustrious and most reverend lordship.

Later on these and various other rumours eventually spread into the territory of Lecco, and consequently reached Agnese's ears. The poor woman did her utmost to find out which was the true version by trying to get to the origin of one after the other, but she never succeeded in tracing one further than that *they say*, which, even nowadays, is considered as proof of so many things. Sometimes she had scarcely been told one story before someone came along and said that it was all quite untrue; but only to produce another one in exchange which was equally strange or sinister. All that was just gossip; here are the facts.

The governor of Milan, and Captain-General in Italy, Don Gonzalo Fernandez de Cordova, had stirred up a great fuss with his lordship the Venetian resident in Milan because a malefactor, a public thief, an organizer of plunder and murder, the notorious Lorenzo Tramaglino, who had fomented a riot to escape when in the very hands of the law, had been received and harboured on Bergamese soil. The resident had answered that this was all quite new to him, and that he would write to Venice, so that he could give His Excellency whatever explanation there might be.

Now, one of the maxims of Venetian policy was the promotion and encouragement of the emigration of Milanese silk-workers into Bergamese territory; to which end the Venetians arranged for them to have many advantages there, particularly the one without which all others are worthless – security. But in any dispute between two important litigants the third party always has to pay some price or other, however small; and so Bortolo was warned in confidence, it is not known by whom, that Renzo was not safe in that village, and would do best to go into some other factory, and also to change his name for a while. Bortolo guessed the reason, asked no questions, and hurried off to tell his cousin, whom he bundled into a trap with him and took to another silk-mill, about fifteen miles away, where he introduced him to the proprietor, an old acquaintance, who had also come from the state of Milan, under the name of Antonio Rivolta. This man, though times were bad, did not wait to be asked twice before taking on a workman recommended as honest and skilful by a trustworthy person who knew the business. And on trying him out he could only congratulate himself on his acquisition; except that at first the young man seemed to be a bit dim, as when he called 'Antonio!' he usually did not reply.

Shortly afterwards the sheriff of Bergamo received an order from Venice, couched in very mild terms, telling him to find and forward information as to whether such a person was to be found under his jurisdiction, and in which particular village. The sheriff had inquiries made in the way which he saw was required, and sent back a negative answer, which was sent off to the resident in Milan, who passed it on to the grand chancellor, who forwarded it to Don Gonzalo Fernandez de Cordova.

There were, of course, a few inquisitive people who asked Bortolo why that youth was no longer there, and where he had gone. Bortolo answered the first query, 'Why, he's just disappeared.' But afterwards, to get rid of the more insistent, without letting them suspect the truth, he had thought it best to hand out to them one or another of the stories which we have mentioned above; but always as uncertain reports which he had heard himself, without having any positive authority for them.

But when the inquiry was made on the cardinal's behalf, without his being named and with some show of mystery and importance and hints that they were being made in the name of some important personage, Bortolo got more suspicious than ever, and decided that he had better give the usual answer, with the exception that, as an important personage was concerned, he handed out in one go all the various rumours which he had distributed one by one on the various different occasions.

Let it not be thought, however, that a nobleman of Don Gonzalo's degree had a very strong grudge against the poor silk-worker from the mountains; or that he had been informed of the disrespectful jest made by the latter about the Moorish king chained by the throat, and wanted to pay him back for it; or that he considered him a person dangerous enough to persecute even as a fugitive, and to prevent him living even at a distance, like the Roman senate with Hannibal.* Don Gonzalo had far too many important matters on his hands to bother himself very much about the doings of Renzo; and if he did appear to worry over them, this was due to a singular combination of events by which poor Renzo, without wanting to, and without being aware of it either then or later, was linked with those same important matters by the thinnest and most invisible of threads.

CHAPTER 27

We have already had occasion more than once to mention the war then raging for the succession to the states of the Duke Vincenzo Gonzaga, second of his name; but this has always been in moments of great haste; so we have never been able to give it more than a cursory glance.* Now, however, some more detailed description of this is needed for the understanding of our story. They are things that any student of history is bound to know; but as we must presume, from a just estimate of ourselves, that this work is unlikely to be read by any but the ignorant, it will not be amiss for us to say enough here to give those who need it some smattering of the facts.

We have already said that on the death of the former duke, the first in the line of succession, Carlo Gonzaga, head of a cadet branch established in France, where he held the duchies of Nevers and Rhetel, had entered into possession of Mantua; and, we may now add, of Montferrat, which we had forgotten in our hurry. The Court of Madrid, which wanted at all costs (we have also mentioned this) to exclude the new prince from these two fiefs, and needed a reason for excluding him (for to make war without a reason would be unjust), had declared itself upholder of the claims on Mantua of another Gonzaga – Ferrante, Prince of Guastalla – and on Montferrat of Carlo Emanuele I, Duke of

Savoy, and Margherita Gonzaga, Dowager Duchess of Lorraine. Don Gonzalo, who was of the family of the 'Gran Capitan', and bore his name, had already waged one war in Flanders, was most eager to wage another in Italy, and was perhaps the person calling most loudly for it to be declared; in the meanwhile, interpreting the intentions and anticipating the commands of the above-mentioned Court, he had concluded a treaty with the Duke of Savoy for the invasion and division of Montferrat, for which he had easily obtained the Count-Duke's ratification by leading him to believe that the conquest of Casale, the most strongly defended point on the sector allotted to the King of Spain, was an easy matter. He protested, however, in the king's name, that he did not intend to occupy a single village except as trustee pending the emperor's decision; for the latter, partly because of the influence of others and partly for reasons of his own, had meanwhile refused to invest the new duke, and had ordered him to give up the contested states in sequestration; the emperor would then, on hearing both sides, hand them over to whoever had a right to them. To this Nevers had refused to submit.

The latter, too, had important friends: Cardinal Richelieu, the Venetian signory, and the pope – who, as we have said, was Urban VIII. But the first of these, since he was engaged at the time in the siege of La Rochelle and a war with England, and was thwarted by the party of the queen-mother, Maria de' Medici (who was opposed to the house of Nevers for certain reasons of her own), could give nothing but hopes. The Venetians would not make a move, nor even declare themselves until the French army came down into Italy; they helped the duke surreptitiously as best they could, by making protests, suggestions, and exhortations, peaceful or threatening according to circumstances, to the Court of Madrid or the governor of Milan. The pope was recommending Nevers to his friends, interceding in his favour with his enemies, and making proposals for a settlement; but he would not hear of putting any men in the field.

Thus the two partners in aggression were able to begin their concerted operations all the more securely. The Duke of Savoy had, on his part, entered Montferrat; Don Gonzalo began with great alacrity to lay siege to Casale; but he did not find it quite as satisfactory as he had anticipated; for it should not be thought that everything in war is roses. The Court did not give him the help he wanted, and even left him without the most necessary equipment. His ally, on the other hand, was helping too much –

by which I mean that, after taking his own sector, he kept nibbling at the one assigned to the King of Spain. Don Gonzalo ground his teeth with rage at this; but he feared that if he made any fuss Carlo Emanuele, who was as active in his intrigues and as fickle in his treaties as he was valiant in arms, would go over to France; so he was forced to shut his eyes, swallow it down, and keep quiet. Then the siege was going badly, dragging on too long, sometimes slipping back, owing partly to the steady, wary, resolute conduct of the besieged, partly to his lack of men, and partly, if one is to believe the historians, to his many blunders. The latter we will leave an open question, being inclined to find it a very happy circumstance if true, and if because of this a few less men were killed, maimed, or lamed in that enterprise, and even, *ceteris paribus** a few less roof-tiles damaged in Casale. In these straits he received the news of the riots in Milan, and hurried off there in person.

In the report submitted to him there mention was made of Renzo's rebellious and clamorous fight and of the real and supposed facts which had caused his arrest; and he was also told that this person had taken refuge in Bergamese territory. This circumstance caught Don Gonzalo's attention. He had been informed from a quite different quarter that the Venetians had been elated at the insurrection in Milan, and that they thought at first that he would be forced to raise the siege of Casale, and still considered him to be very shaken and worried about it; all the more so as on the heels of this came the news for which the Venetians were longing and which he was dreading – the fall of La Rochelle. Highly mortified, both as a man and as a politician, that these gentlemen should have such a low opinion of his affairs, he was on the look-out for every chance to make them see that he had lost none of his former confidence; for to say expressly 'I am not afraid,' is the same as saying just nothing at all. One good way is to take umbrage, pick a quarrel, and put up a complaint; and so when the Venetian resident came to pay him his respects and also to judge by his face and manner what he felt like inside (note all this; for it is the subtle old diplomacy), Don Gonzalo first talked about the riots, in the light tone of voice of one who has already set everything to rights, and then made that fuss about Renzo of which the reader already knows, as he also knows what happened in consequence. After that he took no further interest in such a trivial matter, which was over and done with so far as he was concerned; and when, a long time afterwards, the reply reached him in his camp above Casale, whither he had returned and where he had quite different preoccupations, he got up and threw back his head like a silkworm looking for a leaf, stood there a moment to bring back into his mind a matter of which only a vague shadow now remained, recalled the episode, had a dim, fleeting idea of the person involved, passed on to something else, and thought no more about it.

But Renzo, who from the few hints which he had been given was prepared for anything rather than this kindly indifference, spent some time with no other thought, or rather care, than hiding himself away. He longed to send news of himself to the women and to get theirs; but there were two great difficulties. One was that he would have to confide in a scribe, for the poor boy could not write, or even read in the broader sense of the word. If when asked, as the reader may remember, by Doctor Quibble-weaver, he had replied that he could, it was not a boast, or a bluff, as the saying is: it was true that he could read print, taking his time about it; but handwriting was quite another thing. So he was forced to confide his affairs, and a close secret like this, to a third person; and a man who could wield a pen and was also to be trusted was not so easy to find in those days, particularly in a village where he had no old acquaintances. The other difficulty was to find a messenger: someone who was going to those very parts, who was willing to be charged with the letter, and who would really take the trouble to deliver it – all things difficult, too, to find in one single person.

Finally, after a great deal of searching, he found someone to do the writing for him. But not knowing if the women were still at Monza, or where, he thought it best to enclose the letter to Agnese in another addressed to Fra Cristoforo. The writer also undertook to get the packet delivered, and handed it over to someone who was to pass not far from Pescarenico; the latter left it, with an earnest request that it should be sent on, at an inn at the nearest point on his journey; as the envelope was addressed to a monastery, it reached there; but what became of it after that was never known. Finding that he got no reply, Renzo sent off a further letter, more or less the same as the first, and enclosed it in another to a friend or relation of his at Lecco. Another bearer was sought and found; this time the letter reached the person to whom it was addressed. Agnese went hurrying over to Maggianico, and had it read and explained by that cousin Alessio of hers;

together they thought up a reply, which he put down on paper; a way was found of sending it to Antonio Rivolta at his place of residence. All this was not, however, done as quickly as we have described it. Renzo got the reply, and had another letter written back. In the end, a correspondence began between the two parties, which was neither rapid nor regular, but was yet, by fits and starts, continuous.

To form some idea of this correspondence, however, one should know a little about how such things were carried on then, indeed how they still are now; for I believe that in this particular there has been little or no change.

The peasant who cannot write and needs something written has recourse to one with a knowledge of that art, choosing him, as far as he can, from his own walk in life; for he is either diffident or distrustful of others. He tells him the circumstances with more or less coherence and clarity, and in the same way explains what he wants put on paper. The man of letters understands part of it, misunderstands the rest, gives some advice, suggests a few changes, and says: 'Leave it to me.' Then he takes his pen, transfers the other's thoughts into written form as best he can, correcting them, improving them, touching them up or toning them down and leaving things out, as he thinks most fitting; for – there's no help for it – those who know more than others are never willing to be a mere material instrument in their hands; and when they enter into others' affairs they want things to be done a little their own way. For all that, the aforesaid man of letters does not always succeed in saying everything that he would like; at times he says something completely different; it even happens to us who write for the press. When the letter composed in this way reaches the hands of the correspondent, who is equally unpractised in his ABC, he takes it to another learned person of the same type, who reads and expounds it to him. Questions arise as to how it is to be understood; for the interested party, basing himself on his knowledge of past facts, asserts that certain words mean one thing; while the reader, basing himself on his experience in composition, asserts that they mean another. Finally the one who does not know puts himself into the hands of the one who does, and entrusts him with the reply; which, being put together in the same way as the original one, is subject to a similar interpretation. And if, furthermore, the subject of the correspondence is a little delicate; if secret matters come into it which a third person should not understand in case of the letter going astray; if, with this possibility in view, there is even a definite intention of not putting things too clearly – then, however brief the correspondence, the two parties end by understanding each other about as well as two scholastic philosophers did in the olden days after arguing for four hours about the entelechy* – not to take a more modern example, in case we stir up a hornet's nest.

Now, the case of our two correspondents was exactly like the one we have described. The first letter written in Renzo's name dealt with a number of matters. First, after a much more concise but also much more jumbled account of his flight than the one which you have read, came a report on his present situation, from which Agnese and her interpreter were very far from getting any clear or complete picture; there were secret warnings, a change of name, his being safe but having to hide – things anyway unfamiliar to them, apart from the fact that in the letter they were put more or less in code. Then there were anxious, passionate inquiries about Lucia's misadventures, with obscure and agonized hints of the rumours that had reached Renzo. Finally there were uncertain and distant hopes, plans flung into the future, and promises and entreaties meanwhile to keep the faith plighted, not to lose patience or courage, and to wait for better days.

After some interval Agnese found a trustworthy means of sending Renzo a reply and the fifty *scudi* assigned to him by Lucia. Renzo was at a loss what to think at the sight of all that gold; and, his mind gripped by surprise and suspense that left no room for gratification, he rushed off to find his scribe, to have the letter interpreted and discover the key to so strange a mystery.

In the letter Lucia's scribe, after some complaint about the obscurity of Renzo's reply, went on to describe with about the same degree of clarity the tremendous story of that 'person' (as he called him); and here he accounted for the fifty *scudi*. Then the scribe went on to talk of the vow, but in a roundabout way, adding, in more direct and explicit terms, the advice to set his heart at rest and to think no more about her.

Renzo very nearly came to blows with his reader and interpreter. He trembled, horror-struck, shaking with rage at what he had understood, and at what he could not understand. Three or four times he had the terrible letter read over to him, now seeming to understand it better, and now finding what had at first seemed clear become obscure. And in this fever of passions, he insisted on the scribe taking up his pen at once and writing a reply. After the strongest imaginable expressions of pity and horror at Lucia's misfortunes, 'Write,' he went on dictating – 'write that I don't want to set my heart at rest, and never will; and that that's not the kind of advice to give a man like me; and that I won't touch the money; that I'll put it by and keep it aside for her dowry; that she ought to have been mine already; that I don't accept that vow; and that I've often heard of the Madonna intervening to help those in trouble and obtain favours for them, but never of her doing it to vex them and make them break their word; and that the pledge can't hold; and that with this money there's enough for us to set up house here; and that, if I seem in a bit of a mess at the moment, it's only a squall that'll soon pass over'; and other things of the kind.

Agnese received this letter, and had it answered; and so the correspondence went on, in the way we have described.

Lucia felt greatly relieved when her mother was able to tell her (I do not know by what means) that Renzo was alive and safe and had been informed. All she wanted now was for him to forget her; or, to be more exact, for him to try and forget her. She, on her side, made a similar resolution about him a hundred times a day; and made use of every means to put it into effect. She was assiduous at her work, and tried to occupy her mind with it entirely. When Renzo's image came up before her, she would recite or chant prayers to herself. But that image, just as if it had evil designs did not usually come to her so openly; it would introduce itself stealthily behind others, so that her mind did not realize that it had entered until it had been there some time. Lucia's thoughts were often with her mother (how could they have been otherwise?), and the imagined Renzo would come creeping in softly to make a third, as the real one had so often done. So he came to insinuate himself among all the people, all the places, all the memories of the past. And if the poor girl ever let herself indulge at times in day-dreams of the future, he would appear in them too, if only to say, 'Anyway, I won't be there!' Yet, if it was a hopeless undertaking not to think of him at all, Lucia did succeed, up to a point, in thinking of him less, or less intensely than her heart would have wished. She might have succeeded even better had she been alone in wanting to do so. But there was Donna Prassede, who, all bent, on her side, on banishing the young man from her mind, had found no better

expedient than to talk about him incessantly. 'Well?' she would
say, 'we're not thinking about that fellow any more, are we?'

'I'm not thinking about anybody,' Lucia would reply.

Donna Prassede was not to be appeased by an answer like that;
she would reply that deeds and not words were wanted, then go
on to dilate on the habits of young women, who, she would say,
'when they have set their hearts on some good-for-nothing (that's
the type they're always sweet on), will never shake him off. If an
honest, sensible engagement with a decent, steady citizen goes
wrong by some accident, they're soon resigned; but with a
dangerous rascal, the wound's incurable.' And then she would
launch into a philippic against the poor absent youth, the rogue
who had gone plundering and blood-letting in Milan; and she
would try and get Lucia to admit to villainies which he must have
committed in his own village as well.

Lucia, her voice trembling with shame, pain, and such indignation as her gentle nature and humble station allowed her,
would go on declaring and protesting that the poor boy had
never had anything but good said of him in his own village; she
only wished, she would say, that someone from there were
present to bear her witness. She even defended him as to his
adventures in Milan, of which she knew little, on the strength of
her knowledge of him and of his behaviour since childhood. She
defended him, or meant to defend him, out of pure charitable
duty and love of truth, and as (to use the word with which she
explained her feelings to herself) a neighbour. But Donna
Prassede would find fresh arguments in these apologies to convince Lucia that her heart was still lost to him. And, in fact, I am
not sure myself how things stood at those moments. The unworthy picture which the old woman drew of the youth conjured up
in contrast more vividly and clearly than ever the idea of him
which long association had formed in the girl's mind; the
memories which she had forcibly repressed now came crowding
back; this aversion and contempt recalled so many reasons for
esteem; this blind, unreasoning hatred made her pity well up
stronger than ever. And with these emotions, who can ever tell
how much there might or might not be of that other feeling
which so easily slips behind them into people's hearts – let alone
in the case of those hearts which are already having to keep it
out by force. Be that as it may, the conversation on Lucia's part
never lasted very long, for her words soon ended in tears.

If Donna Prassede had felt urged to treat her in this way from some inveterate hatred for her, those tears might perhaps have touched her heart and made her desist; but as she was speaking for good ends she would push on ruthlessly, just as groans and imploring cries might possibly stay the weapon of an enemy but not the instrument of a surgeon. When, however, she had done her duty thoroughly for the time being, she would pass on from reproaches and reprimands to exhortations and advice, seasoned with a few praises, to temper the bitter with the sweet, and to achieve her purpose more effectively by working on every impulse in Lucia's mind. Certainly these confrontations (which nearly always had the same beginning, middle, and end) left in the kindly girl no resentment against the harsh preacher, who treated her very sweetly in every other way, and whose good intentions could be seen even here. Yet they left her in such agitation, in such a flurry of thoughts and emotions, that much time and effort were needed to bring her back to her former indifferent calm.

Luckily for her, she was not the only one to whom Donna Prassede had to do good; so that these discussions were not very frequent. Apart from the other servants, all of whom were more or less in need of correction and guidance; apart from all the other occasions (which she would go out of her way to find if they did not offer themselves) when she lent the same offices, out of the goodness of her heart, to people towards whom she had no obligation at all, she also had five daughters, none of whom was at home, though they gave her more worry than if they had been. Three were nuns, and two married; hence Donna Prassede naturally found herself with three convents and two households to superintend – a vast and complicated undertaking, and all the more arduous as two husbands, backed by fathers, mothers, and brothers, and three abbesses, flanked by other dignitaries and by numerous nuns, were not anxious to accept her superintendence. It was a war – five wars, rather – that were concealed and courteous up to a point, but for ever active and without truce; in each of these places there was a continual effort to elude her solicitude, to close the door on her suggestions, to evade her inquiries, and keep her in general as much in the dark as possible about everything. I will not mention the opposition and difficulties with which she met in managing other affairs which concerned her even less; it is well known that good has, more often than not, to be done to people against their will. Where her zeal could have full play was at home; there every person was completely subject to her authority, except Don Ferrante, with whom things went in a very particular way.

He was a man of study, and liked neither to command nor to obey. His lady wife could rule everything in the house – well and good; but he was not going to be a slave. And if, when asked, he sometimes lent her the service of his pen, this was because he had a particular talent for it; and anyway, he was quite capable of saying 'no' to this too. When he did not agree with what she wanted him to write, 'Try it yourself,' he would say on these occasions, 'Do it yourself, as it seems so clear to you.' Donna Prassede, after vainly trying for some time to draw him out of this aloofness, had finally restricted herself to grumbling at him frequently, and calling him a lazy-bones, a man fixed in his ideas, a man of letters; a title into which, though pronounced with contempt, there also went a certain satisfaction.

Don Ferrante spent long hours in his study, where he had a considerable collection of books – just under three hundred volumes; all choice works, all by the best-reputed authors on various subjects, in each of which he was more or less versed. In astrology he was generally considered, and rightly, to be more than an amateur; for he not only had the generic conceptions and the common vocabulary of the influences, aspects, and conjunctions, but he knew how to talk of them aptly, and as if *ex cathedra*;* of the twelve houses of the heavens, of the great circles, of the degrees of light and shade, of exaltations and dejections, of transits and revolutions – in fact of the most sure and the most recondite principles of the science. And for twenty years or so he had up held the system of Cardano in long and frequent disputes against another learned man who was fiercely attached to that of Al-Qabisi* out of sheer obstinacy, as Don Ferrante would say, since, although he readily acknowledged the superiority of the ancients, he could not abide this unwillingness to yield to the moderns, even when they obviously had right on their side. He also had a more than mediocre acquaintance with the history of the science, and could, on occasion, quote the more celebrated predictions that had come true, and reason subtly and eruditely about other celebrated predictions that had gone wrong, and show that the fault lay not with the science, but with those who had not known how to apply it properly.

He had learned enough ancient philosophy to suffice him, and was continually learning more by reading Diogenes Laertius.* But these systems, however fine they may be, cannot all be held at once; and as one must settle on some author if one wants to become a philosopher, Don Ferrante had settled on Aristotle, who, as he said, was neither ancient nor modern, but just the philosopher. He also had various works by the most learned and subtle of his modern disciples; those of his opponents he had always refused either to read (so as not to waste time, he would say) or to buy (so as not to waste money). As an exception, however, he found room in his library for the celebrated twenty-two volumes *De subtilitate*, and for some of Cardano's other anti-peripatetic works, in consideration of his knowledge of astrology; for he would say that anyone who could write the treatise *De restitutione temporum et motuum coelestium* and the book *Duodecim geniturarum** was worth listening to, even when he erred; and that the man's great defect was having too much talent; and that no one could guess where might have got to, even in philosophy, if he had always kept to the right road. For the rest, though Don Ferrante passed in the judgement of the learned for a consummate peripatetic, he did not himself consider that he knew enough about it; and more than once was heard to say with great modesty that the essences, the universals, the spirit of the world, and the nature of things were not as clear as might be supposed.

Natural history he had cultivated more as a recreation than a study; even the works of Aristotle and Pliny on this subject he had read, rather than studied; and yet, on the basis of this reading, and with information gathered casually from the treatises of general philosophy, with a few cursory glances at the *Magia Naturale* of Porta, at Cardano's three histories, *Lapidum, animalium, plantarum,* at the treatise on herbs, plants, and animals of Albertus Magnus,* and a few other works of lesser note, he could keep up a reasonable conversation on the more remarkable virtues and the stranger properties of many simples; describe in detail the forms and habits of mermaids and of the unique phoenix; explain how the salamander can stay in fire without burning; how the *remora*, diminutive fish though it be, has the power and ability to stop a ship of any size on the high seas; how drops of dew turn to pearls in the hearts of shells; how the chameleon feeds on air; how crystal is formed by the gradual hardening of ice in the course of centuries; and others of the more wonderful secrets of Nature.

Into the secrets of magic and witchcraft he had penetrated rather more deeply, these being sciences which according to our chronicler are much more popular and necessary, and ones in which facts are of much greater importance, and more accessible for verification. It is hardly necessary to say that his only object in studying these was to inform himself about the sinister arts of sorcery, so as to be able to guard against them and defend himself. Under the guidance chiefly of the great Martin Del Río* (the expert on that science) he was able to discourse *ex professo* on love-spells, hate-spells, and the infinite varieties of these three principal spells which, as our chronicler says, are still practised daily with such lamentable results. Equally vast and profound was Don Ferrante's knowledge of history, particularly universal history; in which his authors were Tarcagnota, Dolce, Bugatti, Campana, Guazza* – in fact the most esteemed.

But what is history, Don Ferrante would often say, without politics? A guide who walks on and on with no one following to learn the road, so that his every step is wasted; just as politics without history is like a man who walks along without a guide. So there was a shelf on his bookcase dedicated to political writers, where, among many others of lesser bulk and renown, there stood out Bodin, Cavalcanti, Sansovino, Paruta, and Boccalini.* But there were two books on this subject which Don Ferrante put a long way before all others; two books which he had been accustomed up to a certain period to call the first, without ever being able to decide which of the two deserved priority in this rank. One was the *Principe* and the *Discorsi* of the celebrated Florentine secretary (a great rascal, to be sure, Don Ferrante would say, but a deep one), the other the *Ragion di Stato* of the no-less-celebrated Giovanni Botero* (an honest man, to be sure, he would also say, but a shrewd one). Shortly before the period of our story, however, a book had appeared which put an end to the discussion of which was first, and surpassed even the works of those two matadors, as Don Ferrante would say; a book which collected and condensed every trick of statecraft, so that they could be avoided, and all its virtues, so that they could be practised; a small book, but pure gold all through – in a word, the *Statista Regnante* by Don Valeriano Castiglione;* by that most celebrated man, whom it might be said that the greatest scholars rivalled each other in praising and the greatest personages in contending for, by the man whom Pope Urban VIII honoured, as is well known, with magnificent praises; whom Cardinal Borghese and the Viceroy of Naples, Don Pedro de Toledo, begged respectively to describe the deeds

of Pope Paul V, and the wars of the Catholic King in Italy – both
in vain; the man whom Louis XIII, King of France, at the
suggestion of Cardinal Richelieu, named as his historiographer;
on whom Carlo Emanuele of Savoy conferred the same office; in
whose praise the Duchess Cristina, daughter of the Most Christian King Henry IV, could in a diploma list, along with many
other titles to fame, 'the unchallenged reputation which he has
achieved in Italy as the foremost writer of our days'.*

But if Don Ferrante could call himself learned in all the above
sciences, there was one in which he deserved and enjoyed the title
of professor – the science of chivalry. Not only did he argue
about it in a really masterly manner, but he was frequently asked
to intervene in affairs of honour, and always had some decision
to give. In his library, and one might almost say in his head, he
had the works of the most renowned writers on this subject –
Paride dal Pozzo, Fausto da Longiano, Urrea, Muzio, Romei,
Albergato, the first and the second *Forno* of Torquato Tasso, all
the passages from whose *Gerusalemme Liberata* and *Gerusalemme Conquistata** that could be used as a text on chivalry, he
always had at his finger's end and could quote from if need be.
The author of authors, however, in his opinion, was our celebrated Francesco Birago,* with whom he was associated more
than once in giving judgement in affairs of honour; and who, on
his part, spoke of Don Ferrante with particular esteem. And
when this illustrious author's *Discorsi Cavallereschi* appeared,
Don Ferrante foretold, without hesitation, that this work would
make Olevano's authoritative work obsolete, and would remain,
together with its other noble sisters, as the code of paramount
authority for posterity; a prophecy, says our anonymous chronicler, whose fulfilment can be observed by anyone.

From this he goes on to polite letters; but we are beginning to
doubt if the reader has really any very strong desire to follow
him any farther in this review, and even to fear that we may
ourselves be blamed as a servile copyist, and, together with our
anonymous author, as a bore, for having followed him so far in
things quite outside the principal story, in which he has probably
been so diffuse only in order to parade his knowledge and show
that he was not behind his age. Therefore leaving what has been
written so far to stand, so as not to waste our labour, we will
omit the remainder, in order to get back on our road; all the
more as we have a long stretch to travel before we meet any of
our characters again, and a longer stretch still before meeting the

ones whose doings must certainly interest the reader most – if there is anything that interests him in all this.

Up to the autumn of the following year, 1629, they all remained, some of their own accord, and some because they had to, in more or less the same condition as we left them, without anything happening to them, and without anyone else doing anything worth recording. The autumn, when Agnese and Lucia had counted on meeting again, came round; but a great public event sent these hopes up in the air (which was certainly one of its most trifling effects). There followed other great events which, however, brought no important change in the destinies of our characters. At length new and more general, graver, extremer disasters involved even them, even the lowest of them, according to the world's scale – just as a vast, sweeping, wandering hurricane, which uproots and strips trees, unroofs houses, untops spires, tears down walls and scatters rubbish everywhere, even stirs up the bits of straw hidden in the grass and searches out of corners the light dry leaves that a gentler wind had borne there, and whirls them off on its headlong course of destruction.

Now, in order to make clear the remaining private events which we have to relate, we simply must preface them by some account of these public ones, and turn back a little way to do so.

CHAPTER 28

After those riots on St Martin's Day and the day after, it seemed that abundance had returned to Milan, as if by a miracle. There was plenty of bread in all the shops, its price was as low as in the best years, and that of flour was in proportion. Those who had gone round during the two days shouting or worse, now (except for the few arrested) had reason to congratulate themselves; and they did not stop doing so, believe me, once the first terror of arrest was over. In the squares, at the street corners, in the taverns, there was undisguised rejoicing and self-congratulation, and muttered boasts at having found the way to bring down the price of bread. In the midst, however, of the gaiety and exultation there was (as there was bound to be) a feeling of disquiet, a presentiment that this state of things could not last. They besieged the bakeries and vendors of flour, as they had done once before during that other, artificial and passing abundance produced by Antonio Ferrer's first tariff; everyone consumed without saving; anyone who had a little money set aside invested it in bread and flour, which was stored in chests, casks, and kettles. So, by vying with each other to make the best of the present market, they made – I will not say its long duration impossible, for it was that anyway – but even its momentary continuation more and more difficult. Then on the 15th November Antonio Ferrer *'De Orden de Su Excelencia'** published an edict, by which anyone with any flour or corn at home was forbidden to buy any, however little, and everyone was forbidden to buy more than two days' supply of bread 'under pain of pecuniary or corporal punishment, as His Excellency may decide'. The competent officials, and everyone else as well, were enjoined to denounce the transgressors; the judges were ordered to search any houses that might be reported to them; and at the same time the bakers were commanded to keep their shops well stocked with bread, *'under pain, in case of failure to do so, of five years of the galleys, or more, as His Excellency may decide'*. Anyone who can imagine such an edict being executed must have a pretty good imagination; and certainly, if all the edicts issued at that time had been executed, the duchy of Milan would have had as many of its citizens on the high seas as England has today.

Be that as it may, the bakers had not only to be ordered to make all that bread, they also had to be supplied with the materials for making it. They had decided (since in time of famine an effort is always made to find a way of turning into bread materials which are usually eaten under another form) – they had decided, I say, to put rice into the so-called 'mixed bread'. On the 23rd November a proclamation was issued sequestrating, at the order of the Commissioner of Supply and his Council of Twelve, half the unpolished rice (*risone* as they called it and still call it here) in everyone's possession, and imposing a penalty on whoever disposed of it without those gentlemen's permission, of the loss of his stocks and of a fine of three *scudi* a bushel. Nothing, as everyone can see, could be fairer.

But this rice had to be paid for, and at a price vastly disproportionate to that of bread. The burden of making up the enormous deficit had been laid on the city; but the Council of Ten, which had assumed this responsibility for the city, decided on the same 23rd November to lay before the governor the impossibility of maintaining it any longer. In a decree of the 7th

December the governor fixed the price of the aforesaid rice at twelve *lire* the bushel; anyone asking more, and anyone refusing to sell, was threatened with confiscation of the goods and a fine of the same value, '*and such greater punishment, pecuniary and corporal, even to the galleys, as His Excellency may decide, according to the nature of the case and the rank of the offender*'.

The price of polished rice had already been fixed before the riots, as probably had also been the tariff, or to use the term celebrated in modern annals, the '*maximum*',* for wheat and other more ordinary grain, by other decrees which we have not come across.

As a consequence of bread and flour being made so cheap in Milan, people came flocking in from the country to buy it. To obviate this inconvenience, as he called it, Don Gonzalo, by another decree of the 15th December, forbade anyone to take out of the city bread beyond the value of twenty *soldi*; under pain of confiscation of the same bread, and of a fine of twenty-five *scudi*, '*and in case of inability to pay, of two strokes of the lash in public and such greater punishment*', as usual, '*as His Excellency may decide*'. On the 22nd of the same month (and one cannot see why it was so late) he published similar regulations for flour and grain.

The people had tried to create abundance by sacking and burning, the government was trying to maintain it by the galleys and the rope. Such means were linked to each other, but the reader can see how little they had to do with the ends; and in a moment he will see just how effective they were in attaining them. It is easy to see, and not uninteresting to observe, how there was a necessary connexion between these strange measures; each was an inevitable consequence of its predecessor, and all a result of the first decree which fixed the price of bread so far from its real price – from the price, that is, that would have resulted naturally from the relation between supply and demand. To the people an expedient like this has always, and must always, seem to be as just as it was simple to put into execution; and so it is a natural thing for them, during the agonies and miseries of a famine, to want it, ask for it, and, if they can, enforce it. But then, as the consequences gradually begin to be felt, it becomes the duty of those responsible to come to the relief of each decree with a law forbidding people to do what they had been encouraged to do by the preceding law. Here we would like to call attention, in passing, to a singular coincidence. In a country and at a period close to our own* at the most clamorous and notable period of modern times, recourse was had to similar expedients in similar circumstances (in substance the same measures, one might almost say, with some difference of proportion, but in roughly the same order) in spite of the changed conditions and all the advance of knowledge in Europe which affected that country perhaps more than any other; and this happened chiefly because the great mass of the people, whom this knowledge had not reached, were able to make their judgement prevail for a long time, and force the hands, as they said there, of those making the laws.

Thus, to return to our subject, when all was said and done, the chief results of the insurrection were twofold: loss and destruction of foodstuffs in the riots themselves, and a great, reckless, immeasurable consumption while the tariff lasted, at the expense of the small amount of grain that was supposed to tide over until the next harvest. To these general effects may be added the hanging of four wretches as leaders of the tumult; two in front of the 'Bakery of the Crutches' and two at the end of the street in which stood the house of the Commissioner of Supply.

For the rest, the historical accounts of the period are so incomplete that not even information as to how and when that arbitrary tariff ceased is to be found in them. If, in the absence of any positive information, we may be allowed to make suggestions, we are inclined to believe that it was abolished shortly before or shortly after the 24th December, which was the day of the executions. And as for the decrees, after the one we have cited of the 22nd of the same month, we can find none which deal with foodstuffs; maybe they have perished or escaped our researches, or maybe the government, finally discouraged if not made wiser by the futility of its remedies, and overwhelmed by events had abandoned them to their own course. We find, in fact, in the accounts of a number of historians (more inclined, as they were, to describe great events than to note their causes and development) a picture of the duchy, and chiefly of the city, in the late winter and spring, by which time the cause of all the harm – the disproportion, that is, between the supply of food and the demand for it – had been increased rather than eliminated by the remedies which temporarily suspended its effects. It could not even be wiped out by a sufficient importation of grain from abroad, for this was prevented by the insufficiency of public and private funds, the poverty and scarcity in the surrounding countries, the slowness and restrictions of commerce, and the very laws that tended to produce and maintain low prices; by this time, too, the real cause of the famine, or rather it would be better to say the famine itself, was raging in full force and without a check. And here is a copy of that mournful picture.*

At every step there were closed shops; the factories mostly deserted; the roads an indescribable spectacle – an endless flow of miseries, a perpetual abode of suffering. The professional beggars, now in a small minority, were confused and lost amid throngs of new ones, and reduced to contending for alms with those from whom they had sometimes received them in other days. There were clerks and apprentices dismissed by shop-keepers, whose daily earnings had either dwindled or stopped entirely, and who were now living sparingly on their savings and capital; there were shopkeepers themselves, for whom the slump in business had meant failure and ruin; workmen, and even master craftsmen of every trade and art, from the commonest to the most sophisticated, from the most necessary to the most luxurious, wandering from door to door, from street to street, leaning against the door-posts, lying stretched out on the pavements in front of the houses and churches, begging piteously for alms, or hesitating between their want and a shame still unsub-dued; emaciated, weak, and trembling with cold and hunger in their scanty rags, which in many instances still showed the traces of a former prosperity; just as a sign of former habits of industry and independence would occasionally show through their present apathy and despair. Mingling in the deplorable throng and forming a large part of it, were servants dismissed by masters who had either sunk from well-to-do circumstances into poverty, or who, however wealthy, had become unable in such a year to maintain their former pomp of retinue. And add to all these different indigent people a number of others attached to them who had been used to living on their earnings – children, women, old folk, grouped around their former supporters, or wandering about in search of alms elsewhere.

There were also – and they were easily distinguishable by their tangled quiffs and showy dress, as well as by something in their bearing and gestures, and those marks that habits stamp on the face (the more deeply and clearly, the stranger and more unusual the habits) – many of the breed of bravi, who, having lost their infamous livelihood in the general calamity, were now begging their bread from charity. Subdued by hunger, they now contended with the others only in entreaties; cowed, as if in a dream, they dragged themselves through the streets which they had so long tramped with their heads in the air, with looks fierce and suspicious, dressed in sumptuous and fantastic liveries, with great plumes, hung with rich arms, elegant and perfumed; and humbly held out hands which had so often been raised insolently to threaten or treacherously to wound.

But perhaps the ghastliest as well as the most pitiful sight was that of the peasants, alone, in pairs, or in entire families: husbands, wives with babies in their arms or bound on their backs, leading little children by the hand, with their old folk behind them. Some had had their homes broken into and pillaged by the soldiery billeted or passing through, and had fled in desperation; and among these were some who, to arouse more pity and make their misery more striking, showed the scars and bruises they had received in defending their last few possessions or in escaping from a blind and brutal licence. Others had not been touched by that particular scourge, but had been driven away by two others from which no corner of the country was immune, the famine and the special levies (now more exorbitant than ever, to meet what are called the necessities of war), and had come, and were still coming, into the city, as the ancient seat and last refuge of wealth and of pious munificence. More than by their hesitating gait and embarrassed manner, the newcomers could be distinguished by their air of amazement and vexation at finding this excess, this competition in misery, in the goal where they had counted on being outstanding objects of compassion and on attracting all eyes and help towards themselves. The others, who had tramped and haunted the streets of the city for some time, kept alive by food which they had obtained or rather hit on by sheer chance amidst so great a disproportion between supplies and needs, bore on their faces and in their gestures a look of deeper and more hopeless consternation. Their dress was varied – those of them who could still be called dressed – and their looks were varied too: there were pale faces from the plains; bronzed faces from the uplands; ruddy faces from the mountains. But all were pinched and wasted, all had sunken eyes and fixed part-idiot, part-surly stares; matted hair, long shaggy beards; bodies, once sturdy and hardened by toil, now wasted by want; skin drawn tight over sunburnt arms and shins and skinny chests, showing through their disordered rags. And no less painful than this sight of wasted vigour, though in a different way, was the sight of nature succumbing more quickly, sinking into lower depths of listlessness and exhaustion, in those of weaker sex and age.

Here and there along the streets and against the walls of the houses were heaps of dirty straw, trampled and mixed with filthy refuse. Yet this filth was the gift and provision of charity; they were couches prepared for some of those wretches to lay their heads on at night. Every now and again could be seen lying or sprawling there, even in daytime, some whose legs had been robbed of the strength to carry them by exhaustion and lack of food; sometimes one of those wretched couches would bear a corpse; sometimes a man could be seen suddenly to fall like a rag and remain on the paving-stones dead.

Beside some of these couches could also be seen stooping some neighbour or passer-by, drawn by a sudden impulse of compassion. In some places there were also evidences of relief organized with greater foresight and set in motion by a hand both rich in resources and practised in doing good on a large scale; it was the hand of the good Federigo. He had chosen six priests, whose eager and persevering charity was seconded and served by a robust constitution. These he divided into pairs, and assigned a third of the city for each to patrol, with porters following, laden with various kinds of food, other subtler and more rapid restoratives, and clothes. Every morning these three pairs took to the streets in different directions, went up to those they saw lying abandoned on the ground, and ministered to each what help he needed. Such as were already on the point of death, and no longer in a state to take nourishment, received from them the last help and consolation of religion. To the hungry they dispensed soup, eggs, bread, and wine; while to others enfeebled by longer fasting they offered jellies, extracts, and stronger wines, first reviving them, if need be, with cordials. At the same time they distributed clothes to those most indecently and miserably clad.

Nor did their succour end there. The good shepherd wanted a more effective and lasting relief to be given wherever possible. Those poor creatures who had recovered enough strength from the first restoratives to be able to stand up and walk, were given a little money, so that their reviving needs and lack of other help should not quickly reduce them to their former plight; for others shelter and maintenance were sought in the neighbouring houses. In the more prosperous ones they were usually received from charity and because they were recommended by the cardinal; in others, where there was the goodwill without the means, the priests asked for the poor creatures to be taken in as boarders, fixed the terms, and paid a first instalment in advance. Then they gave a list of these refugees to the parish priests, so that they could go and visit them; and also went back to visit them themselves.

It goes without saying that Federigo did not confine his care to these extremes of suffering, nor wait for it to reach that point before taking action. His ardent, comprehensive generosity could not but feel every call, busy itself with each of them, prevent suffering where possible, and otherwise hasten to relieve it; take, so to say, as many forms as there were varieties of need. In fact, by putting all his means together, making still more stringent economies, and appropriating savings destined for other good works now reduced to only too secondary an importance, he had done everything he could to raise money so as to spend it all to relieve the starving. He had made big purchases of corn, and sent off a great part of it to the places in the diocese that were most destitute; and as this succour was too little for their needs, he also sent salt, 'with which,' Ripamonti[†] says, describing this, 'the grass of the fields and the barks of the trees were converted into food.' He had also distributed corn and money to many of the parishes in the city, which he visited himself, district by district, dispensing alms and helping many a poor family in secret. In the archiepiscopal palace (as a contemporary writer, the physician Alessandro Tadino, says in his *Ragguaglio*, which we shall often have occasion to quote as we go on) two thousand plates of soup and rice were distributed every morning.[‡]

These charitable achievements can certainly be termed grandiose when we consider that they all came from a single man and from his own resources alone (for Federigo made it a rule to refuse to dispense the liberality of others); yet these, together with the numerous, if not so open-handed bounty of other private persons, and the subsidies decreed by the Council of Ten, which the Tribunal of Supplies was appointed to dispense – all these were very little in comparison to the need. While a few peasants near starving to death had their lives prolonged by the cardinal's charity, others were reaching the same depths; the former fell

† *Historiae Patriae*, Decadis V, Lib. VI, p. 386. (M.)

‡ *Ragguaglio dell'origine et giornali successi della gran peste contagiosa, venefica et malefica, seguita nella citta di Milano,** etc. Milan, 1648, p. 10. (M.)

back into them on finishing their small succour. Meanwhile in other districts where help had not been forgotten but was postponed as less urgent by a charity forced to make priorities, the distress was becoming fatal; everywhere people were perishing, and yet still they came flocking into the city from every direction. Here two thousand starving people, the strongest and most experienced in surmounting competition, might get hold of a plate of soup, just enough to keep alive that day; but thousands more had been left behind envying the more fortunate – if indeed they could be called more fortunate when among those left behind there were often their own wives, children, and parents. And while in some parts of the city a few of the most destitute and desperate were being picked up, revived, sheltered, and provided for temporarily, in a hundred other parts there were others languishing, or even expiring, without help or comfort.

All day a confused murmur of begging voices echoed in the streets; at night there was a chorus of groans, broken every now and then by sudden loud wails, shouts, or solemn invocations, which ended in piercing screams.

It is a notable thing that amid all this extreme want, amid all this variety of grievances, there was not one attempt, not one cry of revolt – or, at least, no mention at all of it is to be found. And yet, there was a large number of men among those living and dying in that way who were brought up to anything rather than patient endurance; hundreds of them were the same men who had made themselves so much felt on St Martin's Day. Nor should we think that they were held back by the example of those four wretches who had been scapegoats for all. What effect could, not the sight but the memory of punishment have on the minds of a vagrant though united mob which saw itself condemned to death by slow torture, and was already suffering its pains? But we mortals are generally like that: we rebel furiously and violently against mediocre evils, and bow down in silence under extreme ones; we endure, not from resignation but from stupidity, the very extremes of what we had at first called quite unendurable.

The gaps daily made by death in that dreadful throng were more than filled up again every day; there was a continual flow, first from the villages nearby, then from the whole countryside, then from the other towns in the state, and finally even from other states. And meanwhile the former inhabitants were leaving the city itself every day; some to get away from the sight of so much suffering; some because they saw their places taken, as it were, by these fresh competitors for charity, and went off in a last desperate effort to find help elsewhere, anywhere – anywhere, at least, where the swarm was not so thick nor the rivalry in begging so intense. Both kinds of pilgrims would meet going opposite ways, each a spectacle of horror for the other, and a painful presage, a sinister omen of what awaited both at their respective journeys' ends. But both pursued their ways, if no longer in the hope of changing their lot, at least so as not to return under a sky that had become so odious, so as not to see again the scenes of their despair. Some, however, found their strength failing them altogether, sank down by the roadside, and died there; an even gloomier sight for their companions in misfortune, and an object of horror, perhaps of reproach, to other wayfarers. 'I myself saw,' says Ripamonti, 'in the road that girdles the walls, the corpse of a woman ... half-eaten grass hanging from her mouth, and her lips still set in a sort of convulsive effort.... She had a bundle on her shoulder, and swathed to her breast was a baby, which was crying and begging for the pap.... Some compassionate folk had come along, picked the poor little creature up from the ground, and were carrying it away, and at the same time fulfilling a mother's first office.'

The contrast of rags and luxury, of misery and superfluity, so frequent in ordinary times, had now ceased altogether. There were rags and misery almost everywhere; and an appearance of even frugal mediocrity stood out at once. The nobles were seen walking about in plain and modest, or even mean and shabby clothes; some because the common causes of distress had reduced their fortunes to this pass, or given the final blow to fortunes already shaky; others because they were afraid of provoking the public desperation by display, or ashamed of insulting the general calamity. Those hated and respected tyrants who usually went about with a trail of bravi at their heels now went almost alone, with their heads down and looks that seemed to offer and to ask for peace. Others who even in prosperity had been of more humane disposition and more modest bearing now seemed confused, bewildered, almost overwhelmed now by the constant sight of a misery that surpassed not only the possibility of relief, but I might almost say, the forces of compassion. Those with the means of giving alms had to make a melancholy choice between hunger and hunger, between urgency and urgency. And no sooner was a pitying hand seen stretching out towards the hand of some poor wretch than a competition arose between the other wretches around. Those with most strength left would push ahead and ask with most insistence. The prostrate, the old, and the children would hold out their skinny hands. Mothers would lift up and show from afar their weeping infants, miserably swathed in filthy rags, who out of weakness had collapsed into their arms.

So passed the winter and the spring. For some time now the Tribunal of Health had been pointing out to the Tribunal of Supply the danger of disease hanging over the city because of all the squalor increasing in every part of it; and it suggested that the beggars should be gathered together in various refuges. While this proposal was being discussed, while they were approving and considering ways and means of putting it into effect, the corpses were accumulating in the streets day by day; and all the other mass of miseries were increasing proportionately. Another suggestion put forward in the Tribunal of Supply, as being easier and quicker, was to collect all the beggars, both sick and healthy, into one place, the lazaretto, where they could be fed and cared for at the public expense. So it was decided, against the advice of the Tribunal of Health, who objected that in such a vast gathering of people the danger which they wanted to avoid would only increase.

The lazaretto of Milan (if by chance this story should fall into the hands of someone unacquainted with it either by sight or description) is a four-sided, almost square, enclosure, outside the city, to the left of the Porta Orientale, and separated from the city wall by the moat, a surrounding road, and a stream encircling the building itself. The two biggest walls are about five hundred yards long; the other two perhaps fifteen less; all of them are divided on the outside into little rooms of one storey; round three sides of the interior runs a continuous vaulted colonnade, supported on small, slender columns.

There were two hundred and eighty-eight rooms or so; in our own day* a number of them have been replaced by a large opening made in the middle, and a smaller one in a corner of the façade on the side flanking the highway. At the time of our story there were only two entrances: one in the middle of the side looking towards the city wall, and another facing it opposite. In the centre of the enclosed area there stood, and still stands, a small octagonal church.

The original object of the whole building, begun in the year 1489 with money from a private bequest and then continued out of public funds and other legacies and donations, was, as the name itself suggests,* to give a refuge, if need be, to those stricken with the plague; which, already long before that period and for a long time after it, usually appeared two, four, six, or eight times in a century, now in one European country and now in another, sometimes attacking a large part of it, or even sweeping over its whole length and breadth. At the moment of which we speak, the lazaretto was used merely as a depository for merchandise held in quarantine.

To free it quickly now the sanitary regulations were not properly enforced, the prescribed purges and fumigations were rushed through, and all the merchandise held there released at one time. Straw was spread in all the rooms, provisions were laid in, in whatever quantity and quality was available, and all beggars were invited, by public edict, to take shelter there.

Many went flocking along willingly; all those who were lying ill in the streets and squares were carried there. In a few days, between one and the other, there were more than three thousand people in it. But far more remained outside. Whether it was the fact that each was waiting for the others to go and so leave fewer to enjoy the city's charity, or a natural aversion to being confined, or the distrust of the poor for anything suggested them by the rich and powerful (a distrust always proportionate to the mutual ignorance of those who feel it and those who inspire it, to the number of the poor, and to the stupidity of the laws), or their knowledge of what in fact were the real benefits offered them – whether it was all these put together, or for some other reason, the fact remains that most of them paid no attention to the invitation, and went on dragging themselves painfully about the streets. Seeing this, it was thought best to pass from invitation to coercion. Bailiffs were sent round, who drove all the beggars into the lazaretto and carried those who resisted there in chains; and for each beggar they were given a prize of ten *soldi* – a proof that even in times of greatest scarcity public money can always be found for foolish uses. And, in spite of the fact (as had been foreseen, and even expressly intended, by the Tribunal of Supplies) that a certain number of beggars left the city, to go and live or die somewhere else, at least in freedom, the drive was so successful that in a short time, between guests and prisoners, the number of inmates was approaching ten thousand.

It is to be presumed that the women and children were put into separate quarters, though the memoirs of the time make no mention of this. Rules and regulations for maintaining good order, too, were certainly not lacking, but anyone can imagine the kind of order that could be established and maintained, particularly in such times and in such circumstances, among such a vast and varied concourse of people, where the willing inmates were mingled with the forcibly, restrained, professional beggars with those to whom begging was a necessity, a sorrow, and a shame; where side by side with those who had grown up amidst the honest toil of the field and workshop were many others brought up on the streets, in taverns, in tyrants' castles, to idleness, trickery, scorn, and violence.

How they all fared for food and lodging could be sadly conjectured, even if we had no positive knowledge; but we have. They slept crammed together in twenties and thirties in each of those little cells, or lay under the arcades on little foul and fetid straw, or on the bare ground. For though there had, of course, been orders for the straw to be fresh and abundant, in effect there was very little of it; it was bad and never changed. There had also been orders that the bread was to be of good quality (for what administration ever decreed that bad materials should be used or distributed?). But how could things which could not even have been obtained in normal circumstances, for a more restricted demand, be obtained at such a crisis and for such a vast multitude? It was said at the time, as we find in the memoirs of the period, that the bread of the lazaretto was adulterated with heavy, unnutritious material; and it is only too likely that this complaint was not imaginary. There was even a scarcity of water – that is to say, of wholesome fresh water. The common reservoir must have been the stream surrounding the walls, and it was shallow, sluggish, sometimes muddy, and soon became what the use and vicinity of such a vast and varied crowd made it.

To all these causes of mortality, which were the more effective as they acted on bodies already sick or sickening, was now added the most perverse of weather; incessant rain, followed by even more incessant drought, and with it a violent and premature heatwave. Added to these evils were the feelings growing from them, the tedium and frenzy of captivity, the memory of former habits, the grief for dear ones lost and the worry for dear ones absent, the mutual horror and disgust, and all the many other passions due to despair and rage either imported or born in there; finally there was the fear and the continuous spectacle of death, made frequent by so many causes, and itself become a new and potent cause. Nor is it to be wondered at that mortality should so grow and rule in that confined space that it took on the aspect – and with many the name – of plague. Whether it was that all these causes growing and working together only increased the action of a simple epidemic of influenza; or whether (as often happens even with famines less severe and prolonged than this one) some prevailing contagion found its own soil and as it were climate there, in bodies already disposed and prepared for it by suffering and malnutrition, bad weather, dirt, exhaustion, and dejection; found, that is, all the conditions necessary for its birth, nourishment, and growth (if a layman may be allowed to make the suggestion, following the hypothesis propounded by certain doctors, and lately re-propounded, with many arguments and with much caution, by a doctor who is as diligent as he is talented)[†] – whether, then, the contagion broke out at first in the lazaretto itself, as, according to an obscure and vague account, the doctors of the Health Tribunal seemed to have thought; whether it was already in existence and hovering about before that time (which seems more likely if one considers how chronic and widespread the famine had been, and how high the death rate), and that, once introduced into that stationary mob, it spread with a new and terrible rapidity; whichever of these conjectures may be the right one, the fact is that the number of deaths in the lazaretto every day had in a short time passed a hundred.

While in that place all was languor, suffering, terror, horror, and lamentation, at the Tribunal of Supply there was mortification, amazement, and uncertainty. They discussed it, they listened to the advice of the Tribunal of Health; the only course on which they could hit was to undo what had been done at so much show, trouble, and expense. They opened up the lazaretto, and released all the remaining paupers there who were not sick, and who came rushing out with riotous delight. Once again the city resounded with all the old lamentations, but rather more feebly and sporadically; once more it saw that scattered throng, but all the more pityingly, says Ripamonti, at the thought of how it was diminished. The sick were carried off to Santa Maria della Stella, then a poorhouse; and there most of them perished.

---

† *Del morbo petecchiale . . . e degli altri contagi in generale, opera del Dott. F. Enrico Acerbi,** Chap. III, paras. 1 and 2. (M.)

Meanwhile, however, those blessed crops were growing golden. The beggars from the country went off, each to his own home, for that longed-for harvest. The good Federigo saw them on their way with a last effort and a new invention of charity; every peasant who came to the archiepiscopal palace was given a giulio* and a reaping-hook.

With the harvest the famine finally came to an end; mortality, whether epidemic or contagious, decreased from day to day, but continued until the autumn. It was just about to finish when along came a new scourge.

Many important events, of the kind more particularly dignified by the word 'historical', had happened meanwhile. Cardinal Richelieu had taken La Rochelle, as we have said, patched up a peace with the King of England, and proposed and carried through by his powerful voice in the Council of the King of France that the Duke of Nevers should be given effective support; at the same time he had persuaded the king himself to lead the expedition in person. While the preparations were being made, the Count of Nassau, the Imperial commissioner, was warning the new duke in Mantua that unless he handed over the states to Ferdinand, the latter would send an army to occupy them. The duke, who had managed to parry so drastic and suspect a condition in more desperate circumstances, and was now encouraged by the approaching help from France, parried it all the more this time; but his refusal was disguised and diluted as much as possible and made with proposals for other acts of submission which would be more ostentatious, although less costly. The commissioner had departed, threatening that they would have to use force. In March, Cardinal Richelieu had come down with the king at the head of an army. They had asked the Duke of Savoy for a passage, started to negotiate, and come to no conclusion. After a brush in which the French had the advantage, they had negotiated again, and concluded an agreement in which the duke, among other things, had stipulated that Cordova should raise the siege of Casale, pledging himself, in case of refusal, to join the French and invade the duchy of Milan. Don Gonzalo, reckoning that he was getting off cheaply, had raised the siege of Casale, which was immediately entered by a group of French to reinforce the garrison.

It was on this occasion that Achillini* addressed his famous sonnet to King Louis:

Sweat, ye fires, in forging metals:

and another exhorting him to go off at once to the liberation of
the Holy Land. But it is the fate of poets to find that their advice
goes unheeded; and if there are any instances in history of things
conforming to their suggestions, you can be safe in saying that
they had been decided beforehand. Cardinal Richelieu had
arranged instead to return to France for affairs which he considered more urgent. In vain Girolamo Soranzo, the Venetian
envoy, urged various reasons against this decision; but the king
and the cardinal paid as little heed to his prose as they had to
Achillini's verses, and returned with the main body of the army,
leaving only six thousand men in Susa to hold the pass and
guarantee the treaty.

While this army was withdrawing on one side, that of Ferdinand was approaching on the other. It had overrun the canton of
Grisons and the Valtellina, and was preparing to descend upon
the Milanese provinces. Besides all the damage to be feared from
this passage, definite news also reached the Tribunal of Health
that in that army there was lurking the plague, of which there
were always traces in the German troops at that time, as Varchi*
says, when talking of the one which they had brought to Florence
a century before. Alessandro Tadino, one of the commissioners
of the Tribunal of Health (there were six, besides the president,
four magistrates, and two doctors), was charged by the Tribunal,
as he himself describes in his *Ragguaglio*,† already quoted, with
the task of pointing out to the governor the appalling danger
threatening the country if those troops passed through it on their
way to besiege Mantua, as rumour said. Don Gonzalo's whole
behaviour shows that he had a great desire to cut a figure in
history, which could not, in fact, very well avoid mentioning him;
but (as often happens) history does not know, or did not trouble
to record, his most memorable contribution to it – the reply he
gave Tadino on this occasion. He replied that he did not know
what was to be done about it; that the motives of interest and
prestige which had caused that army to move outweighed the
danger it represented; that, for all that, they must try to take
what precautions they could, and put their trust in Providence.

In order, therefore, to take what precautions they could, the
two doctors of the Tribunal of Health (the Tadino mentioned

† P. 16 (M.)

above and Senator Settala, son of the celebrated Lodovico)*
proposed that it should be forbidden under the severest penalties
to buy anything at all from the soldiery about to pass through.
But it was impossible to make the president realize the necessity
for such an order. 'He was a very good man,' says Tadino, 'who
just could not believe that the death of so many thousands of
people could depend on their trafficking with these soldiers and
their goods.' We quote this extract as one of the oddest of the
period; for it certainly can never have happened, since boards of
health existed, that any president of such a body has used a
similar argument – if argument it can be called.

As for Don Gonzalo, shortly after making that reply, he left
Milan; and his departure was as cheerless for him as its cause.
He was removed from his post because of the ill success of the
war of which he had been the promoter and commander; and the
people blamed him for the famine suffered under his rule. (What
he had done for the plague was either not known or, if it was,
certainly no one cared except for the Tribunal of Health and the
two doctors in particular.) When he left the governor's palace in
his travelling-coach surrounded by a guard of halberdiers, with
two trumpeters on horseback preceding him, and other coaches
full of nobles escorting him, he was greeted by loud whistles from
groups of boys collected in the cathedral square, who came
crowding along behind him. When the procession entered the
street leading to Porta Ticinese, by which he was to leave, it
began getting into the middle of a crowd of people, some of
whom had been there waiting for it, while others came hurrying
along towards it – the more so as the trumpeters, punctilious
creatures, never ceased playing, from the palace courtyard to the
city gate. And during the inquiry which was afterwards made
into this tumult, one of them, on being told that he had probably
increased it with that trumpeting of his, answered, 'Your worship, that is our profession; and if His Excellency had not wanted
us to play he should have given us orders to keep silent.' But Don
Gonzalo, either from reluctance to do anything that showed fear,
or from fear that this might make the crowd bolder than ever, or
because he was in fact rather overwhelmed, gave no order at all.
The mob, which the guards had tried in vain to push back, was
preceding, surrounding, following the carriage, shouting, 'The
famine's leaving; the bloodsucker of the poor's leaving,' and
worse. As they drew near the gate they began throwing stones,
bricks, cabbage-stalks, and rubbish of every kind – the usual

ammunition, in short, of such expeditions. Some scrambled up
on the walls, and from there let off a final volley against the
carriages as they were going out. Then they quickly dispersed.

In place of Don Gonzalo came the Marquis Ambrosio Spinola,
whose name had already acquired, in the wars in Flanders, the
military renown which it still enjoys.*

Meanwhile the German army, under the supreme command of
Count Rambaldo di Collalto,* another Italian *condottiere*, of
lesser but not negligible fame, had received definite orders to
proceed towards the siege of Mantua; and in the month of
September they entered the duchy of Milan.

At that time armies were still composed mainly of soldiers of
fortune enrolled by professional *condottieri*, sometimes on commission of this or that prince, sometimes also on their own
account, so as to sell their troops and themselves later. Men were
attracted to this calling not so much by the pay as by the hope of
plunder and all the allurements of licence. Fixed and general
discipline there was none; nor would this ever have harmonized
very easily with the semi-independent authority of the various
condottieri. These were no great sticklers for discipline themselves, nor, even had they wanted to, can one see how they could
ever have succeeded in establishing and maintaining it; for
soldiers of this type would either have mutinied against an
innovating commander who took it into his head to abolish
looting, or at least would have left him to guard his banners
alone. Besides that, the princes who, as it were, hired these bands,
were more concerned with mustering big enough numbers to
ensure the success of their enterprises than with getting the
number of men proportionate to their means, which were usually
very scanty – so that pay was always late, and then in dribbles on
account, and the spoils of the place they overran became a sort
of tacitly agreed supplement. Hardly less celebrated than Wallenstein's name is his dictum: it's easier to keep an army of a
hundred thousand men in the field than one of twelve thousand.
And this army of which we are speaking was very largely
composed of men who had ravaged Germany under his command
in the war so celebrated among other wars, both for its importance and its effects, which afterwards took its name from the
thirty years it lasted; it was then in its eleventh. There was also a
regiment of his very own, led by one of his lieutenants. Most of
the other *condottieri* had served under his command, and there

were many among them who were to help him four years later towards that sorry end that is known to all.

There were twenty thousand foot, and seven thousand horse. In coming down from the Valtellina to reach Mantuan territory, they had to follow the whole course of the Adda, first through the two branches of the lake and then as a river again until it emptied into the Po, a good stretch of which they also had to follow; in all eight days in the duchy of Milan.

A large part of the inhabitants took refuge in the mountains, carrying the best of what they had, and driving their livestock before them. Others stayed behind either to tend some sick person, to preserve their homes from fire, or to keep an eye on valuables which they had buried or concealed; still others because they had nothing to lose, or even because they had hopes of gain. When the first detachment arrived at the village at which they were to halt, they at once spread out over it and the neighbouring hamlets and sacked them outright. Anything that could be used or taken away disappeared; the remainder they destroyed or ruined. Furniture was turned into firewood, houses into stables; without mentioning the beating, the wounding, the raping. All shifts and ruses used to conceal things were useless, and sometimes caused even more damage. The soldiers, expert in the stratagems of this kind of war too, searched every hole in the houses, tore down walls, even demolished them altogether. They easily recognized the freshly moved soil in gardens. They even climbed up into the mountains to steal the cattle. They went into the caves, led by some rascal in the village, to search for some rich fugitive who might be cowering there, dragged him back home, and forced him by threats and torture to show them where he had hidden his treasure.

Finally they were going; they had gone; the sound of their drums and fifes was heard dying away in the distance. There followed a few hours of terrified quiet. And then another hateful rumble of drums, another hateful blare of trumpets, would announce a new squadron. These, not finding anything more to plunder, would make havoc of what was left with all the greater fury, burn the casks emptied by the others, the doors of rooms which no longer contained anything; set the houses on fire, and of course maltreat the inhabitants with more ferocity than ever. And so on from bad to worse for twenty days; for such was the number of squadrons into which the army was divided.

Colico was the first district in the duchy to be invaded by these demons. Then they hurled themselves on Bellano; from there they entered and spread through the Valsassina, whence they poured forth into the territory of Lecco.

CHAPTER 29

Here, among the poor panic-stricken inhabitants, we shall find persons of our acquaintance.

Anyone who did not see Don Abbondio on the day when all at once the news spread of the army's descent, of its approach, of its behaviour, can have little idea of what fear and consternation really are. 'They're coming!' 'There are thirty, forty, fifty thousand of 'em!' 'They're devils.' 'They're heretics!' 'They're antichrists!' 'They've sacked Cortenuova!' 'They've set fire to Primaluna!' 'They've devastated Introbbio, Pasturo, and Barsio!' 'They've reached Balabbio!' 'They'll be here tomorrow!' Such were the rumours passing from mouth to mouth; and with them the villagers went scurrying to and fro, stopping each other for hurried consultations, hesitating between fleeing and remaining, while the women flocked together, tearing their hair. Don Abbondio – who had decided on flight before and more than anyone else – was finding insuperable obstacles and terrifying dangers in every road to take, in every place to hide. 'What shall I do?' he kept exclaiming. 'Where shall I go?' The mountains, quite apart from the difficulties of getting up them, were not safe. It was already known that the *landsknechte** clambered over them like cats wherever there was any chance or hope of booty. The lake was rough. There was a high wind blowing. Besides, most of the boatmen, fearing they would be forced to ferry soldiers and equipment, had taken refuge with their boats on the other side. The few who had remained with had gone off later overloaded with people; and, what with their cargo and the storm, were said to be in danger of sinking from one moment to the next. It was impossible to find a vehicle, a horse, or any other means of transport to get far away from the route which the army had to use; Don Abbondio could not manage any great distance on foot, and was afraid of being overtaken on the way. The Bergamese territory was not too far for his legs to take him at a stretch; but it was known that a squadron of *cappelletti* * had been hurriedly

sent off from Bergamo to patrol the frontier and keep the
landsknechte off; and these were just as much devils incarnate as
the others, and would stick at nothing themselves. The poor man
was running round the house half out of his wits. He kept
following Perpetua about so as to concoct some plan with her.
But Perpetua was busy collecting the household valuables and
hiding them in the attic or any out-of-the-way place, and kept
rushing past him, breathless and preoccupied, with her hands or
arms full, and replying, 'I'll just finish putting these things away
safely, and then we'll do what the others do.' Don Abbondio
wanted to detain her and discuss various alternatives with her,
but what with her flurry and hurry, the fears she was also feeling
herself, and her irritation at her master's, she was less tractable
at this juncture than she had ever been before. 'Others are shifting
for themselves, and so must we. Excuse me, but all you do is get
in my way. D'you think others haven't got skins to save too?
And that it's you the soldiers are coming to fight? You might give
a hand at a moment like this, instead of getting in my way,
whining and fussing.' With such answers and others like them
she would rid herself of him, having already decided that once
she had got her tumultous operations over as best she could, she
would take him by the arm like a child and drag him up a
mountain. Left to himself in this way, he went and looked out of
the window, straining his ears; and whenever he saw anyone pass
he would shout out in a half-plaintive, half-chiding voice, 'Do
please, in all charity, help your priest to find a horse, or a mule,
or a donkey. What, is it really possible that no one'll help me?
Oh, what people! Do at least wait for me to come with you. Wait
until there are fifteen or twenty of you, and take me along with
you, so I'm not left entirely on my own. Will you leave me in the
hands of those swine? Don't you know they're nearly all
Lutherans, who hold that killing a priest is a good deed? Will
you leave me here to be martyred? Oh, what people! Oh, what
people!'

But to whom was he saying these things? To men passing
bowed under the weight of their humble possessions, thinking of
what they had left at home, driving their few cows before them,
dragging their children along behind them – also heavily laden –
while the women were carrying at their breasts those who could
not walk. Some were just trudging on, without answering or
looking up; others would say, 'Oh, sir! You must fend for

yourself too! You're lucky not to have a family to think of. Help yourself. Do the best you can.'

'Oh, poor me!' exclaimed Don Abbondio. 'Oh, what people! What a heartless lot! There's no charity left; no one's thinking of anything but themselves; and no one gives a thought to me.' And back he went to look for Perpetua.

'Oh, by the way,' she said to him, 'what about the money?'

'What shall we do?'

'Give it to me, and I'll go and bury it in the garden with the spoons and forks.'

'But . . .'

'But, but! Give it me here. Keep a little back for any emergency and leave it to me.'

Don Abbondio obeyed, went to his chest, extracted his little treasure, and handed it over to Perpetua. 'I'll just go and bury it in the orchard, at the foot of the fig-tree,' she said, and went out. Presently she reappeared with a basket full of provisions and another small empty one, in the bottom of which she hurriedly thrust a change of linen for herself and her master, saying as she did so, 'You'll carry your breviary, at least.'

'But where are we going?'

'Where are all the others going? First of all we'll get out into the road; and then we'll see and hear what's the best thing to do.'

At that moment in came Agnese, with a basket on her shoulder and the air of one who comes to make an important proposal.

Agnese had also been determined not to wait for guests of that kind, alone in the house as she was, and with a little of that money of the unnamed's left, and she had been wondering for some time where was the best place to go. The chief cause of her anxiety and irresolution was the remainder of the *scudi* that had stood her in such good stead during the months of famine; for she had heard that, in the places already overrun, those with any money had found themselves in the most unpleasant position, exposed both to the violence of the invaders and to the treachery of their fellow-villagers. It was true that she had not confided the secret of her windfall, as the word goes, to anyone but Don Abbondio, to whom she had applied from time to time to change a gold piece, always leaving him a little to give to one poorer than herself. But hidden money, particularly with someone not used to handling much, keeps the possessor in a continual state of suspicion of being suspected by others. Now, as she, too, went about doing her best to hide what she could not manage to take with her and thinking of those gold pieces sewn into her bodice, she remembered that with them the unnamed had also sent the most generous offers of service; she recalled how she had been told that that castle of his was in such a safe position that nothing except birds could reach it against the owner's wish: and she decided to go and ask for shelter there. Wondering, then, how she could make herself known to the nobleman, Don Abbondio had at once occurred to her. He had always made a great fuss of her after that interview with the archbishop, all the more heartily as he could do it without compromising himself with anyone, and as, the two young people being both far away, there was only a remote chance of his being asked to do anything which would put that benevolence to a severe strain. She presumed that, in all this pandemonium, the poor man was bound to be even more fussed and frightened than herself, and that he might find this an excellent idea too; and she had now come to suggest it. Finding him with Perpetua, she put the suggestion to them both.

'What d'you say to it, Perpetua?' asked Don Abbondio.

'I say that it's a heaven-sent inspiration, and that we mustn't waste time, and ought to get ourselves on the road right away.'

'And then . . .'

'And then, and then, we'll be very glad when we're there. We know that lord wants to do nothing but help his neighbours now; and he'll be very glad to have us too. The soldiers certainly won't get there – so high up and so close to the frontier. And then, and then, we'll also find something to eat there, for once this little store's finished' – and so saying, she put it into the basket on top of the linen – 'we'd find ourselves pretty badly off up in the mountains.'

'He's converted, eh? He really is converted?'

'How can there still be any doubt, after all that's known about him and all you've seen yourself?'

'And what if we're just going and putting ourselves in a trap?'

'Trap? Nonsense! With all these hemmings and hawings of yours, excuse me, we'll never come to any conclusion. Well done, Agnese! It's a really good idea.' And she put the basket on the table, passed her arms through the straps, and hoisted it onto her shoulders.

'Couldn't we,' said Don Abbondio, 'find some man to come with us, to be an escort for his parish priest? If we meet some ruffian on the way – and there are plenty about – what help can you two give me?'

'Another idea that'll just waste time!' exclaimed Perpetua – 'going to look for a man now, when everyone's got his own affairs to think about. Buck up! Go and get your hat and breviary; and let's be off!'

Don Abbondio went, and came back a moment later with his breviary under his arm, his hat on his head, and his staff in his hand; and the three of them left the house by a small door giving on to the square. Perpetua locked it, more for form's sake than from any faith she had in those bolts and doors, and put the key in her pocket. Don Abbondio gave a glance at the church as he passed, and muttered to himself, 'It's up to the people to look after it; it's for them it's there. If they've got any feeling for their church, they'll see to it; if not – it's their own look-out.'

They went across the fields very quietly, each thinking of their own affairs and looking around – particularly Don Abbondio – for any suspicious face, anything unusual. They met no one: people were either indoors guarding their homes, or packing up, or hiding things away, or else on the tracks leading straight up the mountains.

After sighing over and over again, and then letting out some ejaculations, Don Abbondio began to grumble more coherently. He grumbled at the Duke of Nevers, for not staying on in France and enjoying life and living like a prince, instead of wanting to be Duke of Mantua in contempt of all the world; he grumbled at the emperor, for not having been more sensible than the others and let things take their course, instead of standing on all his rights; for, after all, he would still be emperor if Tom, Dick, or Harry were Duke of Mantua. But most of all he grumbled at the governor, whose business it was to do everything possible to keep such pests away from the country, and had been the very one to attract them; all just for the fun of waging war. 'Those gentry ought to be here and see for themselves what fun it is. They've got a lot to answer for! But meanwhile it's those who aren't to blame that have to suffer.'

'Do let those people alone, for they're not the ones who'll come to our help,' said Perpetua. 'That's just the usual chatter, if you'll excuse me, that doesn't lead anywhere at all. What does worry me, though . . .'

'What's that?'

Perpetua, who had been going over her hasty packing in her mind during that bit of the road, now began to lament having forgotten such and such a thing, and having put another away badly; and how she had left traces here that might give thieves a clue, and there . . .

'Good work!' said Don Abbondio, now feeling sufficiently sure of his life to be able to worry about his possessions. 'Good work! What've you gone and done? Where was your head?'

'What!' exclaimed Perpetua, stopping short a moment, and putting her arms akimbo as well as her basket allowed her. 'What! You come and reproach me like this, when it was you who flustered me, instead of helping and encouraging me! I've probably taken more care of the house-things than I have of my own. I hadn't a soul to lend me a hand; I had to be both Martha and Magdalene.* If anything goes wrong, I can't help it; I've done even more than my duty.'

Agnese would interrupt these disputes, and begin talking in turn about her own troubles. She did not lament the damage and discomfort so much as the vanished hopes of soon holding Lucia in her arms again; for, as you may remember, this was the very autumn when they had been counting on meeting; and it was most unlikely that Donna Prassede would want to come and stay at her country house in those parts in such circumstances; she would probably have left, had she been there, as had all the other visitors.

The sight of the places they were passing brought these thoughts more vividly to Agnese's mind, and made her feel her disappointment more acutely. On leaving the footpaths they had taken to the main road, the same one by which the poor woman had come to bring her daughter home for that short visit after staying with her in the tailor's house. And now the village came into sight.

'Let's go and say how-d'you-do to those good people,' said Agnese.

'And rest a little too; for I'm beginning to have enough of this basket; and also to have a bite to eat,' said Perpetua.

'So long as we lose no time; for we're not travelling for pleasure,' concluded Don Abbondio.

They were welcomed with open arms and looks of delight; they were reminders of a good deed. Do good to as many people as you can, says our author here; and you will the more often meet faces that gladden you.

Agnese, as she embraced the good matron, burst into a flood of tears, which was a great relief to her. To the questions which the woman and her husband asked about Lucia, she replied only with sobs.

'She's better off than we are,' said Don Abbondio. 'She's in Milan; out of danger away from all these devilries.'

'You're making off, are you, your reverence, you and the others?' said the tailor.

'Of course we are,' chorused master and servant together.

'You have my sympathy.'

'We're. on our way,' said Don Abbondio, 'to the castle of * * *.'

'That's a good idea; it's as safe as a church.'

'And aren't you afraid here?'

'I'll tell you, your reverence. Those people aren't likely to come here as guests, shall we say; we're too far off their road, thank Heaven. At the very most there may be some little raid, though God forbid. But, anyway, there'll be time. We'll first hear the news from the other wretched villages where they'll go and stop.'

It was decided to stay on a little and get their breath; and as it was dinner-time, 'Friends,' said the tailor, 'you must all honour my poor table; just pot-luck: there should be one decent dish.'

Perpetua said she had brought some food with her to break their fast. After some protestations on both sides they agreed to pool their resources and all dine together.

The children had gathered round their old friend Agnese in great glee. 'Quick, quick,' the tailor ordered one of the little girls (the one who had taken the food to the widow Maria, if you remember that episode) to go and shell a few early chestnuts that were laid up in a corner and put them on to roast.

And you,' said he to one of the little boys, 'go into the orchard and give the peach-tree a shake to make a few of them fall, and bring them here; the lot, mind you. And you,' said he to another, 'go up the fig-tree and gather some of the ripest ones. You know how to do it only too well already.' He himself went to tap a small cask of his, and his wife to fetch a clean cloth. Perpetua brought out her provisions. The table was spread. A napkin and a majolica plate were put at the seat of honour for Don Abbondio, with a knife and fork that Perpetua had in her basket. They sat down at table, and dined, if not with great gaiety, at least with much more than any of the guests had expected that day.

'What d'you say, your reverence, to all this upset?' asked the tailor. 'One might be reading the history of the Moors in France.'*

'What can I say? That this, too, should go and happen to me!'

'Well, you've chosen a good refuge,' went on the first. 'Who the devil could ever get up there against the owner's will? And you'll find company; for I've already heard that a lot of people have taken shelter there, and more are arriving all the time.'

'I only hope,' said Don Abbondio, 'that we'll be well received. I know that worthy nobleman; and when I had the honour of being in his company once before he was most affable.'

'And to me,' said Agnese, 'he sent word by his illustrious grace the cardinal that whenever I needed anything, I only had to go to him.'

'What a marvellous conversion!' went on Don Abbondio. 'And he's keeping it up, isn't he? He's keeping it up?'

The tailor began to expatiate on the unnamed's holy life, and how, from being the scourge of the countryside, he had become its model and benefactor.

'And those people he had with him? . . . all those servants?' went on Don Abbondio, who had heard something about them more than once, but was never sufficiently assured.

'Dismissed most of them,' replied the tailor. 'And the ones who've stayed have turned over a new leaf; they really have. In fact, the castle's become a regular Thebaid* – you know about these things.'

Then he began to talk to Agnese about the cardinal's visit. 'A great man!' said he. 'A great man! A pity he spent such a short time here, so that I couldn't do him the honours. How glad I'd be to talk to him again, with a little more time!'

On rising from table he showed her a print of the cardinal which he kept hung to one of the door-posts in veneration of that personage, and also to be able to tell anyone who saw it that it was not a good likeness, as he had had ample opportunity of studying the cardinal in person at close quarters, and in that very room.

'Is that meant to be him, that thing there?' said Agnese. 'The clothes are like him; but . . .'

'It's not like him at all, is it?' said the tailor. 'That's just what I always say; they can't deceive us, can they? But it's got his name underneath, if nothing else; it's a memento.'

Don Abbondio was in a hurry. The tailor undertook to find a cart to carry them to the foot of the slope. He went off at once to look for it, and soon after came back to say it was on the way. Then he turned to Don Abbondio, and said, 'Your reverence, if you should happen to want any books up there to pass the time, I can serve you in my poor way; for I amuse myself with a bit of reading too. Not things up to your standard, of course; they're all in the vernacular. But if . . .'

'Thank you, thank you,' replied Don Abbondio. 'In circumstances like these one's hardly able to read one's office.'

While thanks were being proffered and refused, greetings and good wishes, invitations and promises to call in there on the way back were being exchanged, the cart had reached the door. The baskets were put on it, they got in, and, feeling a little more at ease and tranquil in mind, began the second half of the journey.

The tailor had told Don Abbondio the truth about the unnamed. From the day we left him he had steadily pursued the course he had set himself then, of repairing wrongs, seeking peace, helping the poor, and always, in fact, doing any good work when the occasion arose. The courage he had formerly shown in offence and defence he now showed in refraining from either. He always went about alone and unarmed, ready to accept anything that might happen to him after the outrages he had committed, and persuaded that to use force to defend a life which was owed to so many would be to commit another outrage: persuaded, too, that any injury done to him would be an offence to God, but only a just retaliation to himself; and that he less than anyone had a right to punish such an injury. In spite of this, he had remained as inviolate as when he had kept himself and so many men armed for his safety. The memory of his former ferocity and the sight of his present meekness – ferocity which must have left so much longing for a revenge which his meekness made so easy – combined instead to arouse and maintain an admiration for him which was his chief safeguard. He was the man no one had been able to humble, and who had humbled himself. All the rancour which had at one time been increased by his own disdain and by others' fear now vanished before this new humility of his; those whom he had harmed had obtained a satisfaction beyond all their expectations and without any danger to themselves – the satisfaction of seeing such a man repent of his wrongs, and share, as it were, in their own indignation. Many whose bitterest and strongest regret for many years had been that they saw no likelihood of ever finding themselves stronger than he was, so as to be able to revenge some great wrong he had

done them, now, meeting him alone, unarmed, with the air of
one who would offer no resistance, found their only impulse was
to greet him with demonstrations of respect. By this voluntary
abasement his face and bearing had acquired, without his being
aware of it, something indefinably loftier and more noble; for it
showed, even more clearly than before, a contempt of every
danger. Even the roughest and fiercest hatreds were as if tamed
and overawed by the public veneration for a man so penitent and
beneficent. This went to such lengths that often he found it
embarrassing to avoid the demonstrations made him, and he had
to be careful not to show his inward compunction too openly in
his face and actions, and not to abase himself too much, lest he
be too much exalted. He had chosen the humblest place in the
church; and there was no danger of anyone taking it from him,
for it would have been like usurping a place of honour. To
offend, or even to treat this man disrespectfully, would have
seemed not so much insolence and cowardice as sacrilege; and
even those never usually held back by the feelings of others
shared it in more or less degree.

These same reasons and others also saved him from the
vengeance of the law, and procured for him, even in this quarter,
the safety to which he had never given a thought. His rank and
connexions, which had always been of some protection to him,
availed him more than ever now that the praises of his exemplary
conduct and the glory of his conversion were added to his already
illustrious and famous or rather infamous name. Magistrates and
grandees had rejoiced at the change as publicly as had the people;
and it would have seemed very strange to take action against a
man who was the object of such congratulations. Besides this, a
government occupied in a perpetual and often unsuccessful
struggle against spirited and recurrent rebellions must have been
well-satisfied to be freed from the most unmanageable and
irksome rebel of them all, without going out of their way to look
for other reasons; particularly as this conversion brought with it
reparations which they were not used to obtaining, or even
demanding. To torment a saint did not seem a good way of
cancelling the shame of having been incapable of suppressing a
rebel; and the example they would have made by punishing him
could only have had the effect of dissuading others like him from
becoming harmless too. Probably also the part Cardinal Federigo
had played in his conversion, and the association of his name
with the new convert, had served the latter as a sort of sacred

shield. And in the state of things, and ideas then, in the peculiar relationship between spiritual authority and civil power which were so often at loggerheads without ever trying to destroy each other, which were always mingling protestations of gratitude and deference with their hostilities, and which often ended up co-operating towards a common aim without ever making peace – in this state of things it might almost seem that, in a certain way, a reconciliation with the spiritual authority carried with it the indulgence, if not the absolution, of the lay power, when the one had succeeded alone in achieving results desired by both.

Thus the very man whom great and small would have contended to trample underfoot had he fallen, now that he had humbled himself to the dust of his own free will, was spared by all, and reverenced by many.

It is true that there were also many to whom this sensational transformation brought anything but pleasure; many hired agents, many associates in crime, who lost a powerful support on which they were accustomed to depend, as well as finding the threads of some deep-laid plot snapped perhaps at the very moment they were expecting news of its completion. But we have already seen what varied feelings this conversion excited in the ruffians who were with him at the time and who heard it announced from his own lips: amazement, grief, gloom, anger – a little of everything, in fact, except contempt and hatred. It was the same with the others whom he kept scattered in different parts, the same with his accomplices of higher rank, when they heard the terrible news, and all for the self-same reasons. Much of the hatred, as I find in the part of Ripamonti I have quoted from above,* fell on Cardinal Federigo. They regarded him as a meddler in their affairs in order to spoil them. The unnamed had wanted to save his own soul; and no one had any reason to find fault with that.

Gradually, then, most of the ruffians in the household, finding they could not get themselves used to the new discipline, and seeing no probability of its ever changing, had gone off. Some tried to find another master, perhaps among the former friends of the one they had left; some enlisted in a regiment (or *terzo*, as it was then called) of Spain or Mantua, or of one of the other belligerents; some took to infesting the highways to wage a smaller war on their own; some were even content to become freelance vagabonds; and the others under his orders in different countries did the same. Most of those who had been able to accustom themselves to the new way of life or who had embraced it willingly, were natives of the valley, and had returned to the fields or to the trades they had learnt in their early years and then abandoned; some of the foreigners had stayed on in the house as domestic servants. Both natives and foreigners, almost as if they had been blessed at the same time as their master, got along, like him, unarmed and respected, without giving or receiving any injury.

But when, on the descent of the German hordes, fugitives from the villages threatened or overrun began coming up to the castle and asking for shelter, the unnamed, delighted that his walls were being sought as a refuge by the weak who had so long regarded them from afar as a kind of vast scarecrow, received those refugees with expressions of gratitude rather than of courtesy. He had it spread around that his house was open to anyone wanting to take refuge there, and began at once to put not only it, but the whole valley, in a state of defence, in case *landsknechte* or *cappelletti* should feel like trying to come and get up to any of their tricks. He collected his remaining servants, who were few but able, like the verses of Torti,* made them a speech on the great opportunity that God was giving them and him of employing themselves for once to help the fellow-creatures whom they had so often oppressed and terrified; and in that natural tone of command of his, which expressed the certainty of being obeyed, he gave them a general idea of what he wanted them to do, and, above all, impressed on them how they were to behave so that the people coming up there to take refuge should see in them only friends and protectors. Then he had all the firearms and other weapons brought from the attic, where they had been deposited for some time, and distributed them; he sent down to his peasants and tenants in the valley to say that any of them who wanted could come up to the castle with their arms; he gave arms to those who had none; he chose some to act as officers, with others, under their command; he established pickets at the entrance and at other points of the valley, on the ascent, and at the castle gates; he laid down hours and methods for relieving the guard, as in an armed camp, and as had been the custom before in that very same castle in the days of his life of outlawry.

Set aside in one corner of that attic, and divided from the rest, were the arms he alone had borne: that famous carbine, his muskets, swords, rapiers, pistols, knives, daggers, either lying on the ground or propped against the wall. None of the servants touched these; but they agreed to ask their master which he wanted brought down. 'None,' was his reply, and whether it was from a vow, or a resolution, he remained always unarmed at the head of this kind of garrison.

At the same time he had set all the other serving-men and women or dependants to preparing accommodation for as many additional people as possible in the castle, to putting up beds, and arranging mattresses and sacks filled with straw in the rooms and drawing-rooms, which were now turned into dormitories. He had also ordered an ample supply of provisions to be laid in, to maintain whatever guests God might send him, and who now came thronging in daily in increasing numbers. He himself meanwhile was never still; in and out of the castle, up and down the slope, round the valley he went, organizing, fortifying, visiting the different posts, seeing and being seen, putting and keeping everything in order by his words and looks and presence. He would welcome the new arrivals in the house and on the way to it; and all, whether they had seen him before or were seeing him now for the first time, gazed at him ecstatically, forgetting for a moment the misfortunes and the fears that had driven them up there; and they would turn to look at him again when he was past them and pursuing his way.

CHAPTER 30

Although the main influx was not from the side by which our three fugitives were approaching the valley, but from the opening at the other end, they were beginning, in spite of that, to meet companions in travel and misfortune who had come or were coming out on to the highway from side-roads at bypaths. All those who meet in such circumstances seem to know each other already. Every time the cart overtook a pedestrian there was an exchange of questions and answers: some had made their escape like our friends, without waiting for the soldiers' arrival; some had heard their drums and trumpets; some had seen them, and described them as terrified people usually describe things.

'We've been in luck again,' said the two women. 'Thank Heaven for it. Our belongings can go; but at least we're safe.'

But Don Abbondio did not find there was so much to rejoice

at; in fact, he was beginning to be worried at the crowds, and the still bigger ones he heard were coming from the other direction.

'Oh, what a mess!' he would mutter to the women at a moment when there was no one near. 'Oh, what a mess! Don't you see that collecting such a lot of people together in one place is just asking the soldiers to come up there? Everyone's hiding their things, taking them away; there's nothing left in the houses; they'll think it'll be full of treasure up here. They're bound to come; they're bound to. Oh, poor me! What've I got myself into!'

'Oh! They've other things to do than come up here,' said Perpetua. 'They've their own way to go too. And then, I've always heard that in danger there's safety in numbers.'

'In numbers? In numbers?' replied Don Abbondio. 'Poor woman! Don't you realize a single *landsknecht* could eat up a hundred of these people? And then, if they felt like trying any of their tricks, it'd be fun, wouldn't it, to find ourselves right in the middle of a battle? Oh, poor me! It'd have been the better of two evils to have taken to the mountains. Why do they all want to come and hide in one place!... Nuisances!' he muttered in a lower voice then. 'All here; and on and on they come, one behind the other, like senseless sheep.'

'As for that,' said Agnese, 'they could say the same about us too.'

'Keep quiet, will you, for a bit?' said Don Abbondio. 'Chattering's no use now. What's done is done. Here we are, and here we must stay. It's all in the hands of Providence; let's hope to Heaven it turns out all right.'

But it was much worse when, at the entrance of the valley, he saw a big picket of armed men, some at the door of a house, and others in the rooms on the ground floor: it was like a barracks. He looked at them out of the corner of his eye. They were not the faces he had had to see on his last painful journey up here, or, if they were, they were much altered; but, in spite of that, the sight made him feel unspeakably uneasy. – Oh, poor me! – thought he. – So they are going to get up to some tricks! I oughtn't to have expected anything else from a man like that. But what does he want to do? Make war? Play the king? Oh, poor me! Circumstances when one'd like to be able to hide underground, and this man goes and tries every way of getting himself noticed and attracting attention; he might almost be wanting to invite them! –

'You can see now, your reverence,' Perpetua said to him, 'what stout lads there are to defend us. Just let the soldiers come along now. Here they're not like the dithering folk round our part, who're only good at taking to their heels.'

'Shut up!' replied Don Abbondio in a low but angry voice. 'Shut up! You don't know what you're talking about. Pray Heaven the soldiers are in a hurry, and never get to know what's happening here – that the place's been turned into a fortress. Don't you know taking fortresses is the job of soldiers? They like nothing better. Going into an assault for them is like going to a wedding: for all they find is theirs, and the people they put to the sword. Oh, poor me! Anyway, I'll see if there's a chance of getting away up one of those crags. They won't catch me in a battle! Oh, no, they won't catch me in a battle!'

'If you're afraid of being defended and helped . . .' Perpetua was beginning again; but Don Abbondio interrupted her sharply, though still in an undertone, 'Ssssh! And take care not to repeat what we've been saying. Remember, here we must always keep a smiling face and approve of everything we see.'

At Malanotte they found another group of armed men, to whom Don Abbondio doffed his hat, saying to himself, 'Oh dear, oh dear, oh dear! I've come right into an armed camp.' Here the cart stopped; they got down: Don Abbondio hurriedly paid and dismissed the driver, and set off up the slope with his two companions, without a word. The sight of those places had re-awakened in his imagination, and mingled with his present anguish, the memory of his sufferings here before. Agnese, who had never set eyes on these scenes, and had conjured up an imaginary picture which appeared every time she thought of Lucia's ghastly journey, now, on seeing them in reality, felt those cruel memories with a new and sharper pang. 'Oh your reverence!' she exclaimed. 'To think my poor Lucia came up this path!'

'Will you keep quiet now? You silly woman!' hissed Don Abbondio in her ear. 'Are those the sort of remarks to make here? Don't you realize we're in his home? It's lucky no one heard you; but if you talk in that way . . .'

'Oh!' said Agnese. 'Now he's a saint . . .!'

'Be quiet!' replied Don Abbondio. 'D'you think one can say anything that comes into one's head to saints, without consideration? You'd better be thinking, instead, of thanking him for all his kindness to you.'

'Oh, I'd thought of that already. D'you think I don't know how to behave properly?'

'Behaving properly isn't saying things that are offensive, particularly to those not used to hearing them. And just you both make sure you understand that this is no place to go chattering about and saying anything that comes into your heads. This is a great lord's house, as you know. You can see what the company around us is like. People of all sorts come here. So be prudent, if you can. Weigh your words, and above all say little, and then only when you need to. For one never goes wrong when one's silent.'

'You're worse, with all your . . .' Perpetua was beginning again.

But 'Sssh,' hissed Don Abbondio at her in an undertone, doffing his hat hastily at the same time, and making a deep bow; for he had looked up and seen the unnamed coming down towards them. The latter, in turn, had seen and recognized Don Abbondio, and quickened his steps to meet him.

'Your reverence,' said he when he was near, 'I would have preferred to offer you the hospitality of my house on a better occasion; but in any case I am very glad to be able to be of some service to you!'

'Trusting in the great kindness of your most illustrious lordship,' answered Don Abbondio, 'I have ventured to come and intrude on you in these unhappy circumstances; and as your most illustrious lordship sees, I have also taken the liberty of bringing some company with me. This is my housekeeper . . .'

'She's welcome,' said the unnamed.

'And this,' said Don Abbondio, 'is a woman your lordship has already been very good to – the mother of that . . . of that . . .'

'Of Lucia,' said Agnese.

'Of Lucia !' exclaimed the unnamed, turning to Agnese with bowed head. 'I, been good to! Eternal God! It's you, you who are being good to me, by coming here . . . to my home . . . to this house. You are welcome indeed! You bring a blessing with you.'

'The idea!' said Agnese. 'I'm coming to disturb you. And also,' she went on, drawing close to his ear, 'I must thank you . . .'

The unnamed cut short these words by anxiously inquiring for news of Lucia, and on being told, turned back to accompany his new guests up to the castle, and did so in spite of their polite remonstrances. Agnese gave the priest a glance which meant: –

You see now if there's any need of your meddling and giving advice. –

'Have they reached your parish?' the unnamed asked him.

'No, your lordship; I didn't want to stay and wait for the devils,' answered Don Abbondio. 'Heaven only knows if I'd have got out of their hands alive and come to trouble your most illustrious lordship.'

'Well, take heart,' went on the unnamed. 'For you're safe now. They won't come up here; and if they feel like trying, we're ready to receive them.'

'Let's hope they don't come,' said Don Abbondio. 'And I hear,' he added, pointing to the mountains which enclosed the other side of the valley – 'I hear another gang of soldiers is roving about there, too, but . . . but . . .'

'True,' said the unnamed. 'But don't worry; we're ready for them too.'

– Between two fires – said Don Abbondio to himself – right between two fires. Wherever have I let myself be dragged to? And by two chattering women! And this man seems to be absolutely revelling in it! Oh, what people there are in this world! –

When they entered the castle, the nobleman had Agnese and Perpetua ushered to a room in the quarters assigned to the women, which occupied three sides of the second courtyard in the rear part of the building, situated on a jutting and isolated bluff overhanging a precipice. The men were lodged to the right and left of the other courtyard, and in the part facing on to the terrace. The block between, which separated the two courtyards and connected one with the other by a vast passage opposite the main gate, was partly taken up by the food supplies and partly used as a deposit for any belongings the refugees might bring up there for safe keeping. In the men's quarters there were a few rooms reserved for any clergy who might come. There the unnamed personally accompanied Don Abbondio, who was the first to take possession of them.

For twenty-three or twenty-four days our refugees stayed in the castle, in the midst of continuous movement and surrounded by a large company, which at first was always on the increase; though nothing untoward happened. Not a day passed, perhaps, without a call to arms; *landsknechte* were coming over there; *cappelletti* had been seen over here. At each alarm the unnamed sent men off to explore; and if necessary he would take with him some who were always kept in readiness for this, and sally out of the valley with them, in the direction in which the danger had been reported: and it was a strange thing to see a band of men armed from head to foot going along in military formation led by an unarmed man. Usually it was only stray foragers and looters, who made off before they were surprised. But once, when they were chasing away some of these, to teach them not to come to those parts again, the unnamed got a report that a village nearby was being invaded and sacked. It was *landsknechte* of various regiments who had loitered behind to look for booty, joined forces, and were making sudden swoops on the villages nearest those where the army was quartered, despoiling the inhabitants and committing every kind of outrage. The unnamed made his men a short speech, and led them to the village.

They arrived unexpectedly. The rascals, who had thought they were only going out looting, seeing armed men deployed in battle order and ready to fight coming at them, abandoned their prey and took to their heels in the direction from which they had come, without even waiting for one another. The unnamed chased them a short way, then called a halt, waited for a time for any new developments, and finally turned back. And as he passed again through the rescued village it is impossible to describe the applause and blessings that followed the liberating standard and its commander.

Within the castle, in all that great crowd of people assembled there by chance, and differing in rank, manners, sex, and age, no disorder of any consequence ever occurred. The unnamed had posted guards in various places, who watched to see nothing untoward happened with all the care that everyone takes about things for which they have to render an account.

Besides this, he had also asked the clergy and the most authoritative of the refugees to go around and keep an eye on things. And he would go round too as often as he could and show himself everywhere. But even in his absence the memory of whose house it was served as a restraint to anyone who might need it. And besides, they were all refugees, and so generally inclined to quiet: the thoughts of their homes and possessions, sometimes also of their relatives and friends left in danger, the news coming from outside, depressed their spirits and maintained and increased this disposition all the more.

There were, however, a few light-hearted spirits – men of a firmer temper and fresher courage – who sought to pass these days in gaiety. They had abandoned their homes because they were not strong enough to defend them; but they saw no use in weeping and sighing for things that could not be helped, or in brooding and picturing to themselves in their imagination the havoc they were only too sure to see with their own eyes. Families who were friends with one another had gone there in company or been reunited up there, or new friendships had sprung up; and the crowds had split into groups according to habits and dispositions. Those with money and discretion went to eat down in the valley, where inns had been rapidly improvised for the occasion. In some of these each mouthful alternated with sighs, and nothing could be talked of but disaster: in others disasters were never mentioned, except to say that it was best not to think of them. Bread, soup, and wine was distributed in the castle to anyone who could not or did not want to buy his own food; there were also a few tables laid daily for guests expressly invited by the master of the house; among whom were our friends.

Agnese and Perpetua, so as not to eat the bread of idleness, had asked to be employed in the services which such lavish hospitality required; and in this they spent a good part of the day; the rest was passed chatting with friends they had made, or with poor Don Abbondio. The latter had nothing to do, but he was not bored; fear kept him company. The fear of an actual assault had, I think, passed, or, if there was any left, was the one that worried him least; for he had only to think it over to realize how little foundation it had. But the picture of the surrounding country swarming in all directions with the riff-raff of the soldiery, the arms and armed men he saw around him all the time, the idea of his being in a castle, and that particular castle, the thought of all the things that might happen at any moment in such circumstances – all this kept him in a state of vague, general, continuous alarm: this was apart from the acid in his soul at the thought of his poor home. The whole time he spent in that asylum he never went more than a musket-shot away from it, and never once set foot on the descent. His only promenade was to go out on to the terrace and walk from one end of the castle to the other, looking down over the crags and gullies to see if there was any little track, any little path practicable enough for him to use for finding a hiding-place in case of a hand-to-hand fight. He did a great deal of bowing and greeting to his fellow-refugees, but associated with very few. His most frequent conversations were with the two women, as we have mentioned. To them he would pour out all his woes, at the risk of being snubbed by Perpetua, or put to shame even by Agnese. At table, then, where he sat but little and talked still less, he would hear the latest news of the terrible progress as it arrived day by day, either passing from village to village and from mouth to mouth, or brought up there by someone who had tried to stay at home in the beginning and escaped at the last moment without succeeding in saving anything, and after being beaten up into the bargain; every day there was some new tale of disaster. Some, professional newsmongers, were diligently collecting all the rumours, sifting through all the accounts, and passing the gist of them on to others. There were disputes about which of the regiments was the most fiendish, whether the infantry or the cavalry were worse. They would repeat, as best they could, the names of some of the leaders, and recount their past exploits. They would specify the halting-places and the daily marches; that day, such and such a regiment was spreading over such and such a village, tomorrow it would engulf certain others, where in the meantime such and such another regiment had been playing the devil and worse. Above all, they tried to get information and to keep count of the regiments as they crossed the bridge at Lecco, for these could be considered as having really gone, and being out of the country. The cavalry of Wallenstein passed, the infantry of Merode passed, the cavalry of Anhalt passed, the infantry of Brandenburg passed, and then the cavalry of Montecuccoli and those of Ferrari; Altringer passed, Furstenburg passed, Colloredo passed; the Croats passed, Torquato Conti and numbers of others passed; and finally, in Heaven's good time, Gallas also passed, who was the last of them.* The flying squadron of Venetians finally made off as well; and the whole country around found itself free. Already those who came from the parts first invaded and evacuated had left the castle; and more were leaving every day like birds flying out after an autumn storm from all over the leafy branches of a great tree where they had taken refuge. Our three friends were, I think, the last to leave; and this because of Don Abbondio, who feared that if they went back home at once they might meet stray *landsknechte* lurking behind in the rear of the army. In vain Perpetua kept saying that the longer they delayed the more chance they gave the local rascals to get into the house and take away what was left. When it was a question of saving his skin Don Abbondio invariably carried the day – unless of course the imminence of danger had made him lose his head entirely.

On the day fixed for their departure the unnamed had a coach ready at Malanotte, in which he had already caused a supply of house-linen to be packed for Agnese. And, drawing her aside, he also made her accept a number of *scudi* to repair the damage she would find at home; although she kept repeating, patting her breast with her hand that she still had some of the old ones left there.

'When you see that good, poor Lucia of yours,' he said finally, 'I'm sure she says a prayer for me already, as I did her so much harm – anyway, tell her that I thank her, and trust in God that her prayers will bring many blessings to her too.'

Then he insisted on accompanying all three of his guests as far as the carriage. The reader can imagine Don Abbondio's obsequious and profuse thanks, and Perpetua's compliments. Off they set. They made, as agreed, a short halt – but without even sitting down – at the tailor's cottage, where they heard dozens of stories of the troops' passage; the usual tale of robbery and violence, havoc and defilement; but by good luck no *landsknechte* had been seen in that village.

'Ah, your reverence,' said the tailor, as he handed Don Abbondio back into the carriage, 'books ought to be printed about an upset like this.'

After another short stretch of road, our travellers began to see with their own eyes something of what they had so often heard described: vineyards stripped, not as at the harvest, but as if a combination of hail and hurricane had swept over the countryside; branches torn off and lying tossed about on the ground; props uprooted; ground trampled and scattered with twigs, leaves, and suckers; trees broken and branches lopped; hedges full of gaps; gates taken away: then in the villages doors burst in, windows smashed, and straw, rags, rubbish of all kinds heaped and scattered over the streets. The air was foul, with whiffs of stronger stench coming from the houses. The people were flinging out filth, or repairing the doors and windows as best they could, or standing about in groups lamenting to each other; and as the carriage passed, hands were held up here and there towards the windows, begging for alms.

With such scenes either before their eyes or in their minds, and with the expectation of finding their own homes in the same state, they arrived; and found, in fact, what they expected.

Agnese had her bundles put down in a corner of her little yard, which was now the cleanest spot in the house. Then she set to work to sweep it out and collect and put in order the few things that were left. She called a carpenter and a blacksmith to come and mend the worst damage, and then, as she inspected piece by piece the linen she had been given, and counted over her new coins, she said to herself, 'I've fallen on my feet; may God, Our Lady and that good lord be thanked for it; I can really say I've fallen on my feet.'

Don Abbondio and Perpetua entered their house without any need of keys. Every step they took in the passage they smelt a fetid odour, a poisonous, pestilential stench driving them back; holding their noses, they made towards the kitchen door and entered on tiptoe, picking their way carefully to avoid as much as possible the filth covering the floor. They looked around. There was not a single thing whole. In every corner were to be seen bits and pieces of what had been there and in other parts of the house; quills and feathers from Perpetua's chickens, scraps of linen, sheets of Don Abbondio's calendars, fragments of plates and cooking-pots, were all heaped up or scattered about indiscriminately. In the fireplace alone could be seen the vestiges of wholesale looting all heaped up together, like so many ideas hinted in the prose of a subtle writer. There were, I say, a few remains of burnt-out cinders and embers which showed they had once been the arm of a chair, the foot of a table, the door of a cupboard, the board of a bed, or a stave of the cask once containing the wine that was so settling for Don Abbondio's stomach. The rest was just ashes and charcoal; and with that same charcoal the wreckers had for amusement scrawled faces on the walls, trying with birettas and tonsures and broad bands to turn them into priests, doing their utmost to make them look horrible and ridiculous – an intention in which, to tell the truth, such artists could not possibly have failed.

'Ah, the swine!' exclaimed Perpetua. 'Ah, the brigands!' exclaimed Don Abbondio, and both made, as if in flight, for another door giving on to the orchard, where they breathed again. They went straight for the fig-tree; but even before reaching it they saw the earth had been stirred, and both let out a cry together; they reached it, and found, in fact, no treasure, but just the empty tomb. This started more trouble. Don Abbondio began to scold Perpetua for not having hidden the things better; and you can guess whether she remained silent. After shouting loud and long at each other, both with their arms raised and their fingers pointing at the empty hole, they turned back to the house together grumbling. Suffice it to say that they found things more or less in the same state everywhere. They worked hard and long at cleaning up and disinfecting the house, all the harder and longer because it was difficult to get any help for those days; and they had to camp in it for I do not know how long, making the best or worst of it, and gradually putting doors, furniture, and utensils together again, with money lent by Agnese.

On top of it all this disaster was the source of more troublesome bickering. For Perpetua, by dint of asking about and questioning, of spying and sniffing around, came to learn that certain of her master's household goods, which they had thought looted or destroyed by the soldiery, were instead safe and sound in the houses of people in the village; and she kept on pressing her master to do something about it, and ask for his property back. No chord more odious to Don Abbondio could have been touched; for his property was in the hands of rascals – that is of the kind of people with whom he was most anxious to be at peace.

'But what if I don't want to hear anything more about these things?' he kept on saying. 'How many times must I go on repeating that what's gone has gone? Must I be crucified, too, just because my house has been robbed?'

'I tell you,' Perpetua would reply, 'you'd let the very eyes be taken out of your head. It's a sin to steal from others, but it's a sin not to steal from you.'

'What nonsense you're talking!' would answer Don Abbondio. 'Will you be quiet?'

Perpetua would hold her tongue, but not absolutely straight away; and would use any pretext to start all over again. So much so that the poor man, when he found something missing at the moment he needed it, was reduced to having to forgo his lamentations. For more than once he had had the retort back: 'Go and ask such and such a person who's got it, and who wouldn't have kept it up to now, if he hadn't had such an easy man to deal with.'

Another and livelier source of worry for him was the rumour that stray soldiers were still continuing to pass, as he had foreseen only too well. So he was in continual suspense in case one, or even a company of them, should appear at his door, which he had hurriedly had repaired before anything else, and kept carefully locked; but by the grace of Heaven this never happened.

These terrors, however, had not yet passed before a new one followed on their heels.

But here we will leave the poor man on one side. For now there is a far more important matter to deal with than his private apprehensions, than the troubles of a few villages, or than a passing disaster.

CHAPTER 3 I

The plague which the Tribunal of Health had feared might enter the Milanese provinces with the German troops had in fact done so, as is well known; and it is also well known that it did not stop there, but invaded and depopulated a large part of Italy. Following the thread of our story, we now pass on to describe the principal events of that calamity; in the Milanese provinces, of course, and almost exclusively in Milan itself; for the records of the period deal almost exclusively with the city, as nearly always happens everywhere, for various good and bad reasons. And our aim in this account is to tell the truth, not only to represent the conditions in which our characters will find themselves, but to make known at the same time, as far as our restricted space and limited abilities allow, a page of our country's history which is more celebrated than it is known.

Of the many contemporary accounts, there is not one which gives a clear and connected idea of it; but at the same time there is not one which cannot help us form one. In each of these accounts, without excepting that of Ripamonti,[†] which surpasses them all, both in quantity and choice of facts and still more in its ways of observing them, essential facts are omitted which are recorded in others; in each of them there are material errors which can be detected and rectified with the aid of one of the others, or of one of the few official acts, published or unpublished, which survive. Often in one can be found the causes of something whose effects can be seen, vaguely, in another. Then in all of them there reigns a strange confusion of times and facts; it is a continual coming and going, as if at random, without any

---

† *De peste quae fuit anno 1630,** in five books, by Joseph Ripamonti, Canon of La Scala, Chronicler of the city of Milan. Malatesta, Milan, 1640. (M.)

general design, without any design in the details; one of the most common and obvious characteristics, by the way, of the books of that period, particularly of those written in the vernacular, in Italy at least; the learned will know if this was the same in the rest of Europe, as we suspect. No writer of a later period has tried to examine and collate these memoirs with a view to extracting from them a connected series of events, a story of that plague: so the idea that is generally held of it must necessarily be very uncertain and somewhat confused, a vague impression of great evils and great errors (and there were, in fact, both one and the other beyond anything that could possibly be imagined), an impression made up more of opinions than of facts, with a few facts scattered about, often divested of their characteristic details and without any chronological setting – that is, without an understanding of cause and effect, of sequence and progression. On our part, by examining with a great deal of diligence, if nothing else, all the published and a number of unpublished accounts, and many (of the few remaining) so-called official documents, we have tried to produce from them not perhaps what is required, but at least something that has not hitherto been done. We do not propose to give an account of all the public acts or even of all the events worthy of being recalled in some way or other. Still less do we pretend to make the reading of the original documents useless to whoever wants to get a more exact idea of the subject; we are too well aware of the lively, original, and as it were incommunicable force there always is in works of that kind, however they may be conceived and executed. We have only tried to bring out and to verify the most general and important facts, to arrange them in the real order in which they happened, so far as reason and their nature will allow, to observe their influence on each other, and to give for the present, and until someone else does it better, a succinct, but honest and continuous, account of the disaster.

Throughout the whole strip of territory crossed by the army there were a few corpses found in the houses and lying on the roads. Shortly afterwards in this or that village individuals and entire families began to fall ill and die of violent, strange complaints, with symptoms unknown to most people then alive. There were only a few to whom they were not entirely new – the few, that is, who could remember the plague which, fifty-three years before, had ravaged the greater part of Italy and particularly the Milanese provinces, where it was – and still is – called the plague of San Carlo.* Such is the power of charity! It could make the memory of one man stand out over the varied and solemn memories of a general disaster, because it inspired that man with feelings and actions more memorable even than the evils themselves: it could stamp him on people's minds as a symbol of all their misfortunes, because it had urged and thrust him forward into all of them as their guide, help, example, and voluntary victim; it could turn a general calamity into a personal triumph for him; and name it after him as if that calamity had been a conquest or a discovery.

The leading physician, Lodovico Settala, who had not only seen that plague, but had been one of the most active and intrepid doctors in it, and though very young at the time, one of its most successful healers, and who, his suspicions very much aroused, was now on the alert and collecting information, reported to the Tribunal of Health on the 20th October that the epidemic had undoubtedly broken out in the Chiuso district (at the far end of the territory of Lecco adjoining the Bergamese frontier). No decision whatsoever was taken about this, as we learn from the *Ragguaglio* of Tadino.†

And then along came similar news from Lecco and Bellano. The Tribunal now made up its mind to take action, but contented itself with sending out a commissioner who was to pick up a doctor at Como on the way, and take him with him to visit the places indicated. Both of them, 'either from ignorance or from some other reason let themselves be persuaded by an old and ignorant barber of Bellano that that kind of disease was not Plague'‡; but in some places the usual result of autumnal exhalations from the marshes, and in others the result of the privations and hardships suffered during the passage of the Germans. This assurance was reported to the Tribunal, and seems to have set its heart at rest.

But when more and more reports of deaths came pouring in ceaselessly from different directions, two delegates – the abovementioned Tadino, and one of the auditors of the Tribunal – were sent off to look into them, and take steps. When these arrived, the disease had already spread so much that proofs of it obtruded themselves without their having to go and look for them. They hurried through the territory of Lecco, the Valsassina,

† P. 24. (M.)
‡ Tadino, ibid. (M.)

the shores of Lake Como, and the districts called Monte di Brianza and Gera d'Adda. Everywhere they found towns and villages with their entrance gates shut, and others almost deserted, with their inhabitants fled, and camping out in the country or scattered: 'And they seemed,' says Tadino, 'just like so many savages, carrying in their hands sprigs of mint, or rosemary, or rue, or phials of vinegar.' They made inquiries about the number of deaths; it was appalling. They visited the sick and the dead, and everywhere found the hideous and ghastly marks of the pestilence. They at once sent this sinister news off by letter to the Tribunal of Health, which, on receiving it on the 30th October, 'arranged' says the same Tadino, to proclaim quarantine so as to keep out of the city any persons coming from the places where the plague had appeared; 'and while the decrees were being compiled' gave some summary orders to the sentries in anticipation.

Meanwhile the delegates in great haste took what measures they thought best; and returned with the melancholy conviction that they would not be enough to remedy or stop a disease already so far advanced and so widely diffused.

They arrived on the 14th November, and after making a verbal and then another written report to the Tribunal, were instructed by the latter to present themselves before the governor and lay the state of things before him. They went; and reported back that he had once more expressed a great deal of regret at the news and shown deep feeling about it, but that the preoccupations of war were still more pressing; *sed belli graviores esse curas*. Thus says Ripamonti, after ransacking the registers of the Health Tribunal and consulting Tadino, who had been specially charged with this mission – the second one, if the reader remembers, with the same purpose and the same result. Two or three days later, on the 18th November, the governor issued a proclamation ordering public festivities for the birth of Prince Carlos, eldest son of King Philip IV, without suspecting or bothering about the danger of crowding together in such circumstances – all just as if times were normal, as if nothing had been said to him at all.

This man, as we have already mentioned, was the celebrated Ambrosio Spinola, who had been sent out to put the war to rights, repair the mistakes of Don Gonzalo, and, incidentally, to govern; we may mention here also, incidentally, that he died a few months later in the same war that he had so much at heart; died not of wounds, in battle, but in his bed, of chagrin and

[margin handwritten note: but the troubles of war are more grievous]

vexation at the reproaches, wrongs, and disappointments of every
kind received at the hands of those he served. History has
deplored his fate, and censured the ingratitude of the others. It
has described his political and military enterprises with great
diligence, extolled his energy, foresight, and perseverance. It
might also have asked what he did with all these qualities of his
when the plague was threatening and actually invading a population committed to his care, or rather to his mercy.

But what, without diminishing the blame, rather lessens our
surprise at his behaviour, what arouses a different and even
stronger surprise, is the behaviour of the population itself – of
those, I mean, who were still untouched by the plague and so had
all the more reason to fear it. Would not anyone think that the
arrival of such news from districts so badly infected, from villages
almost forming a semi-circle round the city – at some points not
more than eighteen or twenty miles from it – would have created
a general stir, a wish to take some sort of precautions, or at least
a barren disquiet? Yet if there is one thing in which the records
of the time agree, it is in stating that nothing of the kind happened
at all. The famine of the year before, the exactions of the soldiery,
the general worry and strain, seemed more than enough to
account for the death-rate. Anyone in the squares, or shops, or at
home who threw out a hint of the danger, anyone who mentioned
the word plague, was greeted with either incredulous jeers or
angry contempt. The same incredulity, or it would be truer to say
the same blindness and obstinacy, prevailed in the Senate, in the
Council of Ten, and throughout the whole of the magistrature.

I find that Cardinal Federigo, as soon as he heard of the first
cases of contagious disease, enjoined his parish priests in a
pastoral letter, among other things, to impress on the people over
and over again the importance and strict obligation of reporting
every case of the kind and of handing in any infected or suspect
belongings† – something else to count among his praiseworthy
singularities.

The Tribunal of Health asked, begged, for co-operation; but
obtained little or none. And in the Tribunal itself the concern
was far from equalling the urgency of the occasion. As Tadino
repeatedly affirms, and as the whole context of his account shows
even more clearly, it was the two doctors in it who, convinced of

† *Vita di Federigo Borromeo*, compiled by Francesco Rivola, Milan, 1666,
p. 582. (M.)

the gravity and imminence of the danger, were urging on that body, which then had to urge on others in its turn.

We have already seen how indifferent it had been at the first announcement of the plague, both about acting and even about keeping itself informed; here is another example of its dilatoriness which is no less portentous, unless indeed it was forced on it by obstacles put up by superior officials. That decree about quarantine, which was decided on the 30th October, was only drawn up on the 23rd of the following month, and not published until the 29th. The plague had already entered Milan.

Tadino and Ripamonti have tried to record the name of the person who brought it in first, and other details about him and about the circumstances. In fact, when observing the beginnings of a mortality so vast that the victims, so far from being distinguishable by name, can scarcely be indicated by number of thousands, a kind of natural curiosity is aroused to know the first few names that could be noted and kept; this kind of distinction, this precedence in extermination, seems to invest them and all the details about them, which would otherwise be quite unimportant, with something fateful and memorable.

Both historians say that it was an Italian soldier in the service of Spain: but they do not tally very much on anything else, even on the name. According to Tadino, he was a certain Pietro Antonio Lovato, quartered in the territory of Lecco; according to Ripamonti, a certain Pier Paolo Locati, quartered at Chiavenna. They differ also as to the day of his entering Milan; the first putting it at the 22nd October, the second at the same date of the following month: yet it cannot have been either. Both dates contradict others that are much better authenticated. And yet Ripamonti, writing by order of the General Council of Ten, must have had many means at his command of getting the necessary information; and Tadino, because of his occupation, should have been better informed than anyone else on a fact of this nature. Anyway, by comparing it with other dates, which seem, as we have said, to be more authentic, it would appear to have been before the publication of the edicts about quarantine; and it could also be proved, or almost proved, if it were worth while, that it must have been early in that month; but the reader will surely dispense us from this task.

Whatever the date may be, this unfortunate foot-soldier and bearer of misfortune entered the city with a large bundle of clothes bought or stolen from German troops. He went to stay at the house of relations in the district round the Porta Orientale, near the Capuchin convent. Scarcely had he arrived when he fell ill. He was carried to the hospital, where a bubonic tumour found under the arm-pit made the attendant suspect what was, in fact, the truth. On the fourth day he died.

The Tribunal of Health had his family isolated and quarantined at home: his clothes and the bed he had used at the hospital were burned. Two of the attendants who had been nursing him and a good friar who had helped him also fell ill within a few days, all three of the plague. The suspicion at the hospital from the very first as to the nature of the disease, and the precautions taken in consequence, prevented the contagion spreading further there.

But the soldier had left a seed outside which did not take long to sprout. The first to catch it was the owner of the house at which he had lodged, one Carlo Colonna, a lute-player. Then, by order of the Tribunal of Health, all the tenants in the house were taken to the lazaretto, where most of them fell ill: some died shortly afterwards, of obvious infection.

In the city, the infection already scattered by these, by their clothes and by the furniture that relations, lodgers, and servants had hidden away from the searching and burning ordered by the Tribunal, and also the new infection entering through the inadequacy of the decrees, negligence in carrying them out, and adroitness in eluding them, went slowly infiltrating and circulating for the whole of the rest of that year and the first months of the following one of 1630. From time to time, now in one quarter of the city and now in another, someone would be attacked by it, someone would die of it; and the very infrequency of the cases contributed to lulling suspicion of the truth and to confirming the public even more in that stupid and fatal conviction of theirs that there was no plague, that there never for a moment had been. Many doctors, too, echoing the voice of the people (and was it the voice of God this time?), derided the ominous predictions and threatening warnings of the few; and they always had ready the names of common ailments to qualify every case of plague that they were called on to attend, whatever the symptoms or the signs with which it had appeared.

The accounts of these incidents, if they ever reached the Tribunal, usually reached them late or in a vague form. The dread of quarantine and the lazaretto sharpened all wits. The sick were not reported, undertakers and their superiors were bribed, and junior officials of the Tribunal itself, deputed by it to visit the corpses, issued false certificates, at a price.

As, however, at every case it succeeded in finding the Tribunal ordered the burning of household goods, the sequestrating of homes and the sending of whole families to the lazaretto, it is easy to infer how much anger and discontent there was against it among the public; 'among nobility, merchants, and plebs,' says Tadino: convinced as they all were that these were groundless and pointless oppressions. The chief odium fell on the two doctors, the aforesaid Tadino and Senator Settala, the son of the leading physician; it reached such a point that they could not even cross the square without being assailed with insults, if not with stones. Certainly the situation in which these men found themselves for some months was a singular one and worthy of record; of seeing a terrible scourge advancing, labouring in every way to prevent it, yet meeting only obstacles where they were looking for help; and of finding themselves targets for abuse, and being called enemies of their country; *pro patriae hostibus*, says Ripamonti.

Part of this odium also fell on other doctors, who, convinced like them of the reality of the contagion, were suggesting precautions and trying to communicate their fearful certainty to all. The mildest people taxed them with credulity and obstinacy; to all the rest it was an obvious imposture, an intrigue to profit from public terror.

The leading physician, Lodovico Settala, who was then just short of eighty, and had been professor of medicine at the University of Padua, then of Moral Philosophy at Milan, the author of many books then in high repute, honoured, too, for the offers he had received of chairs at other universities – Ingoldstadt, Pisa, Bologna, Padua – and for the refusal of these offers, was certainly one of the most authoritative men of his day. The high repute of his life was added to that of his learning, and affection to admiration for his great generosity in tending and helping the poor. There is one thing which for us today rather disturbs the esteem inspired by these merits and tinges it with regret, but which must at that time have made it stronger and more general than ever, and this is that the poor man shared the commonest and darkest prejudices of his contemporaries. He was ahead of them, but without leaving their ranks, which is what invites trouble, and often makes people lose the authority acquired in other ways. And yet the very great authority he enjoyed was not only insufficient to overcome the general opinion of those whom poets called the profane vulgar* and playwrights the gentle public, but it could not save him from the animosity and insults of that section of it which passes most easily from opinions to demonstrations and to actions.

One day, when he was going in a litter to visit his patients, crowds began to gather round it and shout that he was the chief of those who were determined there was a plague; that it was he who was throwing the city into alarm, with that frown and beard of his; all just to make work for the doctors. The crowd grew and so did its fury; the bearers, seeing how nasty things looked, took their master to shelter in a friend's house which was luckily nearby. This happened to him for having seen clearly, said what the facts were, and tried to save thousands of people from plague. And yet when, by his deplorable advice, he was instrumental in getting a poor wretched woman tortured, branded with red-hot tongs, and burnt as a witch, because her master suffered from strange pains in his stomach and a former master had been wildly in love with her,† then he had increased his reputation for wisdom with the public and, what is intolerable to think, his renown as a benefactor.

But towards the end of the month of March the cases of illness, of deaths with strange spasms, palpitations, coma, delirium, and those fatal symptoms of livid spots and tumours, began to grow frequent, first in the quarter round the Porta Orientale, and then in every part of the city; deaths for the most part sudden, violent, often even immediate, without any previous sign of illness. The doctors who had been opposed to the idea of the contagion, not wanting to admit now what they had derided before, and having to find some generic name for the new disease, which had become too common and too obvious to go without one, adopted the name of malignant and pestilential fever – a miserable expedient, in fact a swindle in words, which yet did a great deal of harm; for while it appeared to acknowledge the truth, it had the effect of preventing people believing what it was most important they should believe and realize, that the disease was caught by contact. The magistrates, as if waking from a deep sleep, began to pay a little more attention to the warnings and suggestions of the Tribunal of Health, and to see that the orders about segregation and quarantine issued by the Tribunal were carried out. The

† *Storia di Milano* by Count Pietro Verri. Milan, 1825, Vol. 4 p. 155. (M.)

latter was also continuously asking for money to defray the daily-growing expenses of the lazaretto and of many other services; and it asked the Council of Ten to decide (which they never did, I think, except *de facto*) whether these expenses were to be charged to the city or to the royal exchequer. The Council of Ten was also being pressed by the Grand Chancellor, on orders from the governor, who had gone off once more to lay siege to poor Casale. The senate was pressing them to find a way of supplying the city with food before, in the unhappy event of the contagion spreading, trade was prevented with other countries; and to find some means of maintaining the large part of the population who were out of work. The Ten tried to raise money by loans and taxes; and they allotted part of what they collected to the Tribunal of Health, part to the poor, and part to buying grain; this met some of the necessities. The worst hardships were yet to come.

In the lazaretto, where the population, though decimated daily, was daily on the increase, another arduous task was to ensure services and order, to preserve the prescribed segregation between the sexes, to maintain in fact, or rather to establish, the regime laid down by the Tribunal of Health: for, from the very first moment, everything had been in confusion owing to the indiscipline of many of the inmates, and the carelessness and connivance of the attendants. The Tribunal and the Ten, not knowing which way to turn, thought of applying to the Capuchins, and begged the Father Commissioner of the province, who was acting for the Father Provincial, dead a short time before, to give them someone capable of ruling that desolate kingdom. The commissioner suggested as head of it a Fra Felice Casati, a man of mature age, who had a great reputation for charity, energy, and gentleness combined with strength of character, a reputation which subsequent events showed to be well deserved; and as companion and assistant to him a Fra Michele Pozzobonelli, who was still young, but was as grave and austere in mind as he was in mien. They were accepted very gladly; and entered the lazaretto on the 30th March. The president of the Tribunal of Health took them around as if to hand over possession; and, assembling all the attendants and officials of every rank, proclaimed Fra Felice before them all as president of that place, with full and primary authority. Then, as the wretched assembly in there grew, other Capuchin monks were brought in, and acted as supervisors, confessors, administrators, nurses, cooks, storemen, launderers, and whatever was required. Fra Felice, ever diligent and ever watchful, patrolled day and night the arcades, the rooms, and that vast internal court, sometimes carrying a staff, sometimes armed only with a hair-shirt: he animated and organized everything; he calmed tumults, settled quarrels, threatened, punished, reproved, comforted, dried tears, and shed them himself. He caught the plague at the beginning, recovered, and resumed his former duties with fresh alacrity. Of his brethren, most sacrificed their lives there, and all did so gladly.

A dictatorship like that was certainly a strange expedient, as strange as the calamity, as strange as the times. And even if we knew nothing else about them, yet seeing who was responsible for such an important piece of organization, and how the authorities could do nothing with it but hand it over, or find anyone else to hand it over to than men who were from their very nature most alien to it – all this would be enough to show, almost to prove, what a very crude and ill-regulated state society was then in. But at the same time, seeing these men bearing such a burden so superbly is also a not ignoble proof of the energy and ability which charity can inspire at any time and any juncture. And it was fine too, their very acceptance of it, for no other reason except that no one wanted it, with no other aim except to serve, with no other hope in this world except a death much more enviable than envied; it was fine, too, their being offered it only because it was difficult and dangerous and they were presumed to have the energy and courage so necessary and so rare in those moments. And that is why the work of these monks deserves to be remembered with admiration, with tenderness, and with that kind of gratitude which is due, in solidarity, to the great services rendered by man to man, and particularly to those which are not undertaken for a reward. 'For if these friars had not been found,' says Tadino, 'assuredly the whole City would have been annihilated, for it was miraculous how much these friars did for the public benefit in so short a time, without having any assistance, or at least very little, from the City, and how they contrived to maintain, by their industry and prudence, so many thousands of poor folk in the lazaretto.' The number of persons admitted to that place during the seven months it was run by Father Felice was about fifty thousand, according to Ripamonti; who rightly says that he would have given such a man the same mention had his account not been of the miseries of a city but of its grandeurs.

Now gradually, too, the obstinacy of the public in denying the plague was naturally giving way and losing ground as the disease went on spreading; and spreading by contact and association. All the more when, after being confined to the poor for some time, it began to affect the notable; the most notable of whom, the leading physician Settala, deserves another special mention here. Did people at last admit that the poor old man had been right? Who knows? He, his wife, two sons, and seven servants all caught the plague. He and one of his sons recovered, the rest died. 'Such cases,' says Tadino, 'occurring in the City in the Noble houses, disposed the Nobility and the Plebs to think, and the sceptical doctors and the rash and ignorant rabble began to purse lips, to set teeth, and to raise eyebrows.'

But sometimes the stratagems – the revenges, so to say – of obstinacy finally convinced are such as to make one wish it had held out firm and unshaken to the last against all reason and evidence; and this was a real example of one of these times. Those who had so firmly and for so long refused to admit that there was a germ of disease near or among them which could propagate itself and make havoc by natural means, could now no longer deny that it had propagated, but were unwilling to attribute it to those means, which would have meant confessing at the same time to a great deception and to a great responsibility; they were more inclined than ever to find some other cause for it, and to accept the first that was suggested. Unhappily there was one ready to hand among the ideas and traditions current at the time not only here but all over Europe: magical arts, diabolical practices, and persons sworn to spread the plague by means of contagious poisons and sorcery. Such things, or others like them, had already been presumed and believed during many other plagues, and particularly during the last one of half a century before. It may be added that the previous year a dispatch had arrived for the governor, signed by King Philip IV, warning him of the escape of four Frenchmen from Madrid, who were being sought under suspicion of spreading poisonous and pestilential ointments; and warning him to be on the alert in case they should happen to arrive in Milan. The governor had passed the dispatch on to the Senate and the Tribunal of Health; no one seems to have taken very much notice of it at the time. But when the plague broke out and was acknowledged by everyone, that warning may have come back to people's minds and served as a confirmation of the vague suspicion of a felonious plot; it may also have been the first cause in creating it.

But two incidents, one due to blind and undisciplined fear, the other to some incomprehensible perversity, were what converted that vague idea of a possible attempt into the suspicion, and for many the certainty, of a definite plot and a genuine conspiracy. Some people fancied they had seen persons in the cathedral on the evening of the 17th May anointing a screen which was used as a partition between the parts assigned to the two sexes; and at night they had the screen and some benches it enclosed carried out of the church: although the president of the Tribunal of Health had hastened to inspect it with four members of his department, and after examining the screen, the benches, and the holy-water stoups without finding anything to confirm the ignorant suspicion of an attempt at poisoning, he had decided, rather to humour people's fancies *and from exaggerated caution rather than from necessity*, that it was enough to give the screen a scrubbing. This mass of lumber piled up made a great impression of terror on the mob, with whom a thing can so easily become a proof. It was said, and generally believed, that all the benches in the cathedral, the walls, and even the bell-ropes, had been anointed. Nor was this said only at the time. All the contemporary records (some written many years later) which allude to this incident speak of it with equal assurance; and the true story of the episode would have been left to guesswork, had it not been found in a letter from the Tribunal of Health to the governor, which is preserved in the archives of San Fedele;* from which we have extracted it, and from which are taken the words we have put in italics.

The following morning a new, even stranger, more significant spectacle struck the eyes and minds of the citizens. Doors and walls of houses in every part of the city were seen to be daubed for long stretches with some dirty yellowish filth, that seemed applied with sponges. Whether this was some stupid prank to create a wider and more general consternation, or whether it was a more criminal design to increase the public confusion, or whatever it might have been, the fact is attested in such a way that it would be less reasonable to attribute it to the dreams of the many than to the action of a few, particularly as this would not be the first or last of its kind. Ripamonti, who on this subject of the anointing often derides and more often deplores the popular credulity, asserts in this case that he had seen these

smears, and describes them.[†] In the letter quoted above, the
gentlemen of the Tribunal of Health describe it in the same terms.
They speak of visits, of experiments made with that material on
dogs, all without any bad results; and add that in their opinion
'*such temerity proceeded rather from insolence than from any
evil intent*'; an opinion which shows they had enough calm of
mind up to that time not to see what did not exist. Other
contemporary records also mention, when describing this, that
many people's opinion at first had been that it was done as a
joke, as a freakish prank. None of them say that anyone denied
this, which they would certainly have done if anyone had, if only
to call them cranks. I have thought it not out of place to relate
and put together all these details, some of which are little known
and others completely unknown, of a celebrated hallucination;
for what, it seems to me, is most interesting and most useful to
observe in mistakes, and particularly in the mistakes of the many,
is the path that appearances have taken, and the ways they can
enter people's minds and dominate them.

The city, already in agitation, was turned upside down. House-
holders burnt off the smeared parts with lighted straw; passers-
by stopped and looked on, appalled and horror-struck. Foreigners, who could then easily be distinguished by their dress, fell
under suspicion just for being foreigners, and were arrested by
people in the streets and taken off before magistrates. Captors,
captured, witnesses were examined and interrogated; no one was
found guilty; minds were still capable of doubting, of weighing
up, and understanding. The Tribunal of Health issued a proclamation in which it promised a reward and immunity to anyone
who brought the author or authors of the deed to light; '*In any
wise, not thinking it expedient*,' say these gentlemen in the letter
we have quoted above, which carries the date of 21st May but
was evidently written on the 19th, the date on the printed decree,
'*that this crime should in any way go unpunished specially in
times so perilous and suspicious, we have for the consoling and
quieting of the People, and to gain information about the deed,
today published a decree*,' etc. There was, however, no hint, or
anyway no clear hint, in the proclamation itself of the reasonable

---

† '. . . et nos quoque ivimus visere. Maculae erant sparsim inaequaliterque
manantes, veluti si quis haustam spongia saniem adspersisset, impressissetve
parieti: et ianuae, passim, ostiaque aedium eadem adspergine contaminata
cernebantur.* P. 75. (M.)

and soothing hypothesis which they had suggested to the governor – an omission which denotes both a fierce prejudice in the people and a compliance with it on the part of the Tribunal which was as blameworthy as it must have been pernicious.

While the Tribunal was making inquiries, many of the public, as is apt to happen, had already found an answer. Among those who thought it a poisonous ointment, some maintained it was a revenge taken by Don Gonzalo Fernandez de Cordova for the insults he had received at his departure, some that it was a device of Cardinal Richelieu to depopulate Milan and make himself master of it without a struggle; others, for what reason is not known, would have it that the author was the Count of Collalto, or Wallenstein, or this or that noble of Milan. There were also, as we have said, those who saw nothing in the incident but a stupid joke, and attributed it to schoolboys, to nobles, or to officers bored with the siege of Casale. No infection, nor any universal slaughter followed, as had been feared; this was probably the reason why that first wave of terror subsided for the moment, and the matter fell, or seemed to fall, into oblivion.

There were, however, still a number of people who were not yet convinced that there really was this plague. And because a few recovered from it both in the lazaretto and the city, 'it was said' (the last arguments in favour of an opinion contradicted by the evidence are always curious to know) – 'it was said by the Plebs, and also by many biased doctors, that it was not real plague, or they would all have died of it.'[†] To remove all doubts, the Tribunal resorted to an expedient proportionate to the need, an object-lesson such as the times might demand or suggest. On one of the feastdays of Pentecost the citizens were in the habit of flocking to the cemetery of San Gregorio, outside the Porta Orientale, to pray for the victims of the former plague who were buried there; and, taking advantage of their devotions to enjoy some diversion and display, everyone would go out in their holiday clothes. That day an entire family had died of the plague. At the hour when the throngs were thickest, amid the press of coaches, horsemen, and pedestrians, the corpses of this family were, by order of the Tribunal of Health, drawn naked on a cart to the aforesaid cemetery, so that the crowds could see the obvious marks of pestilence on them. A cry of horror and terror went up wherever the cart passed; a prolonged murmur could be

† Tadino, p. 93. (M.)

heard wherever it had already gone by; another murmur went ahead. The plague was more believed in after that; but belief in it was growing anyway every day; and that same throng must have served not a little to propagate it.

At first then, it was not the plague – absolutely not, not on any account; the very word was taboo. Then it was pestilential fever; the idea was admitted indirectly in the adjective. Then it was not real plague – that is to say, it was plague, but only in a certain sense; not true plague, but something for which no other name could be found. Finally it was plague without any doubt or contradiction. But already another idea – the idea of poison and sorcery – had become attached to it, which altered and confused the meaning of the word that could no longer be suppressed.

It is not, I think, necessary to be very deeply versed in the history of words and ideas to perceive that many others have followed a similar course. Heaven be praised that there are not many of such a nature and of such importance and which acquire their evidence at such a price, and to which accessories of such a character can be attached. But, in little as much as in great things, this long and winding path could be avoided by following the method laid down for so long, of observing, listening, comparing, and thinking before speaking.

But speaking by itself is so much easier than all the others put together, that we, too – I mean we humans in general – ought to some extent to be forgiven.

CHAPTER 32

As it was becoming more and more difficult to meet the melancholy needs of the situation, on the 4th May the Council of Ten decided to apply to the governor for help. And on the 22nd two members of that body were sent off to his camp to lay before him the misery and the shortages in the city, the enormous expenditure, the empty treasury, the revenues pledged for years ahead, the current taxes unpaid as a result of the general poverty produced by so many causes, and by military wastefulness in particular. They were also to submit to his consideration that by uninterrupted law and precedent, and by special decree of Charles V, the expenses of the plague should be borne by the state exchequer; and that in the plague of 1576 the governor, Marquis d'Ayamonte, had not only suspended all government exactions, but given the city a subsidy of forty thousand *scudi* from the same revenues. Finally they were to ask four things: that the exactions should be suspended as they had been before; that the Crown should make a grant of money; that the governor should inform the king of the wretched state of the city and province; and that the countryside, already ruined by the military billeting of the past, should be dispensed from any more. In reply the governor sent his regrets and fresh exhortations; said he was sorry not to be able to be in the city to use all his efforts for its relief, but that he hoped this would be compensated in every way by their lordships' zeal; and that these were times for them to spend freely and to strain every possible resource. As for the requests made '*proueeré en el mejor modo que el tiempo y necesidades presentes permitieren*':* and underneath a hieroglyphic standing for Ambrosio Spinola which was about as clear as his promise. The Grand Chancellor Ferrer wrote that this reply had been read by the Ten '*con gran desconsuelo*'.* There were more comings and goings and questions and answers; but I do not find that any more definite conclusions were reached. Some time later, at the height of the plague, the governor transferred his authority by letters patent to the same Ferrer, as he had, he wrote, to attend to the war; which, it may be said here incidentally, after carrying off by the contagion it spread a million people at least, not counting soldiers, between Lombardy, the Veneto, Piedmont, Tuscany, and part of Romagna, after laying waste the places it passed, as we have seen above – and what it did in the battle area can be imagined – after the capture and ghastly sack of Mantua, ended with everyone recognizing the new duke, to exclude whom the war had been undertaken. It should be said, however, that he was obliged to cede a piece of Montferrat to the Duke of Savoy, with an income of fifteen thousand *scudi*; and other land with an income of six thousand to Ferrante, Duke of Guastalla; and that there was another most secret treaty apart, by which the aforesaid Duke of Savoy ceded Pinerolo to France – a treaty which was carried out some time later, under other pretexts and amid wholesale trickery.

Together with this resolution, the Council of Ten had taken another: to ask the cardinal archbishop to hold a solemn procession bearing the body of San Carlo through the city.

The good prelate refused, for many reasons. He did not like

this faith in an arbitrary measure, and he feared that if the results did not come up to expectations – as he was also afraid they might not – faith might turn into outrage.[†] He also feared that '*if these anointers really exist*' the procession would be only too convenient an opportunity for their crimes. '*If they do not exist,*' the crowding together of so many people was bound to spread the contagion even more – '*a much more real danger*'.[‡] For, after a lull, suspicion of anointing had meanwhile revived more generally and violently than before.

Once again people had seen, or this time fancied they had seen, walls and entrances to public buildings, doors, and knockers anointed. The news of these discoveries flew from mouth to mouth; and, as so often happens when minds are troubled, hearing had the effect of seeing. People's minds, more and more embittered by the sight of suffering and impatient at the persistence of danger, were all the readier to accept that belief; for anger always needs something to punish; and, as a man of genius[§] has acutely observed in this connexion, it would rather attribute ills to human wickedness, upon which it can vent its revenge, than acknowledge them as coming from a source about which people can do nothing but resign themselves. A subtle, instantaneous, most penetrating poison was more than enough to explain the violence and all the obscure and more disordered symptoms of the disease. The poison was said to be concocted from toads and snakes and saliva and matter from infected persons, of worse still – in fact, of all the foulest and vilest things that wild and distorted fantasies could invent. Then to this was added sorcery, by which every effect became possible, every objection lost its force, and every difficulty was removed. If the effects had not been seen immediately after that first anointing, the reason was obvious: it had been an abortive attempt by novices in poisoning; now their art had been perfected, and their wills become more relentless in their hellish project. Now too anyone who still maintained that

[†] *Memoria delle cose notabili successe in Milano intorno al mal contaggioso l'anno 1630, etc.* Raccolte da D. Pio la Croce. Milan, 1730. This is evidently drawn from the unpublished manuscript of a writer living at the time of the plague: if indeed it is not simply a printing of that manuscript rather than a new compilation. (M.)

[‡] 'Si unguenta scelerata et unctores in urbe essent. . . . Si non essent. . . . Certiusque adeo malum.' Ripamonti, p. 185. (M.)

[§] P. Verri, *Osservazioni sulla tortura: Scrittori italiani d'economia politica, parte moderna*, Vol. 17, p. 203. (M.)

it was all a joke, anyone who denied the existence of a plot was considered as blind and obstinate, if he did not also fall under suspicion of being an interested party in diverting public attention from the truth, an accomplice, an *anointer* – the word very soon became general, solemn, portentous. With such a conviction that poisoners existed, the discovery of them was almost inevitable. Every eye was on the alert; every action liable to suspicion. And suspicion easily became certainty, and certainty fury.

Ripamonti cites two incidents in illustration, telling us that he had chosen them, not because they were the most atrocious of those happening daily, but because he had had the misfortune to be an eye-witness of them both.

In the church of Sant' Antonio one day during some service, an old man over eighty, after kneeling for some time in prayer, wanted to sit down; and before doing so, dusted the bench with his cloak. 'That old man's anointing the benches,' some women who saw the action cried out all together. The people in the church (in church!) fell on the old man, seized him by the hair, white as it was, loaded him with blows and kicks, and half-pushed, half-pulled him outside. If they did not finish him off at once, it was only in order to drag him off, half dead already, to prison, judge, and torture. 'I saw him as they were dragging him along like that,' says Ripamonti, 'and heard nothing more about him; but I am sure he could not have survived more than a few minutes.'

The other instance (which happened the following day) was equally strange, but not equally fatal. Three young Frenchmen, a scholar, a painter, and an artisan, who had come to see Italy to study its antiquities and to look for a chance of earning money, had gone up to one of the outer walls of the cathedral, and were standing gazing at it attentively. A passer-by saw them and stopped; he pointed them out to another, and then to others arriving; a group formed, staring and eyeing the trio, whose dress, hair style, and knapsacks proclaimed them to be foreigners, and, what was worse, Frenchmen. As if to assure themselves that the wall was marble, they put out a hand to touch it. That was enough. They were surrounded, seized, rough-handled, and pushed and beaten off to prison. By good luck the Palace of Justice was not far from the cathedral; and by still greater luck, they were found innocent and released.

Nor was this sort of thing confined to the city: the frenzy had spread like the contagion. The traveller whom peasants met off the main road, or who was dawdling along it looking about, or who flung himself down on the ground to rest, the stranger who was thought to have something odd or suspicious about his face or dress, were all anointers. At the first warning from anyone, even at the cry of a child, the bells would ring the alarm and people come rushing up. The unlucky wretch was pelted with stones, or seized, beaten, and taken off to prison by the angry crowd. So says the same Ripamonti. And prison, at least for the moment, was a haven of safety.

But the Council of Ten, not dissuaded by the wise prelate's refusal, went on pressing him, loudly backed by public opinion. Federigo held out for some time still, trying to persuade them; that is all the good sense of one man can do against the pressure of the times and the insistence of the many. With opinions as they then were, with the ideas of the danger so confused, so contradictory, and so far from the evidence known now, it is not difficult to understand how his good reasons might be overwhelmed, even in his own mind, by the bad ones of others. Whether any weakness of will had any part in his yielding is one of the mysteries of the human heart. Certainly, if there is any occasion when one can attribute all the errors to the intellect and absolve the conscience, it is when dealing with one of the rare people (of whom he was certainly one) whose whole life shows a resolute obedience to conscience without regard to temporal interests of any kind. When the entreaties were renewed, then, he yielded and consented to the procession being held, also consenting to the desire and general eagerness that the casket containing the relics of San Carlo should remain exposed for eight days afterwards on the high altar of the cathedral.

I cannot discover that the Tribunal of Health, or anyone else, made a protest or objection of any kind. The said board merely ordered a few precautions which showed their fear of the danger, without doing anything to prevent it. It issued stricter regulations for the entry of people into the city; and had all the gates shut to ensure they were carried out. Also, to keep infected and suspect persons away from the assembly as much as possible, they had the doors of the quarantined houses nailed up; the number of which, for what the simple assertion of one writer (and one writer of that period) may be worth, numbered about five hundred.[†]

[†] *Alleggiamento* * *dello Stato di Milano*, etc. by C. G. Cavatio della Somaglia. Milan, 1653, p. 482. (M.)

Three days were spent in preparations. At dawn on the 11th June, which was the day fixed, the procession left the cathedral. In front went a long line of people, chiefly women, their faces covered with wide shawls, many barefoot and dressed in sack-cloth. Then came the guilds preceded by their banners, and the confraternities in habits of various shapes and colours, then the monks and friars, then the secular clergy, each wearing the insignia of their rank, and carrying a taper or torch in their hands. In the middle, where the lights clustered thickest and the singing rose loudest, beneath a rich canopy, came the casket, borne by four priests sumptuously robed, who changed relays every now and again. Through the glass could be seen the venerable form, dressed in splendid pontifical robes, and the mitred skull. In the mutilated, decayed features there was still some trace of his former appearance as shown in the pictures of him, and as some could remember seeing and honouring it in life. Behind the mortal remains of the dead shepherd (says Ripamonti, from whom we have mostly taken this description), and near him, as he was in merit, blood and dignity, came Archbishop Federigo. Then followed the rest of the clergy; then the magis-trates in their full robes of state; then the nobles, some dressed magnificently, as for a solemn religious ceremony, and some in mourning, as a sign of penitence, or barefoot and in sackcloth with their faces hooded; all bore tapers. The rear was brought up by a mixed crowd.

The whole way was decked as for a festival. The rich had brought out their most precious hangings. The fronts of the poorer houses had been decorated by their wealthier neighbours or at the public expense. Here and there in place of hangings there were leafy branches. Pictures, inscriptions, coats-of-arms, dangled down on every side; on the window-sills were displayed vases, antiques, and various rarities; there were lights everywhere. The sick in quarantine looked down at the procession from many of these windows, and followed it with their prayers. The other streets were silent and deserted, save where some, also from their windows, strained their ears to catch the wandering sound. Others, among whom even nuns could be seen, had climbed up on the roofs, hoping to catch a glimpse from afar of casket, procession, anything.

The procession passed through every quarter of the city. It stopped at each of the cross-roads or small squares where the main streets came out on to the suburbs (and which then had their old name of *carrobi*, now kept only by one). The casket was set down by the cross erected at each of these points by San Carlo during the last plague, some of which are still standing; so that it returned to the cathedral some time after midday.

And then next day, while the presumptuous confidence and indeed in many the fanatical certainty that the procession had ended the plague was at its height, the death-rate suddenly increased to such an extent in every class and every part of the city, with such a sudden leap, that no one could fail to see the cause or the occasion of it in the procession itself. But oh, the wondrous and awful power of general prejudice! Not to so many people being together for so long, not to the infinite multiplication of chance contacts, did most people attribute the increase. They attributed it to the opportunity which the anointers had found in it to carry out their nefarious designs. It was said that they had mingled in the crowd and infected as many people as they could with their ointment. But as this did not seem a sufficient or a proportionate means of producing a mortality so vast and so diffused among every class of person; as it seemed that not even the watchful and deceptive eye of suspicion had been able to detect any smears or marks of any kind on the walls or anywhere else; so they had to fall back on that other refuge already time-honoured and accepted in the common science of Europe – poisonous and magical powders. It was said that powders of this kind scattered along the streets, and particularly at the halting-places, had attached themselves to the hems of robes, and particularly to the feet, many of which had gone bare that day. 'Hence,' said a contemporary writer,[†] 'the very day of the procession witnessed piety contending with impiety, perfidy with sincerity, loss with gain.' Instead it was the poor human mind that was contending with the fantasies it had itself created.

From that day the plague raged with constantly increasing violence. Within a short time there was scarcely a house left untouched. Within a short time, too, the population of the lazaretto, according to Somaglia, whom I quoted before, rose from two thousand to twelve thousand; later, according to almost everyone, it reached as much as sixteen thousand. On the 4th July, as I find in another letter from the Tribunal of Health to the governor, the death-rate exceeded five hundred a day. Still later,

† Agostino Lampugnano, *La pestilenza seguita in Milano, l'anno* 1630. Milan, 634, p. 44. (M.)

at the very height, it reached, according to the most common computation, one thousand two hundred, one thousand five hundred, and more than three thousand five hundred, if we are to believe Tadino. The latter also affirms that, 'according to investigations', the population of Milan, which had before been more than two hundred and fifty thousand, was reduced after the plague to little more than sixty-four thousand souls. According to Ripamonti, it had been only two hundred thousand; he says the number of deaths on the civic registers came to one hundred and forty thousand, apart from those that could not be counted. Others say less or more, but still more at random.

Imagine now the plight of the Council of Ten, on whom rested the burden of providing for the public needs and remedying what was remediable in such a disaster. The public servants of various kinds had to be replaced and increased every day – *monatti, apparitori*, commissioners. *Monatti* were employed in the ghastliest and most dangerous duties of the plague – removing the corpses from the houses, streets, and lazaretto, carting them to graves and burying them; taking or leading the sick to the lazaretto, and controlling them; burning or fumigating infected and suspect matter. Ripamonti says the name came from the Greek *monos*; Gaspare Bugatti (in a description of the preceding plague), from the Latin *monere*;* but he wonders at the same time, with more reason, if it was a German word, as most of these men were enrolled in Switzerland and the Grisons. Nor would it be too far-fetched to think it a shortening of the word *monathlich* (monthly); for it is probable that in the uncertainty of how long the need might last, agreements were only made from month to month. The special task of the *apparitori* was to go ahead of the carts and warn passers-by to get out of the way, by ringing a hand-bell. The commissioners controlled both under the immediate orders of the Tribunal of Health. They also had to keep the lazaretto furnished with doctors, surgeons, medicines, food, and all the necessities of a hospital; they had to find and prepare new quarters for the sick flowing in every day. For this purpose they had huts of wood and straw hurriedly erected in the space inside the lazaretto; and they built a new lazaretto, made up of shacks, surrounded by a simple fence, and capable of holding four thousand people. And as this was not enough, two others were decreed, and even begun, but never finished, owing to lack of means of every kind. Means, men, and energy decreased as the needs increased.

And not only did execution always fall short of the plans and decrees; not only were many necessities, however obviously needed, insufficiently provided for, even on paper; things reached such a pitch of impotence and desperation that many of the most deplorable as well as the most urgent cases were never provided for at all. For example, a great number of babies whose mothers had been carried off by the plague died from neglect. The Tribunal of Health proposed that a refuge should be formed for these and for destitute women who were lying-in, and that something should be done for them; but could not obtain anything. 'Even so the Council of Ten,' says Tadino, 'should be pitied; for they found themselves afflicted, harassed, and sorely tried by the unruly Soldiery, who had no respect for anyone, and even less in the unhappy Duchy, as no help or provision could be had from the Governor, except to say that it was a time of war, and that the Soldiery must be well-treated.'[†] How important it was to take Casale! How fine seems the glory of victory, independently of the cause or object for which one is fighting!

So also when an ample but single grave that had been dug out near the lazaretto was found to be completely full of corpses, and when fresh corpses, becoming more numerous every day, were being left unburied not only in the lazaretto but in all parts of the city, the magistrates, after searching in vain for the labour to carry out this grisly task, were reduced to saying that they no longer knew where to turn. Nor was it easy to see how things would have ended, had not help been forthcoming from an unusual quarter. The president of the Tribunal of Health came and appealed with tears in his eyes to the two good friars who were superintending the lazaretto; and Fra Michele pledged himself to clear the city of corpses within four days, and within eight days to open up sufficient graves not only for present needs, but for the very worst predictions of the future. With a brother friar and some officers of the Tribunal given him by the president he went out into the country to look for peasants; and, partly by the Tribunal's authority, and partly by the influence of his habit and words, he succeeded in collecting about two hundred, whom he set to digging three enormous graves. Then he sent *monatti* from the lazaretto to collect the dead; so that, on the appointed day, his promise was fulfilled.

Once the lazaretto was left without doctors; after great diffi-

† P. 117. (M.)

culty and delay some were found by offers of high pay and rewards; but many fewer than were needed. Often food was just on the very point of running out, so that it was feared people would have to die of hunger there as well. More than once, just when no one knew where to turn to find what was needed, ample supplies would arrive unexpectedly from private charity; for amidst the general stupor and indifference to others born of continuous fear for themselves, there were hearts still awake to the call of charity, and others whose charity had been aroused by the stopping of all earthly gaiety. In the same way, amidst the havoc and flight of many of those whose duty it was to superintend and provide there were at their posts a few still sound in body and unshaken in courage and there were others who, urged on by pity, assumed and perseveringly sustained tasks to which they were not called by their offices.

Those who showed the most general, ready, and constant devotion to the difficult duties of the occasion were the clergy. Their help in the lazaretti, in the city, never failed. They were wherever there was suffering. They were always to be seen mingling, merged, with the faint and dying, sometimes faint and dying themselves. To spiritual help they added such temporal as they could. They freely rendered any service the circumstances required. More than sixty parish priests in the city alone died of the disease; about eight in every nine.

Federigo, as was to be expected, was an inspiration and example to all. After almost all the archiepiscopal household had died around him, and relations, high magistrates, and neighbouring princes were urging him to get out of danger and retire to some country house, he rejected all this advice and resisted the pressure in the same spirit that made him write to his clergy: 'Be ready to abandon this mortal life, rather than abandon this family, these children of ours; go out and meet the plague lovingly, as if you were going to a reward or to a new life, while there is one soul to be saved for Christ.'† He neglected no such precautions as did not interfere with his duties, and also gave his clergy rules and instructions on these. At the same time he was careless of danger, and almost appeared not to notice it, when he had to go through it on an errand of mercy. Apart from the clergy, whom he was constantly with, commending and directing their zeal, spurring on anyone who was lukewarm in his work,

† Ripamonti, p. 164. (M.)

sending others to posts where a priest had perished, he allowed
free access to anyone who needed him. He visited the lazaretti to
comfort the sick and to encourage the attendants; he hurried
about the city, bearing relief to the wretched in quarantine at
home, pausing at the doors and under the windows to listen to
their laments and offer words of consolation and comfort in
exchange. In short he flung himself into the pestilence and lived
in the midst of it, and was amazed himself, when it ended, to find
that he had come through unscathed.

So, in public calamities and prolonged disturbances of any
normal order, one always sees an increase, a sublimation of
virtue. But, unhappily, with it always and without fail goes an
increase, far more general in most cases, of crime. And this
happened now, too. Rogues whom the plague spared and did not
frighten found new chances of activity, together with new certainty of impunity, in the common confusion following the
relaxation of every public authority; in fact the very exercise of
public authority came to be very largely in the hands of the worst
among them. The only men who generally took on the work of
monatti and *apparitori* were those more attracted by rapine and
licence than terrified of contagion or susceptible to natural
feelings of revulsion. The strictest rules were laid down for these
men, the severest penalties threatened them. Posts were assigned
them by commissioners placed over them, as we have said. Above
both were magistrates and nobles delegated for every quarter,
with authority to punish summarily every breach of discipline.
This organization kept going effectively for some time, but with
the number of those dying, leaving, or losing their senses growing
from day to day, the *monatti* and *apparitori* began to find there
was almost no one to hold them back. They made themselves,
particularly the *monatti*, the arbiters of everything. They entered
houses as masters, as enemies, and (not to mention their thieving
or treatment of the wretched creatures reduced by plague to
passing through their hands) they would lay those foul and
infected hands on healthy people, on children, parents, wives, or
husbands, threatening to drag them off to the lazaretto unless
they ransomed themselves or got others to ransom them with
money. At other times they set a price on their services, and
refused for less than so many *scudi* to carry away bodies that
were already putrefying. It was said (and the irresponsibility of
the one and the viciousness of the other make belief and disbelief

equally uncertain) – it was said, and asserted also by Tadino,[†] that *monatti* and *apparitori* let infected clothes drop from their carts on purpose, in order to propagate and foster the plague, for it had become a livelihood, a reign, a festival for them. Other shameless wretches, pretending to be *monatti* by wearing bells attached to their feet, as the latter were supposed to do for recognition and to warn others of their approach, would introduce themselves into houses and commit every sort of crime. Some houses, which were open and empty of inhabitants or occupied only by some feeble dying creature, were entered by robbers with impunity and sacked. Others were broken into and invaded by bailiffs who did the same and worse.

As crime grew, so did panic also. All the errors already more or less rampant gathered extraordinary strength from the general dismay and agitation, and produced even quicker and vaster results. They all served to reinforce and intensify that predominating terror about anointers, the effects and expression of which were often, as we have seen, another crime in themselves. The idea of this imaginary danger beset and tortured people's minds far more than the danger that was real and present. 'And while,' says Ripamonti, 'the corpses always strewn about and lying in heaps before our eyes and underfoot made the entire city seem like an immense charnel-house, there was something even more ghastly, even more appalling in that mutual frenzy, that unbridled orgy of suspicion … not only was a neighbour, a friend, or a guest distrusted; even those names that are the bonds of human love, husband and wife, father and son, brother and brother, became words of terror; and (horrible and infamous to tell!) the family board and the nuptial bed were feared as traps or hiding-places of the poisoner.'

The imagined vastness and strangeness of the plot upset all judgement and all reasons for mutual confidence. At the beginning it was believed that the only motives of those supposed anointers were ambition and cupidity; but as time went on it was imagined and believed that there was some diabolical pleasure in that anointing, some overpowering attraction. The ravings of the sick, who accused themselves of what they had feared from others, were taken as revelations, and made it possible to believe anything of anyone. And what must have had even more effect than such words were the demonstrations, if it happened that

[†] P. 102. (M).

some of the plague-ridden in their delirium imitated the actions which they imagined the anointers had been through. This seems quite a probable development, and would help to explain the general conviction, as well as the statements of many writers. In the same way, during that long and melancholy period of trials for witchcraft, the confessions of the accused – not always extorted either – served not a little to promote and maintain the prevailing opinions; for when an opinion prevails for a long time over a good part of the world, it ends by expressing itself in every way, by trying every outlet and running through every degree of conviction; and when all, or many, believe for a long time that a certain strange thing is being done, it is almost certain that someone will come along who believes he has done it himself.

Among the stories to which this mania about anointing gave rise, there is one worth mentioning for the credit it acquired and for the way in which it spread. It was said – not by everyone in the same way (which would be too strange a privilege for fables) but nearly – that a certain person, on a certain day, had seen a coach and six arrive in the cathedral square, and inside, among others, sitting a great personage with a swarthy fiery visage, blazing eyes, bristling hair, and lips menacingly set. While the spectator was gazing at it, the coach was stopped, and the coachman invited him to get in; he had not dared refuse. After various detours they had alighted at the gates of a certain palace; and when he entered it, with the others he had found himself among delights and horrors, deserts and gardens, caverns and halls; and in them ghosts sitting in council. Finally he had been shown great chests filled with money, and told to take as much as he liked, on condition, however, that he accepted a small jar of ointment and went round the city anointing with it. But when he refused he had suddenly found himself, in the wink of an eye, back in the same spot where he had been taken up. This story was generally believed here by the people, and, according to Ripamonti, not sufficiently ridiculed by anyone of authority,[†] and circulated throughout the whole of Italy and outside it. In Germany it was printed. The Elector and Archbishop of Mainz wrote to Cardinal Federigo ask him what was to be believed of the marvellous prodigies recounted about Milan; in reply he was told that they were just dreams.

[†] 'Apud prudentium plerosque, non sicuti debuerat, irrisa.' *De peste*, etc., p. 77. (M.)

Of equal value, if not altogether of the same nature, were the
dreams of the learned, and equally disastrous in their effects.
They saw, most of them, the announcement and also the cause of
all these misfortunes in a comet which had appeared in the year
1628, and in a conjunction of Saturn with Jupiter, 'the aforesaid
conjunction,' writes Tadino, 'inclining so clearly over this year
1630, that everyone could understand it.' '*Mortales parat morbos
miranda videntur.*'* This prophecy, taken, they said, from a book
called *Specchio degli Almanacchi perfetti,** printed in Turin in
1623, was on everyone's lips. Another comet which appeared in
the June of the same year as the plague was taken as a new
warning, indeed, as an obvious proof of the anointing. They
searched their books, and found only too many examples of what
they called manufactured plagues; they quoted Livy, Tacitus,
Dion, even Homer and Ovid,* and the many others of the
ancients who have described or alluded to similar things; and of
modern ones there was an even greater abundance. They cited a
hundred other authors who have treated at length or spoken
incidentally of poisons, sorcery, ointments, and powders: Cesal-
pino, Cardano, Grévin, Salio, Paré, Schenk, Zacchia, and finally
that fatal Del Río,* who would surely be one of the most
renowned of authors if their fame was in proportion to the good
or evil produced by their works: that Del Río, whose fantasies
cost more human lives than the campaigns of many conquerors;
that Del Río, whose *Disquisizioni Magiche* (an anthology of everything that men had dreamed about this subject up to his own
times) became the most authoritative, most irrefutable text on it,
and was for more than a century the rule and powerful impulse
for an uninterrupted series of horrible and legal massacres.

From the inventions of the ignorant, the educated took whatever they could fit into their own ideas; from the inventions of
the educated, the ignorant took whatever they could understand,
in whichever way they understood it; the result of both was a
vast and confused mass of public folly.

But what is even more surprising is to see the doctors (the very
doctors who had believed in the plague from the beginning, and
Tadino in particular, who had foretold it, seen it come, watched
its progress, who had said and preached that it was plague and
was passed on by contact, and that the whole country would get
infected unless something was done about it) – to see them now
using these very effects as a conclusive argument for the existence
of poisonous and magical ointments. The same man who had

noted the delirium of Carlo Colonna, the second to die of plague in Milan, as a symptom of the disease, now advanced as a proof of anointings and diabolic plots a story like the following: that two witnesses had sworn to having been told by one of their friends who had the plague, that one night some persons had come into his room and offered him health and wealth if he would consent to anointing the houses in the neighbourhood; and how on his refusal they had gone away, and in their place left a wolf under the bed, and three great cats on it, 'which remained there till daybreak'.[†]

Had it only been one person fantasizing in this way, it might have been said that he was a bit wild, or rather it would not have been worth mentioning. But as many – in fact, almost everyone – did so, it is a part of the story of the human mind, and gives us occasion to observe how an orderly and rational series of ideas may be overwhelmed by another series of ideas being thrown across them. Also, Tadino was one of the most highly reputed men of his day in Milan.

Two illustrious and trustworthy writers have affirmed that Cardinal Federigo had some doubts about the anointings.[‡] We should like to give that distinguished and lovable memory an even fuller meed of praise, and show that the good prelate was superior to most of his contemporaries in this as in everything else; but we are forced instead to note in him another example of the strength, even on the noblest minds, of public opinion. He was seen to be in real doubts from the beginning, or so at least Ripamonti says. He held throughout also that a considerable share of the general opinion was due to credulity, ignorance, fear, and a wish to make up for having been so late in recognizing the disease and in applying remedies, and that there was a good deal of exaggeration about it, but with it a certain amount of truth too. There is a short work about this plague, written in his own hand, preserved in Ambrosian library; and this view is often alluded to, and even once expressly stated. 'The common opinion,' he says more or less, 'is that these ointments are prepared in various places and many tricks are used to spread them; some of which seem to me true and some invented.'[§]

---

† Pp. 123, 124. (M.)

‡ Muratori, *Del governo della peste*. Modena, 1714, p. 117. – P. Verri, op. cit., p. 261. (M.)

§ These were his words: 'Unguenta uero haec aiebant componi conficique

There were, however, some who thought right up to the end and as long as they lived that it was all imagination; and we learn this not from them (for none of them was rash enough to expose publicly an opinion so opposed to the general belief) – we learn it from the writers who ridiculed or rebuked or refuted it as the prejudice of a few, an error which none ever dared bring out into open controversy, but which still existed. We know it, too, from those who had it handed down by tradition. 'I found intelligent folk in Milan,' says the good Muratori in the passage quoted above, 'who had received full accounts from their grandparents, and were not greatly convinced that those poisonous ointments had really existed.' There was, we see, a secret outlet for the truth – in domestic confidence. Good sense existed; but it was kept hidden for fear of public opinion.

The magistrates, reduced in numbers day by day, and more and more disheartened and confused, used all, as it were, of the little resolution they could summon up, in looking for these anointers. Among the documents of the period of the plague which are kept in the archives named above, there is a letter (without any other document related to it) in which the Grand Chancellor most seriously and urgently informs the Governor of his being warned that in a villa belonging to the brothers Girolamo and Giulio Monti, noblemen of Milan, poison was being manufactured in such quantities that forty men were occupied '*en este exercicio*' with the help of four nobles of Brescia who had material sent from the Veneto '*para la fábrica del veneno*'.* He adds that he had taken measures in great secrecy to send the Mayor of Milan and the auditor of the Tribunal of Health out there, with thirty cavalrymen; that, unfortunately, one of the brothers had been warned in time to be able to hide the traces of the crime, and that probably by the auditor himself, who was a friend of his; that the latter had made excuses for not starting out; and that in spite of this the Mayor had gone with the soldiers '*a reconocer la casa y a ver si hallara algunos vestigios*',* and to get information and arrest all those who might be guilty.

This must have come to nothing, as the records of the period which speak of the suspicions about these two nobles do not

---

multifariam, fraudisque uias fuisse complures; quarum sane fraudum, et artium aliis quidem assentimur, alias uero fictas fuisse commentitiasque arbitramur.' *De pestilentia quae Mediolani anno 1630 magnam stragem edidit.** Chap. V. (M.)

mention any proof. But unfortunately they thought they had found it on other occasions.

The trials which took place in consequence were certainly not the first of their kind; nor can they be considered a rarity in the history of jurisprudence. For without mentioning antiquity, and just glancing at the instances nearest the times we are dealing with – in Palermo in 1526; in Geneva in 1530, in 1545, and again in 1574; at Casal Montferrato in 1536; in Padua in 1555; in Turin in 1599 and again in that same year 1630 – in some places a few and in others a large number of wretches were tried and condemned to tortures generally atrocious, as guilty of spreading the plague with powders or ointments or sorcery or all these put together. But the case of the so-called ointments of Milan was the most celebrated, and perhaps the easiest to observe; or at least there is a larger field for observation on it, as the most detailed and authentic documents on it have been preserved. And although a writer whom we have praised a little before has interested himself in it, he intended not so much to write the story of it as to draw arguments from it for a work of greater or certainly of more immediate importance, and it has seemed to us that the story could be the material for a new work. But it is not a thing that can be dealt with in a few words; and this is not the place to treat it with the fullness it deserves. Besides, the reader, after stopping at all these details, will certainly not have any more interest in what happens in the rest of our story. So, reserving the story and examination of these documents for another work,† we will finally return to our characters, and not leave them again until the end.

CHAPTER 33

One night, towards the end of August, just at the very height of the plague, Don Rodrigo was on his way back to his house in Milan, accompanied by the faithful Griso, one of the three or four who had remained alive out of his whole household. He was on his way home from a gathering of friends who were in the habit of carousing together to banish the gloom of the times; and

† See the short work at the end of this volume (M).

on every occasion there were new faces present and old ones missing. That day Don Rodrigo had been one of the merriest; and, among other things, had made the whole company laugh by a sort of funeral oration on Count Attilio, who had been carried off by the plague two days before.

As he walked along, however, he felt a sort of uneasiness, a heaviness, a weakness of the legs, a difficulty in breathing, a burning feeling inside him which he would have liked to attribute to the wine, the late hour, or the season of the year. He never opened his mouth the whole way; and his first words on reaching home were to order Griso to light him to his room. When they got there, Griso noticed his master's face – distorted, inflamed, with his eyes starting out and shining brilliantly. And he kept his distance, for in those circumstances every ragamuffin had had to acquire what is called the doctor's eye.

'I'm all right; go on,' said Don Rodrigo, reading in Griso's attitude the thought that was passing through his mind. 'I'm quite all right; but I've drunk – I may've drunk a bit too much. There was a great white wine! . . . But it'll pass off with a good night's sleep. I feel so sleepy. . . . Take that light a little farther away, it's dazzling me . . . worrying me . . .!'

'Just tricks of that white wine,' said Griso, still keeping his distance. 'But you should go to bed at once, for the sleep'll do you good.'

'You're are right; if I can sleep. . . . After all, I'm quite well. Put that bell near me, anyway, just in case I need anything during the night. And be sure you hear if I happen to ring. But I shan't need anything. . . . Take that cursed light away quickly,' he went on then, while Griso was carrying out the order, going as little near him as possible. 'The Devil! Why does it bother me like this?'

Griso took the lamp, and wishing his master good night, hurried away, while the latter got under the covers.

But the covers seemed like a mountain. He threw them off, drew up his knees and tried to rest; for he was, in fact, very sleepy. But scarcely had he shut his eyes than he woke up with a start, as if someone had come and shaken him out of spite; and he felt the heat getting more oppressive, the frenzy increasing. He fell back again on the thought of August, the white wine, his debauchery; and he longed to put all the blame on them; but these ideas invariably gave way to the one which was then associated with every thought, which entered, as it were, in every sense, which had infiltrated even into the talk during the revelry, as it was easier to turn it into a joke than to pass it over in silence – the plague.

After tossing and turning for a long time, finally he fell asleep; and began to have the most confused and awful dreams in the world. One followed another until he seemed to be in a great church pushing on into the middle of the crowd, and to be there without knowing how he got there, how he had ever thought of going there, particularly at that time; and this exasperated him. He looked at the people around him. They all had pale, emaciated faces, with bleary vacant eyes, and sagging lips; all were dressed in rags hanging from them in shreds, through which could be seen frightful blotches and tumours. 'Make way, you rabble,' he seemed to be shouting, looking at the door that was so far, far away, and accompanying the shout with a threatening look, but without making any move – in fact, shrinking back instead to avoid touching those foul bodies, which were pressing him only too closely on every side. But none of those insensate people gave any sign either of moving off, or even of having heard him; instead they crowded in on him closer still. Then, above all, he felt that one of them must be pressing his elbow or something into his left side between the heart and the arm-pit, where he felt a painful, heavy pounding. And when he twisted round to try and free himself from it, immediately a new unknown something began to press him in the very same place. Enraged, he tried to lay his hand on his sword; and then it seemed that it had been forced up from its scabbard by the throng and that it was its hilt that was pressing on him in that place. But on putting his hand there he could not find the sword, and felt instead a more piercing pain than ever. He shouted out, breathless, and was trying to shout out louder, when suddenly all the faces seemed to turn in one direction. He looked, too; saw a pulpit, and above its parapet rise up something round, smooth and shining; then a bald head could be distinctly made out, then two eyes, a face, a long white beard, a friar standing up rising above the parapet as far as the girdle. It was Fra Cristoforo. He gave a swift glance around the whole audience and seemed to Don Rodrigo to fix it on his face, raising his hand at the same time, in the exact attitude he had taken up in that ground-floor room at his mansion. Then he, too, raised his hand impetuously, and made an effort as if to fling himself forward and seize that uplifted arm. His voice, which had been muffled and struggling in his throat, burst out into a great shriek; and he awoke. He dropped the arm he had lifted in reality, struggled for some time to collect himself and open his eyes, for the daylight which was already bright troubled him as much as the candle had the night before. He recognized his own bed, his own room. He realized it had all been a dream. Church, crowd, friar had all vanished – all except one thing: that pain in his left side. At the same time he felt a violent, laborious throbbing of the heart, a buzzing of the ears, a continuous whistling, a fire raging within him, a heaviness in all his limbs worse than when he had gone to bed. He hesitated some time before looking at the place where he felt the pain. Finally he uncovered it, and gave it a fearful glance; and saw a hideous tumour of a livid purple hue.

He realized he was lost. The terror of death seized him, and with it perhaps even more strongly the terror of falling a prey to the *monatti*, of being carried off and flung into the lazaretto. And as he was casting about for some way of avoiding this horrible fate, he felt his thoughts going dark and confused, and realized the moment was approaching when he would be conscious of nothing but despair. He seized the bell and shook it violently. Griso, who was on the alert, appeared at once. He stopped a certain distance from the bed, looked at his master attentively, and became certain of what he had suspected the night before.

'Griso!' said Don Rodrigo, raising himself up with a great effort, 'you've always been my trusty one.'

'Yes, your lordship.'

'I've always done well by you.'

'Of your kindness.'

'I can count on you . . .'

'Of course!'

'I'm ill, Griso.'

'So I'd noticed.'

'If I recover, I'll do even more for you than I've ever done in the past.'

Griso made no reply, and stood waiting to hear where all these preambles were leading.

'I wouldn't trust myself to anyone but you,' went on Don Rodrigo. 'Do me a favour, Griso.'

'I'm at your command,' said the latter, using his usual formula in reply to the other's unusual one.

'D'you know where Chiodo the surgeon lives?'

'Very well.'

'He's a decent fellow, and keeps his patients secret if he's paid well. Go and call him: tell him I'll give him four, no six *scudi* a visit – more if he asks for it. But he's to come at once; and do it all so that no one notices.'

'Good idea, that,' said Griso; 'I'll go, and be back at once.'

'Listen, Griso; give me a little water first. I feel such a thirst I can't stand it any longer.'

'No, my lord,' replied Griso. 'Nothing without the doctor's advice. These ills are treacherous: there's no time to lose. Keep calm, now, and in three shakes I'll be back with Chiodo.'

So saying, he went out, leaving the door half shut.

Don Rodrigo, back under the covers, accompanied him in his imagination to Chiodo's house, counting his steps and calculating the time. Every now and again he would look at his tumour again, but quickly turn his head away with a shudder. After some time he began to strain his ears for the sound of the surgeon arriving; and this effort of the attention numbed the pain and kept him in his senses. All of a sudden he heard the faint tinkling of a bell, which seemed, however, to come not from the street, but from inside the house. He listened intently. He heard it get louder, more regular, and with it a shuffling of feet. A horrible suspicion crossed his mind. He sat up and listened still more intently. He heard a muffled sound in the next room, as if some weight was being carefully put down; then flung his legs out of bed, as if to get up, looked at the door, saw it opening, and at it appear and advance towards him two filthy red uniforms, two diabolical faces – in a word, two *monatti*. He saw half of another face, Griso's, who was hiding behind the half-closed door, and stopping there to look on.

'Ah, you foul traitor! . . . Get out, you scum! Biondino! Carlotto! Help! Murder!' shouted Don Rodrigo; and thrust his hand under the pillow to find a pistol: he seized it, pulled it out. But at his first cry the *monatti* had rushed towards the bed. The quickest was on him before he could do anything, and had wrenched the pistol from his hand, flung it away, pushed him down on his back, and held him there, shouting, with a grimace of mingled rage and contempt: 'Ah, you villain! Attack the *monatti*! Attack the servants of the Tribunal! Attack those who're doing the work of mercy!'

'Hold him fast, till we take 'im away,' said his companion,

going towards a chest. And at that in came Griso, who proceeded
to force the lock with him.

'Scoundrel!' shrieked Don Rodrigo, glaring at him from under
the man who was holding him, and writhing in his sinewy arms.
'Just let me kill that swine,' he said to the *monatti*, 'and then do
what you like with me.' Then he began shouting again for his
other servants with what voice he had left; but in vain, for the
abominable Griso had sent them all a long way off, with false
orders from their master, before going to the *monatti* and
proposing that if they dealt with this job they could share the
spoils.

'Be good, now, be good,' his jailer kept on saying to the
wretched Don Rodrigo as he held him pinioned on the bed. Then,
turning towards the pair who were looting, he shouted, 'Do it
like gentlemen, now.'

'You! You!' Don Rodrigo was bellowing towards Griso, whom
he saw busy breaking things open, pulling out money and
valuables and dividing them up. 'You! After . . .! Ah, you devil in
hell! I may still recover! I may recover!' Griso did not breathe a
word, or even turn, if he could avoid it, in the direction from
which the words were coming.

'Hold him tight,' said the other *monatto*. 'He's raving.'

And this was true by now. After a loud scream, after a last and
more violent effort to release himself, he suddenly fell back in an
exhausted swoon; his eyes were still staring, however, as if he
were in a trance, and every now and again he would give a start
or a moan.

The *monatti* took hold of him, one by the feet and the other
by the shoulders, and proceeded to lay him on a stretcher they
had left in the next room. One of them came back to fetch the
loot; then, taking up their miserable load, they carried it off.

Griso stayed behind, choosing hurriedly whatever else could
be useful to him. He made a bundle of the lot and went off. He
had carefully avoided touching the *monatti* or letting himself be
touched by them. But in that last frenzied search he had taken his
master's clothes up from the bedside and shaken them to see if
there was any money in them, without thinking of anything else.
He was forced to think about it, however, next day, when, as he
was carousing in a tavern, he was suddenly seized with shivers,
his eyes went dim, his strength failed him, and he collapsed.
Abandoned by his companions, he fell into the hands of the
monatti, who despoiled him of whatever he had on him worth

having and threw him on a cart, on which he died before reaching the lazaretto, where his master had been taken.

Leaving the latter now in this abode of horror, we must go in search of another whose story would never have become involved with his, had he not been determined that it should (indeed we can say for certain that neither of them would have had any story at all). I mean Renzo, whom we left working at the new silk-mill under the name of Antonio Rivolta.

He had been there about five or six months, when those hostilities began between the republic and the King of Spain; this meant that every fear of his being looked for and disturbed by the latter was over, and Bortolo had gone off eagerly to fetch him back and have him with him again. This was both because he liked Renzo and because he thought him a talented youth, skilful at his job, and a great help to the foreman of a factory without ever aspiring to supplant him, because of that blessed misfortune of his not being able to wield a pen. As this last consideration had in fact weighed a certain amount with him, we thought we ought to mention it. Perhaps you, reader, would prefer a more ideal Bortolo? If so, then all I can say is, make one up for yourself. This one was like that.

Since then Renzo had stayed and worked with him. More than once, and particularly after getting one of those blessed letters from Agnese, he had been tempted by the idea of turning soldier and ending it all. There was no lack of opportunities: for it was just at this time that the republic needed more men. The temptation had been particularly strong for Renzo at one time, when there was talk of invading the states of Milan: it had naturally seemed to him a fine thing to return to his own home as a conqueror, see Lucia again, and have it out with her once and for all. But Bortolo, with his persuasive ways, always managed to talk him out of this resolution.

'If they've got to go there,' he would say, 'they'll do it just as well without you, and you can go along afterwards in your own time. If they come back with broken heads, won't it be better that you stayed at home? There'll be no lack of vagabonds to go along. And before they manage to set foot there . . .! As for me, I'm sceptical. They do a lot of barking, of course they do, but the state of Milan isn't a mouthful to be swallowed so easily. Spain's what they've got to deal with, my lad; and d'you realize what Spain means? St Mark is strong enough at home; but he's not up to this. Be patient. Aren't you all right here? . . . I see what you're getting at; but if Heaven has decided it's to succeed, you can be sure it'll succeed all the better for your not doing anything silly. Some saint or other's bound to help you. Believe me, it's not your sort of job. D'you really think it's worth your while leaving silk-spinning to go off killing? What d'you think you're going to do among people like that? Men have to be made for that sort of thing.'

At other times Renzo had made up his mind to go off secretly, in disguise, and under a false name. But from this, too, Bortolo managed to dissuade him every time, with arguments that can easily be guessed.

Then the plague broke out in the duchy of Milan and, as we have said, just on the Bergamese border. It did not take long to cross it, and ... but don't be alarmed, for I don't intend to write the history of this too. It is written, for anyone who wants it, on orders of the state, by a certain Lorenzo Ghirardelli.* It is a rare and almost unknown book, although it probably has more information in it than all the famous books about the plague put together. How many things the fame of books depends on! What I was going to say is that Renzo caught the plague, too, and cured himself – that is, he did nothing. He was at death's door from it, but his strong constitution defeated the disease; in a few days he was out of danger. With the return of life, the memories, desires, hopes, and plans that go with life reasserted themselves more vigorously than ever. In other words, he thought more than ever about Lucia. What had become of her during this period, when to live was almost the exception? To know nothing of her and yet to be so near! And to stay in this state of uncertainty for God knew how long! And even if all this was removed and all the danger was over and he heard Lucia was still alive, there was still that other mystery, that complication about the vow. – I'll go myself, I'll go and clear it all up at once – he said to himself, even before he could stand properly on his feet. – If only she's alive! As for finding her, I'll find her all right. I'll hear what this vow is once and for all from her, tell her it can't hold, and bring her away with me – she and that poor Agnese, too, if she's alive! She's always loved me, and I'm sure she still does. That warrant? Ah! They've got other things to think of now, those who're still alive. There are people going about safely even here with a warrant out against them. ... It's not only rascals who can make the most of this freedom. And then in Milan everyone says the confusion's worse. If I miss such a fine opportunity – (the plague!

Just see the use to which words are sometimes put by that blessed instinct of ours to refer and subordinate everything to ourselves!) – I'll never get another one like it! –

Don't give up hope, my dear Renzo.

As soon as he could drag himself about, he went off to see Bortolo, who had managed to avoid the plague up till then, and was keeping himself apart. Renzo did not enter the house, but gave him a hail from the street which made him come to the window.

'Ah! ah!' said Bortolo. 'So you've got over it, have you. Good for you!'

'I'm still a little weak in the legs, as you see, but as for danger, I'm out of that.'

'Ah! I'd like to be in your shoes. Once the great thing to be able to say was, "I'm well," but that doesn't count for much now. Anyone who's got to the point of saying, "I'm better," is really saying something!'

Renzo wished his cousin good luck, and told him of his resolution.

'Go off, this time, and Heaven bless you,' replied the other. 'Try and avoid the law, as I'm trying to avoid the contagion, and if God looks after us both, we'll meet again.'

'Oh, I'm sure to come back; and if only I don't come back alone! Anyway, I'm full of hopes.'

'Come back together, do. For, God willing, there'll be work for everyone, and we'll make a happy party. I only hope you find me still there, and this devil of an epidemic over.'

'We'll meet again, we'll meet again; we must meet again.'

'I repeat: if God's willing.'

Renzo exercised for a few days, to try out and increase his strength; and as soon as he thought he could make the journey, he made ready to set off. Under his clothes he strapped a belt with those fifty *scudi* in it which he had never touched and about which he had never breathed a word to anyone, even to Bortolo. He took a little other money he had set aside day by day by saving on everything; put in his pocket a letter of recommendation which as a precaution he had got his second master to make out under the name of Antonio Rivolta; thrust a dagger – the least an honest man could carry in those days – in a pocket of his breeches, and set off, in the last days of August, three days after Don Rodrigo had been carried to the lazaretto. He took the road to Lecco so as to pass by his own village, where, as he did not want to go quite blindly to Milan, he hoped to find Agnese alive, and to begin to hear from her some of the many things he was longing to know.

The few people who had recovered from the plague were really like a privileged class among the rest of the population. Most of the others were either sickening or dying of it, while those still untouched by the disease lived in continual terror of it. They went about warily and aloofly, with measured steps and suspicious looks, hastily and hesitatingly at the same time; for anything at all might be the weapon that dealt them a mortal wound. Those who had recovered, on the other hand, feeling more or less secure (for to catch the plague twice was more of a prodigy than a rarity), went about boldly and firmly in the midst of the contagion; they were like knights in the Middle Ages clad in as much iron as could be lifted, and mounted on chargers protected, as much as possible, in the same way, who roamed about at random (whence their glorious name of knight errant), at random and at a venture, amid a poor rabble of burghers and peasants on foot, who had only their rags to ward off or deaden any blows. What a fine, wise, and useful job! A job that really ought to take first place in a treatise on political economy.

It was with this confidence, tempered, however, by the anxieties of which the reader is aware, and sobered by the frequent sight and the incessant consciousness of the general calamity, that Renzo went towards his home, under a beautiful sky and through beautiful country, though meeting nothing, after long tracts of the most dismal solitude, but some wandering shadow rather than living being, or corpses being carried to the grave without funeral rites, without a dirge, without a mourner. At about midday he stopped in a little wood to eat some bread and meat he had brought with him. As for fruit, there was more of that at his disposal along the road than he could eat – figs, peaches, plums, apples, as many as he wanted. All he had to do was to go into a field and pick them or gather them off the ground, where they lay as thick as hail. For it was an unusually abundant year, particularly for fruit; and there was scarcely anyone to do anything about it. Even the grapes almost hid their leaves, so to say, and were left to the first who bothered to pick them.

Towards evening he descried his village. At the sight, however much he must have been prepared for it, he felt a kind of tightening of the heart. He was assailed all at once by a host of painful memories and painful presentiments. His ears seemed to ring with that sinister tolling of the alarm bell which had accompanied him, or rather pursued him, when he had fled from those parts. And at the same time he heard as it were, the death-like silence which reigned over it now. He felt a stronger agitation than ever on coming out upon the square in front of the church; and still worse awaited him at the end of his walk; for the place he had decided to stay at was the cottage he had been wont before to call Lucia's. Now at best this could only be Agnese's; and the only favour he hoped from Heaven was to find her alive and well. And there he intended to ask for lodging, foreseeing only too well that his own house would now only be the home of mice and weasels.

Not wanting to be seen, he took a by-path, the same by which he had come in such pleasant company that night to take the priest by surprise. His own vineyard and cottage lay about half-way down on either side of the path; so that he could enter both for a moment to see what state they were in.

As he went along he kept looking ahead, longing to meet someone and at the same time fearful of doing so; and a few steps farther on he did, in fact, see a man in shirt sleeves, sitting on the ground with his shoulders leaning against a hedge of jasmine, in an attitude of listlessness. From this and from the face, too, he thought he recognized that poor half-wit Gervaso who had come as second witness on that ill-fated expedition. But as he neared him he realized that instead it was the lively Tonio who had looked after him. The plague, by robbing him of the vigour of both body and mind, had brought out in the face and everything about him a small hidden germ of resemblance to his idiot brother.

'Oh, Tonio!' Renzo said to him, stopping in front of him: 'is it you?'

Tonio raised his eyes, without moving his head.

'Tonio! Don't you recognize me?'

'What comes, comes,' replied Tonio, and then stayed with his mouth agape.

'You've got it, eh? Poor Tonio; but don't you recognize me any more?'

'What comes, comes,' replied the other, with a kind of inane grin. Renzo, seeing he could get nothing more out of him, went on his way, feeling more disconsolate than ever. And then round a corner, and making towards him, he saw a black object which he recognized at once as Don Abbondio. He was walking along very slowly, carrying his stick as if it was carrying him instead; and the nearer he came, the more it could be seen in his pale, shrunken face and his every action that he, too, had passed through the storm. He, in his turn, looked hard. Were his eyes deceiving him? He noticed something foreign about the clothes; but, then, they were foreign clothes from Bergamo, of course.

– It's certainly him! – he said to himself, and raised his hands to Heaven in a movement of peevish amazement, letting the stick he held in his right hand dangle in the air; his thin arms could be seen flapping about in the sleeves which at one time they had filled to bursting. Renzo hastened towards him and made him a bow; for even though they had parted on the terms we know, he was still his parish priest.

'You here? You?' exclaimed Don Abbondio.

'I'm here, as you see. D'you know anything about Lucia?'

'What d'you expect me to know about her? Nothing's known. She's at Milan, if she's still in this world. But you . . .'

'And Agnese, is she alive?'

'She may be; but how should I know? She's not here. But . . .'

'Where is she?'

'She's gone to stay in the Valsassina, with those relations of hers at Pasturo, you know; for they say the plague's not as rampant there as here. But you, I say . . .'

'I'm sorry to hear that. And Fra Cristoforo . .?'

'He's gone away some time ago. But . . .'.

'I knew that; they wrote and told me so; I asked in case by any chance he'd come back to these parts.'

'Oh, yes; well, nothing more's been heard of him. But you . . .'

'I'm sorry to hear that, too.'

'But you, I say, what're you doing in these parts, for Heaven's sake? Don't you know about that business of the warrant?'

'What do I care about that? They've got other things to think of. I wanted to come along myself and see to my affairs. So absolutely nothing's known . . .?'

'How d'you expect to see to anything? There's no one, there's nothing left any more. And, I mean, d'you think it's sensible to come here, right into the village, right into the lion's mouth, with that warrant out for you? Just take the advice of an old man who's had to be more sensible than you, and is talking from the affection he's got for you. Just you do your shoes up tight and go back the way you came, before anyone sees you. And if you *have* been seen, just go back all the quicker. D'you think this is the place for you here? D'you realize they came looking for you, that they ransacked, they turned everything upside down . . .'

'That I know only too well, the rascals.'

'Well, then . . .'

'But I tell you I don't care about that. And that fellow, is he still alive? Is he here?'

'I tell you there's no one here; I tell you you mustn't think about things here; I tell you . . .'

'I asked if he's here, that fellow?'

'Oh, Heavens above! Do be a bit more careful what you say. Can you still be as hot-headed as ever, after all that's happened?'

'Is he here or isn't he?'

'He isn't, there. But the plague, my lad, the plague! No one ought to travel these days.'

'If there was only the plague to worry about . . . I'm speaking for myself; I've had it, and got over it.'

'Well, then! Well, then! Isn't that a warning? When one's escaped something like that, one ought to thank Heaven, it seems to me, and . . .'

'I do thank it very much.'

'And not go looking for other trouble, I say. Do what I tell you, now . . .'

'You've had it, too, your reverence, if I'm not mistaken.'

'Had it! And most vicious and deceitful it was too. It's a miracle I'm still here. I can only say it's left me in the state you see me in. What I really needed now was a little quiet to set me to rights again; I was just beginning to feel a little better. . . . Why have you come here, for Heaven's sake? Go back . . .'

'Always on about that going back, you are. If I go back now, I may as well have stayed where I was. You say: why have you come? Why have you come? What a question! I've come home.'

'Home . . .'

'Tell me; have many died here . . .?'

'Ah! ah!' exclaimed Don Abbondio; and, beginning with Perpetua, he gave a list of individuals and entire families. Renzo had been only too prepared for something of the kind, but on hearing the names of so many people he knew, of friends and relations, he stood there grief-stricken, with his head bowed, and exclaiming again and again, 'Poor fellow! Poor girl! Poor things!'

'There, you see!' exclaimed Don Abbondio. 'And it's not over yet. If those who are left don't get some sense in them this time, and get the bees out of their bonnets, there's nothing for it but the end of the world.'

'Don't you worry, I'd no intention of staying here, anyway.'

'Ah! Thank Heaven you've got that into your head! And of course you mean to go back to Bergamo?'

'Don't you worry yourself about that.'

'What! You're not going to do something even sillier than this, are you?'

'You mustn't worry about that, I tell you. It's my business, I'm not a child any longer; I can use my head. I hope, anyway, you won't tell anyone you've seen me? You're a priest and I'm one of your flock. You won't be wanting to betray me?'

'I see,' said Don Abbondio, sighing pettishly, 'I see. You want to ruin yourself and ruin me, too. What you've been through isn't enough for you; what I've been through isn't enough for you. I understand, I understand.' And muttering these last words between his teeth again and again, he went on his way.

Renzo was left standing there, sad and dispirited, wondering where to go and lodge. In that list of dead made by Don Abbondio was a family of peasants who had all been carried off by the plague, except for a youth of about Renzo's age, who had been his comrade since childhood; the cottage was a few yards outside the village. He decided to go there.

On his way he passed by his vineyard; and even from the outside he could guess at once the state it was in. Not a branch, not a leaf of any trees he had left showed above the wall. Whatever could be seen had all grown up during his absence. He went up to the gap (there were not even the hinges of the gate left) and glanced around. Poor vineyard! For two winters running the villagers had gone for firewood 'at poor Renzo's place', as they used to say. Vines, mulberries, fruit-trees of every kind, had all either been roughly torn up or cut down to the ground. But the vestiges of former cultivation could still be seen: ragged lines of young shoots which showed where the devastated rows had stood; here and there sprouts and stumps of mulberry, fig, peach, cherry, and plum-trees; but these, too, were scattered and choked amidst a new, thick, and varied generation which had come up without the help of human hand. There was a riot of nettles, ferns, tares, couch-grass, quaking grass, wild oats, amaranth, dandelion, sorrel, foxtail, and other plants of the kind – the kind, I mean, which the peasants of all countries have made into a great class on their own, and called 'weeds' or something similar.

There was a tangle of stems, each trying to grow higher in the air than the others, or crawl past each other on the ground and get the best place at any cost; a jumble of leaves, flowers, fruits, of a hundred different colours, shapes, and sizes; ears of wheat and Indian corn, tufts and bunches and clusters with little heads of white and red, yellow and blue. Amid this confusion of plants there were some which stood out more clearly, though they were none the better for that, at least, most of them; higher than all the rest was the pokeweed, with its splayed-out reddish tendrils, its majestic dark-green leaves, some of them already fringed with purple, with its drooping clusters of grapes, peacock-blue at the bottom, then purple higher up, then green, and tipped with little whitish flowers: the mullein with its great shaggy leaves trailing on the ground and its stiff upright stem and long spikes scattered and as if starred over with bright yellow flowers; thistles, with their prickly branches, leaves, and calices, from which issued little tufts of white and purple flowers, or else light and silvery down which the breeze wafted away. Here was a mass of bindweed clambering and twining round the young branches of a mulberry-tree, which it had entirely covered with its dangling leaves, its delicate little white bells quivering at the top; there a wild pumpkin had twined itself with its scarlet berries among the new shoots of a vine, which, after searching in vain for firmer support, had ended by winding its own tendrils around it, and, merging together their delicate stems and rather similar leaves, were dragging each other down, as often happens to the weak who take one another for support. There were brambles everywhere; running from one plant to the other, going up, down, bending back or stretching branches where they could. They even went across the entrance, and seemed to be there to prevent anyone passing, even the owner himself.

But Renzo had no desire to go into such a vineyard; and perhaps he spent less time looking at it than we have taken to make this little sketch. He plodded on. Nearby was the house. He crossed the garden, wading up to his knees in the weeds, with which, like the vineyard, it was crowded and overgrown, and set foot on the threshold of one of the two rooms on the ground floor. At the sound of his footsteps, at his looking in, there was a scattering and scampering of mice in all directions, rushing to hide under the filth that covered the whole of the floor: this was what was left of the *landsknechte*'s beds. He glanced at the walls; flaking, stained, blackened with smoke. He raised his eyes to the ceiling; a mass of cobwebs. There was nothing else. He turned away tearing his hair, and went back along the path he had opened up himself a moment before. A few yards farther on, he took a track off to the left through the fields, and arrived close to the cottage where he had thought of stopping, without seeing or hearing a living soul. It was already beginning to grow dark. His friend was sitting on a wooden stool at the door, with his arms crossed and his eyes raised to the sky, like a man over-whelmed by misfortune and grown savage with solitude. Hearing a foot-step, he turned to see who it could be, and cried out to the person he thought he saw through the twilight between the leaves and branches and rising and throwing up his hands: 'Is there no one else but me? Haven't I done enough yesterday? Leave me alone a bit, and that'll be a work of mercy, too.'

Renzo, not knowing what this meant, in reply called him by name.

'Renzo! . . .' said the other, in exclamation and inquiry together.

'The same,' said Renzo; and they rushed towards each other.

'It's really you!' said his friend, when they were close. 'Oh, how glad I am to see you! Who'd have thought it? I'd taken you for Paolino the sexton, who's always pestering me to come and dig graves. D'you know I'm left all alone? Alone! Alone as a hermit!'

'I know, only too well,' said Renzo. And so, quickly exchanging and mingling greetings, questions, and answers, they went into the cottage together. And there, without interrupting their talk, the friend busied himself in getting something ready to do the honours for Renzo as best he could at such short notice and in such times. He set some water on the fire, and began making *polenta*; then he handed the ladle over for Renzo to stir; and went off, saying, 'I'm left all alone. Ah, left all alone!'

He came back with a small pail of milk, some dried meat, a couple of cream cheeses, and some figs and peaches. And when it was all on the table and he had ladled out the *polenta* into a bowl, they sat down to eat together, exchanging thanks, one for the visit, and the other for the hospitality. And they suddenly found that they were greater friends, after an absence of nearly two years, than they had ever been when they saw each other every day; for meantime, says our manuscript, things had hap-pened to both of them which showed what a comfort warmth of heart can be – both what we feel ourselves, and what we find in others.

Of course no one could have taken Agnese's place with Renzo, or console him for her absence, not only because of his long and particular affection for her, but also because she alone had the key to one of the puzzles he was anxious to solve. He hesitated for a time whether to continue his journey, or go and see Agnese first, as she was so near; but considering that Agnese would know nothing about Lucia's health, he kept to his original intention of clearing up his doubt and hearing his sentence first, and then bringing the news back to her mother. But he also learned from his friend many things he did not know, and got others clear that he was vague about, Lucia's adventures, and the persecution against himself, and how Don Rodrigo had gone off with his tail between his legs, and not been seen in those parts again – about the whole tangle, in short. He also learned (and it was knowledge of no small importance to Renzo) the exact surname of Don Ferrante. Agnese had got her secretary to write it; but Heaven knows how it was spelt; and the Bergamese interpreter had read it in such a way, and made such a word out of it, that if Renzo had gone to Milan with it to try and find the address of that family, he would probably not have met a single person who could have guessed whom he meant. And yet this was the only clue he had for finding Lucia. As for the law, he was confirmed still more in his idea that this risk was remote enough not to worry him very much. The mayor had died of the plague, and who knew when another one would be appointed? Most of the bailiffs had been carried off too, and those who remained had quite other things to think about than old scores.

In his turn, he told his friend about his various ups and downs, and in exchange heard dozens of stories about the passage of the army, the plague, the anointers, and other prodigies. 'They're awful things,' said his friend, as he led Renzo to a room left tenantless by the plague – 'things we never thought to see; things to prevent one's being happy again for the rest of one's life. But it is a relief to talk about them between friends.'

At daybreak they were both in the kitchen; Renzo all ready for his journey, with his belt hidden under his doublet and his dagger in his breeches' pocket. The bundle he left with his host, so as to travel lighter. 'If all goes well with me,' he said, 'if I find her alive . . . if . . . anyway . .I'll come back this way; then I'll run over to Pasturo to give poor Agnese the good news, and then, and then

... But if by ill-luck – by ill-luck, which God forbid ... then I don't know what I'll do or where I'll go. One thing for sure is that you won't see me in these parts again.' As he said this, he was standing at the door, with his head thrown back, gazing with a mixture of tenderness and sadness at the dawn over his native village, which he had not seen for so long. His friend told him, as people do, to hope for the best, insisted that he took something to eat with him, accompanied him a short way, and then left him with renewed good wishes.

Renzo walked leisurely along, feeling it was enough for him to get near Milan that day, so as to enter it early the next morning and begin his search. The journey was uneventful, and without anything to distract Renzo from his thoughts, except for the usual spectacles of misery and gloom. He stopped for a time in a copse to eat and rest, as he had done the day before. On his way through Monza he passed an open shop with loaves of bread on show, and asked for a couple, so as not to be unprovided, whatever happened. The baker called to him to keep outside, and held out a bowl of vinegar and water on a little shovel, telling him to drop his money into it, and on his doing so, handed him with a pair of tongs two loaves, one after the other, which Renzo put into his pocket.

Towards evening he arrived at Greco without, however, knowing its name. But, from his memory of the places on his former journey, and by calculating the distance he had walked from Monza, he guessed that the city could not be far away; so he left the high road to turn into the fields and find some little hut to spend the night in; for he did not want to get involved with inns. He fared better than he expected. He came on a gap in the hedge round a farmyard, and went in on the off-chance. There was no one about: in one corner he saw a big barn with a pile of hay in it, against which was leaning a ladder: he glanced round, and then mounted it at a venture: he settled down to sleep, and quickly dropped off, not to wake till dawn. Then, crawling to the edge of his huge bed, he put his head out, and seeing no one, came down the way he had gone up, went out the way he had come in, and set off along the lanes, taking the cathedral as his pole star. After a very short walk he came out under the walls of Milan, between the Porta Orientale and the Porta Nuova, and very close to the latter.

CHAPTER 34

As for how to enter the city, Renzo had heard in a general way that there were very strict orders to admit no one without a certificate of health, but that on the other hand anyone who used his wits and seized the right moment could enter quite easily. Such was, in fact, the case; apart from the general reasons for every order at that time being carried out carelessly, and apart from the particular reasons which made the rigid execution of this one so impracticable, Milan was in such a state by then that it was hard to see that there was any point in guarding it, or anything to guard against: whoever came in was likely to be more careless of his own health than a danger to that of the citizens.

Acting on this news, Renzo's plan was to try and get in by the first gate he happened to come across, and, if he found any obstacle, to go on round the outside wall until he found another easier of access. Heaven knows how many gates he thought Milan had! On arriving under the walls, therefore, he stopped and looked about him, like someone who does not know which way to turn, and seems to be asking some guidance from everything. But all he saw to left and right were two stretches of winding road; in front, a piece of wall. There was no sign of a living being anywhere, except that from one point in the ramparts rose a column of dense black smoke, expanding and curling into wide circles as it rose, then dispersing in the still grey air. This was clothing, bedding, and other infected household goods being burned; and there was a continual succession of these dismal bonfires, not only there, but on various points on the wall.

The weather was close, the air heavy, the sky veiled all over by an even cloud, or rather haze, which seemed to blot out the sun without giving any promise of rain. The countryside around was partly uncultivated, and entirely parched. All the vegetation looked discoloured, and there was not even a drop of dew on the withered, drooping leaves. This solitude, this silence so near a great city, added a new disturbance to Renzo's disquiet, and made his thoughts gloomier than ever.

He stood there some time, then turned right at a venture, going, without knowing it, towards the Porta Nuova, which, although it was close at hand, he could not see because it was hidden behind a bastion. After going a few steps he began to hear the tinkle of little bells stopping and starting again at intervals, and then men's voices. He went on, and turned the corner of the bastion. The first thing he saw was a wooden sentry box, with a guard on the door leaning on a musket, in an attitude of weary carelessness. Behind him was a palisade, and beyond that again a gate – that is, two pieces of wall with an arch over them to shelter the two doors, which were wide open, as was also the wicket in the palisade. But on the ground right in front of the opening was a dismal obstacle – a stretcher on which two *monatti* were laying some poor wretch to take him away. It was the chief excise-man, who had been found to have the plague a short time before. Renzo stopped and waited for them to finish. When the procession had set off and he saw no one shutting the gate, he thought this was his chance, and hurried towards it. But the guard shouted 'Hey, there!' with a threatening gesture. Renzo stopped short again, and, giving the man a wink, pulled out a half-ducat and showed it to him. The fellow, who had either already had the plague, or feared it less than he loved half-ducats, motioned Renzo to throw it to him, and on seeing it roll at his feet, at once whispered, 'Quick, go ahead!' Renzo did not wait to be told twice. He passed the palisade, he passed the doors, and went on without anyone seeing him or taking any notice of him; save for another 'Hey, there!' shouted by an excise-man behind him after he had gone forty yards or so. This time he pretended not to hear, and quickened his pace without even turning round. 'Hey, there!' shouted the excise-man again, in a tone, however, which showed more irritation than determination to get himself obeyed; and, finding he was not, he shrugged his shoulders and went back into his hut, like a man more concerned to keep travellers at a safe distance than to inquire into their affairs.

The street Renzo had taken ran then, as it does now, straight down to the canal called the *Naviglio*. It was flanked by hedges or garden walls, churches, monasteries, and a few houses. At the end of this street, and in the middle of the one running alongside the canal, stood a column with a cross on it called the Cross of Sant' Eusebio. And however much Renzo looked ahead of him, all he could see was that cross. On reaching the cross-roads that divides the street about half-way down, and looking each way, he saw a citizen coming towards him along the street to the right, called the street of Santa Teresa. – A human being at last – he said to himself; and turned towards him at once, intending to ask him the way. The latter had also noticed a stranger approaching, and was eyeing him from a distance with suspicion; this grew deeper on seeing that instead of going about his business the stranger was going to accost him. Renzo, when he had got near, took off his hat like the respectful country dweller he was, and holding it in his left hand, put the other into the crown, and made straight for the unknown man. But the latter stepped back with his eyes starting from his head, raised a knotty stick and pointed the iron tip at Renzo's waist, crying, 'Keep off! Keep off! Keep off!'

'Oh, oh!' cried the youth in his turn. Then he put his hat back on his head, and, having no desire at all (as he used afterwards to say when describing the incident) to start a brawl at that moment, turned his back on this eccentric and went on his way, or rather went on in the direction he was already going.

The other man also went on his way, trembling all over from head to foot, and turning round again and again. And on getting home he said he had been accosted by an anointer with a meek and humble air, but the face of a vile impostor, carrying a little box of ointment or a packet of powder (he was not quite certain which) in one hand in the crown of his hat, and all ready to fling it into his face if he had not managed to keep him at a distance. 'If he'd come one step farther,' he added, 'I'd absolutely have run him through, the scoundrel, before he'd had time to touch me. It was bad luck we were in such a lonely spot; if it had only been right in the middle of Milan I'd have called people and got 'em to help me catch him. I'm sure we'd have found that vile poison in his hat. But, alone there as I was, all I could do was to frighten him off without risking disaster. For it's easy to throw a bit of powder, and these people are highly trained at it, besides having the devil behind them. He'll be going round Milan now; who knows the harm he's doing.' And as long as he lived – which was a good many years – he would repeat his story every time anointers were mentioned, and would add, 'Now don't let people who hold it's not true come and say so to me; for seeing is believing.'

Renzo, far from imagining what a narrow escape he had had, and feeling more angry than frightened, was brooding about this reception as he walked along, and more or less guessed what the unknown man had thought he was; but it seemed so completely unreasonable that he came to the conclusion that the man must have been a half-wit. – A bad beginning – thought he – there seems to be an unlucky star over me in Milan. It's always dead easy for me to get in, and then, once in, I run into trouble everywhere. Ah, well, ... with God's help ... If I find ... if I succeed in finding ... Ah! then nothing'll matter at all. .... –

When he reached the bridge he turned to the left, without hesitation, into the street of San Marco, which he rightly thought must lead towards the centre of the city. And as he went along he kept looking about to try and find some human being, but all he saw was a disfigured corpse in the little ditch running between the scattered houses (then fewer still), and part of the street. Just after passing this, he heard a shout of 'Hey, young man!' Looking in that direction, he saw, a short way off, on the balcony of an isolated house, a poor woman with a cluster of children round her, beckoning with a hand as she went on calling. He hurried towards her, and when he was near, 'Oh, young man,' said the woman, 'do, in the name of all your dead dear ones, go and tell the commissioner that we're here, all forgotten. They've gone and shut us up in the house as suspects because my poor husband died; they've nailed up the door, as you can see, and no one's come to bring us anything to eat since yesterday morning. In all the hours we've been here I've not been able to find a single soul to do us this charity; and these poor innocents here are dying of hunger.'*

'Of hunger!' exclaimed Renzo; and thrusting his hands into his pockets, 'Here, here you are,' said he, pulling out the two loaves. 'Let me down something to put them in.'

'May God reward you! Just a moment,' said the woman, and went to find a basket and a cord to lower it by. Renzo was meanwhile remembering the two loaves he had found near the cross on his other entry into Milan, and said to himself – There, see, it's a restitution, and probably a better one than giving them back to their owner; for this is a real work of charity. –

'As for the commissioner you talk of, my good woman,' he said then, as he put the loaves into the basket, 'I can't be of any use about that; for, to tell you the truth, I'm a stranger, and don't know my way about this town at all. But if I meet some man who looks kind and civil enough to talk to, I'll tell him.'

The woman implored him to do so, and gave him the name of the street, so that he could say where she was.

'You, too, I think,' Renzo went on, 'can do me a service, a real kindness, without putting yourself out. Can you direct me to the house of some nobles who're great folk here in Milan, the * * * house?'

'I know there is that house,' replied the woman, 'but where

I've no idea. If you go straight on here, someone will show you and you'll find it. And don't forget to tell them about us too.'

'Never fear,' said Renzo, and went on.

At every step, certain noises which he had first heard as he stood there talking were growing louder and nearer; the rumble of wheels and the clatter of horses, with a tinkle of little bells, and every now and again the crack of whips, to an accompaniment of curses. He looked ahead of him, but saw nothing. On reaching the end of the street and coming out into the square of San Marco, the first things to meet his eye were two upright beams with a rope and various pulleys; and he did not take long to recognize an object familiar enough in those days, the abominable instrument of torture. It had been erected not only there, but in all the squares and wider streets, so that the deputies for each district, who had been furnished with all the most arbitrary powers to this end, could apply it at once to anyone whom they thought deserved punishment, to people who had broken quarantine, or subordinates who had not done their duty, or anyone else. It was one of those extreme and ineffectual remedies which at that time, and particularly in such moments, were used so very prodigally.

While Renzo was looking at this instrument, and wondering why it had been put up in such a place, he heard the noise drawing nearer and nearer, then round the corner by the church saw a man appear, ringing a bell. It was an *apparitore*. Behind him came two horses pulling ahead with difficulty, their necks straining and their hoofs pawing; drawn by these came a cartful of corpses, and after it another, and then another, and another, with *monatti* walking at the horses' flanks on either side, urging them on with lashes, prods, and curses. The corpses were mostly naked, a few roughly wrapped in rags; they were heaped up and entwined with each other, like a nest of snakes slowly uncoiling to the warmth of spring; for at every jolt and jar those ghastly heaps could be seen quivering and slithering revoltingly over each other, and heads dangling, and maidenly tresses unwinding, and arms sliding out and bumping against the wheels, showing the already horrified eye how much ghastlier and fouler a spectacle like that could become.

The young man had paused at the corner of the square near the canal railings, and was sending up a prayer for these unknown dead. An appalling thought flashed into his mind: – She may be there, there with those . . . under those . . . O Lord, may it not be so! Help me not to think of it! –

When the funeral procession had passed, Renzo moved on, crossed the square, and turned left along the canal, with no other reason for the choice except that the procession had gone in the opposite direction. After covering the few yards between the side of the church and the canal, he saw the Marcellino bridge on his right; and, going over it, came out in Borgo Nuovo. And, looking up it, always with that hope of finding someone who would show him the way, he saw at the end of the street a priest clad in a doublet, with a stick in his hand, standing by a partly open door, with his head bent and his ear to the opening; and presently saw him raise his hand in a blessing. He guessed, what was in fact the case, that he had just finished confessing someone, and said to himself, 'That's the man for me. If a priest who's carrying out his duties hasn't a little charity, a little kindness and civility, then all I can say is, there's none left in the world.'

Meanwhile the priest had left the door, and was coming in Renzo's direction, walking very carefully in the middle of the street. When he drew near, Renzo took off his hat and made signs that he wished to talk to him, stopping at the same time to make him realize that he would go no nearer. The other stopped too, with the air of one prepared to listen, planting his stick down on the ground in front of him, as if to form a barrier. Renzo asked his question, and the priest gave him a satisfactory answer, not only telling him the name of the street in which the house was situated, but also giving him, as he saw the poor lad needed it, some account of how to get there, showing him, by left and right turns, churches and crosses, the six or eight streets he had to pass to get there.

'May God keep you healthy, in these times and ever after,' said Renzo, and then, as the other was beginning to move away, he added, 'One more act of charity,' and told him about the poor forgotten woman. The worthy priest thanked him for giving him an opportunity of doing so pressing an act of charity, and went on, saying he was going to warn the proper authorities. Renzo also started on his way, trying as he went along to remember all the details of the route, so as not to have to ask all over again at every corner. But you cannot imagine how hard this was, not so much from its inherent difficulties as from a new disquiet which now began coming over him. The naming of that street and the tracing of the route had upset him thoroughly. It was the information he needed and asked for and could not do without; nothing else had been said to suggest any sinister premonitions of disaster. And yet – such is the way things go – it was the clearer realization that he was near the end of his uncertainty, near the time when he would hear the words 'She's alive' or the words 'She's dead,' that hit him just then with such force that he almost wished he was still in the dark about everything, or back at the beginning of the journey whose end was now so near. But he pulled himself together and said to himself, 'Ah! If I start being childish now, how will it all end up?' So, cheered as best he could, he pursued his road, and plunged deeper into the city.

What a city! And what it had been the year before because of the famine was nothing compared to it now!

Renzo was in fact just beginning to pass through one of its most squalid and desolate quarters; the network of streets called the *Carrobio* of Porta Nuova. (There was a cross in the middle of it at that time, and opposite, near the present site of San Francesco di Paola, was an old church called Sant' Anastasia.) So violent had been the epidemic in that neighbourhood, and the stench from the abandoned corpses so appalling, that the few inhabitants left alive had been forced to evacuate it; so that to the melancholy which the passer-by felt at its aspect of solitude and desolation, was added horror and disgust at the traces and remains of recent habitation. Renzo quickened his step, heartening himself with the thought that his goal could not be so very close and hoping that he would find the scene changing, at least partly, before reaching it; and in fact a little farther on he came out into a part that could be called a city of living beings. But what a city still; and what living beings! Either from suspicion or terror, all the street doors were locked, except for those that were hanging open because the house had been either abandoned or broken into. Others were nailed or sealed up because there were dead or plague-stricken people inside. Others were marked with a cross in charcoal to show the *monatti* that there were corpses to be taken away. All this was more haphazard than anything else, depending on whether a commissioner of health, or other official, had happened to pass here rather than there, and whether he had tried to carry out orders, or had violated them. Everywhere there was a litter of rags, and, still more revolting, of purulent bandages, of infected straw, or of bedding flung from the windows. Here and there lay corpses, either of people who had suddenly died in the streets and been left until a cart passed to take them away, or which had fallen off the carts themselves, or even been thrown out of the windows, so much had the persistence and virulence of the disaster brutalized men's minds, and made them impervious to every consideration of piety or decency. Silenced everywhere were all sounds from shops, all noise of carriages, all cries of street vendors, all chatter of passers-by; only very rarely was that deathly quiet broken by anything but the rumble of funeral carts, the lamentations of the poor, the moaning of the sick, the shrieks of the delirious, and the shouts of the *monatti*. At dawn, at midday, and at evening, a bell would toll from the cathedral as a signal for reciting certain prayers that had been assigned by the archbishop; the bells of the other churches would reply to this toll; and then one might have seen people coming to the windows to pray in common, and heard a murmur of voices and sighs breathing sadness mingled with a certain consolation.

By that time about two-thirds of the citizens were dead; most of the rest were either fled or sick; the influx of people coming from outside had been reduced almost to nothing; and in a prolonged tour of the streets one was unlikely to meet anyone who had not something odd about him, or showed traces of dire changes of circumstance. The most prominent citizens were to be seen going about without cloak or cape, then a most essential part of civilized dress. Priests went without cassocks; even friars were in doublets. In fact, every article of dress was dispensed with which could touch anything with its folds, or (what was feared more than anything else) give facilities to the anointers. Apart from this care to be as closely and as shortly dressed as possible, everyone was neglected and disorderly in their persons. Those who usually wore beards now had them long, while they had grown on those accustomed to shaving. Hair was also long and tangled, not only from the neglect that comes from prolonged despondency, but also because the barbers had fallen under suspicion ever since one of them, Giangiacomo Mora,* had been borne off and condemned as a notorious anointer. This name was for long afterwards remembered with execration throughout the city; but it deserves a far wider and more lasting pity. Most people carried a stick, some even a pistol in one hand, as a threatening warning to anyone inclined to get too near them: in the other they carried perfumed pastilles, or perforated balls of metal or wood, filled with sponges soaked in medicated vinegar; and as they went along they would put them to their noses or hold them there continuously. Some carried a little phial around their necks with quicksilver inside, convinced that this had the virtue of stopping and absorbing every pestilential exhalation; and they were very careful to renew it every few days. The nobles not only went about without their usual retinues, but could even be seen with baskets on their arms, going to buy the necessities of life. Even when friends met in the street, they greeted each other at a distance with silent and hasty gestures. Everyone had difficulty as they walked along in avoiding the foul and deadly encumbrances scattered all over the ground, and in some places completely blocking the way. Everyone tried to keep in the middle of the street from fear of other filth or some ghastlier weight coming down from the windows; from fear, too, of the poisonous powders which were said to be often thrown on passers-by from above; or from fear of the walls, which might perchance be anointed. Thus ignorance, which had been bold and then careful at the wrong times, now added misery to misery and incited false terrors to balance the reasonable and salutary ones which it had discarded at the beginning.

Such were the least deformed and pitiable sights to be seen around – those of the healthy and well-to-do; for, after all the scenes of misery, and remembering the still more painful ones through which we have yet to guide our readers, we will not stop now to describe the sight of the plague-ridden dragging themselves through the streets or lying in them; the beggars, the children, the women. So appalling was it that onlookers might almost find a desperate consolation in the very thing that made the strongest and most painful impression on those far away or on posterity – in thinking, I mean, and seeing how few were the survivors.

Renzo had already gone a good part of his way amidst this desolation when a few yards away from a street down which he had to turn he heard a confused noise in which he could distinguish that familiar and horrible tinkling.

When he reached the corner of the street, which was one of the widest, he saw four carts standing in the middle of it; and the bustle around them was like a corn-market, with its comings and goings, its sacks being loaded and emptied. There were *monatti* going into the houses, *monatti* coming out carrying burdens on their shoulders and putting them into one or other of the carts; some in their red uniforms, others with no distinctive badges, many with more odious ones still – plumes and tassels of various colours, which these depraved creatures were wearing as a sign of gaiety amidst all this public mourning. A lugubrious cry 'Here, *monatti*,' would come now from one window, now from another. And with an even more sinister sound, a coarse voice would reply 'Coming, coming,' from amidst that dismal bustle. Or tenants would call out complaints and tell them to hurry up; to these the *monatti* would reply with curses.

On entering the street Renzo quickened his step, trying not to look at the encumbrances there any more than was necessary to avoid them; when his eye fell on a strange and pitiable sight – so pitiable that it inveigled the mind into contemplating it: and he stopped, almost without wanting to.

Coming down the steps of one of the doorways and advancing towards the convoy was a woman whose countenance proclaimed her to be in late but still flourishing youth. It showed a beauty which was dimmed and blunted but not destroyed by deep passion and mortal languor; that beauty at once soft and majestic which shines in the Lombard race. Her step was weary but still upright, her eyes showed no tears, though they bore signs of having shed many. There was something calm and deep about her sorrow which showed a mind all conscious and present to feel it. But it was not only her appearance that marked her out for special compassion among so much misery, and revived a feeling that had by now been quenched and exhausted in men's hearts. In her arms she carried a small child of perhaps nine years of age, dead. It was all neatly arranged, with its hair parted on its forehead, and dressed in the purest white, as if those hands of hers had decked it for a party long-promised and given as a reward. Nor did she hold it lying down, but sitting on one arm, with its breast leaning against her breast, as if it was still alive; except that a delicate little hand like wax dangled limply down one side with an inert weight, and that its head rested on its mother's shoulder with an abandon deeper than sleep – on its mother's, I say, for even if the resemblance of the faces had not proclaimed it, the face that could still express feeling would have shown it clearly.

A filthy *monatto* went up to her to take the child from her arms, with a kind of unusual respect and involuntary hesitation. But she drew back, not, however, with any sign of scorn or contempt. 'No,' she said. 'Do not touch her just yet. I must put her on to the cart myself. Take this.' So saying, she opened a hand and showed a purse, which she dropped into the one the *monatto* stretched out. Then she continued, 'Promise not to take a thread off her, or to let anyone else dare to, and to lay her in the ground like this.'

The *monatto* put a hand to his heart; and then, eagerly, tenderly, and almost obsequiously, more because of the new feeling by which he was, as it were, subdued, than because of the unexpected gift, hastened to make room on the cart for the dead child. The mother kissed its forehead, then laid it down as if putting it to bed, arranged it, stretched a white linen cloth over it, and said her last words, 'Good-bye, Cecilia! Rest in peace! We will join you this evening, and stay together for ever. Pray for us meanwhile; and I will pray for you and for the others.' Then she turned to the *monatto* again. 'When,' she said, 'you pass this way tonight, come up and fetch me too, and not me alone.'

So saying, she re-entered the house, and a moment later appeared at the window, holding in her arms another smaller child, alive, but bearing the marks of death on its face. She stood there contemplating those unworthy obsequies of the elder child, until the cart moved and she could see it no longer; then she withdrew. And what else was there for her to do now but lay the only child remaining down on the bed, and stretch herself out beside it, so that they could die together? As the full-blown flower falls with the bud on its stem at the passing of the scythe that levels all the grass in the meadow.

'O Lord,' exclaimed Renzo, 'hear her. Draw her to you – her and her little one; they have suffered enough! They have suffered enough!'

He was just recovering from this overpowering emotion, and was trying to remember his route to decide whether to turn at the next street, and, if so, whether to right or left, when he heard a mixture of different noises coming from that direction – a confused sound of imperious shouts, feeble laments, sobbing women, and moaning children.

He went on ahead, with that same gloomy, dark foreboding in his heart. On reaching the cross-roads he saw a confused crowd coming towards him, and stopped to let it pass. It was a party of sick being led to the lazaretto. Some were being driven against their will and were vainly resisting, were vainly crying that they wanted to die in their own beds, and answering the curses and commands of the *monatto* conducting them with useless imprecations. Others were walking in silence without showing pain or any other feeling, like people out of their minds. There were

women with babies in arms, children terrified by the shouts and
orders and the company rather than by the confused thought of
death, shrieking loudly for their mother and her trusted arms and
their homes. Ah! perhaps the mother they thought they had left
asleep on her bed had flung herself down there, suddenly overcome by the plague, and was lying there senseless, waiting for a
cart to bear her off to the lazaretto, or to the grave if the cart
came too late. Perhaps (oh, tragedy worthy of even more bitter
tears) the mother was entirely taken up with her own sufferings,
and had forgotten everything, even her children, and now had
only one thought – to die in peace. And yet even amidst so much
confusion there were still examples of constancy and family
piety to be seen: fathers, mothers, brothers, sons, husbands and
wives, supporting their loved ones, and cheering them on their
way with words of comfort; and not adults only, for there were
even little boys, even little girls, leading their younger brothers
and sisters along, exhorting them to be obedient, and with all
the wisdom and compassion of grown-ups, assuring them that
they were going to a place where they would be cared for and
cured.

Amidst these melancholy and touching sights there was one
thing that worried our traveller even more, and kept him in a
state of suspense. The house must be near here, and who knew
whether perhaps among those people ... But when the whole
group had passed, and this doubt was removed, he turned to a
monatto going along behind, and inquired for the street and
house of Don Ferrante. 'Go to hell, you lout,' was the reply he
got. He did not bother about giving the fellow what he deserved,
but seeing at the rear of the convoy a commissioner a few yards
away, who looked more human than the rest, he asked him the
same question. This man pointed with a stick in the direction
from which he had come, and said, 'The first street on the right,
the last large house on the left.'

His heart filled with a new and deeper anxiety, the youth goes
in that direction. He reaches the street, and picks out the house
at once among others lower and meaner. He goes up to the door,
which is shut, puts a hand on the knocker, and holds it suspended
there, as if just about to draw from an urn the lot on which is
written his life or death. Finally he raises the knocker and gives a
resolute knock.

After some moments a window opens slightly; and a woman

puts her head out to see who it is, with a suspicious air which seems to say, *Monatti?* vagabonds? commissioners? anointers? or devils?

'Ma'am,' said Renzo, looking up, and in a rather uncertain voice, 'is there a country girl in service here, called Lucia?'

'She's not here any more. Go away,' said the woman, making as if to shut the window.

'Just a moment, for pity's sake! She's not here any more? Where is she?'

'In the lazaretto,' and again she tried to shut the window.

'One moment, for the love of Heaven! With the plague?'

'Of course. Surprise, eh? Go away.'

'Oh, woe is me! Wait! Was she very ill? How long ago was it . . .?'

But meanwhile the window really had shut.

'Ma'am! ma'am! Just one word, for pity's sake! For the sake of you own poor dead. I'm not asking for anything of yours. Hey! hey!' But he might have been talking to the wall.

In his affliction at this news and anger at the way he had been told it, Renzo seized the knocker again, and, leaning against the door, squeezed and twisted it about in his hands, then raised it to give another desperate knock, but held it suspended. In his agitation, he turned round to see if there was anyone near who could give him some more precise information, some indication, some ray of light. But the first and only person he saw was another woman about twenty yards away, who, with a face full of terror, hate, flurry, and cunning, with eyes staring and trying to look towards him and away at the same time, with mouth open as if just about to shout something at the top of her voice but holding her breath, was raising a pair of skinny arms and stretching and closing two shrivelled, claw-like hands, as if in an attempt to catch something, and was evidently trying to call people without his noticing. When their eyes met, she started back as though caught in the act, and looked wilder than ever.

'What on earth . . .?' began Renzo, also raising his fists towards the woman; but she, having lost hope of catching him unawares, now let out the shriek she had up to then restrained, 'The anointer! Catch 'im, catch 'im! Catch the anointer!' 'Who, me? You lying witch! Shut up!' yelled Renzo, and made a jump towards her to frighten her to silence. But suddenly he saw he had better be looking after his own affairs instead. At the old woman's shriek people were hurrying up on every side; not the crowds that would have collected in a similar case three months before, but more than enough to do whatever they liked to one man alone. At the same time the window above opened again, and the same unmannerly woman as before leant out this time, and began shouting too: 'Catch 'im! Catch 'im! He must be one of those rascals who go round anointing honest people's doors.'

Renzo didn't waste any time. He decided at once that his best course was to get away from them at once, rather than stay and explain himself. He cast a glance to left and right to see where there were least people, and made off in that direction. . . . He pushed back one man who was trying to bar his way; made another who had been running towards him reel back eight or ten yards with a great punch in the chest; and away he went at full speed with his fist in the air clenched and ready for anyone else who got in the way. The street in front of him was still clear; but behind him he heard a pounding of feet, and, louder than the pounding, that bitter cry, 'Catch 'im! Catch 'im! Catch the anointer!' He did not know when they would stop; he did not see where he could escape. His anger changed to rage, his anguish to desperation; and, going blind to all around him, seized his dagger, unsheathed it, stopped short in his tracks, and turned round with the fiercest and most savage face he had ever made in his life, brandished the gleaming knife at arm's length, and shouted, 'Come on who dares, yer swine! And I'll anoint 'im good and proper with this.'

But with surprise and a confused feeling of relief he saw that his persecutors had stopped, and were standing there in hesitation; and that, still shouting, they were waving their hands about and making frantic gestures, apparently at people some way behind him. He turned round again and saw (what his extreme excitement had prevented him seeing a moment before) a cart, or rather a row of the usual funeral carts advancing with their usual escort; and some way behind them another group of people, also wanting to get their hands on the anointer and catch him between them; but they were held back by the same obstacle. Finding himself between two fires, it suddenly occured to him that he might use as his salvation the very thing that terrified them; this was not the time to be squeamish, he thought. He sheathed his dagger, got to one side and ran towards the carts, passed the first, and found a good empty space on the second. He judged his

distance, jumped, and landed safely with his right foot in the
cart, his left in the air, and both arms raised.

'Well done! Well done!' exclaimed the *monatti* in chorus, some
of whom were following the convoy on foot, while others were
sitting on the carts, and others, to tell the horrible truth as it was,
were sitting on the corpses, quaffing from a large flask that was
going round from hand to hand. 'Well done! Well jumped!'

'You've come and put yourself under the *monatti*'s protection.
Reckon yourself as safe as in church,' said one of the pair on the
cart he had mounted.

His enemies, as the convoy drew near, had most of them turned
their backs and fled, still shouting, 'Catch 'im! Catch 'im! Catch
the anointer!' Some of them drew back more slowly, stopping
every now and again, and turning round with curses and threatening gestures to Renzo, who replied from the cart by shaking
his fists at them.

'Leave it to me,' said one of the *monatti*; and tearing a filthy
rag off one of the bodies, he quickly tied it in a knot, took it by
one of the ends, raised it towards that stubborn group like a
sling, and made as if to throw it, shouting, 'Just you wait, yer
rabble!' At the gesture, they all fled in terror; and Renzo saw
nothing but his enemies' backs, and their heels glancing in the air
like hammers in a clothing-mill.

A howl of triumph went up among the *monatti*, a stormy burst
of laughter, a prolonged 'Uh!', as a sort of accompaniment to the
flight.

'Aha, you see we know how to protect decent blokes,' said the
monatto to Renzo. 'One of us is worth more than a hundred of
these cowards.'

'Sure, I can say I owe you my life,' replied Renzo. 'And I thank
you with all my heart.'

'What for?' said the *monatto*. 'You deserve it; one can see
you're a good young bloke. You're quite right to anoint those
swine; anoint away, and exterminate all these people, who aren't
worth a thing until they're dead. For all the reward we get from
them for the life we're leading is curses; they keep saying that
when the plague's over they'll have us all hanged. They'll be
finished before the plague is; and the *monatti*'ll be left alone,
singing victory and rollicking all round Milan.'

'Long live the plague, and death to the rabble!' exclaimed the
other; and with this fine toast he put the flask to his mouth, and
holding it there with both hands against the jolting of the cart,

gave it a good swig, then offered it to Renzo, saying: 'Drink to our health.'

'I wish it to you with all my heart,' said Renzo. 'But I'm not thirsty; I really don't feel like a drink at this moment.'

'You've had a pretty good fright, it seems to me,' said the *monatto*. 'But you look harmless enough; anointers ought to look quite different.'

'Everyone tries to do what he can,' said the other.

'Give it me here,' said one of those walking along beside the cart. 'For I want to drink another mouthful, too, to the health of its owner, who finds himself in such capital company here ... Just there, I think, in that grand carriage ahead.'

And with a ghastly and evil guffaw he pointed at the cart in front of the one in which poor Renzo was sitting. Then he composed his face into a serious expression that was even more twisted and rascally, made a bow in that direction, and went on, 'D'you mind, my lord, a poor little *monatto* taking something from your cellar? You see, we're working very hard; we're the ones who put you in your carriage to take you for a bit of country air. And then, of course, wine does you gentlemen harm right away; the poor *monatti*'ve got strong stomachs.'

And amid the laughter of his companions he took the flask and lifted it up; but before drinking he turned to Renzo, fixed him in the eyes, and said with a certain air of contemptuous pity, 'That devil you made your pact with must be new on the job, for if we hadn't been here to save you, you'd not have got much help from him,' and amidst a fresh burst of laughter, he put his lips to the flask.

'Hey, what about us? What about us?' bawled a number of voices from the cart in front.

The rascal swallowed as much as he wanted, and then with both hands handed the big flask over to his comrades, who went on passing it to each other until one of them emptied it, then took it by the neck, twirled it round his head, and dashed it down on the paving-stones with a shout of 'Long live the plague!' Then he began singing one of their rough songs; and at once the whole vile chorus joined in. The infernal chant, mingling with the tinkling of the bells, the rattling of the carts, the tramping of the horses, resounded in the empty silence of the streets, and, echoing among the houses, wrung with bitterness the hearts of the very few still inhabiting them.

But is there anything that cannot be turned to advantage sometimes? Is there anything that does not please in certain circumstances? The danger he had been in a moment before had made the company of these dead and living bodies more than tolerable to Renzo: and now he found those sounds that saved him from the awkwardness of conversation almost like sweet music to his ears. Still half breathless and all in a turmoil, he thanked Providence meanwhile as best he could for having got him out of such a pass without receiving or doing injury. He begged it now to help deliver him from his deliverers too; and from his perch he kept one eye on his companions and another on the road, to seize an opportunity of sliding quietly down without provoking them to make any noise, any scene which might stir up mischief with passers-by.

All of a sudden, at a corner, he seemed to recognize the place; he looked more carefully, and was sure of it. Do you know where he was? On the road to the Porta Orientale, in the very street which he had come along so slowly, and gone back along so quickly, about twenty months before. He remembered at once that it led straight to the lazaretto; and this finding himself on the right road without looking or asking for it struck him as a special act of Providence, and a good omen for the future. At that point a commissioner came towards the carts shouting to the *monatti* to stop and I know not what besides; anyway, the convoy stopped, and the singing changed into a noisy discussion. One of the *monatti* on Renzo's cart jumped down. 'Thank you for your kindness; may God reward you,' Renzo said to the other, and down he went too, on the other side.

'Go on, off with you, poor little anointer,' the other answered. 'You're not the man to ruin Milan.'

Luckily, there was no one to overhear him. The convoy had stopped on the left of the street. Renzo quickly crossed to the opposite side, and, keeping close to the wall, went running off towards the bridge, passed it, went on by the street of the *borgo* and recognized the Capuchin convent. From near the gate he saw the projecting corner of the lazaretto, and passed the palisade. The scene outside the enclosure unfolded before his eyes; this was just an indication or a foretaste; but it was in itself a scene vast, diverse, and indescribable.

The two sides visible to anyone from that point were swarming with people. There were groups of sick going towards the lazaretto; others were sitting or lying along the side of the

encircling moat, either because their strength was not enough to
take them right into the refuge, or had failed, when they had left
it in desperation, to take them any farther away. Others were
wandering about singly, as if in a stupor, and many were in
complete delirium. One was excitedly telling his hallucinations to
a wretch lying there in the grip of the disease; another was raving;
another was looking around with a beaming face, as if he was
assisting at some happy festival. But the strangest and noisiest
part of this melancholy jollity was a loud and continuous singing,
which did not seem as if it could possibly come from that
wretched crowd, and yet could be heard above all the other
voices – it was a merry and playful folk-song about love, of the
type called a *villanelle*; and if you followed the sound with your
eyes to find out who could possibly be so cheerful at such a time
and in such a place, you found a poor wretch calmly sitting in
the bottom of a ditch, with his head thrown back, singing at the
top of his voice.

Renzo had scarcely gone a few yards along the south side of
the building when he heard an unusual noise from the crowd,
and voices shouting in the distance, 'Look! Stop 'im!' He stood
up on tiptoe, and saw a rough-looking horse galloping along,
spurred on by an even stranger rider; it was a madman, who had
seen the animal loose and unguarded near a cart, clambered
quickly on to its back, and by beating him on the neck with his
fists, and spurring him with his heels, was driving him madly on;
behind him came *monatti*, shouting at him; then all was envel-
oped in a cloud of dust, which flew off in the distance.

So, already confounded and weary of seeing miseries, the youth
reached the gate of the place in which more miseries were
concentrated, perhaps, than had been scattered over the whole
area he had already crossed. He walked up to the door, went
under the arch, and stood there motionless a moment in the
middle of the portico.

CHAPTER 35

The reader must picture to himself the precincts of the lazaretto
filled with sixteen thousand plague-stricken people; the whole
area cluttered with cabins and sheds, with carts and human

beings; those two unfinished ranges of arcades to right and left filled, crowded, with a confused mass of sick and dead, sprawling on mattresses or heaps of straw; all over this immense sty a perpetual movement like waves on the sea; here and there a coming and going, a stopping, a running, a bending and rising of convalescents, of madmen, of attendants. Such was the spectacle which burst all of a sudden on Renzo's field of vision, and held him rooted there, appalled and overwhelmed. It was a spectacle we certainly do not propose describing in any detail, nor would the reader desire it. But as we follow our young man on his dolorous tour, we will pause where he pauses, and say as much about what he chanced to see as may be necessary to explain his actions and what followed from them.

From the gate where he stood up to the chapel in the middle, and from there to the gate opposite, there was a kind of alley clear of sheds and other permanent obstacles. On looking at it again, Renzo saw carts moving about in this, and things being dragged away to clear space; he saw Capuchins and laymen directing these operations, and also ordering off anyone who had no business there. Fearing lest he be turned out in the same way, he plunged straightway in among the shacks to the right, which was the direction in which he chanced to be facing.

He went on from shack to shack, as he found space to set his feet, putting his head into each of them, surveying the beds in the open outside, peering into faces, haggard with suffering, distorted by spasms, or motionless in death, longing for a glimpse of what he was afraid of finding. But he had already gone a good way and repeated that dismal inspection again and again, and had as yet seen no women at all; from which he deduced that they must be in some separate part. And he had guessed right; but he had no indication or clue to guide him as to where they were. Every now and again he met attendants, each differing as much in bearing, manners, and dress as did the sources which gave them all strength enough to live through their duties – in some the extinction of all feeling of compassion, in others a compassion that was superhuman. But he did not dare ask questions of either, for fear of getting himself into difficulties, and decided to go on and on until he succeeded in finding women. He did not neglect, as he went, looking carefully about him; but every now and again he was forced to avert eyes saddened and as if dazzled by so much suffering. But where could he turn them, where rest them, save on more suffering?

The very air and sky increased, if anything could, the horror of all around him. The mist had gradually thickened and woven into big clouds, which as they grew darker would have looked like warnings of a stormy night, had there not appeared in the very midst of that glum and lowering sky and as if through a thick veil, the pale disk of the sun, diffusing a dim, feeble light, but pouring out a heavy suffocating heat. Every now and again, amidst the continual buzzing of that confused multitude, could be heard a rumble of thunder, deep, jerky, as if irresolute: and even if you strained your ears, you would not have been able to tell the direction from which it was coming; or you might have thought it a distant rumbling of carts which were stopping abruptly every now and again. In the country around not a branch of a tree could be seen moving, not a bird perching or taking wing; only a swallow, appearing just above the roof of the enclosure, glided down on outstretched wings as if about to skim the ground, but taking fright at the noise, soared quickly up and fled. It was the sort of weather in which travelling companions trudge on without any of them breaking silence, in which the hunter walks deep in thought with his eyes bent on the ground, and the peasant girl digging in the fields stops singing unawares; the sort of weather which foreruns a storm, when Nature, outwardly calm but in the grip of an inward travail, seems to oppress every living thing and add an indefinable heaviness to every action, even to idleness, even to existence itself. In that place particularly dedicated to suffering and death men already gripped by disease could be seen succumbing under this new oppression. By hundreds they could be seen taking a sudden turn for the worse; and at the same time death-struggles became more ghastly and groans more stifled by fresh access of pain. It was perhaps the cruellest hour that had yet passed over that abode of suffering.

The youth had already been threading his way fruitlessly for some time through the maze of huts, when he began to distinguish among the variety of confused mutterings and lamentations a strange mixture of cries of babies and bleats of animals. Finally he reached a splintered, disjointed palisade from behind which these extraordinary sounds were coming. He put his eye to a wide crack between two planks, and saw an enclosure scattered with huts, and inside them and on a small open space, instead of the usual patients, infants lying on mattresses, pillows, sheets, and quilts, with nurses or other women busily attending them.

But what caught and held his eye were the she-goats scattered among them, being made to help in their ministrations; it was an orphanage such as the place and times afforded. It was a singular thing to see some of those beasts standing quietly up above one baby and then another, giving them suck; and another of them running to a crying child, as if with a maternal instinct, and stopping beside their little charges and trying to get into position over them, bleating and fussing, almost as if they were invoking aid for both.

Nurses were sitting here and there with babies at their breasts, some in such loving attitudes that the spectator might doubt whether they had been drawn to that place by the offer of pay or by that spontaneous charity which goes in quest of the needy and afflicted. One of them, in desperation, was removing a little weeping wretch from her exhausted breast and going sadly to find an animal that could take her place. Another looked with loving eyes at the babe who had fallen asleep as it gave suck, then kissed it gently and went to a shed to lay it on a mattress. But a third had abandoned her breast to a little stranger, and was gazing fixedly up at the sky with an air of preoccupation rather than of carelessness. What was she thinking of, in that attitude, with that look, if not of one born of her own womb who had suckled – and perhaps died on – that breast a short time before? Other older women were attending to other services. One ran to answer the call of a hungry babe, took it up, carried it to a goat that was eating a heap of green grass, and put it to its paps, chiding and coaxing the inexperienced animal at the same time so that it should lend itself gently to the office. Here a woman was hurrying to the rescue of a poor infant who was being trampled by a goat which was all intent on suckling another; there another was carrying her charge up and down, dandling it, and trying alternately to croon it to sleep and to calm it with soothing words, calling it by a name that she herself had given it. At that moment a Capuchin with a snow-white beard arrived, carrying on either arm two yelling infants that he had just gathered from beside their dead mothers. A woman hastened to receive them, and went searching among the other women and the goats for someone to take the mother's place straight away.

More than once the youth, urged by his chief and overpowering thought, had torn himself from the opening and prepared to go away, and had then put his eye back again to look another moment.

Finally he dragged himself away from there, and went along the palisade, until a group of huts leaning up against it forced him to turn. He skirted around them, intending to regain the palisade, reach the end of it, and find new country. Then, just as he was looking ahead to reconnoitre his path, a sudden fugitive, instantaneous apparition struck his eye and sent his mind into a ferment. A hundred yards or so away, passing and then quickly lost among the huts, he saw a Capuchin friar – a friar who, seen even from that distance and so fleetingly, had all the gait, the bearing, the form of Father Cristoforo. In a frenzy which you can imagine, he rushed in that direction, and began turning and searching about backwards and forwards, inside and out, through that labyrinth, until finally, with a rush of delight, he saw that same form, that same friar again. He saw him a short distance away, coming away from a cauldron over a fire, and making his way towards one of the huts with a bowl in his hand; then, sitting down at the entrance, hold out the bowl, make the sign of the cross over it and, looking around like someone who is always on the alert, begin to eat. It was indeed Father Cristoforo.

His story, from the point where we had lost sight of him until this meeting, can be told in a few words. He had never moved, and had never thought of moving, from Rimini, until the plague breaking out in Milan gave him a chance of doing what he had always desired: to give his life for his fellow-creatures. He begged with great insistence to be sent there to help and serve those with the plague. The right honourable uncle was dead; and in any case there was greater need of nurses than there was of politicians; so that his request was granted without any difficulty. He came to Milan at once, entered the lazaretto, and had now been there about three months.

But Renzo's joy at finding the good friar was not for an instant unmixed: at the very moment that he recognized him for certain, he was also forced to see how changed he was. His stooping and painful posture, his wan and haggard features – everything about him showed the exhaustion of nature, a failing and broken strength, held together and supported only by a continual effort of the will.

He, too, was gazing fixedly at the youth coming towards him, who was trying to make himself recognized by his gestures, not daring to do so by his voice.

'Oh, Father Cristoforo!' he said then, when he was near enough to be heard without raising his voice.

'You here!' said the friar, putting the bowl down on the ground and rising from his seat.

'How are you, father? How are you?'

'Better than lots of other poor wretches you see here,' replied the friar, and his voice was feeble, hollow – changed like all the rest of him. Only his eye was the same as before, and indeed had something livelier and more splendid about it, as though the spirit of charity, sublimated at the supreme moment of its task, and exulting at feeling near its source, had kindled a brighter, purer flame in him than the one being gradually extinguished by infirmity.

'But you,' he went on. 'What brings you here? Why have you come to brave the plague like this?'

'I've had it, thank heavens. I've come ... to look for ... Lucia.'

'Lucia! Is Lucia here?'

'She's here – at least, I hope to God she's still here.'

'Is she your wife?'

'Oh, my dear father! No, alas! she's not my wife. Don't you know about all that's happened?'

'No, my son; since God took me away from you all, I've heard nothing more; but now that He has sent you to me, I won't hide from you that I very much want to know it. But ... what about your banishment?'

'You know, then, all the things they did to me?'

'But you, what had you done?'

'Listen. I'd be telling a lie if I said I'd been very sensible that day in Milan; but I never did anything wrong at all.'

'I believe you, and believed it before too.'

'Anyway, now I can tell you all about it.'

'Wait,' said the friar, and going a few steps outside the hut he called out, 'Father Vittore!' After a minute or two a young Capuchin appeared, to whom he said: 'Would you be so kind, Father Vittore, as to look after those poor creatures of ours for me too, while I draw aside for a bit; but if anyone wants me, above all that particular person, call me. If he gives the slightest sign of coming to, tell me at once, please.'

'Don't worry,' answered the young friar; and the old one turned towards Renzo and said: 'Let's go in here. But ...' he suddenly added, stopping, 'you look quite shattered; you must need something to eat.'

'That's true,' said Renzo. 'Now that you make me think of it, I remember I haven't eaten anything yet.'

'Wait,' said the friar; and taking up another bowl, he went to fill it at the pot, came back, and gave it, with a spoon, to Renzo. He sat him down on a mattress that served as his bed, then went and drew a glass of wine from a barrel in a corner, and put it on a little table before his guest; after which he took up his own bowl again, and sat down beside him.

'Oh, Father Cristoforo!' said Renzo, 'you shouldn't do all this! But you're always the same. Thank you from the bottom of my heart.'

'Don't thank me,' said the friar. 'This is the property of the poor. But you're one of the poor too just now. Now tell me what I don't know, tell me about our poor girl; and try and be brief, for time is short and there's a lot to do, as you see.'

Renzo began, between one spoonful and the other, to tell Lucia's story, how she had taken refuge in the convent of Monza, how she had been kidnapped. . . . At the idea of such sufferings and such dangers, at the thought that it was he himself who had directed the poor, innocent girl to that place, the good friar's breath was taken away; but it came back when he heard of her miraculous liberation, of her return to her mother, and of her being lodged with Donna Prassede.

'Now I'll tell you about myself,' went on Renzo; and he gave him a brief account of that day in Milan and of his flight; and how he had been away from home all the time, until, now that everything was upside down, he had risked coming back; how he had not found Agnese; how he had heard in Milan of Lucia's being at the lazaretto. 'And here I am,' he concluded. 'I'm here to look for her, to see if she's alive, and if . . . she still wants me . . . because . . . sometimes . . .'

'But,' asked the friar, 'have you any indication where she was put when she came?'

'None, dear father; none except that she's here – if she still is here, which God grant!'

'Oh, my poor boy! But what search have you made so far?'

'I've been going round and round; but, among all the other things, I've seen almost nothing but men. I guessed the women must be in some place apart but have never succeeded in finding it; if that's so, you can show me now.'

'Don't you know, my son, that all men but those with an official job are forbidden to go in there?'

'Well, what could happen to me?'

'The rule is a just and holy one, my dear son; and if the number and gravity of the disasters prevent it being carried out with the proper rigour, is that a reason why a decent person should transgress it?'

'But, Father Cristoforo,' said Renzo. 'Lucia ought to've been my wife by now. You know how we were separated; I've been suffering and patient for twenty months now. I've come all this way, risking so many things, one worse than the other, and now . . .'

'I don't know what to say,' went on the friar, answering his own thoughts rather than the young man's words. 'You're going with good intentions; and may it please God that all those who have free access to that place behave as I am sure you will behave. God, who certainly blesses this constancy of yours, this faith of yours in wanting and seeking her whom He gave you; God, who is more severe but also more indulgent than men, will not notice what may be irregular in your way of searching for her. Remember only that we will both have to render account of your conduct in that place; not to men, very possibly, but certainly to God. Come here. . . .'

So saying, he got up, as also did Renzo; the latter, while not ceasing to listen, had meanwhile decided to himself not to mention Lucia's vow, as he had thought of doing before. – If he hears this too – he thought – he's sure to make other difficulties. Either I find her, and then there'll always be time to discuss it, or . . . and in that case! What's it matter? –

Drawing him to the door of the hut, which faced north, the friar went on, 'Listen. Our Father Felice, who is the president of the lazaretto here, is today leading out to do their quarantine elsewhere the few people who've recovered. You see that church there in the middle . . .' and, raising a gaunt and trembling hand, he pointed to the left through the murky air at the dome of the chapel towering up over the miserable array of huts; and went on, 'They're gathering round there now so as to leave in procession by the gate you must have entered.'

'Ah! that was why, then, they were working at clearing the path.'

'Just so; and you must also have heard a toll or two of that bell.'

'I heard one.'

'That was the second; at the third they'll all be assembled.

Father Felice will make them a short speech, and then he'll set off with them. You go there at that toll. Try to get behind those people on the edge of the path, so, without disturbing anyone or drawing attention to yourself, you can watch them pass; and just see . . . see . . . if she's there. If God has not willed it so, then that part,' and, raising his hand again, he pointed at the side of the edifice facing them – 'that part of the building, and part of the ground in front of it, is assigned to the women. You'll see a fence dividing this area from that, which is interrupted in some places, and open in others, so that you'll have no difficulty in getting in. Once you are inside, probably no one will say anything to you, if you do nothing to cause any suspicion. If, however, anyone makes any objections, say that Father Cristoforo of * * * knows you, and will answer for you. Search for her there; search for her with faith . . . and with resignation. For remember what you've come to look for here is no small thing – you are asking to find a person alive in the lazaretto! Do you realize how many times I've seen my poor flock here renewed? How many of them I've seen carried away! How few walk out . . .! Go and be prepared to make a sacrifice.'

'Ah, yes, I realize that, too,' interrupted Renzo, with his eyes starting and his face all changing; 'I realize that! I'll go, I'll look, I'll search high and low over every corner of the lazaretto . . . and if I don't find her . . .!'

'If you don't find her?' said the friar, with a grave air of interrogation and an admonishing look.

But Renzo, whose rage, re-kindled at the idea of that doubt, had made him lose the light of reason, repeated the words and then went on, 'If I don't find her, there's someone else I'll try to find. Either in Milan or at that cursed mansion of his, or at the end of the earth, or in hell, I'll find the swine who separated us, the scoundrel but for whom Lucia'd have been mine these twenty months; and if we'd been destined to die, at least we'd have died together. If the fellow's still alive, I'll find him. . . .'

'Renzo!' said the friar, seizing him by the arm, and looking at him sternly.

'And if I find him,' went on Renzo, quite blind with rage – 'if the plague hasn't already done justice . . . The time's past when a coward with his bravi around him could drive folk to desperation, and get off all free; the time's come when men meet each other face to face; and . . . I'll do my own justice, I will!'

'Miserable wretch!' cried Fra Cristoforo, in a voice which had recovered all its old fullness and sonority. 'Miserable wretch!' And his head drooping over his chest became erect again, his cheeks flushed with their former life once more, and the flash of his eye had something terrible about it. 'Look, miserable wretch!' and as with one hand he gripped Renzo's arm and shook it hard, he swept the other around him to encompass as much as he could of the ghastly scene around. 'Look and see who is the One who punishes. The One who judges, and is not Himself judged. The One who chastises and who pardons. But you, you worm of the earth, you want to do justice. D'you know, you, what justice is? Be off, wretch, be off with you! I had hoped ... yes, I had hoped that before I died God would give me the joy of hearing that my poor Lucia was alive – perhaps of seeing her, and hearing her promise me that she would send up a prayer towards that ditch where I shall be lying. Go. You have snatched away that hope. God has not left her on earth for such as you; and surely you cannot have the hardihood to think yourself worthy of God's consolation. He'll have thought of her, for she is one of those for whom the eternal consolations are reserved. Go! I've no more time to listen to you.'

And so saying, he flung Renzo's arm from him and began moving towards a hut full of sufferers.

'Ah, father!' said Renzo, following him with a supplicating air. 'D'you want to send me away like this?'

'What!' said the Capuchin, in a voice no less severe. 'Can you expect me to take time away from these afflicted creatures, who are waiting for me to talk to them of God's pardon, to listen to your words of rage, to your plans for revenge? I listened to you when you asked me for consolation and help; I left one act of charity for another; but now you have your vengeance in your heart, what do you want of me? Be off with you. I've seen the oppressed here forgiving as they died; and I've seen oppressors bewailing that they could not humble themselves before those they had oppressed: I have wept with both of them; but what have I to do with you?'

'Ah, I forgive him! I really do forgive him! I forgive him for ever!' exclaimed the youth.

'Renzo,' said the friar seriously, but more calmly, 'think it over, and just tell me how many times you have forgiven him.'

And after standing there some time without receiving a reply, all of a sudden he lowered his head, and then went on in a deep slow voice, 'You know why I bear this habit?'

Renzo hesitated.

'You know why!' insisted the old man.

'I know,' answered Renzo.

'I also have hated; I, who have rebuked you for a thought, for a word, I killed the man I hated deeply, whom I had hated for a long time.'

'Yes; but a bully, one of those . . .'

'Quiet,' interrupted the friar. 'D'you think that if there had been a good reason I would not have found it out in thirty years? Ah! If only I could now instil into your heart the feeling I have always had, and still have, for the man I hated. If only I could! I? But God can do it. May He do so. . . . Listen, Renzo. He loves you more than you love yourself. You might have planned your vengeance, but He is strong and merciful enough to prevent your carrying it out. He does you a favour of which another, whom we know, was too unworthy. You know – you have said so many times – that He can stay the hand of a bully; but you must also know that He can stay the hand of an avenger. And because you're poor, because you've been wronged, do you think He cannot defend against you a man whom He has created in his own image? Do you think He would let you do whatever you want? No! But d'you know what you can do? You can hate, and be lost; you can, with that feeling in you, alienate every blessing from yourself. For, however things go with you, however much you prosper, you can be sure that it will all turn into a penance until you have forgiven him, and in such a way that you need never repeat again: I forgive him.'

'Yes, yes,' said Renzo, all deep emotion and confusion. 'I realize I had never really forgiven him; I realize that I spoke like a dog and not like a Christian; and now, by the Lord's grace, yes, I forgive him from the bottom of my heart.'

'And if you were to see him?'

'I'd pray the Lord to give me patience, and to touch his heart.'

'You would remember, wouldn't you, that the Lord did not only tell us to forgive our enemies, He told us to love them?* You would remember, wouldn't you, that He loved him enough to die for him?'

'Yes, with His help.'

'Well then, come with me. You said "I'll find him"; and you will find him. Come, and you'll see who it was you hated, who it was you wanted to harm, what the life is you wanted to take.'

And, taking Renzo's hand, and gripping it tight as any healthy young man, he set off. The other followed him, without daring to ask anything more.

After a few yards the friar stopped at the opening of a cabin, fixed his eyes on Renzo with a mixture of gravity and tenderness, and led him inside.

The first thing he saw on entering was a sick man sitting on the straw on the floor, who seemed to be not seriously ill, but on the way towards convalescence; on seeing the friar, he shook his head, as if to say no; the friar bowed his in an act of sorrow and resignation. Renzo, meanwhile, turning his glance with restless curiosity on the other objects around, saw three or four patients, and one of them lying apart on a mattress, wrapped up in a sheet, with a nobleman's cloak over him as a blanket. He gazed at him, recognized Don Rodrigo, and started back a step. But the friar, gripping him strongly again by the hand he was holding, drew him to the foot of the bed, and stretching his other hand over it, pointed at the man who was lying on it.

The unhappy wretch lay quite still. His eyes were staring wide, but without seeing. His face was pale and covered with black blotches; his lips were black and swollen; you would have taken it for the face of a corpse, had not a series of violent spasms borne witness to a tenacious vitality. The chest was heaving every now and again with painful breaths; the right hand was outside the cloak and pressed down on it near the heart, with a clawing movement of its fingers which were all livid and already black at the tips.

'You see!' said the friar, in a low and solemn tone. 'It may be a punishment, or it may be a mercy. What you feel now for this man who has wronged you – yes, God, whom you, too, have wronged, will feel the same for you one day. Bless him, and you will be blessed yourself. He's been here four days in the state you see, without giving any sign of life. Perhaps the Lord is ready to grant him an hour of consciousness; but He wanted to be asked for it by you; perhaps He wants you and that innocent girl to pray to Him. Perhaps He is reserving His grace for your prayer alone – the prayer of a heart that is afflicted but resigned. Perhaps the salvation of this man and your own now depends on you, on your feelings of forgiveness, of pity . . . of love.'

He fell silent; and, joining his hands, bowed his face over them and prayed. Renzo did the same.

They had been in this position for a few moments, when the bell tolled. Both of them moved, as if in concert, and went out.

Neither asked any questions or made any protests; their faces spoke.

'Go now,' went on the friar. 'Go, prepared either to receive a grace or make a sacrifice; to praise the Lord whatever the result of your quest may be. And whatever it may be, come and tell me of it, and we will praise Him together.'

Here, without saying any more, they parted. One turned back whence he had come; the other went towards the chapel, which was not more than a hundred paces away.

CHAPTER 36

Who would ever have thought, an hour or so before, that at the very height of his search, just as its most anxious and decisive moments began, Renzo's heart would be divided between Lucia and Don Rodrigo? And yet so it was. That face came thrusting itself into all the tender or terrible images that hope or fear brought up alternately during that walk. The words he had heard at the foot of the bed kept on thrusting themselves between the conflicting 'Yes' and 'No' struggling in his mind; and he could not finish any prayer for the happy issue of this great test without the prayer merging into the one he had begun in the hut, and which the tolling of the bell had interrupted.

The octagonal chapel which arises, raised on a few steps in the middle of the lazaretto, was open in its original construction on all sides with no other support than pillars and columns – a building, as it were, in filigree. In each façade there was an arch between two columns, while inside, round what might be called the church proper, ran an arcade composed only of eight arches, corresponding to those on the façades, with a cupola on top; so that the altar erected in the centre could be seen from the window of every room in the enclosure, and from almost any point in the courtyard. Now that the building is converted to quite other uses, the apertures on the façades are walled up; but the old framework has remained intact, and shows its former state and purpose quite clearly.

Renzo had scarcely started towards it when he saw Father Felice appear in the chapel arcade, and come out under the arch on the side looking towards the city. The company had assembled in front of this, down on the centre path; and at once, from his attitude, Renzo realized that he had begun his sermon.

He wound round among the alleys so as to come out at the rear of the audience, as had been suggested. On getting there he stopped, and, standing quite still, looked it all over; but all he saw was a layer – I might almost say a pavement – of heads. In the middle there were a certain number covered with handkerchiefs or veils. He fixed his eyes more attentively on that section, but, not being able to make out anything more, he, too, raised his eyes where everyone had fixed theirs. The preacher's venerable features touched him to compassion; and with what attention he could muster at such a moment of suspense, he heard this part of the solemn discourse.

'Let us give a thought to the thousands and thousands who have gone out that way,' and he pointed over his shoulder behind him to the gate leading to the cemetery of San Gregorio, which was then, one might almost say, all one vast communal grave. 'Let us give a glance around at the thousands and thousands who are remaining here, only too uncertain which way they are to go out. Let us give a glance at ourselves, and see how few there are of us going out safe and sound. Blessed be the Lord! Blessed in His justice, blessed in His pity! Blessed in death, blessed in health! Blessed in this choice He has made of us! Oh, why, my children, has He wished to, unless it be to reserve for Himself a few who have been purged by affliction and made fervent by gratitude? Unless it be that, feeling more vividly that life is His gift, we may esteem it as a gift from Him merits, and use it in doing good actions which can be offered up to Him? Unless it be that the memory of our sufferings may make us compassionate and helpful towards our neighbours? Let those in whose company we have suffered, hoped, and feared, among whom we are leaving friends and relations, though all of them are our brethren, let those who will watch us passing through their midst find some encouragement from our bearing, as well as perhaps some solace in the thought that a few can also leave here alive. God does not want us to show them any boisterous or worldly joy at having escaped that death with which they are still struggling. Let them see us leave thanking God on our own behalf and praying to Him on theirs; and let them say that even when out of here we will remember them, and will continue to pray for them in their misery. Let us with this journey, from the very first steps we take, begin a life full of charity. Let those of us who have got their former vigour back give a brotherly arm to the weak; young folk, sustain the old; those of you who have been deprived of children, see how many children there are around you deprived of parents. Be parents to them. And this charity, covering your sins,* will also sweeten your sorrows.'

Here the stifled murmur of groans and sobs increasing in the assembly was suddenly hushed as the preacher was seen putting a cord around his neck and throwing himself on his knees; and in deep silence they waited for what he was going to say.

'On behalf of myself,' he said, 'and of all my companions who, through no merit of their own, have been chosen for the high privilege of serving Christ in you, I humbly ask pardon if we have not worthily fulfilled so great an office. If laziness and the stubbornness of the flesh have made us less attentive to your needs, less prompt in answering your calls; if an unjust impatience and a culpable weariness have wrongly made us appear before you with looks of boredom and irritation; if sometimes the mean thought that we were necessary to you has made us fail to treat you with all the humility that was proper; if our frailty has carelessly made us commit some action that has offended you; forgive us! And may God likewise forgive you all your trespasses, and bless you.' And making a great sign of the cross over the audience, he got up.

We have been able to set down, if not the precise words, at least the sense, the theme of his words; but the manner in which they were delivered cannot be described. It was the manner of one who called it a privilege to serve those stricken with the plague because he really considered that it was so; who confessed that he had not responded to it worthily because he really felt that he had not responded to it worthily; who asked for forgiveness because he was really convinced that he needed it. But imagine what sobs and tears these words aroused in people who had seen the Capuchins going about intent only on serving them, who had seen so many of them die, and seen him who now spoke for all of them himself always foremost in toil as in authority, until he, too, had been brought to the doors of death. The admirable friar then took a great cross which was leaning against a pillar, raised it before him, and, leaving his sandals on the threshold of the portico, descended the steps, and made his way through the crowd, that fell back respectfully, to put himself at their head.

Renzo, weeping just as if he, too, had been one of those asked for this singular pardon, drew back also, and took up a position by one of the huts; and he stood there waiting, half hidden, with his body back and his head forward, with his eyes starting from his head, and his heart beating wildly, but at the same time with a certain new and definite sense of confidence, born, I believe, of the tenderness inspired in him by the sermon and by the spectacle of the general emotion.

And now along came Fra Felice, barefoot, with that rope around his neck, and that long heavy cross raised up before him; his face pale and haggard, a face inspiring courage and compunction at the same time; his step slow but steady, as if his only thought was to spare the weakness of others; in every way like a man who acquires strength from extra hardships and fatigue to sustain all the others that are necessary and inherent in his office. Immediately after him came the older children, most of them barefoot, very few of them entirely clothed, some clad only in shirts. Then came the women, almost all holding a child by the hand, and chanting the *Miserere** in alternation; and the feebleness of those voices, the pallid languor of those faces were enough to engross completely the attention of anyone there as a simple spectator. But Renzo was busy scanning row after row, face after face, without missing a single one; for which the slow movement of the procession gave him ample opportunity. On and on they came; on and on he looked. Every now and again he gave a hurried glance at the rows still to come; there were very few left now; now the last one came; they had all passed; all were unknown faces. With his arms hanging down limply beside him, and his head sagging over one shoulder, he followed the column with his eye, while the rows of men passed before him. A new attention, a new hope revived in him as he saw a few carts appear after these, which carried convalescents who were not fit to walk. The women came last in these; and the convoy went by so slowly that Renzo could examine them all, too, without a single one escaping him. But what of that? He examined the first cart, the second, the third, and so on, always with the same result, until the last came along, followed only by another Capuchin friar with a serious mien and a staff in his hand, marshalling the convoy. This was the Fra Michele whom we have already mentioned as having been given to Fra Felice as an assistant in running the lazaretto.

So that fair hope completely vanished; and with it, as it went, it carried off the solace it had inspired, leaving him, as so often happens, in a worse state than before. The very best he could hope for now was to find Lucia ill. And although his hopes were now undermined by growing fears, the poor youth grasped at this cheerless and feeble straw with all the powers of his mind. He went out into the alley, and walked in the direction from which the procession had come. On reaching the foot of the chapel, he went and knelt down on the bottom step, and there offered up to God a prayer, or rather a medley of broken phrases, exclamations, entreaties, laments and promises – one of those pleas that are never made to other human beings, who have not the penetration to understand them or the patience to listen to them, and are not big enough to feel compassion at them without contempt.

He rose up somewhat more heartened, went round the chapel, and found himself in another alley that he had not yet seen and that led to the other gate. After a few steps he saw the fence that the friar had spoken of, interrupted here and there, just as he had said. He went in by one of these openings, and found himself in the women's quarters. At almost the first step he took in it he saw a small bell lying on the ground, such as the *monatti* carried on one foot. It occured to him that this article might act as a sort of passport for him inside there. He took it up, glanced around to see that there was no one looking, and then tied it on in the same way as they did. And then he set straight away about his quest – a quest made difficult enough by the very number of objects to be examined, even had those objects been of an entirely different kind. He began to run his eye around him, only to find it lighting on new scenes of misery, in some ways so exactly like the miseries he had already seen and in others so very different; for the same general calamity here showed other forms of suffering, of languor, lamentation and resignation, and other forms of mutual sympathy and mutual help, which excited in the spectator a different kind of pity and revulsion.

He had already gone some way through this, without any success or any incident, when he heard a 'Hey, there,' being called behind him, which seemed to be directed to him. He turned round and saw, some distance off, a commissioner with a hand raised, pointing straight at him, and shouting, 'There's help needed in the rooms there; here they've just finished clearing away.'

Renzo realized at once what he had been taken for, and that it was the bell that had caused the mistake. He cursed himself for

having thought of the difficulties which that insignia might save
him from, and not of those it might draw him into; but at the
same time he thought of a way of getting away from him. He
nodded his head hurriedly and repeatedly as if to say he had
understood and was obeying, and got out of his sight by diving
in among the huts to one side.

When he considered that he was far enough away, he thought
of freeing himself from the cause of the mischief; and to do this
without being observed, he went and got into a narrow space
between two cabins which were standing back to back. He bent
down to take the bell off, and as he stooped there with his head
leaning against the straw wall of one of the huts, a voice from
inside it reached his ear. . . . Oh, heavens! Was it possible? His
whole soul went into that ear; his breathing stopped. . . . Yes!
Yes! It was her voice . . .! 'Fear of what?' that gentle voice was
saying. 'We've been through much more than any storm. He who
has looked after us up to this, will look after us now, too.'

If Renzo did not let out a cry, it was not for fear of being
discovered, but because he lacked the breath. His knees were
failing him, his sight was clouding over; but that was just the first
moment. The second he was standing upright and more alert and
vigorous than before. In three leaps he had gone round the hut,
he was at the door, he saw her who had spoken, saw her standing
leaning over a bed. She turned at the sound, looked, thought she
was mistaken, that she was dreaming, looked more closely, and
cried, 'Oh, blessed Lord!'

'Lucia! I've found you! I've found you! It's really you! You're
alive!' exclaimed Renzo, coming towards her, trembling all over.

'Oh, blessed Lord!' replied Lucia, trembling even more. 'You?
What's this? How? Why? The plague!'

'I've had it. And you? . . .'

'Ah! So have I. And my mother? . . .'

'I haven't seen her, as she's at Pasturo; I think she's all right.
But you . . . how pale you still are! How weak you look! But
cured, though, you're cured?'

'The Lord has thought fit to leave me here below still. Ah,
Renzo! Why are you here?'

'Why?' said Renzo, drawing closer and closer. 'You ask me
why? Why I had to come? D'you need me to tell you? Who else
have I to think of? Aren't I still called Renzo? Aren't you still
Lucia?'

'Ah, what are you saying? What are you saying? But didn't my mother get someone to write to you? . . .'

'Yes; she did indeed get someone to write to me. Fine things to write to a poor chap who's in trouble, in exile, to a chap who'd never done you any harm – on purpose, anyway!'

'But, Renzo! Renzo! As you knew . . . why did you come? Why?'

'Why did I come? O, Lucia! Why did I come, you say? After all those promises! Aren't we ourselves any more? Don't you remember any more? What was wanting?'

'Oh, Lord!' exclaimed Lucia in agony, joining her hands and raising her eyes to heaven, 'why did you not grant me the favour of taking me to you . . . Oh, Renzo! What have you done now? There, I was beginning to hope that . . . in time . . . I might forget. . . .'

'A fine hope! A fine thing to tell me right to my face!'

'Ah, what have you gone and done! And in this place! Among all these miseries! Among all these sights here! Here where there's nothing but death, how could you . . .'

'One may pray for the dying and hope they'll go to a better place; but that's no reason, even that, why the living should have to live in despair . . .'

'But, Renzo! Renzo! You're not thinking of what you're saying. A promise to Our Lady! . . . A vow!'

'And I tell you there are promises that count for nothing.'

'Oh, Lord! What are you saying? Where have you been all this time? Who've you been mixing with? How've you learned to talk like this?'

'I'm talking like a good Christian; and I think better of Our Lady than you do; for I think she doesn't want promises that harm other people. If Our Lady had spoken, ah, then! But what was it? Just an idea of yours? D'you know what you ought to promise Our Lady? You ought to promise her that we'll give the name of Maria to the first daughter we have; and I'm here to promise that too. Those are the things that do Our Lady much more honour; those are the devotions that are most constructive and don't do anyone harm.'

'No, no, don't talk like that. You don't know what you're saying; you don't know what it is to make a vow; you've never been in that situation yourself; you've never been through such a thing. Go away, go away, for the love of Heaven!'

And she tore herself impetuously from him and went back towards the bed.

'Lucia!' said Renzo, without moving. 'Tell me, tell me this at least; if it weren't for this reason . . . would you feel the same towards me?'

'You heartless man!' replied Lucia, turning round, and holding the tears back with difficulty. 'If you got me to say words that are useless, words that would hurt me, words that might perhaps be a sin, would you be content? Go away, oh, go away! Forget me; it's plain we weren't destined for each other. We shall see each other again above; we haven't got long in this world, anyway. Go; try and let my mother know that I've recovered; that God has always helped me here, too; that I've found a dear soul in this good woman here, who's like a mother to me. Tell her that I hope she's been spared, and that we'll see each other again when God wills, and where He wills. . . . Go, for the love of Heaven, and don't think of me any more . . . except when you pray to the Lord.'

And, like one who has no more to say or no more that she wants to hear, like one trying to get away from some danger, she drew back still nearer to the bed where the woman she had mentioned was lying.

'Listen, Lucia, listen!' said Renzo, but without going any closer to her.

'No, no; please go away.'

'Listen. Father Cristoforo . . .'

'What?'

'Is here.'

'Here? Where? How d'you know?'

'I was talking to him just a little while ago; I was with him some time; and a priest of his quality, it seems to me . . .'

'He's here! To help the poor people with plague, of course. But he? Has he had the plague?'

'Ah, Lucia! I'm afraid, I'm afraid, alas . . .' and as Renzo was hesitating to speak words so painful to him, and which would be so painful also to Lucia, she had left the bedside again and drawn near to him, 'I'm afraid he has it now!'

'Oh, the poor holy man! But what am I saying – poor man? Poor us! How is he? Is he in bed? Is he being looked after?'

'He's up and going around, looking after others; but if you saw him, how pale he is, how he holds himself. I've seen so many, so many, that alas . . . it can't be mistaken.'

'Oh, God help us! And he's right here?'

'Here, and just a little way away; little farther than from your house to mine . . . if you remember . . .'

'Oh, Most Holy Virgin!'

'Well, not much farther. And you can just imagine if we talked about you! He's told me things.... And if you knew what he showed me! You'll hear; but now I want to begin telling you what he told me before – he, with his own mouth. He told me I'd done right to come and look for you, and that the Lord likes a young man to behave like that, and that he'd help me find you; as he really has done in truth; but of course he's a saint. So you see. . . !'

'But, if he said that, it's because he doesn't know . . .'

'What d'you expect him to know about things you've gone and done on your own, without paying any attention to rules or asking any advice? A good man, a sensible man like him isn't going to think up things of that sort. But let me tell you what he showed me!' And here he described the visit he had paid to that hut. Lucia, although her mind and senses must have become used, during her stay there, to the strongest impressions, was filled with horror and compassion.

'And there, too,' went on Renzo, 'he talked like a saint. He said perhaps the Lord intended to take pity on that poor wretch (for I really can't give him any other name now), and that He's waiting for a good opportunity; but that He wants us to pray for him together. . . . Together! D'you understand?'

'Yes, yes, we'll pray, each wherever the Lord calls us; He can put the prayers together.'

'But if I tell you his very words . . .!'

'But, Renzo, he doesn't know . . .'

'But don't you understand that when a saint talks, it's the Lord who's making him talk? And that he wouldn't have talked like that if that wasn't just how it was to be . . .? And what about that poor fellow's soul? I prayed for him fervently, and will pray again. I prayed from the bottom of my heart, as if he were my own brother. But how d'you expect him to get on in the next world, poor chap, if this business isn't settled in this, if the harm he's done isn't undone? For if you'll only listen to reason, then everything will be as it was before. Let bygones be bygones; he's made his penance down here . . .'

'No, Renzo, no. The Lord does not want us to sin so that He can take pity. Leave this to Him; our duty is to pray to Him. If I had died that night, would He not have been able to forgive? And since I did not die, since I have been freed . . .'

'And your mother, poor Agnese, who's always loved me so much, and who was so longing to see us man and wife, hasn't she told you, too, that your idea is all wrong? She, who's made you listen to reason at other times, too, because in certain things she is more sensible than you are . . .'

'My mother! D'you want my mother to advise us to break a vow? Renzo! You're not in your right senses.'

'Oh! D'you want me say it? You women can't understand these things. Father Cristoforo told me I was to go back to him and tell him if I had found you. I'm going; we'll hear him; what he says . . .'

'Yes, yes, go to that holy man. Tell him I'm praying for him, and ask him to pray for me, for I need it so very, very much. But, for the love of Heaven, and for your own soul, for my soul's sake, don't come here any more, making me miserable, and . . . tempting me. Father Cristoforo will know how to explain things to you and bring you back to your senses; he'll set your heart at peace.'

'Set my heart at peace! Oh, you can get that idea out of your head. Those are the words you got them to write to me; and I know how they made me suffer; and now you even have the heart to say them to my face. And instead I tell you flatly that I won't ever set my heart at peace. You want to forget me; and I don't want to forget you. And I promise you, see, that if you make me lose my senses I won't get them back again. My job can go to the devil, and so can my good behaviour! You want to condemn me to a life of rage and despair – then I'll live like a desperate man. . . . And that wretch there! The Lord knows I've forgiven him from the bottom of my heart; but you . . . D'you want me to go on thinking for the rest of my life that if it hadn't been for him . . .? Lucia! You've told me to forget you. I, forget you? How can I? Who d'you think I've been thinking of all this time? . . . And after so much! After so many promises! What harm have I done to you since we parted? Is it because I've suffered that you treat me like this? Is it because I've had misfortunes? Because the world has persecuted me? Because I've been homeless and sad and far away from you for so long? Because I came back to look for you the very first moment I could?'

Lucia, when her sobs allowed her to form words, exclaimed,

joining her hands together again and raising her tear-filled eyes to heaven, 'Oh, Most Holy Virgin, help me. You know I haven't been through a moment like this since that night. You helped me then, help me now too.'

'Yes, Lucia; you do well to invoke Our Lady; but why will you believe that She who is so good, who is the Mother of pity, can take pleasure in making us suffer . . . or me suffer, at least . . . for a word let out at a moment when you didn't know what you were saying? Will you believe that She helped you then, so as to leave us all in difficulties afterwards? . . . But if this is just an excuse, if it really is that I've become hateful to you . . . tell me . . . tell me frankly.'

'Please, Renzo, please, for love of your own dead, stop it, stop it: don't kill me . . . not at such a moment. Go to Fra Cristoforo, commend me to him, and don't come back any more, don't come back any more.'

'I'm going; but I'll be coming back, believe me! I'd come back if this was the end of the world, I would.' And he left.

Lucia went and sat, or rather fell on the ground beside the bed, and leaning her head against it broke into a flood of tears. The woman, who had been lying there breathless, with her eyes and ears open, now asked what was the meaning of that apparition, of that dispute, of those tears. But perhaps the reader may ask in his turn who she was: here also only a few words are needed to satisfy his curiosity.

She was a prosperous merchant's widow of about thirty years of age. In the space of a few days she had seen her husband and all her children die at home. Shortly afterwards she had caught the plague herself, and had been carried off to the lazaretto and put into this hut, just at the time when Lucia, after overcoming, without realizing it, the crisis of the disease, and changing room-mates a number of times also without realizing it, was beginning to revive and come to her senses, which she had lost ever since she had first been taken ill when she was still at Don Ferrante's. The hut could only hold two people; and between these two afflicted, abandoned, terrified women, alone amid that multitude, an intimacy, an affection had soon sprung up, which could scarcely have come from years of living together. In a short time Lucia had been in a fit state to minister to the other, whose condition had become desperate. Now that she, too, was out of danger, they kept each other company and watched over each other by turns; they had promised each other only to leave the lazaretto together; and they had made other plans so as not to separate even after that. The merchant's widow, who had left her well-stocked house, shop, and till in charge of one of her brothers who was a commissioner of health, now found herself sole mistress of much more than she needed to live on comfortably, and wanted to keep Lucia with her as a daughter or sister. Lucia had accepted, with what gratitude to her and to Providence can be imagined, but only until she could get news of her mother and learn, as she hoped, her wishes. Apart from that, being naturally reserved, she had never said a word about her betrothal, or anything about her other extraordinary adventures. But now, with all her emotions boiling up in her, she felt at least as much need to unburden herself as the other did to hear her. And, pressing her friend's right hand in both of hers, she began to answer her questions at once, with no other restraint than that imposed by her sobs.

Renzo meanwhile was hurrying back towards the quarters of the good friar. With some difficulty, and not without retracing his steps now and again, he finally succeeded in reaching them. He found the hut: but he did not find him; but after wandering and searching around near it, he saw him in a tent, bent double and almost prostrate on the ground comforting a dying man. Renzo stopped and waited there in silence. Shortly after he saw him close the poor man's eyes, then kneel down and pray a moment. As he got up Renzo moved towards him.

'Oh,' said the friar, on seeing him coming. 'Well?'

'She's here; I've found her.'

'In what condition?'

'Recovered, or at least up.'

'Thanks be to the Lord.'

'But . . .' said Renzo, when he was close enough to talk in an undertone, 'there's another difficulty.'

'What's that?'

'I mean that . . . you know what a good girl she is, but sometimes she's apt to be stubborn. After all the promises, and all the things you know about, too, now she says she can't marry me, because – well – that night she was so frightened she got into a frenzy and – so to speak – vowed herself to Our Lady. Things like that don't mean anything, do they? All right for those who've got the knowledge and grounds for doing them, but for ordinary

folk like us who don't know how to set about them properly . . .
they aren't binding, are they?'

'Tell me; is she very far from here?'

'Oh, no; a few yards the other side of the church.'

'Wait for me here a moment,' said the friar; 'and then we'll go
there together.'

'Does that mean you'll get her to realize . . .?'

'I don't know anything yet, my son; I must hear her side too.'

'I see,' said Renzo, and stood there with his eyes fixed on the
ground and his arms crossed on his chest, brooding in his
uncertainty, which was still complete. The friar went to find Fra
Vittore again, asked him to take his place once more, went into
the hut, and came out with a basket on his arm; then, turning to
Renzo, he said, 'Let's go,' and went ahead of him towards the
same hut which they had entered together shortly before. This
time he went in alone and reappeared after a moment saying,
'Nothing new. We must pray! We must pray!' Then he added,
'Now you lead the way.'

And, without saying anything more, they set off.

The sky had been growing darker all the time, and now
heralded a certain and imminent storm. Flash after flash of
lightning was piercing the deepening gloom, and showing up
with momentary brilliance the long roofs and arches of the
colonnades, the cupola of the chapel, and the low tops of the
huts; and sudden crashes of thunder were rolling and reverberating from one quarter of the sky to the other. The youth went on
ahead, intent on finding the way, filled with impatience to arrive,
but slowing down his pace to suit it to the strength of his
companion; who, wearied by toil, weakened by disease, and
oppressed by the sultry air, was walking along with difficulty,
every now and then raising his haggard face towards the sky, as
if to breathe more freely.

When he saw the hut, Renzo stopped, turned round, and said,
'Here it is,' in a trembling voice.

They went in. . . . 'There they are!' cried the woman from the
bed. Lucia turned round, started up, and went towards the old
man, crying, 'Oh, who do I see! Oh, Father Cristoforo!'

'Well, Lucia. What a lot of dangers the Lord has delivered you
from! How glad you must be that you always put your hopes in
Him!'

'Oh yes! But, you, father? Ah me, how changed you are! How
are you? Tell me, how are you?'

'As God wishes, and as, by His grace, I wish too,' the friar replied, with a serene face. Then, drawing her into a corner he added: 'Listen; I can only stay here a few minutes. Are you disposed to confide in me, as you used to do before?'

'Oh! Aren't you always like a father to me?'

'Then, my daughter, what is this vow Renzo has told me about?'

'It's a vow I made to Our Lady.... Oh! When I was in great trouble ... never to marry.'

'My poor child! But did you think at the time that you were bound by a promise?'

'As Our Lord and Our Lady were concerned.... No, I didn't think of that.'

'Our Lord, my daughter, willingly accepts sacrifices and offerings when what we offer is our own. It is our heart, it is our will He wants; but you cannot offer Him the will of another to whom you were already bound.'

'Have I done wrong?'

'No, my poor child, don't think that. I believe in fact that the Holy Virgin has accepted the intention of your afflicted heart, and has offered it to God for you. But tell me: have you ever asked anyone's advice about this?'

'I never thought it was wrong, or anything I had to confess; and one knows one mustn't tell others the little good one does.'

'You haven't any other motive that prevents you from keeping the promise you made to Renzo?'

'As for that ... for myself ... what motive? ... I couldn't really say ...' answered Lucia, with a hesitation which showed anything but an uncertainty of thought; and her face, still pale with illness, suddenly flushed quite scarlet.

'Do you believe,' went on the old man, lowering his eyes, 'that God has given His Church the authority to remit or retain the debts and obligations which humans may have contracted with Him,* according to the greater good?'

'Oh, yes, I believe that.'

'Know, then, that we who are entrusted with the care of souls in this place have the fullest powers of the Church for all those who have recourse to us, and that in consequence I can, if you ask for it, absolve you from any obligation, whatever it may be, that you may have contracted by this vow.'

'But isn't it a sin to turn back and repent of a promise made to Our Lady? I made it then from the bottom of my heart ...' said

Lucia, violently agitated by the assault of this unexpected feeling for which the only word was hope, and the opposing uprush of a terror strengthened by all the thoughts that had been in the forefront of her mind for so long.

'A sin, my daughter?' said the friar. 'A sin to have recourse to the Church, and to ask its minister to use the authority he has received from her, and that she has received from God? I have seen how you two have been drawn to each other; and certainly if ever two people ever seemed united by God, you were those two. I do not see why God now should want to see you separated. And I bless Him for granting me, unworthy as I am, the power to speak in His name, and to give you back your words. If you ask me to absolve you from this vow, I will not hesitate to do so. What is more, I want you to ask me.'

'Then . . .! Then . . .! I do ask you,' said Lucia, with a face now clouded only by modesty.

The friar beckoned the youth who had been standing in the farthest corner, looking on (as that was all he could do) with a fixed stare at the dialogue which so closely concerned him; and when he came up, he said to Lucia in a louder voice, 'With the authority which I have from the Church, I declare you absolved from the vow of virginity, annulling what might have been ill-considered in it, and freeing you from every obligation you might have contracted by it.'

The reader can imagine how those words sounded to Renzo's ears. His eyes eloquently thanked him who had uttered them, and then quickly sought those of Lucia, but in vain.

'Return now, in certainty and peace, to your former thoughts,' went on the Capuchin. 'Ask the Lord once more for the grace you asked Him before, to be a holy wife; and be confident that He will grant it more abundantly, after all your troubles. And you,' he said, turning to Renzo. 'Remember, my son, that if the Church gives you this companion, it is not in order to afford you a temporal and worldly joy which, even if it could be complete and unalloyed with any disappointment, would anyway end in great pain at the moment of separation; but in order to put both of you on the road to the joy that knows no end. Love each other as fellow-travellers, with the thought that you must leave each other, and with the hope of finding each other again for ever. Thank Heaven that you have been led to this state not through turbulent and transitory joys, but through suffering and agony, so as to dispose you for a tranquil and collected happiness. If

God grants you children, remember to bring them up for Him, to instil the love of Him and of humanity in them; and then you will be sure to be training them well in everything else. Lucia, has he told you' – and he pointed at Renzo – 'who he has seen here?'

'Oh, father, he has told me!'

'You must pray for him! Pray for him tirelessly. And pray for me too. . . . My children, I should like you to have a memento of the poor friar.' Here he took out of his pocket a little box made of common wood, but turned and polished with a certain Capuchin refinement, and went on, 'In here are the remains of that bread, the first I ever asked of charity, the bread you have heard me speak of. I leave it with you. Keep it: show it to your children. They'll come into a sad world and in sad times, in the midst of the arrogant and the high-handed. Tell them always to forgive; always. Everything, everything! And may they, too, pray for the poor friar.'

And he handed the box to Lucia, who took it with the respect with which she would a relic. Then he went on, in a calmer voice, 'Now tell me, have you anyone in Milan you can apply to for help? Where are you thinking of going to stay as soon as you leave here? And who will take you back to your mother, whom I pray that God will have preserved in health?'

'This kind lady here has been like a mother to me here. We two will leave here together, and then she'll look after everything.'

'May God bless her,' said the friar, approaching the bed.

'I thank you, too,' said the widow, 'for the happiness you have given to these poor creatures; although I counted on having dear Lucia always with me. But I'll have her with me for a while, and then I'll accompany her to her own village and deliver her over to her mother; and,' she added then in a whisper, 'I want to give her her trousseau. I have too many things myself; and none left of those who should have enjoyed them with me.'

'By doing so,' said the friar, 'you will be making a great offering to the Lord, and doing good to your fellow-creatures, too. I will not commend this girl to you, as I see that she is already like your own child to you. It only remains to praise the Lord, who can show Himself a father even amidst afflictions, and who, by bringing you together, has given such a clear sign of His love for you both. Now,' he went on, then, turning to Renzo and taking him by the hand, 'we two have nothing more to do here; and we have stayed too long already. Let us go.'

'Oh, father,' said Lucia, 'shall I see you again? I, who am so useless in this world, am cured, and you . . .'

'For a long time,' replied the friar in a sweet and serious tone, 'I've been asking the Lord for a favour – a great favour: to end my days in the service of my fellow-men. If He wishes to grant me this now, I'll want all those who have any love for me to help me thank Him. Come; give Renzo your messages for your mother.'

'Tell her what you've seen,' Lucia said to her betrothed – 'tell her I've found another mother here, and that I will come out with her as soon as I can, and that I hope – oh, I do so hope – to find her well.'

'If you need any money,' said Renzo, 'I've got here all you sent me, and . . .'

'No, no,' interrupted the widow: 'I've got too much of it.'

'Let us go,' went on the friar.

'Good-bye for the present, Lucia . . . and you, too, kind lady,' said Renzo, not finding words to express what he felt.

'Who knows whether the Lord will grant that we all see each other again,' exclaimed Lucia.

'May He be always with you, and bless you,' said Fra Cristoforo to the two friends, and left the hut with Renzo.

It was almost nightfall, and the weather seemed to be drawing nearer and nearer a crisis. The Capuchin once more urged the youth to shelter in his hut for the night. 'I won't be able to keep you company,' he added. 'But you'll be under cover.'

But Renzo felt a longing to be off; and he was loath to remain any longer in such a place when he could not see Lucia, and not even spend a little time with the good friar. As for the time and the weather, one might say that night and day, sun and rain, breeze and hurricane, were all one to him at that moment. So he thanked the friar, saying he wanted to go off and find Agnese as soon as possible.

When they were in the central path the friar grasped his hand and said, 'If you find that good Agnese – as God grant you will – give her my greetings, and tell her and all who remain and remember Fra Cristoforo, to pray for him. May God be with you, and bless you for ever.'

'Oh, dear father. . . . We'll see each other again? We'll see each other again?'

'Up above, I hope.' And with these words he left Renzo; who stood there waiting until he was lost to sight, and then hurriedly set off towards the gate, casting to left and right final looks of compassion at that place of woe. There was an unusual bustle: *monatti* running, things being lugged about, the entrance flaps of the huts being pegged down, and convalescents dragging themselves towards those or under the arcades, to shelter from the impending storm.

CHAPTER 37

Hardly had Renzo crossed the threshold of the lazaretto and turned to the right to find the lane from which he had emerged that morning under the city walls, than a few big scattered drops began coming down, hitting and bouncing on the parched white road like hailstones, each raising a tiny cloud of dust; a moment later they were falling thick and fast, and before he had reached the lane they were coming down in torrents. Renzo, instead of being put out, wallowed in it, rejoicing in the freshness of the air, in that murmur and stir among the grass and leaves, all quivering, dripping, reviving, and glistening; he drew long, deep breaths; and this sudden change of Nature's made him realize more freely and vividly the one that had taken place in his own destiny.

But this feeling would have been even more intense and complete if Renzo had been able to guess what could be seen a few days later: that this rain was washing the contagion away, and that after it the lazaretto, if it did not return all its inmates to the land of the living, would at least not swallow up any more; that within a week doors and shops would be seen reopening, no one would talk of anything worse than quarantine and only a few scattered traces of the plague would remain here and there – the aftermath which a scourge like that always leaves in its wake for some time.

So our traveller walked gaily along, without having made any plans as to how or where or when or if he was to stop for the night, intent only on pressing ahead, reaching his native village quickly, and finding someone to talk to, to tell his tale to, and, above all, on getting under way again for Pasturo to find Agnese. He walked along with his mind all in a whirl with the things that had happened that day; but among the miseries and horrors and dangers, one thought kept on coming to the surface – I've found her; she's cured; she's mine! – Then he would give a little skip, scattering drops of rain around him like a poodle coming out of water. Sometimes he would just rub his hands together; and then go on, more eagerly than ever. As he looked around him on the way, he collected up, as it were, the thoughts that he had dropped that morning and the day before on his journey in, finding the most pleasure in the very ones which he had then tried hardest to banish from his mind: the doubts, the difficulties of finding her, of finding her alive, among all those dead and dying! – And I've found her alive! – he would end up. He called back to his mind the worst moments of that day; he pictured himself with that knocker in his hand; will she be here or won't she? – And then that dismal reply; and then, before he could even take it in, being set on by that pack of mad rascals. And then the lazaretto, that sea of misery! Hoping to find her there! And then finding her! He recalled the moment when the procession of convalescents had just passed by. What a moment! What anguish not to find her in it! And now it didn't matter at all. And the women's quarters! And to hear her very own voice from behind that hut, when he least expected it! And see her, see her on her feet! And then? Then there was still that tangle of the vow, more a knot than ever. That had been undone too. And that hatred for Don Rodrigo – that ceaseless gnawing hatred which had aggravated all his worries and poisoned all his satisfactions; that had gone too. So that it would be difficult to imagine a more perfect contentment than his, were it not for the uncertainty about Agnese, the sad foreboding about Fra Cristoforo, and his still being in the midst of the plague.

He reached Sesto towards dusk; nor did the rain show any signs of stopping. But he was feeling more energetic than ever, and as there were so many difficulties in finding a lodging, and he was already soaked to the skin, he did not even consider stopping. The only thing that bothered him was a hearty appetite; for a joy like his would have made him digest much more than the Capuchin's thin soup. He looked about to see if he could find a baker's here, too, saw one, and had two loaves given him with the pincers and the usual ceremonies. With one in his pocket and the other in his mouth, on he went.

When he passed through Monza it was quite dark; but he succeeded in finding the gate that put him on to the right road. But great as it was, this was the road's only merit; for you can imagine what state it was in, and how it was becoming worse every moment. It was sunk (as they all were – we must have mentioned this before) between two banks like a river-bed, one might by that time have said, or if not a river, at least a canal; and every now and again there were great puddles from which it was only by heaving and pulling that the feet, let alone the shoes, could be dragged out. But Renzo got out as best he could, without any impatience or cursing or regrets, thinking that every step, however much it cost him, was carrying him forward, and that the rain would cease when God willed it, and that, in its own good time, the day would dawn, and that then the distance he was now travelling would be behind him.

But, to tell the truth, he only thought about all that when he couldn't help it. It was just a distraction. The main occupation of his mind was going over the story of the gloomy years that had passed; so many troubles and disasters, so many moments in which he was on the point of losing hope and throwing it all up; and contrasting this with the picture of a very different future – Lucia's arrival, and the wedding, and setting up house, and telling each other all their adventures, and then their whole lives ahead of them.

How he managed when he came to forks in the road – whether his slight knowledge and the faint light helped him always to choose the right one, or whether he always guessed it by chance – I could not say; for he himself, who was wont to describe his story in detail and at almost too great a length (and everything points to our anonymous chronicler having heard it from him more than once) – he himself, at this point, used to say that he only remembered that night as if he had spent it in bed dreaming. The fact is, however, that towards the end of it he found himself on the bank of the Adda.

It had never stopped raining; but at a certain moment the deluge had turned into thin rain and then into a very fine, very soft, very even drizzle; the few high clouds formed a continuous but thin and diaphanous veil; and by the dawning light Renzo could make out the surrounding countryside. His own village was among it; and what he felt at seeing it would be impossible to describe. Suffice it for me to say that those mountains, that *Resegone* nearby, the Lecco district, had all become a sort of personal property to him. He gave himself a look-over, too, and found he was, to tell the truth, rather different from what he had expected, given how he was feeling. All his clothes were bedraggled and sticking to him; from head to waist he was a sodden mass, dripping like a gutter; from waist to feet he was all mud and mire; the few clean patches looked as though they were the stains and splashes. And if he had seen the whole of himself in a mirror, with his hat-brim flopping limply and his hair sticking in lank strands to his face, he would have had even more of a shock. As for being tired, he must have been that, but he did not notice it at all; and the coolness of the dawn, combined with that of the night and of the bath he had had, only induced in him a fiercer longing to press on quicker than ever.

Now he was at Pescate. He skirted the lower stretch of the Adda, not without giving a melancholy glance at Pescarenico; he passed the bridge; a moment later, over the tracks and fields, he had reached his friend's cottage. His host, who was already up, and standing at his door looking at the weather, raised his eyes to that soaked, muddy, in one word – filthy – figure, which was yet so lively and carefree. Never in his life had he seen a man in a worse state or more cheerful.

'Hallo,' he said. 'Back already? And in this weather? How did it go?'

'She's there,' said Renzo. 'She's there; she's there.'

'Well?'

'Cured, which is even better. I'll have to thank the Lord and Our Blessed Lady as long as I live. But the things I've seen, the fearful things; I'll tell you all about it later on.'

'But what a state you're in!'

'I'm a beauty, aren't I?'

'To tell you the truth, you could use the upper half of you to wash the lower. But wait, just wait; and I'll make up a good fire for you.'

'I won't say no to that. D'you know where it caught me? Right at the very gates of the lazaretto. But it's nothing; the weather's got its job to do and I've got mine.'

His friend went off, and came back with two armfuls of brushwood. He put one on the ground and the other on the fireplace, where, with a few embers left over from the night before, he soon made a good blaze. Renzo meanwhile had taken off his hat, and after shaking it two or three times, threw it on the ground; with rather more difficulty he also pulled off his doublet. Then he took his knife, with its sheath as wet as if it had been put to soak, out of his breeches' pocket, put it on a bench, and said, 'That's in a fine state, too; but it's with water, with water, thank the Lord. . . . I very nearly . . . I'll tell you all about it afterwards,' and he rubbed his hands together. 'Now do me another favour,' he added. 'That bundle I left up in your room, do go and fetch it for me, for before these clothes on me get dry . . .'

When he came back with the bundle, his friend said, 'You must have an appetite, too; You can't have lacked drink on the way; but food . . .'

'I managed to buy a couple of loaves late last night; but to tell you the truth, they just slipped down without my feeling them.'

'Leave it to me,' said his friend. He put the water in a pot, which he then hooked to the chain, and added, 'I'm going milking; when I come back with the milk, the water'll be ready; and we'll make a good *polenta*. Meanwhile make yourself at home.'

Renzo, left alone, took off the rest of his clothes, not without a certain amount of difficulty, as they were almost glued to his back, dried himself, then dressed himself anew from head to foot. The friend came back and went to his pot; Renzo meanwhile sat down to wait.

'Now I feel I'm tired,' he said. 'It was a long haul. But that's nothing! I'd take a whole day to tell you everything. What a state Milan's in! The things you have to see! The things you have to touch! Enough to make you feel disgusted at yourself. Really I needed the good soaking I had. And what those gents down there tried to do to me! You'll hear the whole story. But if you could see the lazaretto! Miseries enough to drive you crazy! Anyway, I'll tell you all about it. . . . And she's there, and will come here, and will be my wife; and you must be best man, and, plague or no plague, I mean to spend at least a few hours of gaiety.'

Anyway, he carried out the promise he had made his friend of describing his adventures the whole day long; particularly as the other spent all day indoors, as it was raining so hard, part sitting beside his friend, part busy preparing his little vat and cask for the vintage, in which work Renzo did not fail to lend a hand; for, as he used to say, he was one of those who got more tired doing nothing than working. He could not refrain, however, from running over to Agnese's cottage to see a certain window again, and rub his hands a little there too. He got back without being seen by anyone, and went to bed at once. Before dawn he was up, and seeing the rain had stopped, though the weather had not yet settled, he set out for Pasturo.

It was still early when he arrived; for he was no less eager to

bring things to a head than the reader may be. He asked for
Agnese, heard that she was well, and was shown an isolated
cottage where she was living. He went there and called to her
from the road. Hearing that voice she rushed to the window; and
as she was still standing there gaping and trying to get some word
out, Renzo forestalled her by saying, 'Lucia's cured; I saw her the
day before yesterday; she sends her love, and will soon be coming.
And then I've got lots and lots to tell you.'

What with her surprise at his appearance, and her delight at
the news, Agnese set about making exclamations, and asking
questions, without finishing any of them; then, forgetting the
precautions she had been in the habit of taking for a long time,
she said, 'I'll come and open the door for you.'

'Wait; what about the plague?' said Renzo. 'You haven't had
it, I think?'

'I haven't, no; have you?'

'I have; but you ought to be careful then. I've come from
Milan, and, as you'll hear, I've been right up to the eyes in the
contagion. It's true I've changed all my clothes from top to toe;
but it's a filthy thing, that can stick to you like witchcraft. And
as the Lord's preserved you up to now, I mean you to be careful
until the epidemic's over; for you're our mother; and I want us to
live long and happily together, after all we've suffered, or I have
at least.'

'But . . .' interrupted Agnese.

'Ah!' interrupted Renzo, 'there's no "buts" about it now. I
know what you mean; but you'll hear, you'll hear how there
aren't any more "buts". Let's go to some place in the open air,
where we can talk at our ease and without danger, and you'll
hear all about it.'

Agnese pointed to a garden behind the house, and added, 'Go
in there, and you'll see there are two benches facing each other,
which might have been put there specially for us. I'll come at
once.'

Renzo went and sat on one of them; a moment later Agnese
was on the other; and I'm sure that if the reader, knowing as he
does all that happened before, could have been there as a third
person, and seen that animated conversation with his own eyes
and heard those accounts with his own ears, and the questions
and explanations and exclamations and condolences and congratulations; and about Don Rodrigo and Father Cristoforo and
all the rest; and those descriptions of the future as clear and

definite as those of the past – I am certain, I say, that he would
have enjoyed it all very much and been the last to come away.
But I think he would not much care to have all that conversation
merely on paper, in silent words of ink, without a single new fact
in it, and that he would prefer to imagine it all for himself. The
upshot was that they would go and set up house all together in
the Bergamese village where Renzo had already made a good
start. As to when, nothing could be decided about that, as it
depended on the plague and on various other circumstances. As
soon as the danger was over, Agnese was to go back home and
wait for Lucia, or Lucia would wait for her there. Meanwhile,
Renzo was to make other trips over to Pasturo, to see his mother,
and keep her informed of anything that happened.

Before he left he offered money to her as well, saying, 'I've got
it all here, you see, that lot. I'd made a vow, me too, not to touch
it, until things were all cleared up. So, if you need some, fetch a
pitcher of water and some vinegar; and I'll throw the whole fifty
shining new *scudi* into it.'

'No, no,' said Agnese. 'I've still got more than I need for
myself. Keep yours, as they'll be useful for setting up house.'

Renzo went back to his village with the added relief of having
found a person so dear to him safe and sound. The rest of the
day and that night he stayed in his friend's house. The day after
he set off on his travels again, but in another direction – towards
his adopted village.

He found Bortolo also in good health and less afraid of losing
it; for in those few days things had taken a big turn for the better
there too. Only a few were falling sick, and the disease was no
longer what it had been; there were no more fatal blotches, nor
those violent symptoms; it was just a fever now, usually rather
an intermittent one, with at the most some small discoloured spot
which healed like an ordinary boil. The appearance of the village
was already changed. The survivors were beginning to come out,
to count their numbers and exchange mutual condolences and
congratulations. There was already talk of starting work again;
employers were already beginning to look out for workmen and
engage them, particularly in those trades which had been short-
handed even before the epidemic, such as silk-spinning. Renzo
promised his cousin without making any difficulties (but subject
to due approval) to return to work when they had all come and
established themselves in the village. Meanwhile he busied himself with the most necessary preparations. He found a bigger

house, which had become only too easy and economical, and stocked it with furniture and utensils, breaking into his treasure this time, but without making any great hole in it, for everything was going cheap, there being more goods than there were people to buy them.

After some days he returned to his native village, which he found still more notably changed for the better. He hurried off to Pasturo at once, where he found Agnese completely recovered in spirits, and ready to go home as soon as possible; so he took her back with him. And we will pass over in silence what they felt and said at seeing all those familiar scenes together once again.

Agnese found everything as she had left it. She could not help remarking that this time, as they were a poor widow and a poor girl, the angels had watched over them. 'And that other time,' she added, 'when it looked as if the Lord was looking elsewhere, and not thinking of us, as He had let our few things be carried off, he showed us it was quite the contrary, by sending me a fine lot of money from another quarter, with which I was able to replace everything. Everything, I say; but that's not quite right, for Lucia's trousseau, which those people had taken away all fine and new with the rest of the things, that was still lacking; but now here it comes from another quarter still. If anyone had told me when I was working myself to death getting that other lot ready – You think, poor soul, you're working for Lucia! but you don't know who you're working for! Heaven knows what kind of creature this linen and these clothes will end up with. Lucia's trousseau, the one she'll really use, will be provided by a good soul whose very existence is unknown to you now!'

Agnese's first care was to provide the best accommodation for this good soul that her poor cottage could provide; then she went to look for some silk to spin, and beguiled away the time by working.

Renzo, on his side, did not pass in idleness those days which were already so long for him; he was lucky enough to have two trades, and he went back to that of a peasant. Part of the time he helped his host, for whom it was a great piece of luck to have a labourer at his disposal at such a time, and particularly one so able; part of the time he cultivated, or rather reclaimed, Agnese's little garden, which had been completely neglected in her absence. As for his own plot, he did nothing about it at all, saying it was too tousled a wig to comb, and that more than one pair of arms was needed to put it to rights again. And he did not even set foot in it, or in the house either; for the desolation of it all would have hurt him too much; and he had already decided to get rid of everything at any price, and to invest in his adopted country whatever he got out of it.

If the survivors seemed to each other like people risen from the dead, Renzo seemed doubly so to his fellow-villagers. Everyone welcomed him and congratulated him, everyone wanted to hear his story from his own lips. 'And how did he deal with that warrant?' the reader may ask; he dealt with it splendidly by not bothering about it at all, and by presuming that those who might have enforced it were not bothering about it at all either. Nor was he mistaken; this was not only the result of the plague, which had put an end to so many things; it was quite common in those days, as various parts of this story show, for decrees both general and particular to remain a dead-letter unless they had been put into effect at once, or unless there was some powerful private animosity to keep them alive – they were rather like bullets which once they have missed their target lie on the ground where they worry no one any longer. This was a necessary consequence of the great facility with which such decrees were scattered about. Man's activity is limited; and the more of it is put into giving orders, the less goes into carrying them out. What goes into the sleeves cannot go into the gussets.

To anyone who also wants to know how things went between Renzo and Don Abbondio during this period of waiting, I will only say that they kept away from each other: Don Abbondio for fear of hearing the topic of the marriage being broached, the very thought of which brought up a picture of Don Rodrigo with his bravi on one side and the cardinal with his arguments on the other; Renzo because he had decided not to mention it until the last moment, not wanting to risk putting the wind up in him beforehand, of his raising – who could ever tell? – some difficulty, or entangling things with useless discussion. His discussions he had with Agnese. 'Do you think she'll come soon?' would ask one. 'I hope so,' would reply the other; and often the one who had replied would ask the same question a little later. By these and other ruses of the kind they tried to beguile the time, which seemed to get longer and longer the more of it passed.

For the reader, however, we will make it all pass in a moment, simply stating briefly that some days after Renzo's visit to the lazaretto, Lucia left it with the good widow, and that, a general quarantine being ordered, they passed it together shut up in the widow's house; that part of the time was spent in putting together Lucia's trousseau, which, after some remonstrances, the latter insisted on working on too; and that as soon as the quarantine was finished the widow left her shop and house in the hands of her brother, the commissioner, and preparations were made for the journey. Here, too, we might just say that they set out, they arrived, and what happened next; but, willing as we are to defer to the impatience of the reader, there are three things that happened during this interval which we would not like to pass over in silence; and as regards two at least we believe the reader himself will agree that we would have been wrong to do so.

The first was this: when Lucia talked her adventures over with the widow in more order and detail than she had in the excitement of her first confidences, and made more express mention of the Signora who had given her refuge in the convent at Monza, she learnt things about the latter which, by giving her the key to many mysteries, filled her with the most painful and fearful amazement. She learnt from the widow that the wretched woman had fallen under suspicion of committing the most atrocious crimes, and been transferred by order of the cardinal to a convent in Milan; that there, after much raging and resistance, she had finally repented and confessed all; and that her present life was such a voluntary torture that short of ending it altogether no severer one could be imagined. Anyone who wants to know this tragic tale in more detail will find it in the book and place we have cited elsewhere[†] in connexion with the same person.

The second thing was that Lucia, when she asked after Father Cristoforo from all the Capuchins she could find in the lazaretto, heard with more sorrow than surprise that he had died of the plague.

The third and final thing was that before leaving she also wanted to find out something about her former master and mistress, and pay her respects, if either of them were still alive. The widow accompanied her to the house, where she heard that both of them had joined the majority. As for Donna Prassede, when one has said that she was dead, one has said everything: but on Don Ferrante, as he was a man of learning, our anonymous chronicler has thought fit to dilate rather more fully; and we will transcribe, at our own risk, more or less what he wrote about him.

† Ripamonti, *Hist. Pat.*, Dec. V, Book VI, Chap. III. (M.)*

He says, then, that from the first mention of plague, Don Ferrante was one of the most resolute in denying its existence, and that he maintained that opinion constantly till the end – not noisily like the mob, but with arguments which at least no one could tax with any lack of logical sequence.

'In rerum natura,' he would say, 'there are only two kinds of things: substances and accidents;* and if I prove that the contagion cannot be one or the other, I shall have proved that it does not exist – that it is a chimera. And here we go. Substances are either spiritual or material. That the contagion is a spiritual substance is an absurdity that no one would venture to maintain; so that it is useless to discuss it. Material substances are either simple or compound. Now, the contagion is not a simple substance, as can be proved in a few words. It is not an aerial substance; for if it were, instead of passing from one body to the other, it would fly off at once to its proper sphere. It is not aqueous; for it would wet things and be dried by the wind. It is not igneous; for it would burn. It is not terreous; for it would be visible. Nor is it a compound substance; for then it would at any rate be sensible to the eye and the touch; and who has ever seen this contagion? Who has ever touched it? It remains to be seen if it could be an accident. Worse and worse. These medical gentlemen say it is communicated from one body to the other; this is their Achilles, their pretext for issuing so many useless orders. Now, if we suppose it to be an accident, it would mean that it was a transferable accident – two words which contradict each other completely, for there is nothing plainer and clearer in the whole of philosophy than this: that an accident cannot pass from one subject to another. And if, to avoid this Scylla, they are reduced to saying it is a produced accident, they fall into Charybdis; for if it is produced, then it cannot be communicated, it cannot be propagated, as people go round blathering. These principles being laid down, what is the use of talking so much of blotches, of exanthemata, of carbuncles? . . .'

'A lot of nonsense,' someone once let out.

'No, no,' rejoined Don Ferrante. 'I don't say that. Science is science; only one must know how to use it. Blotches, exanthemata carbuncles, parotitis, violet tumours and black swellings are all respectable words, each with its own definite meaning. But I say they have nothing to do with the question. Who denies that these things may exist, in fact that these things do exist? The whole point is to see what they come from.'

This was the beginning also of Don Ferrante's troubles. As long as he did nothing but jeer at the opinion that there was a plague, he found ready and willing ears everywhere; for it is amazing how great the authority of a learned man is when he wants to prove to others things of which they are already convinced. But when he came to making distinctions, and trying to prove that the mistake of the doctors lay not in their affirming that a terrible and widespread disease existed, but in their assessment of its cause, then (I am speaking of the early period when no one wanted to hear the word 'plague' mentioned) – then, he found himself up against sharp and stubborn tongues instead of ready ears: then his long sermons were all over; and his doctrine could now only be expressed in jerks and snatches.

'The real cause of it is only too plain,' he would say. 'And even those who uphold those other vague causes are bound to recognize it. . . . Let them just deny, if they can, that fatal conjunction of Saturn and Jupiter. And when have influences ever been known to propagate. . . . ? And do these gentlemen want to deny the existence of heavenly influences? Can they deny the existence of the stars? Or do they mean to tell me they are just up there doing nothing, like so many pins stuck into a pin-cushion . . .? But what I cannot understand is these medical gentlemen one moment admitting we are under a malignant conjunction, and the next saying brazenly – Don't touch this, don't touch that, and you'll be safe. – As if avoiding contact with earthly bodies could prevent heavenly bodies from having any virtual effect. And all this fuss about burning rags. Poor fools! Will you burn Jupiter? Will you burn Saturn?'

His fretus – that is to say, on these excellent grounds – he took no precaution against the plague, caught it, and went to bed to die, like a hero of Metastasio, blaming the stars.*

And that famous library of his? Maybe it is still scattered around on the bookstalls.

CHAPTER 38

One evening Agnese heard a vehicle stop at her door. – It's her, for sure! – And sure enough it was Lucia, with the good widow. The greetings on all sides can be left to the reader to imagine.

Early the next morning along came Renzo, who knew nothing, and intended only to relieve his feelings a little with Agnese about Lucia's long delay. What he did and said at finding her before him can also be left to the reader's imagination. Lucia's demonstrations, on the other hand, do not call for much description. 'Good morning. How are you?' she said, with downcast eyes and an unruffled air. It should not be thought that Renzo found this reception too cold, or that he took it amiss. He understood exactly what it meant; and just as compliments are discounted among refined people, so he, too, realized that these words did not express all that was passing in Lucia's heart. Besides, it was noticeable that she had two ways of pronouncing them: one for Renzo, and another for all the other people she knew.

'I'm well when I see you,' went on the young man, using a hackneyed phrase, which, however, he might have invented himself at that moment.

'Our poor Fra Cristoforo...' said Lucia. 'Pray for his soul; though we can be almost sure that by now he's praying for us up above.'

'I'm afraid I expected it,' said Renzo. Nor was this the only sad chord touched in that conversation. But what of that? Whatever the subject, the conversation seemed just as delightful to him. Time for him had become like one of those capricious horses which first stand stock-still, raising one hoof after the other and pawing the same spot and rearing up again and again without moving a single step, and then all of a sudden start off and are away and going like the wind. Before the minutes had seemed hours, now the hours seemed minutes.

The widow, far from spoiling the party, entered into it very well; and certainly Renzo, when he saw her lying on that pallet, could never have imagined her in such a sociable and jovial humour. But lazaretto and countryside, death and a wedding, are very different things. She had at once made friends with Agnese; then it was a pleasure to see her with Lucia; tender and at the same time playful, teasing her with a graceful raillery, without ever going too far – just enough to make Lucia show all the happiness that she had in her heart.

Finally Renzo said he was going to Don Abbondio's, to make arrangements for the wedding. He went there, and with an air that was part bantering and part respectful, 'Your reverence,' he said to him, 'have you quite got over that headache that kept you from marrying me before? Now we've time; the bride's here; and

I've come to find out when it would be convenient to you; only this time I do beg you to be quick about it.' Don Abbondio did not say no; but he began to hesitate, to find certain other excuses, to make certain other insinuations. Why put himself in the public eye and have his name bandied about, with that warrant hanging over him? And then could it not be done just as well elsewhere? And so on and so forth.

'I see,' said Renzo. 'You've still got some of that headache. But listen, listen.' And he began to describe the state in which he had seen the wretched Don Rodrigo, and how by that time he must certainly have departed this life. 'Let us hope,' he concluded, 'that the Lord will have been merciful to him.'

'That's got nothing to do with it,' said Don Abbondio. 'Have I said no? I don't say no. I'm speaking . . . I'm speaking for good reasons. And anyway, you see, while there's life . . . Look at me; I'm just a broken shell; I've had more than one foot in the grave myself too; and I'm here . . . and . . . if no other troubles come my way . . . well . . . I can still look forward to staying here a little while longer. So just think that someone with a constitution like . . . But, as I say, that's got nothing to do with it.'

After a few other interchanges, which were no more nor less conclusive, Renzo made him a fine bow, and went back to report to his party. 'I came away,' he ended up, 'because I'd had enough, and was afraid of losing my patience and being disrespectful. At some moments he seemed just exactly like last time – just the same sour looks, the same excuses. I'm sure if he'd gone on much longer he'd have brought some Latin words out at me again. I see it looks like dragging on once more; it's better to do what he suggested straightaway, and go and get married where we're going to settle.'

'D'you know what we'll do,' said the widow. 'I'd like us women to go and have another try, and see if we succeed any better. That way I'll also have the fun of meeting this man, if he's really what you say. I suggest we go after dinner, so as not to set on him again straight away. Now, Mr Bridegroom, take us two women out for a little walk, while Agnese's busy; and I'll act as mother to Lucia. I'm really longing to see a bit more of these mountains and this lake I've heard so much about; the little I've seen of it looks very pretty indeed.'

Renzo took them first of all to his host's cottage, where they had another great welcome; and they made him promise to come and have dinner with them not only that day, but every day if he could.

After the walk and the dinner, Renzo went off, without saying where he was going. The women stayed some time discussing and planning the best way to take Don Abbondio; finally they sallied out to the assault.

– Here they come – said the latter to himself. But he put a bold face on it, and produced warm congratulations for Lucia, greetings for Agnese, and compliments for the stranger. He made them sit down, and at once began talking about the plague, asking Lucia to tell him how she had fared through all the calamities. The lazaretto gave him an opportunity of bringing her companion into the conversation; then, as was only fair, Don Abbondio talked about his own troubles; then came great congratulations to Agnese for having got through it scot-free. Things were beginning to lengthen out. From the very first moment the two matrons had been on the watch for a chance to broach the main subject; finally, one of the two – I am not sure which – broke the ice. But what do you think happened then? Why, Don Abbondio went deaf in that ear. Not that he said so; but there he was again at his old twisting and turning, and hopping from one branch to another. 'That ban,' he said, 'would have to be lifted first. You, madame, who are from Milan, must know how these things go, and are sure to have some protector, some person of influence . . . for that's the way every wound's healed. But if you want to do it the quickest way, without going into all these complications, why, as the young couple and our Agnese here already intend to leave the country (and all I have to say about that is that one's own country is where one's best off), everything, it seems to me, could be done there, where no warrant holds. I'm really longing to see this match concluded, but I'd like to see it done in the right way, peacefully. I'll tell you the truth: to come out openly with the name of Renzo Tramaglino at the altar here – with that warrant still out – I couldn't do it with an easy mind – I'm too fond of him; I'd be afraid of doing him a bad turn. You can see that; you can all see that.'

Here Agnese and the widow each began to refute these reasons, and Don Abbondio to put them forward again in other forms. They were always back where they were before, when in came Renzo with a resolute step and a look of having news on his face and said, 'His lordship the Marquis * * * has arrived.'

'What d'you mean by that? Arrived where?' asked Don Abbondio, getting up.

'He's arrived at his mansion, which was Don Rodrigo's; for this marquis is his heir by entail, as they call it; so there's no more doubt about it. Personally, I'd be very glad to know that poor man died a good death. Anyway, I've said some "Our Fathers" for him now, and now I'll say some "*De Profundis*".* This marquis is a real decent fellow.'

'Of course,' said Don Abbondio. 'I've more than once heard him called a really good gentleman, one of the old school. But can it really be true . . .?'

'D'you believe the sacristan?'

'Why?'

'Because he's seen him with his own eyes. I only went nearby, and to tell you the truth, I went because I thought something might be known there. And more than one person told me the same thing. Then I met Ambrogio, who was coming right from there, and who had seen him, as I say, behaving as master. Would you like to hear him, Ambrogio, I mean? I made him wait outside here on purpose.'

'Let's hear him,' said Don Abbondio. Renzo went to call the sacristan, who confirmed it entirely and completely, added other details, and dispersed all doubts; then he went away.

'Ah! So he's dead, then. He's really gone,' exclaimed Don Abbondio. 'Just see, my children, if Providence doesn't get people like that in the end. D'you know, it's a wonderful thing. A great relief for this poor neighbourhood. For the man was impossible to live with. This plague's been a great scourge, but it's also been a great broom: it's swept away certain folk, my children, whom we never thought we'd be rid of any more; in their prime and vigour and prosperity, too; and we'd thought the man who'd conduct their funeral was still doing his Latin exercises at the seminary; and then in the twinkle of an eye they've disappeared in hundreds at a time. We shan't see him going round any more with that pack of cut-throats behind him, with his arrogance and his haughty airs, and his stuck-up way of looking at people as if we were all in the world just by his gracious permission. Anyway, he's not here any more, and we are. He won't send honest folk any more of those messages. He's given us all a great deal of trouble, you see; we can say that now.'

'I've forgiven him from the bottom of my heart.'

'And very proper, too,' rejoined Don Abbondio. 'But one can

also thank Heaven for ridding us of him. Now, to get back to ourselves, I repeat, do just what you think best. If you want me to marry you, here I am; if you find it more convenient any other way, just suit yourselves. As for the warrant, I, too, can see that as there's no one with his eye on you now and wanting to do you any harm, it's not worth worrying about it very much; particularly as there's been that gracious amnesty for the birth of the Most Serene Infante.* And then there's the plague. The plague! A lot that cancelled out, the plague did. So that, if you like . . . today is Thursday. . . . On Sunday I'll call your banns in church; for the ones before aren't valid after so long; and then I'll have the satisfaction of marrying you myself.'

'You know quite well that's just what we came for,' said Renzo.

'Excellent, and I'm at your service; and I want to let His Eminence know at once.'

'Who's His Eminence?' asked Agnese.

'His Eminence,' answered Don Abbondio, 'is our cardinal archbishop, whom God preserve.'

'Oh, you must excuse me about that,' answered Agnese. 'A poor ignorant woman though I may be, I can assure you that's not the way to call him. For just before we were going to talk to him the second time, as I'm talking to your reverence now, one of the priests there drew me aside, and taught me how to behave with the cardinal, and that I was to call him "Most Illustrious Lordship, and Your Grace".'

'And now if he was to teach you again he'd tell you to call him Your Eminence; d'you see? For the Pope – whom God preserve, too – has laid down ever since June that cardinals are to have that title. And d'you know why he came to that decision? Because Most Illustrious Lordship, which was reserved for them and for certain princes – well, even you can see what it's become, and how many people get called it; and how they lap it up! What was the Pope to do? Take it away from all of them? That would have meant complaints, protests, bad feeling, and trouble, and on top of it all, everything going on as it did before. So he's found a capital solution. Gradually, though, they'll begin calling bishops "Your Eminence", then the abbots will want it; then the provosts – for human beings are like that – always wanting to rise, wanting to rise – then the canons . . .'

'Then the parish priests,' said the widow.

'No, no,' rejoined Don Abbondio. 'The parish priests are the ones who pull the cart along; the parish priests won't ever get into bad habits, never you fear. It's "your reverence" for them till the end of the world. No, but I wouldn't be at all surprised if the nobles, who are used to hearing themselves called Most Illustrious and being treated like cardinals, should not one day claim the Eminence for themselves. And if they want it, depend on it they'll find people to call them by it. And then whoever's pope at the time will find something else for the cardinals. Ah well! Let's get back to our own affairs. On Sunday I'll call your banns in church; and d'you know what I've thought of to help it on? We'll ask meanwhile for a dispensation from the other two banns. They must be very busy giving dispensations down there at the curia, if things are going everywhere like they do here. Next Sunday I've already got one ... two ... three, without counting yours. And others may still come in. And you'll see how many more there'll be shortly; there won't be a bachelor left. What a blunder Perpetua made by going and dying now; for even she would find a customer at a time like this. And I imagine, madame, things are the same in Milan.'

'Yes, indeed. Just think that in my parish alone last Sunday, fifty banns were called.'

'There you are; the world doesn't want to end yet. And you, madame, haven't you had the bees buzzing round you?'

'No, no; I don't think of these things; I don't want to.'

'Yes, yes; you want to be all alone. Even Agnese, see; even Agnese ...'

'Pooh! You're in joking mood, you are,' said the latter.

'To be sure I'm in joking mood, and it's time one was, it seems to me. We've been through some bad times, haven't we, my children, some bad times? Let's hope these few days we've still got in the world will be better. Ah, well! You're lucky in having a bit of time to talk over your past troubles, if no new ones come up; but I, on the other hand, am three-quarters past the eleventh hour, and ... rogues may die, and one may recover from the plague, but there's no remedy for the years; and, as they say, *senectus ipsa est morbus*.'*

'Now,' said Renzo, 'you may talk Latin as much as you like, for it doesn't bother me at all.'

'You've still got it in for Latin, have you? Good, good! I'll sort you out. When you come up before me with this girl here, just precisely to say a few words in Latin, I'll say to you, "You don't like Latin? Then go in peace." How'll you like that?'

'Ah! I know what I mean,' rejoined Renzo. 'That's not the Latin that frightens me: that's an honest, sacrosanct Latin, like that of the Mass; and you have to read what's in the book, too. I mean that rascally Latin outside church, that comes at one unawares in the middle of a conversation. For example, now that we're here, and that it's all over – that Latin you went spouting out right there in that corner, so as to make me think you couldn't do it, and that more things were needed, and I don't know what else. Do translate it for me now.'

'Quiet, you fool, quiet! Don't begin stirring up all that again; for if we had to make up accounts now, I don't know who'd come out on top. I've forgiven everything; don't let's talk about it any more; but you've certainly played me some tricks. I wasn't surprised at you – for you're a young rascal, anyway – but what about this deep one here, this little saint, this model madonna, whom it'd seem a sin to suspect of anything! But ah, yes, I know who put her up to it, I know, I know.' So saying, he pointed at Agnese the finger he had first directed at Lucia; and the good humour with which he made these reproaches is impossible to describe. The news had made him gayer and more talkative than he had been for a long time; and we should still be a long way from the end of our story if we described the rest of the conversation, which he kept on prolonging, more than once holding the party back when they wanted to go, and then keeping them again some time on the doorstep, talking nonsense the whole time.

Next day he received a visit that was as welcome as it was unexpected – the marquis mentioned before. He was a man between his prime and his old age, whose aspect was a kind of confirmation of what rumour said of him; open, courteous, quiet, unassuming and dignified, and with something that showed a resigned melancholy.

'I've come,' he said, 'to bring you the greetings of the cardinal archbishop.'

'What condescension on the part of both of you.'

'When I took leave of that incomparable man, who honours me with his friendship, he talked about two young people of this parish who were betrothed, and who had been through a lot of suffering on account of that poor Don Rodrigo. His Grace wanted to have news of them. Are they alive? Are their affairs all settled?'

'Everything's settled. In fact, I had intended to write to His Eminence; but now that I have the honour . . .'

'Are they here?'

'Yes, here; and as soon as possible they'll be man and wife.'

'I would like you to let me know if I can help them at all, and also the best way to do so. I've lost my only two sons and their mother in this calamity, and come into three considerable legacies. In any case, I had more than I needed before; so you see it's really doing me a service to give me an opportunity of using it, particularly one like this.'

'Heaven bless you. Why aren't they all like you, the . . .? Anyway, I, too, thank you from the bottom of my heart in the name of these children of mine. And as your most illustrious lordship encourages me so much – yes, I have an expedient to suggest which may meet with your lordship's approval. Let me tell you, then, that these young folk have decided to go and set up house elsewhere, and to sell the little they possess here. The young man has a vineyard of about nine or ten hectares, I think, but it's completely run wild, and is only worth the ground in it. He also has a cottage, and the bride has another, both of them just mouse-holes, you see. A gentleman like your lordship can't know how the poor fare when they want to get rid of any possessions. They always end by falling into the hands of some sly rascal who may already have had his eye on their few yards of land for some time, backs out when he knows the other needs to sell it, and pretends he's lost interest; then he has to be run after, and gets it just for a crust of bread; particularly in circumstances like these. Your lordship will already have seen what I'm leading up to. The greatest charity your most illustrious lordship could do these people is to get them out of this difficulty by buying their little bits of property. I, to tell the truth, have an eye to my own interest in it, as I would like to acquire a landowner like my lord marquis in my parish; but your lordship will decide as he thinks best; I've only spoken from obedience.'

The marquis praised the suggestion highly, thanked Don Abbondio, and asked him to decide the price and to fix it good and high; and then he quite petrified Don Abbondio with amazement by suggesting they should at once go together to the bride's house, where they would probably also find the bridegroom.

On the way, Don Abbondio, in high glee as you can imagine, thought of something else, and added, 'As your most illustrious lordship is so inclined to help these people, there is another thing that could be done for them. The young man has a warrant out against him – a sort of banishment – for some prank he got up to in Milan two years ago, that day of the great riots, in which he got involved without meaning any harm, out of sheer ignorance, like a mouse in a trap. Nothing serious, I assure you; just a boyish lark – he's not capable of really doing any harm, as I can vouch, who've baptized him and seen him grow up. And besides, if your lordship cares to amuse himself a bit by listening to the muddled talk of these poor folk you could get him to tell you the story and hear it for yourself. Now, as it's an old business, no one bothers him; and, as I said, he's thinking of leaving the country; but in time, if he ever comes back here, or anything else, you never know, it's always best, you'll agree, to have his name off the books. The lord marquis has influence in Milan, as is right and proper, both as a great nobleman and as the fine man he is. . . . No, no, let me go on; for the truth must out at times. A word of recommendation from a person like yourself would be more than is necessary to obtain a complete discharge.'

'There are no serious charges against this young man?'

'No, no; I shouldn't think so. They made a great fuss about it at first; but now I think it's nothing but a mere formality.'

'If that is so, the thing will be easy; and I'll willingly take it on myself.'

'And then you don't want to hear me call you a fine man! I say so, and I want to say so; in spite of you, I want to say so. And even if I was silent, it wouldn't be any avail, for that's what everyone says; and *vox populi, vox Dei*.'*

As they had hoped they found Renzo and the three women at home. Their surprise I leave the reader to imagine. I, for my part, believe that even those rough walls, windows, stools and pots and pans, were amazed at having such an unusual visitor. He led the conversation, talking of the cardinal and other subjects with frank cordiality, and at the same time with delicate tact. Then he went on to make the proposal that had brought him there. Don Abbondio, on being asked to fix the price, came forward, and after some compliments and excuses, saying it wasn't his line, that he could only do it at random, and that he only spoke out of obedience, and that it was just as the other liked, named what he himself thought was an exorbitant sum. The purchaser said that for his part he was quite content, and then, as if he had misunderstood, doubled the figure; he would not hear of any correction, and cut short and ended all further discussion by inviting the company to dine at his mansion the day after the wedding, where the deeds would be executed in form.

– Ah! – Don Abbondio said to himself when he had gone back home – if the plague did things like this always and everywhere, it would be a real shame to speak ill of it. You might almost say that one was needed every generation – even on condition that you had to catch it yourself, so long as you got better.

The dispensation arrived, the discharge arrived, and finally that blessed day arrived. The two betrothed marched in triumphal security to that very church where, from Don Abbondio's own mouth, they were married. The trip to that mansion was another and even more extraordinary triumph; and I leave the reader to guess the thoughts that went through their minds as they climbed that slope and entered that gateway; and the things they said, each according to their natures. I will only mention that several times amidst the gaiety one or other remarked that all that was lacking to complete the festivities was poor Fra Cristoforo. 'But for sure,' they would say then, 'he's better off than we are.'

The marquis gave them a great welcome, conducted them to a nice servants' hall, and saw the bridal couple with Agnese and the merchant's widow to their seats; and before withdrawing to dine elsewhere with Don Abbondio, he stayed for some time mingling with his guests, and even helped to wait on them. The thought, I hope, has not occurred to anyone that it would have been simpler to make up one single table. I have described him as an excellent man, but not as an eccentric, as they would say nowadays; I have said that he was a humble man, but not that he was a prodigy of humility. He had enough to put himself beneath these good folk, but not enough to be on an equality with them.

After the two banquets the contract was drawn up at the hands of a lawyer who was not Quibble-weaver. The latter, or rather, his mortal remains, was, and still is, at Canterelli. And for those of you who do not come from these parts, I feel that some explanation may be necessary here.

About half a mile or so above Lecco, and almost on the borders of another village called Castello, is a place called Canterelli, where two roads cross; and on one side of this cross-road may be seen a mound like an artificial hillock, with a cross on the top, which is in fact nothing else than a great heap of dead from that plague. Tradition, in truth, merely says that they are the dead from a plague; but it must undoubtedly be that one, which was the last and most murderous of any on record. And we know that traditions, unless they are helped out a bit, always say too little by themselves.

The only difficulty on the return journey was that Renzo was rather hampered by the weight of the money he carried away with him; but our young man, as you know, had put up with far worse troubles. I will say nothing of the work – by no means light – that his mind was put to in thinking of the best means of laying it out profitably; watching the plans, reflections, fancies, passing through his mind, listening to the pros and cons for agriculture or industry, was like observing two academies of the last century in debate. And the quandary was a much more real one to him; for, being just one man alone, no one could say to him – What need is there to choose? Why not both? – For the means are the same in both cases; and the two are like legs, which get along better in twos than in ones.

Nothing else was thought of now than packing up and getting under way; the Tramaglino family for their adopted country, and the widow for Milan. Many were the tears, the thanks, the promises to visit each other often. No less tender, apart from the tears, was the parting of Renzo and his family from his hospitable friend; nor should it be thought that the leave-taking with Don Abbondio was cold. Those good creatures had always kept a certain respectful affection for their parish priest; and he had always wished them well at the bottom of his heart. It's these blessed matters of business that mess up the affections.

Some may ask if there was no sorrow at tearing themselves away from their native place, from those beloved mountains? To be sure there was; for there is some sorrow, I venture to say, in almost everything. It could not, however, have been very deep, or they could have spared it to themselves by staying at home, now that the two great obstacles – Don Rodrigo and the warrant – had been removed. But all three had for some time now grown used to considering the village they were going to as their own. Renzo had reconciled the women to it by describing the easy circumstances for workers, and a hundred other things about the fine life that people lived there. Besides, they had all been through some very bitter moments in the one they were leaving behind; and sad memories always in the end spoil the places that recall them. And if these places are the ones where we were born, perhaps there is something even sharper and more poignant about such memories. So, says our manuscript, will a baby rest willingly on its nurse's bosom and reach eagerly and confidently for the pap that has nourished it sweetly hitherto; but let the nurse apply wormwood to wean it, and the baby will withdraw its mouth, then try again, but finally break away – weep, but break away.

What will the reader say after all this when he hears that they had scarcely arrived in the new village and settled in than Renzo found new vexations all ready and waiting for him? They were just trifles; but so little is needed to disturb a state of happiness! Here, in a few words, is what they were.

The talk that had gone on in that village about Lucia long before she arrived; the knowledge that Renzo had suffered so much for her sake, and had always been constant, always faithful; a word perhaps dropped by someone warmly inclined to him and to his affairs, had all aroused a certain curiosity to see the girl and a certain expectation of her beauty. Now, you know what anticipations are like – fanciful, credulous, positive, then in the event captious and disdainful, never finding enough to satisfy them because they never really knew what they expected; and withdrawing without pity the sweets they had given without reason. When this Lucia appeared, many who had perhaps expected to find her hair all gold, and her cheeks all roses, and each eye more beautiful than the other, and I don't know what besides, began shrugging their shoulders and turning up their noses and saying, 'Eh! Is this her? After all this time, after all this talk, we expected something better. What is she, after all? Just a peasant girl like lots of others. Eh! There are plenty like her, and better than her, everywhere.' And coming down to details, one noted one defect and one another; and there were even some who found her downright ugly.

As, however, no one went and told these things to Renzo to his face there was no great harm so far. Those who did the harm were certain people who passed them on to him; and Renzo – what could you expect? – was touched to the quick. He began to brood about it and complain loudly about it, both with anyone who talked to him and at greater length with himself. – And what concern is it of yours? And who's told you to expect anything? Have I ever come and talked to you about her? And told you she was beautiful? And when others said so did I ever reply anything except that she was a good girl? She's a peasant girl! Did I ever tell you I was bringing a princess back here?

Don't you like her? Then don't look at her. You've got beauties of your own, look at them. –

How a trifle is sometimes enough to decide a man's fate for life! If Renzo had had to spend his in that village as he had first planned, it would not have been a very happy one. From constant annoyance, he had become annoying himself. He was gruff with everyone because everyone might be one of Lucia's critics. Not that he was ever downright rude; but you know how much can be done without offending the proprieties: quite enough to get yourself skewered. Every word he spoke had something sardonic about it; he too found things to criticize in everything, so that he got to the pitch, if there was a bad weather two days running, of saying at once, 'Oh, well, in a place like this!' Quite a number of people were getting tired of this, even, I must own, among those who had liked him at first; and in time, with one thing leading to another, he would have found himself up against almost the entire population, without even realizing himself, perhaps, the origin of the trouble.

But it seemed that the plague had undertaken to remedy all his mistakes. It had carried off the owner of another silk-mill situated at the gates of Bergamo; and the heir, a young madcap, finding nothing to amuse him in the whole concern, was determined – in fact, eager – to sell even at half-price; but he wanted to be paid cash down, so as to turn it at once into unproductive consumption. When this came to Bortolo's ears he hurried off to see about it; started negotiations; better terms could not have been hoped for; but that condition of cash down spoilt everything, for what he had put aside, little by little, by saving, was still far from reaching the sum. He left the deal open and hurried back, told his cousin about the affair, and suggested going halves with him. Such a good offer cut short Renzo's economic doubts, which decided at once in favour of industry; and he agreed. They went together, and the contract was made. When, later on, the new owners came to settle on their property, Lucia, about whom there were no expectations at all, not only was not found fault with, but was even rather admired; and Renzo in time came to hear of more than one person saying, 'Have you seen that pretty block-head who's come here?' The adjective made the noun pass muster.

Even the annoyances which he had been through in the other village were a useful lesson to him. Before then he had been rather glib in giving an opinion, and quick to criticize other people's women and everything else. Now he realized that words are one thing on the tongue and another in the ear; and he got rather more into the habit of listening internally to his own before uttering them.

But you should not suppose that he had no little worries even there. Man (says our anonymous chronicler; and you already know by experience that he had rather a strange taste in similes, but bear with this one for it is likely to be the last), man, as long as he is in this world, is like an invalid lying on a more or less uncomfortable bed who sees other beds around him which look outwardly smooth, level, and better made, and imagines he would be very happy on them. But if he succeeds in changing, scarcely is he lying on the new bed than he begins, as his weight sinks in, to feel a twig pricking into him here, and a lump pressing into him there; so that, in fact, he is more or less back where he started. And for this reason, adds our anonymous chronicler, we should think more of doing well than of faring well, and we will end by faring better too. This simile is somewhat far-fetched, laboured, and very seventeenth-century; but it is true on the whole. Anyway, he goes on, there were no more troubles for our friends as great and severe as those we have described; from then onwards they led one of the most tranquil, most happy, and most enviable of lives; so that, were I to describe it, it would bore you to death.

Business went like a charm. At the beginning there was a little difficulty owing to the scarcity of workers and the pretensions and indiscipline of the few who remained. Edicts were published limiting the workers' wages. In spite of this effort to help, things picked up again, because things are bound to pick up eventually. Another rather more judicious edict then arrived from Venice granting foreigners who came to live in the state exemption for ten years from all general and personal taxes. This was another windfall for our friends.

Before the first year of marriage was over a fine baby saw the light; and, as if on purpose to afford Renzo an early opportunity of fulfilling that magnanimous promise of his, it was a girl; and, as you can guess, it was given the name of Maria. Then in the course of time came I know not how many others of both sexes; and Agnese was busy carrying them here and there one after the other, calling them naughty little things and planting big kisses on their faces which left a white mark on them for some time afterwards. And they were all very good-tempered and obedient;

and Renzo was determined that they should all learn to read and write, saying that, as the swindle existed, they ought at least to profit by it themselves too.

The fun was to hear him recount his adventures; and he would always end by enumerating the great things which he had learnt from them so as to improve his conduct in the future. 'I've learnt,' he said, 'not to get into riots; I've learnt not to make speeches in the street; I've learnt to watch who I talk to; I've learnt not to raise my elbow too much; I've learnt not to hold door-knockers when there are excited people about; I've learnt not to fasten a bell to my feet before thinking of the consequences.' And a hundred other things of the kind.

Lucia, however, without finding these doctrines false in themselves, was not satisfied with them; it seemed to her, in a confused sort of way, that something was missing. By dint of hearing the same refrains repeated again and again, and thinking them over each time: 'And I,' – she once found herself asking her moralist – 'what d'you think I've learnt? I never went looking for troubles; they came looking for me. Unless you mean to say,' she added smiling sweetly, 'that my mistake was to love you, and to promise myself to you.'

Renzo at first found himself in rather a difficulty. After discussing the question and casting around together a long time for a solution, they came to the conclusion that troubles often come to those who bring them on themselves, but that not even the most cautious and innocent behaviour can ward them off; and that when they come – whether by our own fault or not – confidence in God can lighten them and turn them to our own improvement. This conclusion, though it was reached by poor people, has seemed so just to us that we have thought of putting it down here, as the essence of the whole tale.

And if this has not entirely displeased you, do feel a little warmth for the man who wrote it, and a little, too, for the man who patched it together. But if we've succeeded in boring you instead, believe me, we didn't do it on purpose.

HISTORY OF THE
COLUMN OF INFAMY

AUTHOR'S INTRODUCTION

The judges who, in Milan in 1630, condemned to death by atrocious sufferings certain persons accused of spreading the plague by methods no less stupid than disgusting, thought they were doing something so worthy of record that, in the very sentence of condemnation, along with a clause ordering the destruction of the house of one of their victims, they decreed that in the space where this house had stood a column be erected, to be called the 'Column of Infamy', and an inscription written where all posterity might read of the crime which they had prevented and the punishment they had imposed. And they were right: that judgement of theirs was indeed memorable.

In the course of the preceding work the author stated his intention of publishing the history of this affair. And this promise he now fulfils; but in offering his account to the public he is uncomfortably aware that some of his readers were expecting something much longer and more learned. Yet, while he is ready to be mocked by those whom he has disappointed, he feels free to disclaim responsibility for their expectations: if he has only a mouse to offer, he never said that mountains were giving birth.* All he said was that while a concern for brevity prevented him from including the affair as an episode, and though he was aware that it had already been discussed by a deservedly famous writer (Pietro Verri, *Osservazioni sulla tortura*), he considered nevertheless that the subject might very well be studied afresh and from a different point of view. Let this difference suffice to explain why the present work was undertaken. Whether it has been usefully undertaken is another question; this, alas, depends more on the execution than the intention.

Pietro Verri was concerned, as the title of his book suggests, to draw from the affair in question an argument against torture, by showing that the effect of torture had been to extort confessions to a crime that was physically and morally impossible. And his argument was as cogent as his intentions were noble and humane.

But from the history of a matter so complex as this (however briefly it may be described) and of so much evil inflicted without reason by men on their fellow men it should, I think, be possible to draw conclusions of a more general character and of an equal, if less immediate, utility. Indeed there is a danger in restricting one's comments only to such points as are most relevant to the particular argument referred to above; the danger, I mean, that the reader might come to take a view of the episode that would be not only incomplete but also false; for he might ascribe it to the ignorance prevalent in those times and to a barbarous legal system, and so come to think of it as necessary and inevitable; which would be to derive a harmful error from data which could be most instructive. Ignorance of natural science may have undesirable effects, but it cannot cause wickedness. Nor do bad institutions function automatically. It was certainly no necessary result of believing in the infectiousness of certain unguents to believe that Guglielmo Piazza and Gianciacomo Mora had used them; and the fact that the law in those days had recourse to torture did not compel the judges in this case to apply torture to all the accused, nor to find guilty all whom they tortured. This is a truth that may seem too obvious to be interesting; but it not infrequently happens that the most obvious truths, which ought to be taken for granted, are in fact forgotten; and it is only by not forgetting the truth I have stated that one can form a right judgement on that appalling sentence. What I have attempted, then, is to bring this truth into the light of day; to show clearly that those judges were guilty of condemning men who were innocent and men whose innocence they were perfectly capable of recognizing, notwithstanding their conviction of the infectiousness of the unguents and notwithstanding the laws permitting the use of torture. I will go further and say that in order to find those persons guilty, in order to suppress the truth which appeared and reappeared all the time in many forms and on every side, and with features as visible then as they are now and always will be, the judges had continually to exercise the utmost ingenuity and have recourse again and again to expedients of the injustice of which they could not have been ignorant. It would of course be absurd, and underhand, to attempt to deny that ignorance and torture had their share in the vile business. A deplorable ignorance gave the evil its chance in the first place, and torture was the cruel weapon it found ready to hand (though not, certainly, the only nor the chief one). But what matters, I think, is that we grasp the real and effective causes of what was done, which were iniquitous actions. And what could have produced these if not perverse passions?

Only God could see which of these causes was predominant in the hearts of those judges and subjugated their wills. Was it anger, stirred up by a vague sense of undefined dangers; an anger that desired an object on which to vent itself and so clutched at the first that came to hand; an anger impatient for evidence and that would not listen to the thought that the evidence in fact presented might be false; which had cried 'At last!' and now absolutely refused to say 'We must start again': an anger made pitiless by prolonged fear and now become a self-righteous hatred of its poor struggling victims? Or was it the fear of seeming not to respond to what the public was expecting, with an expectation as confident as it was hasty and rash; the fear of seeming less intelligent if the accused were found innocent; the fear that if the clamour of the crowd were not heeded it would turn against themselves; the fear too, perhaps, that resistance to that clamour might provoke a serious disturbance of the peace – which may seem a more respectable sort of fear but which is really no less evil and ignoble, if it usurp the place of that other, that genuinely wise and noble fear of committing an injustice? Only God could tell whether those magistrates who found people guilty of a crime they had never committed, but which others desired them to have committed,[1] were more the accomplices or the tools of a public blinded not by ignorance but by malignity and rage, and whose clamour for revenge was directly opposed to the divine law which it professed to revere. But lying, and abuse of power, and violation of the ordinary and obvious rules of behaviour, and playing tricks with the scales of justice – such things we can recognize in human actions too; and, having recognized them, we can relate them with absolute certainty to the passions which pervert the will. Nor need any other passions be looked for, as we seek to explain the objective iniquities of that judgement, than the anger and the fear I have mentioned: both natural enough, and both vile.

Such causes are not, unfortunately, confined to a particular age; nor can the fact that those passions, like all the others, drove men who were anything but wicked by profession to public or private wickedness be attributed solely to such ignorance of

---

[1] *Ut mos vulgo, quamvis falsis, reum subdere.* Tacitus, *Annales*, I, 39.*

natural science as may have occasioned their evil actions, or to their having had the power to inflict torture. 'If,' wrote Verri, 'only one torture the less be inflicted in future, as an effect of my having described these horrors, I shall consider that the grief that impels me to write will not have been in vain; and in this hope I find my consolation.'[2] And for my part I shall consider it well worth while to have reminded my readers of horrors they already know if, by so doing, I can stir their indignation also, and chiefly, against the influence of evil passions – which cannot indeed be discarded like false ideas, nor abolished like harsh institutions, but which can at least be rendered less potent and deadly by recognizing and detesting their effects.

Moreover this way of looking at the matter has its consoling side. If we regard a complex series of cruelties inflicted by man on man merely as the effect of times and circumstances, the horror and pity we feel is accompanied by a sense of discouragement, by a sort of despair. We seem to see human nature driven irresistibly to evil by forces beyond its control, caught in the coils of some perverse and exhausting dream which it can neither throw off nor even become clearly conscious of. And so the indignation that spontaneously springs up in us against the men who did such things begins itself to appear unreasonable, even while, at the same time, we feel it to be noble and religious. Our horror remains, but the deed itself seems to have lost its guilt; and our mind, seeking the true culprit, the right object for its revulsion, is dismayed to find itself hesitating between two alternatives, equally blasphemous and insane: a denial, or an indictment, of Providence. But if, on a closer examination of the facts, we are able to discern an injustice which those who committed it could themselves have recognized; a violation of rules which they themselves accepted; an acting in clean contradiction to principles not only admitted in that age but also evidently respected, in similar circumstances, by the very men who acted in this way – then we can with relief conclude that if these men knew not what they did it was because they did not choose to know, and that theirs was the kind of ignorance which man adopts and discards as he pleases: not an excuse for crime, but itself a crime; and that such things as they did may indeed be suffered, but not done, under compulsion.

With all this I do not want to suggest that Pietro Verri was

[2] Verri, *Osservazioni sulla tortura*, ch. vi.

entirely unaware of the personal and voluntary injustice of the judges in this case; but only that he did not make it his business to study this aspect of the matter, still less to prove that such injustice was the chief – or, more precisely, the sole – cause of the sentence which they passed. I would add that he could not have carried out this demonstration without, in effect, spoiling his case against torture; the upholders of which (for the most irrational institutions never lack supporters so long as there is life in them at all, and even when dead they often still find upholders for the same reasons which once kept them alive) would have turned the proof of the judges' wickedness into a defence of torture. 'Don't you see,' they would have replied, 'the fault is not in the system but in those who abuse it.' A strange defence indeed – to point out that something in any case absurd has also, in certain cases, served the passions as an instrument to commit deeds both absurd and atrocious. Such, however, is the usual reasoning of prejudiced minds. But in any case those who aimed, like Verri, at the abolition of torture had no wish to complicate their case with distinctions, nor to make torture itself seem less horrible by denouncing anything else. Experience shows that whoever strives to inculcate a truth which is in dispute is apt to find his own supporters, as well as his adversaries, a hindrance to its elucidation in a pure form. True, there is always that very numerous third party of the neutral, those with no concerns, no passions, for whom that truth has no interest whatsoever.

As regards the materials for the story I am about to relate, I must say at the outset that all my efforts to discover the original minutes of the trial – efforts which have met with the most courteous and diligent co-operation on the part of those who seemed best able to help me – have only led me to the conclusion that this document is irretrievably lost. A considerable portion of the minutes, however, survives in a copy. It happened that one of the accused, Don Juan Padilla (who I am sorry to say owed this unhappy position to one of his fellow victims), was a man of some importance, being the son of the governor of the Castle of Milan, a Knight of St James, and a captain in the cavalry. This gentleman was able to have a copy of his defence printed, to which he added an abstract of the trial communicated to him in his capacity as one formally charged with the crime in question. And certainly the judges had no suspicion, when they permitted the printing of this record, that they were erecting a monument more solid and enduring than that which they commissioned an architect to build.

There is also extant another copy, handwritten, in some places less complete, in others more so, of this abstract. It belonged to Conte Pietro Verri and was placed at my disposal, with a courtesy both generous and patient, by his son Conte Gabriele. It is this copy that was used by Verri in writing his book and it has marginal jottings in his hand reflecting the thoughts that passed through his mind, and the feelings of pity, distress, and indignation that moved him as he read it. It is entitled *Summarium offensivi contra Don Johannem Cajetanum de Padilla.* Many points are more fully reported in this copy than in the printed abstract. Numbers in the margins refer to the pages of the original minutes of the trial, and there are brief notes in Latin in the same handwriting as the text: *Detentio Morae; Descriptio domini Johannis; Adversatur commissario; Inverisimile; Subgestio,* etc. – obviously, notes made by the lawyer who was defending Padilla. From all this it appears that we have here a literal copy of the official abstract communicated to the defending counsel; and that when the latter had the text printed he left out certain matters as unimportant and gave a mere *résumé* of others. But why does the printed version include things omitted in the manuscript? A likely explanation is that the defending counsel had been able to re-read the original minutes and so make a fresh selection of material which he thought might be useful to his client.

From these two abstracts then, the printed one and the manuscript, I have naturally drawn most of my materials; and since the former has recently been reprinted (it had hitherto been extremely rare) the reader may, if he likes, use it to check the facts which I have culled from the manuscript copy.

The speeches for the defence, referred to above, have also provided certain facts and the material for some observations. As these have never been reprinted and very few copies are extant, I shall be careful to quote *verbatim* such passages from them as I shall have occasion to use.

Finally, a few details have been picked up from sundry scattered documents surviving from that confused and rather careless epoch, and now preserved in the archives to which reference was made, more than once, in the foregoing work.

To my account of the trial I thought it worth while to subjoin a brief history of the opinion held with regard to it down to the time of Verri, that is for a century and a half; I mean, the opinion which found expression in books, which is for the most part the only one of which subsequent generations can have any knowledge and which, in any case, has a special importance of its own. It will, I think, be found curious to watch a succession of writers following one after the other, like the sheep in Dante, without taking the slightest trouble to inform themselves about the matter on which they were writing. I say 'curious', not 'amusing'; for the spectator of that bitter conflict, which ended so horribly with a victory of error over truth and powerful rage over unarmed innocence, can feel nothing but distaste, I almost said exasperation, as he reads those words, by whichever author, which confirm and praise the error, those confident assertions on the basis of such unthinking credulity, those denunciations of the victims, that inverted indignation. Yet the distaste will not be futile if it serve to increase any reader's aversion from and distrust of the old and never sufficiently discredited habit of repeating things without examining them; of – if I may so express myself – serving the public with wine of its own making, and which has sometimes gone to its head already.

With this in mind I thought at first of putting before the reader all the judgements on the matter in hand of all the writers I had read who had anything to say about it. But on second thoughts I decided to spare the reader's patience. Better, I thought, to limit myself to a few authors, of whom none is completely obscure, and most are renowned: those, in other words, of whom even the errors are most instructive, when they can no longer be contagious.

At about half past four in the morning of 21 June 1630 it unfortunately happened that a woman was looking from the window of a sort of bridge which at that time crossed the Via della Vetra de' Cittadini at the end where it meets the Corso di Porta Ticinese, almost opposite the columns of San Lorenzo. The woman's name was Caterina Rosa. As she stood there she noticed a man in a black cloak with his hat pulled down over his eyes and in his hand a piece of paper on which, so she says in her deposition, 'he seemed to be writing'. She watched the man enter the street 'and draw near the wall immediately after turning the corner', and then 'from time to time draw his hands along the wall'. It was then, she said, 'that it occurred to me he might perhaps be one of the people who had recently been going about smearing the walls'. Her suspicions aroused, she went into another room, to a window that looked down the length of the street, in order to keep the stranger in view; 'and I saw', she said, 'that he kept on touching the walls with his hands'.

There was another watcher, at the window of a house in the same street, a woman called Ottavia Bono. Whether she formed the same crazy suspicion on her own account, or only after Caterina Rosa had started the rumour, we cannot say; in any case, on being interrogated, she too declared that she had seen the man from the moment of his entering the street, though she did not mention his touching the wall as he went along it. 'I saw him stop,' she said, 'at the end of the garden wall of the Crivelli's house, and I saw a paper in his hand on which he seemed to be writing with his right hand, and then I saw him raise this hand from the paper and rub it on the garden wall where there is a white patch.' The man was probably rubbing ink off his fingers, for he seems in fact to have been writing: at his interrogation the next day, when asked whether 'his actions that morning had anything to do with writing', he answered, 'Yes, my lord.' And as for his keeping close to the wall, a good enough reason for this was that it was raining, as Caterina herself mentioned, though she drew her own conclusion from the fact, saying: 'And mind you, this is important; it was raining yesterday when he was doing the smearing, and he must have chosen the time on purpose as then more people would get the stuff on their clothes, because they would go close to the wall for shelter.'

After stopping (as Ottavia said) the man turned back down the street again; he reached the corner and was about to pass out of sight when, again unfortunately, he was met by another man who entered the street and greeted him. Caterina Rosa, who by this time, to keep the 'smearer' in sight, had returned to her first window, asked the second man who it was he had greeted. The second man, as he was to declare later at the trial, replied that the other was someone he knew only by sight but that he knew he was a Health Commissioner. 'And I then said to him,' reports Caterina in her deposition, 'that I had seen the other man doing things I didn't like the look of at all. And then the news got around' (chiefly through her, of course), 'and people came out and saw the walls smeared with a sort of thick yellowish paste; and especially the people who live in Tradate said they had found the walls of the approach to their gate all smeared.' The other woman said the same. Asked if she knew why the man rubbed his hand on the wall, she answered, 'the walls were found smeared afterwards, especially round the Tradate gate.'

There are things here that would be reckoned implausible in a novel, though alas the blinding of reason by passion accounts for them only too well. It never occurred to either of these witnesses that in thus describing (especially the first witness) step by step the man's walk up the road and back, neither was able to say that he had entered that particular street; nor did it seem to them 'important' that he appeared to have taken no precautions not to be observed – despite the fact that he had waited until the sun was risen before starting his peculiar business; that he never even glanced up at the windows; that having passed up the street he calmly turned round and came down it again, as though criminals were in the habit of loitering in the place where they have just committed a crime; that he was handling with apparent impunity stuff that was supposed to kill those who 'got it on their clothes'; and many other equally strange improbabilities. But the strangest and most dreadful feature of all was that such things did not seem improbable to the official who interrogated the accused; that he asked for no explanations. Or, if he did, it is still worse that no mention of this was made in the trial.

The people of the neighbourhood hurriedly began to apply burning straw to the walls to burn off heaven knows how much dirt that had probably been there, under their eyes, for heaven knows how long before panic brought it to their notice. Giangiacomo Mora, the barber at the corner of the street, agreed with the rest that the walls of his house had been smeared; unaware, poor wretch, of the very different danger that threatened him from the aforesaid and, as it turned out, equally unlucky Health Commissioner.

The story told by the two women was quickly enriched with fresh details – or at any rate what they were afterwards to say to the Chief of Police did not exactly tally with what they had said to their neighbours. The son of the unfortunate Mora, on being asked later 'whether he knew for himself, or had heard, how the said Commissioner smeared the walls and houses', answered, 'I heard that one of the women who live in the arch that crosses Via Vetra (I don't know her name) said that he smeared with a pen, having a small jar in his hand.' And very likely Caterina Rosa did mention having seen a pen in the man's hand; and as for her 'small jar', its nature may easily be guessed; to a mind obsessed with smearing a pen must have seemed much more directly related to jars than inkpots.

Unfortunately, however, all the babble and chatter conveyed at least one true fact, that the man was a Health Commissioner, a clue which pointed at once to a certain Guglielmo Piazza, 'the son-in-law of midwife Paola', who must have been well known in the neighbourhood. The news spread to other quarters of the city, carried in part by someone who had happened to find himself where the hubbub began. It came to the ears of the Senate, which at once ordered the Chief of Police to collect information and take such action as was required. 'A report has come to the Senate,' said the Chief of Police to the notary whom he took with him on his investigations, 'that yesterday morning the walls and houses of Via Vetra de' Cittadini were smeared with a deadly paste.' With these words – so full already of a lamentable assurance, passing as they did, without the slightest correction, from the mouth of the people to that of the authorities – the case was opened.

So firm a conviction, such insane terror of a crime that was never committed, may well remind my readers of events which took place a few years ago, in various parts of Europe, at the time of the cholera epidemic. But there is this difference, that in the latter case no one with any education (with a few exceptions) shared that disastrous belief; indeed most people did what they could to combat it. And no one was arrested by the authorities on suspicion of similar 'crimes', unless it was to save the person suspected from the fury of the mob. A great improvement, certainly; but even were it greater, even if one could be sure that similar pretexts would never again give rise to the same sort of persecution, still one cannot be certain that the danger of such follies – which would differ indeed as to their subject matter, but not necessarily as to their mode of expression – is altogether a thing of the past. Man can, alas, deceive himself, and terribly deceive himself, on much less absurd presuppositions. A similar fear and fury can equally well be provoked by evils that may really be, and sometimes are, an effect of human depravity; and fear and fury, when not controlled by reason and charity, are unhappily liable, on the flimsiest pretexts and following the wildest assertions, to presume the guilt of men who are simply unfortunate. For example, not so long ago – a little before the cholera epidemic – when there was an outbreak of fires in Normandy, what was it led the mob to fix the guilt, immediately, on one particular man? Simply that he was the first they found on the spot or near it; that he was a stranger and could give no satisfactory account of himself (a thing doubly difficult when a man is terrified and his interrogators angry); that he was accused by a woman of the type of Caterina Rosa and by a boy who, himself suspected of being an accomplice and being ordered to say who had told him to start the fires, gave the first name that came into his head. Happy the juries appointed to try the accused (when there *was* a trial, for more than once in fact the mob itself carried out its own sentence), if they entered the court fully persuaded that so far they knew nothing at all; if their minds were deaf to the clamour outside; if their thought was not: 'We are the People' (one of those abstractions which only too often blind men to the particular and proper nature of the facts before them, and are especially odious and cruel when the People have already made up their ignorant minds on the matter) – but rather: 'We are a group of men entrusted with the sacred, necessary, and fearful authority – and with this authority only – of deciding whether other men are guilty or innocent.'

The man whom the Chief of Police had been advised to interrogate had nothing to say, except that on the previous day he had seen people scorching the walls of Via della Vetra, and that he had heard that these had been smeared that morning by 'the son-in-law of midwife Paola'. The Chief, with his notary, went to the place indicated, saw the fire-blackened walls, and noticed that those of one house, the barber Mora's, had just been whitewashed. And they too were told, by people there, the reason for the scorching: the walls had been smeared. 'The Chief of Police and I,' wrote the notary, 'saw, in fact, on the burnt patches traces of a yellowish pasty stuff, as if someone had been smearing with his fingers.' What a way to check evidence of crime!

A woman in the house of the Tradati was questioned: she had found the walls of the street 'dirtied with some yellow stuff, a lot of it'. Caterina Rosa and Ottavia Bono were questioned, and we know how they replied. Some other persons were questioned who had nothing to say that threw any light on the facts; among these, the man who had met and greeted the Health Commissioner; asked whether 'he had seen dirt on the walls of Via Vetra' he said, 'I didn't take any notice, because nothing had yet been said about it.'

An order was already out for the arrest of Piazza, and this was easily effected. On the same day, the 22nd, 'one of the Baricello di Campagna guard reported to the aforesaid Chief of Police, the latter being still in his carriage on the way home . . . how he had found the aforesaid Guglielmo standing at the doorway of the Lord Senator Monti, President of the Tribunal of Health, and had taken him off to prison as ordered'. That this evident unconsciousness of peril on the part of the Commissioner did nothing to diminish the judges' suspicion of him is a fact that can certainly not be explained away by the ignorance of those times. Those judges knew that the flight of a suspected person was technically an indication of guilt; odd then that this man's *not* fleeing, and so obviously not fleeing, was not taken as indicating the contrary! But it would be ridiculous to demonstrate that men could see things that one could not help seeing: one can always choose to ignore them.

Piazza's house was immediately and thoroughly searched, *in omnibus arcis, capsis, scriniis, cancellis, sublectis,* for jars of unguent and for money. Nothing was found; *nihil penitus compertum fuit.* But not even this was of the least use to him, as became only too clear at his first examination, that very day, by the Chief of Police, assisted by an auditor supplied, probably, by the Tribunal of Health.

He was questioned about his profession, his usual occupations, the walk he had taken the previous day, the clothes he had been wearing. Finally he was asked: 'Whether he knew anything about any fouling of the walls of the houses of the city, especially in the neighbourhood of Porta Ticinese.' He answered: 'I know nothing about it; I never spend any time in Porta Ticinese.' They replied 'Not plausible'; they wanted to prove he knew something. Four times they asked, four times he gave the same answer in different words. They then passed to other matters, but keeping the same end in view. And we shall see why presently; we shall see what cruel cunning was concealed in their insistence on that 'implausibility', and their hunt for others like it.

Among the events of the previous day mentioned by Piazza in his replies was his having met with some 'parochial deputies' – gentlemen chosen from each parish by the Tribunal of Health to see that its orders were carried out. Asked for the names of these deputies, Piazza answered that he knew them only by sight, not by name. Again the reply came: 'implausible'. A terrible word. To make its full meaning clear I must ask the reader now to bear with some rather general considerations on the criminal law procedure of those times. I shall be as brief as the matter allows.

CHAPTER 2

As everyone knows, that procedure was regulated principally, both in this country and nearly everywhere else in Europe, by the authority of the writers on the law; and for the simple reason that in most cases it was the only authority available. For the absence of any accepted legal system framed for society as a whole had two consequences: that those who interpreted the law became in effect its makers; and that their authority to do so was pretty generally admitted. When what needs doing is left undone by those whose business it is to do it – or, if done at all is incompetently done – then there will always be found people who think they can supply the lack, and others who are prepared to accept whatever is provided, regardless of who provides it. Nothing is harder and more wearisome than to live without rules of some kind.

For example, the Statutes of Milan* laid down no other rules or conditions with regard to the power to torture a man accused of crime (a power itself admitted implicitly by everybody, as a natural consequence of the right to put such a man on trial) than that the accusation be supported by public opinion; that the crime in question be punishable by death; and that there be some evidence of guilt – the degree of evidence being, however, left vague. On this last point the Roman law itself, which operated in cases not foreseen by the Statutes, was no more precise, though it had more to say. 'The judges,' it declared, 'must not begin with torture; they must first have recourse to arguments both plausible and probative. But if, having weighed the matter, they consider that they have sufficient grounds to warrant the use of torture in order to find out the truth, then let them use it, having regard to the condition of the accused.'[1] In fact the Roman law explicitly left it to the judges' discretion to decide as to the quality and force of the evidence in each case; and this power of the judiciary was presupposed by the Statutes of Milan.

The so-called New Constitutions*, promulgated by order of Charles V, do not even mention torture; and thenceforward, down to the period of our trial and for a long while after, though many decrees were passed mentioning that torture could be used as a punishment, there was not one, so far as I know, that regulated its use as a means of obtaining proof.

And here again the reason is not far to seek. What was at first an effect had become a cause; a substitute had been found, here as elsewhere, for the legislative authority, and especially in the sphere of judicial procedure; a substitute that operated in such a way as to make the need for any intervention of that authority to be felt less and less, to the point of being almost forgotten. The writers on the law, particularly from the time that mere commentaries on Roman law began to decrease and works of a more independent character, whether on criminal procedure as a whole or on this or that special point, began to increase, took to elaborating their material systematically and at the same time with a minute attention to detail; creating new laws by reinterpretations of the old; extending their application by comparing case with case, and so drawing general rules out of particular decisions. And where all this still seemed insufficient they provided rules of their own in line with what they thought reason or equity or natural law required; and doing this sometimes concordantly – one writer copying and quoting the others – and sometimes not. And the result was that the judges – men trained in the subject and sometimes themselves writers of this kind –

[1] *Codex*, IX, tit. 41, 'De quaestionibus', l.8.

came to have to hand, in almost every case and for every detail of each case, a set of ready-made conclusions to follow or to choose from. Law, in fact had become a body of knowledge, a science. And it was to this science, that is, to the Roman law so interpreted, and to such ancient customs of various regions as had not been obliterated by the authority of Roman law, and were interpreted in the same way, as well as to such customs as were approved by the jurists, along with the latters' precepts now become customary, it was to all this that the name 'Law' came to be almost exclusively applied; whereas the acts of the ruling authority in the State were merely entitled 'orders', 'decrees', 'proclamations', and so forth, and had about them an air of things vaguely contingent and temporary. To give one example, the proclamations of the government of Milan (which was certainly a legislative authority) were valid only so long as a particular government held office; so that the first act of its successor was always provisionally to confirm them. Each *grida-rio*, as it was called, was a sort of Praetor's Edict made for the time being, as the occasion required. But legal science, on the other hand, was continually operative and over the whole field. It developed indeed and changed, but only by degrees too small to be noticed. Those who were masters in it had always started their careers as pupils. One might almost call it a continual revision, in part a continual recompilation, of the original Twelve Tables, entrusted, or rather relinquished, to a perpetual Decemvirate.

Now this age-long and extensive authority of private persons over public law came in time to be regarded – and, if I am not mistaken, is still regarded – as a thing anomalous in itself and pernicious in its effects; especially in the sphere of the criminal law, and more particularly in that of the procedure of the courts. Opposition to it began when men became aware of the desirability and the possibility of abolishing it and of replacing it by a new legal system more complete and precise and logical than the old. Yet we have seen that the old system was in its way a natural product; nor had it arisen as a novelty, but rather as a sort of extraordinary extension of a very ancient practice destined perhaps, in one form or another, to go on forever; for let laws be as precise as you please, they will always, perhaps, require interpretation; and perhaps judges will always be inclined – at one time more, at another less – to have recourse, for the law's interpretation, to writers who have established themselves as the acknowleged experts on the subject as a whole. And for my part

I am not at all sure that, on a calmer and more thorough examination of the facts, we should not have to conclude that the authority of those old jurists was, relatively and comparatively speaking, beneficial; for the state of affairs that preceded it had been far worse.

For after all it is improbable that men accustomed to take into consideration a great number of possible cases, and to endeavour to regulate these either by existing positive law or by more general and higher principles, should recommend procedures more unjust and more unreasonable, more violent and more capricious than such as are only too likely to commend themselves to an authority which deals *ad hoc* with one case after another, in a field so wide open to the passions. The very number of volumes and authors, the multiplicity and ever-increasing particularization of the rules they prescribed are themselves some indication of a desire at work to set limits to the play of arbitrary power and to guide it, so far as was possible, towards reason and justice. Men do not need minute instructions on how to abuse power. If you want a horse to run wild, you don't lecture him on the art of running; just off with his bridle, if he has one!

But so it is as a rule with reforms that are brought in by degrees (I mean real and just reforms, not everything so named). To those who first embark on a course of reform some slight alteration of the *status quo* seems already much – a correcting this or that particular abuse, an adding here, a removing there. But for those who come on the scene later, and sometimes much later, and who find, rightly, much still to blame in the system as it stands, it is only too easy to stop short at a superficial judgement as to the causes of the system; to denounce as its creators those whose name it bears, and which it bears only because they were the men who gave it the form in which it continues to exist and be powerful.

A mistake such as this was made, I think, by the author of *Osservazioni sulla tortura*, along with other distinguished men of his time. It was almost an enviable mistake, the kind of error that sometimes accompanies great and beneficent innovations. But the force and cogency with which Pietro Verri demonstrated the irrationality, injustice, and cruelty of the hideous practice of torture was only equalled by the rashness, as I would call it, with which he attributed all that was worst in it to the authority of those writers of the law. And certainly it is not as claiming any superiority to so justly celebrated a man, nor as ignoring the nobility of his work, that I venture to criticize Verri on this point. It is merely that I have had the luck to be born later and that I have the advantage (taking as my principal theme a point which for him was quite secondary) of being able to study dispassionately, and with an eye to its effects as a whole and in its historical setting, a system which he had to challenge at a time when it still held the field and stood as a powerful obstacle to novel and urgently-needed reforms. And in any case the matter I speak of here is so much part and parcel of our common theme that neither he nor I could avoid discussing it – not Verri, because, the authority of the writers on the law being acknowledged by the men responsible for that iniquitous sentence of the court of Milan, he regarded it as an accomplice and part cause of the iniquity itself; not I, because, having closely studied what this authority prescribed and taught, I am in a position to use it as a subsidiary but very important standard of comparison to bring out the *peculiar* iniquity, as I would call it, of that sentence.

'It is certain,' wrote Verri (his judgement a little disturbed by strong feeling), 'that our laws give no ruling as to who may be tortured, nor as to the circumstances which may justify torture, nor as to the manner of its application (whether by burning, dislocation, or wounding), nor as to the duration of the agony, nor as to the number of times it may be repeated. All this tormenting of human beings depends purely on a decision of the judge, guided by nothing but the teaching of the aforesaid criminal jurists.'[2]

But those laws of ours explicitly prescribed torture; and not our laws only but those of a great part of Europe, not to mention the Roman law which for so long had the name and authority of a universal code; all explicitly prescribed torture.[3] Hence the real question is whether the writings of the interpreters* (as I shall call the old jurists, to distinguish them from those who were to

[2] Verri, op. cit., ch. xiii.

[3] England was an exception. In the English criminal courts the guilt or innocence of an accused person did not depend on his answers to interrogation; and this indirectly ruled out the cruel and deceptive method of extracting confession of guilt by torture. In the kingdom of Aragon, too, Francesco Casoni and Antonio Gomez bear witness to the fact that, at least in their day, torture was not employed; and the same can be said of Sweden, on the evidence of Giovanni Loccenio as quoted by Ottone Tabor. I do not know whether any other European country was immune from this evil, or had succeeded in getting rid of it, before the eighteenth century.

have the merit, and the good fortune, of finally discrediting
them), whether these writings were such as to tend to make
torture more or less cruel than it actually was in the hands of the
judges to whom the law almost entirely, in fact, committed its
execution. And the strongest argument in those writers' favour is
hinted at, to say the least, by Verri himself when he says: 'the
same Farinacci, speaking of things that occurred in his own time,
says that the judges used to devise new tortures in order to gratify
the pleasure they took in inflicting pain on those accused of
crime, *judices qui propter delectationem quam habent torquendi
reos inveniunt novas tormentorum species*'.[4]

I say in those writers' favour because such appeals to the
judiciary to cease inventing new methods of torture – along with
other more general reproaches and complaints which bear witness both to the ingenious and unbridled cruelty of those who
had the power to pass sentence and to a desire, at least, to expose
this cruelty and stop it – are to be found not in Farinacci only
but in nearly all the writings of the criminal jurists. The very
words quoted above were borrowed by Farinacci from an earlier
writer, Francesco da Bruno, who in turn took them from another
still earlier, Angelo d'Arezzo, together with other and yet stronger
expressions which I give here in translation: 'corrupt and savage
judges whom God will punish; ignorant judges, whose doings are
abhorrent to every enlightened and virtuous mind'.[5]

Again, as early as the thirteenth century, earlier than any of
the writers already cited, we find Guido da Suzara declaring his
desire 'to put some check on the excessive cruelty of the judges'
(this in a discussion of torture where the writer refers to a rescript
of Constans on the detention of criminals).[6] Again, in the century
following, Baldo turned the famous rescript of Constantine about
masters who killed their slaves against 'judges who mangle the
bodies of prisoners in order to extort confession of guilt'; if the
prisoner, he says, dies under torture the judge should be beheaded
for murder.[7] Later, Paride dal Pozzo inveighed against those
'blood-thirsty judges who love to inflict torture, not as a just
retribution for crime, nor to deter others from crime, but only to

---

[4] Verri, op. cit., ch. viii. Farinacci, *Praxis et theoricae criminalis*, I, tit. 5, Q.
xxxviii, 56.
[5] Fr. a Bruno, *De indiciis et tortura*, Part 2, Q. ii, 7.
[6] G. de Suzara, *De tormentis*, I, Cod.IX, tit.4, l.2.
[7] B. de Ubaldis, commenting on *Codex*, IX, tit.14, 3.

exalt themselves (*propter gloriam eorum*). They are no better than murderers.'[8] Again, Giulio Claro writes: 'let the judge beware of applying strange tortures not approved by custom; otherwise he were better called a butcher than a judge'.[9] 'We must vehemently denounce (*clamandum est*),' says Antonio Gomez, 'those pitiless judges who devise new tortures for prisoners brought before them; their motive is mere glory and self-interest.'[10] Pleasure and glory! What extraordinary passions to have in such a matter! To enjoy inflicting pain on a fellow man and take pride in humiliating one who lies at your mercy! But at least the writers who drew attention to such motives cannot be supposed to have favoured them.

Let me remark in passing, *à propos* of these texts and of others that I shall adduce, that in all the relevant literature known to me I have not found a single complaint against a judge for using torture too leniently. Should a text of this kind be brought to my notice I would regard it as a genuine curiosity.

Some of the authors I have cited or shall cite are included in a list drawn up by Verri of 'writers who, if they had expressed their inhuman principles in the vernacular, and their careful descriptions of nicely calculated torments in a style less insufferably barbarous to any sensitive and civilized reader, could hardly have escaped that abhorrence and contempt with which we regard tortures themselves'.[11] Well, certainly the things these authors describe are quite horrible; and the things they acquiesced in we rightly abhor; but whether what they themselves contributed, or wished to contribute, to the system be matter for abhorrence and contempt is a question concerning which there may, even on the evidence so far adduced, be two opinions.

In their books – or rather in some of them – it is true that the various methods of torture are set out in greater detail than they appear in the legal codes; but as accepted and customary practices, not as inventions of our authors. And Ippolito Marsigli, a jurist and judge of the fifteenth century who gives, in part from his own experience, a ghastly and grotesque and disgusting list of such methods, nevertheless calls those judges 'bestial' who seek to devise new ones.[12]

---

[8] P. de Puteo, *De Syndicatu*, 'Crudelitas officialis', 5.

[9] J. Clarus, *Sententiarum receptarum*, V, Q. lxiv, 36.

[10] A. Gomez, *Variarumque resolut.*, III, ch. 13, 5.

[11] Op. cit., ch. xiii.

[12] Hipp. de Marsiliis, *Ad tit. Digest. de quaestionibus*; § 'In criminibus', 29.

Again, it was, to be sure, these writers who brought up the question how often a torture might be repeated; but, as we shall see, they did so precisely to set some limits and conditions on arbitrary power; taking advantage of the vagueness and ambiguity of Roman law on this point. Again, it was they who discussed the length of time appropriate to each application of a given torture; but once more, this was to impose limits, to put some control (the law itself putting none) on the tireless cruelty of 'certain judges, as ignorant as they are wicked, who will go on torturing a man for a space of three or four hours'. So wrote Farinacci,[13] and a century earlier Marsigli had inveighed against 'certain unjust judges, infamous wretches from the dregs of society, without knowledge, virtue or reason: when they get a man in their power perhaps in error (*forte indebite*) they refuse to speak to him until he is actually under torture, and if he does not reply as they wish they leave him hanging at the rope's end all day and night'.[14]

The reader will have noticed, in these passages and in others I have quoted, that the idea of cruelty is linked with that of ignorance. Knowledge, no less than conscience, is invoked on the side of moderation, humanity, kindness – all infuriating words I admit, in a context such as this, but they do at least show that those who used them aimed at taming the monster, not goading it on.

As for the statement that 'our laws' gave no rulings as to who could be subjected to torture, I cannot see that this matters in view of the relative abundance of directives on this unsavoury point provided by the Roman law, which was in effect ours also.

Verri continues his indictment:

Ignorant and brutal men, indifferent to those questions of principle without a firm grasp of which it is impossible to frame a system of laws in harmony with nature and reason and conducive to the good of society; men who never thought of asking themselves whence comes the right to punish crime, or what is the purpose of punishment, or how to gauge the gravity of crimes and their relation to punishment, or whether a man may ever be constrained to surrender his right to self-defence; men of no standing in society, mere private individuals, they took it on themselves to elaborate

---

[13] *Praxis*, Q. xxxviii, 54.
[14] *Practica causarum criminalium*; § 'Expedita', 86.

with ignoble subtlety a system for inflicting the maximum pain on their fellow men, and then solemnly to publish their conclusions with all the impassivity of physicians recommending remedies for disease; and such men were set up as authorities, nay as legislators, and the books in which they give careful instructions as to how to dislocate living bodies and how precisely to prolong its agonies and add pain to pain, these inhuman writings found a welcome in all legal libraries and were seriously and calmly studied.

But really, is it credible that men of no social standing or culture – I mean, social standing in their own day and culture by the standards of their time – should have been allowed so much authority? For the question is necessarily a relative one; it is not whether those writers were as enlightened as one would wish legislators to be, but whether they were more or less so than the men who had formerly applied, indeed to a large extent invented, the law on their own bare authority. And how can the man who works out theories in the abstract and then debates them in public be more brutal than the man who exercises his judgement in private on those who resist it?

As for Verri's series of questions, it would be extremely awkward if the first one, 'Whence comes the right to punish crime?', had to be answered before anyone could draft a reasonably satisfactory penal code. No doubt Verri's contemporaries thought they had found the right answer, but today the question is more controversial than ever – and a good thing too, for it is better to be perplexed and uncertain than peacefully in error. And the other questions, those of more immediate and practical importance, were they answered and answered correctly, had they even been examined and discussed, when our writers came on the scene? Are we to believe that the emergence of these writers upset some juster and more humane system? That their follies replaced a long heritage of wisdom? Put out of court a better reasoned and more reasonable jurisprudence? The answer, obviously, is no; and this suffices for my immediate argument. But I could wish that some competent scholar would take the matter further; would examine, that is, whether it was not on the contrary our jurists who, precisely because they were private persons and not legislators, and so were perforce obliged to back their conclusions with reasons, were not in fact the first to relate the whole matter to general principles, by collecting and co-ordinating such principles as lay scattered through the body of

Roman law and seeking to complete them by others drawn from the abstract idea of justice; whether it was not these writers who, in their endeavour to form a complete and coherent system of criminal practice out of old and new materials, did in fact adumbrate the concept and indicate the possibility – and in part the pattern – of a complete and coherent criminal law; whether, in short, their conception of an ideal order in this matter did not open the way to other writers – by whom they have been too summarily condemned – to conceive the idea of a general reform.

As for the accusation, so sweeping and unqualified, that our authors 'took it on themselves to elaborate with ignoble subtlety a system for inflicting the maximum pain', we have seen, on the contrary, that this is what most of them expressly detested and did their utmost to prevent. Many too of the texts cited could serve to acquit them of a cold impassivity in their treatment of the matter; let me quote once more from Farinacci: 'I cannot contain my fury (*non possum nisi vehementer excandescere*) against the judges who keep a man bound in chains day after day before putting him to torture; this is adding cruelty to cruelty.'[15] Words that seem to protest in advance against Verri's charge.

In fact, from the evidence adduced and from all we know of the practice of torture in its latest period, we can in all sincerity conclude that the interpreters of the criminal law left that practice a great deal less barbarous than they found it. It would of course be absurd to attribute this improvement to one cause alone, but it also seems to me unreasonable not to reckon among its many causes the censures and warnings repeated publicly, time and again down the centuries, by writers who, as their critics themselves point out, did have a certain authority over the practice of the courts.

Verri goes on to cite some of their statements, though not enough to support a general historical judgement, even were these all cited accurately. Here, for example, is an important one cited inaccurately: 'Claro asserts that, to put a man to torture, it suffices that there is some evidence against him.'[16] If Claro had really said that, it would be an oddity rather than an argument, so much opposed is it to what a host of other interpreters said. But in fact Claro says just the contrary. Verri was probably misled by a misprint: he read *nam sufficit adesse aliqua indicia*

[15] *Praxis*, Q. xxxviii, 38.
[16] Op. cit., ch. viii.

contra reum ad hoc ut torqueri possit,[17] instead of the *non sufficit*, etc., which I find in two earlier editions of the text.* But in order to become aware of his error Verri did not need to compare texts; he had only to continue reading the one before his eyes, which goes on: 'if such evidence be not legally proved', a phrase which would clash with the antecedent clause if this were in the affirmative. And note how Claro continues:

> I have said that it does not suffice that there is evidence (*dixi quoque non sufficere*); but even legal proof does not make such evidence sufficient, if this be not of a kind sufficient to justify torture; which is a point that God-fearing judges ought always to bear in mind lest they inflict torture unjustly. And if they do such injustice then they themselves must answer to the court of appeal; and de Afflictis tells of a reply that he made to King Frederick, that not even the king had authority to order a judge to put a man to the torture, against whom there was no sufficient evidence.

So speaks Claro, and his words make it fairly clear that Verri has misunderstood another sentence which he renders as follows: 'in the matter of torture and evidence of guilt, since one cannot prescribe a definite rule, everything is left to the decision of the judge.'[18] Verri understands this as allowing an absolute authority to the judiciary. But the contradiction would be too glaring if this were the true meaning of Claro's words; and it becomes, if anything, still more so in the light of another passage: 'although it belongs to the judge to give judgement, he must respect the common norms of justice ... and let the agents of justice take care not to proceed too boldly (*ne nimis animose procedant*), on the pretext that the decision lies with them'.[19]

What then is the sense of that *remittitur arbitrio judicis* which Verri renders as 'everything is left to the decision of the judge'?

It means ... but good heavens, why look for Claro's personal opinion in these words? In writing them he was merely repeating a commonplace, a conventional tag that turns up in all these writers. Bartolo refers to it as a commonplace: *Doctores communiter dicunt quod in hoc* (the question of what evidence suffices to justify torture) *non potest dari certa doctrina, sed relinquitur arbitrio judicis*.[20]* And for the jurists this was simply

[17] Clarus, op. cit., V, Q. lxiv, 12.
[18] Op. cit., ch. viii.
[19] Clarus, op. cit., V, Q. lxiv, 13.
[20] Bartolus de Saxoferrato, *Ad lib. Digest.* XLVIII, tit. 18, l. 22.

a matter of fact, not of theory or principle: since in fact the law did not specify the evidence required, it left this to the judge to decide in each case. So Guido da Suzara, writing about a century before Bartolo, after stating or repeating the same dictum, that the decision as to the evidence was left to the judge, adds, 'as, in general, every matter that the law leaves undetermined'.[21] Again, to cite a later authority, Paride dal Pozzo, having repeated the same formula, comments: 'where neither law nor custom has fixed the procedure, the wisdom of the judge must supply the defect; which is why this matter of evidence of guilt lays a grave responsibility on his conscience'.[22] And finally Bossi, a fifteenth-century writer on criminal law and a Senator of Milan, writes: 'judgement here only means (*in hoc consistit*) that the judge can look for no definite ruling from the law, which merely states that he must begin with probable and plausible arguments. His business, then, is to discover whether a given piece of evidence is plausible and probable'.[23]

In short, what they called 'decision' or 'judgement' was the same as what later, to avoid that equivocal and fearsome word, came to be called discretionary power; a thing which, though dangerous, is inevitable in the application of laws whether good or bad, and which a wise legislator will always endeavour, not to abolish, for that would be impossible, but to limit to certain well-defined circumstances of minor importance; restricting its application, as far as possible, even in these. And such, I venture to say, was the aim from first to last of our laborious interpreters, and particularly in the matter of torture where the law left a terrifying range of power to the judges. Thus Bartolo, after the words I quoted above, adds, 'but I will give such rules as I can'. Others before him had given rules, and his successors in their turn added more, some proposing rules of their own, others recalling and approving those of their predecessors; but none omitting to repeat the formula which expressed the law as it stood in fact; for they were, after all, only the law's interpreters.

But with the passing of time and as their work progressed, they began to express a desire that the formula itself be modified. We can see this in Farinacci, who wrote after the authors I have been citing in the last few paragraphs, but before the period of the

---

[21] *De tormentis*, 30.
[22] *De Syndicatu*, 'Mandavit', 5, 18.
[23] Aegidius Bossi, *Tractatus varii*, 'De indiciis ante torturam', 32.

trial that we are studying, when he was reckoned a major authority. After repeating and confirming, with a great parade of authorities, the principle that a judge's power of decision 'must not be regarded as free and absolute but as bound by justice and equity'; after deducing and confirming, with more authorities, the consequence that 'the judge ought to lean towards mercy, conform his judgement to the general tenor of the law and the teaching of approved authors, and refrain from manipulating evidence as he pleases'; after discussing, at greater length I believe, and more systematically than anyone had hitherto done, the kinds of relevant evidence, Farinacci concludes in these terms: 'Thus it appears that the traditionally accepted ruling of learned authorities – that whether the evidence justifies torture is to be left to the free decision of the judges – has been so much and so concordantly limited by the same authorities that not without reason many jurists maintain that the contrary ruling should hold, namely that this assessment of the evidence should never be subject to the judge's decision.'[24] And he cites Francesco Casoni: 'It is a common error of judges to think that whether torture is to be used or not depends entirely on their own good pleasure; as though Nature had formed the bodies of prisoners only that judges might inflict pain on them at will.'[25]

With these words we come in sight of an important moment in the history of legal science: it is taking stock of its achievements and is claiming that the time has come to give effect to its findings. Not that it declares openly for reform; it did not presume so far, nor would such presumption have been tolerated. But, declaring itself a real co-operator with the positive law, and appealing in support of its own authority to that of a higher, eternal law, it admonishes the judges to conform their practice to its findings; and this both for the sake of those who would otherwise suffer without cause and for the sake of the judges themselves, who would otherwise be guilty of shameful injustice. We may think these efforts rather pathetic, applied as they were to a practice which of its nature could never be made acceptable; but they do at least make nonsense of Verri's contention that 'what is horrible is not merely the suffering caused by torture . . .

---

[24] *Praxis*, Q. xxxvii, 193–200.
[25] Fr. Casoni, *Tractatus de tormentis*, ch. i, 10.

but also the teaching of the jurists on the circumstances attending its application'.[26]

I have not space to examine all the texts quoted by Verri, though a thorough treatment of the question would require this and more: but I may be allowed one last observation. It concerns his reference to Claro in the following passage:

> Let one horror stand for all, one that we learn of from Claro, the celebrated Milanese jurist and a main authority on this matter. 'When a woman,' he writes, 'is in prison under suspicion of some crime, the judge concerned with her case has the right to have her brought secretly to his room and there caress her and pretend to be in love with her, promising her freedom on condition she confess her guilt. It was thus that a certain judge induced a young woman to confess the crime of murder and so was able to have her beheaded.' And lest anyone imagine that I exaggerate in recounting this horrible violation of religion and virtue and the most sacred principles of human life, here are Claro's very words: *Paris dicit quod judex potest*, etc.[27]

Horrible indeed: but what are the facts? In the first place, this Paris (Paride dal Pozzo) was not stating a private opinion; he was recounting, and alas with approval, something actually done by a judge, one of a thousand misdeeds caused by the arbitrary power of the judiciary and without the slightest encouragement from the jurists.[28] In the second place, observe that Baiardi, who mentions this opinion in his supplement to Claro (Claro himself does not refer to it), does so only in order to express his abhorrence and to denounce the judge in question as a 'diabolical deceiver'.[29] In the third place, Baiardi cites not a single other author in support of Paride's opinion during the hundred years that elapsed between Paride and himself. And it would be stranger still to find it upheld in any later period. And as for Paride, heaven preserve us from calling him, as Giannone* does, an 'excellent jurist'[30], but other words of his which I have already quoted suffice to show that even he is not quite fairly represented by the deplorable passage to which Verri refers.

---

[26] Op. cit., ch. viii.

[27] Op. cit., ch. viii.

[28] Paridis de Puteo, *De syndicatu*, 'Et advertendum est'.

[29] *Ad Clari Sentent. recept.*, V, Q. lxiv, 24; additions 80, 81.

[30] *Istoria civile*, Book 28, last chapter.

In all this I do not of course claim to have proved that the teaching of the interpreters of the law, taken as a whole, was not a factor making for evil, as having been turned to evil uses. A most interesting question this – involving as it does an assessment of the aims and general effects of intellectual labours that extended over several centuries and had to do with matters of vital importance for mankind. It is a question for our own time, for, as I have already remarked and as indeed everyone knows, the moment when one is engaged in overturning a system is not the best one in which to write its history. But this question cannot be resolved, that history cannot be written in a few disconnected observations such as I have offered in this chapter. Let these serve, however, as I think they will, to show that the view of the matter I criticized was one too hastily adopted. In a way, too, they introduce the narrative that follows, for in the course of this we shall often have occasion to regret that the authority of the writers on the law was not more effective. Indeed I feel sure that my readers will join with me in saying, 'If only they had been obeyed!'

CHAPTER 3

To come, finally, to the application, it was the usual, almost universal teaching of the law-writers that if an accused man lied to the judge who was interrogating him this amounted to 'legitimate evidence', as they called it, sufficient to justify torture. Hence the reply made to the unfortunate Piazza, under interrogation, that it was 'not plausible' that he should not have heard of the fouling of the walls around Porta Ticinese, nor have known the names of those deputies with whom he had had dealings.

But did they teach that any lie would suffice?

'To constitute evidence sufficient to justify torture the lie must be connected with the nature of the crime and its essential circumstances (namely such as pertain to the crime in such a way that it could be inferred from them). Otherwise it does not suffice: *alias secus*.' Again: 'A lie is not relevant to the question of torture if it concerns matters which would not be to the disadvantage of the accused had he confessed them.'[1]

---

[1] Farinacci, *Praxis*, Q. lii, 11, 14.

Moreover, was it enough, in the view of the same authorities, to justify torture, if it merely seemed to the judge that the accused had lied?

'To be evidence justifying torture the lie must be conclusively proved, either by the accused's own confession or by two witnesses . . ., it being commonly accepted that two witnesses are required to establish a piece of "remote evidence" such as a lie.'[2] I am citing, and shall often cite, Farinacci, who was reckoned a major authority at that time and was a diligent collector of the more commonly held opinions. Some jurists, it is true, were content with only one witness, provided he or she were thoroughly trustworthy. But that a lie had to be proved by the forms of law, and could not rest merely on the judge's conjecture, was common doctrine contradicted by no one.

These conditions were deduced from the clause in the Roman law which forbade the judge to begin a trial with torture (the things men have to forbid, once other things are allowed!).

> If the judges [wrote Farinacci] were authorized to use torture on prisoners in the absence of legitimate and sufficient evidence, this would amount to allowing them to begin with torture. . . . And by legitimate evidence is meant such as is plausible and probable; not trivial indications nor mere formalities, but weighty, serious, certain, and clear evidence – clear as daylight, as people say. . . . It is a question of handing a man over to torture, and to torture that might prove fatal (*agitur de hominis salute*). Do not wonder then, you severe judges, that the law and the men learned in it require evidence so precise and so definite, and have expressed this requirement so emphatically and so often.[3]

I would not say, to be sure, that such pronouncements as these were rational. How could they be? They involved self-contradiction. They represented a hopeless attempt to combine certainty and uncertainty; an endeavour to avoid the risk of torturing the innocent and of extorting false confessions of guilt, while at the same time admitting torture as precisely the means for discovering whether a man was innocent or guilty by compelling him to confess his guilt. The logical consequence of the underlying intention would have been to say outright that torture was absurd and unjust: but against this stood the barrier of a blind

[2] Ibid., 13.
[3] Op. cit., Q. xxxvii, 2, 3, 4.

reverence for antiquity and the Roman law. That little book *Dei delitti e delle pene* which played a notable part not only in the abolition of torture but in the reform of all our criminal legislation, opened with these words: 'Certain residues of the laws of a race of conquerors'*; a phrase which at the time seemed (as indeed it was) audacious, the bold stroke of a brilliant mind; but a century earlier it would have seemed paradoxical to the point of extravagance. And no wonder: have we not seen a similar reverence survive still longer? First, and with even renewed power, in politics, then in literature, and finally in some branches of the fine arts. There comes a moment, in great matters as in small, when something which men have striven, despite its contingency and artificiality, to perpetuate as natural and necessary, must at last succumb to experience, to rational argument, to satiety or change of fashion – or to some other factor, if any there be, more trivial even than fashion – according to the nature and relative importance of the matter in question. But that moment must be prepared for; and it stands a good deal to the credit of the jurists if they did in fact, as I think they did, prepare for such a moment in the history of jurisprudence, however slowly and unwittingly they did so.

But in the case of our trial, even the rules by that time established were enough to convict the judges of definite illegality. For they chose in fact to begin with torture. Completely ignoring the circumstances, whether 'essential' or not, of the presumed crime, they bombarded their victim with questions from which nothing relevant could result, except only a pretext for them to say 'not plausible' and, on this pretext – giving to asserted implausibilities the character of proved lies – to warn him that they would use torture. They were not in fact seeking the truth at all; their only object was to extort a confession. Uncertain of their advantage if they were to stop to examine the facts, they wanted as quickly as possible to inflict the pain which would give them a certain and swift advantage. They were in a hurry: all Milan knew (that is the word used in such cases) that Guglielmo Piazza had smeared the walls, doorways, and approaches of Via della Vetra – and those who had him in their power, couldn't *they* make him own up?

Some may say perhaps that all this was justified, in law, at least, if not in conscience, by the principle – a revolting one but accepted in those days – that when threatened by a crime of more than usual enormity the public authorities need not scruple to

use illegal methods to suppress it. But in point of fact it was –
and heaven knows, this was only right – the common, nay almost
the universal opinion of the jurists that this principle did not
apply to the investigative procedure, but only to the punishment
eventually imposed. As one of them expressed it, 'the enormity
of the crime one may be concerned with is no proof that the
accused committed it; and until such proof be shown, let all legal
formalities be observed'.[4] And here I should like to put on record
another text, if only because it seems to me to represent one of
those moments that occur from time to time in history when a
gleam of eternal justice itself shows through human speech. I
refer to a phrase used early in the fifteenth century by Nicolò
Tedeschi, Archbishop of Palermo, but more famous, so long as
he had any fame, as the Abate Palermitano, and whom our
ancestors called the 'Bartolo of Canon Law'. 'The graver the
crime,' wrote this author, 'the stronger should be the proofs of
guilt, for where the danger is greater there is the greater need of
prudence.'[5] However, these texts do not – from the strictly legal
point of view – apply to our case, for we have it on Claro's
authority that in the practice of the courts of Milan a contrary
custom prevailed – namely that in such cases (of especially grave
crimes) the judge was permitted to set the law aside, even in
examining the accused; 'A rule,' remarks Rimaldi, another erst-
while celebrated jurist, 'which other nations would do well not
to adopt' – on which Farinacci comments, 'well said'.[6] But
observe how Claro himself interprets this rule: 'Recourse is had
to torture although the evidence be not altogether sufficient (*in
totum sufficientia*), nor proved by altogether unimpeachable
witnesses, and often also without having given the accused a
copy of the minutes of the investigation.' But where he treats
particularly of evidence that would justify torture, he expressly
states the necessity of some such evidence – 'not only in the case
of petty crimes but for the greatest crimes too, not excluding high
treason'.[7] Claro, then, allowed that certain cases called for a less
thorough scrutiny of evidence, but not that it could ever be right
to dispense with such scrutiny altogether. He allowed that in
certain cases one might go ahead without witnesses of the highest

[4] P. Folerius, *Pract. crim.*, § 'Quod suffocavit', 52.
[5] *Commentaria in libros decretalium*, 'De praesumptionibus', ch. xiv, 3.
[6] *Praxis*, Q. xxxvii, 79.
[7] *Sentent. recept.*, V, Q. lxiv, 9.

character; not that there need be none at all; that the evidence could be slighter, but not that none need be adduced – and such as was adduced must, he insisted, be real and relevant. Claro, in short, aimed at making things easier for the judges in their task of discovering crime, but not at giving them power to torture, on whatever pretext they chose, whomsoever might fall into their hands. No abstract theory could ever allow, ever conceive, ever dream of conceiving such a power. The passions, however, are far more practical.

And so Piazza was warned by his iniquitous interrogator: 'that he should tell the truth, why he says he does not know that the walls have been smeared, and does not know the names of the deputies, for otherwise, these statements being implausible, we shall put him on the rope to discover the truth behind the implausibilities.' 'Hang me up if you want to, but I know nothing of the things you have asked me about.' So the poor wretch replied, with that sort of desperate courage with which reason will sometimes challenge violence as though to make it understand that, do what it will, violence can never change its nature and become reasonable.

And notice the paltry cunning of these gentlemen in finding an extra excuse for their proceedings by ferreting out a second 'lie', as though to have the term in the plural gave them more assurance – another zero to swell a sum which so far contained no numbers at all.

He was put to the torture. They told him 'that he should tell the truth at last.' Howling and sobbing, praying and supplicating, he answered, 'My lord, I have told the truth.' They persisted with their questions. 'Ah for the love of God,' he cried, 'let me down my lord and I will tell all I know. . . . Give me a drop of water, please.' He was let down, put in a chair, and questioned again. He again replied, 'I know nothing . . . give me some water, please.'

The blindness of panic! It never crossed their minds that from the very thing which they were determined to force Piazza to say he could have made a very strong argument for his innocence – if it had been true, as they so cruelly insisted it was. 'Yes, sir,' he could have replied, 'I had heard that the walls of Via della Vetra had been smeared; and then I went and lounged about at the door of your house, my Lord President of the Tribunal of Health!' And the argument would have been all the stronger for the fact that the two rumours, of the smearing and of Piazza's responsibility for it, were going around together; so that Piazza must have been aware of his danger, along with the rumour of the smearing. But this obvious consideration, to which the minds of his judges were blinded by passion, could not occur to him either, poor fellow; because they had never told him what he was accused of. Before anything else they wanted to break his spirit with torture. It was this that represented for them the plausible and probable arguments which the law required. They wanted to make him feel the terrible and immediate consequences of answering them in the negative; to make him admit himself a liar once, in order to gain the right not to believe him as soon as he should declare himself innocent. But this particular villainy did not succeed. Put to the torture again, lifted up on the rope, warned that the torture would be repeated, subjected to it again, and still pressed to 'tell the truth', Piazza's answer, screamed out at first and then spoken in a low voice, was still: 'I have told you the truth.' Until at last the judges, seeing that he was past giving any answer at all for the present, ordered him to be let down and taken back to prison.

On 23 June a report of this interrogation was made to the Senate by the President of the Tribunal of Health, himself a Senator, and by the Chief of Police (who could also sit in that assembly when invited). The Senate thereupon decreed, in its capacity as Supreme Court, that 'Piazza be shaved, given a purgative, dressed in clothes provided by the court, and then tortured again', this time 'tied by the rope' – a very cruel addition, since it meant that now his hands, as well as arms, would be dislocated. This torture 'was to be repeated as often as the two aforesaid magistrates thought fit, because of certain lies and implausibilities which the trial has brought to light'.

The Senate alone had, I will not say the authority but the power, to take things so far with impunity. With regard to the repetition of tortures the Roman law[8] was interpreted in two ways; and the legally weaker of the two was the more humane. Many authorities – perhaps following Odofredus[9] who is the only one quoted by Cino da Pistoia[10] and the earliest quoted by the other writers who maintained this view – held that torture

---

[8] Reus evidentioribus argumentis oppressus, repeti in quaestionem potest.* Dig. lib. XLVIII, tit. 18, l. 18.

[9] Numquid potest repeti quaestio? Videtur quod sic; ut Dig. eo. l. Repeti. Sed vos dicatis quod non potest repeti sine novis indiciis.* Odofredi, ad. Cod. lib. IX, tit. 41, l. 18.

[10] Cyni Pistoriensis, super Cod. lib. IX, tit. 41, l. de tormentis, 8.

could not be repeated unless in the meantime new and weightier evidence had come to light; with, later, the added qualification that this evidence should be different in kind from that adduced in the first instance. On the other hand many writers followed Bartolo[11] in holding that torture might be repeated if the original evidence were very plain, clear, and pressing; and if – again a condition added later – the first application of torture had been mild.[12] Now clearly, neither of these interpretations had the slightest relevance to the Senate's decree. No new evidence had been shown. And what was the original evidence? That two women had observed Piazza touching a wall, and that (here 'evidence' and 'crime' became the same thing) the magistrates had seen 'some traces of oily material' on the scorched and blackened walls of a part of the street where in fact Piazza had not been! Moreover, these so evidently 'plain, clear, and pressing' signs of guilt had not been tried out or tested in any discussion with the accused. Discussion indeed! The Senate's decree makes no mention of evidence in regard to the crime: the decree was not even a misapplication of the law; it proceeded as though there were no law. In the teeth of all law and all accepted authorities, not to speak of all reason, it ordered that Piazza be tortured anew 'because of some lies and implausibilities'; that is to say, the Senate ordered its ministers to do again, and still more cruelly, what it ought to have punished them for doing in the first place. For it was a universally admitted principle of jurisprudence (and how could it not have been?) that a subordinate judge who had put a man to torture without due evidence of guilt should be punished by his superiors.

But the Senate of Milan was the supreme court of justice; in this world, that is. And it would not do for the Senate of Milan – to which the public was looking, if not for protection, at least for revenge – to be less adroit, persistent, successful in discovery than Caterina Rosa. For in fact the whole business was going forward under this woman's authority. They were her words which had started the trial on its course – 'then it occurred to me that he might perhaps be one of the people', etc. – and the same words were still controlling and ruling it; except that, while she began with surmises, the judges began with assurance. And let us not be surprised to see a court of justice playing the eager disciple to

---

[11] Bart. ad Dig., loc. cit.
[12] Farinacci, *Praxis*, Q. xxxviii, 72f.

a couple of illiterate women; for when one has set out on the road of passion, it is only natural that the blindest should lead the way. Nor need we be surprised to see men whom we cannot suppose to have been, indeed who certainly were not, of the kind that choose evil for its own sake, so cruelly and blatantly violate every rule of justice; for once a man allows himself to think unjustly he will proceed to act unjustly and continue down this road as far as the unjust thought can take him; and if conscience hesitates, and grows uneasy, and starts to send out warnings – well, it is all too easy for popular clamour to smother remorse, or even prevent it from arising, in the mind of one who forgets that he has to answer to another judge.

As for the humiliating, indeed cruel, directions with regard to shaving, clothing, and purging the accused, they are sufficiently explained by Verri. 'It was the belief of those times,' he writes, 'that a criminal might have some diabolical charm or some pact with the devil concealed on his person, in the hair of his head or body, or in his clothes, or even in his stomach; so that shaving, stripping, and purging were employed to render him defenceless.'[13] And it is true, such was the belief of those times; violence was a fact (in various forms) of all times, but a doctrine of none.

Piazza's second interrogation was only a repetition of the first one – just as absurd, still more cruel, and equally ineffective. The poor wretch was first questioned, his answers being contradicted with captious objections which one would call childish if such a term could apply to anything done in this affair; and the questions still bore on circumstances irrelevant to his presumed crime, and did not even mention it. This done, they began to torture him again, and more cruelly, in obedience to the Senate's decree. All they obtained were cries of anguish, cries for mercy – not a word of what they desired to hear, and to extort which they had the nerve to cause such cries and to listen to them. 'Oh my God! Oh, my Lord, what are you doing to me ... get it over quickly, at least ... cut my hand off ... let me die ... give me at least a moment to breathe. . . . Ah, Lord President! For the love of God give me something to drink. . . .' Yet still, with all this: 'I don't know anything; I have told you the truth.' Having answered thus again and again, to their coldly and yet furiously repeated demand, 'Tell us the truth', Piazza's voice failed him, he went

[13] Op. cit., ch. iii.

dumb; during four repetitions of the torture he was silent. Then, at last, he found strength to say once more in a low voice: 'I know nothing, I've already told you the truth.' and with this they had to make an end, and return him, unconfessed, to prison.

And now they no longer had any reason, any sort of pretext, for beginning again; they had taken a short cut and it had led them astray. Had the torture produced its effect of extorting the confession of a lie, they would have had Piazza at their mercy; and, horrible to say, the less important the subject of the lie, the more indifferent and trivial, the more effectively would it have served them as an argument of his guilt; as showing his need to keep clear of the whole business, to appear completely ignorant of it – in short, to lie. But, having tortured him once, illegally, and then again still more illegally and still more savagely (or, to use their term, 'severely'), it would have been just a little too extravagant to begin a third time to torture a man for denying that he had heard certain rumours or knew the names of some parish functionaries. So they were back at their starting point, as if they had not yet done a thing; obliged after all, with nothing gained so far, to begin the investigation of the supposed crime, and therefore to tell Piazza what he was charged with and commence his cross-examination. And what if he denied the charge? What if, as he had shown himself able to do, he persisted in denying even under torture? And this torture would have had to be absolutely the last, unless the judges chose to bring on themselves the fearful judgement pronounced by a fellow judge, one who had died almost a century earlier but whose authority was stronger now than ever before – I mean that Bossi who has been quoted already: 'I have never,' said Bossi, 'known torture to be ordered more than three times, except by judges who were murderous brutes, *nisi a carneficibus.*'[14]* And he meant torture ordered with due regard for the law!

But unfortunately passion is ingenious and intrepid in finding new ways to take when the right way seems long and unsure. The judges had begun with the 'dislocation torture'; they now continued with torture of another kind. By order of the Senate (as we know from a letter of the Chief of Police to the Governor of Milan, Spinola, who at the time was besieging Casale) the Auditor of Health, in the presence of a notary, promised Piazza his liberty on condition – as was to appear in the course of the

---

[14] *Tractatus varii*, 'De tortura', 44.

trial – that he confessed the whole truth. In this way they managed to tell him about the accusation without being compelled to discuss it; to inform him of it, not in order that his replies might help them to discover the truth, not in order to hear his opinion; but to bring to bear on him a powerful stimulus to say what they themselves wanted to hear.

The letter to which I refer was written on 28 June, that is to say when the trial, as we have seen, was already well on its way. It begins thus: 'I think that Your Excellency should be informed of things that have come to light concerning certain criminals who have recently gone about smearing the walls and gates of this city.' And it will not be without interest, or profit, to see how those in charge of the proceedings represented the facts. 'I was commissioned,' the writer continues, 'by the Senate to set up an inquiry, as a result of which, on the evidence of certain women and a man whose words could be trusted, a certain Guglielmo Piazza (a man of the lower class, but who holds the office of Commissioner of Health) came under suspicion of having, in the early morning of Friday, 21 June, smeared the walls of a district in Porta Ticinese, called the Vetra de' Cittadini.'

And the man whose words could be trusted, thus brought in at once to corroborate the testimony of the women, had said that he had met with Piazza, adding 'and I greeted him and he returned my greeting'. And so Piazza 'came under suspicion'! As thought the crime imputed to him was of having entered the Via della Vetra! Incidentally, the Chief of Police does not mention his own visit to the scene of the crime to verify the facts; nor was it mentioned during the rest of the trial.

'Piazza,' the letter goes on, 'was therefore immediately arrested.' But the writer says nothing of the visit to Piazza's house, where 'nothing suspicious' had been found. 'And since his interrogation by the judges made him still more suspect' (as we have seen!) 'he was severely tortured, but did not confess his guilt.'

If someone had informed Spinola that in fact Piazza had not been interrogated at all about the crime, Spinola would have replied: 'But I have positive information to the contrary. The Chief of Police has written to tell me, not indeed of this precisely, for that was not necessary; but he has informed me of something else which implies that and necessarily presupposes it; for he has written to say that the man, though severely tortured, did not confess the crime.' And if the objector had stuck to his point, that eminent and powerful personage might very well have retorted: 'What! Do you suppose the Chief of Police would make fun of me, to the extent of telling me, as an important item of news, that something did not happen which could not have happened?' And yet this precisely was the case: not, of course, that the Chief of Police had tried to make fun of the Governor; but the authorities had, in fact, done a thing of such a kind that they were unable to present a truthful report of it. For the fact was, and is, that bad conscience more easily finds pretexts for acting than formulas in which to render account of what it has done.

But on the matter of impunity that letter contained another deception which Spinola could – and indeed should – have observed for himself, if he had had a mind for anything except the taking of Casale (which he never took). For the letter continues: '. . . Until by order of the Senate (indeed in execution of the last decree which Your Excellency caused to be published on this matter) Piazza, being promised impunity by the President of the Tribunal of Health, finally confessed,' etc.

In the thirty-first chapter of the foregoing work mention was made of a decree in which the Tribunal of Health promised a reward and impunity to whomsoever should reveal the agents responsible for the smearings found on the doors or walls of houses on the morning of 18 May; and reference was also made to a letter of the same Tribunal to the Governor on this point. This letter, after declaring that the Tribunal's decree had been published 'with the approval of the Grand Chancellor', who was deputizing for the Governor, begged the latter 'to confirm it with a fresh decree which should promise a greater reward'. And in fact the Governor did cause another one to be promulgated on 13 June, in which 'he promises to any person who, within thirty days, should identify the person or persons who have committed, favoured, or aided the said crime a reward of, etc. . . . and in the event of such a person being himself involved in the crime, he is also promised impunity from punishment'. Now it was as in execution of *this* decree, which so explicitly referred to something done on 18 May, that the Chief of Police said that impunity had been promised to a man accused of something done on 21 June; and he said it to the very man who had, at least, signed this decree. Such confidence they had, it seems, in the siege of Casale! For it would be too much to suppose that their own minds were confused to such a degree.

But why did they need to use such a subterfuge with Spinola?

It was because they needed the support of his authority to

disguise an action which was irregular and unjust both by common jurisprudence and by the laws of the country. For it was a commonly accepted principle that a judge could not, on his own authority, grant impunity to an accused person;[15] and the Constitutions of Charles V, while conceding very wide powers to the Senate, nevertheless did not concede the power 'of granting pardons for crime, remission of punishment or safe-conducts; these things being reserved to the Sovereign'.[16] And Bossi, from whom I have already quoted, and who was among those who compiled the Constitutions, being a Senator at the time, says expressly, 'the promise of impunity pertains exclusively to the Sovereign'.[17]

But why should they have involved themselves in subterfuge when they could have had recourse to the Governor in the first place for the power to grant the impunity? For the Governor certainly had this power, as the Sovereign's representative, together with authority to delegate it; and the proof that the judges could have obtained this power from him is the fact that they did so later on with regard to another unfortunate man who was to be involved in this same inhuman trial. The Governor's reply is registered in the Acts of the trial:

> Ambrosio Spinola, etc. In conformity with the views expressed by the Senate in a letter of the 5th instant, we herewith authorize you to concede impunity to Stefano Baruello, condemned for distributing and manufacturing certain pestilent unguents which have been disseminated in this city for the destruction of the populace if, within a period of time to be fixed by the said Senate, he shall reveal the agents of the said crime and their accomplices.

The promise to Piazza of impunity was not made in writing and officially; but informally, by the Auditor of Health, outside the trial. Naturally enough; for a formal assurance would have been obviously false, if based on the Governor's decree; and clearly a usurpation of authority if based on nothing. But why, I repeat, did the judges renounce, as it were, the possibility of giving a proper official form to so important an action?

These questions cannot be answered with certainty, but we

[15] See Farinacci, *Praxis*, Q. lxxxi, 227.
[16] *Constitutiones dominii mediolanensis*; 'De Senatoribus'.
[17] Op. cit., 'De confessis per torturam,' 32.11.

shall see presently the advantage the judges gained from acting in this way.

In any case the irregularity of their procedure was so evident that Padilla's counsel liberally drew attention to it. Although – as he very rightly protested – he did not need, in order to disprove the charges against his client, to refer to matters in which the latter was not directly concerned; and although – wrongly and inconsistently – he conceded that a real crime and real criminals were involved in all this muddle of fantasy and invention; nevertheless for good measure, as they say, and with the general object of weakening the case against his client, he made various objections to the conduct of the trial as this had affected others of the accused. And in connexion with the impunity, without impugning the Senate's authority in the matter (for men are sometimes more touchy on the subject of their power than of their honesty), the advocate objected that Piazza 'was brought only before the said Auditor who had no jurisdiction ... and whose actions were therefore null and void and contrary to law'. And referring to the mention that was made in passing, later on, of that impunity, he said: 'And yet there had been nothing said or written hitherto, in the course of the trial, about any impunity, though according to law there ought to have been some such record of it before it was claimed.'

In this part of the defence a very significant remark was made in passing. Reviewing the actions which had preceded the promise of impunity, the advocate, without directly expressing any disapproval of the tortures inflicted on Piazza, nevertheless referred to them in these terms: 'He was tortured on implausible pretexts.' This seems to me a fact worth noting – that the thing should have been called by its true name even at that time, even in the presence of those responsible for it, and by one who was not in the least concerned to defend the innocence of the man who suffered by it.

This promise of impunity must have been little known to the general public: Ripamonti does not mention it in his history of the plague, which gives the main facts of this trial; indeed he indirectly denies its existence. It was not in Ripamonti's nature to misrepresent things deliberately; but he is inexcusable for not having read either Padilla's defence or the digest of the trial which was printed with it, and for having believed instead the loose talk of the public and the lies of certain interested parties. He says that Piazza, immediately after he had been tortured and while they were unbinding him to take him back to prison, came out with a spontaneous and quite unexpected revelation.[18] This false revelation was certainly made, but not until the following day, after Piazza had spoken privately with the Auditor; and it was made to men who very much expected it. Thus if the few documents mentioned above had not survived, if the Senate had only had to do with the public and with historians, it would have succeeded in its attempt to conceal a fact which was of fundamental importance in the trial and was the starting point of all that took place subsequently.

No one knows what took place in that meeting between Piazza and the Auditor. We are left to conjectures and probabilities. Verri writes:

> It is highly likely that the unhappy man was assured in prison itself that if he persisted in his denials, the torture would be repeated every day; that his guilt was held to be certain, and that there was nothing that he could do now except to accuse himself and give the names of his accomplices. In this way he would save his life and escape from the daily torture prepared for him. Piazza therefore begged for impunity, and it was granted him, on condition that he made a clean breast of the facts.[19]

And yet it does not seem at all probable that Piazza himself asked for impunity; as we shall see as we follow the rest of the trial, he never took a step on his own initiative; he had to be dragged forward all the time; and in order to make him take that first step, and such a strange and horrible one, of calumniating himself and others, it is much more likely that he was offered the impunity by the Auditor. Moreover, the judges would surely not have omitted, when they spoke to him of it later, to mention so important a circumstance and one which gave so much more weight to his confession; nor would the Chief of Police have overlooked it in his letter to Spinola.

But who can imagine the struggle that went on in Piazza, with the memory of the torture so fresh in his mind, making him feel at the same time a terror of suffering again and a horror of causing others to suffer; in whom the hope of escaping a terrifying death only appeared before him accompanied by the terror of bringing it upon some other innocent person! For he could not

[18] G. Ripamonti, *De peste quae fuit anno MDCXXX*, p. 84.
[19] Op. cit., ch. iv.

have believed that they were going to let go one prey without trying to catch another, that they were resigned to doing without any condemnation at all. He yielded; he embraced that hope, although it was horrible and uncertain; he accepted the task, although it was loathsome and difficult; he decided to put another victim in his place. But how would he find this victim? Where should he begin? How could he choose with no one to choose from? In his own case, there had been a real fact to serve as the occasion and pretext for an accusation. He had, after all, gone into the Via della Vetra, he had walked along it touching the wall; and though the woman who saw him was warped in mind, she had at any rate seen something. We shall see that it was another equally innocent and equally trivial fact which suggested both the person he would accuse and the story he would invent.

There was a barber called Giangiacomo Mora who compounded and put out for sale an ointment as medicine against the plague – one of a thousand such things which had gained credit with the populace, as was only to be expected when an evil of which no one knew the remedy was working such havoc and in an age when medicine had as yet so little learned how not to dogmatize and had as yet taught people so little what not to believe. Now a few days before his arrest, Piazza had asked this barber for some of his ointment and the latter had promised to get some ready for him; and then, meeting Piazza on the Carrobio on the very morning of the day after the arrest, he had told him that the jar was ready and asked him to come and take it. But a story about ointment, about agreements between people, about the Via della Vetra, was just what the judges wanted from Piazza; hence these circumstances, all so fresh in his mind, supplied him with the materials to compose such a story – if you can call it composing to take a number of real circumstances and tack on an invention inconsistent with them.

On the day following, 26 June, Piazza was brought before the court of inquiry and ordered by the Auditor 'to declare in the presence of the notary Balbiano, and in conformity with the confession he has made extrajudicially to me, whether he knows who is responsible for compounding the unguents with which the gates and walls of the houses of this city have so many times been smeared'. But the poor wretch, who was lying against the grain, tried to move as little as possible away from the truth; he answered: 'It was the barber who gave me the ointment.' This is a literal translation of his words as recorded, which Ripamonti, as we have seen, places in the wrong context: *dedit unguenta mihi tonsor.** They told him 'to name the said barber'; and the latter's self-styled accomplice and instrument in crime replied: 'I think his name is Giovanni Giacomo, but his family [surname] I don't know.' He only knew for certain where the man's house, or rather shop, was; as was to appear in a later interrogation.

Piazza was then asked whether 'from the barber, thus identified, he has received little or much of the ointment'. He replied: 'He gave me as much of it as could be contained in the inkstand on that table.' If he had received from Mora the little jar of the stuff he had ordered, he would have described it; but, finding his memory empty, he grasped at an object he could actually see, as being at least something real. Their next question was 'whether this barber was a friend of his', and he, without noticing that what he really did remember was quite inconsistent with the story he was making up, answered: 'He is a friend, my Lord, yes, we exchange greetings, my Lord'; which simply meant that they knew one another enough to say 'good morning', if so much.

Without comment, the cross-examiners went on to ask him in what circumstancs 'the barber had given him the unguent'. Piazza replied: 'As I was going along, he called me and said, "I've something for you." So I said, "What?" And he said, "a sort of ointment." And I said, "All right, I will come and get it from you later." And so, two or three days later, he gave it me.' Piazza here altered the facts just enough to fit them in with his story; but he left their imprint; and some of the words he quoted probably had been spoken when the two men met. Phrases spoken in consequence of a previous agreement about a safeguard against disease he now reported as having been used to concoct there and then a plan – as crazy, to say the least, as it would have been wicked – to spread poison in the city.

The judges, nevertheless, proceeded with questions on the place, the date, and the time of day of the proposal, and the acceptance. Then, as though satisfied with Piazza's replies on these points, they asked, 'And what did he say to you when he actually gave you the ointment?' 'He said,' answered Piazza, ' "Take this jar and smear the walls of the streets here behind us; and then come to me and I'll give you a lot of money." ' At this point Verri comments with some impatience: 'But what prevented the barber from safely doing the smearing himself during the night?' And the next reply brings out still more plainly the implausibility noted by this comment. Asked, 'Did the barber tell the witness precisely where he was to smear the stuff?' Piazza answered, 'He told me to do it in the Vetra de' Cittadini, and that I was to start with his front door, which I did.'

'So the barber didn't even smear his own front door!' notes Verri; and to be sure *his* intelligence was hardly required for that observation; either a blindness caused by passion was needed for it not to be made, or downright malice, due to the same cause if, as seems more likely, the same idea occurred to the judges.

It cost the unhappy Piazza such an effort to invent his story, it had to be forced out of him by so many questions, that one is left wondering whether that promised bribe was a mere product of his imagination as it cast about for some likely reason for having agreed to do as he was doing, or whether it had really been suggested to him in that secret interview with the Auditor. The same doubt arises when we find his story stumbling, indirectly, against another difficulty – namely how on earth he could have handled so deadly an ointment without being harmed by it himself. On the judges asking him, 'Whether the barber told him why he was having the said doors and walls smeared', Piazza replied, 'He didn't say anything, but I think the ointment was a poison harmful to the body, because the next morning he gave me a glass of water to drink, saying that it would be a safeguard.'

To all these replies, and to others which it would be tedious to repeat, the judges found nothing to object, or rather they expressed no objection. Regarding one point only they thought fit to require an explanation: why had the witness not confessed all this before? Answer: 'I don't know – I can't think of any reason except perhaps the water you gave me to drink; for Your Excellency knows that, in spite of all the tortures, I couldn't say a thing.' But this time they were not so easily satisfied; they repeated the question: 'Why had he not said this truth sooner, especially in view of the tortures he had undergone both on Saturday and yesterday?'

This truth!

He replied: 'I didn't admit it because I couldn't, and if I had stayed hanging on that rope a hundred years I still couldn't have said anything; I just couldn't speak: whenever I was asked about anything to do with this business it all went out of my head and I couldn't answer.' This said, the judges concluded the interrogation and sent the unfortunate Piazza back to prison.

Yet is it enough merely to call him unfortunate? This is a question one's conscience shies away from and would rather declare itself incompetent to answer: how cruel, how arrogant, how pharisaically presumptuous it seems to pass judgement on a man trapped and tortured as Piazza was! But the question cannot be avoided, and there is only one possible answer: he was also guilty. The sufferings and fears of an innocent man are great things, powerful things, but they do not alter the moral law; they cannot make calumny no longer wrong. And the very pity that makes us wish we could find excuses for the sufferer turns us against the calumniator. Another innocent man has been named; we foresee another's sufferings and fears, and perhaps another's similar sins.

And the men who did the trapping and the torturing – shall we excuse them on the plea that they sincerely believed the tale about the poison, and that to torture was normal procedure at that time? But we too believe that men may be killed with poison; but what should we say of a judge who based the justice of a death-sentence for poisoning on this persuasion? The death-penalty is still inflicted; but what should we say to a man who thereby justified every death-sentence? No, the fact is that torture was not prescribed for Guglielmo Piazza's case; it was his judges who deliberately brought it in, who in a sense invented it for that case. Had he deceived them, the fault would still have been theirs, for he was acting under pressure from them; but we have seen that he did not deceive them. And even supposing they were deceived by his statements in the final interrogation – that they believed the story he told, with all the details that we have heard – what was it that started Piazza speaking in this way? How did they obtain his statement? With a device, the illegality of which they had no business to be deceived about, and in fact were not deceived about, since they did their best to conceal it and disguise it.

And if *per impossibile* all that took place subsequently had been nothing but an accidental convergence of factors tending to confirm them in their deception, they would still have been to blame for having prepared the ground for such a deception in the first place. But we shall see, on the contrary, that the whole affair went forward as the effect of, and controlled by, their intention to maintain that deception to the bitter end; to do which they were prepared not only to dodge the law but also to shut their eyes to evidence, and not only to harden their hearts against pity but also to play fast and loose with justice.

CHAPTER 4

The Auditor hastened to Mora's house with a squad of police. They found him in his shop – this second criminal, untroubled by any thought of flight or concealment, though his accomplice had now been four days in prison. With Mora was his son. They were both arrested by order of the Auditor.

When Verri examined the parish registers of San Lorenzo, he found that the unlucky barber may also have had three daughters, one aged fourteen, one twelve, and one just six. I find it moving that a man like Verri, rich, celebrated, well-born, invested with public authority, should have gone to such trouble to unearth the records of people who were poor, lowly, forgotten, and what is more, technically criminals; that he should have thus gone seeking fresh objects for a wise and generous compassion at a time when his contemporaries still blindly and obstinately repeated the foolish denunciations of an earlier generation. It is, to be sure, unreasonable to pit compassion against justice. Justice must sometimes punish in spite of pity; it cannot condone crime out of compassion for the innocent who may suffer when guilty men are punished. Yet compassion too is a type of reason, when it is directed against violence and bad faith. That first anguish of a wife and a mother, the terror that must have gripped the hearts of those children, so utterly unprepared for what occurred – their grief and horror at seeing a father and a brother suddenly seized and bound and insulted – if the men who caused this had had nothing worse on their consciences it alone had been a grievous thing to answer for. For it exceeded anything that justice required or even that the law allowed.

Because, of course, even to arrest a man, you had to have some evidence against him, and against Mora there was none – neither ill-repute, nor attempted flight, nor complaint of an offended party, nor accusation lodged by anyone worthy of belief, nor testimony of any witness, nor any body of evidence; nothing but the statement of a presumed accomplice; and before a judge could act on such a statement many conditions had to be fulfilled. We shall see that more than one essential condition was in fact lacking, and it would be easy to show the same of many others; but there is no need for this, because, even had every condition been scrupulously observed, there was one circumstance in this case which rendered the accusation absolutely invalid from the start – namely, that it was made in virtue of a promise of impunity. 'Whatever is testified,' says Farinacci, 'as a result of a hope of exemption from punishment (whether such exemption be conceded by the law or promised by the judge) ought not to be received as evidence against the persons named in the testimony.'[1] And Bossi writes:

> That testimony is defective which a witness makes in consequence of a promise of impunity ... considering that a witness ought to speak disinterestedly and not with a view to gaining some advantage. ... And this holds even in cases when, for other reasons, the rule which disallows the evidence of an accomplice is dispensed with. ... The witness who testifies because of a promise of impunity is called 'corrupt' and deserves no credence.[2]

This principle was unopposed.

As the police were about to search his house and shop, Mora said to the Auditor: 'Oh, Your Excellency, I know you have come for that ointment of mine. Your Excellency can see it there – a little jar of it that I got ready to give to the Commissioner of Police, but he hasn't come for it. I've done nothing wrong, thank God. You don't need to keep me bound.' The poor fellow thought that it was for making and distributing the specific without a licence that they were arresting him.

They turned everything upside down, examining big jars, little jars, flasks, casks, every sort of container (at that time barbers practised rudimentary surgery, whence it was only a step to dabbling in medicine and pharmacy). They found two things that roused their suspicion; and, with apologies to the reader, I must speak of them, because it was just this suspicion shown by the police in the course of their examination of his house which led to poor Mora's finding something to accuse himself of when he later came to be tortured. Besides, this whole affair contains something more offensive than disgust.

In time of plague it was natural that a man who had to have dealings with many people, and particularly with the sick, should live apart from his own family as much as possible (an observation which Padilla's advocate was to make, as we shall see, when pointing out to the prosecution the lack of material evidence of crime in this case). Besides, the plague itself had

[1] *Praxis*, Q. xliii, 192.
[2] *Tract. varii*, 'De oppositionibus contra testes', 21.

lowered the standard of cleanliness – not in any case a high one then – in that afflicted population. So it is hardly surprising that in a small room behind the shop the police should have found, as the records say, 'two pots full of human excrement'. But one policeman was surprised by this find and remarked (since anyone was free to speak against the smearers) that 'the privy was upstairs'; to which Mora answered, 'I sleep down here and don't go upstairs.'

The second thing was that in a little yard they found 'an oven and in it, behind a low wall, a brass cooking-pot containing dirty water and at the bottom some sticky yellowish-white stuff which, on being thrown against a wall, stuck to it'. Mora said: 'It is *smoglio*' (lye),* and the records note that he said this very emphatically, an observation which shows the sinister importance the police attach to this discovery. But how did they come to take such risks in handling so mysteriously potent a poison? Their fear, no doubt, was overcome by the fury which was yet one of its causes.

They found also, among Mora's papers, a recipe which the Auditor handed to him, asking him to explain it. Mora tore it up because in the confusion he took it for the recipe of his specific against the plague. The scraps were picked up at once, and we shall see later how this paltry incident was used against the unfortunate man.

The report of the trial does not say how many people were arrested along with Mora. Ripamonti says that the whole household was taken away, including those who worked in the shop – the youths and boys in Mora's employment, wife and children and whatever other relatives happened to be there.[3]

On leaving his house (to which he never returned and which was to be razed to the ground to make room for the Column of Infamy) Mora said: 'I haven't done anything wrong. If anything has been wrong, I am ready to be punished for it; but since I made that ointment I've done nothing else. But if I've done something else wrong, I ask for mercy.'

He was interrogated that same day, chiefly concerning the lye found in his house and concerning his relations with the Health Commissioner. His answer on the first point was: 'My Lord, I know nothing about it. The women must have had it made; ask them, they will tell you. As for me, I had no more idea that it was

---

[3] *De peste*, p. 87: 'Et si qui consanguinei erant.'

there than that I should be taken to prison today.' With regard to the Commissioner, Mora told of the jar of unguent which he had promised to let this man have, specifying its ingredients. He denied having had anything else to do with the Commissioner, except that about a year before the latter had come to his house for a service to do with his trade.

Immediately after Mora they had his son up for questioning, and it was then that this poor lad repeated the stupid story about the little pot and the pen which I mentioned at the beginning. For the rest, they got nothing conclusive out of him. Verri, in a note, observes that they ought to have asked the barber's son about the lye, so as to find out how long it had been in the cooking-pot, and how it had been made, and why. 'But,' he adds, 'they feared to find Mora not guilty.' This is the key to the whole affair.

However, they did question Mora's wife on this point. The gist of her replies was that she had done the household washing ten or twelve days previously; that after every such washing she put aside some lye for certain surgical purposes, which was how the police came to find it; but that this time she had not in fact found any use for the stuff. The lye itself they then had examined by two washerwomen and three doctors. The women said it was lye but that it had been altered in some way; the doctors said it was not lye at all. The reason for both replies was the same: the stuff stuck to the pot and only came off in strands. 'In a barber's shop,' comments Verri, 'where linen soiled by wounds and plasterings has been washed, what more natural than to find a sticky, oily, yellowish sediment, especially in the summer?'[4]

But to conclude, all this searching of Mora's house brought no discovery to light; its only results were negative. And Padilla's counsel was to draw the conclusion quite correctly: 'From my reading of the case for the prosecution,' he was to say, 'I cannot see that it has established circumstantial evidence of crime such as a sentence of guilt of necessity requires.' And he went on to observe that such evidence was the more necessary, in this case, in that the effect which was being ascribed to criminal activity, namely the death of so many people, had its proper natural causes. 'How necessary,' he exclaimed, 'to turn back from such vague ungrounded opinions to the certainties of experience. Men have studied the unfavourable influences of the constellations; the mathematicians have made their prognostications; from

---

[4] Op. cit., ch. iv.

which it had become perfectly clear already that the year 1630 would bring plague – the plague which has desolated and destroyed so many fine cities of Lombardy, not to speak of other parts of Italy, without any thought or fear of unguents ever crossing anyone's mind.' Here, even error, we see, comes to the aid of truth, although truth needed no such assistance. But one is sorry to hear this advocate, after this and other equally cogent observations which showed that the crime was non-existent, and after ascribing to the force of torture the depositions which had accused his client, come out at one point with the following strange remark: 'It must be admitted that sheer wickedness caused the said persons and their accomplices to attempt so heinous a crime against the fatherland; for, as the barber himself said on page number 104,* their motive was to enrich themselves by robbery.'

In the letter in which the Chief of Police informed the Governor of these events, we read: 'The barber has been arrested, his house having been found to contain certain compounds which competent judges consider very suspect.' Suspect! A word that a judge may begin with, but never willingly ends with, without first trying every means in his power to change suspicion into certainty. And if there really was anyone who did not know or could not guess what means were available even in those days for establishing the truth, means which certainly could have been adopted had anyone genuinely desired to know exactly how poisonous the filth found in Mora's house was, the President of the Court was there to give such information. In fact, in the letter already referred to, in which the Tribunal of Health told the Governor about the great fouling of walls on 18 May, mention had been made of an experiment with dogs, in order to 'ascertain whether the smearings were poisonous or not.' But when that letter was written the Tribunal had not yet got a man in their clutches on whom to try the experiment of torture, and against whom the mob was yelling 'Tolle!'*

However, before putting Mora to this test, they desired clearer and more precise information (and the reader will agree they needed it) from the Health Commissioner. So they had him brought before them and asked him whether what he had deposed on oath was true and whether he had since remembered anything else. But Piazza only confirmed his previous statement and found nothing to add to it now. Then they said: 'It seems highly implausible that nothing passed between him and the barber other than what he stated in his deposition. For one does not normally entrust a matter of such serious consequence to another's execution in the off-hand way he describes in his statement.'

A remark much to the point; but made too late. Why had they not made it about Piazza's first deposition which did not differ from this one? Why did they call that first deposition 'the truth'? Was their sense of what was plausible so dull and slow that it took them a whole day to wake up to an implausibility? *They* dull and slow? On the contrary! Their sense of the implausible was wonderfully, even excessively, delicate. Had they not immediately found it implausible when Piazza denied having heard of the fouling of the walls in Via della Vetra? When he said he did not know the names of those parish deputies? What made them so hard to please in one case, so quick to decide in the other?

They well knew the reason; and He who sees all things knew it too. And there is something that even we can discern – that they found an implausibility when this served them as a pretext for torturing Piazza, and did not find one when it would have proved too obvious an impediment to the arrest of Mora.

We have, to be sure, already seen that since Piazza's deposition was radically invalid, the judges had no right to make any use of it against Mora. But because they were in any case resolved to use it, they had no choice but to uphold it. If, when Piazza first made his statement they had declared it 'highly implausible'; and if Piazza had not succeeded in getting round this difficulty by putting out a more plausible story, and this without contradicting the first one (an unlikely event); then they would have found themselves faced with the alternatives of either leaving Mora alone or of imprisoning him after having themselves protested, as it were, in advance against such an action.

The remark about implausibility was followed by a terrible admonition: 'If the witness is determined not to speak the whole truth, as he promised to do, then let him take warning that the promised impunity will not avail him – in so far, that is, as his declaration as to what took place between him and the barber be found to come short of the entire truth; whereas on the contrary, if he speaks the truth, the promised impunity will avail him.'

Here, by the way – to recall a point already alluded to – it becomes clear what an advantage it was to the judges not to have had recourse to the Governor for the concession of this impunity. Had he conceded it, on his sovereign authority and with all the

due formalities, there could have been no question of withdrawing it so casually now. But what a mere Auditor said, an Auditor
could unsay.

We may also note here that it was not until 5 September that
an impunity was requested, from the Governor, for Baruello; that
is to say, after the punishment inflicted on Piazza, Mora, and a
few other unfortunates. By that time one could take the risk of
letting someone escape; the animals having been fed, their
bellowings became naturally less impatient, less imperious.

On receiving that warning, Piazza – who was resolved to stick
to the wretched course he had chosen – had fairly to cudgel his
brains for all they were worth; but the only result was a repetition
of his original story. 'I will tell Your Excellency. Two days before
the barber gave me the ointment, he was standing in the street
leading to Porta Ticinese with three other men, and seeing me
pass by, he said to me: "Commissioner, I have some ointment for
you." I said: "Do you want to give it to me now?" He answered,
"No." And just then he did not tell me about the effects of the
ointment. But when he gave it to me later he said that it was for
smearing on the walls to make people die. And I didn't ask him
whether he had already tried it out.' To be sure, in the original
story Piazza did not say: 'he said that it was . . . to make people
die', but rather: 'he didn't say anything, but I think the ointment
was a poison'. However, the judges let this contradiction pass
and asked him, 'Who were the men with the barber and how
were they dressed?'*

Piazza did not know who they were; he only suspected that
they were friends of Mora. As for their dress, he could not
remember. He only insisted that what he had deposed against
Mora was the truth, and on being asked whether he was prepared
to maintain this to Mora's face, he answered 'yes'. They then put
him to the torture again in order to purge his infamy and make it
possible for him to bear witness against the unlucky barber.

The use of torture is, thank God, so much a thing of the past
that these phrases need to be explained. Roman law had laid it
down that 'the testimony of gladiators and suchlike was invalid,
unless corroborated by torture',[5] and later jurisprudence had
specified the persons to whom this rule applied, naming them
'infamous'*. And to this class belonged everyone convicted of
crime, whether by his own confession or by a process of proof.

[5] *Digest*, XXII, tit. 5, 'De testibus'.

But how did torture purge infamy? The jurists reasoned as follows. As an infamous person, an accomplice to a crime is not a believable witness. But if he persist in an assertion that is very much against his own actual and tangible self-interest, then one may admit that he does so as constrained by the force of truth. So then if, after a man convicted of some crime has become the accuser of someone else, the former is told that he must either withdraw his accusation or submit to torture; and if he persist in the accusation, and persist even when the threat is carried out and he actually *is* tortured; then in that case, they said, his testimony becomes credible. Torture has purged his infamy – giving his testimony the authority which it could not get from his personal character.

But then why had they not made Piazza confirm under torture his first deposition? Was it so as not to imperil this deposition – so flimsy in itself but so necessary for the arrest of Mora? The omission, in any case, lent an added illegality to that arrest; for while it was admitted that the accusation of the 'infamous' person, not corroborated by torture, might, like any other weak evidence, be of some use in the process of collecting information, it was not admitted as a ground for taking action against the one who was accused.[6] Claro states this as, without exception, the practice of the courts in Milan: 'For an accomplice to be accepted as a witness, it is necessary that he first be tortured; for as such he is infamous on account of his crime. This is our practice: *et ita apud nos servatur.*'[7]*

Was it then legally correct to torture Piazza, at least this last time? By no means; even in law it was unjust, for their purpose in torturing him was to confer validity on an accusation which, being the effect of a promise of impunity, could never in fact become valid. Why did they not heed their own Bossi's warning on this point? 'Since the harm' he writes, 'done by torture cannot be remedied, care must be taken not to inflict it to no purpose, i.e. when no further presumption or evidence of crime has been found.'[8]

Then whatever they did, they broke the law – torturing or not torturing. Certainly: and why should we be surprised? If one

[6] Farinacci, *Praxis*, Q.xliii, 134, 135
[7] *Sententiarum*, Q.xxi, 13.
[8] *Tractatus*, 'De indiciis . . . ante torturam', 152.

takes a wrong turning one may well come to a choice between two roads that are both wrong.

For the rest, I need hardly tell the reader that the torture used on Piazza to make him withdraw an accusation did not have to be so efficient as that used on him to force him to accuse himself. And in fact they had no howls or groans to record this time; he confirmed his testimony quite calmly.

Then they asked him, and twice over, why he had not made it when they first interrogated him: clearly, they could not get the suspicion out of their minds (and a sting of remorse from their hearts) that perhaps his absurd story had been prompted by their promise of impunity. He answered: 'It was because of the water that I told you I drank.' They would no doubt have preferred a better reason, but they had to put up with this one. They had neglected – indeed shunned and shut out – every means that might have helped them to discover the truth; they had made their choice between the two opposite conclusions to which the inquiry might have led, and had then used one means after another to obtain, at any cost, the conclusion they had chosen: had they now any right to find in this the joy which the sight of a truth that has been sincerely sought for can give? To put out the light is an excellent way to avoid seeing what one does not want to see, but not to see what one does want to see.

When the rope was let down and while they were untying him, the Commissioner said: 'My Lord, please wait until tomorrow, when I will tell you whatever else I can remember about the barber and about other people too.' And then, as they were taking him back to prison, he stopped and said: 'Wait, I have something to say now'; and proceeded to name, as friends to Mora and as shady characters, the aforenamed Baruello and two *foresari*,[9] Girolamo Migliavacca, and his son Gaspare.

In this way the wretched man tried to make names a substitute for the evidence that he knew was lacking. But could his interrogators have possibly failed to see that with this Piazza only gave further proof of not being able to answer their questions? It was they who had asked him to state circumstances that might corroborate his account of what had happened; and presumably he who calls for corroboration sees the need of it.

[9] Grinders of scissors for cutting gold thread. The fact that there was a distinct profession of this kind shows that the industry which it subserved was still flourishing in Milan.

But with these vague new accusations Piazza was as good as saying: You tell me to show you quite clearly the existence of a fact. This I can't do because there was no fact. But after all, what you really want is to get hold of people you can condemn. Very well then, here are some – and now it is up to you to get what you require from them. You are sure to succeed with at least one of them; after all you did so with me.

I shall not mention again the three men named by Piazza – nor others named subsequently, on no better grounds, and condemned with equal assurance – except so far as this may be required for telling the story of Piazza and Mora (who, being the first to fall into the hands of the police, were always regarded as the principal criminals) or so far as they offer an occasion for some particular comment on the affair. I omit also, here as heretofore, various minor happenings, and pass straight to the second examination of Mora; which took place on the same day.

In the course of various questions about his unguent-specific, about the lye, and about some lizards he had had caught by the shop-boys in order to concoct a medicine used at that time (questions which he answered like a man who has nothing to hide and no need to invent) they produced the pieces of the paper that he had torn up when the police visited his home. He said: 'I see it is the paper I tore up without thinking what I was doing, and if you will put the pieces together so that the writing can be read, I will also be able to remember who gave it to me.'

They then asked him: 'How is it that if (as he said in the preceding interrogation) he was not a particular friend of Commissioner Piazza, he so readily had recourse to him for the jar of preservative against the plague, and the Accused so freely and readily agreed to let him have it, and asked him to come and fetch it?'

Notice the appeal, once again, to the *stricter* standard of plausibility. When, the first time, Piazza asserted that his 'friend' with whom he 'exchanged greetings', the barber had offered him, no less 'freely and readily', stuff intended to spread death through the city, the judges accepted the story at once; but not now, on hearing that the stuff was intended as a safeguard. And yet surely one should be less hesitant in looking for the accomplice without whom some minor illegality, and one involving actions in themselves innocent, could not have been committed, than in seeking a superfluous 'accomplice' to a crime both abominable in itself and extremely dangerous to its perpetrators. Nor is this a discovery made in these last two hundred years. The judges' topsyturvy reasoning was not the reasoning of 'seventeenth-century man', but of man driven by passion. As for Mora's answer, it was: 'I did it for the money.'

They asked him next whether he knew the other men named by Piazza; to which he replied that he did, but they were no friends of his, being 'persons better left alone'. Then they asked: Did he know who had fouled the whole city with those smearings? Answer: No, he did not. Did he know, then, who had provided the Commissioner with the unguent to be smeared? No, again he did not.

And then their final question: 'does he know whether anyone offered money to the said Commissioner to induce him to smear the walls of Via Vetra de' Cittadini, and then gave him a glass jar of unguent to be used for the purpose?' To which Mora replied, in a low voice and with his head bowed (*flectens caput et submissa voce*): 'I know nothing about it.'

It was perhaps only now that he began to see to what a strange and horrible conclusion all the twists and turns of these questions might be leading him. But who can tell what exactly the judges did that opened his eyes? Unsure of having discovered what they were seeking, they must have been led to hint that now at last they *were* sure – that now they were forearmed against foreseen denials. But their faces and gestures were not recorded.

They put the direct question to him: 'did he seek out Guglielmo Piazza, Health Commissioner, in order to induce him to smear the walls at the corner of the Via Vetra de' Cittadini, and to this end give him a small glass jar containing unguent for that purpose; promising him a sum of money in payment?'

His reply was more of a cry than an answer. 'My Lord, no! *Maidè*,[10] no! No, no, forever, for eternity! Would *I* do such things?' Words which could be spoken either by a guilty man or an innocent man, but not in the same way by both. But they answered: 'What then will he say when this truth is maintained to his face by Guglielmo Piazza?'

This truth once again! Their entire knowledge of the matter was based on the statement of a presumed accomplice; to whom they themselves, that very day, had replied that the story, as he

---

[10] An old Milanese expression meaning originally 'my God'; it was one of the many forms of legal oath which by corruption entered ordinary speech. But in this case that Name was not being spoken in vain.

told it, was 'most implausible'; and who had since then failed to add to it a single grain of plausibility, unless self-contradiction be such. And now to Mora they coolly say, 'this truth'! Was this due to the grossness of the times? Or to a barbarous legal system? Or to ignorance? Or superstition? Or was it one of those occasions when iniquity gives the lie to itself?

Mora answered: 'If he maintains this to my face, I will tell him he is disreputable, and that he cannot say this, because he has never spoken to me of any such thing, so help me God!'

They summoned Piazza and, in Mora's presence, asked him if this and that and the other were true; one thing after the other, his entire deposition. He answered, 'Yes, my Lord, it is true.' Poor Mora cried, 'God in heaven, this can never be shown to be true!' The Commissioner: 'I have come to this by helping you.' Mora: 'It can never be shown; you cannot prove that you have ever been in my house.' Piazza: 'I wish I never had, but I have been there; and now I've come to this because of you.' Mora: 'You will never prove that you've been to my house.' Then they were taken away, each to his own prison.

In the letter – mentioned more than once above – of the Chief of Police to the governor, this encounter was described as follows: 'Piazza vigorously maintained to his [Mora's] face that he really had received from Mora an unguent of this kind, giving the circumstances of time and place.' Spinola then must have been led to believe that Piazza had specified these circumstances, and, so doing, had been contradicted by Mora on each of them. As for that 'vigorously maintained', all it boiled down to in fact was, 'Yes, my Lord, it is true.'

The letter ended with these words: 'Further inquiries are being made to discover other accomplices and ringleaders. Meanwhile, I thought it well to inform Your Excellency of what is being done in the matter. Humbly kissing Your Excellency's hands, I wish Your Excellency every success in your present undertakings.' There were probably other letters which have not survived. As to the Governor's undertakings, the well-wishing went for nothing: not receiving reinforcements, Spinola lost all hope of taking Casale, fell sick (partly out of chagrin) at the beginning of September and died on the 25th of the same month; having failed in the end to live up to his illustrious title, acquired in Flanders, of 'the taker of cities'; and exclaiming (in Spanish), 'They have dishonoured me.' What 'they' had done was, in fact, worse – placed him in a position involving many grave responsibilities, only one of which he appears to have taken seriously;* this being probably also the only one they had in mind when appointing him.

The day after his confrontation with Mora, Piazza asked to be heard again. Brought before the court, he said: 'The barber has denied that I was ever in his house; so I beg your Lordships to interrogate Baldassar Litta, who lives in Antonio's house in the district of San Bernadino, and Stefano Buzzio, a dyer who lives opposite Sant' Agostino, near Sant' Ambrogio. These men know that I have been in the barber's house and shop.'

Was Piazza acting on his own in saying this? Or on a suggestion from the judges? If the former, it was an odd thing to do, as the result will show; on the other hand the judges would have had a very strong motive for urging him to this step. They wanted a pretext for having Mora tortured; and among the factors which, in the opinion of many learned men, could give to an accusation made by an accomplice the force which it otherwise lacked, and so render it sufficient grounds for torturing the person accused, was a relation of friendship between the latter and his accuser. But not just any kind of friendship or acquaintance; for in that case, as Farinacci observes, 'any accusation by an accomplice could count as sufficient evidence, it being hardly likely that an accuser be wholly unacquainted with the man he accuses. What must be shown is that the two men have been in close and frequent contact, such as to make it plausible that the crime in question was planned by them together'.[11] And this in fact was why the judges had begun by asking Piazza whether the barber were a friend of his. And the reader will remember the answer they received: 'He is a friend ... yes, we exchange greetings.' But more than this bare assertion they could not wring from him, even with threats; so that what they had sought for as a means to the end they were pursuing had become an obstacle in their path. True, it was never, and could never become, a legally valid means; for no friendship, however intimate and however well certified as a fact, could have given validity to an accusation already nullified by the promise of impunity. But this difficulty, like many others not actually raised in the course of the trial, they simply ignored; whereas, having explicitly made an issue of the friendship, or lack of it, between Piazza and Mora, they found themselves now compelled to settle this question once and

[11] *Praxis*, Q.xliii, 172–4.

for all. Thus it is that the records of the trial contain statements by jailers, policemen, and persons who were already in prison for other crimes, statements made in consequence of their being dragged into the affair for the sole purpose of 'getting them to say something' on this point. It is then very probable indeed that the judges had used some such person to tell the Commissioner that his safety might depend on his supplying proofs of his friendship with Mora; and that the poor wretch, to avoid admitting that he had none, had had recourse to a stratagem which would otherwise never have occurred to him. For the actual testimony of the two witnesses cited by him showed how little he could have counted on them: Baldassare Litta, being asked whether 'he had ever seen Piazza in Mora's house or shop', answered, 'No, my Lord'; and Stefano Buzzi, on being asked 'whether Piazza and the barber were friends', answered, 'Perhaps they were; perhaps they exchanged greetings when they met; but I really wouldn't know, my Lord.' And when asked again, 'if he knew whether Piazza had ever been in Mora's house or shop', he said, 'I couldn't say, my Lord.'

After this they called another witness to verify a statement in Piazza's deposition, that a certain Matteo Volpi had been present when the barber had said to him, 'I have something for you.' Questioned on this, Volpi not only replied that he knew nothing about it, but, when his questioners persisted, answered with spirit, 'I am ready to swear that I have never seen them speaking together.'

The next day, 7 June, Mora was examined again; and you would never guess how this interrogation began.

'He is asked to say why, at his last interrogation when he was brought face to face with Guglielmo Piazza, Health Commissioner, he said that he scarcely knew him and that he had never been in his house, although to his face Piazza maintained the contrary; and again, despite the fact that in his first interrogation he showed that he knew him very well, as is also clear from the formal testimony of other witnesses, and as clearly appears from his eagerness in offering Piazza and preparing for him (as he has already admitted) a jar of his preservative.' Mora replied: 'It is true that the Commissioner often passes by my shop; but he is not well known to my household nor to me.' They answered: 'This is contradicted, not only by what you said in the first interrogation, but by the testimony of other witnesses. . . .'

Any comment would be superfluous.

However, they dared not torture Mora simply because of Piazza's deposition. So what then? Why, they went back to the pretext of 'implausibilities'; and, believe it or not, one of these was his having denied that Piazza was his friend and a frequent visitor at his house, while at the same time stating that he had promised Piazza some of the preservative! The other was that he had not sufficiently explained why he had torn up that paper. For Mora persisted in saying that he had done this inadvertently and under the impression that the paper could be of no interest to the police. Perhaps, poor fellow, he feared to make things worse for himself if he admitted to having torn it so as to destroy evidence of an illegality on his part; or perhaps he really could not explain to himself, here and now, what he had done in those first moments of confusion and panic. In any case, those bits of paper were now in the hands of his judges; and if they suspected that the writing on them contained evidence of crime, they had only to put the pieces together and read it, as Mora himself had suggested in the first place. And is it credible that they had not, in fact, already done so?

They ordered Mora, then, with threats of torture, to tell them the truth on the above two points. He replied: 'I have already told you about the paper. As for the Commissioner, he can say what he likes but what he told you is a damned lie, because I gave him nothing.'

He thought – and how could he not have thought? – that this was the truth they finally wanted from him. But of course not! They replied: 'Do not bother us with that point; it is not about that that we are asking you. All that we want to know here and now is why you tore up the piece of paper and why you have denied and still deny that the Commissioner has been to your shop, and so would almost have us believe that you do not know him.'

It would, I think, be hard to find another example of so shamelessly untruthful a respect for legal formalities. Since it was too obvious that they had no right to have Mora tortured on account of the main – indeed the only – charge that had been brought against him, they wanted to make it appear that the torture would be inflicted on other grounds. But wickedness is like a cloak that doesn't fit: pull it down to cover one side of you, it will leave the other bare. For they were now left with only two pretexts for proceeding to physical violence, both entirely unjust:

one which they themselves in effect declared to be such, in preferring not to make out what was written on the paper; the other* shown to be so, and even more flagrantly, by the testimonies with which they had tried to give it the force of legal proof.

As though this were not enough, there is the further point that, even if Piazza's second statement had been fully confirmed by those testimonies, and even had there not been the obstacle of the impunity, Piazza's deposition had no validity at all as legal evidence: 'If,' writes Farinacci, 'the depositions of an accomplice prove inconsistent and self-contradictory, then, as the statements of a perjurer, they cannot render the person whom he accuses liable to torture ... or even to interrogation ... and this is a principle commonly accepted, one can say, by all writers on the law.'[12]

But Mora *was* put to the torture.

He was not so robust, poor man, as his calumniator. For a time, however, the agony only wrung pitiful cries from him and protestations that he had said the truth: 'Oh my God, I don't know the man, we have never been friends, and that's why I can't say ... and that's why it's a lie he tells that he has often visited my house or been in my shop. Oh God! Mercy, my Lord, mercy! I tore up that paper thinking it was the recipe for my preservative ... because all I wanted was the money.'

'That is not a sufficient reason,' they said. He begged to be let down, saying that he would tell the truth. Let down, he said: 'The truth is that I do not know the Commissioner well.' The torture was resumed, with greater severity. To their pitiless questioning he then replied, 'My Lords, tell me what you want me to say, and I will say it'; the same reply that Philotas gave to the man who was torturing him at the command of Alexander the Great ('who himself was behind a curtain listening'[13]): *dic quid me velis dicere*;[14] the same reply of who knows how many other poor wretches.

At last the pain overcame all aversion to self-calumny and all fear of the death-sentence; he said: 'I gave the Commissioner a jar of filth, of excrement, so that he should smear the walls with it. Your Lordships, let me down; I will tell the truth.'

So they had succeeded in making Mora confirm the policeman's

---

[12] *Praxis*, Q.xliii, 185, 186.
[13] From Plutarch's Life of Alexander.
[14] Q. Curtii, VI, 11.*

suspicions just as they had succeeded before in making Piazza confirm the silly woman's fantasies; the means being this time illegal torture, the other time an illegal promise of impunity. The weapons, in both cases, were taken from the armoury of jurisprudence; but were wielded by despots and deceivers.

Seeing that pain had produced its desired effect, they did not heed their victim's plea that at least he be spared further suffering. He was told 'to start talking'.

He said: 'It was human excrement and *smojazzo*' (lye; so here is the result of their discovery of the cooking-pot on visiting Mora's house; that visit begun with such parade of authority and then cut short so cunningly) 'because that Commissioner asked me for it so as to smear on the houses; and also some of the stuff that comes from the mouths of the dead people on the carts.' And not even this last detail was Mora's own invention; for when, on a later occasion, they asked him, 'Where did you learn how to compose your unguent?' his reply was: 'they said in the barber's shop that you use the stuff that comes from dead men's mouths, and then I thought I would add lye and excrement.' He might have answered: 'I have learned a good deal from my murderers – from you and the public.'

But there is something very strange about this confession; for it was not required by the terms of their questions; indeed they had expressly excluded it from the scope of this interrogation by the words quoted above: 'he should not bother us with that point; it is not about that that we are interrogating him.' Since the pain compelled Mora to lie, one might at least have expected that his lie would correspond to their questions. He could have told them that he was a close friend of Piazza; he could have invented some evil motive, one that aggravated his guilt, for having torn up the paper. But why go beyond the limit to which they were pressing him? Was it, perhaps, that during his agony they had suggested other ways by which he might make the agony cease? Did they ask him other questions of which we have no record? If so, then perhaps I myself was deceived when I said, with regard to Piazza, that the judges had deceived the Governor when they induced him to believe that Piazza had been interrogated about the crime. But this suspicion – that perhaps the lie, after all, *was* told in the actual trial, and not in that letter to the Governor – I left unexpressed, as being insufficiently supported by the facts; whereas here, in this matter of Mora's interrogation, it is precisely the strangeness of the fact itself which almost compels one to suspect a further villainy to add to the many already so evident. We find ourselves, I mean, placed between two alternatives: either to believe that Mora, without being asked, accused himself of a horrible crime, which he had not committed, and which would certainly bring him to a terrible death; or to hazard the suggestion that the judges, while admitting *de facto* that they lacked sufficient grounds for compelling Mora by torture to confess the crime, took advantage of the torture which, on a different pretext, they were inflicting, to extort just that confession. I leave the reader to choose the alternative that seems more probable.

The interrogation that followed the torture, like Piazza's after the promise of impunity, was a blend, or, better, a contrasting mix of stupidity and guile – a barrage of questions without any foundation together with an avoidance of matters the examination of which both the case and jurisprudence plainly and imperatively required.

Jurisprudence had established the principle that 'no one commits a crime without some motive', and had acknowledged that 'many persons of weak character have confessed to having committed crimes which later, after sentence has been passed on them and they are about to be executed, they have protested that they did not commit; and of which, afterwards, and too late, they have been found in fact innocent'. On this basis the jurists had formulated the rule that 'no confession is valid unless it contain a statement of the motive that led to the crime, and unless this motive be weighty and plausible in proportion to the crime in question'.[15] Now what had the miserable Mora said? Reduced to the necessity, in that interrogation, of inventing fresh stories to give support to the one which would certainly bring him to a frightful death, he said that the Commissioner had supplied him with saliva from those who had died of the plague and had suggested a criminal use of it; and that Piazza's motive in suggesting this, and his own for accepting the suggestion, was that the two of them would make a large profit as a result of the widespread illness that would ensue; Piazza in his capacity as Commissioner, Mora through the sale of his preservative. I need hardly put it to the reader whether the importance to the two men of such earnings (for which in any case Nature was already providing plentiful occasions) was proportionate to the enormity

[15] Farinacci, *Praxis*, Q. l, 31; lxxxi, 40; lii, 150, 152.

and the dangers of such a crime. But lest the reader suppose that it might have seemed so to those seventeenth-century judges, and that the motive might have seemed to them quite sufficient, let me assure him that he will soon hear the contrary from their own lips.

And there is yet another difficulty in the way of believing the motive stated by Mora; a difficulty perhaps no stronger, but more concrete and material. The reader may remember that when the Commissioner accused himself, he too stated the motive which had led him into crime, namely that the barber had said to him: 'Smear the walls ... and then come to me and you'll get a handful', or, as he said at the next examination, 'a good handful of money'. So there were two motives for the same crime; and two, not only different, but opposed and incompatible motives. The same man, according to one confession, bribes his accomplice with a large sum of money; and, according to the other, agrees to join in the latter's crime in the hope of a paltry profit. Let us put from our minds all we have seen hitherto – how these two motives came to be stated, how the two confessions were obtained – and consider the matter simply as it stands in the situation to which our narrative has brought the persons concerned. How then, in such a situation, would we expect judges to behave whose consciences were not perverted, darkened, and stupefied by passion? Such judges would be horrified at having (even through no fault of their own) gone so far; they would have drawn comfort from the thought that at least they had not yet taken the final, irrevocable step; would have halted at the obstacle that fortunately barred their path to the precipice; have given the difficulty all their attention, fully resolved to unravel its mystery; have exercised all possible diligence, perseverance, and subtlety in interrogating further; have looked up precedents; have not allowed the case to advance an inch until they had discovered (and would this have been so difficult?) which of the two men was lying or whether both were lying. But our judges, on receiving from Mora this reply, 'Because he would have made a good profit from the illness of so many people, and I would have made a good profit with my preservative', turned to other matters.

After this it will be enough, if it is not too much, to touch only in passing and partly on the rest of that interrogation. Asked 'whether there were any other accomplices in this affair', Mora replied 'there may have been Piazza's companions, but I don't know who these are.' They objected: 'This ignorance is not plausible.' At the sound of this word, this fearful herald of torture, the unhappy man at once affirmed in the most positive way, 'They are the scissor-grinders and Baruello'; whose names he had heard at the previous interrogation. As for the poison, he said that he kept it in the oven, that is just where they imagined it might be. He told them how he concocted it, and ended by saying: 'I threw away what was left of it in the Vetra.' Here I cannot refrain from transcribing Verri's marginal note: 'He wouldn't, of course, have thrown this away after the imprisonment of Piazza!'

He answered various other questions they put to him on times and places and so forth, as though now the substance of the matter were quite clear and proved and only certain details were still lacking. Finally, he was tortured again in order to make his testimony valid against those named therein, in particular against the Commissioner – the man they had already tortured to give validity to a testimony which, on essential points, contradicted Mora's! No use citing legal texts or opinions here; for truly no such case was envisaged in jurisprudence.

A confession made under torture remained invalid unless it was ratified without the use of torture and in some other place, where the hideous instruments could not be seen, and on another day. This was an expedient devised by legal science to render an enforced confession, if possible, spontaneous; and to satisfy at once the promptings of common sense, which said only too clearly that words extorted by pain do not merit credence, and the Roman law which upheld torture. Indeed the jurists argued the desirability of such precautions from Roman law itself, referring to the following strange words: 'Torture is a delicate, dangerous, and deceptive thing: for many persons have such strength of soul or body that they heed pain very little, so that it is not a means of getting the truth from them; while others are so susceptible to pain that they will tell any lie rather than suffer it.'[16] I call these strange words in a law that upheld torture; and to understand how it was that the only conclusion drawn from them in fact was that 'one cannot always believe what is said under torture', one needs to remember that originally Roman law was a law made for slaves, and that slaves, in the degraded and corrupt pre-Christian world, could be regarded not as persons

[16] *Digest*, XLVIII, tit. 18, l. 1, 23.

but as things; as objects therefore upon which one might carry out any experiment in order to discover the crimes of others. Later legislators, with other ends in view, made this part of the law apply also to free men; which is one example and a notable one, if by no means unique, of how laws may acquire a wider application than they had at first and, so extended, outlast their origins.

The next day then, in observance of this formality, the judges summoned Mora again. But being now incapable of proceeding without guile, without seeking some advantage, without insinuations, instead of simply asking him whether he meant to ratify his confession, they asked 'whether he has anything to add to what he confessed yesterday after the torture?' Thus they precluded all doubt: jurisprudence required that the confession made under torture should now be open to further question; but they took its truth for granted, only asking that it be added to.

But in those hours (shall we call them of rest?) before they summoned him, the sense of his own innocence, or horror of the death penalty, or the thought of his wife and children, seem to have given Mora some hope of bearing fresh tortures more bravely; for his reply was: 'No, my Lord, I have nothing to add; rather, something to subtract.' So they had to ask him what this was. Then he spoke out more frankly, as it were plucking up courage: 'That unguent I talked about, I didn't make it at all; I only said I did because of the torture.' Immediately they threatened him with a repetition of the torture; and this (apart from other flagrant irregularities) without taking account of Mora's contradiction of Piazza, that is without being themselves prepared to say whether the new torture would be on account of Mora's confession or of the Commissioner's deposition; whether inflicted as on an accomplice or as on the chief criminal; for a crime committed at another's instigation or for one which the sufferer himself had instigated; for a crime for which Mora had been willing to pay lavishly, or for one which he had hoped would yield him a pittance.

To this threat he replied as before: 'I repeat; what I said yesterday is completely untrue; I said it because of the torture'; and then: 'Your Lordships, let me say a *Hail Mary*, and then I will do what God shows me I ought to do'; and he knelt down before an image of the Crucified who would one day judge his judges. After a little he got up and, on their urging him to ratify his confession, said, 'In conscience, it isn't true.' They had the unhappy man taken at once to the torture-chamber and bound, ordering the extra cruelty of the rope. He then said: 'Your Lordships need not torture me again. My confession was true and I confirm it.' Unbound and taken back to the other room, he once more said, 'It is utterly untrue.' So back to the torture-room where again he said what they wanted; and now, the pain having burnt away what little courage was left in him, he upheld what he had said under torture, declaring himself ready to ratify his confession; he did not even want them to read it to him. But to this they would not consent – scrupulously respecting a formality which now meant nothing, while violating greater laws. So they read out the report of the interrogation, and he said, 'It is all true.'

After this, persisting in their method of taking no step in the inquiry, of facing no difficulty, except after using torture (a procedure expressly forbidden in the law itself and one that even Diocletian and Maximian had tried to suppress) they at last thought of asking him whether he had had any purpose other than profit in selling his preservative. 'As far as I know,' he replied, 'I have no other purpose.'

'As far as I know'! Who else, if not he, could know his own private thoughts? And yet these strange words were fitting in the circumstances; no others that the wretched man might have used could have better expressed his self-abdication, so to call it, at that moment; his being ready to say yes and then no, and have only such knowledge, and all such knowledge, as suited the pleasure of those who had the means of torture in their hands.

They continued to press him, saying: 'it is very implausible that he and the Commissioner should have planned, by smearing the gates, to spread death and destruction in the city, simply in order that the one should find work and the other should sell his preservative; therefore, he should tell us why and wherefore they started on this course of action for so trivial a motive.'

Ah, so now it seems implausible! So they had threatened and repeatedly tortured him to make him ratify an implausibility! What I said above can be repeated here: 'a remark much to the point, but made too late'; the circumstances are so similar, they call for the same comment. Just as it had not occurred to these men that there was anything implausible in Piazza's deposition until, as a result of it, they had Mora in prison; so now they see nothing implausible in the latter's confession until after forcing him to ratify it and so obtaining the instrument they needed for his condemnation. Are we really to believe that this was the first time they noticed the implausibility? If so, how are we to explain, how shall we find words to describe, their subsequent upholding of the validity of the confession? Did Mora perhaps give them a more satisfying answer than Piazza had given? Here is Mora's answer: 'If the Commissioner doesn't know, I don't know; but he must know, and your Lordships will get the truth from him, because he started it all.' And clearly, the motive of all this passing on the principal guilt from each to the other and back again was not so much that each wanted to appear less guilty, as that they both wanted to be rid of the task of explaining things which could not be explained.

After that answer of Mora's they gave him to understand that 'having concocted the aforesaid unguent, in agreement with the said Commissioner, and having then given it to the latter to be smeared on the walls of houses (in the mode and manner stated by both in their depositions) in order to make people die (this purpose having been confessed by the said Commissioner), he had incurred the guilt of actively intending the death of people and thus had become liable to the penalties imposed by the law on whomsoever so intends and endeavours'.

To recapitulate. The judges ask Mora: How is it that you – the two of you together – decided to commit this particular crime for this particular motive? Mora answers: the Commissioner certainly knows why we decided; why he did and why I did: ask him. He refers them to another man for an explanation of an event in his own mind; that they might understand how a motive was sufficient to bring him, inwardly, to a decision. And to what other man? To a man who did not admit this particular motive since he attributed the crime to a wholly different cause. And the judges conclude that the difficulty is solved; that the crime confessed by Mora has become plausible; so much so that they find him guilty of it.

Whatever brought them to see implausibility in such a motive, it was not ignorance; and whatever led them to treat in this way the rules and prescriptions of jurisprudence, it was not jurisprudence.

CHAPTER 5

Impunity and torture had produced two stories; and while, for such judges as those, this sufficed to justify two sentences of guilt, nevertheless, as we shall now see, they did all they could to blend the two stories into one; and, all things considered, not without success. Finally, and in conclusion, we shall see them by their actions professing themselves convinced of the truth of this eventual single story.

The Senate confirmed and amplified the decision of its delegates. 'Having taken note of what has come to light from the confession of Giangiacomo Mora; having considered and compared the antecedent facts and all the circumstances' – except that for one and the same crime there were two principal authors; two different causes; two different arrangements of the facts – 'the Senate ordered that the said Mora . . . be once more diligently examined, but without torture, to make him explain more clearly the things he has confessed, and to obtain from him the names of the other authors, ringleaders and accomplices of the crime: and, this examinatioin terminated, that he be pronounced guilty (after all the facts of the case are recounted) of having concocted the poisonous unguent and given it to Guglielmo Piazza; and that he be allowed three days to prepare his defence. And with regard to Piazza, let him be asked whether he has anything to add to his confession, this having been found incomplete; and in the event of his having nothing to add, let him be pronounced guilty of having spread abroad the said unguent; and be granted the same time for his defence.' That is to say: Do your best to get all you can out of both men, and in any case let them both be declared guilty, each on his own confession, in spite of the confessions being contradictory.

They began with Piazza, and on the same day. He had nothing to add and did not know that *they* had something; he had not, perhaps, foreseen that in accusing an innocent he was creating an accuser. They asked him why in his deposition he had not said that he had given the barber saliva from persons dead of the plague with which to make the unguent. 'I didn't give him anything,' was his answer; as though those who had believed his lies had to believe him when telling the truth. After more twists and turns of question and answer they declared that 'since he has not told the whole truth, as he promised to do, he cannot and should not any longer enjoy the impunity that was promised him'. At once he said: 'My Lord, it is true that the barber came and asked me to get him some of that stuff, and I did bring him some, for making the unguent.' He hoped to save his impunity by admitting everything. Then, either to curry yet more favour or simply to gain time, he added that the money promised him by the barber was to have come from 'a great person', and that he learned this from the barber himself, but had never been able to make the latter say who the person was. He had not had time to think of a name.

So they asked Mora the next day; and probably the poor fellow would have thought up some name or other, as best he could, if they had tortured him. But, as we have seen, the Senate had ruled out torture this time – evidently to make the new ratification they desired of his previous confession seem less blatantly enforced. Hence, when asked 'whether the accused took the first step in approaching the said Commissioner ... and promised him a lot of money', Mora answered, 'No, my Lord; and where does your Lordship think I could have found this lot of money?' They might in fact have remembered that when Mora's house was thoroughly searched on the day of his arrest the entire treasure found in it had been 'a *baslotto* (jar) containing five *parpagliole* (twelve and a half *soldi*)'. Asked about the 'great person', he replied, 'Your Lordship wants the simple truth, and this I gave you when I was tortured, and in fact a bit more.'

Neither of the two abstracts of the trial mention that Mora ratified his previous confession; but if, as seems likely, they made him in fact do so, then these words of his amounted to a protest, the force of which he himself did not perhaps realize but which they must have realized. In any case it had always been the common teaching of the jurists, from Bartolo and even before him, from the authors of the Gloss, down to Farinacci, it had become a sort of axiom of jurisprudence, that 'a confession made under torture inflicted on grounds of legally insufficient evidence is null and void and remains so even if later ratified a thousand times without the use of torture': *etiam quod millies sponte sit ratificata.*[1]*

After that, Mora and Piazza received the 'publication', as it was called, of the case (that is to say, its acts were communicated to them) and they were allowed two days in which to prepare

---

[1] Farinacci, *Praxis*, Q. xxxvii, 110.

their defence – why one less than the Senate had decreed is not clear. Each man was assigned an official advocate; but the one assigned to Mora declined the task. Verri suggests that this refusal was due to a cause which unfortunately would not have been unlikely in the circumstances: 'Popular fury,' he says, 'had reached such a pitch that to defend the unhappy victim was regarded as wicked and dishonourable.'[2] However, the true cause is stated in the printed abstract which Verri could not have seen; but it is hardly less strange and, from one point of view, still more deplorable. It was on the same day, 2 July, that the notary Mauri was called upon to undertake Mora's defence; but he said, 'I cannot accept this responsibility, first because I am a criminal notary and so do not undertake defences, and also because I am neither a procurator nor an advocate: I am quite willing to go and speak with him, as a favour, but I will not undertake his defence.' So to a man who now stood in the shadow of death (and what a death! what manner of death!), a man without connexions or education, and who could turn nowhere for help except to them, who had to depend on them entirely, to this man they gave a defender who lacked certain essential qualifications for the task and had some that were incompatible with it! Even supposing no malice was involved, what irresponsibility! And it was left to a subordinate to recall them to respect for the most obvious and most binding rules of procedure.

Mauri returned and said: 'I have been with Mora and he told me frankly that he had done no wrong and that he said what he did because of the tortures; and when I told him frankly that I neither wished nor was able to undertake his defence, he said that he hoped that at least the Lord President would deign to provide him with an advocate and not permit that he should die undefended.' For such favours, with such words, innocence begged from injustice! They gave him in fact another person to defend him.

The one assigned to Piazza 'entered and asked to be shown his client's case; they gave it him and he read it'. Was this as far as they would go to oblige the defence? Not always; for Padilla's counsel (Padilla, as we shall presently see, was to represent in flesh and blood that vaguely indicated 'great person') had the records of the whole case at his disposal; thus being able to make

---

[2] Op. cit., ch. iv.

that copy of a substantial part of it which has survived for our information.

When the period fixed had elapsed the two poor wretches begged for more time. The Senate granted them 'the whole of the day following and no more: *et non ultra*'. Padilla's defence was given three hearings: the first part, on 24 July 1631, was heard 'without prejudice to the rest being heard later'; the next was on 13 April 1632; the last on 10 May of the same year, which was about two years after Padilla's arrest. For an innocent man the slowness of this procedure must have been painful, but compared with the haste used with Piazza and Mora – no lingering for them except in the manner of their death – it represented an outrageous partiality.

However, this new product of Piazza's imagination held up the execution of the death-sentence for some days – days full of deceptive hopes but also of fresh tortures and fresh and deadly calumnies. The Auditor of the Tribunal of Health was commissioned to hear a new deposition from Piazza, but secretly and with no notary present; and this time it was Piazza, through his counsel, who asked to be heard, giving out that he had something further to reveal about the 'great person'. Very likely he thought that if he could succeed in drawing some really big fish into this net, which was so easy to enter and so hard to get out of, that big fish, in its struggle to escape, would tear such a rent in the net that the little fish too could then slip through the hole along with it. And since among the many and various conjectures that were circulating in the city as to those responsible for that disastrous fouling of the walls on 18 May (for the angry excitement, the terrors and accusations caused by this incident were to a large extent themselves the cause of the violence employed by the judiciary, so that those who really did foul the walls were guilty of infinitely more evil than they knew) it was being rumoured that Spanish officers had done it, our miserable story-teller found something to hand that he could clutch at. Probably what caused Piazza to name Padilla in particular was (unless indeed the latter was the only Spanish officer he knew even by name) the fact that Padilla was the son of the governor of the Castle and so had a natural protector who, if he came to his son's assistance, could upset the whole trial. After the interview with the Auditor, Piazza was summoned before the judges to ratify his new deposition. In his other deposition he had said that the barber refused to name the 'great person'. But now he maintained the contrary; and in order somehow or other to soften the contradiction, he said that Mora had not given him the name immediately: 'In the end, after four or five days, he said that this great man was someone or other Di Padiglia. I don't remember the first name although he told me it. I do know and I remember quite clearly that he said that the man was son of the Lord Governor of the Castle of Milan.' He did not, however, say that he had received money from the barber – protesting indeed that he did not even know whether the latter had had any from Padilla.

Piazza was made to sign this deposition, and then immediately the Auditor was sent off with it to the Governor. This the records tell us; and we can safely presume that the Auditor was told to ask the Governor whether, if need be, he would allow Padilla – who was a cavalry captain and at this time serving with the army near Monferrato – to be handed over to the civil authorities. The Auditor came back; Piazza was at once made to ratify his confession afresh; then off went the Auditor again, this time to the unhappy Mora, who, being pressed to say that he had promised Piazza money and told him that he (Mora) had the backing of a 'great person', whose name he had finally revealed to the Commissioner, replied: 'Before God it's all false; and if I could, I would tell him so, as my conscience bears me witness.' So a new confrontation of the two men was arranged, in which Piazza was asked if it was true that Mora had promised him money, 'declaring that he was acting entirely under the orders and direction of Padiglia, son of the Lord Governor of the Castle of Milan'. On this Padilla's counsel very rightly observes that in this way, 'under the pretext of a confrontation', they were letting Mora know 'what they wanted him to say'. Without, in fact, this or some similar device they could certainly never have got Mora to name Padilla. Torture could make him a liar all right, but not a magician.

Piazza maintained what he had said in his deposition. 'You dare to say this?' cried Mora. 'Yes, I do dare to say it, it is true,' answered the other, shamelessly; 'and it's because of you that I've got into this hole, and you know very well what you said to me at the door of your shop.' Mora, who had perhaps hoped that, with the help of his defending counsel, his innocence would be made clear to all, and who now foresaw new tortures to extort a new confession from him, had not even the strength once again to oppose lies with the truth. He only said: '*Pazienza!* It's for you that I shall die.'

And in fact, once Piazza was taken away (which was done immediately) they warned Mora that 'now at last he must tell the truth'; and as soon as he replied, 'My Lord, I have told the truth,' they threatened torture; 'to be inflicted without prejudice to whatever is already proved and confessed'. It was the usual formula; but their using it at this point shows the degree to which their intense desire to find a culprit had deprived them of the capacity to reflect. How on earth could Mora's confession that he had led Piazza into crime with the promise of money from Padilla *not* prejudice his confession that he had let himself be led into it by Piazza in the hope of making a profit from his preservative?

Put to the torture, he at once confirmed everything that the Commissioner had said; and, this not satisfying the judges, added that Padilla had in fact suggested that he make 'an unguent to smear on the doors and bolts', and promised him all the money he might ask for and given him all the money he wanted.

We for our part, of course, who have no fear of unguents or fury against their users, nor around us the fury of others demanding satisfaction, we can easily and clearly see how such a confession took place and what caused it. But if we needed light on the matter, we should have it from the lips of him who confessed. Among the many statements of witnesses which Padilla's counsel managed to collect there is one by a Captain Sebastiano Gorini, who happened at that time (we do not know why) to be imprisoned in the same building as Mora and who often spoke with one of the servants of the Auditor of the Tribunal of Health who had been made the unhappy man's jailer. His testimony was as follows: 'This servant said to me one day, just after the barber had been brought back from an interrogation: "Sir, you don't know what the barber has said to me just now; he said that when they examined him he brought out the name of Don Juan, son of the Lord Governor of the Castle!" And I was amazed to hear this and said, "Is it true?" And the servant replied that it was true, but that it was also true that the barber protested that he could not remember whether he had ever even spoken to a Spaniard, and that if they had shown him this Don Juan he wouldn't even have recognized him. And the servant went on to say, "So I said to him, why then did you give his name?" and the barber replied that he had given it because he heard it from his examiners, and that he answered them according to whatever he heard them say or what they put into his mouth.' This, thank God, is good evidence in favour of Padilla. But are we to believe that the judges who had put Mora, or allowed him to be put, under the guard of a servant of that extremely alert and inquisitive Auditor, only came to know what Mora had said (in words that ring so true, so desperately sincere, compared with those strange ones which pain had wrung from him only a moment before) so much later and from the accidental testimony of a witness at Padilla's trial?

And because it seemed strange even to the judges – among so much else that was strange – that a Milanese barber and a Spanish cavalier should have had such dealings with one another, they asked him who had served as the link between them; and Mora at first only said, 'one of his men', with such and such an appearance and dress: but then, they insisting on giving a name, he said, 'Don Pietro di Saragoza'. And certainly this person, at any rate, was imaginary. Later – after Mora's execution of course – a thorough and persistent inquiry was undertaken: soldiers and officers were interrogated, including even Don Francisco de Vargas, the successor to Padilla's father as Governor of the Castle of Milan. No one had ever heard of that Don Pedro. But in the end a man was found in the city prison, awaiting trial for theft, whose name was Pietro Verdeno and who had been born in Saragossa. Being questioned, he said that he had been in Naples at the time: tortured, he said the same thing. People then dropped the subject of Don Pedro of Saragossa.

Harried by more and more questions, Mora went on to say that he had then put his proposal to the Commissioner; who in his turn had received money for the same purpose 'from someone – I don't know his name'. Of course he didn't know it; but the judges wanted to know: so the poor wretch was tortured again and this time unfortunately brought out the name of a real person, a banker called Giulio Sanguinetti: 'the first name to occur to one inventing in agony'.[3]

Piazza, who had hitherto steadily denied having received any money now, being questioned again, at once said that he had received some (the reader may have a better memory than the judges had, and so be able to recall that when the police visited Piazza's house they found even less money than in Mora's, that is none at all). He had received it, he said, from a banker; and

---

[3] Livy, *History of Rome*, XXIV,5: 'quorum capita ... fingenti inter dolores gemitusque occurrere.'

since the judges had not given him Sanguinetti's name, he gave them another: Girolamo Turcone. And Turcone and Sanguinetti and various subordinates of theirs were duly arrested, questioned, and tortured; but as they stoutly persisted in denying the charge they were finally let go.

On 21 July the supplementary acts of the trial, from its resumption, were communicated to Piazza and Mora, and they were allowed another two days to prepare their defence. This time both chose their own advocates, probably on the advice of those originally assigned to them *ex officio*. On the 23rd Padilla was arrested; that is, as we know from the defence at his trial, Padilla was informed by the Commissioner to the cavalry that Spinola had given orders that he should go to the castle of Pomate and give himself up; which he did. His father, as we know from the same source, petitioned, through his lieutenant and his secretary, that the execution of the sentence on Piazza and Mora be suspended until they had been confronted with Don Juan. The answer sent back to him was: 'No suspension is possible because of the excited state of the public' (so for once they mention it, the *civium ardor prava jubentium*:* and it was only now that they could do so without confessing a vile and vicious compliancy; now that the only question was, not what their judgement would be, but when it would be carried out. But had the public only now begun to show excitement? Or had the judges only now begun to heed its clamour?) . . . 'but in any case the Lord Don Francisco need not trouble himself, for nothing said by such infamous persons as those two could possibly cast a slur on the reputation of Don Juan.' Yet what the 'infamous' persons had said against each other had counted! And how often had the judges called it 'the truth'! And when they passed sentence they decreed that after the publication of the sentence both men should be tortured again to bring to light their accomplices! And what the pair then confessed led to further tortures, and so to more confessions and so to more executions – and, as though this were not enough, to executions where there had been no confession.

'And so,' said the above-mentioned secretary, concluding his deposition, 'we returned to the Lord Governor of the Castle and reported all that had happened: and he said no more, but was mortified; so much so that after a few days he died.'

By the terms of the hellish sentence passed on them, Piazza and Mora were to be taken in a cart to the place of execution, being torn with red-hot pincers on the way; their right hands cut off in front of Mora's shop; their bones broken on the wheel; and, while they were still alive, their bodies twisted into the wheel and lifted from the ground; and after six hours, their throats to be cut, their corpses burned and the ashes thrown into the river. Mora's house was to be demolished and in the space where it had stood a column erected, to be called the 'Column of Infamy'; it being forbidden ever to build on that spot again. And if anything could add to the horror and indignation and pity that such a sentence arouses in us, it would be to hear the two victims, after being informed of it, renewing and even amplifying their confessions; still driven by the same forces which had extorted these: the hope, still not extinguished, of escaping death, and such a death; the violence of the tortures already suffered, which that frightful sentence no doubt made appear, by comparison, almost lenient, but also as things still present and avoidable; these motives made them not only repeat their former lies but extend them by accusing yet more people. Thus did the judges succeed, with their promise of impunity and their torture, not only in bringing innocent men to an atrocious death, but also, so far as the event depended on them, in making those innocent men die guilty.

It is a relief to learn, however, from the records of the defence in Padilla's trial, that Piazza and Mora, once they were perfectly sure that they were to die and would have to answer no more questions, protested their own innocence and that of the persons accused by them. We know this through that Captain Gorini mentioned above. He deposed that, happening to find himself close to the chapel in which Piazza had been put, he heard the latter 'crying out and saying that his death was a crime, and that he was being murdered, and that they had broken their word to him'; and that he refused the ministrations of the two Capuchin friars who had come to help him to die as a Christian. 'And for my part,' added Gorini, 'I saw that he still had some hope that they would withdraw the case against him ... and so I went to the Commissioner, thinking it would be an act of charity if I could persuade him to get ready to die well, in the grace of God; as in fact I can say that I did. Because the Fathers had not touched the point that really mattered, but I did so; which was when I assured him that I had never known or ever heard of an instance of the Senate's withdrawing a case after sentence of condemnation had been passed. ... So at last I was able to calm him ... and after he had calmed down, he sighed for a while and then said that he had unjustly given the names of many innocent persons.' And in fact both Piazza and Mora had a formal retraction written down, by the friars attending on them, of all the accusations which pain or hope had extorted from them. And both of them endured that long death-agony, that series and variety of agonies with a strength which – in men whom pain and the fear of death had so often overcome; in men who were dying as victims, not of some great cause, but of petty accidents and foolish errors and cheap and base deceits; in men who, even when branded with infamy, remained obscure and had nothing to oppose to the execration of the public except the consciousness of a common person's innocence, which no one believed in and which they themselves had repeatedly denied; in men (it hurts to think of this, but how can one put away the thought?) who had families, wives, and children – would be incomprehensible if one did not know that it sprang from resignation; from that gift, I mean, which makes one able to see in the injustice of men the justice of God, and in all punishments, whatever they may be, a pledge, not of pardon merely, but of reward. Both men continued ceaselessly, to the end, and on the wheel itself, to say that they accepted death as a punishment for their sins – their real sins. To accept what cannot be refused! These words may seem meaningless to one who considers things only in their material effects; but they have a deep and clear meaning for one who considers, or without considering understands, that that which may be the most difficult part of any deliberation, and is always the most important – the mind's judgement and the movement of the will – is equally difficult and equally important whether the issue depends upon it or not; whether one is assenting to something done or choosing to do it.

Those protestations of innocence might have struck fear into the consciences of the judges; they might also have roused them to anger. Unfortunately the judges succeeded in getting them in part contradicted, and this in the manner that would have been the most decisive possible had it not been the most illusory; namely, by making many of those persons whom the protestations had so authoritatively exculpated accuse themselves on their own account. Over these further trials, however, as the reader has already been notified, I will pass quickly and selectively, in order to come to that of Padilla – to the trial, that is, which, as it is the principal one in view of the eminence of the person accused, so, by reason of the form it took and of its result, it represents a touchstone by which to judge all the others.

CHAPTER 6

The two scissor-grinders who had had the misfortune to be mentioned by Piazza, and later by Mora, had been in prison since 27 June, but had never been confronted with either of their accusers. Nor were they even judicially examined before the latters' execution, which was on 1 August. On the 11th of that month the father, Girolamo Migliavacca, was interrogated; and the following day tortured, on the usual pretext of having given contradictory and implausible answers. Under torture Girolamo confessed; that is, he made up a story; and did so, like Piazza, by distorting a real fact (they both resembled spiders that stick the ends of their thread on to something solid and then work away in the air). Among Girolamo's things the police had found a phial containing an opiate, given him, indeed composed in his own house, by his friend Baruello; and this, he now declared, 'was an unguent intended to kill people', made of matter extracted from toads and snakes, together with 'certain powders – I don't know what powders they are'. Beside Baruello, he named another fairly well-known person; and, as the chief instigator, Padilla. The judges would have liked to connect this story with that of the two men they had murdered; so they tried to make Girolamo say that he had received 'unguent and money' from Piazza and Mora. Had he simply denied this, they had torture in reserve; but he forestalled them with these remarkable words: 'No my Lord, that is not true; but if you torture me for denying it, I shall have to say it is true, although it isn't.' This checked them: they could not, without too obviously making a farce of justice and humanity, appear to try out a means after being so solemnly assured that its effect was guaranteed in advance.

Migliavacca was condemned to the same death as his accusers. After hearing the sentence he was tortured again, and came out with fresh accusations – of another banker and of some other people. In the prison chapel and on the scaffold he retracted everything.

If all that Piazza and Mora had said about this unfortunate

wretch was that he was a good-for-nothing, enough came out in
the trial to have acquitted them of slander. But his son Gaspare
they did slander, even in this respect. Gaspare was indeed, as the
records show, guilty of an offence; but it was one that he himself
admitted; and at a time and in a manner such as almost to
constitute a proof of the purity and integrity of his entire life. To
the end, under torture and face to face with death, he spoke, not
just like a brave man but like a martyr. After they had failed to
force him to calumniate either himself or others, they sentenced
him (on what pretexts it is impossible to say) as proven guilty;
and having told him of the sentence, went on to the usual
questions, as to whether he had committed other crimes and as
to who had been his associates in that for which he was
condemned. To the first question Gaspare replied: 'I have not
committed this or any other crime. And I am to die because once
in anger I punched a man in the eye.' And to the second: 'I have
had no associates, because I have minded my own business; and
in any case, if I didn't commit the crime, I couldn't have had
associates.' Threatened with torture, he said: 'Your Lordships
can do as you please, because I will never say I have done what I
didn't do; and I will never damn my own soul; I would far rather
suffer three or four hours' pain than go to Hell to suffer eternally.'
Put to the torture, he cried out at the first shock: 'Ah God! I've
done nothing: you're murdering me.' Then he added: 'These
pains will be over quickly, but the next world goes on forever.'
The torture was intensified by degrees, up to the maximum
degree; at every stage they pressed him the harder to tell the
truth; and his reply was always the same: 'I have told it already.
I want to save my soul. I will not have a lie on my conscience; I
have done nothing.'

At this point one cannot help reflecting that if similar senti-
ments had inspired Piazza, poor Mora would have remained
undisturbed in his shop and his home; and this young man also,
even more worthy of admiration than compassion, and many
other innocent people would never have been troubled by even a
thought of the dreadful fate they had escaped. And he himself –
who knows? For certainly to condemn him when he had confessed nothing, simply on the evidence that we have seen, and
when, in default of others' confessions, the crime itself remained
the merest conjecture, the judges had to violate even more
brazenly and boldly every principle of justice and every precept
of the law. At all events, at least they could not condemn him to

the additional horror of making him suffer in company with one the sight of whom must cause him continually to say to himself: I brought him to this! The root cause, then, of such horrors was the weakness. . . . but no! it was the obstinate rage and perfidy of those who, counting it as a disaster and a defeat to discover no culprits, tempted that weakness with an illegal and deceitful promise.

In an earlier chapter I quoted the official decree by which a promise similar to that made to Mora was made to Baruello; and said in passing that I wished to show how the judges' attitudes differed in the two cases. It is chiefly for this reason that the wretched Baruello's story must now be briefly told. As we have seen, he had been accused – without proof – first by Piazza, of being Mora's associate, and then by Mora, of being Piazza's; and then, by both, of having been paid to spread abroad an unguent made by Mora out of muck and worse (and on this point the two witnesses had at first protested ignorance); and then, by Girolamo Migliavacca, of having himself concocted some out of other stuff worse than muck: and now, put on trial for all these things at once, as though they constituted a single charge, Baruello denied everything and stood up stoutly to the ensuing torture. But while his case was still pending, a priest (another of the witnesses to be cited in Padilla's defence), at the request of a relative of Baruello, spoke on the latter's behalf to a barrister employed by the Senate. In due time this official informed the priest that Baruello had been sentenced to death, with all the attendant butchery, but that, at the same time, 'the Senate was prepared to obtain a promise of impunity for him from His Excellency'. The priest meanwhile must go to Baruello and try to persuade him to make a clean breast of everything, 'because the Senate wants to get to the bottom of this affair, and thinks it can obtain the truth from Baruello'. After condemning him to death! And after the execution of Piazza and Mora!

Baruello, on hearing the dire news and the accompanying proposal, said: 'Then are they going to treat me as they treated the Commissioner?' But, being assured by the priest that the promise seemed to be sincere, he launched into the following story. So-and-so (now dead) had taken him to see the barber. The latter, lifting a curtain that hung by the wall of the room and concealed a door, then led Baruello into a large chamber where many persons were seated, among whom was Padilla. The priest, who was not obliged to find culprits, thought this all rather strange; and interrupted the tale, warning Baruello that he ought to take care not to lose his soul along with his body; and then took his leave. Baruello accepted the Senate's impunity and revised his story; and, being brought before the judges on 11 September, informed them that a certain fencing-master (unfortunately alive) had told him that there was a good chance of becoming rich if one was prepared to do a service to Padilla; and that the fencing-master had then taken him to the square in front of the Castle, where they found Padilla waiting with some other men. Padilla had at once invited him to join those who worked under his orders, smearing the city walls for the purpose of avenging the insults offered to Don Gonzalez de Cordova on the occasion of his departure from Milan; and then had given Baruello money and a little jar of the deadly unguent.

To say that this story (of which I give only the beginning) was implausible would be an abuse of language; it was all a tissue of absurdities, as the reader can see from this sample. However, even the judges found implausibilities in it; and, what is more, inconsistencies. Hence, after various questions followed by answers involving ever new complications, they said to him that 'he must express himself more clearly if we are to derive any clear information from his story.' On this Baruello – whether it was that he thought of a trick to get him out of the difficulty, or really suffered a temporary derangement (understandable in the circumstances) – began to tremble and writhe, and shout for help, and roll about on the floor, and try to hide under a table. They had him exorcized and calmed down, and then bade him begin again. So he started another tale, this time bringing in witches and magic circles and incantations and the Devil, whom he said he had taken as his lord and master. Enough for us to note that he had not said these things before; and that among other things he now took back what he had said about a revenge for an offence given to Don Gonzalez, asserting instead that Padilla's aim was to make himself master of Milan; and that Padilla had promised him, Baruello, a very high place in the new régime. After various questions the interrogation, if such it can be called, was declared closed. It was later followed by three more, in which, on their telling him that this assertion of his was not plausible or that one not credible, Baruello either replied that he had lied the first time or else invented some other explanation. And when at least five times they put it to him that, according to Migliavacca's deposition, he had himself given the unguent to as many people, for

them to spread around the city, whereas in his own deposition
these persons were not mentioned, his answer every time was
that this was not true; and every time the judges changed the
subject. The reader who remembers how, in Piazza's case, at the
very first implausibility which the judges thought fit to find in his
deposition they threatened to withdraw his impunity; and how,
on Piazza's first adding a word to that deposition, when Mora
made his first allegation against him and he denied it, they did in
fact withdraw it 'since he has not told the whole truth, as he
promised to do'; will now see clearly – if the point escaped him
before – what an advantage it was to the judges to have played
that trick on the Governor of taking it on themselves to concede
the impunity without obtaining his authorization: they could
make a purely verbal, and void, promise to Piazza. For he had to
be the first victim sacrificed to the public's fury and their own.

Do I mean then that it would have been just to maintain that
promise of impunity? God forbid! That would be as good as
saying that Piazza's testimony was true. I mean only that just as
the impunity had been illegally promised, so it was violently
withdrawn, and that the illegality led straight to the violence. But
then, as I have said before, the judges were not capable of justice
so long as they kept to the path they had chosen; their only
chance would have been to turn back while there was yet time.
They no more had the moral right (quite apart from the legal
authority) to sell that impunity to Piazza than a robber has the
right to concede life to a man on the road, when his simple duty
is to leave the man alone. That impunity was an injustice added
to unjust torturing; both the one and the other being expedients
which the judges deliberately adopted and applied in preference
to the course of action that the law itself, let alone reason or
justice or charity, required of them – namely, to ascertain the
true facts of the case; have these explained to the two women
who had, rightly or wrongly, called attention to them; and to the
man they had, rightly or wrongly, accused; and confront the
latter with his accusers.

Nothing came of the impunity promised to Baruello, because
he died of the plague on 18 September, the day after he had been
confronted with the fencing-master, Carlo Vedano, and had
repeated, shamelessly, his accusations. But when he felt that his
end was near he said to a fellow-prisoner who was nursing him
(and who was to be another of Padilla's witnesses): 'Do me the
kindness of telling the Lord Magistrate that all those I have

accused, I accused unjustly. And it is not true that I got money
from the son of the Governor of the Castle. . . . I'm going to die
of this sickness, and I beg those I have unjustly accused to forgive
me. And please tell the Lord Magistrate this; so I may die in
peace.' 'And I,' added the witness, 'went and told the Lord
Magistrate what Baruello had said to me.'

This retraction was able to help Padilla; but Vedano, who so
far had been mentioned only by Baruello, was tortured atro-
ciously that same day. He had the strength to endure it; and was
then left alone (in prison, of course) until the middle of the
following January. He alone of all these common people had
some acquaintance with Padilla, having fenced with him twice at
the Castle – which clearly was why it occurred to Baruello to
allot him a part in his tale. However, Baruello had not accused
Vedano of concocting or spreading or distributing deadly
unguents; but only of being go-between between him and Padilla.
Hence the judges could not condemn Vedano as guilty without
pre-judging that gentleman's case; which was probably what
saved him. He was not questioned again until after the first
interrogation of Padilla; and the latter's acquittal led to his own.

On 10 January 1631 Padilla, who had been transferred to the
castle of Pizzighettone, was brought to Milan and put in the prison
of the Chief of Police. His interrogation took place on the same
day; and if concrete proof were needed to assure us that even those
judges were capable of interrogating without guile or lies or
bullying; of not seeing implausibilities where there were none; of
being satisfied with a reasonable answer; of allowing, even when
poisonous unguents were in question, that an accused man could
tell the truth, even when he said 'no'; the proof is to be seen in this
interrogation of Padilla and the two that followed it.

Of those who had named Padilla in their depositions, only
Mora and Baruello claimed to have spoken with him; and both
had dated their conversations, the former vaguely, the latter more
precisely. So the judges began by asking Padilla when he had
joined his regiment in the field: he told them the day. The place
from which he had gone there? Milan. Had he returned to Milan
in the meantime? Once only; and only for one day, which he
specified with the same precision. It did not agree with either of
the periods invented by the unhappy pair. Then they asked him,
courteously, using no threats, 'to try to remember' whether he
had been in Milan on such-and-such a day or another day; and
each time he answered 'no', referring back to his first reply. Then

they came to persons and places. Did he know a gunner called Fontana? (This man, who was father-in-law to Vedano, had been named by Baruello as one of those present at his first encounter with Padilla.) Padilla replied that he did. Did he know Vedano? 'Yes' again. Did he know the Via Vetra de' Cittadini and the inn of the Six Thieves (whither Padilla had come, said Mora, accompanied by Don Pedro of Saragossa, to put to him his proposal about spreading poison in the city)? Padilla answered that he knew neither the street nor the inn – not even by name. They asked him about Don Pedro of Saragossa. Padilla did not know him; indeed he could not have known him. They asked him about two men wearing clothes of a French cut and about another dressed as a priest; persons whom Baruello had said had come with Padilla to the meeting in the square in front of the Castle. Padilla had no idea of whom they were speaking.

At the second interrogation, on the last day of January, they asked him about his relations with Mora, Migliavacca, and Baruello – their conversations, the money given, the promises made; but without as yet mentioning the general plan with which these details were connected. Padilla answered that he had never had anything to do with the men in question; he had never even heard of them; and repeated that he was not in Milan at the times referred to.

After more than three months spent in inquiries which, naturally, were quite fruitless, the Senate decreed that Padilla be tried for the crime of which he stood accused, be supplied with the facts of the case and an account of the trial, and given a fixed time in which to prepare his defence. This order led to a third, and last, interrogation on 22 May. After various questions touching all the points on which he was accused – questions Padilla invariably answered in the negative and, for the most part, curtly – they came to 'the facts of the case', that is to say, they threw in his face the crazy story, or rather the two stories, they had collected. And first, that he, the accused, had told Mora, the barber, 'near the inn called the Six Thieves, to make an unguent ... and take the said unguent and go and smear it on the walls', and that he had paid Mora well for his trouble; and that later Don Pedro of Saragossa, acting under his orders, had sent the barber to such-and-such bankers to cash still more money on his account. But this tale is rational compared with the other one: namely, that the accused, having summoned Baruello to the square in front of the Castle, had said to him there: 'Good morning, Signor Baruello, I have been wanting to speak with you for a long time now'; and after various other compliments, had given Baruello twenty-five Venetian ducats and a jar of unguent, telling him that this stuff was made in Milan but that it wasn't quite suitable for its purpose, and that what was needed was to 'take some *ghezzi* and *zatti*' (lizards and toads) and 'some white wine', and put it all in a saucepan and 'boil it *a concio a concio* (very slowly) so that those animals should die in a fury'. Moreover a priest, 'called "the Frenchman" by the said Baruello' and who had come in the accused's company, had caused to appear 'one in the form of a man and dressed like *Pantalone*',* and had made Baruello acknowledge the apparition as his lord; and on its vanishing, Baruello had asked the accused who it was and the accused had replied that it was the Devil. And that on another occasion the accused had given Baruello more money, and promised to make him an officer in his bodyguard, on condition that he served him well.

At this point Verri (so much may exclusive attachment to one point of view cause the noblest minds to err, even after they have seen clearly) concludes thus: 'Such was the series of charges brought against the son of the Governor of the Castle; charges which, though given the lie by all the other persons interrogated – except that unhappy trio, Mora, Piazza, and Baruello, who abandoned truth entirely under the stress of torture – were taken as evidence of an abominable crime.'[1] But, as the reader knows and as Verri himself had related, what led two of the trio to lie was not the stress of torture but the enticement of impunity.

On hearing that contemptible string of accusations Padilla said: 'Of all the persons your Lordship has named I know only Fontana and the *Tegnone* (a nickname for Vedano); and all that your Lordship reports as having been said in the course of the trial by those men is as completely false and untrue as anything possibly could be. It is beyond all belief that a gentleman of my rank should have done, or dreamed of doing, such infamous things. And I pray God and His Holy Mother to send me to Hell here and now if all this be true. And I am confident that God will make it known, and known to the world, that those men were lying.'

The judges replied, as a matter of form and without pressing Padilla, that he must be resolved to speak the truth; and then informed him of the Senate's decree putting him on trial for the

---

[1] *Osservazioni*, end of ch. v.

crime of making and distributing a poisonous unguent and of hiring accomplices. 'I am exceedingly astonished,' was his answer, 'that the Senate should have taken so serious a step when it is clear and proved that all this is nothing but a fraud and a lie – an insult not only to myself but to justice. What! A man of my quality, a man who has spent his life in the service of His Majesty and the defence of this State, a descendant of men who did the same – would I do or think of doing a thing that would bring me such disgrace and dishonour? I repeat: all this is a lie; the biggest fraud ever committed against a man.'

It is gratifying to hear such language from outraged innocence; but horrifying to recall that, before those same judges, innocence had been terrified, bewildered, driven to despair, to lies, to calumny; and also fearless, resolute, loyal to the truth – and condemned just the same.

Padilla was acquitted: the exact date is uncertain, but it must have been more than a year later, since his defence was concluded in May 1632. And certainly the acquittal was not conceded as a favour; but in that case did it not occur to the judges that, acquitting Padilla, and making no further condemnations after his acquittal, they declared all their previous condemnations unjust? When they admitted that Padilla had not paid a penny for those imaginary smearings, did they remember the men they had condemned for being paid by him for that very purpose? Did they remember saying to Mora that that motive (to earn money from Padilla) was 'more plausible . . . than that he would find opportunities for selling his preservative, and the Commissioner find opportunities for work'? Did they remember that in the interrogation which followed, when Mora persisted in denying that motive, they had said to him, 'nevertheless it is evidently true'? That when, confronted with Piazza, he denied it again, they had tortured him to make him confess it, and then tortured him once more to give validity to the confession so extorted? That from then on to the end the whole trial had proceeded on the supposition that that motive was the true one? That it had been expressed or implied in all their questions, and confirmed by every reply, as the motive at last discovered and acknowledged, the true motive, the single and sufficient motive which led Piazza and Mora, and then the others condemned after them, into crime? Did they remember that the Lord Chancellor, at the Senate's request, had caused a proclamation to be published a few days after the execution of Piazza and Mora, declaring them 'to have fallen into so impious a state of mind as to have betrayed their own Fatherland for money'? And when, eventually, they saw that motive eliminated (for there was never any question throughout the trial of anyone but Padilla paying anybody), did it occur to them that now there was no reason left for thinking that a crime had been committed at all, except confessions obtained in such ways as they well knew and retracted between the Last Sacraments and death? And that those confessions, already in contradiction with one another, were now in manifest contradiction with the facts? Did they, in short, realize that in acquitting the ringleader after condemning his accomplices, they showed themselves guilty of condemning the innocent?

Quite the reverse; to judge by what appeared in public, at least. The monument was left standing, the sentence never revoked; and the families of the men it had condemned remained under the imputation of 'infamy'; and the children thus so cruelly orphaned remained legally destitute. And as for the judges' secret thoughts on the matter, who can measure the resistance to fresh evidence of which men are capable, when their deception is wilful and is already toughened in the fight against evidence? Indeed, their deception had now become more dear to the judges, more precious than ever; for if previously to admit the innocence of the accused would have meant only the loss of an opportunity of finding someone guilty, now it would mean that they found themselves guilty, and dreadfully so; and all those deceits, all that flouting of the law, which they knew they had committed and which they wished to believe were justified by the discovery of criminals so depraved and so dangerous, would now not only be unveiled in their own intrinsic ugliness but would be seen by all as the means employed for committing atrocious murder. And, lastly, the deception was upheld and reinforced by an authority that is always powerful, though often wrong and in this case also curiously illusory, since it was to a large extent based on that of the judges themselves; I mean the authority of the public which was proclaiming those judges as wise, zealous, intrepid defenders and champions of the Fatherland.

The Column of Infamy was pulled down in 1778; and when, in 1803, a house was built again on space that it had occupied, the arch over the road was also demolished from which Caterina Rosa,

'the infernal goddess who stood on the lookout'[2]*

---

[2] Caro's translation of the *Aeneid*, VII.

raised the cry that began all the butchery: so that now there is nothing left to remind one either of the frightful effects or of the miserable cause. Where Via della Vetra joins Corso di Porta Ticinese, the house at the corner, to the left as you look from the Corso, stands on ground once occupied by poor Mora's dwelling.

And now, if the reader has patience enough for one final inquiry, let us see how that woman's rash judgement, after proving so powerful in the law-courts, continued, thanks to them, to hold sway in books also.

CHAPTER 7

Of the many writers contemporary with the affair, let us consider the only one who is not now generally forgotten, and whose comments on it were not a mere echo of popular credulity: Giuseppe Ripamonti.* This writer – already so often cited – provides, it seems to me, a curious example of the power which a dominant opinion can retain over the words of those whose minds it has not been able to subdue. Not only does Ripamonti never explicitly deny the guilt of those who suffered in the affair (nor, in fact, did anyone else until Verri, in any work intended for publication) but he more than once seems to want expressly to affirm it. Referring to Piazza's first interrogation, he speaks of his 'evil intentions' and of the judges' 'clearsightedness': he says that Piazza 'by so often contradicting himself, revealed his crime in the act of denying it'. So too when he comes to Mora: 'He denied his guilt as criminals usually do, so long as he could bear the torture; but gave in the end a truthful account of the whole matter (*exposuit omnia cum fide*).' And yet at the same time we find Ripamonti insinuating the contrary view – timidly hinting, in passing, at his own uncertainty as to some of the more important circumstances; dropping phrases here and there that guide the reader's reflections in the right direction; sometimes putting into the mouths of the accused words more calculated to prove their innocence than those they themselves had been able to find; lastly, evincing the sort of compassion that is only aroused by innocence. Alluding to the cooking-pot found in Mora's house, he says: 'This find made a great impression at first, though it may have been, though sordid enough, quite insignificant; but it seemed it could have a bearing on the inquiry.' Speaking of the first confrontation of Piazza and Mora, he says that Mora 'invoked the justice of God against a false and malicious fabrication, against a trap set for unwary innocence.' He calls Mora 'that unhappy father and husband who unwittingly caused his own and his family's ruin'. And all those reflections which, as the reader will remember, I made on the obvious contradiction between the acquittal of Padilla and the condemnation of the others, these and much else that one might say on the subject are all suggested by Ripamonti in a single word: 'The smearers were punished nevertheless, *unctores puniti tamen.*' What a wealth of meaning in that adverb or conjunction! And he goes on: 'The city would have been horrorstruck by the outrageous cruelty of the execution were it not that anything seemed less dreadful than the crime itself.'

But where Ripamonti's real feelings show most clearly is where he protests that he does not wish to show them. After recounting various cases of people who fell under suspicion of being 'smearers' but were not in fact brought to trial, he continues:

Here I find myself at a difficult and delicate point in my discussion of the affair. Can I say that I myself believe that as well as those mistakenly taken for smearers there were real smearers? ... Nor is my difficulty due to an uncertainty in the matter itself, but to the fact that I am not permitted the freedom to which every writer lays claim, viz. that of expressing what one really thinks. For were I to assert that in truth there were no smearers, that imagination has misconstrued as human malice what was really a punishment sent from God, the cry would at once be raised accusing History of impiety and this historian of a want of respect for a solemn judgement of the courts: so firmly rooted in men's minds is the contrary view. And the populace and the nobility, the one, as usual, credulous and the other proud, are united in eager defence of this view as of something exceedingly precious and sacred. To defy so many adversaries would be a most troublesome undertaking and in any case a futile one. Therefore, without either denying or affirming, or even inclining to one side rather than the other, I will limit myself to presenting the opinion of others.[1]

---

[1] *De peste*, pp. 107, 108.

And should it occur to the reader that, in these circumstances, it might have been more reasonable, as well as easier, to say nothing at all, he should know that Ripamonti was the city's official historiographer; that is to say, a man who could sometimes be ordered to write history and sometimes forbidden.

Another historian (though he worked on a wider field), Battista Nani,* who, as a Venetian, was under no constraint in this case to say what was false for fear of giving offence, was led to believe it nevertheless on the authority of an inscription and a monument. 'It may well be true,' he wrote, 'that the terrified populace imagined a great deal, but the fact remains that the crime was discovered and duly punished; witness the inscriptions that are still to be seen in Milan and the memorial marking where the houses stood in which these monsters used to congregate.'[2] The reader not otherwise acquainted with Nani will be greatly deceived if he bases his opinion of Nani's intelligence on this piece of reasoning. On various important embassies abroad and in public office at home Nani had abundant opportunities for observing men and things; and his historical work is there to show that he was no mean observer. But neither the sentences of criminal courts nor the fate of the poor (taken a few at a time) are regarded as a proper subject for history; so it need not surprise us that Nani, when he touched in passing on our affair, did not greatly trouble himself over details. Had anyone referred him to some other Milanese column or inscription as proof of a defeat suffered by Venice* (a defeat that would be as true as the crime of 'those monsters'), Nani most certainly would have laughed.

It is more surprising and more distasteful to find the same argument and similar insults in the work of a much more famous – and very deservedly famous – man. Muratori,* in his *Trattato del governo della peste*, after referring to various accounts of similar cases, says:

> But none is more celebrated than that which occurred in Milan during the plague of 1630, when many persons were arrested and, confessing their hideous crime, were put to death with the utmost severity. A dreadful memorial of this affair survives in the shape of the 'Column of Infamy', which I myself have seen and which stands where once was the house of those inhuman murderers; an object

---

[2] Nani, *Historia veneta*, Part I, Book viii (Venice: Lovisa 1720), p. 473.

deserving the greatest attention lest such execrable scenes be ever re-enacted.

And it does nothing to lessen one's distaste, but only alters it, to find that Muratori was not so firmly convinced as these words make him appear. For later, when he comes to discuss the horrors that can be caused by imagining and believing in such things without regard for evidence (and this, clearly, is what he is really concerned about) he writes: 'It leads to people being thrown into prison and compelled by torture to confess crimes they may never have committed, and then miserably slaughtered on the scaffold.' This looks – doesn't it? – remarkably like an allusion to our poor sufferers. And what gives substance to the suspicion is that Muratori at once continues with words which I quoted in the preceding work and which are few enough to be repeated here. 'In Milan I have met people of good judgement, and who had been well informed on the matter by their elders, who were not much convinced of the truth of that story about the contamination of the city with poisonous unguents which made such a stir during the plague of 1630.'[3] It is, I repeat, impossible not to suspect that in his heart Muratori thought these 'scenes' which he called 'execrable' were really just stupid stories and that – and this is more serious – the men he called 'inhuman murderers' were really innocent and murdered. His case would be one of those, unhappily not infrequent, of men, by no means prone to tell lies, who, desiring to undermine the power of false and pernicious opinions, but fearing to make things worse by a frontal attack, have thought it best to start by lying so as to be able later to insinuate truth.

After Muratori we meet with a writer more famous than he as an historian and one too (which, in a matter of this kind, would make one expect his judgement to be particularly valuable) who was also a lawyer – as he himself said, 'more lawyer than politician'[4] – , Pietro Giannone.* I will not, however, quote Giannone's judgement here, having just done so: his judgement is in fact Nani's, which the reader saw a little while ago and which Giannone copied word for word, this time giving the reference in a footnote[5].

I say 'this time' because Giannone's copying from Nani without

---

[3] Book I, ch. x.
[4] Giannone, *Istoria Civile*, Introduction.
[5] *Istoria Civile*, Book xxxvi. ch. 2.

acknowledgement is a thing worth noting if, as I believe, it has hitherto passed unnoticed. His account, for example, of the rising in Catalonia and the Portuguese revolution in 1640 is a transcript of Nani's, occupying seven quarto pages; with very few omissions, additions, or alterations, the most substantial of these being that the original text, which runs on continuously, has been broken up into chapters and paragraphs. But what would be incredible if it were not true is that when our Neapolitan lawyer comes to deal, not with the risings in Barcelona or Lisbon, but with that of Palermo in 1647 and with the more famous – because it gave rise to stranger happenings and involved Masaniello* – rebellion of Naples in the same year, he can think of no better, of no more detailed way of describing those events than to lift his entire account of them – not just the materials but the complete narrative – from the work of the Knight and Procurator of St Mark! And this after the following words introducing this section of his book:

> The unhappy events which these revolutions involved have been described by a number of writers, some trying to present them as portentous, as exceptions to the ordinary course of Nature, while others confuse the reader with too much petty detail, and so fail to bring out clearly the true causes of what happened and its aims and development and conclusion. Therefore I shall make it my business, guided by the weightiest and most discerning authorities, to present an account of the matter reduced to its just proportions.

Yet, as anyone can see who takes the trouble to compare text with text, Giannone had no sooner written these words than he laid hands on Nani's narrative,[6] mixing a little of his own with it now and then, especially near the beginning, altering a little here and there, sometimes because he really had no choice, just as if you buy second-hand linen you must substitute your own markings for the original owner's. Thus where the Venetian has 'in that kingdom', the Neapolitan writes 'in this kingdom'; where the contemporary writer wrote 'the factions remain almost as they were', the later one says 'the residue of those old factions remained'. True, we do find, in this lengthy section, besides such small additions and alterations, sundry longer pieces in the patchwork that are not from Nani. But, incredibly, they are

---

[6] Giannone, Book XXXVII, chs. ii, iii and iv; Nani, Part II, Book iv, pp. 146–57.

almost all lifted, and almost word for word, from someone else –
from Domenico Parrino,[7] a writer who (reversing the fate of so
many) is now forgotten but still much read, perhaps indeed more
than he himself had ever hoped, if people read as much as they
praise, both in Italy and abroad, the *Storia civile del regno di
Napoli* which bears the name of Pietro Giannone. For – still
keeping to the two periods just mentioned – if, having transcribed
from Nani a description of the Catalan and Portuguese rebellions,
Giannone goes to Nani again for his account of the fall of the
favourite Olivares, it is from Parrino that he copies out his
account of the consequent recall of the Viceroy of Naples, the
Duke of Medina, and the latter's dodges for putting off as long
as possible the surrender of his post to his successor Enriquez de
Cabrera. From Parrino too is copied out most of Giannone's
account of Cabrera's government; after which bits from Parrino
and Nani are fitted together like inlaid work when we come to
the government of the Duke of Arcos and through the rest of the
period, preceding the risings in Palermo and Naples; and, as I
have said, throughout the progress of these to their conclusion
under the government of Don John of Austria and of the Count
of Oñatte. Then it is Parrino alone who is used, still in long
pieces or a lot of little ones, for this last Viceroy's expedition
against Piombino and Portolongone; as also for the Duke of
Guise's attempt on Naples; as also for the plague of 1656. Then
it is Nani for the Peace of the Pyrenees; and then Parrino, finally,

---

[7] *Teatro eroico e politico de' governi de' vicerè del regno di Napoli*, etc.,
Naples, 1692, Vol. II, Duke of Arcos. Nani's text runs, with very few and very
minor changes, for seven paragraphs of Giannone's, the last of which ends with
the words: 'extensive provisions were needed both to make up for losses and to
defend the kingdom'. At this point Parrino comes in with: 'The viceroy, the
Duke of Arcos, straitened because of his need for money', and so on, with very
few changes, for two paragraphs and for nearly half the one after. Then, Nani
comes back and goes on, at first alone, for a good while, then in alternation with
Parrino, like a chequerboard. There are even passages in which pieces of both
are put together after a fashion. Here is an example: 'Thus in an instant that fire
which had threatened to destroy the kingdom was extinguished; and what was
even more wondrous was the sudden change in people's dispositions, which now
went from killing, rancour and hatred to tears of sympathy and tender embraces,
without distinctions between friends and enemies (Parrino, Vol. II, p. 425): apart
from a few who, guided by bad conscience, withdrew by fleeing; all the others
having gone back to their work, cursing the disruptions they had undergone,
gleefully embraced the new tranquillity. (Nani, Part II, Book IV, p. 157)'.
Giannone, Book XXXVII, ch. iv, 2nd para.

for a short appendix on the effects of this peace on the kingdom of Naples.[8]

Voltaire, in his *Siècle de Louis XIV*,[9] speaking of the tribunals set up by that king at Metz and Brisac after the armistice of Nijmegen in order to adjudicate his claims to the territories of neighbouring States, has a footnote mentioning Giannone with high praise, as was to be expected, but also with a rebuke. Here is the footnote translated: 'Giannone, so celebrated for his valuable history of Naples, says that the tribunals were set up at Tournai. He is often wrong on matters that do not concern his own country. He says, for example, that at Nijmegen Louis XIV made peace with Sweden, which was in fact his ally already.' But, leaving aside the praise, the rebuke was not this time deserved by Giannone, who, as on so many other occasions, had not even gone to the trouble of making a mistake. It is true that in this 'so celebrated' author's work occur these words: 'Peace followed between France, Sweden, the Empire, and the Emperor' (which, after all, may be ambiguous rather than wrong); and also the following:

> They [the French] then set up two tribunals, one at Tournai and the other at Metz; and arrogating to themselves a jurisdiction such as the world had never seen over neighbouring sovereigns, they did not merely make over to France, as 'dependencies', every country to which they took a fancy along the frontiers of Flanders and the Empire, but actually and in fact took possession of those territories, constraining the inhabitants to acknowledge the Most Christian King as their sovereign, drawing the frontiers where they pleased and exercising in fact all those rights of overlordship which Princes are accustomed to claim over their subjects.

But it was poor unknown Parrino who penned these words;[10] and Giannone has not even excised them from the narrative where they occurred but has carried them off context and all; because often Giannone cannot wait to pluck a fruit here and a fruit there, but must dig up the whole tree for transplanting in his own garden. His entire account, one may say, of the Peace of

[8] See Giannone, Book XXXVI, ch. vi; all seven chapters of Book XXXVII and the preamble to the next book; Nani, Part I, Book XII, p. 738; Part II, Books III, IV and VIII; Parrino, Vol II, p. 296f., Vol III p. 1f.

[9] Ch. 17, 'Paix de Ryswick', note c.

[10] Giannone, Book XXXIX, last ch. of Vol. IV, pp. 461, 463 (Naples: Niccolò Naso, 1723; Parrino, vol III, pp. 553, 567.

Nijmegen is the work of Parrino; and likewise, in great part, with
much left out and a few additions, his account of the viceroyalty
in Naples of the Marquis de los Veles, during which that Peace
was concluded and with which Parrino ends his narrative and
Giannone the penultimate book of his. And probably (I almost
said certainly) anyone who cared to amuse himself by completing
these comparisons would find that what has been observed with
regard to some decades of the Spanish dominion in Naples held
good for the entire preceding period back to the beginning of
that régime, which is also the point at which Parrino begins his
narrative; nor, if I am not very much deceived, would he ever
find this much-plundered author mentioned by name.[11] From
Sarpi* too (as a kind and learned friend has pointed out to me)
Giannone lifted many passages without acknowledgement and
the whole structure of one of his digressions.[12] And who knows
what other unnoticed thefts would come to light if one cared to
look for them; but so much as we have seen – appropriations,
not merely of other writers' choice and arrangement of materials,
or of their judgements and comments and general spirit, but of
entire pages and chapters and books – this, in a famous and
highly commended author, is surely something of a phenomenon.
Whether due to sterility or to sloth, the result is certainly a rarity,
as the audacity was rare that brought it about: but more than
rare, unique, was Giannone's good fortune – that, for all this, he
remains (while he does remain) a great man. And let this
circumstance, together with the occasion for pointing it out
which our theme supplied, be my excuse to the indulgent reader
for a long digression in what is, after all, only an accessory
chapter of small work.

Who does not know Parini's unfinished poem on the Column
of Infamy?* Yet who would not be surprised to find no mention
of it here?

Here then are the few lines of this fragment, in which the
celebrated poet echoes only too faithfully what the common
people and the inscription said:

[11] He was often cited in footnotes in several editions published after Giannone's death; but readers who knew no better would assume he was cited as
witness of the events, not as author of the text.
[12] Sarpi, *Discorso sull'origine, . . . dell' Uffizio dell' inquisizione*; *Opere varie*,
Helmstat (Venice) vol I, p. 340; Giannone, *Ist civ*. Book XV, last chapter.

When, between mean houses and amid sparse
ruins, I saw an ignoble square open before me.
Here a solitary column rises
among sterile grass and stones and stench,
where no one ever penetrates, for there
the guardian spirit of the Lombard city
turns all away, crying out: keep far,
o good citizens, keep far from here, lest
the wretched infamous ground infect you.[13]

Was this really Parini's opinion? We do not know: and his
having expressed it so affirmatively – but in verse – is no
argument; because at that time it was a rule commonly accepted
that poets had the privilege of making use of any belief, true or
false, that was likely to produce a powerful or pleasing
impression. The privilege! A privilege to keep and spur men on
in error! But then the answer given was that this did not matter
because ... well, poets, nobody believed what *they* said. To
which answer there is no answer; except that it may seem odd
that poets were satisfied with either the permission or the excuse.

Then at last came Pietro Verri, the first writer after one
hundred and forty-seven years who saw and said who had been
the real murderers; the first to speak up for the innocent who had
been butchered with such barbarity and abhorred so obtusely; to
claim for them a compassion so much the more due for being so
long delayed. And yet Verri's *Osservazioni*, written in 1777, were
not published until 1804, when they came out with other works
of his, some already printed and some not, in a collection of
'Italian Classics of Political Economy'.* And in his preface the
publisher explained the delay. 'It was thought,' he said, 'that the
good name of the Senate might suffer from the disrepute that
would attach to the Senate of former times.' A very usual kind of
sentiment, this, in those days; an effect of that *esprit de corps*
which made each member of an institution, rather than ever
admit that his predecessors had made mistakes, assume responsibility even for follies not committed by himself. In our day this
kind of loyalty to institutions has less chance of extending so far
back into the past, because almost everywhere in Europe institutions are of recent origin – with a few exceptions, to be sure,

---

[13] PROCUL. HINC. PROCUL. ERGO. BONI. CIVES.
NE. VOS. INFELIX. INFAME. SOLUM. COMMACULET.

and one in particular which, since it does not draw its origin from man, can be neither abolished nor replaced.* In addition, such institutional loyalty is, now more than ever before, resisted and undermined by individualism: the 'I' thinks itself too rich to beg from a 'We'. And in this respect individualism is beneficial; God forbid I should say in every respect.

In any case, Pietro Verri was not a man to sacrifice truth-telling to human respect of this kind, when the truth to be told was important both because of the credit enjoyed by the contrary falsehood and still more because of the purpose he had in mind in telling it. But there was a circumstance which rendered human respect, in this case, just: the President of the Senate was the illustrious writer's father. And so it happens quite often; good reasons come to the aid of bad ones, and then the combined effect of both is that a truth which has taken a long while to come to birth has to remain concealed a while longer.

NOTES TO THE BETROTHED

p. 3 glorious Firmament: during the period in which the novel is set Milan and its surrounding territory were ruled by the King of Spain, who delegated his powers to a governor. For the names of the various kings and governors concerned, see pp. 9–12 and note.

p. 3 the eyes of Argus and the arms of Briarius: figures in Greek mythology: Argus, surnamed 'Panoptes' (all-seeing) had a hundred eyes (which were transferred to the tail of the peacock when he died); Briarius was a hundred-armed, fifty-headed giant, the son of Uranus and Gaea.

p. 4 enough patience to read it: the device of pretended transcription from a fictional manuscript had previously been employed by several writers, notably Cervantes and Scott. An instance close to M. was Vincenzo Cuoco's *Platone in Italia* (1805). M.'s use of the convention is particularly apt because, while real documents are often quoted in the novel, its main plot involves characters who would have been too humble ('of small import and low degree') to appear in them: the fiction of the source wryly extends the historical record's social reach.

p. 6 too much: M. did in fact begin to write a defence of the style of *The Betrothed* in 1835. Left unfinished at his death, it was published as *Sentir messa*.

p. 9 luxuriant vitality: the quotations which follow are from real proclamations.

p. 10 His Catholic Majesty in Italy: the King of Spain; Philip II (1556–1598) at the time of the first proclamation, then Philip III (1598–1621) and, during the period of the novel, Philip IV (1621–1665).

p. 11 Henry IV: King of France (1589–1610).

p. 11 loss of his head: Charles Emmanuel I (1562–1630), Duke of Savoy, lost three of his dynasty's territories to France in a war of 1600–1601, which was provoked by his seizure of the marquisate of

Saluzzo (1588); Charles de Gontaut (1562–1602), Duke of Biron, was commander of the French forces in the war against Charles Emmanuel; but was at the same time plotting against his monarch. The intrigue was discovered and he was executed in the Bastille.

p. 19 the canonical age of forty: forty was the minimum age prescribed by the Council of Trent (1545–63) for priests' servants.

p. 22 the battle of Rocroi: the tranquillity of Louis II de Bourbon on the eve of his great victory over the Spanish, 19 May 1643, is praised in the funeral oration for him composed by Bossuet, a writer whose works M. knew well: 'jamais il ne reposa plus paisiblement. A la veille d'un si grand jour . . . il est tranquille, tant il se trouve dans son naturel; et on sait que le lendemain, à l'heure marquée, il fallut réveiller d'un profond sommeil cet autre Alexandre.'

p. 23 closed season for marriages: the Council of Trent had decreed that no marriages could be celebrated between the first Sunday in Advent and the Feast of Epiphany (6 January). In 1628 the first Sunday in Advent (according to the Ambrosian calendar) was 12 November, four days after Don Abbondio's interview with Renzo (the date of which we know from p. 8).

p. 25 *Si sis affinis*: Don Abbondio's mnemonic in Latin hexameters lists the following potential difficulties: mistaken identity or legal error; incompatible social status; the possibility that the people involved may have taken disqualifying vows, or be related by blood, or have committed crimes, or be of different religious denominations; or, that they might be forced into marriage against their will, belong to religious orders, be already married to someone else, be dishonest in some way; or that there may be a familial (but not necessarily blood) relation between one of the spouses and a member of the other's family.

p. 25 *antequam matrimonium denunciet*: before the marriage is announced.

p. 36 certificate to say that we are free to marry: a statement certifying that there are no impediments of the kind listed on p. 25, and so enabling them to be married by a priest who doesn't know them.

p. 36 Quibble-weaver: 'Azzecca-garbugli'.

p. 38 a brand-new edict: a real proclamation which M. discovered while reading Melchiorre Gioia's *Sul commercio dei comestibili e caro prezzo del vitto* (1802; *Opere minori* [1832–7], vol. 12, p. 19) in 1821.

He later said to his stepson, Stefano Stampa: 'do you know what it was that gave me the idea of writing the *Promessi sposi*? It was that edict which I came across by chance and which I make Doctor Quibble-weaver read out to Renzo.'

p. 39 valley of Jehoshaphat: the location of the Last Judgement, according to Joel 3: 1–12.

p. 40 there's nothing missing: '*Platonus*' was the signature of Marc'Antonio Platone, secretary of the secret council; Antonio Ferrer was Grand Chancellor. '*Vidit*' means 'approved by.'

p. 43 *Deo gratias*: 'thanks be to God', a liturgical phrase used as a greeting.

p. 46 to whom nothing seemed too low or too high: the Capuchins, an offshoot of the Franciscan order, were founded in the early sixteenth century by Matteo da Bascio with the aim of strictly imitating the poverty and simplicity of the life of St Francis: they were officially recognised by Clement VII in 1528. The movement rapidly increased in size and importance, was constituted an independent order in 1619, and reached the height of its power at about the time in which *The Betrothed* is set. Its distinctive garment, from which it took its name, was a long hood ('*cappuccino*').

p. 47 the building is still standing: the monastery was closed by the French in 1798.

p. 48 who was this Father Cristoforo?: not a historical figure, although M. may have taken some details from the lives of Alfonso III of Este, a famously zealous Capuchin described in Lodovico Muratori's *Delle antichità Estensi* (1717–40; pt. 2, pp. 530–37), one Fra Cristoforo Picenardi of Cremona, mentioned in Pio della Croce's *Memoria delle cose notabili successe in Milano intorno al mal contaggioso l'anno 1630* (1730) and the Blessed Bernardo da Corleone, whose entry into the order resembled that of Fra Cristoforo.

p. 60 their primitive energy: 'dash,' 'cripes,' 'sugar' are English examples.

p. 63 in time to recite sext in choir: at about midday. Sext was so called because it was traditionally sung at the sixth of the twelve hours into which daylight was divided.

p. 66 the challenge to the Christian Knights: Tasso, *Jerusalem Delivered*, canto 6, stanza 17.

p. 66 a proverb which says that ambassadors can't be punished: *'ambasciator non porta pena.'* *Jus gentium*, in ancient Rome, was the law which was taken to govern the world at large.

p. 67 a thrashing in reply: the incident is taken almost word for word from the commentary on canto 7, stanza 20 of Tasso's *The Conquest of Jerusalem* in Francesco Birago's *Dichiarationi et avertimenti poetici, istorici, politici, cavellereschi et morali, nella Gerusalemme conquistata del signor Torquato Tasso* (1616). The substance of the whole argument, including the proverb quoted above and the appeal to *Jus gentium*, is drawn from the same source. Birago supports the opinion here put forward by Count Attilio.

p. 67 a *fetialis* being thrashed: the *'fetiales'* were priests who were concerned with various aspects of foreign relations, such as making peace and declaring war. They would accomplish the latter by throwing a javelin into the territory of the enemy country.

p. 67 *ergo* . . .: the mayor produces his syllogism in strict scholastic form, first stating the major premise – 'to assault an armed man is an act of treachery' – then the minor premise – *'atqui* (well), the messenger, *de quo* (of whom we are speaking), was unarmed' – and finally reaching his conclusion: *'ergo* (therefore) . . .'.

p. 69 expelled from the state: Vincenzo Gonzaga died on 26 December 1627; the Duke of Nevers, Carlo Gonzaga, belonged to a cadet branch of the same family, and was arguably not the legitimate heir. Cardinal Richelieu (1585–1642) was prime minister of France from 1624 until his death. The Count of Olivares (1587–1645) was known as the Count-Duke because he was also Duke of San Lucar; he was chief minister of Spain from 1621 until 1643. The disputed succession to the Duchy of Mantua was a key element in the power struggle between these two countries. Ferdinand II was Holy Roman Emperor (1619–37). 'That year' is 1628, as we know from Chapter 1.

p. 70 the Pope: Urban VIII (1623–44).

p. 70 or whatever his name is: Prince Albrecht Eusebius von Wallenstein (1583–1634); his name was originally the Czech Valdstejna, and he sometimes spelled it Waldstein. He was in this period Commander-in-Chief of the Imperial armies, but by 1628 his personal ambition was making him untrustworthy: he was dismissed in 1630, then recalled, and then murdered on Ferdinand's instructions in 1634.

p. 70 Riciliù: the Mayor's hispanicized mispronunciations of 'Wallenstein', 'Nevers' and 'Richelieu' are indicative of his attachment to the Spanish regime.

p. 71 Henry IV: previously King of Navarre, he had succeeded to the French throne in 1589, although he was not crowned until 1594 after a war with Spain and his conversion to Catholicism ('Paris is well worth a mass,' he is reputed to have said). See also note to p. 11.

p. 72 *censui, et in eam ivi sententiam*: 'I have judged, and agree with that opinion.' Quibble-weaver's expression echoes a common form of statement in the senate of ancient Rome.

p. 72 Heliogabalus: Roman Emperor AD 218–222, a famous debauchee.

p. 76 a way to crush it: Exodus 7–14. Fra Cristoforo's words echo Exodus 7:13: 'And he hardened Pharaoh's heart, that he hearkened not unto them; as the Lord had said.'

p. 80 Proteus: in classical mythology, a marine demi-god, shepherd of the sea's flocks, who would metamorphose himself into all sorts of forms in order to elude people who sought to make him prophesy.

p. 82 *polenta*, made with buckwheat: polenta is a kind of thick porridge, nowadays usually made with maize.

p. 90 *parpagliole*: small coins.

p. 91 a Nathan: in II Samuel 12 the prophet Nathan reproves David for having killed Uriah the Hittite and taken his wife Bathsheba for his own (a crime which resembles Don Rodrigo's designs on Lucia). God strikes David and Bathsheba's first child dead by way of punishment.

p. 92 St Martin's Day: 11 November, and the deadline for the wager. We are now on the evening of 9 November.

p. 97 *mora*: a game in which two players simultaneously shout a number, while at the same time holding out some of their fingers: the aim is to guess the total which your own and your opponent's fingers will add up to.

p. 99 or a hideous dream: Shakespeare, *Julius Caesar*, II.i.63–5. 'A barbarian not devoid of genius' recalls Voltaire's comment on Shakespeare in *Lettre à l'Académie Française* ('la vérité ... m'ordonne de vous avouer que ce Shakespeare, si sauvage, si bas, si effréné, et si absurde, avait des étincelles de génie'); but with ironic intent, as Manzoni explained in a letter to the Revd Charles Swan, first English translator of *The Betrothed*: 'I cannot tell you how much anger I felt at those angry and thoughtless remarks of Voltaire's ... about Shakespeare' (25 January 1828).

p. 100 *berlinghe*: silver coins equivalent to *Lire*.

p. 101 Carneades: Greek sceptical philosopher (214–129 BC); born in Cirene, he became famous after a visit to Rome in 156 BC, during which he helped to arouse the first Roman interest in Greek philosophy. His ethical theories are discussed by Cicero in *De finibus bonorum et malorum*.

p. 101 heard with admiration: the panegyric by Vincenzo Tasca was printed as *La dottrina di San Carlo Borromeo spiegata da Vincenzo Tasca venetiano, chierico regolare della Congregazione di Somasca, nel duomo di Milano* (1626). For more on Saint Charles Borromeo, see pp. 304–5 and note.

p. 101 Archimedes: Greek mathematician, astronomer and inventor (*c.* 287–211 BC). He founded hydrostatics, discovering the law of buoyancy known as Archimedes' principle, did important work on the volume and surface area of spheres and cylinders, and is reputed to have jumped out of a bathtub shouting 'Eureka!'

p. 103 *Deo gratias*: see note to p. 37.

p. 114 the early French kings: in his tragedy *Adelchi*, M. calls Charlemagne 'the long-haired lord' (IV, chorus, 42).

p. 115 *Omnia munda mundis*: 'unto the pure all things are pure' (St Paul, Epistle to Titus 1:15).

p. 120 research for the learned: researchers have since discovered that the family whose name Ripamonti does not mention was called de Leyva, and moved from Spain to Milan in the early sixteenth century. The story of Gertrude, which M. narrates later in this chapter, is loosely based on the life of Marianna de Leyva, Sister Virginia Maria (1575–1650). Giuseppe Ripamonti (1573–1643) was canon and official civic historian of Milan. M. drew on his *Historiae patriae* (10 volumes, Milan, 1641), not only for this episode but also for the account of the food riots and the famine (Chapters 12–13 and 28). He also relied heavily on Ripamonti's account of the Milan plague, *De peste quae fuit anno MDCXXX* (1640), for Chapters 31 and 32, and he discusses its treatment of the 'smearers' case in the *History of the Column of Infamy*, Chapter 7, below).

p. 122 she's sprung from Adam's rib: she comes from an ancient noble family.

p. 122 likely to remember having seen standing: the remains were destroyed in 1814. 'Ten of my readers' – out of the 'five-and-twenty' total envisaged on p. 18.

p. 128 called her Gertrude: M. may have been thinking of the daughter of Pépin, Prince of Brabant, who lived in the 8th century and was abbess of the monastery of Mivelle, or else of St Gertrude the Great, in the 13th century, a Cistercian nun and the daughter of King Andrew of Hungary.

p. 138 the lost sheep: Luke 15: 4–7. Sharply ironic in this context.

p. 142 the *toga virilis* among the ancient Romans: investiture with this garment marked a young man's admission to adult citizenship. Chocolate, in the seventeenth century, was an expensive rarity.

p. 165 a small unpublished work on the Lombards and the Crusades: *I Lombardi alla prima crociata*, by Manzoni's friend Tommaso Grossi (1790–1853), which was in fact published in 1826. The line quoted ('Leva il muso odorando il vento infido') is from canto 10, stanza 16, where it describes a lion, to which the crusading army is being compared.

p. 166 a dear boy: a portrait of M.'s son Enrico, born in 1821.

p. 167 the cloak was bowing before the doublet: wearers of cloaks, the upper classes, were on this day afraid of ordinary people, who wore doublets. The reason will soon be apparent.

p. 170 four great elm-trees: the convent was destroyed in 1812, when Milan was occupied by the French. The 'present fine building' is the Palazzo Belloni-Saporiti.

p. 171 the second year of bad harvests: M.'s fictional narrative here links up with recorded history. The account of the events in Milan on 11 and 12 November 1628 draws on Giuseppe Ripamonte, *De peste quae fuit anno MDCXXX* (1641), pp. 34–50 and Alessandro Tadino, *Raguaglio dell'origine et giornali successi della gran peste . . .* (1648), pp. 6–8. M. mentions these works below, pp. 394 and 429.

p. 176 and still is: it was closed in 1919.

p. 183 when he was carving it: Philip II (1527–1598) King of Spain and Duke of Milan, came to be remembered as an epitome of absolutism, and is portrayed as such in Alfieri's *Filippo* (1783). In 1797 northern Italy was invaded by revolutionary France, and so Philip was (on 7 June) converted into Brutus, tyrannicide and symbol of republicanism. In 1799 the French were temporarily expelled by the Austrian and Russian armies, and so the statue was destroyed (on the morning of 28 April). Andrew Biffi (*c.* 1560–*c.* 1631) was a minor Milanese sculptor.

p. 190 *Por mi vida, que de gente!*: 'on my life, what a crowd!' Ferrer talks to himself and his entourage in Castilian Spanish, his native language.

p. 190 *Si es culpable*: 'If he's guilty.'

p. 190 *Adelante, Pedro, si puedes:* 'Go forward, Pedro, if you can.'

p. 191 *Adelante, presto, con juicio*: 'Go forward, quick, be careful.'

p. 192 *Asi es . . .*: 'so it is.'

p. 192 *Ox! Ox! Guardaos*: 'Shoo! Shoo! Look out!' (Note the difference in register between this brusque expostulation and its polite counterpart in Italian, which the crowd could understand: 'don't get hurt, gentlemen').

p. 194 *Venga usted con migo*: 'Come with me.'

p. 194 *Aqui esta el busilis; Dios nos valga*: 'Now for the hard part; may God preserve us!'

p. 195 *Por ablandarlos:* 'To pacify them.'

p. 195 *Esto lo digo por su bien*: 'I am saying this for your benefit.'

p. 195 *Perdone, usted*: 'I do beg your pardon.'

p. 195 *Animo; estamos ya quasi fuera*: 'Courage; we're already nearly out.'

p. 195 *Beso a usted los manos*: 'I kiss your hands.'

p. 195 *Cedant arma togae*: 'Let arms give way to the toga' (i.e. to civil authority); Cicero, *De officiis*, i, 77.

p. 195 *Levantese, levantese; estamos ya fuera*: 'Get up, get up; we're out now.'

p. 195 *Que dirà de esto su excelencia*: 'What will his excellency say about this;' and then, further on, 'what will the Count-Duke say,' and 'what will our lord the King say.'

p. 196 *Dios lo sabe*: 'God knows.'

p. 196 *Usted ... por el servicio de su magestad*: 'You ... for the service of His Majesty.'

p. 201 *Gratis et amore*: an abbreviation of the saying 'gratis et amore Dei,' 'free, and for the love of God.'

p. 202 **the decree**: of 26 October 1627.

p. 205 **Pindus**: a Greek mountain, sacred to Apollo and the Muses.

p. 209 *siés baraòs trapolorum*: meaningless, although trapolorum joins the traps (trappole) of the powerful to the ending of Don Abbondio's '*latinorum*' (p. 25).

p. 212 **her unknown spouse**: Cupid. He visited Psyche during the hours of darkness on condition that she never looked at him or tried to find out who he was. One night, fearing that he might be a monster, she lit a lamp while he slept, and gazed at him. He awoke, upbraided her and fled. The legend, narrated in books IV–VI of Apuleius's *Metamorphoses* (also known as *The Golden Ass*), was a popular subject for paintings and prints.

p. 219 *extra formam*: without legal formalities (i.e., in this case, without recourse to torture).

p. 228 **a leafy branch**: the sign for an inn.

p. 233 **the Jews of the Via Crucis**: ugly faces in paintings or carvings of the Way of the Cross.

p. 234 *cappa magna*: choral robes.

p. 235 **Turkish-sounding name**: Richelieu (for whom, see notes to pp. 69 and 70).

p. 238 **the clock was striking twenty-four**: the hours were counted from dusk to dusk, so about 5 p.m.

p. 243 **eleven times**: an hour before dawn, or about 6 a.m.

p. 249 **what do the Bergamese do then?**: M. drew the historical information in this paragraph from Lorenzo Ghirardelli, *Il memorando contagio seguito in Bergamo l'anno 1630* (1681), pp. 14–24.

p. 251 *praedicti egregii domini capitanei*: 'afore-mentioned illustrious lord captain.'

p. 251 *palam vel clam*: 'openly or clandestinely.'

p. 251 *ignotum*: 'unknown.'

p. 251 *verum in territorio Leuci*: 'but certainly in the territory of Lecco.'

p. 251 *quod si compertum fuerit sic esse*: 'if this is ascertained to be the case.'

p. 251 *quanta maxima diligentia fieri poterit*: 'with as much care as possible.'

p. 251 *videlizet*: 'that is to say.'

p. 251 ... *et complicibus sumatis*: 'that you should go to the house of the afore-mentioned Lorenzo Tramaglino, and, having carried out the necessary search, requisition anything that may have a bearing on the matter in hand; and also that you should gather information as to his evil character, his life and his accomplices.'

p. 251 *diligenter referatis*: 'you must diligently report.'

p. 265 the Escurial: a huge monastery and royal palace near Madrid, built by Philip II to commemorate the Spanish victory over the French at the battle of San Quintino (1557).

p. 268 *principiis obsta*: 'oppose (an unsuitable love) as soon as it begins:' Ovid, *Remedia amoris*, 91.

p. 272 or even make a guess at them: M. wrote to Cesare Cantù: 'the unnamed is certainly Bernardino Visconti. By the *aequa potestas quidlibet audendi* (equal right of daring to do anything) I have transported his castle to the Valsassina.' Francesco Bernardino Visconti was a bandit lord who was exiled from the state of Milan in 1603, and whose life does correspond, in its broad traits, to that of the unnamed. The Latin quotation in the letter is from Horace, *Ars poetica*, and refers to poetic licence.

p. 272 and leaves it at that: Francesco Rivola, *Vita di Federico Borromeo* (1656), p. 254.

p. 272 as if nothing had happened: Ripamonti, *Historiae patriae decades* (1641–48), 5th decade, p. 308. M. has already mentioned this work on p. 120.

p. 277 Malanotte: 'Evil Night.'

p. 278 what fine names: they mean, roughly, 'Shoot-straight', 'Little Bumpkin', 'Lazy-bones' and 'Screw-loose.'

p. 304 his cousin Carlo: St Charles Borromeo (1538–84), Cardinal and Archbishop of Milan, an important figure in the Italian Counter-Reformation. He was canonized in 1610. The Collegio Borromeo, mentioned in the next sentence, was founded by St Charles in 1561 and still exists.

p. 305 Clement VIII: Pope from 1592 to 1605. He was Tasso's patron and had Giordano Bruno burnt at the stake.

p. 306 the Ambrosian library: founded in 1609; one of the great European libraries.

p. 307 by one Pierpaolo Bosca: *De origine, et statu Bibliothecae Ambrosianae hemidecas* (1672).

p. 309 the *'ne quid nimis'* school: devotees of moderation. The Latin phrase ('nor ever too much') is from Terence, *Andria*, I.i.34.

p. 309 Conclaves: meetings of Cardinals for the election of the Pope. Federigo attended eight of them.

p. 310 not merely ill-founded but odd: he believed in the existence of witches and 'anointers' (for whom see below), and was an active promoter of the persecutions which were meant to eliminate them.

p. 316 the one that was lost: Luke 15:4–7. Gertrude's father quoted from the same parable on p. 138.

p. 317 *Haec mutatio dexterae Excelsi*: 'this change is from the right hand of the Most High' (Psalm 76:11 in the Vulgate; which corresponds to Psalm 77:10 in the Authorized Version).

p. 318 *parcere subjectis*: 'spare the humbled;' from Anchises's great prophetic speech about the destiny of Rome, Virgil, *Aeneid* VI, 853.

p. 320 *perierat et inventus est*: 'was lost, and is found;' the prodigal son, Luke 15:24.

p. 321 *eat straw like the ox*: Isaiah 11:6–7 (from the description of the Last Day).

p. 324 the same job as Michelaccio: eating, drinking and loafing around, according to a popular saying.

p. 325 the next: St Anthony the Abbot (*c.* 251–356) was a famous hermit, often depicted resisting the temptations of the devil; Holofernes was a fearsome Assyrian general whose murder by Judith was likewise a popular subject for artists. His story is told in the apocryphal Book of Judith.

p. 326 Malebolge: the eighth circle of Dante's Inferno (cantos 18–31). It is a rocky landscape, full of ravines (bolge), where the souls who have committed sins of fraud are punished. Dante and Virgil are attacked by the devils there (canto 23).

p. 336 the *Guerrin meschino* and the *Reali di Francia*: chivalrous romances attributed to Andrea da Barberino (1370–1471). The most popular *Lives of the Saints* in seventeenth-century Italy was translated from the *Flos sanctorum, o libro de las vidas de los santos* (1609) by Pedro de Ribadeneyra.

p. 350 like Catiline from Rome: after his plans for revolutioni had been exposed by Cicero in 63 BC, Catiline fled Rome, vowing to return with an army. He was killed in battle the following year.

p. 351 Clerici and Picozzi: the names, as well as the incident, are taken from the *Life* of Federigo by Rivola, which is mentioned on p. 272.

p. 353 Bovo d'Antona or the Desert Fathers: Bovo (in fact 'Buovo') is a hero in the *Reali di Francia*; the Desert Fathers are hermits about whom the tailor would have read in the *Lives of the Saints*.

p. 364 with a finger: Matthew 23: 2–4.

p. 366 let us keep our lamps alight: Matthew 25: 1–13 (the parable of the wise and foolish virgins); 'redeem the time' is from Ephesians 5:16.

p. 374 like the Roman senate with Hannibal: after his defeat by Scipio at Zama, which ended the second Punic war, Hannibal was forced to flee from Carthage to Ephesus, and then to Bithynia, where he committed suicide.

p. 374 a cursory glance: see note to p. 69.

p. 376 ceteris paribus: 'other things being equal'.

p. 379 the entelechy: an Aristotelian term meaning, roughly, that which makes actual what would otherwise be only potential. However, ambiguities in Aristotle's use of the word meant that its precise definition was the subject of abstruse debate by mediaeval ('scholastic') philosophers.

p. 383 *ex cathedra*: 'giving a lecture.' 'Influences': those which were thought to be exerted by the heavenly bodies on the world; 'aspects':

the positions of the planets; 'conjunctions': alignments of stars or planets in ways which might be propitious or maleficent; 'the twelve houses': twelve segments into which the sky was divided; 'the great circles': the lines which separated the twelve houses; 'the degrees of light and shade': measurements of the supposed orbits of the sun ('light') and planets ('shade'); 'exaltations and dejections': the points at which planets have their greatest and least influence: 'transits and revolutions': movements of celestial bodies across particular meridians or around their apparent orbits.

p. 383 Al-Qabisi: (or 'Alcabitius'); a tenth-century Arab astronomer, author of an influential textbook, *Introduction to the Art of Astronomy*. Gerolamo Cardano (1501–1576) was a Milanese polymath: some of his work is described on p. 384. They had different systems for defining the 'twelve houses.'

p. 383 Diogenes Laertius: a Greek from the 3rd century AD, author of an important history of Greek philosophy.

p. 384 *Duodecim geniturarum*: The titles in English are: *On Subtlety, Amendments to the Calculation of the Seasons and Celestial Motion,* and *Twelve Births* (an astrological analysis of the times and dates of birth of twelve great men). 'Anti-peripatetic' means 'opposed to the philosophy of Aristotle'.

p. 384 Albertus Magnus: a Dominican philosopher and saint, lived from *c.* 1200 to 1280, wrote, among many other works, treatises *De vegetalibus* and *De animalibus*, and taught theology at Paris, where St Thomas Aquinas was one of his pupils. Cardano's three histories are *Of Minerals, Of Animals* and *Of Plants*. 'Porta' is Giambattista della Porta (1535–1615), a Neapolitan polymath, author of *Magia naturalis* (1558). Pliny the Elder (23–79 AD) wrote a monumental and celebrated *Natural History*; Aristotle produced several books on the subject, the most important of which is his *Physics*.

p. 385 Martin Del Río: Spanish Jesuit, lived from 1551 to 1608, wrote a six-volume disquisition on the magic arts (1599). He is mentioned again on p. 457. '*Ex professo*' means 'as an expert.'

p. 385 Tarcagnota, Dolce, Bugatti, Campana, Guazzo: Giovanni Tarcagnota (d. 1566), wrote a history 'which contains all that has happened from the beginning of the world until our times' (1561); Lodovico Dolce (1501–1568), was a playwright and poet, and translator of *Historie di Giovanni Zonara dal cominciamento del mondo infino all'imperatore*

Alessio Comneno; Gaspare Bugatti (C16th), was author of an *Istoria universale* (1571); Cesare Campana (1532–1606) and Marco Guazzo (d. 1556) wrote similar works. None of these authors is remembered today.

p. 385 Bodin, Cavalcanti, Sansovino, Paruta, and Boccalini: i.e., Jean Bodin (1530–96); Bartolomeo Cavalcanti (1503–62); Francesco Sansovino (1521–83); Paolo Paruta (1549–98); Traiano Boccalini da Loreto (1556–1613). A more distinguished list.

p. 385 Giovanni Botero: alive from 1543 to 1617, the *Reason of State* (1589) is his most important work. The 'celebrated Florentine secretary' is Machiavelli (1469–1527); the books of his which M. mentions are *The Prince* (1513) and the *Discourses on the first Decade of Titus Livius* (1517).

p. 385 Don Valeriano Castiglione: a Milanese Benedictine, he lived from 1593 to 1668. His *Ruling Statesman* (1628) is, despite the contemporary acclaim which M. goes on to describe, much less distinguished than the works by Machiavelli to which Don Ferrante prefers it.

p. 386 . . .of our days: the diploma is quoted from Argelati, *Bibliotheca scriptorum mediolanensium* (1745), vol. 1, pt. 2, p. 387.

p. 386 *Gerusalemme Liberata* and *Gerusalemme Conquistata*: *Jerusalem Delivered (1600) and The Conquest of Jerusalem*, by Torquato Tasso (1544–95); his 'first and second *Forno*' are dialogues on chivalry. The full (and correct) names of the writers listed are Paride del Pozzo, or Paris de Puteo (1413–93); Sebastiano Fausto da Longiano (author of *Duello . . . regolato a le leggi de l'honore*, 1559); Ximenez de Urrea (who translated Ariosto into Spanish and wrote a *Dialogo de la verdadera honora militar*, 1566); Girolamo Muzio (author of *Le risposte cavalleresche*, 1550); Annibale Romei (whose *Discorsi*, 1586, were translated into English as *The Courtiers Academie* in 1598); and Cardinal Fabio Albergati, author of a *Trattato del modo di ridurre a pace l'inimicitie private* (1583).

p. 386 Francesco Birago: 1562–1640; 'our' because Milanese. Giovan Battista Olevano's 'authoritative work', in the next sentence, was entitled *Trattato . . . nel quale co 'l mezzo di cinquanta casi vien posto in atto pratico il modo di indurre a pace ogni sorte di privata inimicitia, nata per cagion d'honore* (1603).

p. 388 *De orden de Su Excelencia*: 'on the orders of his Excellency,' i.e. of the governor.

p. 389 *maximum*: this term was celebrated after the 'Laws of the Maximum,' passed in France in 1793, which fixed ceilings first on prices and then on wages.

p. 390 close to our own: revolutionary France. M. refers to the above-mentioned 'Laws of the Maximum.'

p. 391 'that mournful picture: M. here draws on Ripamonti's *De peste*, for which see p. 429.

p. 394 . . . *nella città di Milano*: *An Account of the Origins of the Great Contagious, Poisonous and Maleficent Plague which Took Place in the City of Milan*, etc.

p. 397 in our own day: the lazaretto was largely destroyed at the end of the nineteenth century, although part of its wall and the central church which is mentioned below are still standing.

p. 398 as the name itself suggests: from 'a certain beggar named Lazarus . . . full of sores' (Luke 16:20).

p. 400 *Dott. F. Enrico Acerbi*: 1785–1827. M.'s doctor. His book is *On Petechial Sickness . . . and other Contagions in General*.

p. 401 *giulio*: small silver coin so called because it was first minted under Pope Julius II (1503–15).

p. 401 Achillini: Claudio Achillini (1574–1640). The line in Italian is 'Sudate, o fochi, a preparar metalli.' The other sonnet, mentioned in the same sentence, is 'I tuoi colpi devoti, alfin, troncaro . . .'

p. 402 Varchi: Benedetto Varchi (1503–1565), in vol. 12, Chapter 51 of his *Storia Fiorentina*, written between 1527 and 1538 but not published until 1721. He is writing of the plague which struck Florence in 1531.

p. 403 the celebrated Lodovico: see below, p. 436.

p. 404 which it still enjoys: Ambrosio Spinola (1569–1630), a Genovese, famously successful commander of the Spanish troops in the Netherlands. His capture of the fortress of Breda in 1625 is the subject of a painting by Velásquez, 'Las Lanzas.' He died at the siege of Casale.

p. 404 Count Rambaldo di Collalto: 1575–1630. *Condottieri* were mercenary generals.

p. 406 *landsknechte*: 'servants of the fatherland', an irregular army of mercenary troops first instituted by Emperor Maximilian at the end of the fifteenth century.

p. 406 *cappelletti*: Albanian cavalry in the pay of Venice, named after their distinctive helmets.

p. 411 be both Martha and Magdalene: i.e., do both the thinking and the acting. From Luke 10: 38–42.

p. 413 the Moors in France: the Moorish invasion of France, narrated in the tailor's beloved *Reali di Francia*.

p. 413 Thebaid: the area surrounding Thebes in Egypt, a refuge for hermits as the tailor would have known from his *Lives of the Saints*.

p. 416 above: p. 272.

p. 417 Torti: Giovanni Torti (1774–1852), a poet and friend of M.'s.

p. 425 the last of them: the names of the commanders and squadrons in the Imperial army are important for their cumulative rhetorical effect rather than for any biographical or historical details which might be attached to them. The epic feel of this passage is kept up with the bird simile in the next few lines, for which cf. Dante, *Inferno* V, 40–49 and Virgil, *Aeneid* X, 264–66.

p. 429 *De peste quae fuit anno 1630*: 'On the Plague of 1630.'

p. 431 the plague of San Carlo: took place in 1576 and was named after St Charles Borromeo.

p. 437 profane vulgar: 'profanum vulgus,' Horace, *Odes* III.i.1.

p. 441 is preserved in the archives of San Fedele: now in the Archivio Storico di Stato, Milan.

p. 442 . . . cernebantur: 'and we too went to look. There were scattered, uneven stains remaining, as though someone had soaked a sponge in diseased liquid and splashed and pressed it against the walls: and we could see the doors and entrances of houses contaminated with the same substance.'

p. 445 . . . *permitieren*: 'I shall provide for them in the best way that the times and present necessities allow.'

p. 445 . . . *desconsuelo*: 'with great disappointment.'

p. 448 *Allegiamento*: 'The relief.'

p. 451 *monere*: 'to advise'; '*monos*': 'alone.' In fact the term probably derives from the Lombard dialect word 'monàt', grave-digger.

p. 457 . . . *miranda videntur*: the hexameter means 'it is preparing fatal diseases, wonders are seen.'

p. 457 *Specchio degli almanacchi perfetti*: 'The Mirror of Perfect Almanacs.'

p. 457 even Homer and Ovid: Livy (58 BC–AD 17), Tacitus (*c*. AD 56–*c*. AD 115) and Dio (AD 150–235), were famous historians of Rome; plagues are described frequently in their works. There are plagues in Homer's *Iliad*, I, 43–57, and Ovid's *Metamorphoses*, VII, 523–660.

p. 457 that fatal Del Río: for him, see p. 385 above; the other authors listed are all sixteenth-century writers on witchcraft, plague and poisons.

p. 459 *stragem edidit*: 'Of the Plague which in 1630 caused a great Massacre in Milan.' M. drew extensively on this work for the descriptions which follow.

p. 459 *para la fábrica del veneno*: for the manufacture of the poison; '*en este exercicio*' means 'in this business.'

p. 459 . . . *algunos vestigios*: to search the house and see whether any traces are to be found.

p. 467 by a certain Lorenzo Ghirardelli: see note to p. 249.

p. 481 of hunger: M.'s treatment of this episode (which derives from a hint in Borromeo's *De pestilentia*) echoes Dante, *Inferno* XXXIII, where Count Ugolino is imprisoned in a tower with his three small children. The door there, as here, is nailed up ('e io senti' chiavar l'uscio di sotto') and the prisoners die of hunger.

p. 485 Giangiacomo Mora: See *History of the Column of Infamy*, below, pp. 551–650.

p. 505 to love them: Matthew 5:44; 'But I say unto you, Love your enemies, bless them that curse you, do good to them that hate you, and pray for them which despitefully use you, and persecute you.'

p. 509 covering your sins: I Peter 4:8; 'And above all things have fervent charity among yourselves: for charity shall cover the multitude of sins.'

p. 510 the *Miserere*: Psalm 51; 'Have mercy upon me, O God, according to thy loving kindness: according unto the multitude of thy tender mercies blot out my transgressions. Wash me throughly from mine iniquity, and cleanse me from my sin . . .' Cf. Dante, *Purgatory*, V, 22–24: 'E'ntanto per la costa di traverso / venivan genti innanzi a noi un poco, / cantando '*miserere*' a verso a verso' ('Meanwhile traverse along the hill there came, / A little way before us, some who sang / The 'Miserere' in responsive strains': Cary's translation).

p. 520 may have contracted with Him: Christ to St Peter; 'And I will give unto thee the keys of the kingdom of heaven: and whatsoever thou shalt bind on earth shall be bound in heaven: and whatsoever thou shalt loose on earth shall be loosed in heaven' (Matthew 16:19).

p. 533 (M.): see p. 120 and note.

p. 534 substances and accidents: Aristotelian terms; the substance is the unchanging and distinctive essence of a thing, while the accident may alter a thing's appearance, but not its essence. Further on: by 'spiritual substance' Don Ferrante would mean God and the angels; 'simple' substances consisted of only one of the four elements, air, water, earth and fire; the medical gentlemen's 'Achilles' is their strongest argument, after the Greek hero of the Trojan war; 'Scylla,' in classical mythology was a twelve-legged, six-headed monster who lived on one side of the Straits of Messina, and 'Charybdis' a deadly whirlpool which lurked on the other. Don Ferrante's opening, '*In rerum natura*,' means 'in nature,' and echoes, pompously, the title of Lucretius's long philosophical poem *De rerum natura*.

p. 535 like a hero of Metastasio, blaming the stars: for instance Cato ('Almen sia la sorte / ai figli felice / se al padre non è' – *Catone in Utica*, III, xii) or Dido ('Ma che feci, empi numi?' etc. – *Didone abbandonata*, III, xix). The mock-heroic joke is spiced by the way in which Don Ferrante blames, not a generalized fate or the classical gods, but specific astrological conjunctions. Metastasio (1698–1782) was a famous writer of dramas set to music ('melodramme').

p. 539 De profundis: Psalm 130; 'Out of the depths have I cried unto thee, O Lord. Lord, hear my voice . . .'

p. 540 the Most Serene Infante: the amnesty for the birth of Charles, son of Philip IV (which also occasioned the festivities mentioned on p. 432 above) was announced on 30 January 1630.

p. 541 senectus ipsa est morbus: 'old age is itself a disease.'

p. 544 vox populi, vox Dei: 'the voice of the people is the voice of God.'

NOTES TO HISTORY OF THE
COLUMN OF INFAMY

p. 553 he never said that mountains were giving birth: Horace, *Ars poetica*, 139: 'Parturient montes, nascetur ridiculus mus': 'the mountains will go into labour, an absurd mouse will be born'.

p. 555 *Ut mos vulgo, quamvis falsis, reum subdere:* 'With the common propensity of crowds to find someone responsible, however false the charge'. This and subsequent numbered footnotes in the *History of the Column of Infamy* are Manzoni's.

p. 566 Statutes of Milan: the *Statuta civilia Medioliani reformata a Ludovico Maria Sfortia* of 1498 and the *Statuta iurisdictionum et extraordinariorum reformata* of 1502.

p. 567 New Constitutions: the *Constitutiones mediolanensi dominii* of 1541.

p. 570 the interpreters: the jurists (and, where indicated, the works) cited in the *History of the Column of Infamy* are Prospero Farinacci (1544–1618), *Praxis et theoricae criminalis* (1616); Francesco Bruni (15th century), *De indiciis et tortura* (1495); Angelo Gambiglioni d'Arezzo (15th century), *Tractatus de maleficiis* (1472); Guido da Suzara (died 1292), *De tormentis sive indiciis et tortura*; Baldo degli Ubaldi (1319?–1400), *Commentaria in XI Codicis libros* (1541); Paride dal Pozzo (Paris de Puteo, 1413–93), *De syndicatu omnium officiam* (1473); Giulio Claro (1525–75), *Sententiarum receptarum libri V* (1568); Antonio Gomez (16th century); Ippolito Marsigli (Hippolytus de Marsiliis) (1450–1529), *Practica causarum criminalium* (1542); Matteo d'Afflitto (1448–1528), *In utriusque Siciliae Neapolisque sanctiones et constitutiones novissima praelectio* (1580); Bartolo da Sassoferrato (1313?–57); Egidio Bossi, *Tractatus varii qui omnem fere criminalem materiam complectuntur* (1562); Francesco Casoni (died 1564), *De indiciis et tormentis tractatus duo* (1577); Giambattista Baiardi (1530–1600), *Additiones et annotationes ad Julii Clari lib. V receptarum sententiarum sive practicam criminalem* (1603); Pietro Follerio (16th century); Nicolò Tedeschi (1386–1445); Ippolito Riminaldi (1520–89), *Consilia seu responsa in causis gravissimis* (1609); Odofredo Denari (died 1265), *Lecturae in secundum Codicis partem* (1550); Cino da Pistoia (1270?–1336?), known also as a poet contemporary with Dante.

p. 576 *nam sufficit* . . . in two earlier editions of the text: in the first case the meaning is 'for [*nam*] it is sufficient that there is some evidence against the accused in order that he may be tortured' whereas *non sufficit* means 'it is not sufficient'. Manzoni found the latter reading in Venice editions of 1580 and 1595.

p. 576 *Doctores communiter dicunt* . . . *relinquitur arbitrio judicis*: 'It is the common opinion of the learned that in this question [of what evidence suffices to justify torture] there can be no firm principle, but it must be left to the decision of the judge.'

p. 579 Giannone: Pietro Giannone (1676–1748), historian and jurist, had a European reputation as a staunch upholder of the independence of the civil power from the Church. He is exposed below by Manzoni (see ch.7) for plagiarism from other historians: at once a vice of unacknowledged borrowing and a bad practice of reproducing an earlier writer's claim without going back to the primary sources and evidence.

p. 582 Certain residues of the laws of a race of conquerors: the polemical opening sentence of *Dei delitti e delle pene* (*Of Crimes and Punishments*, 1764) by the Milanese Cesare Beccaria (1738–94), Manzoni's maternal grandfather and a close associate of Pietro Verri's. The 'race of conquerors' are the Romans, whose laws, handed down to posterity and mingled with local customs and commentaries, constituted for Beccaria a 'debris of barbarous times', a dead weight of accumulated tradition. Beccaria's treatise, which made a great impact throughout Europe, argued for the abolition of torture and the death penalty and for a penal system matching punishments to crimes on the utilitarian principle of the least punishment necessary in each case to deter a potential offender from a particular crime.

p. 585n *Reus evidentioribus argumentis oppressus, repeti in quaestionem potest*: 'When the accused is burdened by clearer proofs, torture may be repeated.'

p. 585n *Numquid potest repeti quaestio? Videtur quod sic; ut Dig. eo l. Repeti. Sed vos dicatis quod non potest repeti sine novis indiciis*: 'May torture be repeated? . . . But you say it may not be repeated without new evidence.'

p. 588 *nisi a carneficibus*: 'except by slaughterers'.

p. 595 *dedit unguenta mihi tonsor:* 'the barber gave me the unguent'.

p. 600 lye: an alkaline solution used for washing clothes, sometimes leaving a viscous sediment.

p. 602 page number 104: the page number referred to by Padilla's lawyer is that of the transcript of the interrogation, of which he had had a copy made.

p. 602 against whom the mob was yelling *'Tolle!'*: see Luke 23: 18, on the multitude opposing Pilate's proposal to release Christ: *'tolle hunc, exclamavit simul universa turba'* ('Take him away, the whole crowd cried out together').

p. 604 how were they dressed: the suspicion is that they were foreigners, identifiable by their different clothing.

p. 605 infamous: in law, an *infamous* person ('infamy', from Latin *infamia*, means 'ill repute') was one who, as a consequence of being convicted of certain crimes, was disgraced by being deprived of some or all of the rights of a citizen. *Infamy* was thus both a condition of the convicted person and a form of punishment. Beccaria in Chapter 23 of *Dei delitti e delle pene* defines it as follows: 'Infamy is a sign of public disapproval which deprives the convicted person of public esteem, the confidence of his country and that near fraternity which society inspires.' This was the meaning of the Column of Infamy in this case. Erected on the site where the executed Mora's house had been razed to the ground, the accompanying inscription carried a warning to 'good citizens' to keep far from the spot (for the text, see note to p. 648 below).

p. 605 *et ita apud nos servatur:* 'and such is the custom among us'.

p. 610 only one of which he appears to have taken seriously: namely that of extending Spanish domination.

p. 613 the other: i.e. the alleged friendship between Mora and Piazza.

p. 613.: Q. Curtius Rufus, *De rebus gestis Alexandri Magni*.

p. 622 *etiam quod millies sponte sit ratificata:* 'even if it be voluntarily ratified a thousand times'.

p. 628 *civium ardor prava jubentium:* 'the fury of the citizens who demand iniquities' (Horace, *Odes*, III, 3).

p. 638 dressed like *Pantalone*: the cuckold figure in Italian comedy.

p. 640 the infernal goddess who stood on the look-out: Virgil, *Aeneid*,

VII, 511, describing the Fury Allecto: 'At saeva e speculis tempus dea nacta nocendi'; Manzoni quotes the Italian translation by Annibal Caro (VII, 789): 'L'infernal dea che alla veletta stava'.

p. 641 Giuseppe Ripamonti: see note to p. 120 above.

p. 643 Battista Nani: Giovanni Battista Nani (1616–78), ambassador and librarian of the Republic of Venice.

p. 643 some other Milanese column ... a defeat suffered by Venice: the column of San Babila, on top of which stands a lion. It was popularly believed in Milan to record a military victory against the Venetians, whose civic symbol is the lion of St Mark, but it probably just symbolized the San Babila district.

p. 643 Muratori: Ludovico Antonio Muratori (1672–1750), prolific historian, worked at the Biblioteca Ambrosiana from 1695 to 1700. His *Del governo della peste* was published in 1714.

p. 644 Giannone: see note to p. 579.

p. 645 Masaniello: leader of the 1647 uprising of the self-styled *lazzari* or *lazzaroni* (plebs) of Naples, Masaniello (Tommaso Aniello) was a fish-seller whom the uprising brought to temporary power.

p. 648 Sarpi: Paolo Sarpi (1552–1623), historian.

p. 648 Parini's unfinished poem on the Column of Infamy: Giuseppe Parini (1729–99), Milanese poet; the last lines are a translation of the end of the Latin inscription (reproduced by Manzoni here in the footnote) on the plaque which was set alongside the Column and is now in the Musei Civici in the Castello Sforzesco, Milan. The whole inscription translated reads as follows: 'Where this open space now is there formerly stood the barber's shop of Giangiacomo Mora, who plotted with Guglielmo Piazza, public health commissioner, and others, while the atrocious plague raged; by scattering here and there deadly unguents he brought many to a cruel death. Both these men having therefore been judged enemies of the state, the Senate ordered that they first be tortured with red-hot forceps on a high cart and their right hands cut off, that they be broken on the wheel and then threaded onto the wheel, that after six hours their throats be slit and that they be burned, and in order that nothing should remain of such iniquitous men their goods be confiscated and their ashes thrown into the river. In perpetual memory of such a crime, the Senate ordered that this house, the workshop of the iniquity, be razed to the ground and never rebuilt, and a column be erected to be called infamous (*et erigi columnam quae vocetur infamis*). Keep far from here, keep far therefore, good citizens, lest the wretched infamous soil contaminate you. 1 August 1630.'

p. 649 Italian Classics of Political Economy: the *Osservazioni sulla tortura* were included in Volume 17, pp. 193–312, of this series, published by Pietro Custodi.

p. 650 can be neither abolished nor replaced: i.e. the Catholic Church.

MANZONI AND HIS CRITICS

Johann Wolfgang Goethe (as reported by J. P. Eckermann) (1827)

Goethe's admiration for Manzoni's work (he translated *Il cinque maggio* into German and praised *Il Conte di Carmagnola*, which had been poorly received in Italy) was instrumental in launching his European reputation. At the same time, Goethe's remarks on the first edition of *The Betrothed* (he died in 1832 before the second appeared) established a critical view according to which Manzoni the historian got the upper hand over Manzoni the poet, producing an 'excessive preponderance of history' which lessened the novel's poetic value.

Saturday, 21 July 1827

When I went to see Goethe in his room this evening I found him reading Manzoni's novel. 'I am already into volume three', he declared as he laid the book aside, 'and lots of new thoughts have occurred to me in the process... There are preeminently four things which prove useful to Manzoni and contribute to the outstanding quality of his work. In the first place, the fact that he is an excellent historian, by virtue of which his writing has acquired the great dignity and efficacy that raises it far above anything else which one normally understands by a novel. In the second place, the Catholic religion is to his advantage, since it provides him with many situations and occasions of a poetic kind which he would not have enjoyed as a Protestant. Similarly, in the third place, it proves advantageous to his work that the author himself has suffered much in our times of revolutionary friction which, even if he was not personally involved in them, have nonetheless directly affected his friends and in some cases have brought them to destruction. And finally, in the fourth place, it is a favourable circumstance for this novel that the action takes place in the pleasing and attractive area around Lake Como, a place which has made a deep and lasting impression upon the writer from his youth onwards, and which he therefore knows intimately and utterly. For this is also the source of one of the work's principal merits, namely the clarity and the truly remarkable detail it shows in the depiction of locality.'

Monday, 23 July 1827

... 'I recently mentioned to you', Goethe began, 'that the historian in him proved very advantageous to our writer, but now that I am into the third volume, I find that the historian is playing a cruel trick on the poet, in as much as Signor Manzoni all of a sudden divests himself of the poet's garb and stands revealed for some considerable time as a naked historian. And indeed this transpires in a description of war, famine and pestilence, all things which are repulsive in themselves and actually become unbearable through circumstantial detail and dry description in the manner of a chronicle. The German translator must strive to avoid this error; he must condense the description of the war and the famine a good deal, and that of the plague by two thirds, so that only so much remains as is required for the direct involvement of the acting characters. If Manzoni had had a friend at his side to advise him, he would easily have been able to avoid this error of judgement. But as a historian he was filled with too great a respect for reality ... Yet as soon as the characters of the novel make their appearance again, the poet once more stands before us in all his glory, and compels once again all of our customary admiration.'

We stood up and directed our steps towards the house. 'One can hardly comprehend', Goethe continued, 'how a poet like Manzoni, who is capable of producing such a marvellous composition, could fail poetry in this way even for a moment. But the matter is quite simple, and it is this: Manzoni is a born poet, just as Schiller was one. Yet our own time is so poor that the poet no longer encounters within the human life which surrounds him the kind of nature that he can make use of. In order to elevate himself therefore, Schiller turned his attention to two great subjects, namely philosophy and history; whereas Manzoni has recourse to history alone. Schiller's Wallenstein is such a great achievement that we cannot find a second comparable example of its kind; but you will discover that these two mighty aids and accomplices, history and philosophy, really obstruct the work at various places and inhibit its purely poetic success. Thus it is that Manzoni suffers from an excessive preponderance of history'.

From Johann Peter Eckermann, *Gespräche mit Goethe in den letzten Jahren seines Lebens*, in J. W. Goethe, *Gedenkausgabe der Werke, Briefe und Gespräche*, edited by Ernst Beutler, (Artemis Verlag, Zurich, 1948), Vol. 24, pp. 264–5, 266–7.

Etienne Delécluze (1827)

This first long French review of the novel contains some interesting remarks about the 'nullity' of the two main characters and their being upstaged by the minor characters.

> The history or the *novel* of The Betrothed lacks unity in the construction of its plot. This defect results from the fact that the two protagonists around whom the action revolves are constantly being eclipsed by the power and brilliance of the secondary characters. It has to be admitted: these young fiancés, who are so good-natured that even their desires are good, do nothing by themselves which is not blighted by a nullity which neither the flashes of their intelligence nor the strength of their attachment for one another can alleviate. They always demonstrate so much moderation of character, and so complete a trust in Providence, that the reader, reassured by this pious disposition, promptly ceases to feel any anxiety about their fate. In fact, Renzo and Lucia fade from the picture as soon as Father Cristoforo, Don Rodrigo, the unnamed, Federigo Borromeo or Father Abbondio himself, whose cowardice is so amusing and whose character is so skilfully drawn, make their appearance. As for the persecutions suffered by the betrothed, what are they? What emotions can they excite when the reader will necessarily compare them to three disasters such as the famine, the war and the plague?
>
> Nonetheless, the succession of the two fiancés' adventures is like the thread left by the writer for the use of his readers, to help them to travel through the many detours of his work without going astray. This thread (since we have made the comparison) is too thin; it slips out of our hands, it breaks too easily, and we lose it too often.

From *Journal des Débats*, 1 November 1827, p. 3.

Giovita Scalvini (1828)

An early anti-Catholic reaction against the novel by an Italian liberal; its echoes were to carry through to the present (see for instance the extracts from Settembrini, Croce and Moravia below, and, for a Marxist variant, from Gramsci).

> Renzo and Lucia are not characters. They seem to let themselves be carried along by a religious instinct like animals by the instincts of their species. They are children of Providence: and Providence seems to concern itself with them all the more because they are, in themselves, absolutely null. Their thoughts and actions are not the effects of their wills, but of directions and laws which they receive from outside. It is true that they are very lovable little beings, but any interest which they might arouse in us always gives way and turns to He who has placed them on earth and protects them there. They interest us as principles, as ideas, and not as individuals. They interest us as the means which leads us to other thoughts, to enquiries which are beyond them: like a flower, like a butterfly.
>
> ... One might say: the novel is a fiction inspired by the poetic sense; and its morality must therefore take on the tangible and poetic form of religion. This is all very well, but religions, so long as they live and are believed, are not only a form of the universal, but also its substance. Moral sanction ends up by falling back on the material shape of the thing, and the believer says: either you believe in this particular way, or you have no belief at all. . . . In the novel, religion is so closely aligned with morality that it appears that the latter derives from the former, and not that the former is a way in which God has revealed to people the eternal laws on which the latter is founded. It seems that Manzoni wants to say: either you are a Catholic, in which case you are obedient, virtuous and holy, or you are not, in which case you are a criminal, a ruffian, an adulterer, a murderer. Religion, in the book, is identified with morality to such a degree that whoever rejects the first must, if he is to be coherent, also reject the second: the Egidios and Rodrigos seem to be immoral because they have no religion, and they are irreligious because their moral sense is dead.

From *Le note manzoniane di Giovita Scalvini*, edited by Mario Marcazzan (Morcelliana, Brescia, 1942).

Edgar Allan Poe (1835)

Poe reviewed the novel in 1835 in the American translation of G. W. Featherstonehaugh (Washington, 1834), claiming that 'it promises to be the commencement of a new style in novel writing.' Though he recognised Manzoni's debt to Scott, he praised *The Betrothed* for its originality, the fact that it rescued the actions of 'great and good men' from beneath 'the rubbish of revolution' and the stark picture of moral coercion in the episode of Gertrude.

The machinery of the story is not intricate, but each part is necessary to the rest. To leave anything out is to tell nothing. It might be too much to say that this novel is, in every sense of the word, original. The writer is obviously familiar with English literature, and seems to have taken at least one hint from Sir Walter Scott. The use made by that writer of the records and traditions of times gone by, has suggested this hint. It naturally occurred to Manzoni, a native of Italy, that much of the same sort of material was to be found among the archives of the petty Italian states now blotted from the map of Europe. It is obvious that the collisons of small states, though less interesting to the politician than those of mighty nations, must afford more occasion for a display of individual character, and the exercise of those passions which give romance its highest interest. But what is known of the great and good men who nobly acted their parts in these scenes, when the very theatre of their acts is crushed and buried beneath the rubbish of revolution? To drag them from beneath the ruins, and permit the world to dwell for a moment on the contemplation of their virtues is a pious and praiseworthy task. The Cardinal Borromeo is an historical character. The writer obviously means to paint him as he was; and the annals of mankind may be searched in vain for a more glorious example of the purity, the enthusiasm, and the inspiration of virtue.

We might suspect that something of a zeal for the honor of the Romish Church had mingled itself in the rich coloring of this picture. But Manzoni was as much alive, as Luther himself, to the abuses of that church. The moral coercion, more cruel than bodily torture, by which a poor girl, the victim of the heartless pride of her parents, without command, without even persuasion (for both it seems are forbidden), is driven to the cloister, that her brother may have more ample means to uphold his hereditary honors; this was a thing inscrutable and inconceivable to us. In reading such works as Mrs Sherwood's *Nun*, we feel that we are dealing with conjectures. We turn to the scene exhibited in this work, and we *know* it to be real life.

'I Promessi Sposi, or The Betrothed Lovers'; originally in *Southern Literary Messenger*, May 1835; reprinted in *The*

Complete Works of Edgar Allan Poe, edited by James A. Harrison, Vol. VIII (AMS Press, New York, 1965), pp. 15–17.

Luigi Settembrini (1872)

Settembrini, a prominent Risorgimento liberal, criticized the novel retrospectively (this passage was written after Italian Unification and the year before Manzoni's death) as the 'book of Reaction', that is to say of the conservative, monarchic and clerical reaction in Italy which had followed the revolutionary and Napoleonic period (1796–1814) and had been embodied in the so-called Holy Alliance (Austria, Prussia, Russia) of 1815–48. Settembrini found in the novel not only an over-schematic polarization between the representatives and followers of the Church, who are all good, and the other characters, who are all bad or contemptible, but also a moral of forgiveness of one's oppressors which he claims was politically unacceptable for Italian liberals under the yoke of reaction. Silvio Pellico, mentioned here, was a liberal nationalist; jailed by the Austrians for conspiracy, he wrote a widely read account of his sufferings and the spiritual consolation he found in prison (*Le mie prigioni*, 1832); the Five Days uprising was an episode of the 1848 revolution in Milan.

But let us allow the poet to create a world of his own, different from the real world and let us allow his priests and clerics to be the only good characters and true Christians. Let us leave the characters and see what is the essence of the tale, the moral ideas which form the characters and determine their actions.

Faith in God lightens the ills of the world and turns them to our own improvement. One must do God's will in all circumstances and at all times and bear everything which comes from Him. Forgive offences against us; always, always, always forgive.

These maxims are fine and holy; the trouble begins when they have to be converted into actions. Certainly I want to do God's will; but to do it I must know who God is, and what his will is. When you who call yourself God's minister tell me to do something which my reason does not find persuasive, I suspect that this is your will, and that you are putting yourself in God's place and tricking me with God's name. And if you are a wicked person, a supporter of tyrants, an upholder of the Holy Alliance, then I would be doing the will of a wicked man, of my enemy and the enemy of my country. God has given his law to everyone, he has given everyone reason with which to understand it and follow it, and what my reason does not approve is not God's will for me. Yes, I can forgive offences when they are done against me; but when they are done to my country and to many millions of people, I must not forgive them, because in forgiving a single offender I harm many millions of offended. The idea of forgiveness is holy so long as it does not contradict the idea of justice. These fine maxims in their ethereal purity might console good Silvio Pellico in the Spielberg Prison but they can not give rise to the Five Days of Milan. . . .

Today the Germans have gone back over the Alps and are our brothers again. Justice has been done and it is our duty to forgive. But in 1827, in the darkest and fiercest time of Reaction, when the priests played master, Austria held Lombardy-Venetia in a cruel grip and our own enraged petty tyrants tormented us, to write and publish a book which praised priests and friars and counselled patience, submission and forgiveness, meant (Manzoni certainly did not intend this, but it was the necessary consequence of his book) counselling submission in servitude, the denial of one's country and all feelings of civil generosity, it meant that God wanted Austrian rule over Lombardy and Venetia, the Duke in Modena, the Pope in Rome, the Bourbons in Naples, and that he wanted these things to make us suffer in order to deserve a better life.

The Betrothed is the book of Reaction.

From *Lezioni di letteratura italiana*, Naples 1869–72, Vol. III, pp. 302–5.

Francesco De Sanctis (1873)

De Sanctis, the foremost Italian critic of the nineteenth century, was, like Settembrini, a Neapolitan liberal and he too registered the 'propagandist' religious and moral bias of Manzoni's novel. Unlike him, though, he judged it to be a great work of realist art in which the author's abstract ideal (the 'idea') was successfully absorbed into the concrete 'fact': the variegated reality of the represented world. This highly influential view served to redeem and relegitimize Manzoni for many non-Catholic readers and teachers of literature in Italy.

> Lucia, Father Cristoforo and Federigo Borromeo are perfect exemplars of an ideal world, . . . counterbalanced by opposite exemplars,

such as Don Rodrigo and the Unnamed, and in between there wander characters who are more or less close to one of the two poles. The mechanism is such that the ideal world is always victorious in the conflict, so that in the end, with irresistible conviction, it comes to dominate the reader's mind.

The content is new: it is a rejuvenated and modernized world; but the form is old: it is the usual ideal which is postulated and imposed, so that it is superimposed on nature and on history.

In this way, the poetic world of the novel has a propagandist bias in the service of moral and religious ideas, in accordance with the impulse which was given to culture in the eighteenth century and which has lasted until the present day.

. . . But the Manzonian ideal has a great advantage. It is not a purely spiritual world which lives only in the imaginations of cultivated men, a mere aspiration rather than a reality, and therefore lyrical, polemical, satirical, as the idea is when it is in opposition to the fact. It is, rather, a real historical organism, where the ideal lives in the majority of people, altered, perverted, rusty, always differentiated in degree, from the lowest to the highest on the scale, from Don Abbondio to Federigo Borromeo. . . .

The novel's originality, therefore, lies in this: that its ideal is not an idea of the poet's, a moral world of his own which is formed from his spirit and detached from the story, but an effective and organic member of a real and concrete narrative. It is not an ideal which the imagination has realized by an artificial process, but an ideal which has become a true historical reality, and which can be gathered just as it is found at a particular epoch in a particular place. . . . The author does not interfere, except in order to help you, as a kind of guide, who explains and responds to what you see, not without a degree of malice at your expense; but the observant reader will note that his spirit wanders through the story like a harmonious and serene breath, which orders and contains the movements, preserving equilibrium and measure in the tussle between people and things. What Manzoni was trying to achieve, the aim which seemed to him unattained and unattainable, that is to say unity of the composition and homogeneity of its elements, even though some are historical and some are invented, is perfectly accomplished; in fact, this is his originality, this is his great title in the history of our literature. His historical novel is not only a beautiful work of art, but it is a true monument, which occupies the same place in the history of art as the *Divine Comedy* or *Orlando furioso*.

From 'I "Promessi sposi"', originally in *Nuova Antologia*, Vol. XXIV, December, 1873, pp. 742–65; reprinted in F. De Sanctis, *Manzoni*, edited by Carlo Muscetta and Dario Puccini (Einaudi, Turin, 1965), pp. 74–5, 77–8.

Luigi Pirandello (1908)

The character of Manzoni's cowardly priest Don Abbondio had been used by De Sanctis in another lecture of 1873 to illustrate his argument (see above) that in the writing of the novel Manzoni's Christian ideal was 'absorbed' into human reality with all its weaknesses. For Pirandello, in a series of lectures on humour which he gave in 1908, Don Abbondio (along with Don Quixote in Cervantes's novel) was used to illustrate the difference between humour and comedy: for Pirandello, comedy prompts the simple reaction of laughter whereas humour involves a 'sense of contraries', a complex tension between laughter and pity, detachment and sympathy, which can end up displacing laughter altogether.

> Now, I don't deny that Don Abbondio is a chicken. But we know that when Don Rodrigo threatened he didn't threaten in vain, we know that in order to *win the bet* he really was capable of anything; we know what sort of times those were, and we can perfectly well imagine that if Don Abbondio had married Renzo and Lucia nobody would have saved him from a musket shot, and that perhaps Lucia, wife in no more than name, would have been kidnapped as she stepped out of the church, and Renzo killed as well. What good are the intervention and the advice of Fra Cristoforo? Isn't Lucia kidnapped from the convent of Monza? There's a *league of rascals*, as Renzo says. To cut that knot you need the hand of God; not as a figure of speech – the hand of God for real. What could a poor priest do?
>
> Don Abbondio is certainly scared and De Sanctis has written some magnificent pages examining the poor curate's feelings of fear; but he did not take account of the fact that a frightened man is ridiculous, is comic, when he makes up risks and imaginary dangers: but when a frightened man has *a good reason to be frightened*, when we see someone caught up, entangled in a terrible confrontation, someone who by nature and by design wants to avoid all confrontations, even the most gentle ones, and is forced to get involved in this terrible confrontation by his sacred duty, then this frightened man is no longer merely comic. . . .

A superficial observer will pay attention to the laughter which derives from the external comedy of Don Abbondio's acts, gestures, reticent phrases, and so on, and will call him ridiculous and nothing more, a merely comic figure. But anyone who is not satisfied by these superficialities, and who is able to see a bit more deeply, will feel that the laughter here is prompted by something very different, and is not only the laughter of comedy.

But Don Abbondio is the character one is given instead of the character one should have had. But the poet does not despise this piece of reality which he finds because although, as we have said, he has an extremely high ideal of the mission of a priest in this world, he also has the power of reflection which suggests to him that this ideal is incarnated only in very rare exceptions, and which therefore forces him to limit that ideal, as De Sanctis has observed. But what exactly is this limitation of the ideal? – it is the effect of that power of reflection which, going to work on this ideal, suggested to the poet the feeling of its contrary. And Don Abbondio is precisely this feeling of its contrary made concrete and brought to life; and therefore he is not merely comic but frankly and profoundly humorous.

... Laughing at him and sympathizing with him at the same time, the poet also comes to laugh bitterly at this poor human nature of ours, weak with so many weaknesses; and the more sympathetic considerations gather to protect the poor curate, the further the discrediting of human value spreads around him. In short, the poet induces us to have sympathy for the poor curate by making us recognize that what he thinks and feels is only human, and belongs to all of us; and so he makes us look deeply into our own consciences. And what follows from this? It follows that if this particular, by its own power, becomes general; if this mixed feeling of laughter and tears, the more it condenses and fixes itself in Don Abbondio, the more it widens and almost vaporizes in an infinite sadness, it follows, we were saying, that if we look at the representation of Manzoni's curate in this way, we will no longer be able to laugh at it. That pity, deep down, is pitiless: the sympathetic indulgence is not as good-natured as it seemed at first sight.

It is a great thing, as we see, to have an ideal – religious as in Manzoni, chivalrous as in Cervantes – only to watch it being cut down by reflection in Don Abbondio and Don Quijote! Manzoni finds solace by creating alongside the country priest Father Cristoforo and Cardinal Borromeo, but the fact remains that, since he is above all a humorist, his most living creature is the first of these, the one in whom the feeling of contrariety is incarnated. Cervantes cannot find any solace because, in the prison of La Mancha, with Don Quijote – as he himself says – he gives birth to 'someone who resembles him'.

From 'L'umorismo' (1908), in L. Pirandello, *Saggi*, edited by Manlio Lo Vecchio Musti (Mondadori, Milan, 1939), pp. 157–9.

Benedetto Croce (1921)

A counterweight to De Sanctis's positive appraisal of Manzoni by his most influential intellectual successor. For Croce, the 'wisdom of the moralist' limited Manzoni's range as an artist and led him in his novel to compress the complexity of human passions into a schematic view of the world. Croce also judged Manzoni's abilities as an historian to have been compromised by his religious beliefs, his intellectualism and moral rigidity, making him unable to look at the past impartially and sympathetically. Late in his life, Croce partially retracted his earlier negative view of Manzoni's novel.

In his essay of 1829 [sic] on *The Betrothed*, Giovita Scalvini noted that the novel has a uniformity and insistency about it; that one doesn't feel 'the wide variety of the moral world moving freely within it,' and that often one senses that one is 'not under the great dome of the firmament,' which covers 'all the multitudinous forms of existence,' but under that of 'the church, which covers the faithful and the altar.'

However much this judgment has been repeated or renewed by others who have diminished its truth and vigour by importing into it their own biased passions, in its first author it grew from an impression which was undeniably sincere; and, in my opinion, it deserves to be deepened and more precisely defined, because it opens the way to the correct critical interpretation of one of the greatest masterpieces of our literature.

What is the origin of the sense of narrowness which seems sometimes to be felt during the reading of *The Betrothed*, or rather when Manzoni is compared with other poets? In the novel one feels in their full force and free range none of what we call the human passions and desires: the hunger for the truth, the travails of doubt, the longing for happiness, the rapture of the infinite, the dreams of beauty and power, the joys and the anxieties of love, the dramas of politics and history, the ideals and memories of peoples, and so on; all those things, in short, which furnish material for other poets. It is not that the author has not experienced them and does not know them; but that he has passed them by and subdued them to a superior design, because he has risen out of the tumult into the calm, and has arrived at wisdom. But what wisdom! Not the wisdom which feels sympathetically all the different human passions, while at the same time holding itself above them, arranging each one in its place, and composing them into its own harmony; but the wisdom of the moralist, who sees nothing but black and white, on this side justice, on that side injustice, here goodness, there evil, here innocence, there malice, here reason, there distortion and stupidity, and approves of one side and condemns the other, often with the subtle ponderings of a casuist. The world, so various in its colours and its sounds, all its parts so closely linked together, so inexhaustible and so profound, is simplified, not to say impoverished, in this vision; and of all the innumerable notes of the soul here only one is given, the one which, because it sounds alone, gave Scalvini the impression of insistency and uniformity. Manzoni's inspiring theme appears to be the motto: *Dilexi iustitiam, odivi iniquitatem.*

From *Poesia e non poesia. Note sulla letteratura europea del secolo decimonono* (1921) (Laterza, Bari, 1955), pp. 131–2.

In fact, Manzoni always retained more than a little of an eighteenth-century intellectual education, which habitually saw history as a means rather than as an end; and his intellectualism was strength-ened in its anti-historical tendency by his rather Jansenist, morally rigid and meticulous Catholicism. The description of seventeenth-century Italian life in *The Betrothed* is, without doubt, a master-piece, but a masterpiece of satire and of subtle irony rather than of historical intelligence, which consists in sympathy, and always turns its attention to whatever new and positive developments are taking place, even in those historical periods which seem to be characterized by decadence and confusion.

From *Storia della storiografia italiana nel secolo decimonono*, Volume I (Laterza, Bari, 1921), pp. 188–9.

Hugo von Hofmannsthal (1927)

Hofmannsthal's essay is noteworthy for its emphasis on the unobtrusive but careful arrangement of the novel's parts and the restraint of its style, which he compares to the report of a diligent steward.

In order to make his affection for the town [Milan] completely and tangibly felt, it was necessary to select a dismal and terrible episode from its history; for only this would produce the pathos which accompanies the thought that this town really has experienced such things – that this town bears the memories of these things in its very entrails. Now the plague of 1628 [sic] was an event of this kind, in as much as it befell the entire town, threatened the lives of everyone at once, and gave rise to terrible consequences and strange chains of events. At the same time, this period also shared something in common with the present; then as now the town stood under the control of a foreign military power; then it was the Spanish power, whereas now it is the Austrian; – but the beginning of the seventeenth century and the beginning of the nineteenth century are even more profoundly related with one another in their innermost rhythm as epochs of political restoration and reaction. The figures and scenes, though not too many of them, are placed within this framework, but all selected and executed in such a wonderful manner that they comprise the whole range of character which belongs to Lombardy, both with respect to social classes and levels of culture and to the various kinds of individuals with their particular attitudes and sensibilities.

This extreme vitality, which simultaneously represents a maximum of discretion, is accomplished by a narrative exposition which is utterly sober, penetrating and exact. In tone it resembles the kind of report which a good steward (whether it be one entrusted with the care of worldly goods or of human souls) would provide for his superior in order to inform the latter really accurately so that he could form a judgement for himself. To mention only a few examples, something of the depredations suffered by the priest's house at the hands of plundering soldiers is reported in just this tone, and it is exactly the same with the unfolding circumstances which turn the 'Signora' into an arrogant unhappy woman, and finally into a sinner. Or again the author provides a kind of psychological inventory of an average sort of person like Agnese, the mother of Lucia, without making her appear better than she is, but also without particularly emphasizing the less attractive, all too human selfish aspects of her character; and it is in the same way that the world of the followers and bandits who depend upon the 'Unnamed' is reported, that peculiar combination of horror and enjoyment which binds them to him is accurately revealed – without any romantic chiaroscuro, but rather in a completely classical manner. There is absolutely nothing further removed from romanticism than the style of this book, which is ranked amongst the masterpieces of the romantic era. But even Stendhal's anti-romantic 'sobriety' appears almost mannered when measured against the unconditional and natural sobriety and objectivity of this narrative.

From 'Manzoni's "Promessi sposi"' (1927), in H. von Hofmannsthal, *Gesammelte Werke in Einzelausgaben, Prosa*, Vol. IV, edited by Herbert Steiner (Fischer Verlag, Frankfurt, 1955), pp. 419–21.

D. H. Lawrence (1927)

This brief comment on Manzoni is from a preface written by Lawrence in 1927 to his translation of *Mastro-don Gesualdo* (1888) by the Sicilian writer Giovanni Verga. The preface did not in fact appear with the translation and was first published after Lawrence's death.

It seems curious that modern Italian literature has made so little impression on the European consciousness. A hundred years ago, when Manzoni's *I Promessi Sposi* came out, it met with European applause. Along with Sir Walter Scott and Byron, Manzoni stood for "Romance" to all Europe. Yet where is Manzoni now, even compared to Scott and Byron? Actually, I mean. Nominally, *I Promessi Sposi* is a classic; in fact, it is usually considered *the* classic Italian novel. It is set in all "literature courses". But who reads it? Even in Italy, who reads it? And yet, to my thinking, it is one of the best and most interesting novels ever written: surely a greater book than *Ivanhoe* or *Paul et Virginie* or *Werther*. Why then does nobody read it? Why is it found boring? When I gave a good English translation to the late Katharine Mansfield, she said, to my astonishment: I couldn't read it. Too long and boring.

From 'Mastro-don Gesualdo' in *Phoenix: The Posthumous Papers of D. H. Lawrence*, edited by Edward D. McDonald, Heinemann, London, 1936, pp. 223–4.

Antonio Gramsci (1931–3)

During his ten-year imprisonment by the Fascists, the former leader of Italy's Communist Party filled twenty-eight school exercise books with notes on a wide variety of subjects. The notes on literature were influential among Marxist critics in Italy when the *Prison Notebooks* were published after the Second World War. They include a few jottings on Manzoni's novel, criticizing it for its Catholic paternalism and its tone of ironic condescension towards the lower-class characters.

> The 'aristocratic' character of Manzoni's Catholicism is apparent from the jocular 'sympathy' shown towards the figures of the common people (which does not appear in Tolstoy): Fra Galdino (compared with Fra Cristoforo), the tailor, Renzo, Agnese, Perpetua and also Lucia.
>
> ... the point is not that of wanting Manzoni to 'flatter the people'; the question is one of his psychological attitude towards individual characters who belong to the people. It is clearly a caste attitude, even in its religious Catholic form. For Manzoni the people do not have any 'inner life', any deep moral personality. They are 'animals' and Manzoni is 'benevolent' towards them, with exactly that benevolence of a Catholic society for the protection of animals. In a sense, Manzoni reminds one of the epigram about Paul Bourget: for Bourget a woman must have an income of 100,000 francs before she can have an inner life. Manzoni (and Bourget) are in this respect unmitigatedly Catholic. There is nothing in them of Tolstoy's 'popular spirit', of the evangelical spirit of primitive Christianity. Manzoni's attitude to the people is the attitude of the Catholic Church to the people: one of indulgent benevolence, not shared humanity. ... Manzoni sees *all* of the people with 'a severe gaze', while he sees with a severe gaze '*the majority* of those who do not belong to the people': he finds 'magnanimity', 'noble thoughts' and 'great feelings' only in some of the upper class and in none of the people, who as a whole are basely animal-like.
>
> (1931)

There is a disjunction of feeling between Manzoni and the 'humble' people. For Manzoni they are a 'problem of historiography', a theoretical problem that he believes he can solve with the historical novel and the 'verisimilitude' of the historical novel. Hence the 'humble' people are often presented as popular 'caricatures', with good-natured irony, but irony none the less. Manzoni is too Catholic to think that the voice of the people is the voice of God: between the people and God there is the Church. Tolstoy can believe that God is incarnate in the people, but not Manzoni.

Of course, this attitude of Manzoni's is felt by the people and therefore *The Betrothed* has never been popular among them. Emotionally, the people felt that Manzoni was distant from them and felt his novel to be like a book of devotion, not a popular epic.

(1933)

From *Quaderni del carcere*, edited by Valentino Gerratana (Einaudi, Turin, 1975), pp. 895–6 and 1703; translated by William Boelhower in A. Gramsci, *Selections from Cultural Writings*, edited by David Forgacs and Geoffrey Nowell-Smith (Lawrence and Wishart, London, 1985), pp. 291–2 and 296.

Georg Lukács (1936–7)

Lukács, developing Hegel's aesthetics in a Marxist direction, argues that the great historical novels embody, through 'typical' or socially representative characters, the central social conflicts of the period they depict. Manzoni's novel takes one concrete episode – the story of Renzo and Lucia – and transforms it into the general 'tragedy of the Italian people as a whole' in conditions of political fragmentation and foreign domination. Yet at the same time Manzoni's characters do not directly typify the dialectical conflicts of their age and this deprives *The Betrothed*, for Lukács, of the 'world-historical atmosphere' he finds in Scott or Tolstoy.

In Italy historical themes were similarly unfavourable [as in Germany]. Yet here Scott found a successor who, though only in a single, isolated work, nevertheless broadened his tendencies with superb originality, in some respects surpassing him. We refer, of course, to Manzoni's *I Promessi Sposi* (*The Betrothed*). Scott himself recognized Manzoni's greatness. When in Milan Manzoni told him that he was his pupil, Scott replied that in that case Manzoni's was his best work.

As a truly great artist he also discovered a theme which enabled him to overcome the objective unfavourableness of Italian history and to create a real historical novel, that is, one which would rouse the present, which contemporaries would experience as their own pre-history. He sets the historical events even further in the background than Scott, although he draws them with an historical concreteness of atmosphere learned from Scott. But his basic theme is much less a given, concrete, historical crisis of national history, as is always the case in Scott, it is rather the critical condition of the entire life of the Italian people resulting from Italy's fragmentation, from the reactionary feudal character which the fragmented parts of the country had retained owing to their ceaseless petty internecine wars and their dependence on the intervention of the great powers. Thus, while Manzoni's immediate story is simply a concrete episode taken from Italian popular life – the love, separation and reunion of a young peasant boy and girl – his presentation transforms it into a general tragedy of the Italian people in a state of national degradation and fragmentation. Without ever departing from the concrete framework of time, place and the age- and class-conditioned psychology of the characters, the story of Manzoni's lovers grows into *the* tragedy of the Italian people as a whole.

As a result of this superb and historically profound conception Manzoni creates a novel in which the human comes out even more powerfully than in his master. But the inner nature of his theme shows that this had to be an only novel, that it could have been repeated only in a bad sense. . . . Manzoni shows his artistic discretion in striking the one path that could lead to a grand conception of Italian history and in his realization that only one version of it was possible.

But this, of course, had its consequences for the novel itself. We have emphasized here those human and poetic features in Manzoni, wherein in several respects he excels Scott. But the lack of that great historical substratum which Goethe admired in Scott, cannot possibly be confined in its effects to subject-matter alone. It also had inner artistic consequences: the absence of that world-historical atmosphere which can be felt in Scott, even when he is presenting an extensive picture of petty clan wars, manifests itself in Manzoni in a certain limitedness of human horizon on the part of his characters. Despite all the human and historical authenticity, despite all the psychological depth which their author bestows upon them, Manzoni's characters are unable to soar to those historically typical heights which mark the summits of Scott's works.

From *The Historical Novel*, translated from the German by Hannah and Stanley Mitchell (Penguin, Harmondsworth, 1969), pp. 77–9.

Ford Madox Ford (1939)

An illuminating appraisal of the novel for its combination of 'passion' and 'exactitude in the reproduction of an unhappy time'.

There must be some masterliness about a book that has given delight to a whole world for a century – *I Promessi Sposi* was written in 1827. But there is more than just some masterliness about this exuberant book; there is a real clash of passions; a real world is there reconstituted for you. Reading it as a child, if you are in the least bit sophisticated, virtuous Italian peasants, blue Italian lakes, black Italian bravi and tyrants will be apt to have, even to you, a certain air of the cliché. This writer used to question his love for the book; he does so no longer. It is written with a sort of unsleeping fire – which was, perhaps, no more than the fire of the Risorgimento. And the passion of an exciting time will every now and then so influence an author that he will be sedulous to give you always more and more exactitude in the reproduction of an unhappy time. . . .

Manzoni is intent on displaying, through the wrongs done in a past age, the tortures inflicted on the Italy of his own day by a tyranny the heaviest, the most unsleepingly cruel, the most dully insupportable that there has ever been. *I Promessi Sposi* is an historical novel and historical novels are nearly always *tours de force* – inventions of atmospheres more or less specious. But Manzoni, casting back to the eighteenth century, came upon a tyranny identical with, and only less cruel and complete than, the foreign rule that he himself saw in action under the Austrians of the unspeakable Metternich and the unthinkable Holy Alliance. In the days of *The Betrothed* Spain ruled over Italy, with the assistance of Spanish satraps, of the Holy Inquisition, of the usually connivent Italian aristocracy, who in turn were supported by the licenced assassins called "bravi." . . .

Thus, Manzoni could see his story enacted under his eyes and did not need to have recourse to the gloomy inventions and exaggerations that were common to the fiction of all the other true romantics. . . . And his characters are managed with remarkable subtlety, as well as with a great vigour and truth. Practically none of them are stock figures, nor are any of them overdrawn and static like the Pecksniffs and Heeps and Steerforths of Dickens, and the English novelists in general. His virtuous peasants are at times devious, cunning, even unscrupulous; his saintly friars exhibit moments of ill temper; his very bravi and counts feel sometimes remorse and hesitate in the midst of the exploits.

From *The March of Literature: From Confucius to Modern Times* (Allen and Unwin, London, 1939), pp. 665–8.

Jean-François Revel (1958)

One of the most scathing critiques of the novel for its 'asexuality' and its general failure to be a 'novel of opposition', this extract is taken from an alternative guide to Italy and its culture written by Revel (real name Jean-François Ricard) who visited the country in 1957–8, during the conservative regime of the Christian Democrats.

Why, despite all its historical truth and literary value, does *The Betrothed* not figure in the international pantheon of great novels of the nineteenth century? To understand this we need only consider why this new genre, the nineteenth-century novel, originated and developed. Up to the seventeenth century the novel or romance had been devoted to pure escapism and illusion. . . . From the eighteenth century, however, and above all in the nineteenth, the novel became the means of expressing what had never been said before and what could not be said in any other form: it became the means for describing love in its connections with sexuality. . . . Suddenly, with *Moll Flanders* and *Manon Lescaut*, the thing is uttered and called by its true name for the first time. And up to Proust and Joyce the novel strives to speak this truth more and more fully.

There is no need to point out how asexual *The Betrothed* is. This is the sort of literature that can be put into anyone's hands, and preferably those of ten year olds and ninety year olds. The love of Renzo and Lucia is strictly of the engaged couple type – no question that they might want to sleep with one another. Lucia's mother is always present when they are together and Manzoni finds this normal and perfectly acceptable (in his eyes this is not among the abuses of seventeenth-century society). What each of these two young people is really in love with is not the other but what they will attain through the other – marriage. Hence the enthusiasm of all Italian fathers and husbands for Manzoni's novel. In Don Rodrigo's sinful designs on Lucia one does not sense anything related to desire; they are a simple abuse of power by a local tyrant, following a wager with a cousin, and whose object could just as well be the laying waste of a field. In the tale of Gertrude, the nun of Monza, that wonderful short story inserted into the novel, what Manzoni puts at the centre of the drama is the despotism of the father who forces his daughter into the convent to satisfy an absurd aristocratic pride and not the sexual desire that is frustrated, the appetite for life that is stifled. He alludes rapidly, in a couple of pages, to the 'sinful' relations between Gertrude and a local noble, and to the crime they commit together to get rid of a witness. One can imagine what Stendhal would have done with this perverse passion and this murder! Manzoni gives a bare report of them without narrating them. Being the good neo-Catholic he is, what really interests him in this story is to show that one should not send girls to convents if they lack a religious vocation. But convents in themselves seem to him excellent institutions, and he waxes tender over them. The only expression of female amorous emotion he keeps is when Lucia goes 'red, red, red' when she finds herself obliged to tell someone, not that she loves Renzo, but that she has chosen to marry him. All the silliness of the myth of the young girl's innocence – a myth characteristic of societies where women are subjugated – is presented in the character of Lucia as if it were the expression of the sublimest poetry . . .

Ultimately Manzoni, as well as being reactionary in this area, is equally so in politics and religion . . . If he criticizes a society, it is that of two centuries earlier and as an Italian patriot against the Spaniards. But the great novelists of the nineteenth century – Stendhal, Gogol, Dickens or Flaubert – attacked the society they lived in, and with what violence! It has been said repeatedly that Manzoni defends the weak against the strong. It is true. But he does it to illustrate the idea that the weak, thanks to their resignation, can count on the help of Divine Providence. . . .

All the great novels are novels of opposition. Italy has never had its *Dead Souls* or its *Bel-Ami*. It did not take any courage to write *The Betrothed*, and this book is scrupulously silent on the real questions which torment modern man and the real problems which were posed – and still are posed – by the development of a modern Italian society. It is not surprising that official and conformist Italy has never ceased to recognize itself in it without tolerating any discussion of it. Nor is it surprising that foreign readers find it hard to take any interest in it.

From *Pour l'Italie* (Juillard, Paris, 1958), pp. 57–60.

Alberto Moravia (1960)

Moravia reversed De Sanctis's view (see above) that Manzoni's Catholic ideals are absorbed into the novel's realism. In his view, the dosage of religion was 'excessive' for a nineteenth-century novel: it was because Manzoni wanted to promote Catholic values that he set his story in a historical period when the Church was powerful rather than in his own more secularized age. Moravia here sees Manzoni as performing for Catholicism a similar task to that attempted for Soviet communism in the 1930s by 'socialist realism', namely to make realism coincide with propaganda.

> We believe it is easy to guess the underlying reason why Manzoni wrote a novel about an episode of the seventeenth century instead of about an episode of his own time. One need only look at the most obvious aspect of *The Betrothed*: the preponderant, excessive, massive, almost obsessive importance of religion in the novel. This aspect, as we said, is obvious, particularly to Italian eyes, but it is a lot less obvious if we compare *The Betrothed* with other great nineteenth-century novels which are more or less contemporary with it: *Madame Bovary*, *La Chartreuse de Parme*, *War and Peace*, *Pickwick Papers*, *Vanity Fair*, *Le Père Goriot*, etc. If one could measure the dose of each of the different types of content in a novel one would find that religion – Catholic or otherwise – represents no more than five per cent of the total in the novels just cited, whereas in *The Betrothed* the dose rises to no less than ninety-five per cent. And yet the authors of these novels were immersed in the same political and social reality as Manzoni, which was that of European society after the French Revolution. So let us repeat: the importance of religion in *The Betrothed* is hypertrophic, obsessive. It does not correspond in the least to a real condition of Italian and European society in the nineteenth century. And it is precisely this excessive importance which explains why Manzoni, who was not a petty romantic realist like Scott but a great moral and social realist like Stendhal and who therefore could easily have based his novel on an episode of contemporary life, turned to the historical novel. As well as aspiring to represent the whole of Italian reality, Manzoni aspired even more to squeeze this reality, without violence or amputations, into the ideological frame of Catholicism. In other words, as we have already mentioned, a century and a half before socialist realism Manzoni, in his own terms, set himself the problem of an analogous Catholic realism, namely that of a novel in which, by artistic means alone, one might obtain a complete identification between the reality that was represented and the dominant ideology, or the ideology which one wanted to be dominant.

From the introduction to the 1960 edition of *I promessi sposi* published by Einaudi with illustrations by Renato Guttuso; reprinted as 'Alessandro Manzoni o l'ipotesi di un realismo cattolico' in *L'uomo come fine* (Bompiani, Milan, 1964), pp. 305–39.

Kenelm Foster (1967)

In a lecture given to the British Academy in 1967, Kenelm Foster, a lecturer in Italian at Cambridge and a member of the Dominican order, compared the notion of truth in the Christian Manzoni with that of his atheist contemporary Giacomo Leopardi. He argued that Manzoni developed after his conversion a 'humanistic', non-transcendental form of Christian belief in which the emphasis on human reason and on morality in relations between people was central and every human activity was seen as expressing some aspect of truth.

> Everyone knows that Manzoni was a Christian, and discerning readers will know that in him an ardent faith went hand in hand with a very rational cast of mind and a conviction of the rightness, indeed the duty of using reason freely and vigorously on all serious matters, not excluding the issue of religious belief. This rational temper, reflected in the persistent logical finesse of his prose, is a constant in Manzoni's work, in his approach to every topic without exception. His return to the Church in youth was the decisive event of his long life and an absolutely religious event; yet he remained, and consciously so, a child of the Enlightenment, even in a sense, of the Revolution: the *Promessi Sposi* from one point of view is all a searching critique of the *ancien régime*. Indeed in a sense he always remained a rationalist, if this term can be used without its negative connotation of disbelief in revelation. He rejected with horror the idea that Christian faith involves any sort of loss or reduction of rationality; and – given the powers he possessed and the interests he came to pursue – this meant that Christianity, as he conceived it, was not only capable of, but demanded, the utmost extension of those powers and interests; which again meant, in particular, an exploration, both rational and poetic, of what I would call the special manzonian problem, the relation between history and morality, man as he has been and man as he should be.

From 'The Idea of Truth in Manzoni and Leopardi' in *Proceedings of the British Academy*, volume LIII (Oxford University Press, London, 1968), pp. 245–8.

Pier Paolo Pasolini (1973)

A reading of the novel as a homosexual narrative.

Manzoni had a tragic relationship with his parents, and especially with his mother (this obliged him, among other things, to spend long years at boarding school). For us moderns, readers of Freud, it is easy to analyse the consequent neurosis, which is characterised by the typical pattern of complexes with regard to the female sex (of which the vertigo which he felt even when sitting in an isolated chair is a classic symptom): this had to make him crystallize femininity, as without doing so it would have been impossible for him to imagine a sexual relationship. Even this crystallization of femininity has schematic, classic, laboratory symptoms: on the one hand woman is crystallized in Gertrude, the sinner whom one must ignore and keep away from oneself with horror (and apart from everything else, in order to simplify a possible conflict of conscience, she is a nun, and her religious habit is an impassable barrier erected by Censorship): on the other hand, woman is crystallized in Lucia, the immaculate image of the young mother, who cannot – it is inconceivable – have a relationship with a man (and, in fact, here too Censorship, as well as the whole series of obstacles which constitutes the plot of the novel, erects a barrier which is blessed by all the creeds: the vow of chastity). Behind so complicated a relationship with the female sex – as always in such cases – there could not but be a certain tendency, by all means unconscious and totally unrealized, to homosexuality. Sexual life – says Freud – is not a river which runs within its banks, but a stream of sticky liquid, full of secondary branches and stagnant pools, whose main flow reaches its outlet only with difficulty. Manzoni's homosexuality was evidently one of these secondary rivulets, one of these pools: but all the thick weave of personal relationships in *The Betrothed* develops under its influence; Don Rodrigo and the bravi, Don Rodrigo and Griso, Don Rodrigo and his cousin, Cardinal Borromeo and the Unnamed, to mention only the first that come to mind: but, if the reader re-reads *The Betrothed* in this key, he will see that once the male-female relationship has been privileged and placed on an altar, all the relationships which make up the web of the book are characterized by a strange homoerotic intensity (of brotherhood or of hate). This is only natural, and can be seen in all the great novelists. But in *The Betrothed* it also produces Renzo. Renzo is a nostalgic projection on the part of Manzoni, a father-son figure such as he never was nor ever could have been: a possibility for ever lost to the world. Renzo is the symbol of health and wholeness. This love for Renzo's solid and deep-rooted youth – he is the young lad with no problems – means that the relationship between Manzoni and his character is always poetic: reality shines through the pages in which Manzoni writes about Renzo; they merge into the real, they have the absoluteness of the real, and also its substantial lightness.

From 'Inchiesta parlamentare sui personaggi dei "Promessi sposi"', in the magazine *Tempo*, 26 August 1973.

Italo Calvino (1973)

This paper from the early 1970s exemplifies a structuralist reading of the novel. For Calvino, the meanings of the text come not so much from the 'essence' of the individual characters as from their functions in the narrative and the 'relations of force' between them. These relations form a triangle around the central characters (Renzo and Lucia), with a different type of power situated at each corner: civil (or secular) power (Don Rodrigo, the unnamed), true spiritual power (Father Cristoforo, Cardinal Borromeo), false spiritual power (Don Abbondio, Gertrude). This structure, Calvino argues, is particularly effective in a text which displays the workings of power in society.

Around Renzo and Lucia and their obstructed marriage the forces at work are arranged in a triangular figure which has for its vertices three authorities: civil power, false religious power, and true religious power. Two of these forces are adverse and one propitious: civil power is always adverse; the church is divided into a good and a bad church, the first of which strives to overcome the obstacles raised by the second. This triangular figure appears twice in a virtually identical way: in the first half of the novel with Don Rodrigo, Don Abbondio and Fra Cristoforo, and in the second with the Unnamed, the Nun of Monza and Cardinal Federigo.

It is not a distortion to extract a geometrical scheme from a book which is so modulated and complex: no novel is calculated with as much exactness as *The Betrothed*; every poetic and ideological effect is governed by a predetermined but essential clockwork, by diagrams of carefully balanced forces. Certainly, the particularly Manzonian quality of the novel comes not so much from the skeleton as from the flesh, and the same skeleton could have served for a completely different book, for example a *roman noir*: there are ingredients enough to set up even a de Sade, with castles full of tortures and perverted convents, or there would have been if Manzoni were not allergic to the representation of evil. But if Manzoni is to be able to bring into the novel everything that he wants to say, and to leave in the shade everything he prefers to pass over, the skeleton must be completely functional; and there exists no more functional story than the fable in which there is an objective to be reached despite the obstacles created by opposing characters and by means of the aid of sympathetic characters, and the hero and heroine have nothing to worry about apart from doing the right things and abstaining from the wrong ones: just like poor Renzo and poor Lucia.

. . . What Manzoni has really at heart are not so much characters as the forces which act in society and in life, what conditions them and the conflicts between them. Relations of force are the real motor of his narrative, and the crux of his moral and historical interests. When he is representing relations of force – Fra Cristoforo at Don Rodrigo's banquet, or the 'free choice' of Gertrude's vows, or the Commissioner of Supply in Ferrer's carriage surrounded by the angry crowd – Manzoni always has a light and certain hand, he can find the right spot to within a millimetre. It is not for nothing that *The Betrothed* is our most widely read *political* book, which has shaped Italian political life for all parties, a work in which, more than in any other, the politician who day in, day out has to measure general ideals against the objective conditions finds himself reflected. But it is also the *anti-political* book *par excellence*, since it takes as its point of departure the conviction that politics can change nothing, neither with laws which pretend to limit *de facto* power, nor with demonstrations of collective force by the excluded. Not that Manzoni is making things up; on the contrary it is perfectly true that it was down to people like Dr Quibble-weaver to apply the decrees against the bravi; it is perfectly true that if you get involved with a crowd which is attacking the bakeries of Milan you always bump into a provocateur like Ambrogio Fusella who has been let loose by the High Sheriff in order to catch the usual scapegoat. It is an Italian classic in this, too, for it has never ceased shaping reality in Italy according to its model.

From '*I promessi sposi*: il romanzo dei rapporti di forza', lecture given at a conference on Manzoni at the University of Nijmegen,

Netherlands, October 1973; reprinted in *Una pietra sopra. Discorsi di letteratura e società* (Einaudi, Turin, 1980), pp. 267–78 (271–4).

Leonardo Sciascia (1981)

Sciascia, much of whose own writing denounced abuses of the law and of state power, draws an analogy between modern totalitarian forms of evil and those depicted in the *History of the Column of Infamy*.

The figure of the 'smearer,' which had already made its appearance in the plague of 1576, ... had a more tragic, multiple and prolonged apotheosis in that of 1630. And not only in Milan. But it was the Milanese figure, the recollections which remained of it in the city, the documents which described it, which in the next century provoked the scorn of Pietro Verri, the Enlightenment thinker; and again in the next century, the nineteenth, the no less scornful but more sorrowful, anxious and acute meditation of the Catholic Alessandro Manzoni. Today we feel closer to the Catholic than to the thinker of the Enlightenment. Pietro Verri paid attention to the darkness of the times and their fearsome legal institutions, Manzoni to the responsible individuals. We can indicate the justice of Manzoni's vision by establishing an analogy between the Nazi death camps and the trial, torture and death of the smearers. When Nicolini (whose book *Peste e untori* of 1937 we will often have occasion to mention) says that 'the enquiry was entrusted to Monti and Visconti, which is to say to men whose integrity, probity, intelligence, love for the common good, spirit of sacrifice and civil courage were venerated by the whole of Milan,' leaving aside civil courage (and that is to say leaving it out) he makes one think of that book by Charles Rohmer, *The Other*, which is all that is most terrible in the memory and consciousness of all the literature on the Nazi horrors published from 1945 onwards: 'a demonstration *per absurdum*, in which it is precisely the element of humanity that remains in the bureaucrats of evil, their capacity to feel and act like all of us, which gives the exact measure of their wrongdoing' (these words, almost certainly by Vittorini, are from the note introducing the Italian translation). Nicolini does not notice that what is frightening is precisely this: that those judges were as honest and intelligent as Rohmer's prison guards; they were good fathers, sensitive, lovers of music, kind to animals. Those judges were 'bureaucrats of Evil': and they knew that they were doing evil.

From the postscript to the edition of the *Storia della colonna infame* published by Sellerio, Palermo, 1981, pp. 175–7.

Vittorio Spinazzola (1983)

Spinazzola argues that the figure and discourse of the narrator, the 'I' who doubles for Manzoni and tells the story, is so dominant, paternal and authoritative that the reader is drawn into sharing his totalizing viewpoint rather than the partial and limited viewpoints of any of the individual characters. The totalizing viewpoint in turn refers the reader to the authority and equanimity of God, the creator and arbiter of all things. Spinazzola, writing from a Marxist position, is implicitly criticizing an ideological mechanism by which the reader is co-opted into an 'objective' view of the world which coincides with that of both the Church and the liberal state, where the rule of law acts to regulate conflict by balancing diverse interests.

> *The Betrothed* does not allow the reader to identify consistently with any one of its main characters, not even those closest to the author's heart. . . . They are all lacking in one way or another, and the writer is always quick to emphasize their limitations and point out their faults. On the other hand, the text continually invites the reader to identify partially with each of the characters as their various attitudes are unfolded at successive stages of the story. No one of them is so lacking in humanity that one cannot in some way recognize oneself in him or her.
>
> In this way, the reader is continually referred back by the individual narrative figures to the narrating I, who with his explicit presence provides the only key to a proper reading of the text: he allows the reader to situate every aspect of a chaotic panorama on a horizon of totality. The author's relationship with his readers thus assumes the same form as his relationship with his characters: there is a strict functional similarity between them.
>
> In psychological terms, one can say that Manzoni brings his own image into the book to endow it with a sum of unmistakably paternal attributes that are denied, at least to the same extent, to any other of the many characters who crowd its pages. Hence the supreme responsibility which Manzoni gives to the figure of the writer, into which he infuses his demiurge so as to make him the

subject that carries the discourse of the novel. But, at the same time, as a creator he is well aware that he himself is created, a child like all of us of our common Father. . . .

On a sociological level the totalization of the point of view brought into the novel by the Manzoni character implies the transcendence of the limited and fragmented views of individual particularities or supraindividual entities – classes, corporations, associations – who are perpetually struggling to attain their respective privileges. The novel's overall view is shaped by a highly articulated sense of general interests, which the narrating I administers with firm wisdom. In this way the narrating I embodies the just authority which collective institutions must possess when they serve to guarantee equanimity in the relations between rulers and ruled.

From *Il libro per tutti. Saggio sui 'Promessi sposi'* (Riuniti, Rome, 1983), pp. 65–6.

Giovanni Macchia (1983)

Macchia argues that Manzoni used digressions both because they were more 'natural' than the usual artificial devices of plot construction and because they gave him the freedom to mix history, moral comments and reflections on literary form. This procedure culminated in the *History of the Column of Infamy*, a digression which outgrew the novel and yet remained attached to it, sharing its central concerns.

What he rejected was the novel elaborated and held together by external means, where the most disparate facts were stitched together with a heavy thread to propel the action along. In many of the novels he had read, unexpected relationships were constructed between different characters so that they could all be brought onstage together, but for Manzoni this meant forcing the narrative into an artificial unity not to be found in real life. He was aware – he wrote to Claude Fauriel – that readers liked this sort of 'unity', but only because it reminded them of an old habit. . . .

This contempt for artificial unity led him in *Fermo e Lucia* to display such a freedom of composition that it would be difficult to find its like not only in novels of the same period but even, with a few exceptions, in those written before it. . . .

Displaying the most unbridled independence from the facts, he interrupted the action, discussed the opinions of the chronicler he was citing and the features of the novel he was writing, improvising conversations with supposed antagonists, and he added his ideas about literature. . . . In other words, the procedure he used most forcefully in the writing of his novel, imposing it magisterially in the first draft and mitigating it almost to the point of suppressing it in the definitive version, was that of the digression. . . .

This mobility and variety of viewpoints, these continual shifts, were not suggested to Manzoni by novelists like Cervantes or Prévost but by the masters who had tackled the narrative form in the most unusual and adventurous ways. They were essayists and moralists. They were those who in composing their books had decided to destroy every kind of artificial unity and preferred to confront disorder rather than lock themselves in conceptual rigidity.

. . . If the digression had become, in writing, an appendix, the appendix became in time a 'short work'. But this short work which could not be contained, as he had imagined, within the body of the novel, was to remain tied to it to the point of sharing its destiny. . . .

Without inventing anything, following the transcripts of the trial step by step, Manzoni thus entered the great current of trial and inquisition writing of the modern novel, from Stendhal to Dostoyevsky. . . . And it is admirable that the 'timid' Manzoni, just as he was about to conclude his novel, carrying to its ultimate consequences the procedure of the digression, against all those who rushed like sheep behind the twistings of the law and hurled curses at the victims, should have resolved the figure of the judge into that of the writer. Because of these closing pages the 'writer' assumed a stature he might never have attained in the novel. He became the accuser of men and a world and an age in which even a disease, a scourge of nature, became the occasion of unprecedented cruelties, in the desperate search for blame. It is only when one reads the *Column of Infamy* that one realises that Goethe, who admired the 1827 edition of *The Betrothed* but was critical of the chapters on the plague, did not fully understand what Manzoni was trying to do. Manzoni was certainly a poet but he knew well that great poetry is not sufficient to write a great novel. And, using the facts of historical reality, he presented again, in chaos and destruction, the theme he had developed in the novel: the theme of the passions.

From 'Nascita e morte della digressione. Da *Fermo e Lucia* alla *Storia della colonna infame*'; (1983), in *Tra Don Giovanni e Don*

Rodrigo. Scenari secenteschi, second edition (Adelphi, Milan, 1989), pp. 28–30, 37–8, 51, 53–4.

Umberto Eco (1986)

This extract is from a paper given to a conference on the semiotics of *The Betrothed*. Eco claims that Manzoni's novel implicitly and consistently distinguishes two kinds of 'semiosis' (ways of signifying or conveying meaning): a 'natural' (or 'popular') kind, consisting of gestures, facial expressions, etc., and a 'verbal' kind, namely language in all its spoken and written forms. The former, used and understood by the lower classes, is normally reliable; the latter is presented as unreliable and is frequently associated with the deceptions of those in power.

The lower-class characters distrust verbal language because it imposes a logical syntax which natural semiosis abolishes, since the latter works not in linear sequences but in 'pictures', in instantaneous iconological units of meaning. Whereas the plots of linguistic sequences can thicken to infinity, and the simple can lose themselves in this wood, natural semiosis permits, or seems to permit, a more easy access to the truth of things, of which it is the spontaneous vehicle: a true, instinctive gesture can reveal the intentional falsity of an earlier gesture. The notary who arrests Renzo speaks to him encouragingly. Renzo does not trust words but he could be deceived by the tone. However the notary has him handcuffed and by this sign Renzo understands without a shadow of doubt that he is in trouble. . . .

Throughout the novel we always find this same opposition between 'natural' sign and verbal sign, visual sign and linguistic sign. Manzoni is always so embarrassed by the verbal sign, or wants to show he distrusts it, that in all the cases of enunciation he scatters across the novel he apologizes for the way he is telling the story, whereas when he assumes truth-telling tones it is to talk about the credence one needs to give to a proof, a piece of evidence, a trace, a symptom, a clue, an exhibit.

His characters do the same: . . . Renzo may aspire to have his children learn to read and write but he does not fail to point out these verbal and grammatical artifices are a 'swindle' (Chapter 38). As for Latin, the language *par excellence*, Renzo distrusts it and the only time he uses it he improvises a Babelic version of it: ('siés baraòs trapolorum', Chapter 14). Only once (Chapter 38), when

he has by now made his peace with Don Abbondio, does he say he
accepts the Latin of the marriage sacrament and the mass, and it is
because 'that's an honest, sacrosanct Latin, . . . and you have to
read what's in the book, too.' The 'good' Latin of the liturgy is not
a spoken language; it is song, formula, psalmody, gesture, it does
not speak and therefore cannot falsify. It is like an item of clothing,
a gesture of the hand, an expression of the face: all signs (and
Manzoni repeatedly calls them 'signs' – 'segni') which belong to
natural semiosis.

'Semiosi naturale e parola nei "Promessi sposi"' (1986), in
Giovanni Manetti (ed.), *Leggere i 'Promessi sposi'*, Bompiani,
Milan, 1989, pp. 5–6.

Carlo Dionisotti (1988)

Dionisotti, an eminent literary historian and critic, saw the
renewed critical interest in the *History of the Column of Infamy*
in 1970s and 1980s Italy as a sign of the continued relevance of
its critique of a political and judicial system which could arrest
and try scapegoats or petty suspects while failing to combat
large-scale organized crime and corruption.

The revaluation of the *Column of Infamy* has not happened for
literary and ideological reasons, as it has for Manzoni's other
works, but because people have recognized in that text the same
indignation which the maladministration of justice has aroused in
our own time. Concern with the limits and defects of human justice
is predominant in all of Manzoni's work. But only in the *Column
of Infamy*, which for precisely this reason is unique and not simply
rare in the Italian literary tradition, does this concern take the form
of outright protest, the re-reading and re-fighting of a trial by a
writer without legal qualifications but fortified by the right of
human beings to produce history, regardless of privileges. For our
part, the solace we have received from the *Column of Infamy*
requires that a greater effort be made to interpret it, not only
because of its relevance to questions that remain unresolved today
but also for the reasons specific to the work itself and to a remote
age, different from our own. These two aspects of research on the
text are inseparable but distinct. Leaving out the first, which
requires political and not just scholarly competence, I would
remind readers that the maladministration of justice, the inability
to contain, let alone suppress, crime and brigandage, and the

related tendency to lay hands and inflict sufferings on the weak and the poor and even the innocent – in other words the maladministration denounced by Manzoni – is an old wound that has never been healed in Italian society, either in the seventeenth century or, making the necessary changes, in the nineteenth and twentieth, in Manzoni's time or in ours. It has always been and continues to be a scandalous wound, because it is exposed to the gaze of foreign observers, in a country which has played so great a part in the history of European civilization.

From 'Appendice storica alla "Colonna infame"', in *Appunti sui moderni. Foscolo, Leopardi, Manzoni e altri* (Il Mulino, Bologna, 1988), pp. 248–9.

SUGGESTIONS FOR FURTHER READING

Related works by Manzoni

On the Historical Novel is Manzoni's discussion of the genre; it is translated with an introduction by Sandra Berman, University of Nebraska Press, Lincoln and London, 1984. For those able to read Italian, *Fermo e Lucia* exists in various editions.

Biographical

Archibald Colquhoun, *Manzoni and his Times*, Dent, London, 1954; Natalia Ginzburg *The Manzoni Family*, Carcanet, Manchester, 1987.

Criticism

In English, see the Manzoni centenary issue of *Italian Quarterly*, Vol. 17, No. 67, Fall-Winter 1973 and S. Matteo and L. H. Peer (eds), *The Reasonable Romantic: Essays on Alessandro Manzoni*, Lang, New York, 1986; in Italian, in addition to the works represented in 'Manzoni and His Critics' in this edition, there are various useful anthologies of Manzoni criticism, of which the most comprehensive remains Giancarlo Vigorelli, *Manzoni pro e contro*, three volumes, Istituto di Propaganda Libraria, Milan, 1976.

TEXT SUMMARY

The story of *The Betrothed* takes place in northern Italy in 1628–30, during the period of Spanish rule over the Duchy of Milan (see Maps). The opening pages purport that the narrator has transcribed and reworked the story from an authentic manuscript of the period. The plot centres on two young lovers, Renzo Tramaglino and Lucia Mondello, workers in the silk industry in a village near Lecco. They have arranged their wedding for 8 November 1628, but an arrogant Spanish nobleman, Don Rodrigo, has seen Lucia and made a bet with his cousin Attilio that he will capture her and have her in his house by Martinmas, 11 November. The action of the novel starts with Don Rodrigo's hired thugs (known as *bravi*) waylaying the parish priest, Don Abbondio, and threatening to kill him if he performs the wedding (Chapter 1). Don Abbondio makes excuses to delay the wedding, but Renzo finds out the truth about Don Rodrigo's threat (Chapter 2). He attempts to get a lawyer, Dr Quibble-weaver, to intercede on his behalf (Chapter 3) but the lawyer is in league with Don Rodrigo. The couple turn next to a Capuchin friar, Fra Cristoforo, the story of whose conversion many years before is told in a digression (Chapter 4). Fra Cristoforo visits and confronts Don Rodrigo but is unable to make him withdraw the threat to Lucia (Chapters 5–6). Lucia's mother Agnese then tells the couple that they can become legally married simply by standing before a priest and declaring themselves husband and wife in his presence. They hatch and execute a plan in which Agnese distracts Don Abbondio's servant Perpetua while Renzo and Lucia, accompanied by two witnesses, enter the priest's house. Don Rodrigo's *bravi* meanwhile break into Lucia's house hoping to abduct her but find it empty (Chapters 7–8). The surprise wedding fails, the alarm is raised, the *bravi* scatter and the two lovers, assisted by Fra Cristoforo, flee and go in separate directions: Lucia, with Agnese, to a convent in Monza; Renzo to Milan. But their tribulations are not over. In the convent is a nun, Gertrude, a noblewoman whose tyrannical father had intimidated her into entering the cloister; she has since taken a lover, Egidio, and has been involved in the murder of a novice who had threatened to reveal her secret (Chapters 9–10). In Milan, meanwhile, Renzo has been caught up in the

Martinmas bread riots and has subsequently made a speech asserting the rights of the poor and downtrodden against the corrupt and powerful. He is picked up by a disguised police agent and taken to a tavern, where he is arrested (Chapters 11–15). He manages to escape, leave Milan and cross the border to the Republic of Venice, where his cousin, Bortolo, finds him work in a silk-mill near Bergamo (Chapters 16–17). An order for Renzo's arrest arrives at his home village. Meanwhile, Don Rodrigo, through the mediation of Attilio, has used the influence of his powerful uncle to get Fra Cristoforo transferred to Rimini, out of harm's way (Chapters 18–19). He then seeks the help of a local tyrant, 'the unnamed', to get Lucia out of the convent. The unnamed contacts Egidio, Gertrude's lover, who persuades her to give up Lucia. His associates seize Lucia while she is out running an errand for Gertrude and bring her to the castle of the unnamed, who intends to convey her into Don Rodrigo's hands. Lucia prays to the Virgin Mary for salvation, vowing to remain chaste if she is unharmed (Chapters 20–21). The unnamed, his already troubled conscience stirred by Lucia's terror and piety, undergoes a religious crisis, pays a penitent visit to Cardinal Federigo Borromeo and sets Lucia free (Chapters 22–24); he subsequently sends her a large cash gift as a dowry. Cardinal Borromeo, informed of Lucia's story, reproaches Don Abbondio for putting his own safety before his pastoral duty towards his parishioners (Chapters 25–26). Lucia tells her mother about her vow of chastity, and she communicates it in a letter to Renzo, who refuses to accept it as binding (Chapters 26–27). Lucia, still in danger from Don Rodrigo, is taken under the wing of a noblewoman and her husband (Donna Prassede and Don Ferrante) who have a house in Milan. The famine there has worsened, and its effects have been aggravated by maladministration and an influx of starving beggars from the country (Chapter 28). In the villages an invading mercenary army is pillaging houses: Agnese, Don Abbondio and many others flee their homes and stay in the unnamed's castle, which he has opened to refugees, until it is safe to return (Chapters 29–30). The betrothed lovers do not meet again until the summer of 1630, when they are in Milan during the plague epidemic (the spread of the disease, and reactions to it, are the subject of Chapters 31–32). Renzo, who has had plague in Bergamo and recovered, finally finds Lucia, herself recovering from the disease, in the lazaretto on the edge of the city. There too is Don Rodrigo, who is dying, and Fra Cristoforo, who, ill with plague himself, is tending the sick. Fra Cristoforo persuades Renzo to forgive and pray for Don Rodrigo and he declares Lucia's vow of chastity null before dying (Chapters 33–36). The plague's disruption of civil life and the passage of time have made the arrest warrant on Renzo a dead letter. He and Lucia are finally able to marry. They move with Agnese to a village outside Bergamo, where they are assured work (Chapters 37–38).

ACKNOWLEDGEMENTS

The editors wish to thank Oxford University Press for their permission to reproduce Kenelm Foster's translation of the *History of the Column of Infamy* for this edition, Nicholas Walker for translating the extracts from Goethe and Hofmannsthal, Claire Trocmé for her careful copy-editing, Jone Riva in Milan and Philippa Lewis in London for their help with the cover illustration and Hilary Laurie, Andrea Henry and Alex Bulford at Dent for overseeing the project. For the notes they are indebted to various annotated Italian editions: those of *I promessi sposi* by Ettore Bonora (Loescher, Turin, 1972), Piero Nardi (Mondadori, Milan, 1940) and Geno Pampaloni (De Agostini, Novara, 1988); those of *Storia della colonna infame* by Renzo Negri (Marzorati, Milan, 1974) and Carla Riccardi (Monadori, Milan, 1984). Any shortcomings or errors in the present edition remain the editors' responsibility.

The editor and publishers wish to thank the following for permission to use copyright material:

Adelphi edizioni s.p.a. for material from Giovanni Macchia, *Tra Don Giovanni e Don Rodrigo*, 2nd edn (1989), pp. 28–30, 37–8, 53–4;

S. Fischer Verlag GmbH for material from Hugo von Hofmannsthal, 'Manzonis "Promessi sposi"' (1927), in *Gesammelte Werke in Einzelausgaben, Prosa*, Vol. IV, ed. Herbert Steiner (Fischer Verlag, 1955), pp. 419–21;

The Wylie Agency on behalf of the Estate of the author for material from Italo Calvino, 'I promessi sposi', a lecture given at the University of Nijmegen, Netherlands, October 1973.

Every effort has been made to trace the copyright holders but if any have been inadvertently overlooked the publishers will be pleased to make the necessary arrangement at the first opportunity.